Mikhail Sholokhov

Quiet Flows the Don

a novel in two volumes

volume two

translated by Robert Daglish

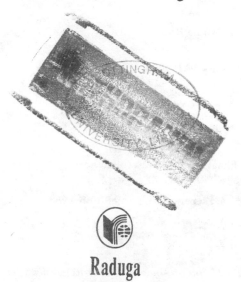

Raduga

Collets

342824

Translation from the Russian

English translation © Raduga Publishers 1984

First unabridged English edition 1984
as part of Mikhail Sholokhov's collected
works in eight volumes.

First unabridged separate English edition 1988

Raduga Publishers, *119859 Moscow, 17 Zubovsky Blvd.*, USSR
Collets, *Denington Estate, Wellingborough, Northants, U.K.*

Printed in the Union of Soviet Socialist Republics

ISBN 0569-08957-3

CONTENTS

BOOK THREE

Oh, Father, fair and peaceful Don,
Don Ivanovich, you are our provider,
Blessed is your name,
Good and great your fame,
But once you swiftly flowed; oh Don,
Swift and clean you flowed,
Yet now, oh Don, you flow so sludgily,
Sludgy through and through you flow.
And then spoke forth the fair and peaceful Don:
'What else but sludgy should I be?
Far away my eagles brave are flown,
My eagles—Cossacks of the Don,
And my steep banks are washed away while they are gone,
While they are gone, my yellow sands grow tresses long.'

(*Old Cossack Song*)

PART SIX

I

In April 1918 a great cleavage took place on the Don. The ex-frontline Cossacks of the northern districts, those watered by the rivers Khopyor and Medveditsa and part of the Upper Don, went with Mironov and the retreating units of the Red Army; while the Cossacks of the Lower Don harassed and pursued them to the borders of the region, fighting for the liberation of every inch of their native soil.

The Cossacks from the Khopyor went with Mironov almost to a man; along the Medveditsa it was half and half, and only an insignificant number came from the Upper Don.

Not until 1918 did history finally divide the Cossacks of the Upper and Lower Don. But the first signs of the rift had begun to show hundreds of years earlier, when the less prosperous Cossacks of the northern districts, not blessed with the rich soils of the Azov littoral, its vineyards, abundant hunting and fishing grounds, would at times break away from Cherkassk and take to raiding the Great Russian lands, while providing a safe and reliable stronghold for all rebels, from Razin to Sekach.

Even in later times, when most of the Don was writhing silently under the imperious hand of the central power, the Upper Don Cossacks rose openly and, led by their own atamans, shook the foundations of the throne, fighting the crown forces, plundering the caravans of barges on the Don, ranging as far as the Volga and inciting the subjugated Cossacks of Zaporozhye to rebellion.

By the end of April 1918, two-thirds of the Don had been cleared of the Bolsheviks and, when the need for it to have its own regional government became obvious, the senior officers of the detachments that had been fighting in the south proposed holding a Cossack Army Council. It was agreed that members of the Provisional Don Government and delegates from the stanitsas and army units should meet on April 28th in Novocherkassk.

The village of Tatarsky heard the news in the form of a message from the Vyoshenskaya stanitsa ataman, stating that on April 22nd a meeting was to be held in the stanitsa to elect delegates for the Army Council.

The message was read out by Miron Grigorievich Korshunov at a village meeting, which decided to send him, Old Bogatiryov and Pantelei Prokofievich Melekhov to Vyoshenskaya.

At the Vyoshenskaya meeting Pantelei was included among the delegates chosen to go to Novocherkassk. He returned home the same day and decided to set out on the morrow with his daughter-in-law's father so as to reach Novocherkassk in good time (Miron wanted to buy kerosene, soap and other household goods in Millerovo and was also hoping to make a little money by buying Mokhov some sieves and a babbitt for his mill).

They left at daybreak. The wagon bowled along lightly behind Miron's black stallions, the two fathers sat together in the gaily painted seat, and by the time they topped the hill they were talking freely. There were German troops stationed in Millerovo and Miron asked not without some apprehension, 'The Germans won't start knocking us about, will they, kinsman? They're a terrible lot, so I've heard!'

'No,' Pantelei assured him. 'Matvei Kashulin was there t'other day and he says the Germans are quiet as mice... They daren't touch a Cossack.'

'You don't say so!' Miron smirked into the foxy russet of his beard and toyed with his cherrywood whipstock; apparently reassured, he changed the subject. 'What kind of government should be set up? What d'you think?'

'We'll have an ataman. One of our own folk! A Cossack!'

'God grant it! Mind you make a good choice! Feel out those generals like a Gypsy feels out horses. Don't pick a dud.'

'We'll choose the right one. The Don hasn't run out of good brains.'

'Ay, kinsman, that's so... But the fools sprout up without our sowing 'em.' Miron screwed up his eyes and a sadness settled on his freckled face. 'I thought to give my Mitka a proper chance in life, wanted him to study to be an officer, but he didn't even finish at the parish school, played truant the second winter.'

For a minute they fell silent, thinking of their sons who had gone off in pursuit of the Bolsheviks. The wagon began to shake feverishly on the bumpy road and the right-hand horse got out of step and began hitching. The seat swayed and the two fathers rubbed up against each other like fish in a spawning bed.

'Where are our Cossacks now, I wonder?' Pantelei said with a sigh.

'They've gone off up the Khopyor. Fedot the Kalmyk has just come back from Kumylzhenskaya, ruined his horse, he did. He says they were heading for Tishanskaya.'

Again they fell silent. The cool breeze was chilling their backs. Behind them, on the other side of the Don the forests, meadows, lakes and clearings burned majestically and soundlessly in the pink fire of the dawn. A sandy ridge glowed like a yellow honeycomb and the camel humps of the dunes gave a grudging gleam of bronze.

Spring was coming in slowly. The faint aquamarine of the forests had deepened to a rich green verdure, the steppe was blooming and the flood waters had drained away, leaving countless glittering lakelets in the meadows, but under the steep slopes of the ravines the ravaged snow still clung to the sandy soil, its whiteness challengingly bright.

On the evening of the second day they drove into Millerovo and put up for the night with a Ukrainian acquaintance, who lived in a house tucked away under the brown wall of the grain elevator. After breakfast the next morning Miron harnessed his horses and set out for the shops. He drove over the level crossing without hindrance, and then for the first time in his life he saw Germans. Three German territorials were making for the road with the obvious intention of intercepting him. One of them, a skinny fellow with a curly chestnut beard growing right up to his ears, signalled to him to stop.

Miron reined in the horses, munching his lips in worried expectation. The Germans came up. One of the three, a tall, fleshy Prussian gave a sparkling white-toothed smile and said to his comrade, 'Here's a real Cossack for you! Look, he's even wearing Cossack uniform! His sons were probably fighting us. Let's send him off alive to Berlin. He'll make a very interesting exhibit!'

'All we need is his horses, he can go to the devil!' the skinny one with the chestnut beard replied unsmilingly.

He circled cautiously round the horses and came up to the wagon.

'Get down, old man. We need your horses to take a load of flour from this mill to the station. Get down, I said! You can go to the commandant for your horses later.' The German glanced towards the mill and with a gesture that left no doubt as to its meaning showed Miron that he had better get off the wagon.

The other two walked away towards the mill, looking back and laughing. A greyish yellow flush spread over Miron's face. He wound the reins round the side-bar of the seat, jumped down youthfully, and walked out in front of the horses.

'I've no one with me,' the momentary thought struck him chillingly. 'They'll take the horses! What a mess I've landed in! The devil tempted me to come here!'

The German compressed his lips and, taking Miron by the sleeve, showed him that he should go to the mill.

'Let go!' Miron jerked his arm away, turning noticeably paler. 'Hands off! I won't give you the horses.'

The German guessed from his tone what the answer was. His lips suddenly parted in a snarl, baring a row of bluish, very clean teeth, his pupils dilated menacingly and his voice rose in a rasping command. His hand went to the rifle slung over his shoulder, and at that moment Miron remembered his young days. Like a skilled boxer with hardly a swing of the arm he struck the German full on the cheek. The punch sent the other man's head back with a click and the helmet strap under his chin snapped. He fell over backwards and, as he tried to rise, a wine-red clot of congealed blood fell from his mouth. Miron hit him again, this time on the back of the head, and with a furtive glance over his shoulder, bent down and snatched the rifle. His mind worked quickly and with surprising clarity. As he swung the horses round, he knew that the German could not shoot him in the back, and his only fear was of being seen by sentries from behind the railway fence or along the track.

Never, even at the races had his black steeds galloped at such a frenzied pace! Even at weddings the wagon wheels had never had such a drubbing! 'Lord, help me to get away! Save me, Lord! In the name of the Father!...' Miron whispered to himself, belabouring the horses with his whip. Inborn cupidity was nearly his undoing; he longed to stop off at his lodgings for the rug he had left there, but reason triumphed and he turned in the other direction. He covered the twenty versts to Orekhovaya, as he himself said afterwards, faster than the Prophet Elijah in his chariot. In the settlement he swerved into the yard of a Ukrainian he knew and, more dead than alive, told him what had happened and begged refuge for himself and his horses. To this the Ukrainian had no objection, but warned him, 'I'll hide you then, but if they start interrogating me, I'll tell them. It's no use, friend! They'll burn my house down and string me up.'

'Hide me, brother! I'll pay you anything you ask! Only save me from death, hide me somewhere! I'll bring you a flock of sheep! I wouldn't grudge you a dozen of the finest!' Miron begged and pleaded as he pushed the wagon under the overhang of the shed.

Scared to death of being pursued, he lay low in the Ukrainian's yard until evening and made off as soon as it grew dark. All the way from Orekhovaya he drove like a madman with foam flying from the horses and the wagon wheels spinning so fast that the spokes were a mere blur. He recovered his wits only when he was nearing Lower-Yablonovskaya. Just before he got there he reached under the seat and pulled out the rifle he had captured, examined the leather sling with its markings in indelible pencil on the under side, and grunted with relief.

'Well, did you catch me, you sons of the devil? Bit off more than you could chew, eh!'

He never did bring the Ukrainian any sheep. In the autumn he stopped on his way past and in response to an expectant look from his host replied, 'Our sheep have all died. We're badly off for sheep... But I've brought you some pears from my own orchard in memory of what you did!' He turned out of the wagon a couple of bushels of pears that had got badly bruised during the journey and said with his rascally eyes averted, 'Lovely pears they are—they've been lying long enough to get nice and ripe.' And with that he took his leave.

While Miron was galloping away from Millerovo, Pantelei was hanging about at the station. A young German officer wrote out a pass for him, questioned him through an interpreter and, lighting a cheap cigar, said patronisingly, 'Well, off you go then, but remember that what you need is a sensible government. Elect a president, a tsar, whoever you like, but it must be a man with a sense of statesmanship, who will pursue a fair policy towards our country.'

Pantelei gave the German a rather surly look. He was in no mood for conversation and, as soon as he received the pass, went to buy his ticket.

In Novocherkassk he was astonished to find the place full of young officers. They were strolling about the streets, sitting together in the restaurants, walking out with the young ladies, and hurrying about round the ataman's palace and the court of justice, where the Council was to be held.

In the hostel for the delegates Pantelei met several other Cossacks, one of whom was an acquaintance of his from Yelanskaya. Most of the delegates were Cossacks; there were not many officers and only a sprinkling of the local intelligentsia. Vague rumours were going around about the election of a regional government. The only clear fact that had emerged was that there should be an ataman. The popular names among the Cossack generals were bandied about and their candidatures discussed.

After evening tea on the day of his arrival, Pantelei sat down in his room to have a bite of the food he had brought from home. He laid out a bunch of dried carp on the table and sliced some bread. Two Migulinskaya men joined him and a few others gathered round. The talk started with the situation at the war front and gradually moved on to the election.

'You won't find anyone better than the late General Kaledin—God rest his soul!' a Shumilinskaya man with a musty-coloured beard said with a sigh.

'True enough,' the Cossack from Yelanskaya agreed.

A captain representing Bessergenevskaya stanitsa broke in rather heatedly, 'No suitable candidate? Really, gentlemen! What about General Krasnov?'

'Who's he?'

'Who is he? Aren't you ashamed to ask, gentlemen? He's famous! Commander of the Third Cavalry Corps, holds the Order of St. George, a very clever man and a gifted general!'

The captain's effusive speech outraged a delegate representing one of the frontline units.

'Well, I can tell you for a fact. We know all about his gifts! As a general he's a wash-out! He didn't do so badly in the German war, but he'd have stayed a brigadier if it hadn't been for the revolution! '

'How can you say that, my dear fellow, when you know nothing about General Krasnov? How dare you speak in this way of a general who is universally respected? You have probably forgotten that you're only a rank-and-file Cossack?'

The officer uttered the icy words with withering sarcasm and the Cossack, taken aback, muttered confusedly, 'I was speaking from what I know of serving under him, Your Honour... On the Austrian front he landed our whole regiment on the barbed wire! That's why we think he's no good... But who knows... Mebbe it's all the other way round...'

'What did they give him the St. George for then, you fool?' Pantelei choked on a fishbone, cleared his throat, and launched into an attack on the frontline man. 'You've stuffed yourselves with daft ideas. You run everyone down, no one's good enough for you... A fine fashion! If you didn't talk so much, things wouldn't be in such a mess. Windbags—that's what you are! Too clever by half.'

The Cossacks of Cherkassk and the Lower Don were all for Krasnov. The old men liked the idea of a general with the Order of St. George; many of them had served under him in the war against Japan. The officers were attracted by his background, his career in the Guards, his social accomplishments, his erudition, his service at court in attendance on the Emperor. The liberal intelligentsia viewed with satisfaction the fact that Krasnov was not just a man of the battlefield and the parade ground, but also something of a writer, whose stories of officers' life had made pleasurable reading in the *Niva;* he must be a civilised person, if he was a writer.

Support for Krasnov was fervently canvassed in the hostel. The names of other generals faded in comparison. Krasnov's supporters among the officers whispered the rumour that Afrikan Bogayevsky was in league with Denikin, and that if Bogayevsky were elected ataman, all the Cossacks' privileges and autonomy would go by the board as soon as they got rid of the Bolsheviks and marched into Moscow.

There were also opponents of Krasnov. One of the delegates, a schoolmaster, tried unsuccessfully to besmirch the general's good name. He roamed from room to room, buzzing venomously, like a mosquito, in the Cossacks' ears, over which the hair now grew lank and long.

'Krasnov? A rotten general and no good as a writer either! A bootlicker at court, a lickspittle! The man wants to acquire national standing, so to speak, and retain his democratic innocence at the same time. Mark my words, he'll sell the Don to the first taker. A mere nonentity. As a politician he simply doesn't exist. Ageyev's the man to elect! He's quite a different quantity.'

But the schoolmaster made no headway. And on May 1, when the Council had been in session for three days, the call went up:

'Invite General Krasnov!'

'Be so kind...'

'Do us the honour...'

'We beg you!'

'He's the man we're proud of!'

'Let him come and tell us how to live!' The large hall stirred with excitement.

The officers clapped resoundingly and the Cossacks followed suit, clumsily batting their hands together. The sound of those black, work-hardened hands was dry and unpleasantly abrasive, in deep contrast to the soft music of applause produced by the sleek palms of the ladies, officers and students who thronged the gallery and corridors.

And when the tall, handsome general, with a figure that belied his years, strode out on to the platform in a uniform bedecked with crosses and medals, with epaulettes and other insignia of his high rank, the first ripple of applause rose to a roar, and the roar grew into an ovation. A storm of approval swept the rows of delegates. In this general, standing in a picturesque pose, his face flushed with emotion, many saw a dim reflection of the empire's former might.

Pantelei's eyes began to water and he blew his nose into the red handkerchief he had taken from inside his cap. 'That's a general! You can see what a man he is right away! Like the emperor himself, very like! Could be the late Alexander!' he thought, gazing sentimentally at the figure of Krasnov at the edge of the stage.

The Council known as the Council for the Salvation

of the Don conducted its proceedings at a leisurely pace. At the suggestion of the Council's president, Major Yanov, a decision was passed on the wearing of shoulder straps and all insignia of military rank. Krasnov made a brilliant, skilfully constructed speech. He spoke emotionally of 'Russia desecrated by the Bolsheviks', of her 'former might' and the destiny of the Don. In outlining the current situation he touched briefly on the German occupation and evoked a roar of approval when he ended his speech with a passionate appeal for autonomy of the Don Region after the defeat of the Bolsheviks.

'The sovereign Army Council will rule the Don Region! The Cossacks, liberated by the revolution, will restore their splendid ancient Cossack way of life, and we, like our fathers before us, will say in a stronger, full-blooded voice, "Long live the white tsar in Moscow's mighty citadel, and we, Cossacks, here on the quiet Don! "'

At the evening session on May 3rd Major-General Krasnov was elected Ataman of the Army Council by a majority of 107 votes to 30 with 10 abstentions. He refused to accept the ataman's feathered mace from the Army Major until the following conditions had been observed: the basic laws he had proposed to the Council must first be approved and he must be vested with full and unrestricted ataman's powers.

'Our country is on the brink of destruction! Only if complete trust is placed in the ataman will I accept the mace. Events demand drastic measures. You can work with confidence and a joyful sense of performing your duty, only when you know that the Council—the supreme expression of the will of the Don—trusts you, when in contrast to Bolshevik dissipation and anarchy there are firmly established legal standards.'

The laws proposed by Krasnov were the hurriedly rehashed laws of the former empire. How could the Council fail to approve them? It approved them with joy. Everything, even the clumsily redesigned flag, recalled the past—blue, red and yellow stripes (signifying Cossacks, outsiders, and Kalmyks); but as a concession to the national spirit the state emblem was radically changed: the rapacious two-headed eagle with wings spread and claws extended was replaced by a Cossack stripped to the waist, wearing a tall sheepskin busby, sabre, gun and other equipment, and sitting astride a wine barrel.

A delegate of the kowtowing, simple kind asked an obsequious question.

'Perhaps His Excellency will propose that something be changed or amended in the fundamental laws that have been passed?'

With a gracious smile Krasnov allowed himself to indulge in a jest. He surveyed the assembly and in the voice of a man gratified by the general attention replied, 'Yes, indeed. Articles 48, 49 and 50, on the flag, the emblem and the anthem. You may propose to me any flag, except the red flag, any emblem but the Jewish five-pointed star or other masonic badge, and any anthem but the *Internationale.*'

Amid general laughter the Council endorsed the laws, and the ataman's jest was repeated time and again for long afterwards.

On May 5th the Council was dissolved. The final speeches were made. Colonel Denisov, the commander of the Southern Group and Krasnov's right-hand man, promised that Bolshevik subversion would soon be eradicated, and the members of the Council departed in a mood of reassurance, encouraged both by the fortunate choice of ataman and the reports from the front.

Pantelei set out from the capital of the Don, deeply moved and charged with an explosive joy. He was unshakeably convinced that the feathered mace had fallen into safe hands, that the Bolsheviks would be defeated and that his sons would return to the farm. The old man sat by the carriage window, his elbow resting on the table. The farewell strains of the Don anthem were still ringing in his ears, the refreshing words were steadily permeating his mind and it did seem that the 'quiet and Christian Don' really was 'awake and stirring'.

But when the train had gone only a few versts from Novocherkassk, Pantelei spotted the advance posts of the Bavarian cavalry. A group of mounted Germans trotted past, seated calmly in their saddles, the well-fed horses with their massive cruppers and short tails glistened in the bright sun. Leaning forward with a pained twist of his eyebrow, Pantelei watched the hooves of the German horses dancing victoriously on the Cossack land, then turned away despondently and sat for a long time breathing heavily, with his broad back to the window.

II

Train after train of red-painted wagons rolled away from the Don across the Ukraine, loaded with wheat flower, eggs, butter and bullocks for Germany. On the observation platforms stood grey-uniformed, round-capped German sentries with fixed bayonets.

German boots made of strong brown leather with iron-tipped heels that would outlast the uppers tramped the steppeland tracks, and the Bavarian cavalry watered their horses in the Don... Meanwhile on the border of the Ukraine young Cossacks, called to the colours as soon as they had finished their training in Persianovka, near Novocherkassk, fought the troops of the Ukrainian nationalist leader Petlyura, and nearly half the newly formed 12th Don Cossack Regiment perished at Starobelsk, trying to win an extra slice of Ukrainian territory for the Don Region.

Further north the stanitsa of Ust-Medveditskaya changed hands time and again. Mironov and his Redguard Cossacks converging from the surrounding country would capture the stanitsa only to be driven out by a detachment of Alexeyev's Whiteguard partisans and within an hour the streets would be thronged with the uniform coats of high school and seminary students, who formed the main strength of the detachment.

Waves of Cossacks of the Upper Don surged northwards. Mironov fell back to the borders of the Saratov Province, leaving almost the whole of the Khopyor district free of Bolsheviks. By the end of the summer the Don Army, whipped together out of Cossacks of all ages capable of bearing arms, took its stand on the borders. Reorganised on the march and reinforced with officers from Novocherkassk, it had begun to look like a real army. The small forces provided by each stanitsa had been merged to form larger units; the old regular regiments were remustered with what was left of their previous complement after the war against Germany, and these regiments were organised into divisions; at headquarters the Cossack cornets were replaced by experienced colonels; and little by little the whole command passed into other hands.

By the end of the summer on the orders of Major-General Alferov units consisting of Migulinskaya, Meshkovskaya, Kazanskaya and Shumilinskaya Cossacks crossed the Don Region's border, occupied the settle-

ment of Donetskoye, in the Voronezh Province, and laid siege to the town of Boguchar.

For four days the squadron of Tatarsky Cossacks commanded by Petro Melekhov had been marching northwards through the Ust-Medveditskaya district. Somewhere to the right of them the Reds under Mironov were withdrawing hastily, without fighting towards the railway, and the Tatarsky men had not even sighted the enemy. Their daily marches were by no means long. Petro himself and all the other Cossacks had quietly decided that there was no sense in hurrying towards death and they kept the day's march down to not more than thirty versts.

On the fifth day they entered Kumylzhenskaya and crossed the River Khopyor at the village of Dundukovo. The meadow was draped with a fine curtain of midges. The vibrant high-pitched hum rose steadily. Swarms of insects swirled blindly round men and horses, crawling into their ears and eyes. The horses fretted and snorted, the Cossacks waved their arms and puffed away furiously at their home-grown tobacco.

'Here's a fine game, dammit!' Khristonya grunted, wiping a streaming eye with his sleeve.

'Got something in your eye?' Grigory grinned.

'It's smarting. Must be a poisonous one, the devil!'

Khristonya rolled back his eyelid, drew a rough finger over the eyeball and, pouting ruefully, gave his eye a long rub with the back of his hand.

Grigory was riding beside him. They had kept together from the start and had later been joined by Anikei, who had put on weight lately and looked even more like a woman.

The detachment numbered not quite a hundred. Petro's second-in-command was Sergeant-Major Latyshev, who had recently married into a Tatarsky family. Grigory was commanding a troop. Nearly all his Cossacks—Khristonya, Anikei, Fedot Bodovskov, Martin Shamil, Ivan Tomilin, the lanky Borshchev and the bearlike Zakhar Korolyov, Prokhor Zykov, the gypsy crowd—Merkulov, Yepifan Maksayev and Yegor Sinilin—and another ten or fifteen young Cossacks in their first year of service, were from the lower end of the village.

The second troop was commanded by Nikolai Koshevoi, the third by Yakov Koloveidin, and the fourth by

Mitka Korshunov, who after the execution of Podtyolkov had been hastily promoted by General Alferov to the rank of senior sergeant.

The squadron was going at a brisk trot. The road skirted flooded ponds, dipped into hollows, overgrown with rushes and willow bushes, and wound its way across the meadowland.

From the rear ranks came the booming laughter of Horseshoe Yakov, echoed by the high-pitched titters of Andrei Kashulin, who had also earned sergeant's stripes with the blood of Podtyolkov's comrades.

Petro Melekhov was riding with Latyshev to one side of the column. They were chatting quietly. Latyshev was toying with the new sword-knot on his sabre, Petro was stroking his horse with his left hand and scratching between its ears. A smile was playing on Latyshev's plump face and his crumbling, badly capped teeth gleamed a yellowish black from under his scanty moustache.

Last of all, on a limping piebald filly came Antip, Son of the Braggart, as he had been nicknamed by the Cossacks after his father.

Some of the Cossacks were chatting, some had broken ranks and were riding five abreast, but the rest kept a keen eye on the unfamiliar country, the meadowland, pockmarked with lakes, and the green walls of poplar and willow. It was clear from their equipment that the Cossacks were on a long march; their saddlebags were bulging with booty, their packs tight, and each had a greatcoat carefully strapped to the back of his saddle. And one could also judge from their harness: every strap had been thoroughly stitched with waxed thread, every piece of equipment fitted well and was in good repair. Only a month ago they had believed there would be no war, but now they rode with a gloomy and resigned awareness that bloodshed could not be avoided. 'You wear you skin today, but tomorrow the crows may be tanning it in the open field,' was the thought in every mind.

They passed through the village of Kreptsy. Scattered rush-thatched roofs showed up on the right. Anikei pulled a bun out of his trousers' pocket, bit off half of it, baring his small sharp teeth, and chewed hurriedly, his jaws working like a hare's.

Khristonya gave him a sidelong glance.

'Feeling hungry?'

'Why not?.. The wife baked it for me.'

'You're good at stuffing yourself! You must have a gut like a hog.' He turned to Grigory and went on in a peevish tone, 'The way he guzzles, the fiend! Where does he put it all? I've been watching him these last few days and it scares me; he's not so big, to look at him, but he swallows everything like a bottomless pit.'

'I'm only eating my own grub—or, at least, I try. If you eat mutton at night, you'll be up at first light. It's all grist to the mill, you know.'

Anikei chortled and winked at Grigory with a nod at Khristonya, who was spitting in annoyance.

'Petro Panteleyevich, where are we going to stop for the night? Our horses are limping!' came a shout from Tomilin.

He was supported by Merkulov.

'Time to knock off for the night, the sun's setting.'

Petro waved his whip.

'We'll stop in Klyuchy. Or mebbe we'll get as far as the Kumylga.'

Merkulov smiled into his black curly beard and whispered to Tomilin, 'He's trying to get into Alferov's good books, the son-of-a-bitch! He's in a hurry.'

Someone in trimming Merkulov's beard had played a trick on him and cut its glorious growth down to a crooked wedge. Merkulov's new appearance made him a constant target for jokes. And even now Tomilin could not resist the opportunity.

'Whose good books are you trying to get into?'

'What d'you mean?'

'You've had your beard trimmed like a general. You reckon they'll give you a division with a beard like that, eh? Anything else you want?'

'Stupid devil! I meant what I said and you twist it.'

Amid talk and banter they rode into the village of Klyuchy. Andrei Kashulin, who had been sent on ahead to find billets for the night, met them by the first house.

'Our troop, follow me! The first goes in those three houses, the second, over to the left, and the third, in this one, by the well, and the next four houses.'

Petro rode up to him.

'Did you hear anything? Did you find out?'

'Not a smell of 'em. But there's plenty of honey, lad. One old woman's got three hundred hives. We'll raid one tonight, that's for sure!'

'None of that nonsense! Or I'll raid you!' Petro

frowned, and gave his horse a touch of the whip.

They found their billets and stabled the horses. It grew dark. Their hosts gave them supper. The local Cossacks and the men on active service sat on last year's alder logs, stacked by the fences, chatted for a while about this and that, and went off to bed.

The next morning the squadron rode out of the village and had almost reached Kumylzhenskaya when it was overtaken by a messenger. Petro opened the envelope and read the contents, swaying in the saddle and holding the sheet of paper at arm's length with a strained look, as if it were too heavy for him. Grigory rode up to him.

'Is it an order?'

'Uh-huh.'

'What does it say?'

'Quite a lot... I've got to hand over the squadron. All the men of my age have been recalled. There's a 28th Regiment being formed in Kazanka. The artillerymen as well, and the machine-gunners.'

'What about the rest?'

'There's what it says, "Report to the commander of the 22nd Regiment in Arzhenovskaya. Without delay". I like that! "Without delay"!'

Latyshev trotted up and took the order from Petro. He read it with his thick lips moving and one eyebrow sharply raised.

'Get going!' Petro shouted.

The squadron started off again at a walk. The Cossacks looked back, keeping a sharp eye on Petro, waiting to hear what he had to say. Petro read out the order when they reached the stanitsa. The Cossacks in the older age-groups started making hasty preparations for the return journey. It was decided that they should spend the day in the stanitsa and set out for their various destinations the following morning. Petro, who had been looking for a chance to speak to his brother all day, came round to his billet.

'Let's go to the square.'

Grigory strode out through the gate in silence. Mitka Korshunov was about to follow them, but Petro objected coldly.

'Go away, Mitka. I want to talk to my brother.'

'That's all right then,' Mitka grinned understandingly, and dropped behind.

Grigory, who had been observing Petro from the side,

saw that he wanted to talk seriously and tried to put him off by affecting a lively conversation.

'It's a funny thing. We've only gone a hundred versts from home and the people round here are quite different. They don't speak the same way and their buildings are different, a bit like the Old Believers'. Look at that gate, it's got a ridged roof, like a roadside cross. We don't have that kind. And look over there,' he pointed to the nearest house, 'the coping's covered too. To keep the wood from rotting, I suppose?'

'Never mind that,' Petro frowned. 'You're on the wrong subject... Let's stand by the fence. People are looking at us.'

Cossacks and housewives coming from the square glanced at them curiously. An old man in a blue unbelted shirt and a Cossack cap with a band that had turned pink with age stopped as they came by.

'Staying for the day?'

'We want a day's rest.'

'Have ye got enough oats for your horses?'

'Just about,' Petro replied.

'Call on me if ye like, I'll let ye have a bushel.'

'God bless you, Grandad!'

'Praise the Lord... Drop in. That's my place over there, the one with the green iron roof.'

'What was it you wanted to talk about?' Grigory asked, frowning impatiently.

'Everything.' Petro gave a forced, half-guilty smile and tucked one wheaten whisker into the corner of his mouth. 'With the times we're living in now, Grisha, boy, we may never see each other again...'

The lurking hostility to his brother that had been about to sting Grigory suddenly disappeared, banished by Petro's wretched smile and the 'Grisha, boy' that had stayed with them since childhood. Petro eyed his brother affectionately, still with that lingering, lop-sided smile. Then he drove the smile away and his face hardened.

'Look how they've divided the people, the swine! Like with a plough. Some on this side of the coulter, others on that. It's a hell of a life, a terrible time to be living in! You can't tell what's in another man's mind... You, for instance,' he suddenly came to the point. 'You're my own brother but I can't make you out, honest to God, I can't! I feel you're somehow drifting away from me. That's the truth, isn't it?' And he answered himself, 'Yes, it is. You're wobbling. I'm afraid you'll be going over to the Reds. You still haven't found your way in life, Grisha, boy.'

'Have you?' Grigory asked, watching the sun sink behind a chalky headland on the distant Khopyor, and the scorched flakes of cloud flying out of the afterglow.

'Yes, I have. I've found my furrow and I'll stick to it! I'm not going to wobble like you, Grisha.'

'Oh no?' Grigory forced a bitter smile.

'No, I won't!' Petro tugged crossly at his moustache and blinked as if he had been dazzled. 'You couldn't drag me over to the Reds with a rope round my neck. The Cossacks are against 'em, and so am I. I don't want to change sides and I won't! How can I put it? There wouldn't be any sense, their road's not my road!'

'Don't let's talk about it,' Grigory said wearily.

He was the first to make for his billet. He walked away with determined strides, swinging his hunched shoulders.

Petro followed, but dropped behind at the gate and asked, 'Just tell me, so that I'll know, Grisha... Will you go over to them?'

'I don't think so... I don't know.'

It was a listless, reluctant answer. Petro sighed but asked no more questions. He walked away looking disturbed and drawn. To both brothers it was as clear as day that the paths that had once linked them were overgrown with the thickets of their past lives and there was no way to reach the other's heart. Just as when a smooth path, well trimmed by goat's hooves, winds along the side of a ravine, then suddenly, at a bend plunges to the bottom and breaks off, there was nothing but a wall of tangled weeds, a spiky forbidding barrier.

The next day Petro set off back to Vyoshenskaya with half the squadron. The remaining youngsters, commanded by Grigory, headed for Arzhenovskaya.

From early morning the sun had been beating down relentlessly. The steppe was simmering in a brownish haze. Behind them lay the lilac spurs of the Khopyor hills and a saffron sweep of sand. The sweating horses plodded along under their riders. The Cossacks' faces were dark and drained of colour by the sun. The saddle seats, the stirrups, the metal of the bridles were too hot to touch. Even in the woods there was no relief from the heat; the air was stuffy and humid and smelled strongly of rain.

A deep despondency had taken possession of Grigory. All day, as he sat swaying in the saddle, he thought disconnectedly about the future; in his mind he toyed with Petro's words, as with the beads of a glass necklace, and brooded bitterly. The tart tang of the wormwood stung his lips, the road seemed to smoke in the heat. The brown, gold-tinted steppe lay prostrate in the sun and the dry winds groped across it, crushing the shaggy grass and kicking up the sand and dust.

By evening the sun was wrapped in a translucent haze. The sky looked faded and grey. Heavy clouds appeared in the west. They hung motionless with their drooping corners touching the dim, finely woven thread of the horizon, and then, as the wind caught them, they began to advance menacingly, dragging their brownish tails tauntingly low, their rounded crests glistening like sugar.

The detachment recrossed the River Kumylga and rode in under the canopy of a poplar grove. The leaves fluttered their milky-blue undersides in the wind and kept up a low harmonious rustle. Somewhere beyond the Khopyor driving rain and hail from a dazzlingly white cloud, girdled with a bright rainbow, was lashing down.

They spent the night in a small, almost deserted village. Grigory stabled his horse and went to the hives. The owner, an aged curly-headed Cossack, who was rescuing bees from his beard, engaged him in anxious conversation.

'I got this hive only a day or two back and the young brood has all died. See, the bees are carrying them out.' He stooped beside a hive hollowed out of a log and pointed to the hole; the bees were steadily dragging the small bodies of the young out on to the entrance platform and flying away with them, buzzing quietly.

The bee-keeper screwed up his reddish eyes and smacked his lips regretfully. He walked in a quick, jerky manner, waving his arms. He seemed too erratic and hurried in his movements to be looking after a place like this, where a huge family of bees was steadily and harmoniously performing its wise unhurrying labour. Grigory watched the broad-shouldered old Cossack with a slight feeling of hostility, involuntarily evoked by his fidgety manner and quick, grating voice.

'We'll have a good yield this year. The thyme bloomed well and they were gathering from it. The frame boxes are better than hives. I'm starting them now...'

Grigory drank his evening tea with thick, glutinous

honey. It smelled sweetly of thyme, trinity, and meadow blossom. The tea was poured by his host's daughter, a tall handsome woman. Her husband had gone off with Mironov's Redguards, so the host was obliging and submissive. He seemed not to notice his daughter glancing quickly at Grigory from under lowered lashes and pursing her thin pale-red lips. As she reached out for the teapot Grigory noticed the jet-black curly hair under her arms. More than once he encountered her probing, curious glance and it seemed to him that she flushed when their eyes met and nursed a hidden smile at the corners of her mouth.

'I'll make up your bed in the front room,' she told Grigory after tea, as she walked past with a pillow and rug and scorched him with an openly avid glance. Puffing up the pillow, she murmured quickly, 'I'll be sleeping outside by the shed... It's so stuffy in the house and the fleas bite you...'

Grigory took off only his boots and, as soon as he heard his host snoring, went out to where she was lying under the overhang of the shed. She made room for him on an up-ended wagon and, pulling her sheepskin over them, let her legs touch his and lay still. Her lips were dry, hard and smelled of onion and an unspoiled freshness. Grigory lay in the embrace of her slim dark arms until dawn. All night she hugged and caressed him insatiably, with little laughs and jokes biting his lips till they bled and leaving on his neck, chest and shoulders the blue marks of the love-bites made by her small, sharp teeth. After third cock-crow Grigory was about to go back to his room but she restrained him.

'Let me go, love, let me go, sweetheart!' Grigory urged her, smiling into his black, drooping moustache and trying gently to free himself.

'Stay awhile yet. Just a little while!'

'But we'll be seen! Look, it's getting light!'

'Never mind that!'

'What about your father?'

'Dad knows.'

'How does he know?' Grigory's eyebrow quivered in surprise.

'He just knows...'

'That a fine way to talk! Who told him then?'

'It was last night, you see. He told me, if the officer makes up to you, go and sleep with him. Be nice to him, or they'll take the horses or something else because of

Gerasim. My husband, Gerasim, is with the Reds...'

'So that's it!' Grigory said with an amused smile, but underneath he was offended.

She dispelled the unpleasant feeling herself. As she fondled the muscles in his arm, she gave a little gasp.

'My dear husband isn't like you!'

'What's he like then?' Grigory inquired, looking up at the paling rim of the sky with more sober eyes.

'He's no good. He's flabby.' She nestled up to him trustingly and dry tears sounded in her voice. 'I never had it real sweet from him all the time we lived together. He's no good with women.'

She opened her innocent young heart to Grigory as simply as a flower opens to drink the dew. It was intoxicating, and wakened a faint sense of pity. Grigory fondled his chance love's dishevelled hair and closed his tired eyes.

The fading light of the moon filtered through the rush roof of the overhang. A shooting star dived for the horizon, leaving a cool phosphorescent trail in the ashen sky. In the pond a wild duck started quacking and her mate answered with loving huskiness.

Grigory walked back to his room, carrying his drained, deliciously aching body lightly. He fell asleep with the salty tang of her lips on his and cherishing the memory of the Cossack girl's love-hungry body and its mingled smells of thyme honey, sweat and warmth.

Two hours later he was awakened by his men. Prokhor Zykov saddled his horse and led it out of the gate. Grigory took leave of his host, firmly withstanding his smoulderingly hostile stare and nodded to the daughter as she walked past into the house. She bowed her head, nursing a smile and the faint bitterness of regret in the corners of her thin, pale-red lips.

Grigory rode away down the lane, looking back. The lane skirted the yard where he had spent the night and through the fence he saw the woman he had befriended watching him from under her slim brown hand and turning her head as he rode by. He felt an unexpected surge of yearning and tried to picture the expression on her face, her figure, all of her, but saw only the woman's head in its white kerchief turning slowly as her eyes followed him. Just like a sunflower, as it traces the slow course of the sun across the sky.

Mikhail Koshevoi was marched under escort from Vyoshenskaya to the front. But when he had gone as far as Fedoseyevskaya, the local ataman detained him for a day, then sent him back to Vyoshenskaya.

'Why are you sending me back?' Mikhail asked the clerk.

'Orders from Vyoshenskaya,' was the reluctant reply.

It turned out that Mishka's mother had pleaded on her knees before the elders of the village and they had written a letter on behalf of the community, requesting that Mikhail Koshevoi, his family's only provider, should be made a herdsman. Miron took the letter to the Vyoshenskaya ataman himself and the request was granted.

Mishka stood at attention in the office while the ataman bawled at him, then the ataman lowered his pitch and ended crossly, 'We don't trust Bolsheviks with the defence of the Don! You shall go off to the range and serve as a herdsman, then we'll see. And watch out, you son-of-a-bitch! I'm sorry for your mother, or I'd... Get out now!'

Mishka set off along the scorching streets without an escort. His rolled greatcoat was chafing his shoulder. His feet, sore from the hundred and fifty versts he had already marched, refused to obey him. He only just managed the distance to his own village and on the next day, wept over and caressed by his mother, rode off to the range with a memory of his mother's ageing face and the grey strands he had noticed in her hair for the first time.

To the south of Karginskaya lay a tract of virgin steppe, twenty-eight versts long and six versts across, that had never known the plough. This great stretch of land was reserved for grazing the stanitsa's stallions and was known as the range. Every year on St. George's Day the herdsmen led the restless stallions out of their winter stables in Vyoshenskaya and drove them out to this huge grazing ground. In the middle of the range a stable with open summer stalls for eighteen stallions had been built at the expense of the stanitsa. Close by there was a long log hut for the herdsmen, the overseer and the veterinary surgeon. The Cossacks of Vyoshenskaya District would bring out their young mares and the surgeon and the overseer would make sure that no mare was less than fourteen hands high or younger than four years.

The healthy ones were assigned to herds of forty. Each stallion took his herd out into the steppe and guarded it jealously.

Mishka rode out to the range on the only mare his family possessed. When seeing him off, his mother had said as she wiped her tears on her apron, 'That mare might give us a foal, you know... Mind you look after her, don't ride her too hard. We need another horse, that we do!'

At noon Mishka caught a hazy glimpse of the iron roof of the hut, the fence, and the grey, weathered roof of the stables. He urged on the mare and, on reaching the top of the next ridge, spotted the buildings of the camp and the milky flood of grassland beyond them. Far away to the east a moving reddish-brown spot indicated a herd of horses making for a pond; the mounted herdsman trotting at their side looked like a toy rider glued to a toy horse.

Mishka rode into the yard, dismounted, tied the reins to the porch and entered the building. In the wide corridor he ran into one of the herdsmen, a shortish freckled Cossack.

'Who're you looking for?' he asked abruptly, surveying Mishka from head to foot.

'I'd like to see the overseer.'

'Strukov? He's off somewhere. Sazonov's here, his assistant. Second door on the left... What do you want him for? Where're you from?'

'I'm to be a herdsman here.'

'They push all kinds on to us.'

He walked muttering towards the door. The lasso looped over his shoulder dragged on the floor behind him. He opened the door and, standing with his back to Mishka, waved his whip and said more amicably, 'Our job's a tough one, mate. Sometimes you're in the saddle for two days at a stretch.'

Mishka stared at his stooped back and bandy legs. The Cossack's ungainly figure stood out in sharp relief against the light of the doorway. The bow legs amused Mishka. Looks as if he'd been sitting on a barrel for forty years, he thought, chuckling to himself as his eyes searched for the doorhandle.

Sazonov received the new herdsman with majestic indifference.

Soon the overseer himself, Sergeant-Major Afanasy Strukov, a burly Cossack guardsman, arrived. He had

Koshevoi enrolled for allowances and walked out with him into the white sultry heat of the porch.

'Do you know how to break in horses? Ever done it?'

'Never had to,' Mishka confessed frankly and at once noticed a flash of disapproval on the overseer's heat-bemused face.

Twisting his mighty shoulders to scratch his sweating back, the overseer stared stolidly into Mishka's eyes.

'Can you throw a lasso?'

'Yes.'

'Are you good to horses?'

'Yes, I am.'

'They're like people, only they're dumb. Be good to 'em,' he ordered and, with a sudden fury, shouted, 'And mind you are! Don't just rely on your whip!'

His face became intelligent and animated for a moment, but the animation soon disappeared and every feature acquired a hard husk of stolid indifference.

'Married?'

'No.'

'Then you're a fool! You ought to get married,' the overseer retorted joyfully.

He paused expectantly, gazing at the great exposed bosom of the steppe, then yawned and walked back into the hut. In a whole month's service on the range Mishka never heard another word from him.

Altogether there were fifty-five stallions on the range. Each herdsman had to mind two or three herds. Mishka was given a large one, led by a powerful old stallion named Bakhar, and another, smaller herd of about twenty mares under a stallion called Banalny. The overseer summoned one of the most efficient and fearless herdsmen, Ilya Soldatov, and gave him his instructions.

'Here's a new herdsman, Mikhail Koshevoi, from Tatarsky village. Show him Banalny's and Bakhar's herds and give him a lasso. He'll be living in your shelter. Show him round. Dismiss.'

Soldatov lighted a cigarette in silence and nodded to Mishka.

'Come on.'

On the porch he glanced at Mishka's little mare standing sleepily in the sun.

'Is that your nag?'

'Yes, she's mine.'

'Is she with foal?'

'No.'

'Mate her with Bakhar. He's from the Korolyov stud. He's got English blood in him. Real fast he is!.. Well, mount up.'

They rode along side by side, their horses knee-deep in the grass. The hut and stables lay far behind. Ahead stretched the silent and majestic steppe, veiled in a gossamer-fine haze. In the zenith the sun languished behind a curl of small opal clouds. A rich clinging aroma rose from the hot grass. To the right, in a vaguely outlined dip a pond gave an inviting pearly-white smile. And all around, as far as the eye could see, lay a green boundless expanse, quivering streams of haze, the ancient steppe held fast by the noonday heat, and on the horizon, dreamlike and inaccessible, a beetling, blue-grey look-out mound.

From the root up the grass was a rich green turning to verdigris only at the sunlit tips. The unripe feathergrass waved its shaggy plumes, the curly imurka made rings across it, the couchgrass reached up greedily towards the sun, lifting high its seed-heavy spikelets. Here and there a stunted shrub, interspersed with sage, clung blindly to the ground, then again the feather-grass spread in a flood, giving way to a variety of grasses—wild oats, yellow winter cress, spurge and chingis grass, a stern unsociable herb, loving only its own kind and ousting all others from its domain.

The Cossacks rode on in silence. Mishka was experiencing a sense of resigned contentment that he had not known for many a day. He was overawed by the stillness and grandeur of the steppe. His companion was simply asleep in the saddle, leaning towards the horse's mane, his freckled hands clasped over the saddle-bow as though he were about to take the sacrament.

A bustard flew up right in front of them and swept away across a ravine, its white underfeathers sparkling in the sun. A breeze, which perhaps only that morning had rippled the Azov Sea, blew from the south, flattening the grass.

After half an hour they reached a herd grazing near Aspen Pond. Soldatov woke up, stretched himself and said lazily, 'That's Pantelei Lomakin's herd. Can't see him anywhere tho'.'

'What's the stallion's name?' Mishka asked, admiring the long-backed light chestnut Don stallion.

'Frazer. He's a fierce bastard! Look at the way he rolls his eyes! There! Off he goes!'

The stallion had swung away with the mares following him in a bunch.

Mishka took over the herds assigned to him and put his few belongings in the shelter. Before his arrival, there had been three men living in the shelter: Soldatov, Lomakin, and a hired herdsman, an elderly taciturn Cossack named Turoverov. Soldatov was the senior man there. He willingly introduced Mishka to his duties, told him about the characters and habits of the stallions and, with a knowing smile, advised him 'By rights you're supposed to do your work on your own horse, but if you keep her at it day after day you'll soon wear her out. Put her in with the herd, saddle up one of the others and keep changing.'

While Mishka watched, he drove one of the mares out of the herd, went into a gallop and lassoed her with practised skill. When he had put Mishka's saddle on her, he led the trembling, resisting horse up to him.

'Get on her! Looks as if she's not been ridden before, the devil! Get on!' he shouted angrily, holding the reins tight with his right hand and squeezing the mare's distended nostrils with his left. 'Go easy with 'em. This isn't the stables, where you can bark at a stallion to move over and he moves. No nonsense here! And be very careful of Bakhar. Don't ride up close or he'll kick you,' he said, holding the stirrup for Mishka and fondling the restlessly stamping mare's tight satiny black udder.

III

For a week Mishka took it easy and enjoyed himself, spending days on end in the saddle. The steppe humbled him. Imperiously it forced him to lead a primitive, vegetable existence. The herd would be roaming somewhere not far away, while he either sat dozing in the saddle or lay in the grass and thoughtlessly watched the flocks of frosty-edged clouds being herded across the sky by the wind. At first this state of abnegation satisfied him. He even liked this remote, secluded life. But by the end of the week, when he had grown used to his new circumstances, he felt a dimly awakening fear. 'Out there people are deciding how they and others should live, and I'm here just grazing a lot of mares. I can't go on like this. I must get away or it'll drag me

31

down,' he thought more soberly. But then a different, lazy whisper seeped into his brain. 'Let them fight it out. Death is on the prowl out there, but here you have freedom, the grass and sky. Out there it's all hate, but here there's peace. Why should I bother about the rest of the world?' Such thoughts gnawed persistently at Mishka's new-found peace of mind and drove him to seek the company of others. More often than at first he went out of his way to meet Soldatov, who was grazing his herds near Dudarev Pond, and tried to make friends with him.

Apparently Soldatov was not burdened by loneliness. He seldom spent the night in the hut and was nearly always to be found with the herd or by the pond. He led an animal-like existence, providing for himself, and did so with remarkable skill, as though he had been doing it all his life. One day Mishka noticed him plaiting a line out of horse hair.

'What's the line for?'

'Fish.'

'Where is it?'

'In the pond. Carp.'

'What's the bait—red worm?'

'Red worm and bread.'

'Do you boil your fish?'

'I dry it and eat it. Here, have some,' he said hospitably, taking a dried carp out of his trousers' pocket.

One day when he was following his herd, Mishka came across a trapped bustard. Nearby stood a skilfully made decoy with carefully concealed traps staked out all round it in the grass. That evening Soldatov baked the bustard in a pit filled with hot embers. He invited Mishka to have supper with him and, as he pulled apart the fragrant flesh, said, 'Don't take it out next time, or you'll spoil my work.'

'How do you come to be here?'

'I'm my family's only provider.'

Soldatov was silent for a while then asked suddenly, 'Is it true what the lads say about you being a Red?'

The question took Mishka by surprise.

'No... Well, how shall I put it... I was going off to join 'em... But I got caught.'

'Why did you go? What were you after?' Soldatov asked softly, stern-eyed, chewing more slowly.

The campfire was at the top of a waterless ravine. The dried dung was smoking heavily and a flame was trying to break out of the ash. Behind them the night breathed the dry warmth and scent of the fading wormwood. Shooting stars were slashing the black sky. When one of them fell, its fluffy trail lingered in the sky like the mark of a whip on a horse's crupper.

Mishka cautiously scanned Soldatov's face as it caught the golden light of the fire, and replied, 'I wanted to get some rights.'

'Who for?' Soldatov cut in quickly.

'The people.'

'What kind of rights? Tell me.'

Soldatov's voice was low and stealthy. For a moment Mishka hesitated, thinking that Soldatov had deliberately put some fresh fuel on the fire to hide the expression of his face. He made up his mind and spoke.

'Equal rights for all—that's what! No masters and no slaves. Understand? They'll do away with all that.'

'Don't you think the Cadets will win?'

'No, I don't.'

'So that's what you want...' Soldatov drew a deep breath and suddenly jumped to his feet. 'You bastard, you want to sell out the Cossacks to the Yids?!' he cried fiercely. 'You... I'd like to smash you and all your kind— you want to uproot us?! Ah, so that's it!... You want the Yids to build their factories all over the steppe? And take our land away?!'

Mishka rose slowly to his feet. He was astounded. Was Soldatov going to hit him? He recoiled and the other man, seeing his frightened step backwards, swung his arm. Mishka caught it in mid-air and, squeezing the wrist, warned him,

'Drop it, man, or I'll clout you! What's all the noise about?'

They stood facing each other in the darkness. The fire they had trampled on went out; only a lump of dung that had rolled aside still glowed smokily. Soldatov grabbed the front of Mishka's shirt with his left hand and hoisted it up, trying to free his right.

'Hands off!' Mishka gasped, twisting his powerful neck. 'Let go, I tell you! I'll hurt you, d'you hear?'

'Hurt me, would you? No, I'll... Just wait!' Soldatov panted.

Breaking free, Mishka pushed him hard and, experiencing a hateful desire to knock him down and give free play to his fists, stood back nervously pulling his shirt straight.

Soldatov did not approach him. Grinding his teeth and swearing, he shouted, 'I'll report you!.. I'll have you up before the overseer! I'll get you gaoled!.. You snake! Scum!.. Bolshevik!.. You ought to be dealt with like Podtyolkov! Strung up! On the gallows!'

'He'll do it. He'll make up all kinds of things and they'll put me in prison. They won't send me to the front, so I won't be able to desert to my own side. It's all up with me!' Mishka went cold and his thoughts threshed about desperately, like a fish cut off from the river by the receding flood. 'I'll have to kill him! I'll choke him... There's no other way...' And in obedience to this momentary decision, his brain found an excuse. 'I'll say he flew at me with his fists, I got him by the throat and it happened by accident... In the heat of the moment.'

Mishka took a trembling step towards Soldatov and if the other man had run at that moment there would have been blood and death between them. But Soldatov stood there swearing and Mishka weakened; his legs began to tremble feebly and sweat broke out on his back and under his arms.

'Wait a bit, Soldatov... D'you hear? Don't shout. After all, you started it.'

And Mishka began to plead abjectly, jaw quivering and shifty-eyed.

'We were only talking like friends... I didn't hit you... And you grabbed my shirt... Did I say anything very terrible? You'd have to prove it, wouldn't you?.. If I offended you, I'm sorry... Honestly I am! Come on now?'

Gradually Soldatov calmed down and stopped shouting. About a minute later he said turning away and wrenching his hand out of Koshevoi's clammy grip, 'You wriggle like a snake! All right then, I won't say anything. I pity your foolishness... But keep out of my way, I never want to see you again! You're a swine! You've sold out to the Yids and I don't like people who sell themselves.'

Mishka smiled wretchedly in the darkness, although Soldatov could not see his face—any more than he could see the swelling veins in Mishka's clenched fists.

They parted without another word. Koshevoi lashed his horse furiously and galloped off to look for his herd. Lightning flared in the east and there was a rumble of thunder.

That night a storm broke over the range. Towards

34

midnight the wind came panting up like an overridden horse and brought with it an invisible wave of cool air and bitter dust.

The sky grew murky. Lightning cut a slanting furrow through a towering cloud that was as black as the black earth; then came a long pause and far away the thunder rolled warningly. Big granular drops of rain flattened the grass. A second, circular flash of lightning showed Koshevoi a menacing brownish cloud with black charred edges spread across half the sky, and on the earth below, a knot of tiny horses bunched together. There was a terrifying clap of thunder and lightning raced to earth. After another thunderclap rain gushed out of the cloud, the steppe gave a faint mutter, and a whirling gust of wind whipped Koshevoi's wet cap off his head and bent him over his saddle-bow. For about a minute there was swirling darkness, then the lightning again caracoled across the sky, making the darkness even more intense. The next stroke of thunder was so violent and came with such an explosive crack that his horse fell back with a snort and then reared on its hindlegs. The horses in the herd began to stampede. Holding the reins with all his strength, Koshevoi shouted in an attempt to calm them,

'Whoa there! Steady!'

In the sugar-white glare of lightning that went bounding across the cloud crests Koshevoi saw the herd charging towards him. The horses were straining forward in a wild gallop, their gleaming muzzles almost touching the ground. Their distended nostrils drew snorting breaths, their unshod hooves beat a soggy tattoo on the damp earth. Bakhar was out in front, coming on at full speed. Koshevoi dragged his horse round and just managed to ride clear. The horses dashed past and halted not far away. Not knowing that the herd, excited and frightened by the storm, had charged in response to his shout, Koshevoi shouted again, even louder,

'Whoa! Steady there!'

And again—this time in darkness—the rumble of hooves came towards him at terrifying speed. In sheer terror he lashed his mount between the eyes but it was too late. A fear-maddened horse charged his mare from behind and Koshevoi was catapulted out of the saddle. By a miracle he was not trampled to death; the main herd passed to the right and only his hand was stamped into the mud by a mare's hoof. Mishka rose to his feet and walked away as quietly as possible. He could feel the herd only a short distance away, just waiting for his shout, to come at him again in a mad stampede. He could make out Bakhar's distinctive snorting.

It was nearly daybreak when he reached the herdsmen's shelter.

IV

On May 15th, Ataman of the Grand Don Army Krasnov, accompanied by Major-General Afrikan Bogayevsky, chairman of the Council of Heads of Departments, and head of the Department for Foreign Affairs, Colonel Kislov, Quartermaster-General of the Don Army, and Ataman of the Kuban Filimonov, arrived by steamship at the stanitsa of Manychskaya.

While the ship was being moored, the masters of the Don and Kuban lands looked down languidly at the bustling sailors, and at the brownish waves foaming and falling back from the gangway. They disembarked, watched by the hundreds of eyes of the crowd assembled round the pier.

The sky, the horizon, the day, the shimmering haze were all blue. Even the Don had an unusual light-blue tint and reflected the snowy summits of the clouds like a convex mirror.

The wind was charged with the scents of sunshine, dried-up salt marshes and last year's rotting grass. A rustle of talk rose from the crowd. The generals were met by the local authorities and drove off to the square.

An hour later a conference between representatives of the Don Government and the Volunteer Army began in the house of the stanitsa ataman. The Volunteer Army was represented by generals Denikin and Alexeyev, accompanied by General Romanovsky, the army's chief of staff, and colonels Ryasnyansky and Evald.

The atmosphere of the meeting was cool. Krasnov was heavily dignified. Alexeyev greeted the assembled company and at once sat down at the table, resting his pendulous cheeks on his lean white hands and closing his eyes indifferently. The car journey had made him feel sick. He seemed to have shrunk with age and the shocks he had experienced. There was a tragic curve in the lines of his thin mouth, and his blue, veined eyelids were bloated. A multitude of fine wrinkles fanned towards the temples. The fingers clamped to the flabby skin of the cheeks ran their tips into the yellowing short-clipped hair. Colonel Ryasnyansky, helped by Kislov, carefully spread out a stiff, crackling map on the table. Romanovsky stood over them, holding a corner of the map with the nail of his little finger. Bogayevsky leaned back against the low window, watching Alexeyev's exhausted face with keen sympathy. It was as white as a plaster mask. 'How he has aged! How terribly aged he looks!' Bogayevsky thought to himself, keeping his liquid almond-shaped eyes fixed on Alexeyev. They were not all seated, when Denikin addressed Krasnov in sharp emotionally charged tones.

'Before opening the conference, I must tell you that we are extremely surprised to see it indicated in your plan for the capture of Bataisk that your right-hand column is to be supported by a German battalion and battery. I must confess that I find such collaboration more than strange... May I be informed of your motives in entering into relations with enemies of our country — with utterly dishonourable enemies!—and availing yourself of their assistance? You must, of course, be aware that the Allies have offered us their support?.. The Volunteer Army regards alliance with the Germans as betrayal of the cause of the restoration of Russia. The actions of the Don Government are similarly regarded in broad Allied circles. Will you, pray, give us an explanation.'

With one eyebrow angrily arched, Denikin waited for the reply.

Only thanks to his self-control and polished manners was Krasnov able to maintain an appearance of composure; but indignation claimed its own and under the greying moustache a nervous tick pulled at his mouth. Very calmly and very politely he replied, 'When the fate of the whole cause is at stake, the help even of former enemies is not to be scorned. And in any case the Don Government, the government of a sovereign nation of five million people, which is under no one's protection, has the right to act independently, in accordance with the Cossack interests it is called upon to defend.'

At these words Alexeyev opened his eyes and, evidently with a great effort, tried to listen attentively. Krasnov glanced at Bogayevsky, who was nervously twisting the waxed tip of his moustache, and went on.

'Your reasoning, Your Excellency, appears to be predominantly of an ethical nature. You have committed yourself to a statement about what you choose to call our betrayal of the Russian cause, betrayal of the Allies... But I assume you are aware of the fact that the Volunteer Army has received from us shells that were sold to us by the Germans?'

'Will you kindly distinguish between things of an entirely different character! It is no concern of mine how you get ammunition from the Germans, but to rely on their troops for support!..' Denikin shrugged angrily.

Krasnov concluded his speech by hinting guardedly but firmly that he was no longer the same brigade general that Denikin had known on the Austro-German front.

Breaking the awkward silence that ensued, Denikin wisely turned the conversation to the subject of merging the Don and Volunteer armies and setting up a joint command. But the preceding altercation was, in effect, the beginning of a further steady deterioration in the relations between them, which, by the time Krasnov resigned from the government, had broken down completely.

Krasnov gave no direct answer to Denikin's proposal and, instead, suggested a combined attack on Tsaritsyn with the object first of capturing a vital strategic centre and, second, when this had been achieved, of linking up with the Cossacks of the Urals.

A brief exchange took place.

'I need hardly speak of the colossal importance Tsaritsyn has for us.'

'The Volunteer Army might run into the Germans. I won't march on Tsaritsyn. My first duty is to liberate the Cossacks of the Kuban.'

'Yes, but the capture of Tsaritsyn is a task of paramount importance. The Government of the Don Army has instructed me to ask Your Excellency.'

'I must repeat that I cannot abandon the Kuban.'

'The question of a joint command can be discussed only on the condition that we attack Tsaritsyn.'

Alexeyev bit his lip disapprovingly.

'Unthinkable! The Kuban Cossacks won't go beyond their own borders until their territory has been completely cleared of Bolsheviks. The Volunteer Army has only two and a half thousand infantry and a third of them are out of action, either sick or wounded.'

Over a modest meal the talk consisted of a few insignificant remarks and it was clear that no agreement would be reached. Colonel Ryasnyansky described an amusing, almost anecdotic exploit by one of Markov's men, and gradually, under the combined influence of the meal and the merry tale the tension relaxed. But after dinner, when they retired to the front room to smoke, Denikin touched Romanovsky on the shoulder and, indicating Krasnov with narrowed eyes, whispered, 'A provincial Napoleon... Not a very intelligent man, I think.'

Romanovsky smiled and replied quickly, 'He longs to rule and hold sway... A brigade general revelling in a monarch's power. I believe he has no sense of humour...'

They parted full of enmity and dislike. From that day on the relations between the Volunteer Army and the Don Government deteriorated rapidly and the deterioration reached its climax when the contents of Krasnov's letter to the German Emperor Wilhelm became known to the command of the Volunteer Army. Wounded volunteers convalescing in Novocherkassk laughed at Krasnov's aspirations to autonomy and his weakness for the restoration of Cossack traditions, and among themselves referred to him in scornful and rustic accents as 'the master', and substituted 'all-merry' for 'almighty' in the official title of the Don Army. The devotees of Donland autonomy responded by calling them 'wandering minstrels' and 'rulers without territory'. One of the 'great men' in the Volunteer Army remarked caustically that the Don Government was 'a prostitute earning her keep in a German bed'. And in reply to this came General Denisov's remark: 'If the Don Government is a prostitute, the Volunteer Army is the ponce living on her earnings.'

The reply was an allusion to the Volunteer Army's dependence on the Don, which shared with it the military supplies obtained from Germany.

The cities of Rostov and Novocherkassk in the rear of the Volunteer Army were swarming with officers, like carrion with maggots. In their thousands they profiteered, served in the innumerable rear-support establishments, lodged uncomfortably with relatives and acquaintances, or stayed in hospital with forged papers saying they had been wounded... All the bravest had been killed in action or died from wounds or typhus, and the rest, who through the years of revolution had lost both honour and conscience, skulked like jackals in the rear, floating like scum, like horse manure on the surface of that heroic time. These were the unscathed, mummified officer personnel whom Chernetsov had in his time thunderously exposed and held up to shame in his calls to defend Russia. For the most part they were the nastiest specimens of the so-called 'thinking intelligentsia' in uniform. Having fled from the Bolsheviks without joining the Whites, they led a hole-and-corner existence, arguing about Russia's destiny, trying to make ends meet, and wishing only for the war to end.

It was all the same to them who ruled the country — Krasnov, the Germans, or the Bolsheviks. All they wanted was an end to the war.

But every day brought a fresh explosion of events. The mutiny of the Czechoslovak troops in Siberia, the anarchist Makhno in the Ukraine, who was now talking to the Germans more maturely in the plain accents of artillery and machine-guns. The Caucasus, Archangel, Finland... All Russia was ringed with fire... All Russia was enduring the torment of the great remaking.

In June, rumours that the Czechoslovaks were occupying Saratov, Tsaritsyn and Astrakhan in order to form an Eastern Front for an offensive against the Germans, swept the Don like an east wind. The Germans in the Ukraine showed reluctance to grant safe-conducts to officers escaping from Russia to serve with the Volunteer Army.

Alarmed by the rumours of an 'eastern front', the German command sent its representatives to the Don. On July 10th three majors of the German army—von Kokenhausen, von Stefani and von Schleinitz—arrived in Novocherkassk.

On the same day they were received at the palace by Ataman Krasnov with General Bogayevsky in attendance.

Major Kokenhausen recalled the fact that the German command had given every assistance, up to and including armed intervention, to the Grand Don Army in the struggle to expel the Bolsheviks and restore its borders, and asked how the Don Government would react if the Czechoslovaks launched military operations against the Germans. Krasnov assured him that the Cossacks would observe strict neutrality and, of course, not allow the Don to become an arena of war. Major von Stefani expressed the hope that the ataman's reply would be confirmed in writing.

At this point the audience ended and the next day Krasnov wrote the following letter to the German Emperor.

40

Your Imperial and Royal Majesty!

The bearer of this letter, the envoy of the Grand Don Army at the court of Your Imperial Majesty, and his comrades, are authorised by me, the Don Ataman, to convey greetings to Your Imperial Majesty, the mighty monarch of great Germany, and to communicate the following:

Two months of the struggle which the valiant Don Cossacks are waging for the freedom of their country with the same courage that in recent times was displayed by the Boers, a nation related to the German people, in their struggle against the British, have been crowned with complete victory on all the borders of our country, and the land of the Grand Don Army is now nine-tenths liberated from the barbaric Red Guard bands. Order has been strengthened within the country and complete legality has been established. Thanks to the friendly assistance rendered by the troops of Your Imperial Majesty calm has been restored to the south of the Army's territory and I have prepared a corps of Cossacks to maintain law and order in the country and prevent any enemy encroachment from outside. It is difficult for a young body politic such as the Don Army represents at the moment to exist alone and it has therefore concluded a close alliance with the leaders of the Astrakhan and Kuban Armies, Colonel Prince Tundutov and Colonel Filimonov, so that when the lands of the Astrakhan and Kuban Armies have been cleared of Bolsheviks, a strong state formation based on principles of federation may be organised out of the Grand Don Army, the Astrakhan Army with the Kalmyks of Stavropol Province, the Kuban Army, and also the peoples of the North Caucasus. The consent of all these powers has been granted and the newly formed state, in complete agreement with the Grand Don Army, has decided not to allow its lands to become an arena of conflict and bloodshed, and has undertaken to observe strict neutrality. Our envoy at Your Imprerial Majesty's court has been authorised by me:

To request Your Imperial Majesty to recognise the right of the Grand Don Army to independent existence and, as the lands of the remaining Kuban, Astrakhan and Terek Armies and the North Caucasus are liberated, the right of the whole federation to independent existence under the title of the Don-Caucasus Alliance.

To request Your Imperial Majesty to recognise the borders of the Grand Don Army in its former geographical and ethnographical dimensions to help resolve the dispute between the Ukraine and the Don Army over Taganrog and its military district in favour of the Don Army, which has been in possession of the Taganrog district for more than 500 years and which regards the Taganrog district as part of Tmutarakan, from which the Don Army land originated.

To request Your Majesty to assist in annexing for strategic reasons to the Don Army Region the cities of Kamyshin and Tsaritsyn of the Saratov Province and also the city of Voronezh, and the stations of Liski and Povorino, and to define the border of the Don Army Region as it is defined on the map in the Don Army's embassy.

To request Your Majesty to bring pressure to bear on the Soviet authorities in Moscow and force them by your order to clear the territory of the Grand Don Army and other powers intending to join the Don-Caucasus Alliance of the marauding bands of the Red Army, and make it possible to restore normal peaceful relations between Moscow and the Don Army. All the losses incurred by the population of the Don Army Region, trade and industry, in the course of the Bolshevik invasions, shall be reimbursed by Soviet Russia.

To request Your Imperial Majesty to help the young state with guns, rifles, ammunition and engineering equipment and, should you see this as being to your advantage, to build arsenals and ammunition factories on the territory of the Don Army.

The Grand Don Army and other countries of the Don-Caucasus Alliance will not forget the friendly services of the German nation, with whom the Cossacks fought shoulder to shoulder at the time of the Thirty Years' War, when there were Don regiments in the Wallenstein army, and in 1807-1813, when the Don Cossacks under their Ataman Count Platov fought for the freedom of Germany, while now in nearly three and a half years of bloody warfare on the fields of Prussia, Galicia, Bukovina and Poland the Cossacks and Germans have learned mutual respect for the bravery and endurance of their troops and today have shaken hands like two noble warriors and are fighting together for the freedom to our native Don.

The Grand Don Army undertakes in return for the services of Your Imperial Majesty to observe complete neutrality during the world conflict of nations and not to allow on its territory any armed forces hostile to the German nation; the Ataman of the Astrakhan Army, Prince Tundutov, and the Kuban government, have agreed to this, as will the remaining members of the Don-Caucasus Alliance upon their unification.

The Grand Don Army grants the German Empire the right of preference to export stocks exceeding local requirements of such products as grain and flour, leather goods and raw materials, wool, fish products, vegetable and animal fats and oils, and their products, tobacco and tobacco goods, cattle and horses, grape wine and other produce of horticulture and agricultural products, in return for which the German Empire will supply agricultural machinery, chemicals and tanning agents, equipment for the manufacture of state documents and adequate supplies of material, and equipment for woollen, cotton, leather, chemical, sugar and other factories, and also electrical machinery and appliances.

In addition the Government of the Grand Don Army will grant German industry special privileges for the investment of capital in Don industrial and commercial enterprises, particularly in the building and exploitation of new waterways and other communications.

Close agreement promises mutual advantages, and the friendship sealed with the blood that has been shed on the common battlefields by the martial German and Cossack peoples will be a powerful force for combating all our enemies.

This letter to Your Imperial Majesty comes not from a diplomat, not from a scholar versed in all the subtleties of international law, but from a soldier, who has learned in honourable battle to respect the strength of German arms. I therefore beg Your Majesty to excuse a forthrightness of tone to which all subterfuge is alien, and to believe in the complete sincerity of my feelings.

> *Yours respectfully,*
> *Pyotr Krasnov,*
> *Ataman of the Don,*
> *Major-General*

* * *

On July 15th the letter was considered by the Council of Heads of Departments and, although the attitude towards it was generally restrained and, on the part of Bogayevsky and some other members of the government clearly negative, Krasnov lost no time in handing it to the Duke of Lichtenberg, the Cossack envoy in Berlin, who took it to Kiev, and from there, accompanied by General Cheryachukin, to Germany.

Not without Bogayevsky's knowledge the Foreign Department made copies of the letter before sending it. These copies were circulated widely and then, with suitable commentaries, made the rounds of the Cossack units and stanitsas. The letter acted as a powerful propaganda weapon. Louder and louder grew the voices saying that Krasnov had sold out to the Germans. Protest flared up at the front.

Meanwhile the Germans, elated by their successes, took the Russian General Cheryachukin to the battlefields near Paris, where in the company of high-ranking officers of the German general staff he observed the impressive performance of Krupp's heavy artillery and the routing of the British and French forces.

V

During Kornilov's retreat from Rostov that afterwards became known as the Ice March, Yevgeny Listnitsky was wounded twice, first in the fighting for the stanitsa of Ust-Labinskaya, and a second time in the assault on Yekaterinodar. Both wounds were slight and he was soon back in action. But in May, when the Volunteer Army halted for a brief rest in the area of Novocherkassk, Listnitsky began to feel unwell and managed to obtain two weeks' leave. Much though he would have liked to go home, he decided to stay in Novocherkassk and rest without wasting time on travelling.

Major Gorchakov, a fellow officer in his platoon, went on leave with him and invited him to stay at his house.

'I have no children and my wife will be glad to see you. She knows about you from my letters.'

At noon on a day when the sun was blazing as hot and white as in summer they drove up to a squat little mansion in a street near the station.

'Here it is, my residence of days gone by,' the lanky, black-moustached Gorchakov said, striding forward with a glance over his shoulder at Listnitsky.

His prominent bluish-black eyes were moist with joyful excitement and a smile pulled at the tip of his big Grecian nose. He strode into the house with the worn leather patches on his khaki riding breeches rustling drily and at once filled the room with the smell of the trenches.

'Where's Olga? Olga Nikolayevna?' he called to the smiling maid who had hurried out of the kitchen. 'In the garden? Come with me.'

The apple-trees in the orchard spread a tigerskin of shadows and the air smelled of bee-hives and sun-charred earth. Sunbeams caught in the lenses of Listnitsky's pince-nez splintered like shrapnel. Somewhere in a siding a locomotive was bellowing insatiably; Gorchakov's voice broke through its monotonous clamour.

'Olga! Olga! Where are you?'

A tall woman in a pale-yellow dress appeared momentarily behind some bushes of sweet briar, then stepped out from a side path. For a second she stood motionless with her hands clasped to her breast in a frightened and lovely gesture, then held them out and ran forward with a cry. She ran so fast that Listnitsky noticed only the roundness of the knees pushing at her skirt, the pointed toes of her shoes and her hair that fluffed like golden pollen as she threw back her head.

Reaching up, she flung her bare, sun-pink arms round her husband's neck and kissed his dust-grimed cheeks, nose, eyes, lips and dark, weatherbeaten neck. Her quick smacking kisses came in bursts, like machine-gun fire.

Listnitsky wiped his pince-nez, breathing in the scent of verbena that rose around him and, quite consciously, allowed a strained utterly foolish smile to take possession of his face.

When the explosion of joy had subsided, Gorchakov tenderly but firmly unlocked his wife's fingers, put his arm round her shoulders and gently turned her.

'Olga, this is my friend Listnitsky.'

'Ah, Listnitsky! I'm so glad! My husband has told me about you—' she paused for breath and glanced at him with laughing, unseeing eyes.

They walked back to the house together. Gorchakov's hairy hand with its ill-kempt nails and scarred fingers held his wife's girlish waist. Listnitsky glanced sideways at it as he walked along, drinking in the scent of the verbena and the woman's sunwarmed body, and felt deeply and childishly unhappy, as though he had been bitterly and for no reason offended by someone. He glanced at the pink lobe of Olga's small ear, half-concealed by a golden-russet lock of hair, at the silky skin of her cheek only an arm's length away from him; his eyes darted lizard-like to the low neck of her dress and focused on the small milk-yellow mounds of her breasts and a brown, compressed nipple. Occasionally Olga turned her light-blue eyes towards him; their glance was affectionate and friendly, but he was stung with disappointment when they raced back to Gorchakov's grimy face, radiating a quite different light.

Only over dinner was Listnitsky able to examine the mistress of the house as thoroughly as he wished. In both her shapely figure and her face there was the fading beauty of a woman who had seen her thirtieth autumn. But her mocking, rather cold eyes and her movements still retained an unspent reserve of youth. Her face with its soft, attractively irregular features was, perhaps, quite ordinary, except for one striking contrast: the thin, dark-red, passion-parched lips that should have belonged to a southern brunette and the cheeks with their pink translucent skin and colourless brows. She laughed readily but in the smile that showed her small, close-set teeth there was something slightly affected. Her deep voice was rather dull and toneless. To Listnitsky, who apart from a few dowdy overworked army nurses had not seen a woman for two months, she seemed inordinately beautiful. He gazed at Olga's proudly poised head with its heavy knot of hair, answered questions absent-mindedly and soon withdrew to his room, saying that he was tired.

The sweet wistful days dragged on. Later Listnitsky recalled them reverentially, but at the time he suffered unreasoningly and foolishly, like a small boy. The Gorchakovs were too fond of each other to want his company. From the room adjoining their bedroom they moved him to the far corner of the house. Gorchakov made the excuse that repairs were needed, chewing his moustache and keeping an expression of smiling seriousness on his face, which had suddenly regained its youth. Listnitsky realised that he was in the way, but could not bring himself to go and stay with someone else. He spent the days lying in the dusty orange shade of the apple-trees, reading newspapers hastily printed on coarse wrapping paper, and dozed off into oppressive, unrefreshing sleep. His frustration was shared by a splendid chocolate-and-white pointer. Silently jealous of its master, the dog would lie down sighing at Listnitsky's side and he would stroke it, whispering sympathetically:

> *Dream on, my friend ... while dimmer grows*
> *The gaze of golden-tinted eyes...*

Lovingly he went over in his mind all the rich, honey-scented lines of Bunin's poetry that he could remember, then fell asleep again.

With a woman's instinct Olga sensed the cause of his despondent mood and became even more restrained in her attitude towards him. One evening when they were walking back from the municipal gardens alone (Gorchakov had been detained at the park gate by some officer friends from another regiment) Listnitsky took Olga's arm and disturbed her by pressing her elbow closely to his side.

'Why do you look at me like this?' she asked smiling.

Listnitsky thought he detected a playful, challenging note in her low voice. Otherwise he would never have risked a melancholy line of poetry. (For days his head had been full of verses, and his thoughts carried, like bees to the honeycomb of memory, the haunting song of another's sorrow.)

He leaned forward smiling and whispered:

> *By a strange intimacy possessed*
> *I sought to pierce the veil's dark frond,*
> *And there an enchanted shore I guessed*
> *And enchanted lands beyond.*

She gently freed her arm and said in a merrier tone, 'Yevgeny Nikolayevich, I know enough to... I can't help seeing how you feel about me. Aren't you ashamed! No, wait a minute! I imagined you as rather a—a different kind of person. So let's drop all this. Otherwise it's rather a sham. I'm a poor subject for such experiments. You wanted just a passing affair? Well, let's not break off our friendly relations, but give up the silliness. After all, I'm no "beautiful stranger". Don't you agree? Give me your hand then.'

Listnitsky tried to feign a noble indignation but could not keep it up and eventually joined in her laughter. When Gorchakov caught up with them, Olga became even merrier, but Listnitsky grew silent and mocked himself bitterly all the way home.

Intelligent woman though she was, Olga sincerely believed that after this explanation they would stay friends. Outwardly Listnitsky encouraged her belief, but in his heart he almost began to hate her and a few days later, catching himself desperately trying to find fault with Olga's character and appearance, realised that he was on the verge of falling well and truly in love.

His furlough expired leaving a sediment of unspent feelings in his mind. The Volunteer Army, rested and reinforced, was preparing for new thrusts; centrifugal forces were driving it towards the Kuban, and it was not long before Gorchakov and Listnitsky left Novocherkassk.

Olga saw them off. A black silk dress brought out her unobtrusive beauty. She smiled with wept-out eyes and her swollen lips gave her face a touchingly childlike expression. And so she remained in Listnitsky's memory. Amid the blood and filth of all he had yet to go through he cherished that radiant, unfading image, crowned with a halo of unattainability and adoration.

In June the Volunteer Army went into action. In the very first engagement Major Gorchakov's stomach was gouged by a splinter from a three-inch shell. He was dragged out of the line and an hour later, as he lay on a cart with the last blood and urine oozing out of him, he said to Listnitsky, 'I don't think I'll die... They'll operate on me in a minute. They say there's no chloroform... It'd be a pity to die. What do you think?.. But just in case... I hereby, while in full possession of my senses, and so on... Yevgeny, don't leave Olga... Neither of us has any relatives. You're a fine, honest man. Marry her... Don't you want to?..'

He looked up at Yevgeny with entreaty and hatred, his unshaven bluish cheeks were trembling. With some care he pressed a grimy blood-stained hand to his gaping stomach and licked the pinkish sweat from his lips.

'D'you promise? Don't abandon her—unless you get the same beauty treatment that Russia's soldiers have given me. D'you promise? She's a good woman.' His face twisted in a scowl. 'A woman of the Turgenev breed... They don't exist any more... Do you promise? Have you nothing to say?'

'I promise.'

'All right then, and to hell with you!.. Goodbye!'

He seized Listnitsky's hand in a trembling grip, and with an awkward, desperate effort that made him even paler raised his damp head and pressed his parched lips to it, then turned away hastily, drawing his greatcoat over his head. Listnitsky, shaken to the core, caught a glimpse of his coldly quivering lips and the grey moist smudge on his cheek.

Gorchakov died two days later. The day afterwards Listnitsky was sent off to hospital in Tikhoretskaya with a badly wounded left arm and thigh.

At Korenovskaya a long and stubborn battle had developed. Listnitsky's regiment had attacked and been thrown back twice. His battalion rose for a third attempt. Urged on by the shouts of their company commander, 'Keep going! Forward, my eagles!' 'Forward for Kornilov!' he stumbled through unreaped wheat, a spade in his left hand, to shield his head, rifle in his right. A bullet pinged off the sloping surface of the spade and as he steadied the handle Listnitsky felt a spurt of joy. That one missed me! Then his arm was jerked aside by a quick but stunningly powerful blow. He dropped the spade and in the heat of the moment ran another twenty paces without protection for his head. But when he tried to take his rifle in both hands, he found he could not lift his left arm. Pain flooded into every joint, like boiling lead into a mould. He dropped down in a furrow and, losing control, cried out several times. While he was lying there another bullet bit into his thigh and he slowly and painfully lost consciousness.

In Tikhoretskaya his shattered arm was amputated and a splinter of bone extracted from his thigh. For two weeks he lay in a torment of pain and misery, then he was moved to Novocherkassk and passed another thirty agonising days in hospital. Changing of dressings, the bored faces of the nurses and doctors, the stench of iodine and carbolic... Occasionally Olga came to see him. Her cheeks were sallow. Her mourning dress deepened the misery of her stricken colourless eyes. Listnitsky stared up at them in silence, furtively hiding his empty sleeve under the blanket. As if reluctantly, she asked for details of her husband's death. When he told her, she looked away at the other beds and seemed to listen without attention. On being discharged from hospital, he went to see her. She met him at the porch and turned aside when he bowed his head with its mass of short sunbleached curls to kiss her hand.

He had shaved carefully, his elegant tunic fitted him as perfectly as ever, but the empty sleeve was a torture—

49

the short bandaged stump kept moving spasmodically inside it.

They entered the house. Listnitsky spoke without sitting down.

'Before he died, Boris asked me ... made me promise that I would not abandon you...'

'I know.'

'How?'

'From his last letter.'

'His desire that we should be together... If, of course, you can accept marriage to an invalid... I beg to assure you... For me to speak of my feelings now would be... But I sincerely desire your happiness.'

She was touched by Listnitsky's confusion and faltering speech.

'I have thought about it already... I agree.'

'We'll go to my father's estate.'

'Very well.'

'And we can arrange the formalities later?'

'Yes.'

He respectfully pressed his lips to her hand, which was as light as porcelain, and as he looked up submissively, noticed the shadow of a smile dart from her lips.

Listnitsky was drawn to Olga by love and by lustful desire. He came to see her every day. His war-weary heart was eager for high romance... When alone, he would argue with himself like the hero of a classical novel, patiently seeking elevated feelings that he had never had for anyone, hoping perhaps that they would hide or adorn the nakedness of plain sensual desire. One wing of the romantic tale touched reality, however; he was bound to this woman whom chance had brought into his life, not only by sexual attraction but by some other invisible thread. Scarcely able to understand his own emotions, he sensed only one thing with absolute clarity: though disabled and out of action, he was still ruled by the savage, unbridled instinct 'I can do as I like'. Even while Olga was in mourning, while she was still pregnant with the grief of her irreplaceable loss, he allowed himself to be inflamed by jealousy of the dead Gorchakov and desire her with a frenzied longing. Life was a madly foaming whirlpool. Hard-bitten men, blinded and deafened by what was going on around them, lived fast and greedily, only for the present. And was not this the reason why Yevgeny had hastened to join his and Olga's lives together, perhaps sensing the inevitable failure of the cause for which he had more than once faced death.

He wrote his father a long letter to say that he was getting married and would soon bring his wife to Yagodnoye.

'...I have done my share. I could still go on with only one arm destroying these rebellious swine, this accursed "people" whose fate the Russian intelligentsia has bewailed and slobbered over for decades, but now, I must admit, it all seems utterly senseless... Krasnov can't get on with Denikin, and in both camps there is backbiting, intrigue, calumny and filth. Sometimes I am horrified. What of the future? I am coming home to embrace you with my one arm and live with you for a while, watching the struggle from the sidelines. I am no longer a soldier but a cripple, physically and morally. I am tired, I capitulate. This may be partially the reason for my marriage and the desire to find a "quiet haven",' he concluded in a sadly ironic postscript to the letter.

They were to leave Novocherkassk in a week's time. A few days before their departure Yevgeny finally established himself at Olga's. After the night that made them man and wife Olga seemed to droop and fade. She continued to yield to his demands but found the situation repugnant and was inwardly insulted. Yevgeny did not know or did not wish to know that people may have different measures for the love that binds them but only one for hate.

Before their departure Yevgeny thought of Aksinya unwillingly, in snatches. He shielded himself from such thoughts as a man shields his eyes from the sun. But against his will, like shafts of light, memories of their liaison, which over the years had grown into a firm bond, more and more often broke through and worried him. At one point he told himself that he would not break with her. She would accept the situation as it was. But his sense of decency prevailed and he decided that as soon as he arrived, he would explain things to her and, if the opportunity offered, they should part.

They reached Yagodnoye after a four-day journey. The old master met the young couple a verst from the estate. In the distance Yevgeny saw his father swing round stiffly to climb out of the light carriage, and take off his hat.

'We drove out to meet our dear guests. Now then, let me look at you,' the old man boomed, awkwardly embracing his daughter-in-law and thrusting his greenish-white nicotine-stained moustache against her cheeks.

'Come in with us, Father! Off we go, coachman! Ah, Grandad Sashka, hullo! Still alive? Take my seat, Father, and I'll go up on the box with the driver.'

The old man sat down beside Olga, dabbed his moustache with a handkerchief and surveyed his son restrainedly but with seemingly youthful vigour.

'Well, my boy?'

'I'm so glad to see you!'

'You're disabled, you say?'

'Can't be helped. That's what I am.'

The general tried to hide his sympathy under a mask of severity and kept his glance averted from the empty sleeve tucked into the belt of the green uniform.

'Never mind, I've got used to it.' Yevgeny's shoulder jerked involuntarily.

'Of course, you will,' the old man hastened to agree. 'You still have your head, that's the main thing. You've come home with your shield, haven't you? Yes, indeed you have. And even with a beautiful captive?'

Yevgeny took pleasure in his father's delicate, if rather old-fashioned gallantry. He gave Olga a look, asking what she thought of the old man, and by her animated smile, by the warmth in her eyes realised, without being told, that his father was to her liking.

The grey hunters whisked the carriage along down the slope. The buildings of the estate came into view—the white-walled house, the straggling mane of the poplar grove behind it and the maples shading the windows.

'Oh, how lovely!' Olga exclaimed excitedly.

The black borzoi wolf-hounds came bounding towards them and surrounded the carriage. From the droshky following behind Sashka lashed out at one of them that tried to jump up and bawled at it to keep away from the wheels. 'Down, ye devil!'

Yevgeny was sitting with his back to the horses and, when they snorted, the wind sprinkled his neck with a fine spray.

He looked smilingly at his father, Olga, the road strewn with ears of corn, and the hillock rising behind them that hid the distant ridge and the horizon beyond.

'How remote and secluded! And so quiet...'

Olga sent a smile after the rooks flying across the road and the clumps of wormwood and sweet clover dropping away behind them.

'They've come out to meet us,' the general exclaimed, screwing up his eyes.

'Who?'

'The servants.'

Yevgeny glanced round. Before he could distinguish the figures in the distance, he sensed that one of the women was Aksinya, and flushed purple. He had expected Aksinya's face to betray her emotion, but when the carriage swept in through the gate and he glanced at her in trepidation, he was struck by the calm and smiling cheerfulness of her expression. A huge weight fell from his shoulders and he nodded a greeting.

Olga glanced admiringly at Aksinya. 'What a wanton beauty! Who's that?.. Challengingly beautiful, isn't she?'

But Yevgeny's courage had returned and he responded coolly enough, 'Yes, she's a beautiful woman. She's our parlour-maid.'

Olga's presence had its effect on the whole household. The old master, who had been in the habit of going about all day in a night-shirt and warm knitted underpants, ordered his frockcoats and general's trousers to be taken out of mothballs. Formerly careless of his personal appearance, he now scolded Aksinya for the slightest crease in the linen she had ironed and made a terrible face if his boots were not properly polished in the morning. He looked much fresher and Yevgeny was pleasantly surprised to see that he shaved regularly.

As though sensing the worst, Aksinya did all she could to please the young mistress and was ingratiatingly obedient. Lukerya went out of her way to cook better dinners and excelled herself in thinking up tasty sauces and gravies. Even Old Sashka, who had aged badly and gone all to pieces, was affected by the changes on the Yagodnoye estate. One day the master met him by the porch, looked him over from top to toe, and wagged his finger ominously.

'What's all this, you son-of-a-bitch? Eh?' he asked, rolling his eyes furiously. 'What state are your trousers in?'

'Anything wrong with 'em?' Old Sashka replied impudently, though even he was rather taken aback by the unusual interrogation and his master's tones.

'There's a young woman in the house, and you, you ruffian, d'you want to drive me mad? Why don't you button your fly, you stinking goat? Now then?!'

53

Old Sashka's grimy fingers touched one then another of the long row of large-sized buttons, as if fingering the stops of a silent accordion. He was about to say something really insolent, but his master stamped his foot as in the days of his youth, and so hard that the pointed toe of the old-fashioned boot gaped open, and bellowed, 'Back to the stables! Quick march! I'll have Lukerya pour boiling water all over you! Scrape the dirt off yourself, you old nag!'

Yevgeny enjoyed himself roaming with a gun along the dry ravines and flushing partridges out of the millet stubble. Only one problem weighed on his mind and that problem was Aksinya. But one evening his father called him in. Casting apprehensive glances at the door and avoiding his son's eyes, he said, 'It's like this... Forgive my intruding in your personal affairs. But I want to know what you intend to do about Aksinya.'

Yevgeny gave himself away by the haste with which he lighted a cigarette. He felt his face redden as it had on the day of his arrival, and the awareness made it redden even more.

'I don't know... I simply don't know,' he confessed frankly.

The old man said firmly, 'Well, I know. Go and speak to her at once. Offer her money, pay her off,' he let a smile hover under his moustache, 'and ask her to go away. We'll find someone else.'

Yevgeny went to the servants' quarters at once.

Aksinya was standing with her back to the door, kneading dough. The shoulder blades were working in her cleanly grooved back. Muscles rippled in the brown shapely arms, which were bare to the elbow. Yevgeny looked at her neck with its fluffy ringlets and said, 'Please, Aksinya, I want to speak to you.'

She turned quickly and her face lit up. She tried to put on an expression of indifferent obedience, but Yevgeny noticed her fingers tremble as she rolled down her sleeves.

'I won't be long.' She shot a frightened glance at the cook and, unable to hide her joy, came up to Yevgeny with a happy pleading smile.

On the porch he said, 'Let's go into the orchard. We must talk.'

'Let's,' she complied joyfully, thinking that this was to be a resumption of their former relationship.

As they made their way to the orchard Yevgeny

asked quietly, 'Do you know why I wanted to see you?'

She smiled in the darkness and clasped his hand but he shook himself free and she knew at once what this meant. She halted.

'What was it you wanted, Yevgeny Nikolayevich? I won't go any further.'

'Very well. We can talk here. No one will hear us...' Yevgeny rushed on, stumbling in an invisible net of words. 'You must try to understand. Things can't be the way they used to be... I can't live with you. You understand? I'm married and it would be against my honour to deceive... My conscience wouldn't allow it...' The high-flown words were a torture to utter.

Night had just come out of the dark east.

In the west a strip of sunset-kindled sky still glowed purple. In the barn the corn was still being threshed by lantern light and a thresher was pulsing on a high, passionate note amid the shouts of the labourers; the man who was feeding the sheaves into the ravenous machine kept up his husky happy cry, 'Come on! More! More! More!' A ripening stillness filled the orchard. The air smelled of nettles, wheat and dew.

Aksinya stood silent.

'Well, what do you say? Why don't you speak, Aksinya?'

'I've nought to say.'

'I'll give you money. You must go away from here. I think you will agree... It will be difficult for me to see you constantly.'

'My month will be up in a week's time. May I stay on till then?'

'But of course!'

Aksinya waited a minute in silence, then sidled up to him timidly, as though she had been beaten, and said, 'All right then, I'll go away... Won't you be good to me just for one last time? It's my need that makes me so shameless... It's such torture being alone... Don't judge me, love.'

Her voice was dry and throbbing. Yevgeny tried in vain to decide whether she was serious or joking.

'What do you want?'

He coughed in annoyance, then suddenly felt her timidly groping for his hand.

Five minutes later he emerged from behind a damp, richly scented black-currant bush, walked to the fence and stood pulling at a cigarette and rubbing the grass stains off his trousers with a handkerchief.

As he walked up the steps in front of the house, he looked back. In the servants' quarters Aksinya's splendid figure was framed in the yellow light of the window. With her hands raised to tie back her hair she was looking at the fire and smiling.

VI

The feather-grass has ripened. For verst upon verst the steppe is clad in its shimmering silver. The wind treads springily across it, rustling and lifting its plumes, driving the bluish-grey opaline waves now south, now west. Where the air flows in a steady stream, the grass bows penitently and a darkening trail lingers long on its grizzled humps.

The other grasses have bloomed and faded. The withered wormwood droops despondingly on the ridges. The short nights burn out quickly and the charred black sky shines with countless stars; the moon—the Cossacks' sun—is on the wane and sheds only a grudging, whitish light; the broad Milky Way has merged with other starry roads. The air is tangy, pungent, the wind dry and wormwood-scented, the earth, drenched in the same all-powerful bitterness of wormwood, yearns for cool. The proud starry roads, untrodden by hoof or foot, heave and ripple; the stars, scattered like wheat seed in the dry blacksoil blackness of the sky, perish without sending up so much as a shoot to delight the eye; the moon is a dry saltmarsh and in the steppe there is nothing but dryness and withered grass, vibrant with the ceaseless frenzied piping of the quails and the metallic twang of the grasshoppers.

The days are all heat, sultriness and a dense haze. High in the faded blue of the heavens there is a ruthless sun, a cloudlessness, and the brown steel arches of a kite's outspread wings. In the steppe the feather-grass shines blindingly, overpoweringly bright and the hot camel-brown turf smokes in the heat; the kite dips a wing as it glides amid the blue and its huge shadow sweeps silently across the withered grass beneath.

The susliks whistle languidly and huskily. The marmots doze on the fresh yellow diggings around their burrows. The steppe is hot but dead, the whole scene translucently still; even the dark-blue burial mound on the horizon is poised on the brink of the visible, as magical and elusive as a dream...

Beloved steppe! A bitter wind settling on the manes of herd mares and stallions. It has made their dry muzzles salty and, as they breathe in this bitter salty smell, their silky lips munch and they whinny their delight in the taste of the wind and sun. Beloved steppe beneath the low-hanging sky of the Don! The windings of your dry valleys, of your red-clay ravines, the feather-grass expanses, pitted with grass-grown nestlike hoofmarks, the ancient mounds guarding in wise silence the buried Cossack glory... I bow low and, as a son, kiss your fresh sweet earth, steppe of the Don, steeped in unrusting Cossack blood!

* * *

He had a small, lean snake-like head. His ears were neat and mobile. His chest muscles were developed to the highest degree. His legs were slim and strong, the pasterns perfect, the hooves finely chiselled and as smooth as a pebble in a stream. The croupe sloped a little and the tail was long and thick. He was a Don thoroughbred. And a very pure thoroughbred at that. Not a drop of alien blood flowed in his veins and his breeding showed in every inch of him. His name was Malbruk.

At the watering place he fought to protect one of his mares against a stronger and older stallion and a kick from the other horse lamed his left foreleg, although the stallions on the grazing lands were never shod. The two horses reared and bit each other, kicking with their forefeet and tearing each other's skin.

There was no herdsman at hand—he was sprawling on the ground asleep, his back and outspread legs in their scorching dusty boots well exposed to the sun. Malbruk was thrown to the ground, then chased to a spot far away from the herd and left there to bleed while his adversary took possession of both herds and led them away along the edge of Bog Ravine.

The wounded stallion was brought in to the stables and the veterinary surgeon treated his injured leg. On the sixth day Mishka Koshevoi, who had come in to report to the overseer, saw Malbruk, driven by the mighty instinct to perpetuate his race, bite through his tether, jump out of his stall, round up the mares belonging to the herdsmen, overseer and vet, and chase them out into the steppe, first at a trot and then forcing the pace by snapping at those that lagged behind. The herdsmen and the overseer rushed out of the hut only in time to hear the sound of the mares' hobbling thongs breaking.

'He's unhorsed us, the son-of-a-gun!'

The overseer swore hard, but watched the horses cantering away into the distance not without secret approval.

At noon Malbruk brought his charges to the watering place. The herdsmen who had followed him on foot took the mares away from him, and he himself was saddled by Mishka, who rode him out into the steppe and let him loose among his own herd.

In the two months of his service as a herdsman Koshevoi studied the life of the horses on the range and, in doing so, acquired a deep respect for their intelligence and more than human nobility. He saw stallions mounting mares and this eternal act, performed in its primeval setting, was so naturally chaste and simple that he could not help drawing comparisons unfavourable to human beings. But there was also much of the human element in the relations between horses. Mishka noticed, for instance, that the ageing stallion Bakhar, uncontrollably fierce and rough in his treatment of the mares, had singled out one chestnut four-year-old with a broad blaze on her forehead and glowing eyes. When he came near her, he was always roused and vibrant, and would always snort in a special restrained and passionate way as he sniffed her loins. When the herd was resting, he liked to put his fierce head on his loved one's croupe and fall into a long doze. Watching him from the side, Mishka would notice the muscles rippling wearily under the stallion's fine skin, and it seemed to him that Bakhar loved this mare with an old man's love, a love that was hopelessly devoted and sad.

Koshevoi performed his duties well and word of his diligence must have reached the ears of the stanitsa ataman, for in the early days of August the overseer received orders to put Koshevoi at the disposal of the stanitsa authorities.

Mishka was ready in no time, handed in the equipment that had been issued to him, and by evening on the same day was on his way home. He kept his mare going at a lively pace and by sunset he topped the rise beyond Karginskaya, and there he came up with a droshky heading towards Vyoshenskaya.

The driver, a Ukrainian, was whipping on a pair of sweating well-fed horses. A tall broad-shouldered individual in a townsman's frock-coat and with a grey slouch hat tilted off his brow was reclining in the back. For a time Mishka rode behind, watching the passenger's gently jiggling shoulders and the dusty white rim of his collar. At his feet lay a yellow travelling-bag and a sack, half covered by a folded overcoat. The unfamiliar scent of a cigar tickled Mishka's nostrils. He must be some official on his way to the stanitsa, he thought, riding his mare level with the droshky. But when he glanced under the brim of the hat, his mouth fell open and a shiver of fear and astonishment raced down his spine. The man reclining in the back of the droshky, impatiently chewing the black stump of a cigar and narrowing his wild light-coloured eyes as he watched the road go by was Stepan Astakhov. Mishka glanced again, incredulously, at the familiar but oddly changed face of his fellow villager and decided that the man swayed by the carriage springs was the real and living Stepan and, breaking into a sweat of excitement, cleared his throat to ask, "Scuse me, sir, but could you be Astakhov?'

The man in the droshky nodded the hat on to his forehead and turned to look up at Mishka.

'Yes, my name's Astakhov. What about it? Haven't you... Wait a minute, aren't you—Koshevoi?' He half rose and, smiling with only his dark lips from under his clipped chestnut moustache, while his eyes and generally aged face retained a stern aloofness, held out his hand gladly but in some embarrassment. 'You are Koshevoi? Mikhail? So we meet again! Glad to see you...'

'But how come?' Mishka dropped the reins and spread his arms in astonishment. 'They said you'd been killed. And now what do I see—it's Astakhov!'

Mishka's face broke into a broad smile and he leaned forward eagerly in his saddle, but Stepan's appearance and precise, toneless way of speaking confused him; he changed to a more formal manner of address and kept it up for the rest of the conversation, vaguely aware of an invisible barrier between them.

They began to talk. The horses walked on side by side. In the west the sunset blossomed flamboyantly with small tulip-bright clouds that marched away across the sky into the night. A quail piped up deafeningly amid the tangled millet stalks at the side of the road, and a dusty stillness settled over the steppe as the flutterings and cries of day abated. At the fork of the Chukarinskaya and Kruzhilinskaya tracks the dim shape of a roadside shrine appeared against the backdrop of the violet sky; above it rose a sheer wall of billowing brick-brown clouds.

'Where've you come from, Stepan Andreich?' Mishka inquired joyfully.

'From Germany. Managed to get home at last.'

'But our Cossacks said they'd seen you killed before their eyes?'

Stepan's replies were guarded, deliberately calm, as though he had no liking for being questioned.

'I was wounded in two places and the Cossacks... What d'you expect of Cossacks? They left me behind... So I was captured. The Germans got me well again and put me to work.'

'You didn't send any letters, did you?'

'There was no one to write to.' Stepan threw away the butt of his cigar and at once lighted another.

'What about your wife? She's well enough.'

'I wasn't living with her—I thought everybody knew it.'

Stepan's voice was toneless, without a single warm note. The mention of his wife left him unmoved.

'Didn't you feel homesick living so far away?' Mishka questioned avidly, leaning almost flat over the pommel of his saddle.

'I was at first, but I got used to it. I lived well over there.' Stepan paused for a moment, then went on, 'I had a mind to stay in Germany for good and take their citizenship. But then I felt the call of home.'

The harsh lines at the corners of his eyes softened for the first time and he smiled.

'And you see what a mix-up we're in here?.. We're fighting amongst ourselves.'

'Yes, so I've heard.'

'What road did you come by?'

'From France, by boat from Marseilles—there's a city of that name—to Novorossiisk.'

'Will they mobilise you?'

'Probably... What is the news in the village?'

'How can a man tell it all? There's news aplenty.'

'Is my house still standing?'

'Just about.'

'How are the neighbours? Are the Melekhov boys alive?'

'That they are.'

'Have you heard any word of my former wife?'

'She's still out there, at Yagodnoye.'

'And Grigory—is he living with her?'

'No, he's with his lawful wife. He's given up your Aksinya.'

'Has he now? I didn't know.'

For a minute they were silent. Koshevoi went on surveying Stepan with eager curiosity. Approvingly and with respect he said, 'It looks as if you had a right good life, Stepan Andreich. You're dressed up fine, like a gentleman.'

'Everyone dresses clean over there,' Stepan frowned, and tapped the driver's shoulder. 'Now then, get a move on.'

The driver swung his whip unenthusiastically and the tired horses pulled unwillingly at the traces. The droshky's wheels muttered softly as they heaved over the ruts and Stepan ended the conversation by turning away from Mishka and asking, 'Are you heading for the village?'

'No, the stanitsa.'

At the fork Mishka turned right and rose in his stirrups.

'Goodbye for now, Stepan Andreich!'

Stepan crushed the dusty brim of his hat with a heavy bunch of fingers and replied coldly and distinctly, pronouncing every syllable, like a foreigner.

'Good-day to you.'

VII

Along the Filonovo-Povorino line the front was straightening out. The Reds were bringing up fresh forces, clenching their fist for a blow. The Cossacks developed their offensive half-heartedly; they were very short of ammunition and had no desire to go beyond the borders of the region. On the Filonovo front, operations proceeded with varying success. In August a lull set in and the Cossacks who came home from the front on short leave spoke of the likelihood of an armistice by autumn.

But meanwhile there was the wheat harvest to be gathered in. Hands were needed. The work was too much for the women and old men and, besides, they were constantly hindered by orders from the authorities, instructing them to cart ammunition and food supplies to the front.

Nearly every day five or six wagons left Tatarsky for Vyoshenskaya. There they were loaded with crates of cartridges and shells and sent on to the transit post at Andropovsky, where sometimes, for lack of other transport, they were ordered to go even further, to the villages along the Khopyor.

Tatarsky lived a busy but restricted life. All thoughts were turned towards the distant front and everyone awaited bad news about the Cossacks there with pain and anxiety. Stepan Astakhov's homecoming stirred the whole village; it was the talk of the day in every house, on every threshing floor. A Cossack had come home, a Cossack long since dead and buried, remembered only by the old women, and by them only in their prayers that he might "rest in peace". Was this not a miracle?

Stepan stopped at Anikei's, carried his belongings into the house and, while the housewife was making supper, went to look at his own cottage. For a long time he paced heavily about the white moonlit yard, groping round the half ruined barns, looking over the house, tugging at the posts of the fence... The eggs that Anikei's wife had fried for him had long since grown cold in the pan but Stepan still went on examining his dilapidated domain, cracking the joints of his fingers and muttering inarticulately under his breath.

That same evening the Cossacks came knocking at his door to have a look at him and ask about his life as a prisoner-of-war. Their womenfolk and children crammed into Anikei's front room. They stood listening to Stepan's tales, forming a solid wall broken only by the black gaps of gaping mouths. Stepan spoke reluctantly and not once did his aged face brighten with a smile. Evidently life had bowed him to the very root and made a different man of him.

The next morning, while Stepan was still asleep in the best room, Pantelei came round to see him. He coughed deeply into his cupped hand and waited for the returned soldier to wake. The air from the room was a mixture of cool freshness from the earthen floor, a strange, suffocatingly strong smell of tobacco, and all the odours of a long journey that linger upon the traveller.

Stepan was awake. Pantelei heard the scrape of a match as he lit up for a smoke.

'May I come in?' Pantelei asked and, as though appearing before his commanding officer, hurriedly straightened the folds of the stiff new shirt that Ilyinichna had insisted on his wearing for the occasion.

'Come in.'

Stepan had begun to dress and was puffing at the stub of a cigar, his sleepy eyes half closed against the smoke. Pantelei crossed the threshold with some trepidation and, equally astonished by Stepan's changed face and the metal attachments to his silk braces, came to a halt with his dark work-blackened hand stiffly outstretched.

'Hullo to you, neighbour! Glad to see you alive...'

'Good morning!'

Stepan slipped the braces over his powerful sloping shoulders, shrugged them and with some dignity placed his hand in the old man's rough grip. They scanned each other quickly. Blue sparks of hostility flared in Stepan's eyes; Melekhov's protruding orbs expressed respect and a faint surprise mingled with irony.

'You've aged a bit, Stepan... That you have, my lad.'

'Yes, I have aged.'

'We'd said our prayers of remembrance for you, like for my Grigory...' Pantelei broke off vexedly; it was hardly the time to recall such things. He tried to make good his slip of the tongue. 'But he came back safe and sound, praise the Lord! Yes, we said our prayers for Grisha and, like Lazarus, he got up and walked. He's got two children now and his wife, Natalya, thank the Lord, has recovered. She's a fine woman now... Well, and you, my boy, how are you?'

'Quite well, thank you.'

'Will you come and see your neighbour? Come now, do us the honour, just for a chat.'

Stepan refused the invitation, but Pantelei was not to be put off and when he showed offence Stepan gave in. He washed his face, combed his short-cut hair, smiled at the old man's question, 'What've you done with your Cossack forelock? Worn it out?' then clamped his hat confidently on his head and was the first to leave the house.

Pantelei was so ingratiatingly affectionate that Stepan could not help thinking, 'He's trying to make up for the old insult.'

Obeying the mute instructions of her husband's eyes, Ilyinichna bustled about the kitchen, hurrying Natalya and Dunyashka, and herself laid the table. Now and then the women shot curious glances at Stepan as he sat in the corner under the icons. They eyed his coat, neat collar, silver watch-chain and carefully combed hair, exchanging glances and barely concealed smiles of astonishment. Darya came in rosy-cheeked from the backyard and, wiping her finely pursed lips with the corner of her apron, surveyed him with a quizzical smile.

'Well, neighbour dear, I hardly recognised you. You don't look like a Cossack any more.'

Pantelei lost no time in putting a bottle of home-brew on the table. He pulled out the rag plug and sniffed the sweetish bitter fumes with appreciation.

'Try a drop. It's our own make. Burns with a blue flame if you put a match to it, upon my word!'

The conversation rambled on. Stepan drank unwillingly but one glass soon made him tipsy and his manner softened.

'Now we'll have to get you married, neighbour.'

'What about my old wife? Where shall I put her?'

'The old one? What about her? D'you think an old one never wears out? A wife's like a mare; you ride her as long as she's got teeth in her mouth. We'll find you a young one.'

'Life's such a mix-up nowadays... I don't feel like marrying. All I've got is ten days' leave, then I'll have to report to the administration. I reckon they'll send me to the front,' said Stepan, gradually losing his foreign manner of speech as he got drunk.

A little while later he left, accompanied by Darya's admiring glances and leaving the family in a welter of argument and conjecture.

'What a change he's made in himself, the son-of-a-bitch! The way he talked! Like a tax-collector or some other man of noble rank... I come into the room and there he stood, putting on these silk breast-bands with brasses on 'em over his vest! All strapped up, chest and back, like a horse, he was. What d'you make of it? Is there something behind it? He's like a real learned man now,' Pantelei proclaimed admiringly, evidently flattered that Stepan had not scorned his hospitality and let bygones be bygones.

From what had been said it appeared that, when his army service was over, Stepan would come back to live in the village and put his house and farm in order. He had mentioned in passing that he had the necessary funds and this set Pantelei thinking and evoked his involuntary respect.

'It looks as if he's in the money,' he declared after Stepan's departure. 'He's got capital, the blighter. Most Cossacks come home from captivity in nothing but rags, but look how he's dressed up... He must have murdered someone or stolen some money.'

For the first few days Stepan rested at Anikei's place and seldom appeared in the street. Watchful neighbours kept track of his every movement and even tried to find out from Anikei's wife what he intended to do, but she only pursed her lips and made a pretence of knowing nothing.

Rumours spread thick and fast through the village when Anikei's wife hired a horse from the Melekhovs and early on a Saturday morning set out for no one knew where. Only Pantelei guessed what it was all about. 'She'll be going off to fetch Aksinya,' he said with a wink at Ilyinichna as he harnessed his lame mare to a tarantas. And he was not mistaken. The woman had driven off to Yagodnoye with a message from Stepan: 'Ask Aksinya if she'll come back to her husband and forget old wrongs.'

That day Stepan parted for ever with his new-found restraint and self-assurance. Till evening he tramped about the village, and then sat for a long time on Mokhov's porch with the merchant and his partner, talking about Germany, about his life there and the journey through France and across the sea. But though he talked and listened to Mokhov's complaints he was glancing avidly at his watch all the time.

Anikei's wife returned from Yagodnoye at dusk. While making the supper in the outdoor kitchen, she related that Aksinya had taken fright at the unexpected news and asked many questions about him, but had flatly refused to return.

'She don't need to come back, she lives like a lady,' the messenger chattered on, swallowing envious sighs. 'In fine fettle she is! And her face is all white and smooth. She never has any heavy work to do. What more could she want? And the way she's dressed—you couldn't imagine. In a snow-white skirt on a weekday and her hands as clean as clean can be.'

Stepan's cheekbones flushed pink. Sparks of anger and longing flared and died out in his lowered light-coloured eyes. He spooned sour milk out of an earthenware bowl, trying to steady his trembling hand and asking questions with a deliberate slowness.

'You say Aksinya boasted of the way she lives?'

'Why shouldn't she! Anybody would like to have a life like hers.'

'Did she ask about me?'

'Of course, she did. She went all pale when I said you'd turned up.'

Stepan finished his supper and went out to the grass-grown yard.

The brief August twilight had faded swiftly. The drums of the winnowers were clattering persistently in the damp cool of the night; sharp voices could be heard. By the light of the spotted yellow moon people were still hard at it in the usual scramble for existence, winnowing the grain that had been threshed during the day and carting it to the barns. The village was wrapped in the hot dry smell of newly threshed wheat and chaff dust. Somewhere near the square a steam thresher was chugging and dogs were barking. On the distant threshing floors a slow song was spinning itself out. A vapid dampness was drifting up from the river.

Stepan leaned on the fence and gazed at the streaming waters of the Don and the fiery zigzag path that the moon had trodden across it. Faint eddies wove themselves into the current. On the far bank the poplars stood in dreamy peacefulness. Quietly and irresistibly a regretful longing took possession of Stepan.

* * *

It rained at dawn but after sunrise the clouds drifted away and two hours later only the mud-spattered wheels of the wagons recalled the bad weather.

That morning Stepan drove over to Yagodnoye. Anxiously he tethered the horse by the gate and strode rapidly towards the servants' quarters.

The spacious yard with its tufts of withered grass was deserted. Some chickens were digging in a pile of dung near the stables. A rooster as black as a rook was stamping about by a fallen fence. As it called the hens, it pretended to be pecking at the red lady-birds crawling over the fence poles. The borzoi hounds, sleek from lack of exercise, were lying in the shade beside the coach-house. Six small black-and-white puppies had pulled down their mother, a young bitch pupping for the first time, and were thrusting forward with their little legs to suck at the limp grey teats. The shady side of the manor's iron roof was glistening with dew.

Stepan paused for a moment to look round, then entered the servants' quarters and asked the portly cook, 'Can I see Aksinya?'

'Who are you?' she asked, wiping her perspiring pock-marked face with her apron.

'Never mind that. Where might Aksinya be?'

'She's with the master. You'd better wait.'

Stepan sat down and with a gesture of utter weariness placed his hat on his knees. The cook pushed her pots into the oven and made a clatter with the pot-holders, taking no notice of the visitor. The kitchen reeked of soured cottage cheese and yeast. A black shroud of flies covered the front of the stove, the walls, and the flour-sprinkled table. Stepan listened with strained attention and waited. The familiar sound of Aksinya's footsteps jerked him off the bench. He stood up, letting the hat fall from his lap.

Aksinya entered carrying a pile of plates. All the life went out of her face and the corners of her full lips began to twitch. She stood stock-still, helplessly clasping the plates to her chest and staring at Stepan with frightened eyes. Then somehow she got moving again, walked to the table, and freed her hands.

'Hullo.'

Stepan was breathing slowly and deeply like a man asleep, his lips had split in a strained smile. He leaned forward silently and held out his hand to Aksinya.

She made a gesture that said, 'Come to my room.'

Stepan lifted his hat as though it were a great weight; the blood rushed to his head and clouded his eyes. As soon as they were in her room and had sat down with the table between them, she asked with a moan, licking her dry lips, 'You? Here?'

Stepan swept his arm in a vague unnaturally cheerful manner, as if he were drunk. His lips remained fixed in the same smile of joy and pain.

'I was a prisoner-of-war... I've come back to you, Aksinya.'

He jumped up in sudden absurd haste, drew a small packet out of his pocket, ripped off the cloth wrapping and, unable to control his trembling fingers, took out a small silver wristwatch and a ring with a cheap blue stone in it. He held them out to her in his sweating hand, but Aksinya could not take her eyes off his face. With its twisted smile of abasement it was the face of a stranger.

'Take them, I kept them for you... We used to be together...'

'What good are they to me? Wait...' Aksinya's dead lips answered.

'Take them... Don't offend me... It's time we gave up our foolishness.'

Aksinya rose covering her face with her hand and walked away to the stove-bench.

'They said you'd been killed...'

'Would you be glad if I had been?'

She made no reply; more calmly now she surveyed her husband from head to foot, aimlessly straightening the pleats of her carefully ironed skirt. She put her hands behind her back.

'You sent Anikei's wife, didn't you?... She said you wanted me to come ... and live with...'

'Will you?' Stepan cut in.

'No,' Aksinya's voice was dry. 'No, I won't.'

'Why not?'

'I've got out of the habit. And anyway it's a bit late... Too late.'

'I want to start farming again. I was thinking about it all the way from Germany, and while I was there too... What will you do then, Aksinya? Grigory's left you... Or have you found someone else? I've heard you're with the master's son... Is it true?'

The blood rushed hotly into Aksinya's cheeks, forcing tears from her shame-burdened eyes.

'Yes, it's true. I'm living with him now.'

'I didn't mean any reproach,' Stepan looked scared. 'What I'm saying is, mebbe you haven't decided what you're going to do? He won't need you for long, you know, he's only amusing himself... You've got wrinkles under your eyes... He'll get tired of you and turn you out. Where will you be then? Haven't you had enough of being a servant? It's up to you... I've come home with money. When the war's over, we'll have a fine life. I thought we could be together again. I want to forget the past.'

'What were you thinking of before, Stepan, my dear?' Aksinya spoke with merry tears and a quiver in her voice as she rose from the stove-bench and came right up to the table. 'What were you thinking of before, when you trampled on my young life? You kicked me into Grigory's arms... You broke my heart... Don't you remember what you did to me?'

'I didn't come here to settle old scores... You ... what do you know? Mebbe I've been through hell because of that? Mebbe I've lived another life remembering...' Stepan stared at the hands he had spread out on the table and put his words together slowly, as though each one had to be forced out of his mouth. 'I used to think of you ... and my heart bled, bled till it choked... You were in my mind day and night... I was living with a widow out there, a German woman, and living well but I threw it all up... I wanted to come home...'

'Felt like a quiet life, did you?' Aksinya asked, her nostrils twitching furiously. 'Like to start farming again? And maybe you want a few children and a wife to wash for you and feed you?' A dark, unpleasant smile came into her eyes. 'No, so help me, Christ! Yes, I'm old, you've spotted my wrinkles... And I've got out of the way of bearing children. My job's being a mistress, and mistresses aren't supposed to have any... Is that the kind of woman you want?'

'You're very sharp nowadays.'

'I'm what I am.'

'So the answer is no?'

'Yes, it is. I won't come.'

'Well, good-day to you then,' Stepan rose, toyed aimlessly with the wristwatch and put it down on the table again. 'If you change your mind, let me know.'

Aksinya saw him as far as the gate, then stood watching the dust rising from under his wheels and shrouding his broad shoulders as he drove away.

Angry tears fought within her and an occasional sob broke from her lips as she thought vaguely of the things that had never come true, and sorrowed over her life that was once again at the mercy of the winds. After being told by Yevgeny that he didn't want her any more, and then learning of her husband's return, she had decided to go back to Stepan to gather up the pieces of a happiness that had never been. And she had waited for him with this decision in her mind. But at the sight of Stepan, humbled and submissive, a dark pride, the same pride that would not allow her to stay at Yagodnoye as a cast-off mistress, had reared up within her. A fierce urge that she could not control had once again guided her words and actions. She had remembered past wrongs, remembered all that she had suffered from this man, from his big iron hands and, without wishing to make the break, inwardly horrified at what she was doing, she had panted out the stinging words, 'No, I won't live with you. Never.'

Her eyes turned once again to watch the disappearing tarantas. Plying his whip, Stepan dropped out of sight behind the fringe of stunted purple wormwood growing beside the road.

The next day Aksinya was paid off and packed up her belongings. She gave a sob as she said goodbye to Yevgeny.

'Don't think ill of me, Yevgeny Nikolayevich.'

'Not for a moment, my dear!.. Thank you for everything.'

Hiding his confusion, his voice sounded affectedly cheerful.

And she left. By evening she was in the village of Tatarsky.

Stepan met Aksinya at the gate.

'So you've come?' he said, smiling. 'Is it for good this time? Can I hope that you won't go away any more?'

'I won't,' Aksinya replied simply, and her heart sank as she looked round at the half-derelict house and yard, choked with goosefoot and tall black weeds.

VIII

Not far from the stanitsa of Durnovskaya, the Vyoshenskaya regiment fought its first battle against the retreating Red Army units.

At noon Grigory Melekhov's squadron occupied a smallish village buried in a wilderness of willow groves. In the damp shade of the osiers Grigory ordered his Cossacks to dismount beside a stream that had cut a shallow channel across the village. The source was not far away, bubbling and gurgling out of the soggy black soil. The water was icy cold and the Cossacks drank thirstily, scooping it up in their caps, then clamping them on their sweating heads with grunts of satisfaction. The sun hung sheer over the heat-bemused village. The scorching earth was veiled in a noonday haze. The grass and willow leaves caught in the venomously hot rays were drooping limply, but by the stream, in the shade of the osiers there was abundant cool and the burdock and other luxuriant grasses fed by the boggy soil grew green and fresh; the duckweed in the little backwaters glowed like a girl's smile; somewhere close by ducks were diving and flapping their wings. The horses snorted and squelched through the mud towards the water, pulling the reins out of their riders' hands and wading out into the middle of the stream, stirring up the silt and seeking with silken lips for a cleaner current. And as they raised their heads the hot wind plucked diamond droplets from those wet drooping lips. A sulphurous smell of churned-up mud and slime mingled with the bitter-sweet odour of soaked and rotting osier roots.

No sooner had the Cossacks stretched themselves out amid the burdock, chatting and smoking, than the advance patrol returned. The word 'Reds' brought everyone to their feet in an instant. They tightened their saddle girths and ran back to the stream to fill their water-bottles and have another drink, each of them probably wondering whether they would ever have another chance to drink such water—pure as an infant's tears.

They crossed the stream and halted.

About a verst away an enemy patrol was moving across a sandy scrub-covered hill.

'Let's grab 'em!' Mitka Korshunov suggested to Grigory.

With half a troop Mitka rode out of the village by a side track; but the Red reconnaissance had already spotted the Cossacks and turned back.

An hour later, when the regiment's two other mounted squadrons had come up, they took the field. The patrols reported that a Red force of about one thousand bayonets was advancing towards them. The Vyoshenskaya squadrons had lost touch with the 33rd Yelanskaya Regiment on its right but nevertheless decided to give battle. They rode across the hill and dismounted. The minders led the horses down into a broad gully that sloped towards the village. Somewhere on the right the patrols clashed and a light machine-gun chattered wildly.

Presently the Reds' wide-spaced skirmish lines appeared. Grigory deployed his squadron at the top of the gully. The Cossacks took up their position among the tousled scrub along the top of the ridge. From under a stunted crab-apple tree Grigory watched the distant enemy through his field glasses. He could clearly distinguish the first two lines advancing and further back, among the brown ungarnered swathes of reaped corn, a dark column was moving out into line.

He and the other Cossacks were astonished to see a figure on a tall white horse—evidently the commander—riding in front of the first line. Two others were out in front of the second. And the third was also led by its commander, with a banner fluttering beside him. The banner glowed scarlet on the greyish yellow background of the stubble, like a small drop of blood.

'They've got their commissars up in front!' a Cossack cried.

'Oho! That's real heroic, eh!' Mitka Korshunov chortled admiringly.

'Look at that, lads! That's what the Reds are like!'

Nearly the whole squadron rose, shouting to one another. Hands went up to shade eyes from the sun. But then the talk died away and a stern majestic silence, preluding death, spread like the shadow of a cloud over steppe and gully.

Grigory looked back. Beyond an ash-grey island of willows to the side of the village he spotted a billowing cloud of dust, where the second squadron was cantering ahead for a flanking attack. Their approach would be concealed for a time by a ravine, but after about four versts it rose in a fork to the crest of a hill and Grigory tried to calculate when and at what distance the squadron would come out on the flank.

'Down!' he shouted to his men, turning sharply and slipping the glasses into their case.

He walked over to his line. The men's faces, now a grimy purple from the heat and dust, turned towards him. There was an exchange of glances and the men took up their positions. At the command 'Ready!' the breach-bolts of their rifles snapped rapaciously. All Grigory could see from above was their splayed legs, the tops of their caps and their dust-caked shirts with sweat stains on their shoulder blades and along the grooves of their spines. The men shifted about, looking for cover and better firing positions. Some of them tried to dig into the hard ground with their sabres.

And it was then that breeze blowing from the Red lines brought the faint sounds of singing.

The lines advanced unevenly, in taut irregular curves, heaving over the rough ground. The voices sounded subdued, lost amid the sultry expanse as they drifted towards the hill.

Grigory felt his heart thump sharply and miss a beat. He had heard this solemn chorus before, he had heard the sailors from Mokrousov's detachment singing it at Glubokaya, their caps off as if in prayer, their eyes shining. A vague anxiety, almost fear rose within him.

'What are they howling about?' an aged Cossack asked, twisting his head worriedly.

'Sounds like a prayer or something,' another lying on his right replied.

'It's a prayer to the devil,' Andrei Kashulin grinned, and looked impudently at Grigory, who was standing nearby. 'You were with 'em, Grigory, I reckon you know what song they're singing? Reckon you've sung it yourself?'

'*...own the land!*' the distant voices surged for a moment, then silence again flooded the steppe. The Cossacks broke into a surly resentful merriment. Someone in the middle of the line roared with laughter. Mitka Korshunov fidgeted impatiently.

'D'you hear that, eh?! They want to own the land!' And Mitka swore obscenely. 'Grigory Panteleyevich! Let me pick off that one on the horse! Just one shot?'

He fired without waiting for Grigory's consent. The bullet alarmed the rider. He dismounted, handed over his horse and marched on ahead of the line, his bared sabre glinting.

The Cossacks started shooting. The Reds dropped to the ground. Grigory ordered the machine-gunners to open fire. After two bursts the first line dashed forward about twenty paces and dropped to the ground again. Through his glasses Grigory saw the Red Army men get to work with their spades as they dug themselves in. A flurry of bluish-grey dust rose over the line and tiny mounds, like a marmot's diggings, grew up in front of it. A ragged volley followed, and then there was a fierce exchange of fire. The action began to look as if it would drag on. After an hour the Cossacks' losses amounted to one man killed outright and three wounded, who had crawled away to the horse-minders in the gully. The second squadron appeared on the flank and threw up the dust in a charge. The attack was beaten off by machine-gun fire. The Cossacks could be seen galloping back in panic, first in a bunch, then fanning out. After its retreat the squadron reformed and silently, without a cheer, charged again. And again a squall of machine-gun fire drove it back, like leaves driven by the wind.

But these attacks shook the resolve of the Red Army men and the first lines wavered and began to fall back.

Without ceasing fire Grigory ordered his men forward. The Cossacks advanced without pausing to seek cover. The hesitation and perplexity they had felt at first seemed to have vanished. Their cheerful mood was encouraged by a battery that had galloped up to the positions. Its first troop mounted its gun and opened fire. Grigory sent for the horses and prepared to attack. By the apple-tree where he had stood observing the early stages of the engagement the third gun was being hoisted off its limber. A tall officer in tight riding breeches, smacking his boot with his whip, shouted in a fierce high-pitched voice at the drivers who were slowly manoeuvring their guns.

'Get moving! Now then?! Devil take you!'

An observer and a senior officer who had dismounted on a hillock about half a verst away from the battery watched the enemy's retreating lines through their field glasses. Signallers came running across with coils of wire to link up the battery with the observation post. The elderly major who was in command of the battery twiddled the focus of his binoculars with big nervous fingers (a gold wedding ring gleamed on one of them) and stumped about aimlessly round the first gun, shaking his head as if to free it from the whining bullets; a shabby map-case jumped at his side with every abrupt movement.

After the flabby, crackling roar Grigory watched to see where the ranging shell would fall, then glanced round; the crew was straining to drag the gun forward. The first shrapnel burst scattered over the field of ungarnered wheat and a white cottony wad of smoke was shredded by the wind and slowly melted into the blue.

The four guns, one after the other, sent their shells across the swathes of wheat, but to Grigory's surprise the artillery fire caused no noticeable confusion in the Red lines. They fell back in an unhurried, orderly fashion and disappeared from the squadron's field of vision into a ravine. Grigory realised that an attack would be pointless, but decided to have a word with the battery commander. With something of a swagger he walked over to him, touched the sun-scorched tip of his reddish curly moustache with his left hand, and smiled amiably.

'I wanted to attack.'

'How can you attack!' The major tossed his head, then dabbed with the back of his hand at the sweat trickling from under the peak of his cap. 'You've seen them withdraw, the bastards! They won't let you get at 'em! It would be absurd. All their commanders are regular officers. A colleague of mine, Lieutenant-Colonel Serov, is there.'

'How do you know?' Grigory frowned unbelievingly.

'From deserters... Cease fire!' the major commanded, and explained apologetically, 'It's no good shooting and we're short of shells... You're Melekhov, aren't you? My name's Poltavtsev.' He jerked his big sweating hand into Grigory's, then snatched it away and felt deftly in the unfastened map-case for cigarettes. 'Have a smoke!'

There was a muffled rumble as the drivers rode up out of the gully. The battery's guns were again hitched to their limbers. Grigory mounted his squadron and led it in the wake of the Reds who had retired beyond the hill.

The Reds had occupied the next village, but they gave it up without resistance. The three Vyoshenskaya squadrons and the battery took up their quarters there, the frightened villagers stayed in their houses and the Cossacks explored the village in search of something to eat. Grigory dismounted by a house on the outskirts, led his horse into the yard and left it by the porch. The master of the house, a tall elderly Cossack, was lying on his bed, groaning and rolling his small birdlike head from side to side on the dirty pillow.

'What's the matter? Feeling ill?' Grigory greeted him with a grin.

'That I am.'

The man was pretending to be ill and to judge by his shifty eyes guessed that he was not believed.

'Will you feed my Cossacks?' Grigory demanded.

'How many?' the man's wife asked, stepping away from the position she had taken by the stove.

'Five.'

'Well, come inside then, we'll give you what God provides.'

When he and his men had eaten, Grigory went out into the street.

The battery was drawn up by the well, fully equipped and ready to go. The harnessed horses were shaking their nosebags as they munched the last of the barley. The drivers and crews were sheltering from the heat beside ammunition crates or under the guns. One of them was lying on his face with his legs crossed, his shoulder twitching in his sleep. He had probably been lying in the shade, but the sun had moved and was beating down on his bare curly head, sprinkled with bits of hay.

Under the broad straps of the leather harness the horses' glistening flanks were yellow and frothed with sweat. The mounts of the officers and gun-crews, tethered to the fence, stood dejectedly with their tails between legs. The Cossacks, dusty and sweating, rested in silence. The officers and the battery commander were sitting on the ground with their backs to the wooden wall of the well and smoking. Not far away a cluster of Cossacks, their legs forming a six-pointed star, were lying on a patch of withered goosefoot, frantically scooping sour milk out of a pail; occasionally one of them would spit out a barley seed that had stuck in his teeth.

The sun blazed down frenziedly. The village streets running out towards the hill were almost deserted. The Cossacks slept under the overhangs of barns and sheds, beside fences and in the yellow shade of the burdock. Their horses, still saddled, clustered round the fences, tormented by heat. A Cossack rode past, lifting his whip lazily to the level of his horse's back. And again the street was like a forgotten steppeland track and the green-painted guns and the sleeping men, exhausted by the sun and the long marches, seemed an accidental and unnecessary presence amid the wilderness.

Overcome by boredom, Grigory was about to go back into the house when three Cossacks from another squadron appeared riding down the street. They were driving a bunch of captured Red Army men. The gunners stirred and rose to their feet, brushing the dust off their tunics and trousers. The officers also stood up. In a neighbouring yard someone shouted joyfully, 'Heh, lads, they're bringing in some prisoners! You think I'm kidding? By the Holy Mother!'

Sleepy-faced Cossacks came hurrying out of the yards. The prisoners, eight young fellows stinking of sweat and grimed with dust, were soon surrounded.

'Where were they captured?' the battery commander asked, surveying the prisoners with cold curiosity.

One of the escorts replied with boastful bravado, 'They call 'emselves soldiers! We caught 'em in the sunflowers near the village. Hiding like quails from a kite they were! We spotted 'em all right from the saddle, and gave chase! We killed one.'

The Red Army men huddled together in a frightened bunch, evidently fearing reprisals. Their eyes roamed helplessly over the Cossacks' faces. Only one man, evidently a little older, with a deeply tanned face and high cheekbones, wearing a greasy tunic and hopelessly tattered leg wrappings, stared contemptuously over their heads with his dark slightly squinting eyes and kept his broken bleeding lips tightly closed. He was stocky and broad-shouldered. A peaked cap, no doubt a relic of the German war, with the mark of a cockade still visible was clamped over his stiff black curls like a green pancake. He stood in an easy posture, touching the unbuttoned collar of his vest and his sharp black-haired Adam's apple with thick dark fingers that were crusted with blood round the nails. Outwardly he appeared indifferent, but the leg he had moved to one side was grotesquely fat in its wrappings up to the knee, and trembling uncontrollably. The others were a pale, faceless lot. Only he caught the eye with his massive shoulders and energetic Tatar face. Perhaps for this reason the battery commander addressed him.

'Who are you?'

The Red Army man's small eyes, like chips of anthracite, sparked into life and almost imperceptibly, yet smartly he drew himself up.

'Red Army man. Russian.'

'Where were you born?'

'Penza.'

'Are you a volunteer, you swine?'

'No. Senior N.C.O. in the old army. Enlisted in 'seventeen and been at it ever since.'

One of the escorts interrupted, 'He shot at us, the devil!'

'Did he?' the major frowned sourly and gave Grigory, who was standing opposite him, a meaningful look, indicating the prisoner with his eyes. 'So that's the kind he is!.. Shot at you, did he? Did you think you wouldn't be captured? Suppose we decide to get rid of you because of that?'

'I wanted to shoot my way out.' The battered lips twitched in a guilty leer.

'A fine specimen! Why didn't you then?'

'I ran out of ammo.'

'A-a-ah!' A cold look came into the major's eyes but he surveyed the soldier with unconcealed satisfaction. 'And you, you young ruffians, where are you from?'

he asked in quite a different tone, scanning the other prisoners with a more cheerful eye.

'We was mobilised, Your Excellency! We're from Saratov, Balashovo...' a tall, long-necked lad began in a whining voice, blinking rapidly and scratching his ginger hair.

With aching curiosity Grigory studied the young men in their greenish-brown uniforms, their plain peasant faces, their shabby foot-soldier's appearance. Only the man with high cheekbones roused his hostility. He addressed him with angry mockery.

'What was the idea of confessing like that? I reckon you were commanding one of their companies? A commander, weren't you? A Communist? Run out of ammo, you say? Well, what if we have a go at you now with our sabres? How about that?'

The Red Army man's nose, which had been pulped by a rifle butt, gave a twitch and he spoke up more boldly.

'I didn't confess just to sound daring. Why should I hide anything? If a man shoots at someone he ought to say why... That's right, isn't it? As for ... well, execute me then.' And he smiled again. 'I didn't expect anything good from you—after all, you're Cossacks.'

At this there were general smiles of approval. Grigory, appeased by the soldier's reasoning tones, walked away. He saw the prisoners go to the well for a drink. A squadron of unmounted Cossacks marched out of a side-lane in platoon order.

IX

Later the regiment entered a period of incessant fighting and the front became a long jagged line instead of an occasional covering operation. And whenever Grigory clashed with the enemy in battle or was in close proximity to him, he always experienced the same intense feeling of huge, insatiable curiosity about the Bolsheviks, about these Russian soldiers whom for some reason he had to fight. It was as if he had retained for ever the naive boyish feeling that had come over him in the first days of the 1914-17 war, when from the hill near Leszniow he had first watched the hurrying Austro-Hungarian troops and their baggage trains. 'Who are these people? What kind of people are they?' It was as if there had never been that period in his life when he had fought Chernetsov's detachment at Glubokaya. Then he had been in no doubt as to the nature of his adversaries; most of them had been officers of the Don Army, Cossacks. But here he had to deal with Russian soldiers, with quite different people, with men who in huge numbers were supporting the power of the Soviets and were bent, so he thought, on seizing the Cossack lands.

On another occasion he had come almost face to face with some Red Army men who had suddenly appeared from behind the spur of a ravine. He had been on reconnaissance patrol with his troop and as he rode along the bottom of the ravine to where the track forked he had suddenly heard the broad vowels and hard 'g' of Russian speech, swearing and a quick patter of footsteps. Several Red Guards, one of them a Chinese, topped the rise and, stunned by the sight of the Cossacks, froze for a second in astonishment.

'Cossacks!' one of them cried in a frightened choking voice and fell over.

The Chinese fired a shot. And the fair-haired one who had fallen over broke into a panting rush of words.

'Comrades! Get the Maxim! They're Cossacks, dang'ee!'

'Come on! Get it... They're Cossacks!'

Mitka Korshunov brought down the Chinese with a shot from his revolver, swung his horse round and, barging Grigory's mount aside, was the first to gallop away down the steep-banked echoing stream-bed, working hard with his reins to guide the horse's startled flight. The others galloped after him, kicking up the dust and bunching as they tried to get past one another. Behind them the machine-gun roared in a deep baritone, bullets snicked the leaves of blackthorn and hawthorn that grew thickly over the slopes and spurs, and pounded and tore rapaciously at the stony bed of the stream.

And several other times he had come face to face with the Reds, watched the Cossacks' bullets tearing the ground under the Red Guards' feet, and seen them fall and quit this life on the fertile yet, to them, alien soil of the Don.

And little by little Grigory had conceived a bitter anger against the Bolsheviks. They had invaded his life as enemies, taken him away from the land! He saw that this feeling was beginning to possess the other Cossacks. To all of them it seemed that the whole blame for this war lay with the Bolsheviks, who were encroaching on their region. And every man, when he looked at the ungarnered swathes of wheat, at fields of unreaped grain trampled by horses' hoofs, at the deserted threshing floors, remembered his own land, where the women were panting from toil that was beyond their strength, and his heart grew hard and brutal. To Grigory in battle it sometimes seemed that his enemies—these Tambov, Ryazan, and Saratov peasants—were also driven on by the same jealous feeling for the land as he. 'We're fighting for it like for a sweetheart,' he thought.

They started taking fewer prisoners, and instances of brutality towards prisoners became more frequent. A great wave of looting swept the front; the victims were anyone suspected of sympathising with the Bolsheviks, the families of men who were with the Red Army; prisoners were stripped naked.

Everything was taken, from horses and wagons to bulky things that could be of no use to men on the march. Both officers and men indulged in the looting. The second-line baggage trains swelled with plunder. The wagons were loaded with everything imaginable! Clothes, samovars, sewing-machines, harness, anything of any value. The loot was sent home. Relatives arrived, gladly bringing ammunition and food, and returned on wagons crammed with loot. The mounted regiments—and they were in the majority—showed the least restraint. A foot soldier had nowhere but his field-bag to put things, but a mounted man could fill his saddle-bags and tie on bundles and the horse would begin to look more like a pack animal than a cavalry mount. The Cossack fraternity let itself go. Plunder had always been the prime inspiration for Cossacks at war. Grigory knew this from the old men's tales about past campaigns, and from his own experience. Back in the days of the German war, when the regiment had been ranging over the rear areas in Prussia, the brigade commander—a general of some merit—had addressed the twelve squadrons drawn up before him and, pointing with his whip at a small town lying amid the hills, had said, 'Take it and the town is yours for two hours. But when those two hours are up, the first man caught looting goes to the wall!'

But Grigory had somehow never acquired the habit. Vaguely apprehensive of touching another man's goods and disgusted by looting, he took only food and fodder for his horse. Any looting by his own Cossacks struck him as particularly revolting. He kept his squadron on a tight rein and, if his men did take anything, it was only seldom and secretly. He never ordered the killing or stripping of prisoners. This undue gentleness roused discontent among the Cossacks and the command of the regiment. He was summoned to divisional headquarters to explain himself. One of the staff officers gave him a rough dressing-down.

'What's all this, Cornet? Why are you spoiling the squadron for me? What's the idea of this sob-stuff? Leaving yourself a loophole just in case? Playing a double game for old time's sake?.. What's that — don't shout at you?.. Now then, none of that talk! Don't you know what discipline means? What? Replace you? We shall indeed. I'll give orders today that you are to hand over the squadron! And you'd better not grumble, my lad!'

At the end of the month the regiment and a squadron of the 33rd Yelanskaya Regiment that was on its flank occupied the village of Gremyachy Log.

The dell below the village was crowded with willow, ash and poplar. About thirty white-walled cottages with low fences of rough-hewn stone were spread out over the slope. Above the village, on the crest of the hill stood an old windmill, exposed to all the winds that blew. Against the backdrop of an approaching white cloud its firmly anchored sails stood out blackly, like a crooked cross. It was a rainy overcast day. A yellow flurry of falling leaves was whispering in the dell. The lush osiers showed up like streaks of crimson blood. The threshing floors were piled high with gleaming straw. The soft canopy of approaching winter was spreading over the fresh-smelling earth.

Grigory and his troop took over the house that had been assigned to them by the billeting officers. The master had gone off with the Reds and the troop was obsequiously served by a stout elderly woman and her teenage daughter. Grigory walked out of the kitchen into the front room. Evidently the family lived well; painted floors, bentwood chairs, a mirror, the usual army photographs and a school diploma in a black frame on the walls. Grigory hung his soaked cape by the stove and made himself a cigarette.

Prokhor Zykov came in, propped his rifle against the bed, and informed him unconcernedly, 'The transport men have arrived. Your father's with them, Grigory Panteleyevich.'

'No?! Tell us another one!'

'I mean it. There're six others from our village besides him. Go and see!'

Grigory pulled on his greatcoat and went out.

Pantelei was leading the horses in through the gate by the bridle. On the wagon sat Darya, wrapped up in a homespun coat. She was holding the reins. Her laughing eyes glistened in a damp smile from under the dripping hood of the coat.

'What brings you here, good folk?' Grigory shouted, smiling at his father.

'Ah, my son, so you're still alive! We're your guests, so we're coming in without asking.'

Grigory flung an arm round his father's broad shoulders as he stepped forward to unhitch the traces.

'So you weren't expecting us, Grigory?'

'Of course, not.'

'We've been commandeered for supply duties... Ay, they grabbed us. We've brought you some shells, so all you've got to do is fight.'

They talked in snatches as they unharnessed the horses. Darya unloaded the food and fodder.

'What did you come for?' Grigory asked.

'To keep Father company. He's poorly, hasn't been well since harvest festival. Mother was afraid something might happen and he'd be all alone in strange country.'

Pantelei tossed the horses some fragrant green quitch, then came up to Grigory and, rounding his dark bloodshot eyes worriedly, asked in a husky whisper, 'How're things going?'

'Not bad. We're still at it.'

'I've heard tell the Cossacks don't want to march any further than their own border... Is that so?'

'That's just talk,' Grigory replied evasively.

'What do you mean by it, you lads?' the old man's voice was confused, almost estranged. 'How can you? And back home, our folk have been hoping... Who is there to defend our Father Don but you? And if you— God forbid!—don't want to fight... But how can that be? Your drivers were saying... They're sowing discord, the bastards!'

They entered the house. The other Cossacks came in and the talk turned at first to news of the village. After a whispered conversation with the mistress of the house, Darya untied her food bag and made the supper.

'They tell me you're a squadron commander no more?' Pantelei asked his son, combing out his matted beard with a homemade comb.

'I'm a troop commander now.'

Grigory's unconcerned reply stung the old man. His brow furrowed and he limped to the table, prayed hurriedly, and wiping his spoon on the hem of his coat, asked offendedly, 'What got you into disfavour? Didn't you please your superiors?'

Grigory had no desire to discuss the matter in the presence of the other Cossacks and he shrugged vexedly.

'They sent us a new commander... He's educated.'

'Well, you'll have to serve them just the same, son! They'll soon find out what they've lost! Them and their education! Tell 'em you got educated on active service in the German war, and much better than any of their lot in spectacles!'

The old man was clearly indignant, but Grigory frowned and glanced out of the corner of his eye to see if the Cossacks were grinning.

The demotion had not worried him. He had handed over the squadron gladly, realising that he would no longer bear the responsibility for the lives of the villagers. But his pride had been hurt and, by talking about it, his father had unwittingly upset him.

The mistress of the house went out to the kitchen and, feeling that he had support in the person of Bogatiryov, a fellow villager who had also come with supplies, Pantelei set the ball rolling.

'So it's true you're set on this idea of not going beyond our borders?'

Prokhor Zykov blinked his gentle calf-like eyes and smiled but said nothing. Mitka Korshunov, who was squatting on his haunches by the stove, went on smoking his cigarette though it had already burnt down to his fingers. The other three Cossacks were sitting or lying on the benches. No one answered the question and Bogatiryov made a despairing gesture.

'They don't trouble their heads much about such things,' he boomed in his deep voice. 'It's all one to them.'

'Why should we go any further?' Ilyin, a quiet sickly-looking Cossack, asked indolently. 'What for? My wife's left me with a house full of orphans. Why should I get myself killed for nothing?'

'We'll drive 'em off Cossack land, then go back home!' another Cossack supported him firmly.

Mitka Korshunov's green eyes flickered in a smile and he twirled his thin wispy moustache.

'We can fight for another five years for all I care!
I like it!'

'Outside!.. Saddle up!..' came a shout from the yard.

'There, you see!' Ilyin exclaimed desperately. 'Look at
that, folk! We haven't had time to get dry and they're
already calling us out! Into the line again! And you talk
about crossing the border! What borders? We ought to
go home! Making peace, that's what we ought to be
doing! And you say...'

It proved to be a false alarm. Thoroughly out of temper, Grigory led his horse back into the yard and for no
reason kicked it in the groin. Glaring at it furiously, he
barked, 'Walk straight, you devil!'

Pantelei was at the door smoking. He made way for
the Cossacks and asked, 'What set you off like that?'

'It was an alarm! They took a herd of cows for the
Reds.'

Grigory threw off his greatcoat and sat down at the
table. The others, grunting and swearing, pulled off
their outdoor clothes and dropped their sabres, rifles
and equipment on the benches.

When they had all bedded down for the night, Pantelei
called Grigory out into the yard. They sat down together
on the steps of the porch.

'I want a word with you.' The old man touched Grigory's knee and whispered, 'A week ago I paid Petro a
visit. Their 28th Regiment is just beyond Kalach... And
I got some good pickings there, son. Petro, he's real
thrifty, he is! He gave me a big sack of clothes, a horse,
sugar... And it's a right fine horse...'

'Just a minute!' Grigory interrupted grimly, stung by
a sudden conjecture. 'Is that what you came here for?'

'Why not? Other people are taking what they can,
Grisha...'

'Other people! Taking what they can!' Grigory repeated, at a loss for words. 'Haven't you got enough of your
own? You're like pigs! During the German war men were
shot for things like that!'

'Don't make all that fuss!' his father checked him
coldly. 'I'm not asking you for anything. I don't need
it. I'm alive today but tomorrow I may give up the ghost...
Think of yourself. You're such a rich man, to be sure!
Only one wagon left on the farm, and he... But why
shouldn't we take what we can get from the ones that
have gone over to the Reds? It'd be a sin not to! And
back home we can do with every bit of it.'

'Cut that out! And if you don't, I'll soon send you packing! Here am I, punching Cossacks on the jaw for that kind of thing and my own father comes to rob other men's families!' Grigory panted, quivering with rage.

'That's why they took your squadron away from you!' his father observed maliciously.

'And to hell with it! I'll give up the troop as well!'

'Why don't you! Very clever of you.'

For a minute neither of them spoke. As he lit a cigarette Grigory caught a glimpse of his father's surprised and insulted face. Only now had he fully grasped the old man's motives. That's why he brought Darya, the old devil! To guard the swag!

'Stepan Astakhov has turned up. Have you heard?' Pantelei said casually.

'What?' Grigory dropped his cigarette.

'Ay, he wasn't dead after all, he'd been taken prisoner. He's come home in fine shape. All the stuff and clothes you could think of! Two wagonloads of it,' the old man lied, boasting as though Stepan were one of his own family. 'He drove out and fetched Aksinya, then went straight off to the army. They've given him a good position, road-stage commandant somewhere—in Kazanskaya, I think.'

'Have you threshed much grain?' Grigory changed the subject.

'Thirty-five bushels.'

'How are your grandchildren?'

'Oho, they're doing fine! You ought to send 'em a present.'

'What presents can you send from the front!' Grigory sighed wistfully but his thoughts were with Aksinya and Stepan.

'You couldn't find a rifle for me, could you? Mebbe you've got one to spare?'

'What do you need it for?'

'To guard our home. Against beast and bad man. Just in case. I've got a whole crate of cartridges. We were carting a load of 'em, so I took one.'

'You can have a rifle. We've got plenty of that kind of thing.' Grigory smiled gloomily. 'Now go to bed! I've got to inspect the outpost.'

The next morning when part of the regiment left the village, Grigory rode away confident that he had shamed his father into abandoning his plans for loot. But as soon as he had seen the Cossacks off, Pantelei marched into the barn as if he owned it, lifted the horse collars and breach-bands down from their pegs and carried them out to his wagon. He was followed by the mistress of the house, her face streaming with tears as she screamed and clung to his shoulders.

'What are you doing! Have a heart! Don't you fear God's punishment! How can you treat orphans so? Give back the collars! Give them back, for God's sake!'

'Huh! You leave God out of it,' Pantelei limped away, waving the woman aside. 'Your lot would have been taking our stuff, I'm sure. Your man's a commissar, isn't he?.. Let go! What's yours is mine and God's as well, so stop whining.'

Then he went into the house, knocked the locks off the chests and, watched in silent approval by the other wagoners, picked out the newer trousers and tunics, examined them against the light, felt them with his black stubby fingers, and tied them up in bundles.

He left before dinner. Darya sat atop the loaded wagon, perched on a pile of bundles, her thin lips tightly compressed. At the back, on top of everything else stood a boiler. Pantelei had wrenched it out of the furnace in the bath-house and had only just managed to carry it as far as the wagon. In reply to Darya's scornful remark, 'Well, Father, you wouldn't part with your own shit!' he had replied wrathfully, 'Shut up, you bitch! Why should I leave 'em a boiler! You're as much use as our good-for-nothing Grisha! That boiler will come in useful to me. That it will! So get moving! And no more yapping!'

To the still weeping mistress of the house, as she closed the gate, he said amiably, 'Goodbye, m'dear! Don't be angry. You'll get some more by-and-by.'

X

A chain of days. One link forged to another. Marches, fighting, rest. Heat. Rain. The mingled smells of horse sweat and hot saddle leather. From the constant strain the blood in a man's veins turned to liquid lead. And from lack of sleep his head grew heavier than a three-inch shell. If only Grigory could have rested, refreshed himself with sleep! If only he could have gone plodding along a soft furrow behind a plough, whistling at his oxen, listening to the trumpeting of the cranes, way up amid the blue of the sky, gently wiping the silver gossamer from his cheeks and drinking in the winy scent of autumn soil upturned by the plough.

But instead, the standing corn was slashed by front-line roads. And along those roads came crowds of half-naked prisoners, black as death from the dust, or a squadron of cavalry trampling a fresh road with its iron hooves, crushing the corn. And in the villages those who enjoyed such pastimes searched the families of the Cossacks that had gone away with the Reds, and scourged the wives and mothers of the apostates with the lash...

The dreary, gelded days dragged on. They evaporated from the memory and even significant events left no trace. Wartime duties seemed even more tedious than in the previous campaign, perhaps because everything that had once been new was now utterly familiar. All those who had taken part in the previous war treated this one with scorn; the scale, the forces involved, the losses were all of toylike dimensions compared with the war against the Germans. Only death was the same as on the fields of Prussia, ever towering to its full height and frightening men into defending themselves like animals.

'Call this a war? It's just chickenfeed. When the Germans started shelling, they'd wipe out whole regiments. But now, if a couple of men in a squadron get scratched, they say it's a big loss!' the veterans reasoned.

But even this midget war was irksome. The discontent, the weariness, the bitterness slowly mounted. More and more voices in the squadron were heard to say, 'We'll knock the Reds out of the Don lands and call it a day! We won't go any further than our own border. Let Russia live in her own way, and we in ours. There's no need for us to force our ways on them.'

Around Filonovskaya desultory fighting continued all through autumn. The key strategic centre was Tsaritsyn, where both Whites and Reds had concentrated their best forces, but on the northern front there was nothing to choose between the opposing sides. Both were building up their forces for a decisive attack. The Cossacks had more cavalry and made use of this advantage to wage a war of manoeuvre, enveloping the enemy's flanks and attacking from the rear. They retained the advantage only while they were opposed by half-hearted, newly mobilised units drawn mainly from the frontline zones. The peasants of the Saratov and Tambov provinces surrendered in thousands. But as soon as the command sent in a workers' regiment, a detachment of sailors or Red cavalry, the balance was restored and again the initiative swung from one side to the other and victories of purely local significance were scored in turn.

Though he himself was a participant, Grigory observed the course of the war with indifference. He was sure that by winter the front would disappear; he knew that the Cossacks were in a mood for peace and there could be no question of a prolonged struggle. Occasionally the regiment received newspapers. With a feeling of hatred Grigory would pick up a number of *Upper Don Country*, printed on yellowish wrapping paper, scan the communiqués from the fronts, and grit his teeth. The other Cossacks would guffaw good-naturedly when he read out to them the bragging reports, full of forced optimism.

On 27 September, fighting continued with varying success in the Filonovskaya sector. On the night of the 25th the valiant Vyoshenskaya Regiment drove the enemy out of the village of Podgorny and in the course of a hot pursuit broke into the village of Lukyanovsky. Much booty and huge numbers of prisoners were captured. The Red units are retreating in disorder. Cossack morale is high. The men of the Don are eager for new victories!

'How many prisoners did we take? Huge numbers? Ho! Ho! The sons-of-bitches! We captured thirty-two! And they... Haw! Haw! Haw!' Mitka Korshunov showed his white teeth in a guffaw, holding his sides with his long hands.

Nor did the Cossacks believe the reports of the successes of the 'Cadets' in Siberia and on the Kuban. The newspaper's lies were too blatant. When Okhvatkin, a tall, burly Cossack, read an article about the mutiny of Czechoslovak troops, he declared in Grigory's presence, 'They'll squash the Czechs first, then they'll have their whole army to smash us with and we'll be for it! We'll have all the muzhiks in Mother Russia against us!' And he concluded ominously, 'Some joke, eh!'

'Don't try to scare us! Your daft talk gives me the belly-ache,' Prokhor Zykov waved him aside.

But Grigory, as he rolled a cigarette, thought to himself with quiet malice, 'He's right!'

For a long time that evening he sat at the table with

his shoulders hunched and the collar of his faded shirt with its equally faded shoulder-straps unbuttoned. His sunburnt face, its deep furrows and sharp cheekbones smoothed by an unhealthy fleshiness, was stern. He sat working his dark muscular neck, thoughtfully twisting the curly sun-rusted tip of his moustache and staring at nothing with eyes that in the past few years had acquired a cold, stony look. His thoughts were unusually sluggish and, as he bedded down for the night, he said aloud, as though answering a general question, 'There's nowhere to go!'

He spent a sleepless night. Several times he went out to see his horse and stood for a long time on the porch, amid the black, silkily rustling darkness.

* * *

Yes, the tiny star under which Grigory had been born was still burning with a faint, tremulous light. The time had not yet come for it to break loose and sear the heavens with its cold descending flame. Three horses had been killed under him that autumn, his greatcoat had been holed in five places. Death seemed to be playing with the Cossack, hovering over him on its black wings. One day a bullet went straight through the brass hilt of his sabre and the sword-knot fell at his horse's feet, as though cut with scissors.

'Someone's praying hard for you, Grigory,' Mitka Korshunov told him and was surprised at the far from cheerful smile that appeared on Grigory's face.

The front moved on beyond the railway line. Every day more wagons arrived bringing coils of barbed wire. Every day the telegraph buzzed messages along the front:

The forces of the Allies may be expected any day now. The positions along the border must be consolidated pending the arrival of reinforcements. The Red advance must be held up at all costs.

Mobilised civilians hacked at the frozen ground with crowbars, dug trenches and stretched barbed wire along them. But at night, when the Cossacks abandoned the trenches and went to the houses to get warm, the Red Army patrols would creep forward, pull down the posts and fix appeals to the Cossacks on the rusty barbs. The

Cossacks would read them eagerly, like letters from home. Clearly the war could not be continued under such circumstances. Fierce frosts alternated with thaws and heavy snowfalls. The trenches were buried in snow and it was hard to stay in them even an hour. The Cossacks shivered and nursed their frostbitten hands and feet. Many of them in the unmounted units had no boots. Some had come to the front as if they had merely stepped out into their own farmyards to feed the cattle, in leather shoes and light trousers. No one had any faith in the Allies. 'They must be drawn by beetles,' Andrei Kashulin complained one day. And when the Cossacks encountered a Red patrol, they would hear shouts of, 'Heh, there! Christ-lovers! While you're waiting for tanks, we'll chase you out on our sledges! So grease your heels well—we'll soon be paying you a visit!'

In mid-November the Reds launched an offensive. They attacked stubbornly, forcing the Cossacks back to the railway, but the turning-point came later. On 16 December after a lengthy engagement Mironov's Red cavalry crushed the 33rh Regiment, but in the Vyoshenskaya Regiment's sector, which was deployed round the village of Kolodezyansky, it encountered desperate resistance. From behind a snowy ridge of threshing-floor fences the Vyoshenskaya machine-gunners met the enemy, now attacking on foot, with a squall of fire. The right-flank machine-gun in the experienced hands of Antipov, a Karginskaya Cossack, carved deep into the advancing enemy lines. The Cossacks' positions were veiled in gun smoke. And on the left flank two squadrons started an enveloping movement.

Towards evening the half-heartedly attacking Red Army units were replaced by a detachment of sailors, who had just arrived at the front. They came straight at the machine-guns without cheering or taking cover.

Grigory fired until the stock of his rifle began to smoke, and the barrel was so hot it burnt his fingers. When he had cooled it, he put in a fresh clip and again trained his sights on the distant black figures.

The sailors drove them out of their positions. The squadrons took to their horses and galloped through the village on to the hill beyond. Grigory glanced back and the reins dropped from his hands. From the hill he could see far across the sombre snow-covered field with its jutting snowdrifts and violet-shadowed ravines. For a verst or more it was covered with a black rash of bodies.

The pea-jackets and leather jerkins of the sailors who had been mown down by the machine-gun fire showed up darkly on the snow like a flock of migrating rooks that had settled on the field to rest.

Towards evening the squadrons, split up by the Red offensive and out of touch with the Yelanskaya Regiment and a regiment from Ust-Medveditskaya that had been on their right, halted for the night in two villages situated on a small stream that flowed into the River Buzuluk.

It was dusk when Grigory, returning from the place where the squadron commander had ordered him to set up outposts, met the regimental commander and his adjutant in a lane.

'Where's the Third Squadron?' the commander asked, reining in his horse.

Grigory replied and the officers rode on.

'Did your squadron suffer heavy losses?' the adjutant called back when he had gone a little distance. Doubtful of the reply, he repeated his query, 'Did you hear me?'

But Grigory rode on without answering.

Transports were coming through the village all night. A battery halted for a long time near the house where Grigory and his Cossacks were lodged. The sound of the drivers' shouting and swearing as they hurried to and fro penetrated the little window. The gun-crews and some orderlies from regimental headquarters who had turned up in the village came in to get warm. At midnight the Cossacks and their hosts were awakened by three gunners from a battery. One of their guns had got stuck in the stream. They had decided to spend the night in the village and drag the gun out with oxen the next morning. Grigory awoke and lay watching the gunners scraping the frozen mud off their boots and hanging their wet footcloths on the edge of the stove. Then a mud-spattered artillery officer entered the house. He asked if he could stay the night, pulled off his greatcoat and sat for some time, carelessly smearing the mud over his face with the sleeve of his tunic as he tried to wipe it off.

'We've lost one gun,' he said, looking at Grigory with the unprotesting eyes of a weary horse. 'The fighting today was as bad as it used to be at Machekha. They spotted us after two shots... And what a wallop they gave us—broke the main axle in one go! And that gun was on a threshing floor. Couldn't have been better camouflaged!..' Habitually, and probably unconsciously, he attached an obscenity to every phrase. 'You from the Vyoshenskaya Regiment? Want some tea? Good woman, could you let us have a samovar, eh?'

He turned out to be a garrulous companion, and his thirst for tea was insatiable. After half an hour Grigory knew that he had been born in Platovskaya stanitsa, had received his education at a secondary modern school, served in the German war and experienced two unsuccessful marriages.

'Now it's Amen for the Don Army!' he said, licking the sweat from his shaven upper lip with the sharp tip of his red tongue. 'The war's nearly over. Tomorrow the front will start breaking up and in a fortnight's time we'll be in Novocherkassk. We thought we'd take Russia by storm with a bunch of barefoot Cossacks! Weren't we idiots? And the regular officers, they're all scoundrels, honestly they are! You're a Cossack, aren't you? Well, they want to use you to do their dirty work for them. While they draw all the grub and bayleaf they want from the stores!'

His colourless eyes blinked rapidly and his massive body shifted from side to side, as he leaned forward over the table, but the corners of his big flabby mouth drooped despondently and his face retained its former expression of an obedient browbeaten horse.

'It was all right fighting in the old days, even in Napoleon's time. The two armies clashed then fell apart again. No fronts, no sticking in trenches. But now try to sort out these operations— it'd fool the devil himself. If the historians used to shoot a line about past wars, what'll they make of this one! It's not a war, it's sheer boredom! No colour. Only mud! And anyhow it's all senseless. If I had my way, I'd get these leaders facing each other and say to them, "Here's a sergeant-major for you, Mr. Lenin, let him teach you to handle a sabre. And as for you, Mr. Krasnov, you ought to know already." And then let them fight it out, like David and Goliath, and the one who wins takes power. The people don't care who rules them. What do you think, Cornet?'

Grigory watched the fleshy shoulders and arms jerking and the red tongue flickering unpleasantly, and made no reply. He wanted to sleep and this troublesome half-witted artilleryman annoyed him and the doggy smell from his sweaty feet was sickening.

The next morning Grigory awoke with a nagging sense of having failed to solve a problem. The outcome that he had foreseen since autumn had nevertheless taken him by surprise. He had not realised that the dissatisfaction with the war, which had at first murmured in tiny streams through the squadrons and regiments, was quietly growing into a mighty flood. But now he could see only this flood, greedily washing away the front.

So it is in early spring, when a man is riding across the steppe. The sun is shining. All around, the violet snow lies virgin fresh. But underneath, invisible to the eye, the wonderful work of freeing the earth goes on, as it always has and always will. The sun eats away the snow, burrows into it and soaks it with moisture from below. A steaming misty night passes and next morning the crust begins to settle with a rustle and roar, the green water from the hillsides bubbles over the roads and tracks, melting lumps of snow spatter from under hooves. The air is warm. The loamy hillocks thaw and grow bare, and there is a primeval smell of clayey soil and rotted grass. At midnight the ravines roar lustily; the snow-choked bottoms gurgle, the bared velvet-black ploughland gives off a languorously sweet vapour. By evening a moaning steppeland stream breaks the ice and carries it away with waters swollen and full as the breast of a nursing mother. And the man, astonished by the sudden end of winter, halts on the sandy bank, looking for a place shallow enough to cross and flicking his sweating, nervous horse with his whip. While all around the snow gleams treacherously and innocently blue, and white winter slumbers still.

All day long the regiment retreated. Transports galloped down the roads. Somewhere to the right, beyond a grey cloud muffling the horizon, artillery rumbled like a fall of loose rock. The squadrons squelched along the melting dung-strewn tracks, their horses mashing the slush that came over their fetlocks. Orderlies galloped past along the verges. Silent rooks, all decked out in gleaming blue-black plumage, awkward as dismounted cavalrymen, strutted importantly along the roadside as if they were taking the salute of the retreating Cossack squadrons, the columns of tattered Cossack infantry, and the straggling baggage trains.

Grigory realised that it was in no man's power to hold back the uncoiling spring of the retreat. And that night, filled with a joyous resolve, he deserted his regiment.

'Where're you off to, Grigory?' Mitka Korshunov asked, quizzically watching Grigory as he pulled on his

cape over his greatcoat and hitched his sabre and revolver to his belt.

'Why d'you ask?'

'I just wondered!'

The muscles in Grigory's flushed cheeks tautened but
he replied cheerfully, with a wink, 'All the way to nowhere. Get me?'

And he walked out.

His horse was waiting as he had left it, still saddled.

Until daybreak he galloped along the frostily steaming
steppeland tracks. 'I'll have a spell at home and then,
when I hear them going past, I'll slip out and join them,'
he thought indifferently of those with whom only the
day before he had been fighting shoulder to shoulder.

Towards evening on the next day he led his horse,
hollow-flanked and staggering after a ride of two hundred versts, into his father's yard.

XI

At the end of November news of the arrival of a military mission of the Entente powers reached Novocherkassk. Persistent rumours spread through the town
that a powerful British naval squadron was anchored in
the roads of Novorossiisk harbour, that a huge expeditionary force of Allied troops from Salonica was being
landed, that a corps of French zouaves had already disembarked and would soon join with the Volunteer Army
in a combined offensive. Rumours snowballed through
the town.

Krasnov ordered a guard of honour from the Ataman's
Life Guards to be sent out to meet the new arrivals.
Two hundred young guardsmen were hastily fitted out
in top boots and white leather equipment and no less
hastily despatched to Taganrog along with a hundred
trumpeters.

The British and French military missions in South
Russia had decided to send a few officers to Novocherkassk to make a political reconnaissance. Their task was
to study the situation on the Don and the prospects of
further struggle against the Bolsheviks. Britain was
represented by Captain Bond and lieutenants Bloom-
field and Monroe, France by Captain Cochin and lieutenants Dupré and Faure. It was the arrival of these
relatively low-ranking officers of the military missions,

elevated to the status of 'ambassadors' by the whim of fate, that caused such a flurry in the Ataman's palace.

The 'ambassadors' were escorted to Novocherkassk in great pomp. Flattered by the excessive servility and obeisance that surrounded them, these unassuming officers suddenly became aware of their 'true' greatness and began to look down condescendingly on the renowned Cossack generals and statesmen of the almighty cardboard-and-tinsel republic.

Chilly notes of condescension and arrogance began to break through the young French lieutenants' outward polish and exaggerated French politeness in their conversation with the Cossack generals.

That evening a banquet for a hundred guests was held at the palace. A Cossack Army chorus draped the hall in the silken tapestries of Cossack songs, richly embroidered with tenor descants, and a brass band impressively blared out the Allies' national anthems. As the circumstances required, the 'ambassadors' ate modestly and with great dignity and, sensing the historic importance of the occasion, the ataman's guests watched them with surreptitious curiosity.

Krasnov began his speech.

'Gentlemen, you are seated in a historic hall, from whose walls the heroes of another national war, that of 1812, look down upon you in silent witness. Platov, Ilovaisky and Denisov remind us of the hallowed days when the people of Paris welcomed their liberators— the Don Cossacks—and when Emperor Alexander I restored beautiful France from the ruins...'

The delegates of 'beautiful France' already had a merrier gleam in their eyes from the good measure of the local sparkling wine they had drunk, but they listened attentively to Krasnov's speech. After expatiating at great length on the desperate hardships endured by 'the Russian people at the hands of the barbarous Bolsheviks', Krasnov ended on a note of high pathos.

'...The best representatives of the Russian people are dying in Bolshevik prisons. They are looking to you; they await your help and it is they, not the Don, that you should assist. We can say with pride: we are free! But all our thoughts, the aim and purpose of our struggle are great Russia, the Russia that is loyal to her allies, defending their interests, the Russia that has sacrificed herself for them and now longs so passionately for their assistance. One hundred and four years ago, in the month of March, the French people welcomed the Emperor Alexander I and his Russian Guards. And from that day on there began a new era in the life of France, an era which brought her to first place among the nations of the world. One hundred and four years ago Count Platov visited London. We are looking forward to seeing you in Moscow! We shall be expecting you, so that together we may enter the Kremlin to the sound of triumphant marches and our national anthem, so that together we may share all the delights of peace and freedom! Great Russia! These words express all our dreams and hopes!'

When Krasnov had concluded, Captain Bond rose to his feet. Dead silence fell upon the assembled guests at the sound of English being spoken. The interpreter applied himself zealously to his task.

'Speaking on his own behalf and on behalf of Captain Cochin, Captain Bond is authorised to inform the Ataman of the Don that they are official envoys of the Entente powers, sent to find out what is happening on the Don. Captain Bond assures you that the Entente powers will help the Don and the Volunteer Army in their courageous struggle against the Bolsheviks with all the forces and means at their disposal, not excluding troops.'

Before the interpreter could utter the last phrase, the walls were shaken by three resounding cheers. Toasts were proposed amid flourishes and fanfares from the band. Glasses were raised to the prosperity of 'beautiful France' and 'mighty Britain' and to 'the granting of victory over the Bolsheviks'... The sparkling wine of the Don foamed in the glasses, the vintage champagne fizzed, and the well-matured port gave off its sweet fragrance...

Everyone was expecting a speech from the representatives of the Allied mission and Captain Bond did not keep them waiting.

'I propose a toast to great Russia and I should like to hear in this hall your beautiful old anthem. We shall not pay attention to the words, I only want to hear the music...'

The interpreter translated and Krasnov, turning his face, now pale with emotion, to the guests, cried in an overpitched voice, 'To a great, united and indivisible Russia—hurrah!'

The band swept smoothly and powerfully into 'God save the Tsar'. Everyone rose to their feet and drained their glasses. Tears rolled down the cheeks of the grey-haired Archbishop Hermogenus. 'How beautiful it is!' the tipsy Captain Bond proclaimed delightedly. In an excess of feeling one of the dignitaries sobbed unaffectedly, plunging his beard into a napkin smeared with squashed caviar...

* * *

That night a fierce wind blowing from the Sea of Azov howled and roared over the town. The dome of the cathedral gleamed deathly pale amid the whirling flurries of the first snowstorm.

That night, at a rubbish dump in the ravines outside the town the Bolshevik railwaymen of Shakhty were shot by order of a court martial. With their hands tied behind their backs they were led in pairs to the edge of a ravine and gunned down at point-blank range with revolvers and rifles. The sounds of the shots were snuffed out by the frosty wind like the sparks from a cigarette.

But at the entrance to the Ataman's palace the guard of honour from the Ataman's Life Guards froze at attention in the searing winter wind. The Cossacks' hands gripping the hilts of their bared sabres grew black and numb, their eyes watered, their feet froze... Drunken cries, the brassy blare of the band and the sobbing flights of the tenors in the Don Army chorus rose from the palace until dawn.

* * *

A week later the worst happened. The front collapsed. The first regiment to abandon its sector, in the Kalach area, was the 28th, in which Petro Melekhov was serving.

After secret negotiations with the command of the 15th Inzenskaya Division the Cossacks decided to withdraw from the front and allow the Red forces to pass unopposed through the territory of the Upper Don district. Yakov Fomin, a Cossack of rather limited intelligence, took command of the insurgent regiment, but he was really only the figurehead and behind him stood a group of Bolshevik-minded Cossacks who held the reins of power.

After a stormy meeting, at which the officers, fearing a bullet in the back, half-heartedly argued the need to fight and the Cossacks unitedly, forcefully and without much rhyme or reason shouted the same old phrases that everyone was tired of hearing about the war being unnecessary and about making peace with the Bolsheviks, the regiment started to withdraw. After the first day's march, at the settlement of Solonki the commander of the regiment, Lieutenant-Colonel Filippov and most of the other officers stayed behind during the night and at dawn joined the retreating battered remnants of Count Molyer's brigade.

The next regiment, after the 28th, to abandon its positions was the 36th. At full strength, with all its officers it arrived in Kazanskaya. The commander, a stunted little fellow with furtive eyes, who was making servile efforts to please his Cossacks, rode up amidst a bunch of horsemen to the house where the roadstage commandant had his office. He strode in, playing belligerently with his whip.

'Who's the commandant?'

'I am the commandant's assistant,' Stepan Astakhov replied, rising with some dignity. 'Close the door after you, sir.'

'I am the commander of the 36th Regiment, Lieutenant-Colonel Naumov. Er ... I have the honour to... My regiment needs boots and clothing. My men are half-naked and barefoot. D'you hear?'

'The commandant is away, without his permission I can't issue a single pair of felt boots from the stores.'

'What?'

'That's what.'

'You! Whose side are you on? I arrest you, damn you! Put him down in the cellar, lads! Where are the keys of the store, you rear rat?.. Wha-aa-at?' Naumov lashed the table with his whip and, pale with anger, pushed his shaggy Manchurian hat to the back of his head. 'Give me the keys and don't argue!'

Within half an hour bundles of sheepskins, felt boots and leather boots were flying out of the doorway of the store and landing on the snow amid clouds of orange dust or in the arms of the waiting throng of Cossacks. Bags of sugar were passed out. For a long time the square buzzed with a cheerful hubbub.

Meanwhile the 28th Regiment with its new commander, Sergeant Fomin, had marched into Vyoshenskaya. In its wake, at a distance of about thirty versts came units of the Inzenskaya Division. That day Red patrols ranged as far as the village of Dubrovka.

Four days before this the commander of the Northern Front, Major-General Ivanov, and his chief of staff, General Zambrzhitsky, had hastily evacuated to Karginskaya. Their car got stuck in the snow. In her anxiety Zambrzhitsky's wife bit her lips till they bled, the children began to cry....

For a few days Vyoshenskaya was in a state of anarchy. It was rumoured that forces were being concentrated in Karginskaya for an attack on the 28th Regiment. But on December 22nd Ivanov's adjutant arrived from Karginskaya and, chuckling to himself, went to the general's quarters to collect a few things that had been forgotten during his hasty departure: a summer cap with a brand-new cockade, a hairbrush, some underwear and a few other odds and ends.

Units of the 8th Red Army poured through the yawning gap in the Northern Front. General Savateyev fell back to the Don, offering no resistance. General Fitskhelaurov's regiments withdrew hastily towards Taly and Boguchar. For a week the north was unusually quiet. No rumble of artillery was heard, the machine-guns were silent. Discouraged by the defection of the Upper Don regiments, the Lower Don Cossacks who had been fighting in the north retreated without a fight. The Reds advanced cautiously, slowly, carefully feeling out the villages ahead with their patrols.

But this huge setback for the Don Government on the Northern Front was compensated by a joyful event. An Allied mission consisting of General Poole, head of the British military mission in the Caucasus, and his chief of staff Colonel Keyes and the French representatives General Franchais d'Espère and Captain Fouquet, arrived in Novocherkassk.

Krasnov took the Allied officers to the front. On a cold December morning a guard of honour was drawn up on the platform of Chir station. General Mamontov, who with his drooping moustache and drink-sodden face usually looked slovenly, spruced himself up for the occasion. His freshly shaven cheeks glowed purple as, surrounded by his officers, he paced up and down the platform waiting for the train. By the station building a military band stood in readiness, stamping their feet and blowing on their chilled blue fingers. The guard of honour was a picturesque array of Lower Don Cossacks of various hues and ages. Grey-bearded grandfathers stood side by side with beardless youth and hairy frontline men. The old men's greatcoats gleamed with the gold and silver of the decorations they had won at Lovcha and Plevna, the younger Cossacks had rows of crosses they had earned in daredevil charges at Geok-Tepe, Sandepa and in the German war, at Peremysl, Warsaw and Lvov. The youngsters had nothing to shine with but they held themselves stiffly to attention and did all they could to imitate their elders.

The train rumbled in amidst milky clouds of steam. Before the Pullman car could open its doors the band-master waved his hands wildly and the band blared out the British national anthem. Holding his sabre to his side, Mamontov hurried towards the carriage. Krasnov, ever the hospitable and attentive host, escorted his guests to the station building past the rigid ranks of Cossacks.

'The whole of Cossackdom has risen to defend the Motherland from the barbaric Red Guard bands. Here you see representatives of three generations. These men fought in the Balkans, in Japan, in Austro-Hungary and in Prussia, and now they are fighting for the freedom of their own country,' he said in his splendid French, smiling graciously and giving a royal nod in the direction of the older Cossacks standing at attention with bulging eyes and bated breath.

Acting on orders from above, Mamontov had not wasted his time in selecting the guard of honour. The goods were displayed to their best advantage.

The Allies toured the front and returned to Novocherkassk well satisfied.

'I am extremely pleased by the splendid turn-out, discipline and fighting spirit of your troops,' General Poole told Krasnov before leaving. 'I shall immediately give orders for the first contingent of our soldiers to be sent here from Salonica. I request you, General, to have three thousand winter coats and pairs of warm boots in readiness. I trust that with our assistance you will be able to eradicate Bolshevism for ever.'

The sheepskins and boots were prepared in all haste. But for some reason the Allied expeditionary force did not arrive in Novorossiisk. Poole went back to London and was replaced by the cold and haughty General Briggs, who brought with him new instructions from London and declared harshly, with a directness befitting his rank, 'His Majesty's Government will give the Volunteer Army on the Don extensive material assistance, but not a single soldier.'

No further comment on this statement was needed.

XII

By the autumn of 1918 the hostility that since the days of the imperialist war had divided officers and Cossacks like an invisible furrow assumed unprecedented dimensions. At the end of 1917, when the Cossack units were slowly returning to the Don there had been few cases of the killing or betrayal of officers, but a year later they became almost a regular occurrence. Officers were forced to follow the example of the Red commanders and lead their troops in attack, and then quietly, without more ado were shot in the back. Unity was still strong only in such forces as the Gundorovsky St. George Regiment, but there were not many of them in the Don Army.

Petro Melekhov, a slow but wily thinker, had long since realised that to quarrel with the Cossacks could mean death, and from the outset had worked hard to break down the division between himself, an officer, and the rank and file. When circumstances permitted, he talked just as they did about the senselessness of the war; his words were forced and insincere, but this was not noticed; he posed as a Bolshevik sympathiser and laid himself out to please Fomin as soon as he saw that the regiment favoured him as its commander. Like any of the others, Petro was not averse to a little looting, to cursing his superiors or to sparing the life of a prisoner, even though his heart might be burning with hatred and his hands twitching with the desire to strike and kill. In the performance of his duties he was unassuming and easy-going—more like a lump of wax than an officer! And by this means Petro had managed to worm his way into the Cossacks' confidence, to change his face before their very eyes.

When Filippov went off with the other officers at Solonka, Petro stayed behind. Quiet and submissive, always keeping in the background, moderate in all things, he rode into Vyoshenskaya with the regiment. But there after only two days his restraint left him and without reporting to headquarters or to Fomin, he made a dash for home.

That morning a meeting had been held in Vyoshen- skaya in the square outside the old church. The regiment was expecting delegates from the Inzenskaya Division. Cossacks in greatcoats and short coats—some of them turned, some made out of old greatcoats—in frock coats and wadded tunics, thronged the square. Petro could scarcely believe that this huge motley crowd was a fighting unit, the 28th Cossack Regiment. He walked despondently from one group to another, looking at the Cossacks with new eyes. At the front their dress had not attracted much attention and, in any case, Petro had never seen the whole regiment assembled together. Biting his wispy blonde moustache with hatred, he stared at the frost-rimed faces and heads in their sheepskin hats of every shape and peaked caps of every shade, then looked down and found the same rich variety of foot- wear: down-at-heel felt boots or top boots, leg-wrappings over the ankle-boots taken from Red Army men.

'Trash! Muzhiks! Bums!' Petro whispered to himself in helpless anger.

Fomin's orders hung in white sheets on the fences. There were no local people about. The stanitsa was lying low. The white breast of the snow-covered Don could be seen at the ends of the side-streets. Beyond it the forest stood out blackly, as though drawn in Indian ink. Beside the grey stone pile of the old church a bunch of women who had come from the villages to meet their husbands huddled together like a flock of sheep.

Petro in his fur-trimmed sheepskin with its huge breast pocket and that wretched officer's Astrakhan busby of which he had but recently been so proud, was constantly aware of the cold, hostile glances cast in his direction. They got under his skin and deepened the apprehensive confusion that already possessed him. Later he would vaguely recall a stocky Red Army man in a good greatcoat and new lambskin cap with untied earflaps climbing on to an upturned barrel in the middle of the square. His hand in its fluffy woollen glove straight- ened the grey tasseled rabbitwool Cossack scarf round his neck as he surveyed the scene.

'Comrade Cossacks!' the man's low husky voice grated on Petro's ears.

Petro looked round and saw the Cossacks, taken aback by this unusual mode of address, exchanging glances and winking at each other expectantly. The Red Army man spoke at length about rule by the Soviets, about the

Red Army and relations with the Cossacks. A thing that impressed itself on Petro's memory was that the speaker was constantly interrupted by shouts:

'Comrade, what's a commune?'

'Will they let us in?'

'What's this commune party then?'

The speaker clasped his hands to his chest, turning to all sides and patiently explained.

'Comrades! The Communist Party is a voluntary organisation. Those who join the party do so at their own wish, because they want to fight for the great cause of freeing the workers and peasants from oppression by capitalists and landowners.'

The next minute a voice from another corner shouted:

'Will ye, please, explain about the Communists and commissars?'

The answer was given and again, within minutes, a strident bass boomed, 'You're not making it clear about the commune. Would you kindly explain it. We're an ignorant lot here, ye know. Put it simple like!'

The next speaker was Fomin, who rambled on, trying to show off with the word 'evacuate', which he could hardly pronounce. A young fellow in a student's cap and fashionably smart overcoat was dancing attendance on Fomin. But as Petro listened to Fomin's incoherent speech he recalled the February of 1917 and the day when his wife Darya had come to visit him and he had first seen Fomin at a station on the line to Petrograd. Mentally he conjured up the stern, moistly glittering gaze in the wide-set eyes of the guardsman deserter, wearing a greatcoat with the frayed number '52' on his sergeant's shoulder straps, and his bearlike walk. 'Couldn't stand any more of it, brother!' that scarcely audible phrase came back to Petro. 'A deserter, a fool like Khristonya, and now he's commander of the regiment and I'm left out in the cold,' Petro thought with a feverish glint in his eyes.

A Cossack with machine-gun belts criss-crossed over his chest took Fomin's place on the barrel.

'Brothers! I was in Podtyolkov's detachment myself and, God willing, I'll see the days when we'll fight together against the Cadets!' he shouted huskily, twitching and waving his arms tipsily.

Petro strode quickly away to his quarters, and while he was saddling his horse, he heard the sound of shots as other Cossacks rode out of the stanitsa, giving the traditional salute to tell the villages of their return.

XIII

The short ominously silent days seemed as long as those of harvest time. The villages lay buried in the vast snowy wilderness of the steppe. It was as though the Don lands had died, as though every district had been deserted by its inhabitants. And now a great cloud seemed to cover these lands with its thick, impenetrably dark wing and spread silently, menacingly until suddenly, like a whirlwind it would twist and bow the poplars to the ground, blaze with lightning, and let loose a dry crackling roar of thunder, tearing and twisting the white forest beyond the Don, ripping rocks from the chalky headlands and howling in all the destructive voices that a storm can command.

In Tatarsky mists had covered the earth since morning. The murmur from the hill presaged a frost. By noon the sun slipped out of the soggy murk but the scene grew no brighter. The mist roamed aimlessly over the Donside hills, plunged into ravines and clefts and perished there, leaving its dampness on the mossy chalk boulders and the bare snow-sprinkled ridges.

Night lifted the huge glowing red shield of the moon over the spears of the stark forest. It shone murkily above the silent villages like a bloody reflection of war and its fires. And its ruthless, unfading light stirred dim anxieties in men's hearts and made animals restless. Horses and oxen stirred restlessly in their stalls until dawn. Dogs howled balefully, and long before midnight the cocks began to crow discordantly. By daybreak the wet branches of the trees were sheathed in ice. When the wind stirred them they rang like steel stirrups. And it was as though an invisible host of cavalry were riding along the left back of the Don, through the dark forest and the blue murk, its weapons and harness clanking.

Nearly all the Tatarsky Cossacks who had been on the Northern Front returned to the village, deserting the units that were slowly falling back towards the Don. Every day one of the latecomers would appear. Some came with the intention of unsaddling their war horses for a long time hence, of hiding their weapons in a rick of straw or under the eaves of a barn and waiting for the

Reds, while others opened their snow-choked gates only to tether the horse in the yard, replenish their supply of dried bread, spend a night with their wives, and in the morning make for the highway and look back for the last time on the dead white expanse of the Don and the land of their birth that they might be leaving for ever.

Who can foresee his death? Who can guess the end of the human journey?.. It was hard for the horses to quit the village. It was hard for the Cossacks to tear from their scarred hearts their love-pity for their near ones. And as they trod this shifting windswept track, many in their minds turned back and made for him. Many were the sad thoughts they pondered on that road... And maybe a tear or two, salty as blood, slipped down a saddle flap and fell on a freezing stirrup or the hoof-hacked road. But no yellow steppeland tulip, flower of parting, would grow there in spring.

* * *

The night after Petro arrived from Vyoshenskaya the Melekhovs held a family council.

'Well?' Pantelei had asked almost before Petro had crossed the threshold. 'Had enough fighting, have you? Come back without your shoulder straps? Go and shake hands with your brother, then, your mother'll be glad to see you, your wife's pining for you... Welcome home m'lad... Grigory! Come down off that stove!'

Grigory let his bare feet dangle, displaying the trouser straps under the instep, and scratched his dark hairy chest with a smile as he watched his brother take off his sword-belt and fumble with numb fingers at the knotted scarves of his hood. Darya stared silently and smilingly into her husband's eyes as she undid the fastenings of his sheepskin, nervously avoiding his right side, where a hand grenade, hitched to his belt, gleamed dully beside his revolver holster.

Dunyashka brushed her brother's frosty moustache with her cheek and ran out to stable the horse. Ilyinichna wiped her lips with her apron in readiness to kiss her 'eldest'. Natalya was busy at the stove with the children clinging to her skirt. Everyone expected Petro to say something but all he did was to utter a husky greeting from the threshold and pull off his outdoor clothes in silence. He was a long time brushing the snow off his boots with the millet-straw besom and when he finally straightened his back his lips suddenly trembled wretchedly. He leaned helplessly against the back of the bedstead and everyone was surprised to see tears on his dark, frost-bitten cheeks.

'Now then, soldier! What's all this?' the old man asked, trying to hide his alarm and the quiver in his own voice with a show of joviality.

'We're finished, Father!'

Petro's mouth drooped and twisted, his blond eye-brows twitched and, lowering his eyes he blew his nose into his dirty, tobacco-fouled handkerchief.

Grigory knocked aside the cat that had come rubbing up to him and with a 'humph!' jumped down from the stove. Their mother burst into tears as she kissed Petro's lice-infested head, then quickly tore herself away.

'My little chit! My poor thing, can't I give you some milk? Sit down and have some soup, dear. You must be hungry?'

Seated at table with his nephew on his knees, Petro recovered a little. Checking his emotion, he described the 28th Regiment's abandoning of the front, the flight of its officers, the appearance of Fomin and the recent meeting in Vyoshenskaya.

'What do you think?' Grigory asked, keeping his dark-veined hand on his daughter's head.

'I don't have to think. Tomorrow I'll rest up during the day, then set off at night. Get some grub ready for me, Ma,' he said turning to his mother.

'So you're clearing out?' Pantelei plunged his fingers into his pouch and stood with a pinch of tobacco sprinkling from his fingers, while he waited for an answer.

Petro stood up and made the sign of the cross before the dim, blackened icons and a sad stern look came into his eyes.

'Christ save us, I have eaten!.. Am I clearing out, you say? What else? Why should I stay? For the Red bellies to come and chop my knob off? You may be thinking of staying, but I... No, I'm going! They don't pardon officers.'

'What about our home? Are we to leave it all here?'

Petro merely shrugged in reply to his father's question. But Darya gave tongue at once.

'So you'll go away while we stay here? You're a fine lot, I'm sure! And we look after your property for you!...

Then get killed for its sake! The whole place can go up in smoke! I'm not staying here!'

Even Natalya entered the discussion. Drowning Darya's clamorous declamation, she exclaimed, 'If the whole village goes, we won't stay behind! We'll go, even if we have to walk!'

'Fools! Bitches!' Pantelei roared frenziedly, rolling his eyes and groping involuntarily for his stick. 'Keep quiet, you yelping bitches! This is men's business and you try to stick your oar in.. All right then, suppose we chuck up everything and go where our fancy takes us! But what about the animals? What do we do with them? Tuck 'em down our shirtfronts? And the house?..'

'You, girls, must be off your heads!' Ilyinichna took her husband's side offendedly. 'You didn't spend your lives building a home and farm, so it's easy for you to throw it away. But your father and me, we were at it day and night—how can we leave it all? And we won't!' She pursed her lips and sighed. 'You can go but I won't budge. I'd rather be killed on my own doorstep than die in a ditch!'

Breathing heavily, Pantelei turned up the wick of the lamp. There was a minute or two of silence. Dunyashka, who had been knitting a new top on to a stocking, looked up from her needles and said in a whisper, 'We can drive the cattle with us... We don't have to stay because of them.'

Another fit of rage seized the old man. He stamped his feet like an impatient stallion, nearly tripped over the little goat lying by the stove and, coming to a halt in front of his daughter, bawled, 'Drive 'em with us! What about the old cow? She'll soon be calving. How far will ye drive her? Sinful mouth! Thriftless creature! Slut! Hussy! All my life I've been working to build a home for them, and this is what I have to listen to!.. What about the sheep? What'll ye do with the lambs?.. You daft bitch! You'd better keep quiet!'

Grigory glanced sideways at Petro and, just as he used to many years ago, noticed in his brother's brown eyes a mischievous, mocking and yet obediently respectful smile, and that familiar twitching of his corn-coloured moustache. Petro gave him a lightning wink and began to shake with laughter. Grigory, too, felt a willingness to laugh that he had lost in recent years and broke into throaty peals of merriment that he made no attempt to hide.

'Now this... Praise the Lord!.. So that's how we talk!'

107

The old man shot a wrathful glance at him and sat down, turning away to the frost-wreathed window.

Not until midnight did they reach a common decision. The menfolk should join the retreat while the women stayed behind to guard the house and farm.

Long before daybreak Ilyinichna lighted the stove and by morning had baked bread, cut it up into small pieces, dried them and filled two bags of them for her sons. Pantelei had his breakfast by lamplight and at the crack of dawn went out to tend the animals and prepare the sledge for the journey. He stood for a long time in the barn with his hand thrust into a bin of first-grade wheat, letting the full-kerneled grain sprinkle through his fingers. When he came out again he was hatless and closed the new resin-streaked door quietly behind him, as though he had paid his last respects to a dead man.

He was still busy under the overhang of the shed, changing the seat of the sledge, when Anikei appeared in the lane, driving a cow down to the watering-place. They exchanged greetings.

'Getting ready to clear out, Anikei?'

'That won't take me long. All my property'd go in one pocket, and there'll be room in the other for someone else's.'

'What's the news?'

'Plenty of that, Prokofievich!'

'What about?' Pantelei asked worriedly, and stuck the axe into the hand-bar of the sledge.

'The Reds'll be here any time now. They're nearing Vyoshenskaya. Someone from Bolshoi Gromok saw 'em. And he didn't like the look of 'em, he says. They're slaughtering a lot of people... There's Yids and Chinese with 'em, may they burn in hell! We didn't get rid of enough o' them squint-eyed devils!'

'Slaughtering people, are they?'

'What did you think? Just sniffing at 'em? And there's the blasted up-river lot as well!' Anikei swore and walked on, calling over his shoulder the last of what he had to say. 'The women across the Don have had their stills going and are giving 'em plenty to drink so they don't cut up rough, but they get tight, then go on to the next village and beat the place up.'

The old man fixed the back seat, walked round all the outbuildings, inspecting every stall and fence that he had built with his own hands, then he took a hay net and limped over to the threshing floor to pull out some hay for the journey. He lifted an iron hook down from its rack and, still not convinced of the necessity of going, began to take the worst hay, with weeds in it (he always kept the good stuff for the spring ploughing), then changed his mind and stumped vexedly over to another rick. It was beyond his comprehension that in a few hours' time he was to leave his farm and village and head for the south, perhaps never to return. He made up a good bale of hay and, obeying an old habit, reached for the rake to clear up after him, then snatched his hand away as if from hot metal and, wiping the sweat off his forehead, said aloud, 'Why should I look after it now? It'll only be trampled by their horses or burnt.'

He broke the rake over his knee, gritted his teeth and carried the bale of hay out into the yard, shuffling and letting his shoulders sag as if age had suddenly got the better of him.

He went only as far as the door of the house, opened it a little way and said, 'Get your things together, I'm just going to harness up. We'll be late starting.'

Only when he had harnessed the horses and hoisted a big sack of oats into the back of the sledge did he begin to wonder why his sons were so long in coming out to saddle their horses, and only then did he go back to the house again.

A strange scene met his eyes. Petro was fiercely flinging open the bundles that had been prepared for the journey and throwing out trousers, tunics and the women's best clothes.

'What's all this about?' Pantelei asked in utter astonishment and pulled off his cap.

'Here's what!' Petro thumbed over his shoulder at the women and explained, 'It's their howling. We're not going anywhere! If one goes, we all go, or not at all! While we're away saving our stuff, the Reds may come raping our women. At least if they kill us here, we'll die before their eyes!'

'Take your coat off, Father!' Grigory smiled as he removed his own greatcoat and sabre, while a weeping Natalya caught his hand from behind and kissed it and Dunyashka, her face poppy-red, clapped joyfully.

The old man pulled on his cap but took it off again at once, walked over to the front corner of the room, kneeled and made the sign of the cross with a wide sweep of the arm. When he had bowed three times, he rose from his knees and looked round at his family.

'Well, if that's how things are, we'll stay. Shield and protect us, Holy Queen of Heaven! I'll go and unharness.'

When Anikei dropped in, he was surprised to see the Melekhovs' laughing and smiling faces.

'What's happened?'

'Our Cossacks aren't going!' Darya answered for them all.

'Well, I'm blowed! You've changed your minds?'

'That's it!' Grigory showed his sugar-white teeth in a slow grin and winked. 'No use looking for death. It'll find us here too.'

'If the officers aren't going, it's God's will for us not to!' And Anikei charged off down the steps of the porch and past the windows, his boots clattering like hooves.

XIV

Fomin's orders were fluttering on the fences in Vyoshenskaya. Red forces were expected at any hour. But in Karginskaya, thirty-five versts from Vyoshenskaya, the headquarters of the Northern Front was still active. On the night of January 3rd a force of Chechens arrived in Karginskaya, and from Ust-Belokalitvenskaya stanitsa a punitive detachment under Lieutenant-Colonel Roman Lazarev set out in all haste to deal with Fomin's rebellious regiment.

The Chechens should have attacked Vyoshenskaya on the 5th. Their patrols had already reconnoitred Byelogorka. But the attack was abandoned when a Cossack who had turned against Fomin rode up to say that formidable Red Army forces had spent the night in Gorokhovka and were expected in Vyoshenskaya on the 5th.

Krasnov, who was busy with the Allied mission that had arrived in Novocherkassk, attempted to influence Fomin with a personal summons. The telegraph in Vyoshenskaya, which had been buzzing persistently with calls for Fomin, finally brought him to the office for the following brief exchange of views.

VYOSHENSKAYA FOMIN STOP SERGEANT FOMIN COMMA I ORDER YOU TO COME TO YOUR SENSES AND MAN YOUR POSITIONS WITH YOUR REGIMENT STOP PUNITIVE DETACHMENT HAS BEEN SENT OUT STOP DISOBEDIENCE WILL BE PUNISHED BY DEATH STOP KRASNOV

Fomin unbuttoned his sheepskin and by the light of

an oil lamp watched the thin stream of tape snaking between the telegraphist's fingers. Breathing a mixture of frost and alcohol fumes down the man's neck he said, 'What's he blathering about? Come to my senses? Is that all!.. Now send him this... Wh-a-a-t? What d'you mean, it's not allowed? It's an order! Send it or I'll have your guts!'

And the message went back.

NOVOCHERKASSK ATAMAN KRASNOV STOP GO TO FOGGIN HELL STOP FOMIN

The situation on the Northern Front had become so critical that Krasnov decided to drive out to Karginskaya himself to direct the 'hand of vengeance' against Fomin and, above all, to restore the Cossacks' shaken morale. With this in mind he invited the Allied representatives to accompany him on a tour of the front.

In the settlement of Buturlinovka the Gundorovsky St. George Regiment which had just come out of the fighting line, was drawn up for inspection. After the march-past Krasnov strode up to the regimental colours, made a smart right turn and bellowed, 'All those who served under my command in the 10th Regiment—one step forward!'

Nearly half the Gundorovsky men stepped forward. Krasnov took off his busby and kissed the sergeant-major standing nearest to him on both cheeks. The sergeant-major, an elderly but still very smart Cossack, wiped his short-clipped moustache with the sleeve of his great-coat and stood with his eyes bulging in astonishment. Krasnov went down the line, kissing all the men of his old regiment. The Allied officers were astounded and exchanged whispers. But their surprise gave way to smiles and restrained approval when Krasnov came up to them and explained.

'These are the heroes with whom I defeated the Germans at Nezwiskaya and the Austrians at Belzhets and Komarovo in aid of our common victory.'

...Two white-belted rainbow pillars stood on either side of the sun, like sentries beside the regimental coffers. A cold north-east wind blew like a bugler in the forests, raced across the steppe, wheeled for the charge and swept down on the bristling ramparts of steppeland scrub. Towards evening on the 6th of January (the Chir was already curtained in twilight) Krasnov, accompanied by His Britannic Majesty's officers Edwards and Alcott and the French officers Captain Bartellot and Lieutenant

Erlich, arrived in Karginskaya. In their fur coats and shaggy hare-skin hats the Allied officers with much laughter, shivering and stamping of feet climbed out of their cars in a cloud of cigar smoke and eau-de-Cologne. After warming themselves and drinking tea at the house of the rich merchant Levochkin, the officers went with Krasnov and the commander of the Northern Front, Major-General Ivanov, to the local school, where a meeting was to be held.

Krasnov spoke at great length to a wary-looking crowd of Cossacks. They listened to him attentively, in a good spirit. But when in the course of his speech he embarked on a colourful account of the 'Bolshevik atrocities' committed in the occupied areas, an irritated voice from the blue haze of tobacco smoke over the back rows shouted, 'That's not true!' and spoiled the effect.

The next morning Krasnov and the Allied officers left hurriedly for Millerovo.

With similar haste the headquarters of the Northern Front was evacuated. The Chechens scoured Karginskaya until evening, rounding up Cossacks who did not want to go. When darkness fell, a munitions dump was set on fire. Until midnight cartridges blazed and crackled like a huge pile of burning brushwood and exploding shells thundered like an avalanche. The next day, when prayers for the retreat were being said on the square, a machine-gun opened fire from Karginskaya hill. The bullets drummed on the church roof like spring hail and there was a general stampede into the steppe. Lazarev's Chechens and a few Cossack units tried to cover the retreat. A line of infantry took up its positions beyond the windmill and the 36th Karginskaya Battery, commanded by a Karginskaya man, Major Fyodor Popov, bombarded the advancing Red forces but soon hitched up its guns. Attacking from the village of Latyshevo, Red cavalry outflanked the defending infantry and drove them into the ravines, where they cut down about twenty old men, whom someone flippantly dubbed 'shock troops'.

XV

The decision not to join the retreat restored Pantelei's faith in the power and importance of worldly goods. When he went out to feed the animals that evening, he had no hesitation about using the worst hay. In the dark shed he walked around the cow, feeling her flanks, and told himself with satisfaction, 'She's mighty big. Mebbe the good Lord will give us twins?' Everything was dear to him once again; everything that he had mentally rejected had regained its former significance. In one brief hour before nightfall he had found the time to scold Dunyashka for spilling chaff out of a bin and for not breaking the ice out of the drinking trough, and to mend a hole that Stepan Astakhov's hog had made in the fence. When Aksinya ran out to close the shutters, he took the opportunity of asking whether Stepan was thinking of leaving. Asksinya drew her shawl round her shoulders and answered with a lilt in her voice.

'No, whatever for! He's laid up, seems to have a fever. His forehead's hot and he says he's got pains inside. Stepan's ill. He won't go.'

'Nor will ours. I mean we won't go either. I'm plagued if I know whether it's for the best or not.'

Dusk fell. Across the Don, beyond the grey blur of the forest the Pole Star was burning fiercely in the green depths. The eastern edge of the sky was rimmed with purple by the after-glow. The sliced-off crust of the moon rested on the branching horns of a black poplar. Vague shadows spread over the snow. The drifts darkened. It was so quiet that Pantelei could hear someone, probably Anikei, pounding the ice at the water-hole on the Don, and the splinters of ice falling with a glassy tinkle. From the yard came the steady munching of the oxen.

A lamp was lighted in the kitchen. Natalya showed up at the window for a moment. Pantelei felt drawn to the warm. He found the whole family at home. Dunyashka had just come back from a visit to Khristonya's wife. She gulped down a cup of sour milk and, anxious not to be interrupted, hurriedly recounted the news.

In the front room Grigory was greasing his rifle, revolver and sabre; he wrapped his field glasses in a towel and called out to Petro, 'Have you got yours ready? Bring it in. We've got to hide it.'

'What if we have to defend ourselves?'

'That's a way to talk!' Grigory gave a dry laugh. 'Mind they don't find it or they'll hook you on to your own gate by the seat of your pants.'

They went out into the yard. For some unknown reason they hid their weapons in different places. But

113

Grigory kept his new black revolver and tucked it away under a pillow in the front room.

They had just had supper and were exchanging a few idle remarks as they made ready for bed when the yard dog broke into a husky barking, straining at its chain and choking on the collar. Pantelei went out to look and came in with a man swathed to his eyebrows in a hood. He was fully armed and wearing a tight white belt. He crossed himself as he entered and steam poured from his frost-rimed mouth.

'So you don't recognise me, eh?'

'Why, it's our kinsman Makar!' Darya exclaimed. And only then did Petro and the others recognise their distant relative Makar Nogaitsev, a Cossack from the village of Singin, known throughout the district for his rare accomplishments both as a singer and a tippler.

'What ill wind brings you here?' Petro asked smilingly, but did not rise.

Nogaitsev clawed the icicles out of his moustache and tossed them on to the threshold, stamped his feet in their huge leather-soled felt boots, and unhurriedly removed his coat.

'It'll be a bit lonesome, I thought, retreating by myself, so I'll drop in and take my kinsmen with me. I'd had word you were both at home. I'll call for the Melekhovs on the way, I told my old woman—the more the merrier.'

He carried his rifle to the stove and put it among the pot-holders, evoking smiles and laughter from the women, then slipped his field bag under the bench by the stove and gave his sabre and whip a place of honour on the bed. As usual Makar's breath was heavy with the aroma of home-brew and his big prominent eyes burned with a tipsy glow; a full set of bluish-white teeth, like the Donside shingle, gleamed through the wet tangle of his beard.

'Aren't the Cossacks retreating from Singin?' Grigory asked, holding out his bead-embroidered pouch.

The guest pushed the pouch aside.

'No tobacco for me... Our Cossacks? Some have left, others are looking for a hole to crawl into. You'll be going, won't you?'

'No, they won't. And don't you try to tempt them!' Ilyinichna exclaimed anxiously.

'You're staying? I can't believe it! Cousin Grigory, is it true? You're taking a fatal step, brothers.'

'What's going to happen...' Petro sighed and suddenly, flushing a fiery red, asked, 'Grigory! What about it? Mebbe you've changed your mind? Shall we go?'

'No.'

A cloud of tobacco smoke veiled Grigory and hung for a time over his curly pitch-black forelock.

'Is Father putting your horse in the stables?' Petro asked inconsequentially.

A long silence ensued, broken only by the drowsy hum of Dunyashka's spinning wheel.

Nogaitsev sat with them till first light, urging the Melekhov brothers to take the road across the Donets. During the night Petro twice ran out hatless into the yard to saddle his horse, but on returning to the house was crushed by Darya's threatening glances and went back to unsaddle it.

The dawn came up and their guest made ready to leave. Muffled in his coat and hood, with his hand on the doorlatch, he coughed meaningfully and said with a treatening undertone in his voice, 'Well, mebbe it's for the best, only you'll regret it later. If we come back from over there, we'll remember the ones on the Don who opened their gates to the Reds and stayed behind to serve 'em.'

In the morning it began to snow heavily. When he stepped out into the yard, Grigory noticed a black swarm of human figures crossing from the far bank. A team of eight horses was towing something and the sound of talk, shouting and swearing floated across the river. The murky figures of men and horses loomed through the whirling mist of snow. Grigory guessed by the four pairs of horses that it was a battery. Surely they weren't Reds? His heart missed a beat at the thought, but further consideration calmed him.

The straggling crowd came nearer, giving a wide berth to a gaping black hole where the ice had thawed. But as it was being towed out on to the bank, the first gun broke through the thin shore ice and one wheel sank. The wind carried the cries of the drivers, the crunch of breaking ice and the scrape and clatter of hooves. Grigory went to the cattle-yard and looked out cautiously. On the greatcoats of the men on horseback he spotted snow-sprinkled shoulder straps and recognised them as Cossacks.

About five minutes later an oldish sergeant-major rode in at the gate on a tall, broad-cruppered horse. He dis-

115

mounted at the porch, hitched the bridle to the rail, and entered the house.

'Who's the master here?' he asked after a greeting.

'I am,' Pantelei replied and waited fearfully for what he thought would be the next question, 'Why are your Cossacks still at home?'

But the sergeant-major straightened the long twisted tips of his snow-whitened moustache with his fist and said, 'Cossacks! For Christ's sake, help us to pull out the gun! It's sunk right up to its axles just by the bank. Mebbe you've got some ropes? What village is this? We're lost. We're looking for Yelanskaya, but we can't see a thing in this snow. We've missed our route and the Reds will be on our tail any time now.'

'I don't know, honest to God I don't...' Pantelei muttered.

'Know what? Look at the Cossacks you've got here. We need men to help us too.'

'I'm sick,' Pantelei lied.

'Now then, lads, what's this!' The sergeant-major surveyed the family like a wolf, without turning his head. His voice seemed to grow younger and clearer. 'Or aren't you Cossacks? Let the army's property go to hell, eh? I'm the only one left to command the battery, the officers have all run away. I've been in the saddle for a week, I've got frost-bitten, I can hardly feel my toes, but I'd take my own life rather than ditch the battery! And you... No argument! If you won't come of your own accord, I'll call in the Cossacks and we'll—' the sergeant-major's voice rose to an angry tearful pitch '—we'll force you, you sons-of-bitches! Bolsheviks! Curse the lot of you! We'll put you in harness too, Grandad, if that's what you want! Go and get some more people and if they won't come, by God, I'll ride back this way and blast the whole village flat.'

He spoke like a man who was not quite sure of his own strength and Grigory felt sorry for him. He grabbed his hat and said grimly, without looking at the infuriated sergeant-major, 'Keep your hair on! We'll help you to save your gun, then you'd better go and God be with you.'

They put down hurdles and brought the battery across. Quite a few men turned out to help. Anikei, Khristonya, Ivan Tomilin, the Melekhovs and a dozen or so women with the gunners' help hauled the guns and caissons ashore and helped the horses to climb the slope.

The frozen wheels would not turn and only slid over the snow. The emaciated horses were too weak to climb the smallest hill. The gun-crews—those that had not deserted—continued their journey on foot. The sergeant-major took off his cap, bowed and thanked his helpers, then turned in the saddle and called out quietly, 'Battery! Follow me!'

Grigory watched him with respect and unbelieving astonishment. Petro came over chewing his moustache and, as though in response to the thought in Grigory's mind, said, 'If only they were all like him! That's the way to defend the quiet Don!'

'You mean that one with the whiskers? The sergeant-major?' Khristonya came up, muddy from head to foot. 'And he'll get his guns there, I reckon. He nearly took a swipe at me with his whip, the old devil! And he would have done too. Real desperate he is. I didn't want to come out but, I admit, he scared me. I haven't got any felt boots but I came. Tell me, what good are those guns to him, the fool? He's like a runaway pig dragging its halter; it's tough for him and no good to anyone else, but he goes on dragging.'

The Cossacks went their way smiling but saying nothing.

XVI

It was well after dinner-time when far away across the Don a machine-gun fired two muffled bursts and fell silent.

Half an hour later Grigory, who had scarcely moved from the front-room window, stepped back, his face tinged ashy blue to the cheekbones.

'Here they come!'

Ilyinichna gasped and hurried to the window. Eight horsemen were cantering in loose formation down the street. They rode as far as the Melekhovs' yard, scanned the crossing place and the dark track between the river and the hill, and turned back. The well-fed horses wheeled about with their bobbed tails swaying and snow spattering from under their hooves. The mounted patrol reconnoitred the village and disappeared. An hour later Tatarsky echoed to the sound of boots crunching through the snow, strange, broad-vowelled northern speech, and the yelping of dogs. An infantry regiment

117

with machine-guns on sledges, baggage wagons and field kitchens crossed the Don and spread out through the village.

Frightening though the first moment of the enemy's entry had been, laughter-loving Dunyashka could not resist her nature; when the patrol turned back, she snorted into her apron and ran out to the kitchen. Natalya met her with a frightened look.

'Whatever's the matter?'

'Oh, Natasha, dear! Oh, lovey! The way they ride! To and fro in saddle they go and their arms are all elbows! They look like bundles of old rags—everything shakes!'

She imitated the awkward way the Red Army men sat their horses so well that Natalya ran shaking with suppressed laughter to the bed and buried her face in a pillow so as not to attract the wrathful attention of her father-in-law.

Shivering feverishly, he was seated in a corner, aimlessly moving thread, awl and a tin of birchwood nails about the bench and peeping out of the window with a hunted look on his face.

And meanwhile in the kitchen the women—surely it was a bad omen—were splitting their sides with laughter. A purple-faced Dunyashka, her eyes wet with tears and shining like dew-sprinkled nightshade berries, was showing Darya how the Red Army men sat in their saddles and unconsciously putting a suggestion of indecency into her rhythmic movements. The steep arches of Darya's pencilled eyebrows cracked with nervous laughter, and through her laughter she gasped, 'They must wear their trousers into holes! A rider like that—would soon flatten his saddle-bow!'

Even Petro, who had come out of the front room looking like misery itself, was cheered for a minute by the laughter.

'Find it funny the way they ride, do you?' he asked. 'They don't care. If they break a horse's back they'll grab another. Muzhiks!' And his hand cut the air in a gesture of total contempt. 'Mebbe they've never seen a horse before. "Let's try it and see if we get there," they says. Their fathers took fright at the creak of wagon wheels and they think they can do trick riding! Pah!' He cracked his knuckles and took himself off into the front room.

A crowd of Red Army men came down the street,

breaking up into groups and turning into the yards. Three of them went in at Anikei's gate, five, one of them mounted, stopped at Stepan Astakhov's house; and the remaining five walked along the fence towards the Melekhovs. They were led by a shortish elderly soldier, clean shaven, with a flat wide nose, very agile and wiry, an old frontline man if ever there was one. He was the first to enter the Melekhov's yard. He halted by the porch and for about a minute stood with his head jutting forward, watching the big tawny dog barking and choking at the end of its chain; then he slung his rifle off his shoulder. The shot tore a white cloud of frost from the roof. Tugging at the collar of his shirt, Grigory watched through the window as the dog rolled about in the snow, spattering it with blood and biting its wounded side and the iron chain in its death agony. When he looked round he saw the women's blanched faces and his mother's fainting eyes. Without bothering to put on his hat, he made for the porch.

'Let it go,' his father shouted after him in a strangely unfamiliar voice.

Grigory flung the door open. An empty cartridge case fell on to the doorstep with a clatter. The other Red Army men came in through the gate.

'Why'd you kill the dog? Was it in your way?' Grigory asked, standing on the threshold.

The Red Army man's broad nostrils sucked in air and the corners of his thin blue-shaven lips curved downwards. He looked round and changed his grip on the rifle.

'Sorry, are you? Well, I wouldn't be sorry to use a bullet on you as well. Want me to? Up against the wall then!'

'Now then! No need for that, Alexander!' a tall ginger-browed Red Army man walked up laughing. 'Good afternoon, master! Never seen Reds before? We want you to billet us. Did he kill your dog? He shouldn't have done!.. Comrades, this way.'

Grigory was the last to enter. The Red Army men uttered cheerful greetings, took off their field bags and leather Japanese cartridge belts, and piled their greatcoats, padded jackets and caps on the bed. And at once the whole house was filled with the pungent all-pervasive stench of soldiery, the odours of human sweat, tobacco, cheap soap and gun oil that make up the smell of long marches.

119

The man called Alexander sat down at the table, lit a cigarette and, as though resuming a conversation he had already begun with Grigory, asked, 'Were you with the Whites?'

'Yes.'

'Ah... I can spot an owl right away, by its flight, and I spotted you by your slobbering. A whitey, eh! An officer? Any gold braid on your shoulder straps?'

He sent up a column of smoke from his nostrils, drilled into Grigory, who was still standing by the door, with cold unsmiling eyes and tapped the butt of his cigarette with a curved nicotine-stained fingernail.

'You're an officer, aren't you? Come on, out with it! I can see it by your bearing; I went through the German war myself.'

'I was an officer.' Grigory forced a smile and, catching Natalya's frightened imploring glance, frowned and raised a quivering eyebrow. He was annoyed with himself for smiling.

'What a pity! So it wasn't the dog I ought to have shot.'

The Red Army man threw down the butt of his cigarette at Grigory's feet and winked to the others.

And again Grigory felt a guilty, pleading smile twisting his lips and blushed with shame at his involuntary, unreasoning display of weakness. Like a dog cringing before its master! The thought scorched him with shame and for a moment he pictured the dead dog's silky black lips writhing in just the same kind of smile when he, its master, with the power of life or death over it, approached and it rolled over on its back, showing its young teeth and wagging its fluffy reddish tail.

In that same unfamiliar voice his father asked if the guests might be wanting some supper. If so, he would tell the mistress.

Without waiting for anyone's assent, Ilyinichna hastened to the stove. Her hands were trembling and she could scarcely lift out the pot of cabbage soup. Darya kept her eyes lowered as she laid the table. The Red Army men took their places without crossing themselves. Pantelei watched them with fear and concealed disgust and in the end could not resist asking, 'So you don't pray to God?'

A shadow of a smile crept across Alexander's lips. Amid general laughter from the others he replied, 'And I don't advise you to either, Father! We packed our gods off long ago to—' he broke off and knitted his brows. 'God don't exist, only fools believe in him and bow down to those bits of wood!'

'Ay, o'course... Learned men ... they've gone far,' Pantelei agreed in fright.

Darya placed a spoon in front of each man but Alexander pushed his aside.

'Haven't you got one that's not wooden? All I need now is to pick up some infection! Call that a spoon? It's just a stump!'

Darya flared like gunpowder.

'Carry your own then, if you don't like other people's!'

'Not so much of that, young woman! You haven't got a spoon? Well, give me a clean towel to wipe this with.'

When Ilyinichna brought the bowl of soup to the table, he also took her to task.

'Eat some yourself first, Mum.'

'Why? Have I put in too much salt?' the old woman asked anxiously.

'Try it yourself! Maybe you've put in a few powders for your guests.'

'Take a spoonful! Go on!' Pantelei ordered sternly and tightened his lips. After that he brought his cobbler's tools out of the corner, moved the alder stump that he used as a seat to the window, lighted a wick in a bottle and fastened his attention on an old boot. He took no further part in the conversation.

Petro stayed in the front room. Natalya was also sitting there with the children. Dunyashka sat knitting a stocking with her back against the stove, but went out after one of the Red Army men had called her 'miss' and invited her to share their supper. The conversation petered out. The Red Army men finished their supper and started lighting up their cigarettes.

'Can we smoke in here?' the ginger-browed man asked.

'We've got plenty of chimney-pots of our own,' Ilyinichna responded grudgingly.

Grigory refused the cigarette that was offered him. He was shivering inwardly and a painful spasm closed round his heart at the sight of the man who had shot his dog and persisted in treating him with such provocative arrogance. He was evidently bent on collision and constantly sought a pretext to goad Grigory into conversation.

'What regiment did you serve in, Your Honour?'

'Several.'

'How many of our men did you kill?'

'No one counts that in war. You needn't think I was born an officer, comrade. I came back as an officer from the German war. They gave me these stripes for distinguished service.'

'I'm no comrade of any officer! We put your kind up in front of a firing squad. I don't mind admitting I've drawn a bead on quite a few myself.'

'Well, what I want to tell you is this, comrade... You're not acting right; you treat us as if you'd captured the village. We left the front ourselves and let you through, but you march in like it was conquered territory. Anyone can shoot dogs. And there's nothing clever either in killing or insulting an unarmed man.'

'Don't try to teach me! We know what you're up to! "Left the front"! You wouldn't have left it, if we hadn't given you a good bashing first. And I can talk to you any way I like.'

'Drop it, Alexander! We've had enough!' the ginger-browed soldier suggested.

But the other had come up to Grigory, nostrils quivering and breath whistling through them.

'Don't start getting at me, you officer, or you'll be sorry.'

'I'm not getting at you.'

'Yes, you are!'

Natalya opened the door a little way and called desperately for Grigory. He stepped round the Red Army man and walked to the front room, swaying at the door as if he were drunk. Petro greeted him in a snarling querrulous whisper.

'What are you playing at? Why the hell get into a fight with him? Why argue? You'll get yourself killed— and us too! Sit down!' he pushed Grigory down on to the clothes chest and went out into the kitchen.

Grigory sat gasping for breath, the dark flush left his cheeks and a faint gleam came into his dulled eyes.

'Grisha! Grisha, dearest! Don't have anything to do with them!' Natalya pleaded, trembling and holding the mouths of the children, who were beginning to cry.

'Why didn't I leave?' Grigory asked with a wretched glance at Natalya. 'All right, I won't. Quiet! I've had enough.'

Later on three more Red Army men arrived. One, in a

tall black lambskin hat, evidently a commander, asked, 'How many men are billeted here?'

'Seven,' the ginger-browed man answered for them all, fingering the keys of an accordion.

'We're setting up a machine-gun post here. You'll have to make room.'

No sooner had they left than the gate creaked and two wagons drove into the yard. One of the machine-guns was dragged into the porch. Someone struck matches in the darkness and swore furiously. Some of the newcomers sat smoking under the overhang of the shed, others pulled hay out of the stacks on the threshing floor and lighted a fire, but no one came out of the house.

'Why don't you go and look at the horses,' Ilyinichna whispered to Pantelei as she passed him.

But the old man only shrugged. All night doors were slamming and steamy air hung under the ceiling and settled like dew on the walls. The Red Army men made up their beds on the floor in the front room. Grigory brought them a rug, spread it out, and gave them his sheepskin as a bolster.

'I've been in the army myself, I know what it's like,' he smiled appeasingly at the man who felt him to be an enemy.

But the man's broad nostrils quivered and his eyes scanned Grigory implacably.

Grigory and Natalya shared the bed in the same room. The Red Army men piled their rifles by the bolster and turned in all together on the rug. Natalya was about to put out the lamp, but a sharp voice checked her.

'Who asked you to put out the light? Don't you dare! Turn down the wick a bit. That lamp's got to burn all night.'

Natalya had made a place for the children at the foot of the bed. She lay next to the wall, without undressing. Grigory stretched out with his hands under his head and was silent.

'If we'd left,' he thought, gritting his teeth and turning over so that his heart pressed into the corner of the pillow. 'If we'd joined the retreat, they'd have had Natalya laid out on this bed and played hell with her, like in Poland, with Frania.'

One of the Red Army men started telling a yarn, but the familiar voice interrupted him and droned on in the murky semi-darkness between expectant pauses.

'It's a dull life without a woman. I'd like to get stuck into one... But the master's an officer... They won't share their wives with scum like us, ordinary folk. Can't you hear me, master?'

One of the Red Army men was already snoring, another gave a sleepy chuckle. The voice of the ginger-browed soldier cut in threateningly, 'I'm fed up arguing with you, Alexander. In every billet you make trouble, playing up like this and disgracing the name of the Red Army. It's not good enough! I'm going to the commissar or the company commander right now. D'you hear? We'll have it out with you!'

There was an icy silence. The only sound was of the ginger-browed soldier panting angrily as he pulled on his boots. A minute later he went out, slamming the door.

Natalya broke down and gave a loud sob. Grigory's hand shook as he stroked her hair, her damp forehead and tearful face. With his other hand he groped calmly over his chest and his fingers worked mechanically, fastening and unfastening the buttons of his vest.

'Hush! Hush!' he whispered to Natalya. And at that moment he knew with utter certainty that he was ready for any trial or humiliation if only it would save his own and his family's lives.

A match lit up the face of Alexander, the broad bridge of his nose and his mouth pulling at a cigarette. Through the sound of the other men's snoring he could be heard muttering to himself and sighing as he stood up to get dressed. Thanking the ginger-browed man with all his heart, Grigory listened impatiently, and a thrill of joy went through him when he heard footsteps and an indignant voice by the window.

'He keeps bullying people!.. What can I do?.. It's terrible, Comrade Commissar.'

The footsteps came up into the porch, the door opened with a creak, and a young authoritative voice commanded, 'Alexander Tyurnikov, get your clothes on and leave this house at once. You will spend the night in my billet and tomorrow we're going to try you for conduct unworthy of a Red Army man.'

Grigory encountered the good-natured penetrating glance of the man in a black leather jacket standing at the door beside the ginger-browed soldier.

He looked young and youthfully stern; his lips with their boyish fluff were drawn together with perhaps a little too much firmness.

124

'So you got landed with a troublesome guest, comrade?' he said to Grigory with a barely perceptible smile. 'Now you can have some sleep, we'll calm him down tomorrow. Good-night. Come along, Tyurnikov!'

They left and Grigory drew a deep breath of relief. The next morning, after paying for their food and lodging, the ginger-browed soldier hung back before leaving.

'You mustn't be offended with us, good folk. That Alexander of ours is a bit touched. Last year in Lugansk—that's where he's from—some officers shot his mother and sister before his eyes. That's what did it. Well, thanks. And goodbye. Oh, yes, I nearly forgot, this is for the kiddies!' And to the children's unspeakable delight he took two lumps of grimy-looking sugar out of his pack and gave them one each. Pantelei gazed feelingly at his grandchildren.

'And here's a present for them! We haven't seen sugar for eighteen months or more... Lord bless ye, comrade!.. Come on, Polyushka, say thank ye to our friend here! That's not the way, love! Why do you stand scowling like that!'

As soon as the Red Army man left, Pantelei turned angrily on Natalya. 'Where's your breeding! Can't you even give him a bun or something for the journey? Show a good man some gratitude? Pah!'

'Run after him!' Grigory ordered.

Natalya pulled her shawl over her head and overtook the ginger-browed soldier at the gate. Flushed with embarrassment, she pushed a doughnut into the gaping pocket of his greatcoat.

XVII

At noon the 6th Mtsensk Regiment marched hurriedly through the village, requisitioning some of the Cossacks' army mounts as they went. From far away beyond the hill came an intermittent rumble of gunfire.

'They're fighting along the Chir,' Pantelei surmised.

In the evening both Petro and Grigory went out into the yard more than once. From somewhere down the Don, not nearer than Ust-Khopyorskaya, they could hear the dull boom of artillery and, if they put their ears close to the frozen ground, the quiet chatter of machine-guns.

'They're having a pretty good set-to out there as well! That's General Guselnikov and the Gundorovsky Regiment men,' Petro declared, brushing the snow off his knees and hat, and added inconsequentially, 'They're commandeering horses in the village. Yours is a fine-looking one, Grigory—they'll take it, sure to God they will!'

But their father was a jump ahead of them. When Grigory led the two army mounts out of the stable to water them for the night, he noticed they were limping on their forelegs. He tried his own, then Petro's—they were both lame. He called his brother over.

'Look at that—both horses are lame! Yours has a limp in his right leg, mine in his left. There was no sign of 'em hitching before. Could it be foot rot?'

On the lilac-tinted snow, under the dim evening stars the horses stood with their heads hanging dispiritedly, neither playing nor kicking after a whole day in their stalls. Petro lighted a lamp but his father, who had just come in from the barn, stopped him.

'What's the lamp for?'

'The horses are lame, Father. Must be foot trouble.'

'What's so bad about that? D'you want some muzhik to saddle 'em and ride off with 'em?'

'In that way it's not bad.'

'Well, tell Grisha I lamed 'em myself. I got a hammer and put a nail in under the gristle. Now they'll limp till the front moves on.'

Petro shook his head, chewed his moustache and went to tell Grigory.

'Take them to the mangers. Father's lamed 'em on purpose!'

Pantelei's ruse saved the horses. That night commotion again reigned in the village. Horses cantered down the streets; a battery clattered past over the ruts and pot-holes and swung round on the square. The 13th Cavalry Regiment halted in the village for the night. Khristonya had just come round to see the Melekhovs. He squatted on his haunches and smoked for a bit.

'Are none of the devils here? No one spending the night with you?'

'The Lord's spared us so far. The ones we had made the whole house stink of muzhik. No wonder they talk of "stinking Russia"! To be sure!' Ilyinichna said grumpily.

'They were at my place.' Khristonya's voice sank to

a whisper and his huge hand wiped away a tear. But then he shook his massive head and cleared his throat as though ashamed of his weakness.

'What's come over you, Khristonya?' Petro asked with a chuckle. He had never seen Khristonya in tears and the sight cheered him.

'They've taken my Raven. I rode to the German war on him. We went through a lot together, you know. Like a human being he was—cleverer! And I had to saddle him myself. "Saddle him," this fellow says, "because he won't let me do it." "Why should I?" I says, "You won't have me to saddle up for you all your life? Now you've taken him, you'd better manage him yourself." But I put the saddle on for him. And this fellow, if only he'd been a man. But he was just a matchstick! Didn't come up any higher than my waist, I reckon, and he couldn't reach the stirrup with his foot. So he led the horse to the porch and got on from there. And I started howling like a kid. "This is too bad," I says to my old woman, "I looked after him, watered him, fed him..." ' Khristonya's voice again dropped to a panting whisper. 'Now I can't bring myself to look inside my own stable! It seems dead now.'

'It's all right for me. I had three horses killed under me, so I won't feel so—' Grigory broke off to listen. Outside the window there was a crunch of footsteps in the snow, a rattle of sabres and a muffled 'whoa!' 'They're coming here too. Like fish to a bait, curse 'em! Or somebody's tipped 'em off.'

Pantelei began to fidget and could find nowhere to put his hands.

'Anyone at home? Show yourself now!'

Petro pulled a homespun coat over his shoulders and stepped outside.

'Where're you horses? Bring 'em out!'

'I'd be glad to, comrades, but they're lame.'

'Lame? How so? Bring 'em out! Don't worry, we don't take 'em for nothing. We leave you our own.'

Petro led the horses out of the stable one by one.

'There's another horse in there. Why don't you show us that?' one of the Red Army men asked, swinging a lantern.

'She's a mare and with foal. A real old 'un, about a hundred years old.'

'Now then, bring out the saddles!.. Half a mo', they *are* lame! By the Lord God and his cross, where're you taking 'em, the cripples?! Put 'em back!' the man holding the lantern shouted fiercely.

Petro tugged at the bridles and turned his face with its pursed lips away from the light.

'Where're the saddles?'

'The comrades took 'em this morning.'

'You're lying, Cossack! Who took 'em?'

'God's truth!.. May the Lord strike me, they did! The Mtsensk Regiment came through and took the lot. And two horse collars as well.'

The three horsemen rode away, swearing. Petro came back into the house, stinking of horse sweat and urine. His firm lips were twitching and there was a bragging note in his voice as he slapped Khristonya on the shoulder.

'That's the way to do it! Our horses are lame and they've taken the saddles already... You're a fine one!'

Ilyinichna turned out the lamp and groped her way into the front room to make up the bed.

'We'd better sit in the dark or the devil will bring us some more night-birds.'

* * *

That night there was a party at Anikei's. The Red Army men asked for the neighbours to be invited. Anikei came round for the Melekhovs.

'Reds?! What do we care if they're Reds? They're not heathens, are they? They're just the same as us, Russians. Honestly they are! Believe it or not!.. I'm real fond of 'em... Why shouldn't I be? There's a Yid with 'em. He's just a human being, like the others. The number of Yids we killed in Poland—huh! But this one poured me a glass of home-brew. I love Yids! Come on, Grigory! Petro! Don't turn up your noses at me.'

Grigory refused the invitation, but his father advised, 'You'd better go or they'll say he thinks it's beneath him. Let bygones be bygones.'

The three men went out into the yard. It was a warm night and promised fine weather to come. The air smelled of ash and dung smoke. They stood for a minute without speaking, then set off. Darya caught up with them at the gate.

The dark sweep of her pencilled eyebrows shone a velvety black in the dim moonlight that filtered through the clouds.

'They're trying to get my wife drunk. But it won't work out the way they want. I've got eyes in my head, chum,' Anikei mumbled, but the drink sent him staggering against the fence and tumbled him off the path into a snowdrift.

The bluish loose-grained snow crunched like sugar underfoot. Snow flurries swept down from the grey blanket of the sky.

The wind carried sparks from the men's cigarettes and sifted the powdery snow. Up under the stars it pounced ferociously on a white cloud (like a hawk driving its distended chest into a swan) and white flakes floated down like feathers on to the submissive earth, covering the village, the crossroads, the steppe, the tracks of man and beast.

At Anikei's there was nothing to breathe. Sharp sooty tongues of flame were darting from the lamp and the room was almost hidden in tobacco smoke. A Red Guard was pumping out a Russian dance on the accordion, flinging the bellows wide apart and his long legs even wider. Red Army men and the women from the neighbouring houses were sitting round on the benches. Anikei's wife was being courted by a burly fellow in padded khaki-coloured trousers and short boots, loaded with a pair of huge spurs that looked as if they had come out of a museum. A grey lambskin cap was perched on the back of his curly head and there was sweat on his blotchy brown face. He had his arm round Anikei's wife and his hot wet hand was scalding her back.

The good woman was well enough cooked already. Her mouth was a slobbery red; she felt she ought to move away from her admirer but she just couldn't bring herself to do so; she could see her husband and the other women's smiling faces, but she lacked the strength to shake off that powerful arm: shame seemed to have deserted her and she kept going off into drunken fits of giggling.

There were uncorked jugs on the table and the whole hut reeked of spirits. The tablecloth was like a rag. In the middle of the room a troop commander of the 13th Cavalry was capering like a green devil on the earthen floor and bawling out a popular ditty. He was wearing smart box-calf boots and officer's breeches. Grigory looked at him from the threshold and guessed where the boots and breeches had come from. His glance shifted to the face: it was swarthily dark and shining with sweat like a horse's croupe. The round ears stuck out, the lips were thick and drooping. 'He may be a Yid, but he can dance!' Grigory told himself. Glasses of home-brew were poured out for Grigory and Petro. Grigory drank cautiously, but Petro quickly got drunk. And after an hour he was drumming his heels on the earthen floor in a Cossack dance, kicking up the dust and hoarsely begging the accordionist to play faster. Grigory sat at the table, nibbling pumpkin seeds. Beside him was a tall Siberian, a machine-gunner. He wrinkled his round boyish face and, speaking with a soft Siberian accent, said, 'We've smashed Kolchak. We'll give your Krasnov a good bashing and everything will be fine! Go and get on with your ploughing, you've got all the land you could wish for here. Take it and make it bear fruit! The earth's like a woman; she won't give of her own accord, you've got to take her. And anyone who stand in your way—kill him. We don't need what's yours. All we want is to make everyone equal.'

Grigory nodded his agreement but kept a wary eye on the men around him. There seemed to be no grounds for misgivings. They were all staring with smiles of approval at Petro, at his easy, flowing movements. A sober voice exclaimed delightedly, 'What a devil, eh! That's fine!' But Grigory happened to notice a curly-headed Red Army man, a sergeant-major, watching him with attentively narrowed eyes. The man's glance alerted him and he stopped drinking.

The accordionist struck up a polka. The women were handed round. One of the Red Army men, his back whitened by the wall, swayed to his feet and invited a young woman who was a neighbour of Khristonya's, but she refused and, picking up her gathered skirt, darted over to Grigory.

'Come and dance!'

'I don't feel like it.'

'Come on, Grisha! My steppeland tulip!'

'Stop fooling, I won't dance!'

She tugged at his sleeve and gave a forced laugh. He frowned and hung back but rose to his feet when he noticed her winking. They went round twice, the accordionist pounded the bass notes and in that brief moment she managed to put her head on Grigory's shoulder and whisper barely audibly, 'They're planning to kill you... Someone said you were an officer... Get away quick.'

130

And then aloud, 'Oh, how dizzy you've made me!'

Grigory suddenly felt more cheerful. He went to the table and drank a mug of spirits, then asked Darya, 'Petro tight?'

'Nearly. He's reeling.'

'Take him home.'

Darya took Petro by the arm, controlling his staggers with a man's strength. Grigory followed.

'Where're you off to? Where to? No, you don't! I'll kiss your hand, but don't go!'

Drunk to the wide, Anikei clung to Grigory but Grigory gave him such a glare that he spread his arms and staggered back.

Grigory waved his cap from the threshold, 'Goodnight all!'

The curly-headed man braced his shoulders, straightened his belt and came after him. On the porch, breathing into Grigory's face and, with a glint in his light dare-devil eyes, he asked in a whisper, 'Where are you going?' And took a firm grip on the sleeve of Grigory's greatcoat.

'Home,' Grigory replied without stopping, dragging the man with him. With a surge of joy he had decided that he would not be taken alive.

The curly-headed man gripped Grigory's elbow with his left hand and kept up with him, breathing heavily. At the gate they paused. Grigory heard the house door creak and at that moment the other man's hand went to his thigh and his fingernails scratched the flap of his holster. For a second Grigory met the blue blade of the other man's glance full face, then swung round and caught the hand that was tearing at the holster catch. He squeezed it at the wrist and with a great heave forced the arm over his right shoulder. As he bent over and threw the heavy body, using a trick he had known for years, he jerked the arm down and heard the elbow joint crack as the bone came out of its socket. The fair-haired head, as curly as a lamb's, hit the snow and plunged into a drift.

Grigory ducked below the fence and ran down the lane towards the Don. His legs carried him springily along the path to the river bank. If only there was no outpost there. For a second he paused. Anikei's yard was in full view behind him. A shot. The bullet whined past viciously. More shots. He ran on down the slope and over the dark crossing. Half way across the Don a snarling bullet gnawed into a clear patch of ice and the flying splinters stung Grigory's neck. On the other bank he stopped and looked round. Shots were still cracking like a herdsman's whip. Far from being overjoyed at his escape, Grigory was discouraged by a feeling of indifference to what had happened. 'They tried to shoot me down like an animal!' he thought mechanically, stopping again. 'They won't come looking for me, they'll be scared of going into the forest... I made a nice mess of his arm. The rotten snake, thought he'd take a Cossack barehanded!'

He headed for the winter ricks, but caution led him past them and for a long time he weaved about, like a hare at feeding time. In the end he decided to spend the night in an abandoned stack of dry rushes. As he pulled off the crown of the stack, a mink slipped away from under his feet. He buried himself in the rot-scented rushes and lay shivering. He had no thoughts. A question rose reluctantly, on the fringe of his mind. 'Why not saddle up tomorrow and make a dash across the front to your own lot?' But he found no answer and let it pass.

Towards morning he began to feel cold and looked out. The world was shimmering in the first light of morning and the blueblack sky above seemed to have opened, like the Don at the rapids, revealing its lower depths; the zenith was a misty blue and all round the edges lay a fading drift of stars.

XVIII

The front moved on. The rumble of gunfire died away. On their last day the machine-gunners of the 13th Cavalry Regiment planted Mokhov's gramophone on a broad-backed Ukrainian sledge and charged about the village streets till the horses were in a lather. When the gramophone croaked and coughed (spatterings of snow from the horses' hooves had gone down its wide-mouthed horn), a machine-gunner in a Siberian cap with long ear-flaps casually cleaned out the horn and wound the carved handle as confidently as he controlled the hand-grips of his gun. And behind him, like a grey bunch of sparrows came the children, clinging to the sides of the sledge and shouting, 'Uncle, play the one that whistles! Play it, Uncle!' The two luckiest were sitting on the machine-gunner's lap delighted beyond bounds, and when he was not turning the handle the gunner would carefully and sternly use his mitten to wipe the youngest lad's peeling nose, which was running like a tap because of the frost and his great good fortune.

The sounds of battle could still be heard from Ust-Mechetka. The transports that supplied the 8th and 9th Red Armies of the Southern Front with food and ammunition passed through Tatarsky from time to time.

On the third day messengers visited every household to tell the Cossacks to attend a village meeting.

'We're going to elect a Red Ataman!' Antip the Braggart's son announced as he left the Melekhov's yard.

'Elect one or have one dumped on us from above?' Pantelei inquired.

'We shall see...'

Grigory and Petro attended the meeting. All the young Cossacks were there, but hardly any of the old men. Only the Braggart had gathered a bunch of scoffers round him and was relating how a Red commissar had lodged with him and invited him to accept a position of command.

' "I didn't know you'd been a sergeant-major in the old army," he says. "Take over command, Father, and we'll be only too glad to have you on the job." '

'Command of what? The bottle-washers?' Mishka Koshevoi suggested sarcastically.

Other suggestions were readily offered.

'He'll be in charge of the commissar's mare. To wipe her arse for her.'

'Bit higher than that!'

'Haw! Haw!'

'Avdeich! Can you hear me? He wants you to look after C Grade supplies.'

'You don't know what was going on in there... While the commissar was talking him round, the commissar's messenger was making up to his old woman. Real handy he was with her. And Avdeich sat there with his mouth wide open.'

Avdeich glared at his audience, swallowed hard and demanded, 'Who made that last statement?'

'I did!' someone at the back spoke up.

'Have you ever seen such a son-of-a-bitch?' Avdeich turned round, looking for sympathy, and there was plenty to be had.

'He's a snake. I've always said so.'

'His whole breed's the same.'

'If I was a younger man...' Avdeich's cheeks blazed like a bunch of guelder-rose berries. 'If I was a bit younger, I'd make you answer for that! Your conduct is pure Ukrainian! You Taganrog tar-brush!'

'Why don't you take him on, Avdeich? He's a weakling compared to you.'

'Avdeich don't go in for such things any more.'

'He's afraid his belly-button might come untied.'

Avdeich retreated with dignity amid a roar of voices. The Cossacks were standing about the square in bunches. Grigory, who had not seen Mishka Koshevoi for ages, came up to him.

'How are you, soldier?'

'Praise the Lord!'

'Where've you been all this time? What flag were you serving under?' Grigory smiled as he shook hands with Mishka, looking into his light-blue eyes.

'Oho! I was out on the range, chum, and in the punishment company on the Kalach front. And goodness knows where. Only just managed to get home. I wanted to desert to the Reds but I was being watched closer than a mother guards her virgin daughter. The other day Ivan came to see me, all dressed up in a cloak and marching equipment. "Well," he says, "off we go a marching." I had only just got home, so I ask, "Surely you're not going to join the retreat?" He gives a shrug and says, "That's my orders. The Ataman sent for me. I used to work at the mill, so I'm on their books." He said goodbye and off he went, and I thought he really had retreated. But the next day the Mtsensk Regiment comes through and there he is, large as life... He's here right now—Ivan Alexeyevich!'

Ivan came over with Davydka, the mill hand. Davydka still had his mouthful of glistening white teeth and looked to be on top of the world. But Ivan gripped Grigory's hand in his horny fingers, that reeked and would always reek of engine grease, and clicked his tongue.

'How come you stayed behind, Grisha?'

'What about you?'

'Well, it's different for me.'

'You mean because I was an officer? It was a risk, but I stayed. They nearly killed me... When they were chasing me and started shooting, I wished I'd cleared out, but now I don't regret it.'

'Why did they pick on you? Were they from the 13th?'

134

'Yes. They were having a party at Anikei's. Someone told them I was an officer. They left Petro alone, but they had it in for me... Because of my rank. I got away across the Don, gave one of 'em a crick in the arm tho'... For that they came to our house and took everything I had. Trousers, coats, everything. I'm left with what I stand up in.'

'If we'd gone off with the Reds then, before Podtyol-kov's... We wouldn't be looking so silly now.' Ivan smiled sourly and lit a cigarette.

People were still arriving. The meeting was opened by Lapchenkov, a Junior Cornet and associate of Fomin's, who had come down from Vyoshenskaya.

'Comrade Cossacks! Soviet power has taken root in our district. Now we've got to set up an administration, elect an executive committee, a chairman and his deputy. That's one question. And besides that I've brought an order from the District Soviet. It's quite short. It says all firearms and cold steel are to be surrendered.'

'That's great!' someone at the back commented sarcastically. After that there was a silence that towered menacingly over the square.

'Now there's no call for that kind of remark, comrades,' Lapchenkov drew himself up to his full height and placed his hat on the table. 'All weapons must, of course, be given up as not being necessary for household needs. Anyone who wants to go and defend the Soviets will be given arms. So within three days from now bring in your rifles. And now we'll begin the elections. It will be the chairman's duty to make this order known to everybody, and he must also take charge of the ata-man's seal and all the village funds.'

'They didn't give us arms! What right have they got to take 'em away?'

Before the questioner had finished speaking, all heads had turned in his direction. It was Zakhar Korolyov.

'What do you need 'em for?' Khristonya asked simply.

'I don't need 'em. But there was no agreement that when we let the Red Army through our district we'd be disarmed.'

'That's right!'

'Fomin promised at the meeting!'

'We paid out our own money for those sabres!'

'Give up the rifle I've had with me since the German war?'

'No giving up of arms!'

'They want to rob the Cossacks! What do I count for when I'm unarmed? A sledge can't go without runners. A Cossack without his weapons is like a woman with her skirt up—he's naked!'

'We're going to keep 'em!'

Mishka Koshevoi asked respectfully for permission to speak.

'Now listen, comrades! I'm a bit surprised to hear this kind of talk. Are we under martial law or aren't we?'

'You bet we are! But so what?'

'Well, what's all the talk about then? If we're under martial law we've got to give up our arms. Didn't we disarm the Ukrainians when we captured their settlements?'

Lapchenkov smoothed the fur of his hat and rapped out,

'Anyone who fails to give up his weapons in these three days will be tried by a revolutionary court and shot as a counter-revolutionary.'

After a minute of silence Tomilin coughed and called out huskily, 'Let's get on with the election then!'

The names of various candidates were shouted out—about ten in all. One of the youngsters shouted, 'Avdeich!'

But the joke fell flat. Ivan was the first candidate to be put to the vote and he was elected unanimously.

'No need for any more voting then,' Petro Melekhov proposed.

The meeting readily agreed and Mishka Koshevoi was chosen as the chairman's assistant without a vote.

The Melekhovs and Khristonya walked home together but had gone only half way when they met Anikei. Under his arm he was carrying his rifle and some cartridges wrapped up in his wife's apron. At the sight of his fellow Cossacks he looked crestfallen and slipped down a side lane. Petro glanced at Grigory and Grigory at Khristonya and they all laughed at once.

XIX

Cossack-like, an east wind is on the march across its native steppe. The gullies are choked with snow. Dells and ravines have been levelled. There are neither tracks nor paths. A bare white plain, licked smooth by the winds, stretches far and wide. The steppe looks dead. Occasionally a raven, as old as the steppe itself, as that ancient mound in its snowy cap with a princely beaver trimming of dry wormwood, flies high overhead cutting the air with its wings and letting fall a throaty despondent cry. The wind will carry its cry far away and for long its sad sound will vibrate over the steppe, like a bass string accidentally plucked in the stillness of the night.

But beneath the snow the steppe still lives. Where the snow-silvered fields stretch in frozen waves, where underneath is the groundswell of furrows that were ploughed and harrowed in autumn, the frost-flattened winter rye clings to the soil with its greedy, tenacious roots. Silkily green, sprinkled with tears of frozen dew, it huddles to the crumbly black soil, feeds on its reviving black blood and waits for spring, for the sun, for the day when it will rise and break through the gossamer-thin, diamond-studded crust to burst into abundant verdure in May. And rise it will, having waited its time! The quails will fight in its greenery, the April lark will sing in the sky above. As ever the sun will shine for it, as ever it will be lulled by the breeze. Until the time when the ripe, full-kernelled ear, battered by rainstorms and rough winds, bows its bearded head, falls under the scythe and humbly sheds its firm, heavy grain on the threshing floor.

The whole Don country was living a furtive, subdued existence. Fearsome days were approaching. Events were on the brink. A grim rumour had spread from the upper reaches of the Don, along the Chir, the Tsutskan, the Khopyor, the Yelanka, all the rivers of the region, big and small, whose banks were sprinkled with Cossack villages. The thing to be feared, folk were saying, was not the front, which had rolled on and come to a halt along the Donets, but the extraordinary commissions and tribunals. Any day now they would appear in the villages, they were already in Migulinskaya and Kazanskaya, meting out summary and unjust punishment to Cossacks who had served with the Whites. It was said that the fact that the Upper Don Cossacks had abandoned the front was not being taken into consideration and the court's method was simple beyond belief: a charge, a couple of questions, a sentence—and a burst of machine-gun fire. In Kazanskaya and Shumilinskaya, it was said, more than one Cossack head was lying uncared for in the bushes... The frontline men made light of it. 'Bollocks! Officers' yarns! The Cadets have always made a bogey of the Red Army!'

The rumours were believed and not believed. Tales had been plentiful in the villages before this. They had driven the weak-minded into retreat. But when the front had passed on, there were still many who could not sleep at night, whose pillows were hot and beds hard, who could find no comfort even in their wives.

Some were already regretting they had not gone away across the Donets, but what was done could not be undone and a tear, once shed, was lost for ever.

In Tatarsky the Cossacks gathered of an evening in the lanes, exchanged their news, and then went off to drink home-brew, first at one house, then another. Life in the village was quiet and rather bitter. Since Shrovetide only one sledge had jingled by with wedding bells tinkling from the harness, when Mishka Koshevoi had given away his sister. And the comment on that occasion had been snide and scornful.

'A fine time to get married! Must have been a matter of necessity!'

On the day after the election every household in the village handed over its arms. The inner porch and corridor of Mokhov's house, which had been requisitioned by the Revolutionary Committee, were stacked with weapons. Petro Melekhov also brought in his and Grigory's rifles, two revolvers and their sabres. The brothers kept their officer's revolvers and handed in only the ones they had brought back from the German war.

Petro went home with a feeling of relief. But in the front room he found Grigory sitting with his sleeves rolled up, stripping down and soaking in kerosene the rusty parts of two rifle bolts. The rifles were propped against the stove-bench.

'Where did you get them?' Petro's moustache drooped in astonishment.

'Dad brought 'em home when he came to see me in Filonovo.'

Small glow-worms flickered in the narrowed slits of Grigory's eyes. He burst out laughing, smearing his thighs with his oily hands. But his laughter broke off just as suddenly, with a wolf-like snap of the teeth.

'This is nothing! You know what,' his voice dropped to a whisper, although there was no stranger in the house, 'Father came out with it today,' another half-suppressed smile crossed Grigory's face, 'He's got a machine-gun.'

'Get away! How? What for?'

'He says the Cossacks on transport work gave it to him for a firkin of soured milk. But I think he's lying, the old devil! He must have nicked it! He's like a dung beetle, he'll drag away anything he can't carry. "I've got a machine-gun buried under the threshing floor," he whispers. "The spring would make good fish hooks, but I haven't used it." "What do you need it for then?" I says. "It was such a good spring, mebbe it will come in handy for something else. It's valuable, made of steel..." '

Petro got angry and wanted to go to the kitchen and tackle his father about it, but Grigory advised him not to.

'Never mind! Help me clean up and put the stuff away. You won't get anywhere with him.'

Petro huffed and puffed as he cleaned the rifle barrels, but after a while he said thoughtfully, 'Mebbe they will come in useful. Let 'em stay there.'

That day Ivan Tomilin turned up with the rumour that there had been shootings in Kazanskaya. While they sat round the stove, talking and smoking, Petro grew pensive. Hard thinking was a strain for him and brought the sweat out in tiny beads on his forehead. After Tomilin had left, he said, 'I'm going to Rubezhin to see Fomin. He's staying with his family just now, so I've heard. They say he runs the Revolutionary Committee. He's not a very big pot, but at least he stands for something. I'll ask him to put in a word for us, just in case.'

Pantelei harnessed the mare to the big sledge. Darya wrapped herself up in her new winter coat and, after a whispered discussion, she and Ilyinichna took themselves off to the barn and emerged with a bundle.

'What's that?' the old man asked.

Petro said nothing and Ilyinichna explained in a hurried whisper.

'I'd been storing up some butter as a stand-by. But we're not likely to need it now, so I've given it to Darya. She can make Fomin's wife a present of it. He may be able to help our dear Petro.' And she began to weep. 'After doing their duty all this time, risking their lives, and now because of their officer's rank, they may be...'

'Stop wailing, woman!' Pantelei roared, throwing his whip into the hay, and went up to Petro. 'Say you'll bring him some wheat.'

'What the hell would he want that for!' Petro blazed. 'You'd do better to go to Anikei's, Father, and buy some home-brew. What's the good of wheat!'

Pantelei came back with a huge flagon of home-brew tucked away under his coat and voiced his approval.

'Fine vodka this! The real stuff!'

'And you've had a swig already, you old dog!' Ilyinichna scolded; but the old man seemed not to hear and strode away youthfully into the house, purring with pleasure and wiping his tingling lips on his sleeve.

Petro drove out of the yard, not bothering to close the gate.

He had a present for his now all-powerful regimental comrade. Besides the home-brew he had with him a length of prewar Cheviot cloth, a pair of top-boots and a pound of expensive jasmine-flavoured tea, all of which he had obtained in Liski, when the 28th Regiment had stormed the station and run riot, pillaging the freight cars and warehouses.

In a train that had been captured he had seized a basket of ladies' underwear and sent it home by his father, who had come out to the front. And Darya, to the great envy of Natalya and Dunyashka, had flounced about in underclothes such as they had never seen in their lives. The fine foreign cloth was whiter than snow and every piece had initials and a coat of arms embroidered on it in silk. The lace on the knickers foamed more luxuriantly than the Don itself. On the first night of her husband's return Darya went to bed in them.

Before putting out the lamp, Petro grinned condescendingly.

'What are you wearing men's pants for?'

'They're warmer and nicer to look at,' Darya replied dreamily. 'But who knows whether they're men's anyway? If they were men's, they'd be longer. And what about all this lace? What would a man need frills for?'

'Gentlemen have 'em, I suppose,' Petro answered, scratching himself sleepily. 'Wear 'em if you like. What do I care?'

He was not particularly interested. But the next night, when he got into bed with his wife, he moved aside warily, squinting sideways at the lace with involuntary respect and anxiety, afraid to touch it and feeling somehow estranged from his wife. And he never did get used to that underwear. On the third night he lost his temper and demanded firmly, 'Come on, off with those devil's pants of yours! They're not the thing for a Cossack woman! You look like the lady of the manor in 'em! You might be a stranger!'

The next morning he rose before Darya and, frowning and coughing, tried on the knickers himself. For a long time he gazed warily at the ribbons and frills and at his own hairy legs. Then he turned round and, spotting himself in the mirror with voluminous folds at the back, started spitting and swearing and struggled like a bear to free his legs from the billowing garment. His big toe caught in the lace, he nearly fell over, and in a final fit of fury tore the ribbons and escaped to freedom. From the bed Darya inquired sleepily, 'What are you up to?'

Petro breathed hard and spat, but maintained an offended silence. And that day Darya consigned the pants that had been made for no one knew what sex to the family chest, where many an object for which none of the women could find a use was hoarded. Eventually they would be cut up for bodices. But Darya did use the petticoats; they were strangely short but, clever woman that she was, she lengthened them so that they showed a couple of inches of lace below her skirt. How Darya enjoyed herself, sweeping the earthen floor with her Flemish lace!

So, when she set out to make this social call with her husband, she was dressed to kill. Her lace petticoat showed under her otter-trimmed sheepskin and her skirt was also new and of fine woollen cloth. Fomin's upstart wife would see that Darya was no ordinary Cossack woman but an officer's wife.

Petro waved his whip and clicked his tongue. The pregnant mare, its back sagging and moulted, took the smooth track along the Don at a slow trot. They reached Rubezhin at dinner-time. Fomin was indeed at home. He greeted Petro affably, invited him to his table and smiled into his reddish moustache when his father brought in from Petro's sledge the frost-coated flagon of vodka still sprinkled with bits of hay.

'Where've you been hiding yourself, chum?' Fomin drawled in his pleasant bass, looking sideways at Darya with the wide-set blue eyes of a woman-chaser, and twirling his moustache with some dignity.

'You know what it's like yourself, Yakov Yefimovich. Troops on the march, troubled times like these...'

'Ay, that's so. Woman! What about some pickled cucumbers and cabbage and a bit of our cured fish.'

The cramped cottage was as hot as a furnace. Two children were sleeping on the ledge above the stove, one a boy with the same light-blue wide-set eyes as his father, the other a girl. After a drink Petro got down to business.

'There's word going round the villages that the Cheka boys are here and getting after the Cossacks.'

'The tribunal of the 15th Inzenskaya Division is in Vyoshenskaya. What about it? What's that to you?'

'Well, Yakov Yefimovich, you know yourself, I'm considered to be an officer. Though I'm an officer, as you might say, only in name.'

'So what then?'

Fomin felt himself to be in command of the situation. The drink had made him overbearing and boastful. He drew himself up, smoothed his whiskers and knitted his eyebrows in an imperious frown.

Petro spotted his weakness and played the poor little orphan. His face wore a smile of humble abasement, but little by little he shifted from the formal to the familiar mode of address.

'We were in the same regiment together. You couldn't have anything bad to say about me. Or have I ever been against our folk? Never in my life! Strike me God, but I've always stood up for the Cossacks!'

'We know that. You needn't have doubts on that score, Petro Panteleyevich. We know all about you. No one's going to touch you. But there's some we'll be after. We'll take some of you by the scruff of your necks. There're plenty of vermin lurking round here. They've stayed behind but they're playing their own game. Burying their weapons... Have you given up yours? Eh?'

After his slow beginning Fomin's sudden thrust was so quick that Petro was taken unawares and the blood rushed to his face.

'Well, have you or haven't you? Why don't you answer?' Fomin forced the question home, leaning across the table.

'Of course, I have, Yakov Yefimovich. You mustn't think... I'm being open and honest with you.'

'Open and honest! We know your lot... I was born here myself,' he winked tipsily and opened a mouth full of flat strong teeth. 'Shake hands with a rich Cossack with one hand and keep a knife in the other, or he'll stab you... The dogs! None of 'em are open or honest! I've seen plenty of men in my time. Traitors! But don't worry, no one will touch you. Take my word!'

Darya tasted the meat jelly and out of politeness ate hardly any bread. The mistress of the house diligently displayed her hospitality.

Petro left towards evening in a hopeful and merrier mood.

* * *

After seeing off Petro, Pantelei paid a visit to Natalya's father Miron Korshunov. His last call had been before the Reds came. Lukinichna had been helping Mitka to pack for the road and the house had been in a turmoil. Feeling that he was in the way, Pantelei had not stayed long. But this time the purpose of his visit was to find out if all was well and, in passing, to bemoan the present state of affairs.

It was quite a long walk for a lame man to the other end of the village. The first person he met on entering the Korshunovs' yard was Grandad Grishaka, looking older and with a few teeth missing. It was Sunday and the old man was going off to church for Evensong. At the sight of his relative, Pantelei nearly dropped. The old man's coat was unbuttoned, revealing a display of all the medals and other decorations he had won in the war against the Turks; red tabs gleamed challengingly on the high collar of the old uniform, the trousers, loose and baggy, with stripes down the sides were neatly tucked into white woolen socks, and on his head, pulled down firmly on to the big wax-like ears, was a peaked cap with a cockade.

'Grandad! Are you in your right mind? Who wears medals and a cockade at a time like this?'

'Eh?' Grandad Grishaka cupped his hand round his ear.

'Take off your cockade, I say! Put away those medals! You'll get yourself arrested! That kind of thing's not allowed under the Soviets, the law forbids it.'

'Young man, I served my tsar loyally and well. And this government is not of God. I don't recognise their power. I gave my oath to Tsar Alexander, mark you, and not to the muzhiks!' Grandad Grishaka munched his pallid lips, wiped his greenish-looking moustache and pointed his stick in the direction of the house. 'Did you come to see Miron? He's at home. But we've seen our Mitka off. He went off with the retreating army. May the Holy Mother of God, Queen of Heaven, protect him! But your two have stayed behind? Eh? Ah, well... That's the kind of Cossacks we've got now! Didn't they swear allegiance to the Ataman? And now when the Army's in need of troops, they stay behind with their wives... Is Natalya, our dear daughter, alive and well?'

'Quite well... Go indoors and take those medals off, kinsman! They're not allowed nowadays. Lord God in heaven, are you crazy, man?'

'Go your way! You're much too young to teach me! Off with you!'

Grandad Grishaka bore down on Pantelei, who had to step off the path into the snow to make way for him and then looked round, shaking his head despairingly.

'Did you meet our old soldier? He's a terror, he is! And the Lord won't take him,' Miron, who had noticeably aged in the past few days, rose to meet his guest. 'Going out with all those medals on his chest and with a cockade in his cap! It's enough to make you use force. He's grown just like a child lately, doesn't understand a thing.'

'Let him have his way. He hasn't got much longer... Well, how are our boys getting on out there? We heard tell those fiends attacked Grisha?' Lukinichna sat down with the Cossacks and cupped her chin in her hand sorrowfully. 'And what a terrible thing has happened to us... They've taken four of our horses, and left us only the mare and a yearling. It's ruination!'

Miron screwed up one eye, as though taking aim at somebody, and a new note, of pent-up anger, sounded in his voice.

'And what is it that's brought our life to ruin? Who caused it? It's this damned government! It's to blame for everything. Make us all equal? How could anyone think of such a thing? You can shoot me, but I won't agree! I've worked hard all my life, sweating and straining. Why should I live equal with someone who's never stirred a finger to rise from poverty? No, by God, we'll just wait a bit! This government is hamstringing the good farmer. That's why we're downing tools. What's the use of working? Who is it for? If you earn something today, tomorrow they'll take it all away from you... And another thing, kinsman. An old regimental comrade of

144

mine from the village of Mrykhin was round here t'other day and we had a talk... You know where the front is, along the Donets. But will it stay there? To tell you the truth, what I say to people I trust is this: our lads, the ones out yonder, across the Donets, have got to be helped...'

'Helped? In what way?' Pantelei asked anxiously, for some reason in a whisper.

'In what way? Get rid of this government, kick 'em out! And kick 'em so hard they'll end up in Tambov province. Let 'em get on with their levelling out there, with the muzhiks. I'd give up every scrap of property I have, to destroy these scoundrels. We must tell people, kinsman, we must make 'em understand! It's high time! Or it'll be too late. The Cossacks, my friend told me, are up in arms in his village too. We've got to set about it together!' And his voice dropped to a rapid, breathless whisper. 'The main army units have passed through, so what's left? Only a few! You could count 'em on the fingers of one hand! In the villages there's only the chairmen. It won't take a minute to send their heads rolling. And as for the Vyoshenskaya lot, if we all go for them together, as one man, we'll tear 'em to bits! Our lads won't let us down, and then we'll link up. It's a sure thing, man!'

Pantelei rose to his feet. Weighing his words, he advised warily, 'Mind you don't slip up or you'll be in trouble! The Cossacks may be wobbling, but I'll be plagued if I know which way they'll go. You can't talk about such things with everyone these days. There's no making out the young ones at all, they seem to live blindfold. Some retreat, others stay behind. These are difficult times! We're all living in the dark.'

'Don't you worry, kinsman!' Miron smiled condescendingly. 'I know what I'm talking about. People are like sheep; where the ram goes they all follow. You've got to show 'em the way! Open their eyes to what kind of government this is! If there's no cloud, there'll be no stroke of lightning. I tell the Cossacks straight out: you've got to rise up. There's a rumour going round that they've given an order to wipe out all Cossacks. What do you make of that?'

The flush in Miron's face showed up through his freckles.

'What are we coming to? They say the shootings have already begun... What kind of life is this? Look at the way everything has gone to rack and ruin these past few years! No kerosene, no matches. The only thing Mokhov has for sale lately is sweets... And what about the crops? How much do they sow nowadays compared with what they used to? They've stripped us of our horses. Surely you remember? Some fine race-horses we had, fast enough to ride down a Kalmyk! There was one chestnut with a blaze on its forehead. I used to ride down hares on it. I'd ride out into the steppe, flush a hare out of the scrub and chase it for two hundred yards or more, then ride it down. I remember it as if it were now!' A rapt smile appeared on Miron's face. 'I rode out one day to the windmills and there he was— a hare hopping along straight towards me. So I went after him and off he ran down the hill and across the Don! It was at Shrovetide. The wind had swept the snow off the ice and it was right slippery. Well, I got into a real gallop after that hare, and then the horse slipped and went down at full speed. And that was the end of him. When I got up I was shaking all over! But I took the saddle off and ran back home. 'Father, my horse got killed under me! I was chasing a hare." "Did you catch the hare?" "No, Father." "Well, saddle up Black and catch it, you son-of-a-bitch!" Ay, those were the days! Lived like kings the Cossacks did! You could kill a horse but it didn't matter as long as you caught the hare. A horse cost a hundred and a hare only a mite... But what's the use of talking!'

* * *

Pantelei left the Korshunovs feeling even more confused than when he had come; his whole being was poisoned with anxiety and despair. Now, at last, he was fully aware that certain strange and hostile elements had taken control of his life. Whereas in former days he had run his farm and managed his life as he would a well-broken-in mount in a steeplechase, life was now whirling him along like a rabid foaming runaway, and he was no longer controlling it but bouncing limply on its heaving back and making pitiful efforts to save himself from falling.

The future was wrapped in murk. The past loomed dimly. It was not long since Miron had been the richest farmer in the neighbourhood. But the past three years had sapped his strength. His labourers had drifted away, his sowings had shrunk to a ninth of what they were before, his horses and oxen had been sold off for a mere promise or for money whose value lurched drunkenly every day. It was as though he had been living in a dream, like the drifting mists over the Don. Only the house with its fancifully carved balcony and faded eaves was left to remind him of times gone by. Too early the foxy ruddiness of Korshunov's beard had given way to grey. And the sprinklings had spread to his temples, at first like a shrub on sandy soil, in clusters, and then in a stubborn assault, hair by hair, until they captured the whole brow. And in Miron himself these two elements were fiercely at war with each other. The good red blood that flowed in his veins was rebelling, driving him to work, forcing him to sow, to build barns, to mend his tools, to make money; but more and more often he was assailed by despondency—'What's the good of getting rich? You'll only lose it all!'—that bathed everything in the deathly pallor of indifference. The ugly old hands no longer reached eagerly for hammer or hand-saw as they had used to, but lay idly on his knees, their grimy disfigured fingers twitching. With this time of chaos came old age. The soil that he had once loved repelled him. And he went to it as to an unloved wife, out of habit, out of duty. Whatever profit he did make brought him no joy and his losses had none of their former sting... When the Reds requisitioned his horses, he scarcely raised an eyebrow. But only two years ago, for a mere trifle, for a haycock that had been trampled by the oxen, he had nearly attacked his wife with a pitch-fork. 'Korshunov's stuffed himself so full it's coming back out of him,' the neighbours used to say.

Pantelei limped home and lay down on his bed. He had a pain in the pit of his stomach and a choking sickness in the throat. After supper he asked his wife to bring him a salted water-melon. When he had eaten a slice, he began to shake all over and hardly managed to reach the stove-bench. By morning he was unconscious in the throes of typhus, consumed by a raging fever. His bloodcaked lips cracked, his face grew yellow, and the whites of his eyes were filmed with a blue enamel. Old Drozdikha, the leachwoman, opened a vein and let out two plate-fuls of dark, tar-like blood. But consciousness did not return, a bluish pallor spread over his face and his black-toothed mouth gaped even wider as he gasped for air.

XX

At the end of January Ivan Alexeyevich Kotlyarov left for Vyoshenskaya in response to a message from the chairman of the District Revolutionary Committee. He was expected back that evening. Mishka Koshevoi sat waiting for him in Mokhov's deserted house, in the former owner's study at a writing-desk as wide as a double bed. There was only one chair in the room and Olshanov, the militiaman who had brough the message from Vyoshenskaya, was lounging on the windowsill. He smoked in silence, spitting with great skill into the fire-place and hitting a fresh tile with every long-range shot. Outside the night was radiant with stars. A resonant frosty stillness hung over the village. Mishka was signing the pages of a report on the search that had been made at Stepan Astakhov's house. Occasionally he glanced through the window at the frost-sugared branches of the maples.

Somebody came up the steps of the porch, his felt boots creaking softly.

'Here he is.'

Mishka rose to his feet. But the cough and the footsteps in the corridor were not Ivan's. The man who entered was Grigory Melekhov, his greatcoat buttoned to the throat, his face ruddy from the cold, his brows and moustache rimed with frost.

'I saw the light and decided to drop in. How are you!'

'Come in. Any complaints?'

'Nothing to complain about. I just dropped in for a word and to say we shouldn't be given transport duties just now. Our horses have gone lame.'

'What about your oxen?' Mishka gave him a cautious look.

'Oxen are no good in this weather. It's too slippery.'

Someone came up on to the porch, scraping the frost-fettered boards with his heavy tread. Ivan swept into the room in a sheepskin cloak with the hood wrapped round his head in woman's fashion. He brought with him a breath of fresh cold air, the smell of hay and tobacco fumes.

'Brrr! I'm frozen stiff, lad! Hullo, Grigory! What are you up to, roaming about at night?.. Devil take these cloaks! They let the wind through like a sieve!'

He took off the cloak and started talking even before he had hung it up.

'Well, now I've seen our chairman,' Ivan came up to the desk with a happy twinkle in his eyes, impatient to tell his story. 'I walk into his office. He shakes hands and says, "Please, take a chair, comrade!" And that's the District Chairman for you! Remember what it was like before? With the Major-General? How did we have to stand in front of him? That's our kind of government for you, bless its heart! We're all equal!'

His animated, happy face, the way he jigged about round the desk, and his enthusiastic talk were incomprehensible to Grigory.

He asked, 'What are you so happy about, Alexeyevich?'

'What about?' Ivan's dimpled chin quivered. 'I've been treated as a human being. That's why I'm happy. He offered me his hand like an equal, asked me to sit down.'

'The generals have also been going about in homespun shirts lately.' Grigory straightened out his moustache with the side of his hand and narrowed his eyes. 'I saw one of 'em—he even had shoulder straps marked in indelible pencil. He was also going around, shaking hands with the Cossacks.'

'The generals do it because they have to, but it comes natural to these fellows. See the difference?'

'There's no difference!' Grigory shook his head.

'So you think there's no difference in government either? What have we been fighting for then? What were you fighting for? For the generals? And you say it's all the same.'

'I was fighting for myself, and not for any generals. To tell you the truth, neither of them are to my liking.'

'Well, who is then?'

'No one!'

The militiaman spat all the way across the room and laughed sympathetically. Evidently no one was to his liking either.

'You didn't always think that way, did you?'

Mishka's remark was meant to sting Grigory but he showed no sign of being affected by it.

'We all had different views.'

Ivan wanted to see Grigory out and tell Mishka the details of his visit to the chairman, but he was carried away by the turn their talk had taken. Still under the impression of all he had seen and heard at the district centre, he plunged into argument.

'You've come here just to argue, Grigory! You don't know yourself what you want.'

'No, I don't,' Grigory agreed readily enough.

'What have you got against this government?'

'And why are you so keen to please it? Since when have you turned so Red?'

'We won't go into that. Talk to me as you find me now. Understand? And you'd better leave the government out of it too, because I'm chairman here and it's not for me to argue with you.'

'Let's drop it then. It's time for me to be going anyway. I just came in about transport duties. As for your government, I don't care what you say, but it's a rotten government. Tell me straight now and we'll leave it at that. What does this government give us, Cossacks?'

'Which Cossacks do you mean? They're different.'

'I mean all Cossacks.'

'Freedom, rights... Now, wait a bit... Just a minute, you seem to be—'

'That's what they said in 1917, but you've got to think up something new now!' Grigory cut in. 'Does it give land? Freedom? Does it make us equal?.. We've got land in plenty, enough to lose ourselves in. We don't need any more freedom or we'll be sabering each other in the streets. We used to elect our own atamans but now they're chosen for us. Who elected the one that overjoyed you with his handshake? For the Cossacks this government means nothing but ruination! It's a muzhiks' government and they're the ones that want it. But we don't want the generals either. Communists or generals, they're both a yoke on our necks.'

'The rich Cossacks don't want it, but what about the others? You muddlehead! There's three rich Cossacks in the village, but how many poor? And the workers— what will you do about them? No, that's not the way for us to reason! Let the rich Cossacks do without some of their wealth and give it to the needy. And if they won't, we'll tear it out of 'em, with their flesh as well! They've lorded it long enough. They stole the land and—'

'They didn't steal it, they won it! That land is soaked in the blood of our forefathers. Maybe that's why it yields so well.'

'All the same, the poor have got to have their share. If we're going to make people equal, we'll do it properly. And you're not pulling your weight. You're like a weathercock, you change with the wind. People like you create confusion in life.'

'All right, you needn't bawl at me! I came in for old time's sake, to tell you what was on my mind. You say make people equal... That's how the Bolsheviks have caught the ignorant. They've sprinkled their fine words around and people go for 'em, like fish to a bait! But what's happened to that equality? Take the Red Army. You saw the way they marched through the village. The platoon commander's in box-calf boots, but it's leg-rags for the rank and file. I saw a commissar all wrapped up in leather, jacket and trousers as well, but for some of the others there wasn't leather enough for a pair of boots. And it's only one year that they've been in power. When they put down roots— what will happen to equality then?.. They used to say at the front: "We'll all be equal. The same pay for commanders and soldiers!" But no! Bullshit! It's just a bait! A lord may be bad, but the upstart, believe you me, is a hundred times as bad! We had some rotten officers, but if you got a jumped-up Cossack from the ranks you might as well lie down and die—you wouldn't find anyone worse! He was no better educated that any other Cossack, all he knew was how to twist the bullocks' tails, but here he was—a man of importance, drunk with power, and ready to flay the hide off anyone else to stay that way.'

'You're talking like a counter-revolutionary,' Ivan said coldly, but without raising his eyes to meet Grigory's. 'You won't turn me into your furrow and I don't want to force you into mine. I haven't seen you for a long time and, I won't hide it, you're like a stranger. You're an enemy of Soviet rule!'

'I never expected that from you... So if I think about the kind of government we've got, I'm a counter-revolutionary, am I? A Cadet?'

Ivan took the pouch Olshanov had offered and his voice grew softer.

'How can I make you see? People think these things out for themselves, with their own brains. Their own hearts! I'm no good with words because I'm ignorant and never had any proper education. And I've had to feel my way to it, groping in the dark...'

'That's enough!' Mishka shouted furiously.

They left the Executive Committee office together. Grigory was silent. Oppressed by the silence and not wishing to justify Grigory's wavering because he himself was well rid of it and now had quite a different view of life, Ivan said in parting, 'You'd better keep such thoughts to yourself. Because although we know each other and your Petro is a kinsman of mine, I'll find a way of dealing with you! Don't try to wobble the Cossacks, they're wobbling enough as it is. And don't stand in our way. Because we'll walk over you! Goodbye!'

Grigory went off with a feeling that he had crossed a dividing line beyond which everything that had seemed confused now revealed itself in stark clarity. As a matter of fact, he had said in the heat of the moment only what had been on his mind for several days, pent up and begging for an outlet. And because he stood between the two conflicting sides, rejecting both of them, he was assailed by a half-suppressed but unrelenting sense of irritation.

Mishka and Ivan walked on together. Ivan again took up the story of his meeting with the District Chairman, but all its colour and importance seemed to have faded. He tried in vain to recover his previous enthusiasm but there was something in the way, something that prevented him from rejoicing in life, from breathing deep of the crisp frosty air. And that something was Grigory, the talk they had just had. At the thought of it, he said with hatred in his voice, 'People like Grigory are just a hindrance when it comes to a fight. The swine! He won't drop anchor, he just floats about like cowdung in a water hole. If he comes round again, I'll turn him out! And if he starts any agitation, we'll find a place to put him away... What about you, Mishka? How are things with you?'

Mishka, who was lost in his own thoughts, merely swore in reply.

They walked to the next cross-roads and Mishka turned to Ivan with a confused smile on his full, girlish lips.

'What a bitter thing politics is, damn it! You can talk about anything but you'll never make as much bad blood as you will with politics. That talk we've just had with Grigory... We're old friends, we were at school together, we ran after the same girls, he's like a brother to me... But when he started going on like that, I got so wild, I thought my heart would burst like a water melon. I was all shaking inside! It was like he was taking the very dearest thing I had. Like he was robbing me! You can kill a man, you get so worked up with that kind of talk. There aren't any brothers or cousins in this war. You have to draw a line and stick to it!' Mishka's voice was

shaking as though he had suffered an unbearable insult.
'I was never so riled with him for any girl he took
off me as I am for the way he talked tonight. That's
how it got me!'

XXI

Snow was falling and melting as it fell. At noon the
ravines rustled with sliding snow. The forest on the other
side of the Don was soughing. The oak trunks had thawed
and darkened. Drops of moisture from the branches
soaked right through the snow to the earth nestling
under its rotting cover of fallen leaves. The warm, heady
scent of spring was in the air and there was a smell of
cherrywood in the orchards. Thaw patches had appeared
on the Don. Along the banks the ice had receded and the
holes in it were awash with the clear green water of the
river's edge.

A transport bringing a load of shells to the Don was to
change its sledges in Tatarsky. The Red Army men escorting it showed they meant business. While the senior
man stood guard over Ivan, having told him, 'I'd better
sit here with you or you might run away!', the others
went out to requisition the sledges. Forty-seven sledges
with two horses apiece were needed.

Yemelyan, Mokhov's former coachman, found his
way to the Melekhovs' farm.

'Harness up, you've got to take shells to Bokovskaya!'

Petro responded with a shrug, 'Our horses are lame
and I used the mare yesterday to take the wounded
to Vyoshenskaya.'

Without another word Yemelyan made straight for
the stable. He was followed by a protesting hatless
Petro.

'Here, wait a bit... Can't you do without 'em?'

'Can't you cut that crap?' Yemelyan stared grimly at
Petro and added, 'I feel like having a look at your horses.
What's made them lame, I wonder. Mebbe it was a hammer that someone accidentally on purpose happened to
clout a joint with? So don't think you can diddle me! I've
seen more horses in my time than you've seen horse-
shit. Harness up! Horses or oxen—don't matter which.'

Grigory undertook to drive the sledge. Before leaving
he slipped into the kitchen and, as he kissed the children,
told them hurriedly, 'I'll bring back something nice.

153

Don't be naughty, do what your mother tells you.' And to Petro, 'Don't worry about me. I won't go far. If they send us on beyond Bokovskaya, I'll leave the oxen and come back. But I won't come to the village. I'll stay awhile in Singin, with our aunt. Come over and see me, Petro, now and then... I find it a bit creepy staying here.' He gave a dry little laugh. 'Anyway, good-bye for now! Don't be sad, Natalya!'

Outside Mokhov's shop, which was now a food store, they transferred the shell crates to the new sledges and set out.

'The Reds are fighting to make a better life for them-selves, and we've been fighting for the good life we had,' Grigory went on thinking as he lay in the sledge with his head muffled in his homespun coat, listening to the steady plodding of the oxen's hooves. 'There's no one truth in life. The man who wins eats the man who loses. I've been looking for a truth that doesn't exist, eating my heart out over it, swinging this way and that... In the old days, they say, it was the Tatars that hurt the Don, trying to take our land and make us slaves. Now it's Russia. No! I won't give in! They're alien to me and to all Cossacks. The Cossacks are waking up to it now. They abandoned the front and now they all see as well as I do—ah, but it's too late!'

His eyes took in the blur of hills and bristling ravines, the tangle of weeds, as they floated past near the road-side, then wandered to the snowy fields rolling away southwards into the distance. The endless winding of the road bored him and made him drowsy.

Now and then he shouted lazily at the oxen or fell into a doze, trying to make himself comfortable on the shell crates. After a smoke he buried his face in the hay, which still smelled of sweet-clover and hot June days, and fell asleep. He dreamt that he was walking with Aksinya through a field of tall rustling wheat. She was carrying a child carefully in her arms and glancing at him with watchful eyes. Grigory heard the beating of his own heart, the lilting murmur of the wheat-ears and saw the fanciful patterns of the grass, the poignant blue of the heavens. Emotion surged within him and he loved Aksinya as utterly and desperately as before. He felt this love with his whole body, with every heartbeat, and at the same time he realised that it was not real, that there was nothing but a lifeless void before his eyes, that it was a dream. And yet he rejoiced in his dream and accepted it as real life. Aksinya was as lovely as she had been five years ago, but colder, more restrained. More vividly than ever before, in reality, Grigory saw the fluffy ringlets on her neck (the wind was playing in them) and the ends of her white kerchief... A sudden jerk and the sound of voices awoke him.

Several sledges were approaching along the road.

'What are you carrying, lads?' Bodovskov, who was at the head of the column, shouted hoarsely.

For a time there was no answer, only the creak of runners and the crunching of the oxen's hooves in the snow. At length someone replied, 'Corpses. They died of typhus...'

Grigory raised his head. The bodies in their grey greatcoats were piled lengthwise on the sledges and partly covered by tarpaulins. On a slippery patch Grigory's sledge hit an arm that was sticking out of one of the oncoming sledges and it responded with a dull metallic sound... Grigory turned away indifferently.

The rich, overpowering scent of the sweet-clover beckoned sleep, gently recalling the half-forgotten past and forcing him once again to bare his heart to the sharpened blade of bygone love. Rending and yet sweet was the pain that Grigory felt as he fell back into the sledge with his cheek pressed to a yellow sprig of sweet-clover. Pricked by memories, his heart bled and for a long time its unsteady pounding kept him from falling asleep.

XXII

The village revolutionary committee was backed by a small group consisting of Davydka, the mill-hand, Timofei, Mokhov's former coachman Yemelyan, and the pock-marked cobbler Filka. These were the men on whom Ivan relied in his daily work, for every day he felt an invisible wall growing up between him and the rest of the village. The Cossacks had stopped attending meetings or, if they did come, it was only after Davydka and the others had gone round four or five times, calling at every house. Those who came kept quiet and agreed with everything. Most of them were young, but there was not a sympathiser among them. Stony faces, estranged, distrustful eyes and sullen looks confronted Ivan at the meetings and sent a shiver through his heart.

His eyes saddened and his voice lost its former strength and confidence. Filka had good reason for the remark he made one day.

'We've parted company with the village, Comrade Kotlyarov! The people are in a terrible mood. Yesterday I went asking for sledges to take wounded Red Army men to Vyoshenskaya—no one would go. It's a bugger, ye know, living in the same house with someone you don't get on with.'

'And they're drinking themselves silly!' Yemelyan added, sucking at his pipe. 'The stills are going in every yard.'

Mishka Koshevoi frowned and kept his thoughts to himself but in the end he too let go. When they were walking home one evening, he asked Ivan to give him a rifle.

'What for?'

'You don't know! I'm scared of going about unarmed. Can't you see what's happening? If you ask me, we ought to take a few people in charge. Grigory Melekhov for one, and Old Boldyrev, Matvei Kashulin, Miron Korshunov. They're all trying to set the Cossacks against us, the scum. They're waiting for their lot to come back from across the Donets.'

Ivan gave a gloomy shrug and chopped the air with his hand.

'Once we start, we'll have so many ringleaders to root out. People don't know their own minds. A few of them would support us if they weren't looking over their shoulders at Miron Korshunov. They're afraid his Mitka will come back from the Donets and have their guts.'

Life had taken a steep turn. The next day a mounted messenger arrived from Vyoshenskaya with instructions to impose a levy on the richest households. The overall figure for the village was forty thousand rubles. They broke it down into contributions. A day passed. The money collected filled two sacks and amounted to only a little over eighteen thousand rubles. Ivan reported back to the district centre and three militiamen arrived with instructions that those who had not paid their share of the levy should be arrested and dispatched under guard to Vyoshenskaya. Four of the old men were temporarily confined in Mokhov's cellar, where the merchant used to store his apples in winter.

The village buzzed like a disturbed beehive. Korshunov refused point-blank to pay, though the money he clung to was rapidly losing its value. But the time had come for the final reckoning. Two more emissaries arrived from the district centre: the local investigator, a young Vyoshenskaya Cossack, who had served in the 28th Regiment and another man who wore a long sheepskin over his leather jacket. They showed the mandates given to them by the Revolutionary tribunal and shut themselves up with Ivan in his office. The investigator's companion, an elderly man with a shaven head, launched the proceedings in a businesslike manner.

'There have been signs of unrest in the district. The White Guard elements who have stayed behind are getting active and sowing confusion among the working Cossacks. The most hostile of them must be cleared out. Let's make a list of the officers, priests, atamans, gendarmes and rich men, of everyone who's been engaged in active resistance to us. Help the investigator. He knows some of them already.'

Ivan looked at his smoothly shaven, womanish face and reeled off the names. When he mentioned Petro Melekhov, however, the investigator shook his head.

'He's our man, Fomin asked us not to touch him. He's pro-Bolshevik. I served with him in the 28th.'

The list, written by Koshevoi on a sheet of squared paper torn out of an exercise book, was completed.

A few hours later the arrested Cossacks were sitting on a pile of oak beams in Mokhov's spacious yard, watched by the militiamen. They were waiting for their families to bring them food for the journey and a sledge for their belongings. Miron, dressed as if for burying in new clothes, a sheepskin, leather shoes and clean white stockings with his trousers tucked into them, was sitting beside Old Bogatiryov and Matvei Kashulin. Avdeich the Braggart was walking nervously about the yard. Now he would glance aimlessly into the well, now he would pick up a chip of wood that was lying on the ground and again hurry from the porch to the gate, wiping his purple, apple-cheeked perspiring face with his sleeve.

The others sat in silence, heads bowed, scratching the snow with their sticks. Their flustered womenfolk hurried into the yard, thrust bundles and bags into their hands and whispered in their ears. A tearful Lukinichna buttoned up her husband's coat, tied a white shawl round his collar and stared beseechingly into his dull, lacklustre eyes.

'Don't be so upset, Grigorich! It may all turn out for the best. You mustn't give up like this! Oh, Lord above!..' A spasm of tears clawed her mouth sideways, but with an effort she pursed her lips and whispered, 'I'll come and see you, I'll bring Agripina with me. You're so fond of her.'

The militiaman at the gate shouted. 'Sledge is here! Put your bags in and get going! Stand aside, women, we don't want any of your sobstuff!'

For the first time in her life Lukinichna kissed Miron's ginger-haired hand and broke away from him.

The ox-drawn sledge crawled slowly away from the square towards the Don.

The seven arrested men and the two militiamen followed behind. Avdeich stopped to tie up his shoe, then ran youthfully to catch up. Matvei Kashulin and his son walked together. Maidannikov and Korolyov lit up cigarettes as they walked. Miron held on to the back of the sledge. Behind all the rest, with his heavy majestic stride, came Old Bogatiryov. The head wind sent his white patriarchal beard streaming out behind him and waved a farewell with the tassels of the scarf he was wearing over his shoulder.

On that same gloomy February day an unbelievable thing happened.

The village had of late grown used to the arrival of officials from the district centre. So no curiosity was aroused by the appearance in the square of a two-horse sledge with a shivering passenger seated beside the driver. The sledge halted outside Mokhov's house. The passenger stepped down and turned out to be an elderly man, unhurried in his movements. He straightened the soldier's belt round his long cavalry greatcoat, loosened the earflaps of his big red-topped fur-trimmed Cossack cap and, pressing the wooden holster of his Mauser pistol to his side, walked unhurriedly to the porch.

Kotlyarov and the two militiamen were in the office of the Revolutionary Committee. The man entered without knocking, stood on the threshold, smoothing down his short grizzled beard, and said in a rather deep voice, 'I want to see the chairman.'

Ivan stared with round, bird-like eyes at the newcomer and tried to jump to his feet, but failed. He sat with his mouth wide open and his fingers scrabbling at the shabby arms of his chair. Stokman, much aged, stood looking at him from under the floppy fringe of his cap.

At first his narrowed eyes did not recognise Ivan, but suddenly they grew lighter and a fan of wrinkles spread from the corners to the greying temples. He strode up to Ivan, who was still trying to rise, took him in his arms, pressed his wet beard to his cheeks as he kissed him, and said, 'I knew it! I thought to myself, if he's still alive, he'll be the chairman at Tatarsky!'

'Osip Davydovich! Strike me! Strike me cold! I can't believe my eyes!' Ivan burst out, almost weeping.

Tears were so unbecoming to his manly face that even the militiaman turned away.

'Well, you'll have to!' Stokman responded in his deep voice, smiling and gently freeing his hands from Ivan's grip. 'What? Haven't you got anything to sit on here?'

'Here, take the arm-chair!.. Tell me now! Where've you come from?'

'I'm in the army's political department. I see you're determined not to believe I'm real. You old chump!'

Stokman smiled ar.d, slapping Ivan's knee, plunged into his story, 'It's all very simple, chum. After they took me away from here, they sentenced me and I was still in exile when the revolution came. Another comrade and I organised a Red Guard detachment to fight Dutov and Kolchak. Yes, we had a fine time of it out there! But now we've driven them across the Urals—did you know that? And here I am on your front. The political department of the 8th Army has sent me to work in your district because I once lived here and am supposed to know the locality. As soon as I got to Vyoshenskaya and talked to the people at the Revolutionary Committee I decided the first place to visit should be Tatarsky. Before I go anywhere else, I thought, I'll live there for a bit and help them to get organised. So you see, old friends don't forget each other, do they? But we'll come back to that. Right now let's talk about you, about the situation; tell me about the people, what's happening. Have you a Party group in the village? Who's working with you? Who's survived?' He turned to the militiamen, 'Well, comrades ... perhaps you'll give the chairman and me a little time to ourselves now. Damn it, if as soon as I drove into the village I didn't feel the smell of the old days... What a time that was! But nothing to what we're living through now... Well, let's hear your story!'

About three hours later Mishka and Ivan took Stokman to his old lodgings at cross-eyed Lukeriya's. As they strode along the brown surface of the road, Mishka kept plucking at the sleeve of Stokman's greatcoat, as if afraid he would suddenly melt away like a ghost.

Lukeriya fed her former lodger on cabbage soup and even produced an aged-looking lump of sugar from some secret hiding-place.

After tea, brewed out of cherry leaves, Stokman lay down on the stove-bench. He listened to the two men's halting stories, put in a question now and then, chewed at his cigarette-holder and eventually fell asleep, dropping the cigarette on his dirty flannel shirt. Ivan went on talking for another ten minutes and realised what had happened only when Stokman answered a remark of his with a quiet snore. He walked out on tip-toe, going purple in the face in his attempts to stifle a cough.

'Feel better now?' Mishka asked as soon as they were in the yard, and broke into quiet laughter, as if he were being tickled.

* * *

Militiaman Olshanov, who had escorted the arrested men to Vyoshenskaya, got a lift on a passing sledge and arrived back in the village at midnight. He went on knocking at the window of the little room where Ivan was sleeping until he woke him.

'What's up?' Ivan came out sleepy-faced. 'Is it a message or something?'

Olshanov toyed with his whip.

'They've shot the Cossacks.'

'You lying bastard!'

'They had 'em up for interrogation as soon as we got there, and even before it was dark they took them out into the pinewood. I saw it myself!'

Fumbling with his boots, Ivan dressed hurriedly and dashed off to see Stokman.

'The men we sent off today—they've been shot in Vyoshenskaya. I thought they'd be given a spell in gaol, but if that's how it is... If that's how it is we won't get anywhere out here! The people will turn away from us, Osip Davydovich! There's something wrong about this. Why did those men have to be destroyed? What's going to happen now?'

He had expected Stokman to be as indignant as he was at what had happened, and as worried about the conse-

160

quences, but Stokman slowly pulled on his shirt.

'Don't make such a noise. You'll wake the landlady,' he said when his head was clear of the collar.

When he had dressed, he lit a cigarette and asked to be told again of the reasons for the arrest of the seven Cossacks, then he began to talk rather coldly.

'You must get this into your head, and keep it there! The front is only a hundred and fifty versts away. The bulk of the Cossacks are hostile to us. They're hostile because your kulaks, your Cossack kulaks—I mean the atamans and the other people at the top—carry a lot of weight with the ordinary working Cossack. They're looked up to, so to speak. Why? Well, you ought to know the reason for that too. The Cossacks form a special group in society, they're a military caste. Respect for rank, for the "officers, our fathers" was cultivated by tsarism... Now then, how does the old Cossack song go? "And as the officers, our fathers, command, so shall we fight with sabre, lance and gun." Isn't that it? Well, there you are! Those father-officers commanded the Cossacks to break up the workers' strike demonstrations. For three hundred years the Cossacks' heads have been fuddled by this poison. Quite a long time! But remember this! There is a great difference between a kulak in, let us say, Ryazan Province and the Don Cossack kulak! If you squeeze the Ryazan kulak, he'll hiss against Soviet power, but he's powerless, he's only dangerous if he can stab you in the back. But the Don Cossack kulak? He's an armed kulak. He's a dangerous and poisonous snake! A powerful one. He won't just hiss and spread rumours against us, slander us, as Korshunov and others—you told me so yourself—were doing. He'll try to attack us openly! Of course, he will! He'll take his rifle and shoot us. He'll shoot you! And he'll try to gain the support of the other Cossacks, the Cossack of average means, so to speak, and even the poor Cossack. He'll use them to fight and kill us! Then what are we waiting for? Was he caught red-handed acting against us? Right then! Don't talk—up against a wall with him! And there's no need for any snivelling pity—what a good man he was, and all that!'

'I'm not pitying them, don't think that!' Ivan waved his hands. 'I'm afraid the others may turn away from us.'

Stokman, who up to now had been rubbing his grizzled chest with apparent calm, suddenly flared up, seized Ivan by the front of his tunic and spoke hoarsely, trying to hold back a fit of coughing.

'They won't turn away if we teach them our class truth! The only road for the working Cossacks is our road, not the kulak's! What's come over you! The kulak lives by their labour,—yes, their labour!—doesn't he? And grows fat on it! Ah, you old muddler! You've lost your fire! The rot's setting in. I'll have to take you in hand! So stupid! A working man with all this intellectual slobber! Like some rotten little Socialist-Revolutionary! You just watch yourself, Ivan!'

He let go of Ivan's collar and smiled faintly with a shake of the head. Lighting a cigarette, he inhaled the smoke and ended on a calmer note.

'If we don't arrest the most active of our enemies throughout the district, there'll be an uprising. If we manage to isolate them now, in good time, an uprising may be avoided. We don't have to shoot all of them. Only the diehards must be destroyed, the rest can be sent away into the heart of Russia. But in any case we can't afford to stand on ceremony with our enemies. Lenin said you can't make a revolution with gloves on. Was it necessary in this particular case to shoot these men? I think it was. Perhaps not all of them, but it would be no use trying to reform Korshunov, for example. That's quite clear! And what about Melekhov? Perhaps not for long, but he's slipped through our fingers. He's the man we ought to have dealt with! He's more dangerous than all the rest put together. Remember that! The talk he started with you at the Executive Committee was the talk of a man who tomorrow will be our enemy. But there's nothing in this to get upset about. The best sons of the working class are dying at the war fronts. Dying in their thousands! That's what we should grieve over, not over those who are killing them or waiting for the chance to stab them in the back. It's them or us! There's no middle course. That's how matters stand, my good Ivan Alexeyevich!'

XXIII

Petro had just fed the animals; he returned to the house and was picking the stalks of hay out of his mittens, when the door-latch clacked in the porch.

Muffled in a thick black shawl, Lukinichna stepped across the threshold. Uttering no greeting, she ran with quick short steps towards Natalya, who was standing by the kitchen bench, and fell on her knees before her.

'Mother dear! What is it?' Natalya cried in alarm, trying to raise her mother's inert body.

Instead of answering, Lukinichna beat her head on the earthen floor and began to moan in a low, broken voice that rose to a howl of lament.

'Oh, my dearest!.. Who will look after us now!..'

The women wailed so concertedly and there was such a chorus of crying from the children that Petro grabbed his tobacco pouch and made a dash for the porch. He had quickly guessed what the matter was. He stood on the porch and smoked. The wailing voices in the house died down and Petro with unpleasant shivers running down his back returned to the kitchen. With her soaking handkerchief still pressed to her face Lukinichna lamented, 'They've shot our Miron Grigoryevich!.. Our dear one's dead!.. We're nothing but orphans now!.. We'll be at everyone's mercy!..' And again she broke into that wolf-like howl: 'His dear eyes are closed for ever!.. They will never see the light again...'

Darya brought the swooning Natalya to her senses with water. Ilyinichna dried her cheeks with an apron. From the front room, where Pantelei was lying sick, came a cough and a rasping moan.

'For the sake of Jesus Christ our Lord! For the sake of the Lord God, our Creator! Go to Vyoshenskaya, dear boy, and bring him back to us, even though he's dead!' Lukinichna seized Petro's hands and pressed them frantically to her breast. 'Bring him back... Oh, merciful Queen of Heaven! I can't let him lie there to rot unburied!'

'For goodness sake, woman!' Petro backed away from her as though she had the plague. 'Bring him back? How on earth! I've got my own life to think about! How could I ever find him over there?'

'Don't refuse, Petro dear! For our Lord's sake! For the sake of Christ!'

Petro chewed the tips of his moustache and in the end agreed to go. He decided to call on a Cossack acquaintance in Vyoshenskaya and enlist his aid in recovering Miron's body. He left at night. The lights were burning in the village and every house was humming with the news. 'They've shot our Cossacks!'

Petro reined in near the new church, called on his acquaintance, an old regimental friend of his father's, and asked for his help in digging up Miron's body. The man readily agreed.

'Come on, then. I know the place. And they don't bury 'em very deep. But how'll we find him? He's not the only one, you know. Yesterday they shot twelve executioners, the ones who'd been executing our boys under the Cadets. But there's one condition. Afterwards you stand me a flagon of home-brew? All right?'

At midnight, equipped with spades and a stretcher of the kind used for carrying dung fuel, they made their way along the outskirts and through the graveyard to the pinewood, on the fringe of which the sentences had been carried out. The snow was crispening up. The hoar-frosted willow leaves crunched underfoot. Petro pricked up his ears at every sound and inwardly cursed the whole enterprise, Lukinichna, and even his deceased kinsman. Beside a high sand dune, on the edge of the first stand of young pines the Cossack halted.

'It's somewhere hereabouts...'

They went on for another hundred paces. A pack of local dogs raced away from them, howling and yelping. Petro dropped the stretcher and whispered hoarsely, 'Let's turn back! He can go to—! What's it matter where he's buried! I've got myself into a right mess... She talked me into it, the hellhag!'

'What are you scared of? Come on!' the Cossack responded with a chuckle.

They reached the spot. Beside an old, branching willow bush there was a patch of trampled snow mixed with sand. Human footprints and the scampering trails of dogs radiated from it in all directions...

...Petro recognised Miron by his reddish beard. He pulled the body out by the belt and heaved it on to the stretcher. Coughing now and then, the Cossack filled in the grave and, as he gripped the handles of the stretcher, muttered vexedly, 'We ought to have driven up to the pines in the sledge. There's a couple of blockheads for you! He must weigh a good thirteen stone, the great hog! It won't be easy walking across the snow.'

Petro parted those stiff legs whose walking days were over and gripped the handles of the stretcher.

He spent the rest of the night drinking with the Cossack at his house, while Miron, wrapped in a rug, lay on the sledge waiting. The tipsy Petro had left his horse tethered to the sledge and the animal stood all night, straining at the bridle, snorting, and twitching its ears in fright. Not a wisp of hay did it touch for fear of the dead man.

In the grey light of dawn Petro reached the village. He had taken the meadow track and forced the pace. Throughout the journey Miron's head had beat a steady tattoo on the crossboards, though Petro had stopped twice to shove a bunch of stringy meadow hay under it. He drove his late kinsman straight home. The gate was opened by the dead man's favourite daughter Agripina, who recoiled from the sledge and flung herself tearfully into a snowdrift. Petro carried the body like a sack of flour into the roomy kitchen and lowered it gently on to the table, which had already been spread with a homespun runner. Lukinichna, who had by this time wept out all her tears, kneeled voiceless and bareheaded, at her husband's feet, which were still clad in the clean white socks he had put on to meet his death.

'I thought you'd come back on your own dear feet, my master, but they had to carry you into your own house,' came her husky whisper amid sobs that sounded grotesquely like laughter.

Petro took Grandad Grishaka by the arm and led him in from the front room. The old man was staggering, as though the floor were heaving like a bog under his feet. But he stepped forward bravely to the table and stood at the dead man's head.

'Well, welcome home, Miron! So this is how we meet, my son!' he made the sign of the cross and kissed the icy forehead smeared with clay. 'Dear, dear Miron, it won't be long now before I...' His voice rose to screech. As though afraid of blurting something out, Grishaka with a deft and by no means old-mannish movement clapped his hand over his mouth and leaned against the table.

A spasm seized Petro's throat in a wolf-like grip. He went out quietly into the yard, where his horse was tethered to the porch.

XXIV

From deep silent backwaters the Don spills out into wider reaches. The current curls and spins and the Don rolls on in a silent steady flood. On the firm sandy bottom the roach graze in shoals; at night the sterlet come out to feed there, while the carp wallow in their haunts amidst the green slime along the bank; the chub and zander chase the small fry, a sheat-fish rummages amongst the shells and shingle; now and then it raises a green billow and shows up under the spacious moon, working its golden gleaming fin, then plunges back again to stir the drifts of shells with its bulbous bewhiskered head and, when morning comes, lies motionless in a torpid doze beside some black corroded snag.

But where the channel is narrow, the captive Don gnaws a deep pathway and drives its foaming white-maned waves along with a muffled roar. In the inlets behind the headlands the current forms whirlpools, where the water turns in awesome bewitching circles that the eye never tires of watching.

From the wide reaches of peaceful days life had rolled on into the narrows. The Upper Don was seething. Two currents had clashed, the Cossacks were torn asunder and the whirlpool was in motion. The young men and the poorer Cossacks hesitated and lay low, still expecting peace from the Soviets, but the older ones rushed into the attack and openly declared that the Reds wanted to wipe out the Cossacks to the last man.

On March 4th Ivan held a village meeting in Tatarsky. Attendance was unusually good, perhaps because Stokman had proposed to the Revolutionary Committee that at the next general meeting the property left behind by the merchants who had fled with the Whiteguards should be shared out among the poorest Cossacks. Before the meeting there had been a violent showdown with a district official, who had come from Vyoshenskaya with an authorisation to collect confiscated clothing. Stokman had explained to him that the Revolutionary Committee could not comply at the moment because only the day before a transport of sick and wounded Red Army men had been supplied with more than thirty items of warm clothing. The young man from Vyoshenskaya had let fly at him in strident tones.

'Who gave you permission to hand out confiscated property?'

'We didn't ask anyone for permission!'

'Then what right had you to embezzle public property?'

'Don't shout, comrade, and don't talk nonsense. No one has embezzled anything. We've got signed receipts, showing that we gave the drivers the wintercoats on condition that they would bring them back as soon as they had delivered the Red Army men to the next staging-point. The sick and wounded were half-naked. If we had sent them off as they were, we'd have sent them to their death. What else could I do? Especially as the clothing was lying in the store unused.'

Stokman, though irritated, had kept his temper and the conversation might have ended peacefully, but the young man put an icy note into his voice and snapped, 'Who are you anyway? Chairman of the Revolutionary Committee? I arrest you! Hand over to your deputy! I'm sending you to Vyoshenskaya at once. Maybe you've stolen half that property already and I—'

'Are you a Communist?' Stokman asked, squinting nervously and turning deathly pale.

'That's none of your business! Militiaman! Arrest this man and take him to Vyoshenskaya at once! Hand him over to the district militia and get a receipt.'

The young man measured Stokman with a perfunctory glance.

'We'll talk to you there! I'll make you sit up, you power-drunk imposter.'

'Comrade! Are you mad? Now, look here—'

'None of that! Silence!'

Ivan, who had not been able to put in a word during the exchange, saw Stokman reach slowly and menacingly for the Mauser pistol hanging on the wall. Terror flooded into the young man's eyes. At astonishing speed he backed out through the door, tumbled down the steps of the porch, scrambled into his sledge and drove away, thumping the driver's shoulders and looking round apprehensively until they had crossed the square, evidently fearing pursuit.

Great bursts of laughter battered the window panes of the Revolutionary Committee's office. Davydka, to whom laughter came easily, writhed on the desk in contortions. But for a long time a nervous tick dragged at one of Stokman's eyelids and kept his eyes squinting.

'What a scoundrel! Eh? The dirty little snake!' he repeated several times as he made himself a cigarette with trembling fingers.

He set off for the meeting with Koshevoi and Ivan. The square was packed. At the sight of so many people, Ivan's heart gave an unpleasant bump. There's something behind this, he thought. The whole village is here. But his misgivings disappeared when, taking off his cap, he entered the circle. The Cossacks willingly made way for him. Their faces were patient, some even had a twinkle

167

in their eyes. Stokman surveyed the Cossacks. He wanted to clear the air and get the crowd talking. Following Ivan's example, he also removed his floppy red-topped hat and said loudly, 'Comrades! Cossacks! It is six weeks now since you began living under Soviet rule. But we, the Revolutionary Committee, are still aware of a certain distrust, even hostility, towards us on your part. You don't turn up to meetings, all kinds of absurd rumours are circulating about wholesale shootings and repressive measures that the Soviet government is said to be perpetrating against you. It's time for us to have a heart-to-heart talk, as people say, it's time we got to know one another better. You yourselves elected your own Revolutionary Committee. Kotlyarov and Koshevoi are Cossacks from your own village, there are no grounds for any misunderstandings between you. First of all I wish to state most firmly that the rumours spread by our enemies about wholesale shootings of Cossacks are nothing but slander. The aim of those who spread this slander is clear. They wish to set the Cossacks against the Soviet government and drive you back into the arms of the Whites.'

'No shootings, you say? What about the seven Cossacks—what did you do with them?' voices shouted from the back rows.

'I am not saying, comrades, that there have been no shootings. We do shoot, and will go on shooting the enemies of the Soviet government, all those who try to impose on us the rule of the big landowners. Not for that did we overthrow the tsar, put an end to the war against Germany and lead the people out of bondage. What did you get out of the war with Germany? Thousands of Cossacks killed, thousands of orphans and widows, your farms ruined—'

'That's true!'

'You're right there!'

'We want to put an end to war,' Stokman continued. 'We want brotherhood among nations! Under the rule of the tsar you Cossacks were used to conquer land for the landowners and capitalists, to make those same landowners and factory-owners rich. Not far from here landowner Listnitsky had a large estate. For the part he played in the war of 1812 his grandfather was given more than ten thousand acres. And what did your grandfathers get? They lost their lives on German land! It is soaked with their blood!'

A hubbub arose, died down for a minute, then rose again to a roar.

'That's true!..'

Stokman wiped the sweat from his balding forehead with his big hat and shouted, 'We shall destroy all those who take up arms against the power of the workers and peasants! The Cossacks from your village who were shot by order of the Revolutionary Tribunal were our enemies. You all know that. But with you, toilers, with those who support us, we shall march together, like oxen pulling a plough, shoulder to shoulder. Together we shall plough the soil of the new life and harrow it to get rid of all the old weeds, our enemies, and throw them away! So that they can never put down roots again! So that they won't choke the shoots of the new life!'

Stokman could tell by the restrained murmur and animated faces that his speech had stirred the Cossacks' feelings. The heart-to-heart talk that he had hoped for was going to take place.

'Osip Davydovich! We know you pretty well because you used to live amongst us and you're like one of our own folk. Don't be afraid, tell us straight what this government wants of us? We're supporting it, of course, our sons left the fronts, but we're ignorant folk, we can't make out what it's all about.'

Old Gryaznov rambled on at great length without coming to the point, weaving words in evasive foxy circles, evidently afraid of speaking his mind. It was too much for one-armed Alexei Shamil.

'Can I speak?'

'Fire ahead!' Excited by the turn things were taking, Ivan gave his permission.

'Comrade Stokman, just tell me beforehand. Can I say all I want to say?'

'Yes.'

'And you won't arrest me?'

Stokman smiled and dismissed the idea with a downward sweep of his hand.

'But promise you won't get angry! I'm a simple man and I'll just put it as best as I can.'

His brother Martin tugged at Alexei's empty sleeve from behind and whispered anxiously, 'Keep quiet, you daft bugger! Drop it, or they'll have you in the clink rightaway. You'll get your name listed, Alexei!'

But Alexei waved him aside and with his disfigured cheek twitching rapidly faced the assembly.

'Gentlemen! Cossacks! I'll speak and you give us the word whether I'm right or, mebbe, getting off track.' He made a smart military turn and faced Stokman with his eye winking cunningly. 'The way I see it is this— if you're going to speak out you might as well make a clean breast of it! Straight from the shoulder! So I'll say right away what all us Cossacks think and what we've got a grudge against the Communists for... You, comrade, said just now you don't go against the ordinary working Cossacks that are not your enemies. You're against the rich and for the poor, like. Well, tell me this then. Was it right to shoot the Cossacks from our village? I won't speak of Korshunov—he was an ataman, he rode on other people's backs all his life. But what was Avdeich the Braggart shot for? Or Matvei Kashulin? Bogatiryov? Maidannikov? Korolyov? They were just ordinary un-learned, straightforward men like us. They were taught to hold plough-handles, not books. Some of 'em couldn't even read or write proper. All they knew was the ABC. If men like them happened to blurt out something wrong, was it a reason for lining them up before a firing squad?' Alexei drew a deep breath and plunged on. The empty sleeve of his long uniform coat fluttered on his chest and his mouth lurched to one side. 'You grabbed the ones that blurted out what was in their stupid heads and shot 'em, but you don't lay a finger on the mer-chants! They've got money and they've bought their lives from you with it! But we've got nothing to buy ours with, we've spent all our lives mucking with the soil, while the big money passed us by. Mebbe the ones you shot would have driven the last bullock from their yards just to save their skins, but no one told them to pay up. You just took 'em and finished 'em off. But all of us here know what's going on in Vyoshenskaya. The merchants and the priests, they're sitting pretty out there. And I reckon it's the same in Karginskaya. We hear what's going on all around. Good news lies buried, while bad news flies!'

'Very true!' came a lonely shout from the back.

A hubbub rose and drowned what Alexei was saying, but he waited and, ignoring Stokman's raised hand, went on shouting in his strident voice, 'And we've come to know that this Soviet government may be very good, but the Communists in the official positions will pick on any little thing to do away with us. They've got their knife into us for 1905; we've heard the Red soldiers say

170

so. And the way we figure it out amongst ourselves is that the Communists want to get rid of us, wipe us out altogether. So there won't be a single Cossack left on the Don! That's what I have to say! I'm talking now like as if I was drunk, saying what's on my mind. And we're all drunk from this fine life we're having, from the grudge we've got against you, Communists!'

Alexei dived away into the crowd of sheepskins and a long confused silence hung over the assembly. Stokman began to speak but he was interrupted by a shout from the back.

'It's true! The Cossacks feel hard done by! You ought to hear the songs they've been making up in the villages these days. Not everyone durst say it outloud, but they put it in their songs—you can't say much against a song. But here's one they've made up:

The samovar's a-boiling and the fish is a-frying.
When Cadets come back, we'll be a-crying.

'So there must be something to cry about!'

Someone gave a jarring laugh. The crowd stirred. Whispers and muttering broke out.

Stokman clamped his big hat on his head and pulled out of his pocket the list that Koshevoi had compiled.

'No,' he shouted, 'it's not true! Those that are for the revolution have nothing to complain of! Here's what the Cossacks from your village, the enemies of the Soviet government, were shot for. Listen!' And in a clear voice, pausing now and then, he read out.

CHARGE-SHEET

Enemies of Soviet Power, Arrested and Placed at the Disposal of Investigating Commission For Revolutionary Tribunal of 15th Inzenskaya Division.

No	Name	Reason for Arrest	Notes
1.	Korshunov, Miron Grigorievich	Former ataman, grew rich on the labour of others	
2.	Sinilin, Ivan Andreyevich	Spread propaganda for overthrow of Soviet government	

3.	Kashulin, Matvei Ivanovich	Same thing
4.	Maidannikov, Semyon Gavrilovich	Wore officers' shoulder straps, shouted anti-government slogans in the street
5.	Melekhov, Pantelei Prokofievich	Member of Cossack Army Council
6.	Melekhov, Grigory Panteleyevich	Captain, hostile to Soviet government
7.	Kashulin, Andrei Matveyevich	Took part in shooting of Podtyolkov's Red Cossacks
8.	Bodovskov, Fedot Nikiforovich	Same thing
9.	Bogatiryov, Arkhip Matveyevich	Churchwarden. Spoke against government in churchyard lodge. Stirs up people and counter-revolution
10.	Korolyov, Zakhar Leontyevich	Refused to surrender his arms. Unreliable

A note against both Melekhovs and Bodovskov, which Stokman did not read out, stated, 'These enemies of the Soviet government have not been taken in charge because two of them are absent, having been mobilised for transport duties to take cartridges to Bokovskaya. And Pantelei Melekhov is down with typhus. On their return the two will be arrested immediately and sent to district headquarters. The third will be sent as soon as he can walk.'

There was a silence for only a few seconds, then the meeting burst into an uproar.

'It's not true!'

'Yes, it is! They did say things agin the government!'

'They deserve it then!'

'Should we just listen to them and do nothing?'

'It's just a pack of lies!'

Again Stokman spoke. The crowd seemed to listen attentively and even uttered a few shouts of approval but, when he concluded with the proposal to share out the property of those who had fled with the Whites, the response was silence.

'What's the matter? Have you lost your tongues?' Ivan exclaimed angrily.

The crowd broke up and trickled away like spilled buckshot. One of the poorest villagers, Syomka, nick-named Anvil, took a hesitant step forward, then changed his mind and turned away with a dismissive wave of his woollen mitten.

'You'd look a bit daft if the owners came back.' Stokman tried to remonstrate with the dispersing crowd, but Koshevoi, his face as white as flour, whis-pered to Ivan, 'I said they wouldn't take it. It'd be better to burn the stuff now than give it to them!'

XXV

Thoughtfully slapping the top of his boot with his whip, head sunk on his chest, Koshevoi walked slowly up the steps of Mokhov's house. There were several saddles piled in the corridor by the front door. Evidently someone had only just arrived, for a dung-yellowed lump of snow on one of the stirrups had not yet melt-ed and there was a small puddle beneath it. Koshevoi saw all this as he crossed the muddied floor of the veran-da. His eyes wandered over the carved blue-painted rail-ing with its broken posts and a fluffy lilac fringe of frost by the wall; he also glanced at the windows, which were so steamed up that they looked like bull's bladders. But nothing registered, everything was vague and hazy as in a dream. Pity and hatred of Grigory Melekhov were all snarled up in Mishka's simple heart.

The front hall reeked of tobacco, harness and melted snow. A maid, one of the servants who had stayed be-hind after the Mokhovs had fled across the Donets, was stoking up the big tiled stove. Militiamen were laughing loudly in the next room. 'What's so funny?' Mishka thought resentfully as he walked past, giving his boot-top a final, angry slap of the whip, and entered the corner room without knocking.

Ivan was sitting at the desk, with his padded jacket open. His black lambskin cap was cocked dashingly to one side, but his perspiring face looked tired and worried. Stokman was sitting near him on the windowsill, still wearing the same long cavalry greatcoat. He greeted Koshevoi with a smile and made room for him on the windowsill.

'Well, how goes it, Mikhail? Take a seat.'

Koshevoi sat down and kicked out his legs. Stokman's calm inquiring voice had a sobering effect on him.

'I've heard from a reliable man,' he said, 'that Grigory Melekhov came home yesterday evening. But I haven't been in to see them.'

'What do you think about this?'

Stokman rolled a cigarette, glancing sideways at Ivan, and waited for his answer.

'Shall we lock him up in the cellar or what?' Ivan replied undecidedly, blinking rapidly.

'You're the chairman of the Revolutionary Committee. It's up to you.'

Stokman smiled and gave an evasive shrug. He had a way of smiling so sarcastically that it stung as painfully as a whip. Beads of sweat broke out on Ivan's chin.

Through clenched teeth he said abruptly, 'Yes, I'm the chairman and I'll arrest both of 'em, Grishka and his brother, and send 'em to Vyoshenskaya.'

'I don't think there's much point in arresting Grigory Melekhov's brother. He's got Fomin to back him up. You know what a fine opinion Fomin has of him. But you must take Grigory today, at once! We'll send him to Vyoshenskaya tomorrow, but the report on him must go off today by mounted militiaman to the chairman of the Revolutionary Tribunal.'

'Mebbe we'll make the arrest this evening?'

Stokman broke into a fit of coughing, then, wiping his beard, asked, 'Why this evening?'

'It'll cause less talk.'

'That—that's just nonsense!'

'Mikhail, take two men with you and go and arrest Grigory right now. Put him away separate. Get me?'

Koshevoi slid off the windowsill and went to the militiamen's room. Stokman paced to and fro for a while, scraping the floor with his battered grey felt boots, then halted by the desk and asked, 'Have you sent off the last batch of confiscated weapons?'

'No.'

'Why not?'

'Didn't have time yesterday.'

'Why not?'

'We'll send it off today.'

Stokman frowned, then raised his brows and said quickly, 'Did the Melekhovs hand in their weapons?'

Ivan's eyes crinkled at the corners as he tried to remember, then he smiled.

'Yes, on the nail—two rifles and two revolvers. But d'you think that was all they had?'

'Wasn't it?'

'They aren't fools, are they?'

'I don't think it was all either.' Stokman drew his lips into a thin line. 'If I were you, I'd make a careful search after the arrest. Tell the commandant that. You're good enough at thinking, but you've got to act.'

Koshevoi returned half an hour later. He ran across the veranda and after a wild banging of doors appeared on the threshold, breathing heavily. 'Like hell!' he shouted.

'Wha-a-t?!' Stokman strode up to him, his eyes bulging menacingly, the long skirts of his greatcoat flapping between his legs and catching on his felt boots.

Either because Stokman's voice was quiet or for some other reason Koshevoi flew into a rage.

'Don't roll your eyes at me!' And he swore violently. 'They say Grishka has gone off to Singin, to his aunt's, so why blame me? Where were you? Twiddling your thumbs? Well, you've let him give you the slip! And you needn't bawl at me! What am I, after all? I just do what I'm told. What were you thinking about?' He backed away as Stokman bore down on him and, leaning on the tiled wall of the stove, burst out laughing. 'Don't come any nearer, Osip Davydovich! Don't come nearer or I'll hit you! Honestly, I will!'

Stokman stood for a while in front of him, cracking his finger joints, then, taking in Mishka's white-toothed grin and his smiling devoted eyes, he snapped, 'Do you know the way to Singin?'

'Yes.'

'Why did you come back then? And you say you fought the Germans—you bungler!' And he narrowed his eyes in affected scorn.

* * *

The steppe lay in a dove-blue haze. A purple moon was rising from behind the Donside hills. Its dim light did not eclipse the phosphorescent radiance of the stars.

Six horsemen were on their way to Singin. The horses were going at a trot. Stokman was riding beside Koshevoi, bumping up and down in his dragoon's saddle. The tall Don bay kept tossing its head sportively and trying to bite its rider's knee. With an imperturbable air Stokman was recounting some amusing tale and Mishka was leaning over his saddle-bow, uttering peals of childlike laughter, gasping and choking, and trying to catch a glimpse of the stern, watchful eyes under Stokman's hood.

A careful search at Singin yielded no results.

XXVI

From Bokovskaya Grigory had been ordered to drive on to Chernyshevskaya. He returned some ten days later and two days before his arrival his father was arrested. Pantelei had only just begun to walk after the typhus. He rose from his bed more grizzled than ever and as bony as a horse's skeleton. The silvery karakul of his hair was moulting as though the moth had been at it, his beard was matted and heavily fringed with grey.

The militiaman took him away after allowing him ten minutes to get ready. Before being despatched to Vyoshenskaya, Pantelei was confined in Mokhov's cellar. Besides Pantelei there were nine other old men and a justice of the peace in the cellar, which smelled strongly of anise apples.

Petro told Grigory the news even before he drove through the gate. 'Turn your sledge around, brother,' he advised. 'They've been asking when you'll be back. Go in and get warm, have a look at the kids and then I'll take you off to Rybinsky. You can lie low there. If anyone asks, I'll tell 'em you've gone to your aunt's in Singin. They've had seven of us up against the wall already—heard that? Let's hope it won't turn out that way for Father. It would with you though—that's for sure!'

Grigory sat in the kitchen for half an hour or so, then saddled his own horse and galloped away through the night to Rybinsky. A distant relative of the Melekhovs, a hospitable Cossack, hid Grigory in a stack of dried dung fuel. There he lived for two days, creeping out of his lair only at night.

XXVII

On the second day after returning from Singin Mishka Koshevoi set off for Vyoshenskaya with Yemelyan to find out when the next meeting of the Communist group would be held there. He, Ivan, Yemelyan, Davydka and Filka had decided to make their party membership offical.

Mishka took with him the last batch of weapons surrendered by the Cossacks, a machine-gun that had been found in the school-house yard, and a letter from Stokman to the chairman of the District Revolutionary Committee. As they were crossing the meadow they kept flushing hares, whose numbers had grown so fast during the war years that they turned up at every step. Hares' tails were as common as bulrush tops. The creak of a sledge would start up a grey white-bellied hare and its black-edged tail would go bobbing away over the virgin snow. Yemelyan, who was driving the sledge, would drop the reins and yell frantically, 'Shoot him! Bring him down!'

Mishka would jump off and from one knee empty his gun after the rolling grey ball and watch disappointedly as the bullets kicked up crumbs of snow all around while the ball got up speed and plunged into the thickets of scrub and thorn, knocking off their white caps as it disappeared.

...The office of the Revolutionary Committee was in a state of wild confusion. People were dashing about anxiously, mounted messengers kept riding up, the streets were strangely deserted. Not knowing what all the fuss was about, Mishka was surprised. The committee's deputy chairman thrust Stokman's letter into his pocket distractedly and, when Mishka asked if there would be any reply, snapped grimly, 'Oh, go to hell! I've no time for you!' Red Army men of the guard company were scurrying about the square. A steaming mobile kitchen clattered by, leaving a smell of beef stew and bay leaf.

Koshevoi went into the Revolutionary Tribunal for a smoke with the lads he knew there and asked, 'What's all the hurry-scurry about?'

One of the local investigators, Gromov, responded unwillingly, 'Seems to be some trouble in Kazanskaya. Either the Whites have broken through or the Cossacks have started an uprising. There've been rumours of fighting out there. The telephone's dead.'

177

'Why don't you send a messenger?'

'We did. He never came back. And a company went off to Yelanskaya today. Things don't look too good there either.'

They sat smoking by the window in the imposing house the Tribunal had taken over from a local merchant. Light powdery snow was falling outside.

From somewhere, near the pinewood beyond the outskirts, in the direction of Chornaya, came the muffled sound of shots. Mishka turned pale and dropped his cigarette. Everyone rushed out into the yard. The shots were now clear and resonant. The scattered firing turned into a volley and whining bullets tore and bit into the woodwork of sheds and gates. One of the Red Army men in the yard was wounded. Gromov ran out into the square, screwing up papers and stuffing them into his pockets. The remaining soldiers of the guard company formed up outside the Revolutionary Committee. Their commander, in a skimpy sheepskin, shuttled to and fro among the ranks, then led them at the double to the path down to the Don. A disastrous panic broke out. Men darted across the square. A saddled but riderless horse galloped past, tossing its head.

Koshevoi hardly knew how he came to be in the square. He saw Fomin in a heavy cloak hurtle out from behind the church like a black whirlwind. A machine-gun was tied to the tail of his tall stallion. Its small wheels could not turn fast enough and it slid from side to side in the wake of the madly galloping horse. Crouching low in his saddle, Fomin disappeared down the slope, leaving a silvery cloud of snow dust behind him.

Mishka's first thought was that he must get to his horses. He made for his lodgings, ducking down as he darted over cross-roads and running all the way. By the time he got there his heart was thumping wildly. Yemelyan began harnessing the horses, but in his fright could not secure the traces.

'What's happening, Mikhail? What's it all about?' he mumbled through chattering teeth. By the time he had finished harnessing he had lost the reins. When he found them, the collar strap had come loose.

The yard of the house where they had lodged gave out on to the steppe. Mishka looked out towards the pines but no line of infantry or charging cavalry appeared. Firing was going on somewhere, the streets were deserted, the place looked as ordinary and drab as ever. And yet something terrbile was afoot; the revolt was coming into its own.

While Yemelyan was struggling with the harness, Mishka kept his eyes on the steppe. He saw a man in a black overcoat run out from behind a roadside shrine, past the spot where the radiostation had been burnt down in December. He was running for all he was worth, bending forward, his hands pressed to his chest. By his overcoat Koshevoi recognised him as the Tribunal investigator Gromov. He also noticed the figure of a horseman appear from behind a fence. Mishka recognised him too. It was a Vyoshenskaya Cossack named Chernichkin, a young out-and-out Whiteguard. Gromov was separated from Chernichkin by a distance of about two hundred paces. As he ran he glanced round once or twice and drew his revolver. A shot rang out, then another. Gromov ran up on to a sandy hillock and fired again. Chernichkin dismounted in a flying leap and, still holding the reins, unslung his rifle and took cover behind a snowdrift. After his first shot Gromov lurched sideways, reaching out to the bushes with his left hand. He staggered round the hillock and fell face downwards in the snow. 'He's killed him!' Mishka told himself and turned cold. Chernichkin was a crack shot and with the Austrian carbine he had brought back from the German war could hit his target at any range. As Mishka got into the sledge and drove out of the gate, he saw Chernichkin ride over to the hillock and slash at the black overcoat lying huddled in the snow.

It would be dangerous to drive across the Don towards Bazki. Horses and driver would make a perfect target against the white expanse of the river.

Two Red Army men of the guard company were already lying there, cut down by fire from the bank. Yemelyan headed across the lake into the forest. The lake ice was covered with slush. Splashes and clots of snow flew from under the horses' hooves and the sledge runners carved deep furrows. They drove at a mad pace until they were opposite Tatarsky. But at the crossing Yemelyan reined in and turned his wind-scorched face towards Koshevoi.

'What'll we do now? Suppose it's all a muck-up there too?'

A look of misery came into Mishka's eyes. He scanned the village. Two horsemen were galloping along the street nearest to the river. Mishka decided they were militiamen.

'Make for the village. We've got nowhere else to go,' he said decidedly.

With great reluctance Yemelyan whipped up the horses. They crossed the Don. But as they drove up the slope, Antip, the Braggart's son, and two old men from the upper end of the village came running towards them.

'Mishka, look out!' Yemelyan spotted the rifle in Antip's hands and swung the horses round.

'Stop!'

A shot. Yemelyan slumped forward without letting go of the reins. The horses veered into a fence. Koshevoi jumped off the sledge. Antip came sliding towards him; he slithered to a halt and aimed his rifle. As he fell against the fence Mishka noticed the white prongs of a pitch-fork held by one of the old men.

'Get him!'

With a searing pain in his shoulder Koshevoi silently dropped to the ground and covered his eyes with his hands. Someone bent over him breathing heavily and jabbed him with the fork.

'Get up, you bastard!'

The rest was like a dream. Antip flew at him, sobbing, and clawed at his chest.

'He put my father to death... Lemme get at him, good folk! Lemme take it out on him!'

He was pulled away. A small crowd gathered. A reasonable voice boomed good-naturedly, 'Let the lad go! Have you no Christian feeling? Drop it, Antip! You won't bring your father back to life, it'll only be another man killed.... Break it up, lads! They're sharing out the sugar up at the stores. That's where to go.'

Mishka came to in the evening. He was still lying by the fence. His side was throbbing where the fork had jabbed him. The prongs had pierced his sheepskin and jacket and not sunk deep into the flesh. But the wounds were sore and caked with congealed blood. Mishka rose to his feet and listened. Insurgent patrols were scouring the village. Shots echoed now and then. Dogs were baying. A murmur of talk was coming nearer. Mishka took the cattle track along the Don, then climbed the ravine until he reached the fences and worked his way along the edge, clawing at the crusted snow with his bare hands, slipping and falling back. Hardly knowing where he was, he crawled blindly. He began to shiver and his hands were frozen. It was the cold that drove him into some-one's back yard. He pushed open the side-gate, which was kept closed only by a faggot, and slipped through into the yard. A chaff shed loomed up on the left. He was creeping into it, when he heard footsteps and a cough.

Someone was heading for the shed, his felt boots scraping on the snow. 'Now they'll finish me off,' Mishka thought indifferently, as though of someone else. The man halted in the dark gap of the door.

'Who's that in there?'

The voice was feeble and seemed afraid.

Mishka drew back against the wall.

'Who's there?' the voice was louder and more urgent.

Recognising it as Stepan Astakhov's, Mishka came out of the shed.

'Stepan, it's me—Koshevoi. Help me, for God's sake! Just don't say a word to anyone, eh? Help me!'

'Oh, so it's you!' Stepan, who had just got on his feet after the typhus, spoke in an enfeebled voice. His mouth, widened by the gauntness of his face, smiled broadly and uncertainly. 'All right then, you can stay here for the night, but you'd better go somewhere else during the day. How come you're here?'

Without answering, Mishka reached out in the darkness for his hand, then crawled into a pile of chaff.

The next night, as soon as dusk fell, he took a desperate step and made his way home. He knocked on the window. His mother opened the door and began to cry. Her groping hands locked round Mishka's neck and her head thumped on his chest.

'Go away! For Christ's sake, Mishka dear, go away! The Cossacks were here today... They turned the whole place upside down looking for you. Antip whipped me. "You're hiding your son," he says. "It's a pity we didn't finish him off right then." '

Mishka had no idea where his comrades were or what was going on in the village. From his mother's brief account he gathered that all the villages along the Don had risen, that Stokman, Ivan, Davydka and the militiamen had got away, but Filka and Timofei had been killed on the square the day before, at noon.

'Go away! They'll find you here.'

His mother was weeping but her sorrowful voice was firm. For the first time in many years Mishka wept too, blubbering like a child with little bubbles round his lips. Then he bridled the mare he had used when he was a herdsman and led her out on to the threshing floor.

The mare's foal and his mother followed him. His mother helped him to mount and made the sign of the cross. The mare started off unwillingly and neighed twice, calling her foal. Each time Mishka's heart seemed to drop and roll away from him. But he rode out safely on to the hill and trotted eastward along the Hetman's highway in the direction of Ust-Medveditskaya. The night opened its arms, dark and inviting, to the fugitive. The mare neighed time and again, afraid of losing her foal. Koshevoi gritted his teeth, thwacked her over the ears with the end of the bridle and often stopped to listen. Was that a rumble of galloping hooves from behind? Was someone coming towards him? Had the mare's neighing roused attention? But all around a magic silence reigned, still as death. Koshevoi heard only the foal sucking and smacking its lips as it took advantage of the halt to seize its mother's black udder, while its thin hind legs puddled the snow and the mare's back shook in response to its demanding nudges.

XXVIII

The fuel shed reeked of dried dung, rotted straw and smattering of hay. In the daytime a grey light seeped through the rush roof. Sometimes a gleam of sunlight pierced the wattle door. At night it was pitch dark and the only sound was the squeaking of mice.

Once a day in the evening the mistress of the house came furtively with food for Grigory. He had a big jug of water buried among the dung bricks, and things would not have been too bad but for the fact that he had run out of tobacco. For a day and a night he suffered acutely. Dying for a smoke, he crawled out the next morning, scraped a handful of dried horse dung off the earthen floor, crumbled it between his palms, and smoked that. In the evening his host sent two mildewed pages torn out of the Bible, a box of matches and a handful of a mixture of dried clover and roots of unripe home-grown tobacco. Grigory was glad to have it, smoked until he felt sick, and for the first time fell fast asleep on the knobbly dung bricks, wrapping his head in the skirt of his greatcoat, like a bird tucking its head under its wing.

In the morning he was awakened by his host, who ran into the shed and shouted, 'Still asleep? Come on out of it! The Don's breaking up!' and roared with laughter.

Grigory scrambled down from the stack, starting an avalanche of heavy dung bricks.

'What's happened?'

'The Yelanskaya and Vyoshenskaya Cossacks have rebelled on this side. Fomin and the rest of the authorities have run away to Tokin. Looks as if Kazanskaya, Shumilinskaya and Migulinskaya have risen too. See the way things are going?'

The veins in Grigory's neck and forehead swelled and greenish sparks gleamed in his eyes. He could not hide his joy, his voice shook, his grimy fingers fumbled aimlessly with the fastenings of his greatcoat.

'What about here, in your village?'

'Nothing so far. I saw the chairman and he was laughing. "It's all the same to me, which God I pray to," he says, "as long as there is one." Come on, lad, out of your burrow!'

They went to the house. Grigory strode along eagerly and his host hurried beside him, telling the story.

'The first to rise in Yelanskaya stanitsa were the Krasnoyarsky Cossacks. Day before yesterday twenty Yelanskaya commies went to Krivskoy and Pleshakovsky to nab some Cossacks there, and when the Krasnoyarsky men heard about it they got together and decided, "How much longer are we going to put up with being kicked around like this. They're pulling in our fathers, soon they'll start on us. Let's saddle up and set 'em free." So about fifteen, all daredevil lads, took the road. Their leader was Atlanov, a real firebrand. They could only muster a couple of rifles between 'em. Some had sabres, some had lances, and the rest had only sticks. They crossed the Don and headed for Pleshakovsky. The commies had halted and were resting in Melnikov's yard, so they went straight at 'em in a proper cavalry charge. But there was a stone wall round the yard and they had to fall back. One of 'em got killed, God rest his soul. The commies fired a volley after 'em and he fell off his horse and was left hanging over a fence. The local Cossacks carried him to the stables. But by the time they got there, he was cold, still holding his whip in his stiff hand... Well, and that started it. This is the end of Soviet power, and good riddance to the bloody thing!'

In the house Grigory greedily ate what was left of breakfast, then went out again with his host. Little crowds of Cossacks had gathered at the street corners as if it were a public holiday. Grigory and his host came up to one of the groups. In reply to their greeting the Cossacks raised their hands to their caps and spoke with restraint, eyeing the stranger with watchful curiosity.

'He's one of us, Cossacks! Have no fears about him! You've heard about the Tatarsky Melekhovs, haven't you? This is Pantelei's son, Grigory. He was hiding at my place to save himself from being shot!' his host said proudly.

They had just got talking, and one of the Cossacks was relating how Fomin had been chased out of Vyoshenskaya by the Reshetovsky, Dubrovsky and Chorny Cossacks, when two horsemen showed up against the white slope of the hill at the end of the street. They cantered down the street, stopping at each group, turning their horses, shouting and waving their arms. Grigory waited eagerly for them to approach.

'They're not ours, they're not from Rybinsky... Must be messengers,' the Cossack took a long look and broke off his story about the capture of Vyoshenskaya.

The two passed by the nearest lane and rode up. The one in front, an old man with his homespun coat flapping open and no hat, his face red and perspiring under a fringe of grey curls reined in his horse smartly, leaned back and held out his right hand.

'Cossacks! What are you standing about at street corners for, like a lot of women?' he shouted in a weeping voice. Angry tears choked him and his purple cheeks shook with emotion.

He was riding a splendid four-year-old filly, a chestnut with white nostrils, a bushy tail and lean legs that looked as if they had been cast out of steel. Snorting and chewing the bit, she danced and reared, begging to be given her head, so that she could again go thundering across the steppe at a gallop, so that the wind would again flatten her ears, and swish through her mane, and the resonant, frost-seared earth would again gasp under her chiselled hooves. Every vein and sinew was playing under the fine skin. The great neck muscles rippled, the pink muzzle quivered, and the protruding ruby eyes showed their bloodshot whites as she squinted at her master with fierce persistence.

'Why are you standing here, sons of the quiet Don?!' the old man shouted again, shifting his glance from Grigory to the other Cossacks. 'The Yid Commissars are shooting your fathers and grandfathers, grabbing your property, and jeering at your faith, while you nibble sunflower seeds and go out for the evening. Are you waiting for them to draw the noose round your throats? How much longer are you going to cling to your women's skirts? The whole Yelanskaya district, young and old, is up in arms. In Vyoshenskaya they've driven out the Reds—and what about you, Rybinsky Cossacks! Or d'you hold your lives cheap now? Or instead of Cossack blood is it peasant kvass that flows in your veins? Arise! Take up arms! The village of Krivskoy has sent us to rouse the other villages. To horse, Cossacks, before it's too late!' He glared with half-crazed eyes at the familiar face of one of the old men and shouted as if he had been bitterly insulted, 'What are you standing here for, Semyon Khristoforovich? The Reds cut down your son at Filonov, and you're skulking here by your warm stove?!'

Not waiting to hear more, Grigory ran back to the yard, led his restless horse out of the chaff shed, then dashed to the pile of dung fuel and, almost tearing off his fingernails, dug out his saddle, and rode out of the yard like a madman.

'I'm off! God bless you!' he managed to shout to his host as the latter approached the gate, then, crouching forward over his saddle-bow, he raised a white whirlwind of snow as he hurtled down the street, lashing his horse on both flanks. Snow trailed behind him like smoke, the stirrups jerked his numbed legs, and his legs rubbed the saddle flaps. The horse's hooves drummed out a wild tattoo. He felt such a huge and fierce joy, such a burst of strength and resolution that a yelping throaty cry broke involuntarily from his throat. It released all his captive, pent-up feelings. From now on, it seemed, his road would be as clear as a moonlit track across the steppe.

Everything had been weighed and decided during those long days of suspense while he was hiding like a hunted animal in his dung-brick lair, starting at every sound, every voice from outside. It was as though the days of truth-seeking, of wavering and hesitation, of painful inner conflict, had never been.

They had billowed and passed away like the shadow of a cloud and now all his questing seemed vain and empty. What had there been to think about? Why should his soul go back and forth like an ambushed wolf at the flag line, seeking a way out, groping for a solution to the contradictions? Life had turned out to be mockingly, wisely simple. Now it seemed to him that there had never been one truth under whose wing all could shelter and find comfort; embittered beyond measure, he told himself that each man had his own truth, his own furrow. For their bit of bread, for their strip of land, for the right to live, men had always fought and always would fight so long as the sun shone upon them and the blood flowed warm in their veins. And against those who wanted to take away that right, he must fight and fight hard, without wavering, as they used to in those village fist fights, and the struggle would fire his hatred and make him strong. No need to hold back his feeling; he must give full rein to their fury, and that was all there was to it.

The Cossacks' road had crossed that of Russia's landless peasants and factory workers. Then fight them to the death! Get back the rich land of the Don, watered with Cossack blood. Drive them out of the region as the Tatars had once been driven! Shake Moscow itself and force it to accept a shameful peace! If the road was too narrow, someone would have to be pushed aside. After all, hadn't they tried the other way? Hadn't they let the Red regiments on to Cossack soil and seen what happened? But now—out with your sabre!

Thus thought Grigory, inflamed by a blind hatred, as his horse whirled him over the white-maned canopy of the Don. For a moment a confusing thought stirred in his brain: 'It's the rich against the poor, not the Cossacks against Russia. Mishka Koshevoi and Kotlyarov are also Cossacks, and they're Red through and through...' But he angrily brushed these thoughts aside.

Tatarsky came into view. Grigory tightened the reins and brought his foam-flecked horse into a light canter. On the outskirts he thrust forward again, forced the gate open with his horse's chest, and pranced into the yard.

XXIX

At dawn, utterly worn out, Koshevoi rode into the village of Bolshoi, way down the Don near Ust-Khopyorskaya. He was stopped by an outpost of the Red Army's 4th Trans-Amur Regiment. Two of the sentries marched him to headquarters, where a clerk interrogated him suspiciously and at great length, trying to catch him out by asking such questions as 'Who was the chairman of your Revolutionary Committee?' 'Why haven't you got any identity papers?' And much more in the same vein. In the end Mishka got tired of answering.

'Don't muck about, comrade! The Cossacks mucked me about a lot more than you could, and it didn't get them anywhere.'

He pulled up his shirt and showed the side and lower part of his belly where the fork had pierced his flesh. He was about to give the clerk the rough edge of his tongue, when the door opened and Stokman entered.

'Why, it's our prodigal son! You young devil!' his deep voice quivered as he flung his arms round Mishka's shoulders. 'What are you interrogating him for? He's one of our lads! This is a fine way to carry on! You could have sent for me or Kotlyarov and there would have been no need for any more questions... Come on, Mikhail! How did you manage to stay alive? How did you manage it? We'd crossed your name off the list. We thought you'd died the death of a hero.'

Mishka remembered his capture, his helplessness, and the rifle he had left lying forgotten in the sledge, and flushed painfully.

XXX

The day Grigory arrived in Tatarsky two Cossack squadrons had already been formed. At a village meeting it was decided to mobilise everyone capable of bearing arms, from the age of sixteen to seventy. Many sensed the hopelessness of the situation. In the north were the hostile, Bolshevik-controlled Voronezh Province, and the Red Khopyor district; in the south was a front that could turn and sweep the rebel off the face of the earth. Some of the more cautious Cossacks did not want to take up arms, but they were forced. Stepan Astakhov flatly refused to fight.

'I won't go! Take my horse, do what you like with me, but I won't take up arms!' he declared on the morning when Grigory, Khristonya and Anikei came to his house.

'So you won't, eh?' Grigory questioned, nostrils twitching.

'No, I won't—and that's flat!'

'And what if the Reds take the village? Where'll you go then? With us or stay behind?'

Stepan slowly turned his steady, penetrating gaze from Grigory to Aksinya and, after a pause, replied, 'We'll see, when it happens.'

'If that's what you think—outside! Take him, Khristonya! We'll have you up against a wall!' Trying not to look at Aksinya, who had shrunk back against the stove, Grigory yanked Stepan forward by the sleeve of his tunic. 'Come on—no mucking about!'

'Grigory, don't be a fool. Drop it!' Stepan resisted weakly, turning pale.

A gloomy-faced Khristonya grabbed him from behind and grunted, 'You'd better come along, then, if that's your tune.'

'Brothers!..'

'We're no brothers of yours! Get moving!'

'Let me go, I'll sign up in the squadron. I'm still weak from typhus.'

With a sneering grin Grigory released Stepan's sleeve. 'Go and draw a rifle. And about time too!'

He wrapped his greatcoat round him and stalked out without another word. Khristonya, however, was not ashamed, even after what had been said, to touch Stepan for a pinch of tobacco, and stayed on chatting for a while as though nothing had happened.

That evening two sledgeloads of weapons were brought in from Vyoshenskaya. Eighty-four rifles and over a hundred sabres. Many of the Cossacks brought out weapons they had stashed away. Altogether the village mustered two hundred and eleven fighting men. A hundred and fifty were mounted.

As yet the insurgents had no unified command. The villages acted individually, forming their own squadrons, choosing the most experienced Cossacks as their commanders on the basis of merit rather than rank; they undertook no offensive operations and confined themselves to making contact with neighbouring villages and reconnoitring the locality with mounted patrols.

Before Grigory's arrival, Petro Melekhov, as in 1918, had been elected commander of the Tatarsky mounted squadron. The foot squadron was taken over by Latyshev. The gunners, under Ivan Tomilin, rode off to Bazki to repair a half-wrecked gun without sights and with one wheel broken, which had been abandoned by the Reds.

From Vyoshenskaya the village's 211 fighting men received 108 rifles, 140 sabres and 14 sporting guns. Pantelei, just released from Mokhov's cellar along with the other old men, dug up his machine-gun. But there were no ammunition belts and it was not accepted.

On the evening of the following day it became known that a Red punitive detachment commanded by Likhachov with 300 bayonets, 7 artillery pieces and 12 machine-guns was on its way from Karginskaya. Petro decided to send out a strong patrol in the direction of Tokin and at the same time inform Vyoshenskaya.

The patrol left the village at dusk. The thirty-two Tatarsky men were led by Grigory Melekhov. They left the village at a gallop and kept it up nearly all the way to Tokin. With about two versts still to go Grigory halted, ordered the Cossacks to dismount and positioned them in a shallow ravine near the highway. The horse minders led their charges away into a dell. The snow was so deep there that the horses sank in up to their bellies; one of the stallions, sensing the approach of spring, whinnied and kicked and a special minder had to be sent to deal with it.

Grigory sent on three of his Cossacks—Anikei, Martin Shamil and Prokhor Zykov—into the village. They set off at a walk. In the distance the road sloped down to where the blue poplar groves of Tokin zigzaged away to the south-east. Night fell. Low clouds closed in over the steppe. The Cossacks waited silently in the ravine. Grigory watched the figures of the three riders going down the hill, merging with the black hump of the road. Soon the horses disappeared and only the riders' heads could be seen. Then they, too, disappeared. A minute later a machine-gun broke into a raucous chatter from that direction. Then another, evidently a light one, struck up on a higher note. After emptying its drum it fell silent, but the first rested only for a moment then hurriedly fired off another belt. Flocks of bullets swept high over the ravine. Their light, cheerful drone spurred the senses. The three horsemen came riding back at full gallop.

'We bumped into an outpost!' Prokhor Zykov shouted from a distance. His voice was drowned by the thunder of hooves.

'Horse-minders—at the ready!' Grigory ordered. He ran up on to the edge of the ravine, as if it were a breastwork, and ignoring the bullets that were now hissing into the snow walked to meet the approaching Cossacks.

'Did you see anything?'

'We could hear 'em messing about. A lot of 'em by the sound of their voices,' Anikei said breathlessly, jumping

189

off his horse. His boot got stuck in the stirrup and he swore as he hopped about on one leg, freeing it with his hands.

While Grigory questioned him, eight Cossacks walked down from the ravine into the dell, found their horses and rode off home.

'We'll shoot them tomorrow,' Grigory said quietly as he listened to the sound of hoofbeats dying away in the distance.

The remaining Cossacks waited for another hour in the ravine, maintaining strict silence and listening. Eventually someone heard the clip-clop of hooves.

'Somebody's coming from Tokin!'

'A patrol.'

'Not on your life!'

They talked in whispers and raised their heads in a vain attempt to see something through the drapes of darkness. Fedot Bodovskov's Kalmyk eyes were the first to penetrate.

'They're coming,' he said confidently, unslinging his rifle.

He carried it in a strange fashion, dangling from his neck like a crucifix. He usually walked and rode like this, resting his hands on the stock and barrel.

About ten horsemen were riding along the road in ragged formation. An imposing warmly dressed figure was a little ahead of the others. His big dock-tailed horse walked with a proud confident gait. From below, against the backdrop of the grey sky Grigory clearly made out the shapes of horses and riders, and even the flat-topped Kuban hat on the leader's head. The horsemen were about twenty paces from the ravine; the distance was so short it seemed they should have heard the Cossacks' husky breathing, the thumping of their hearts.

Grigory had warned his men not to fire until he gave the order. Like a hunter in ambush, he waited with perfect confidence in his timing. A plan had formed in his mind: he would call out to the riders and, when they gathered in a confused bunch, open fire.

The snow on the road crunched peacefully. A spark darted from under a hoof like a yellow glow-worm as the shoe slipped on a bare flint.

'Who goes there?'

Grigory leaped lightly as a cat out of the ravine and straightened up. The Cossacks followed him with rustling strides.

But then something happened that Grigory could never have expected.

'Who do you want?' the leader's deep husky bass asked without a trace of fear or surprise. He turned his horse and rode towards Grigory.

'Who are you?!' Grigory shouted sharply, standing his ground and stealthily raising his revolver with his arm half bent.

The same deep voice thundered back angrily.

'Who dares to shout? I'm the commander of a detachment of punitive troops! I have been authorised by the headquarters of the Eighth Red Army to crush the rebellion! Who's your commander? Bring him to me!'

'I am.'

'You? Aha...'

Grigory saw a dark burnished object in the rider's upraised hand and flung himself to the ground just before the shot; as he fell he shouted, 'Fire!'

The blunt-nosed bullet of a Browning zipped over Grigory's head. Deafening shots crashed out from both sides. Bodovskov seized the fearless commander's bridle. Reaching over Bodovskov, Grigory struck a measured blow with the blunt edge of his sabre at the man's hat and knocked him out of the saddle. It was all over in a couple of minutes. Three Red Army men got away, two were killed and the rest disarmed.

Grigory questioned the captured commander briefly, thrusting the barrel of his revolver into his battered mouth.

'What's your name, you swine?'

'Likhachov.'

'What did you hope to get out of coming here with your nine bodyguards? Did you think the Cossacks would go down on their knees to you? And ask for pardon?'

'Kill me!'

'There'll be time for that later,' Grigory assured him. 'Where're your papers?'

'In the bag. Take them, you bandit!.. Bastard!'

Ignoring Likhachov's curses, Grigory searched him, found a second Browning in the pocket of his sheepskin, and took his revolver and field bag. In the side pocket he found a small bright-coloured leather pouch containing papers and a cigarette case.

Likhachov swore constantly and moaned with pain. His right shoulder had been shot through and his head badly bruised by Grigory's sabre. He was tall, taller than Grigory, heavily built and probably very strong. His face was brown and clean-shaven and the black brows curved steeply and imperiously towards the bridge of the nose. He had a big mouth and square chin. He was wearing a waisted sheepskin and a black Kuban hat, now crumpled by the sabre stroke, and under his sheepskin was a smart tunic and billowing riding breeches. But his feet were small and clad in smart boots with patent-leather tops.

'Take off your coat, commissar!' Grigory ordered. 'You're sleek enough. You've stuffed yourself well on Cossack grub—you won't freeze!'

They tied the prisoners' hands with sashes and bridle reins and put them on their own horses.

'At the trot—follow me!' Grigory commanded, adjusting Likhachov's revolver at his belt.

They spent the night in Bazki. Likhachov lay on a litter of straw by the stove, grinding his teeth and tossing about. By lamp-light Grigory washed and bandaged his wounded shoulder, but asked no further questions. He sat for a long time at the table, looking through Likhachov's credentials, the lists of Cossack counter-revolutionaries he had been given by the fugitive Revolutionary Tribunal, his notebook, letters, the markings on the map. Occasionally he looked at Likhachov and their glances clashed like swords. The Cossacks who were with them stayed up all night, going out to the horses now and then, smoking in the porch or lying on the floor talking.

Grigory dozed off at dawn, but soon awoke and lifted his heavy head from the table. Likhachov was sitting on the straw, tugging at the bandage on his shoulder with his teeth and trying to untie it. He stared at Grigory with bitter, bloodshot eyes. His white teeth were bared in a snarl, like a man in his death agony, and there was such mortal anguish in his eyes that Grigory's drowsiness vanished at once.

'What's the matter?' he asked.

'What the—hell's it got to do with you? I want to die!' Likhachov growled, turning pale and burying his head in the straw.

During the night he had drunk half a pail of water and not closed his eyes once.

In the morning Grigory sent him off on a machine-gun cart to Vyoshenskaya with a brief report and all the papers that had been found on him.

XXXI

The machine-gun cart, escorted by two mounted Cossacks, drove swiftly up to the red-brick building of the Executive Committee. Likhachov was reclining in the back. He stood up pressing his hand to the blood-stained bandage on his shoulder. The Cossacks dismounted and escorted him into the building.

About fifty Cossacks were packed into the room of the provisional commander of the united insurgent forces Suyarov. Protecting his shoulder, Likhachov pushed his way through them to the desk, which was occupied by Suyarov, a small man in no way remarkable save, perhaps, for a pair of unusually malicious yellow eyes in narrow slits. He glanced up at Likhachov and asked, 'So you've brought in the birdie?.. Are you Likhachov?'

'Yes. Here are my papers.' Likhachov tossed the pouch, now wrapped in a piece of sacking, onto the desk and let his eyes rest on Suyarov in a stern, remote stare. 'I'm sorry I didn't succeed in carrying out the task entrusted to me of crushing the lot of you like vermin! But the Soviet Government will give you what you deserve. I request you to shoot me.'

His wounded shoulder and one of his bushy eyebrows twitched.

'No, Comrade Likhachov! Shootings are what we've risen against. Our way's not your way—we don't have shootings. We're going to get you better and then you may be of some use to us,' Suyarov said softly, but with a glint in his eyes. 'Now then, clear the room. And quick about it!'

Only the commanders of the Reshetovskaya, Chernovskaya, Ushakovskaya, Dubrovskaya and Vyoshenskaya squadrons remained in the room, seating themselves by the table. One of them kicked a stool forward for Likhachov, but he merely leaned back against the wall, looking over their heads at the window.

'Now then, Likhachov,' Suyarov began, exchanging glances with the squadron commanders. 'Tell us how many you've got in your detachment?'

'I won't tell you anything.'

'Won't you? Never mind then. We'll find that out from your papers. And if we don't, we'll question your bodyguards. But there is one more thing we'll *ask* (Suyarov stressed the word) you to do: write to your detachment telling them to come to Vyoshenskaya. There's no cause for us to fight each other. We're not against the Soviet Government, we're against the commies and the Yids. We'll disarm your detachment and let 'em go home. And we'll set you free too. So, just write to them that they've got nothing to fear from us, we're not against the Soviets—'

Likhachov's spit landed on the small grey wedge of Suyarov's beard. He wiped his beard and his cheeks reddened slightly. Some of the commanders smiled, but no one made a move to defend their chief's honour.

'You're insulting us, Comrade Likhachov!' Suyarov said, now with patent insincerity. 'The atamans and the officers kicked us around and spat on us, and you—a communist—also spit. And yet you're always saying you're for the people... Hi, anyone out there?.. Take the commissar away. Tomorrow we'll send you off to Kazanskaya.'

'Mebbe you'll change your mind?' one of the squadron commanders asked sternly.

With a quick jerk Likhachov straightened the tunic that he was wearing draped over his shoulders and strode towards the guard at the door.

He was not shot. Hadn't the insurgents said they were fighting against 'shootings and plunder'? The next day he was marched off to Kazanskaya. He walked ahead of his mounted escorts, treading the snow lightly, knitting his bushy brows. But in the forest, as he passed a deathly white birch-tree, his face broke into a quick smile and, stopping for a moment, he reached up with his sound arm to break off a twig. The brown buds on it were already swollen with the sweet sap of March; their subtle, barely perceptible scent promised spring blossom, life repeating itself with every cycle of the sun. Likhachov thrust the swollen buds into his mouth and chewed them. He gazed with misty eyes at the trees, which were growing brighter as they recovered from the frost, and a smile appeared at the corners of his shaven lips.

He died with the black petals of the buds still clinging to his lips. Seven versts from Vyoshenskaya, among the grimly frowning sand dunes he was brutally murdered by the escorts. While he was still alive, his eyes were gouged out, his arms, ears, and nose cut off, his face slashed by sabres. The Cossacks undid his trousers and profaned the big, manly handsome body. They defiled the bleeding stump, and then one of the escorts stood on the faintly heaving chest and with one slanting stroke severed the head from the prostrate body.

XXXII

From across the Don, from the upper reaches, from all sides came news of the wide sweep of the revolt. It was no longer just two districts. Shumilinskaya, Kazanskaya, Migulinskaya, Meshkovskaya, Vyoshenskaya, Yelanskaya and Ust-Khopyorskaya had joined in with hastily mustered squadrons; Karginskaya, Bokovskaya and Krasnokutskaya were clearly swinging in favour of the insurgents. The revolt threatened to spread to the neighbouring Ust-Medveditskaya and Khopyor districts. Discontent was already brewing in Bukanovskaya, Slashchevskaya and Fedoseyevskaya; the villages around Alekseyevskaya, near Vyoshenskaya were seething... As a district centre Vyoshenskaya became the focal point of the revolt. After long arguments and debate it was decided to maintain the existing administrative structure. The most respected Cossacks, mainly young men, were elected to the District Executive Committee. One Danilov, an official of the Board of Artillery, was made chairman of the committee. Soviets were set up in the stanitsas and villages and, strange to relate, the once despised word 'comrade' remained in everyday use. Someone thought up the catchy slogan, 'For Soviet power, but against the commune, shootings and pillaging.' And for this reason, instead of one, white stripe or ribbon on their caps the insurgents wore two: a white crossed with a red.

Suyarov's place as commander of the united insurgent forces was taken by a young, twenty-eight-year-old cornet, Pavel Kudinov, holder of the St.George Cross, 1st, 2nd, 3rd and 4th classes, a clever fellow and persuasive speaker. He was rather a weak character and certainly not the man to rule a rebel district in such troubled times. But the Cossacks were drawn to him by his unassuming and considerate manner. The main thing was that Kudinov, himself a Cossack born and bred, had deep roots among the Cossacks, and was free of the arrogance and officer-like haughtiness usually to be found in upstarts. He was always modestly dressed, wore his hair long and trimmed straight all round, walked with a stoop and talked quickly. His lean long-nosed face was rather common, in no way remarkable.

As their chief of staff the Cossacks elected a captain, Ilya Safonov. He was chosen because he was a bit of a coward but a good hand at writing. At the meeting that elected him someone had put it like this, 'Give Safonov a staff job. He's no good for the battlefield, he'll only land his Cossacks and himself in trouble. You might as well ask a Gypsy to become a priest.'

The small rotund Safonov had responded to this observation by smiling with relief into his whitish yellow moustache and agreeing with great readiness to take over the staff.

But Kudinov and Safonov only gave official shape to what was set in motion independently by the squadrons. As leaders their hands were tied and, in any case, they could never have controlled such a sprawling mass amid the swift onrush of events.

The 4th Trans-Amur Cavalry Regiment, supported by the Bolsheviks of Ust-Khopyorskaya and Yelanskaya stanitsas and part of Vyoshenskaya, fought its way through a number of villages, crossed the Yelanskaya border and struck out westwards across the steppe and along the Don.

On March 5th a Cossack rode into Tatarsky with a message. The Yelanskaya men were in dire need of help. Short of ammunition and rifles, they were falling back almost without resistance. The Trans-Amur regiment was replying to their feeble volleys with a hail of machine-gun fire and bombardment by two batteries. In such a situation there was no time to wait for orders from district headquarters and Petro Melekhov decided to take the field with his two squadrons.

He also took command of another four squadrons from the neighbouring villages. The next morning he led his Cossacks out on the hill above the village. There was the usual skirmishing between patrols, then the battle began.

On that dull winter day eight versts from Tatarsky, near Red Ravine, where Grigory and his wife ploughed until they were caught by the onset of winter, and where Grigory had first confessed to Natalya that he didn't love her, the cavalry squadrons dismounted in the snow and took up their positions while the horse-minders led their mounts to safety. The Reds were advancing in three lines from the lower ground and the white expanse was dotted with moving human figures. Sledges were driving up behind the lines and horsemen were going to and fro. With a distance of about two versts between them and the enemy the Cossacks prepared unhurriedly to do battle.

After positioning the Yelanskaya squadrons, Petro rode over to Grigory on his steaming well-fed horse. He was cheerful and animated.

'Save your ammo, lads! Don't fire till I give the order... Grigory, take your men about three hundred paces to the left. Get a move on! And don't let the horse-minders bunch together!' He gave a few more instructions and reached for his field glasses. 'It looks as if they're mounting a battery on Matvei's Mound?'

'I spotted it long ago. You can see it without glasses.'

Grigory took Petro's glasses and scanned the field. Just below the bare windswept top of the mound there was a dark cluster of sledges with tiny human figures moving about round it.

The Tatarsky infantry—'crawlers' as the mounted Cossacks dubbed them—had ignored the strict order not to bunch together and were standing about in crowds, sharing out their cartridges, smoking and swapping jokes. Khristonya's lambskin busby towered over the heads of the other rather short Cossacks (he was in the infantry now, after losing his horse) and Pantelei's big red-topped cap was also to be seen. Most of the infantry were old men or youngsters. About a verst and a half to the right, beyond an uncut patch of withered sunflower stalks, were the Yelanskaya men. Their four squadrons numbered some six hundred Cossacks, but nearly two hundred were looking after the horses. A third of the whole force was lying low in the ravines.

'Petro Panteleyevich!' someone shouted from the infantry lines. 'Don't leave us, foot-sloggers, in the lurch when the fighting starts!'

'Don't worry—we won't!' Petro responded with a smile and, as he watched the Red lines slowly approaching the hill, he toyed nervously with his whip.

'Petro, come over here,' Grigory called, stepping out of the line.

Petro rode over to him and Grigory, with a frown of unconcealed disapproval, said to his brother, 'I don't like this position. We ought to be clear of these ravines. They'll turn our flank and we'll be in real trouble. Don't you think?'

'What's biting you?' Petro brushed him aside irritably. 'How can they outflank us? I've got a whole squadron in reserve. And if the worst comes to the worst, the ravines may be useful. They're nothing to worry about.'

'Well, watch out, brother!' Grigory warned quietly

and cast yet another searching glance over the surrounding country.

He went back to his line and surveyed his men. Many of them had pulled off their mittens and gloves as their hands grew hot with excitement. Some were fidgeting; one was adjusting his sabre, another tightening his belt.

'Our commander has dismounted,' Fedot Bodovskov announced with an ironic nod at Petro, who was wading through the snow towards the Cossack lines.

'Hi there, General Platov!' bawled one-armed Alexei Shamil, who was armed only with a sabre. 'Order the Cossacks a swig of vodka each!'

'Shut up, you old soak! The Reds'll chop off your other arm, then what will you drink with? You'll have to lap it up out of a trough.'

'Get away!'

'I could do with a drink anyhow!' Stepan Astakhov sighed, and let go the hilt of his sabre to twirl his fair moustache. For a time like this the talk all along the line was right off the mark. It died away at once when a gun struck a booming octave from Matvei's Mound.

The deep resonant sound broke loose from the barrel and hung over the steppe like the white puff of gun-smoke until it melted into the hard, sharp crack of the exploding shell. The shot fell short, half a verst in front of the Cossack line. Black smoke fringed with gleaming white snow spouted slowly over the ploughland and fell back into the scrub. At once the Red machine-guns went into action. Their resonance deadened by the frost, the bursts racketted like a night-watchman's rattle. The Cossacks lay flat in the snow, among the weeds and spiky sunflower stalks.

'That smoke's real black! Like from a German shell!' Prokhor Zykov shouted, looking round at Grigory.

A commotion arose in the neighbouring Yelanskaya squadron. The shouts were carried across by the wind.

'Cousin Mitrofan's been killed!'

Ignoring the fire, squadron commander Ivanov, a red-bearded Cossack from Rubezhin, ran over to Petro. Thrusting his hand under his cap to mop his brow, he gasped, 'That's snow for you! You can't pull your legs out of it!'

'What's up?' Petro blazed at him, knitting his brows.

'I've got an idea, Comrade Melekhov! You ought to send one squadron down to the Don. Take one out of the line. Let 'em go to the village by the lower path and bust into the Reds' rear from there. I bet they've left their transports unguarded—anyway what kind of a guard would it be? And besides it'll cause panic.'

The 'idea' appealed to Petro. He ordered his men to open fire, waved a signal to Latyshev, the infantry commander, standing at full height in the line, and strode over to Grigory. He explained the plan and gave a brief order, 'Take your half-squadron and tread on their tail!'

Grigory took his men out of the line. In a ravine they sorted out their horses, mounted and set off for the village at a trot.

The Cossacks in the line emptied their magazines twice and stopped shooting. The Red lines dropped to the ground. Their machine-guns burst into a choking chatter. Martin Shamil's white-stockinged horse, wounded by a stray bullet, broke away from its minder and charged madly through the line of Rubezhin Cossacks and down the hill towards the Reds. Caught by the spray of machine-gun bullets, it kicked its hind legs high and plunged into the snow.

'Aim at the machine-gunners!' Petro's order was passed along the line.

It was obeyed. Only the sharpshooters went to work and they did some damage. A plain little Cossack from Upper Krivskoy village picked off three machine-gunners one after the other and a Maxim gun fell silent with its cooling jacket boiling. But the crew was soon replaced and the gun rattled again, scattering its deadly seeds. The salvoes came over thick and fast and the Cossacks began to look depressed as they dug themselves deeper and deeper into the snow. Anikei had reached bare earth and was still in a joking mood. He had run out of bullets (he had only had five altogether, in a rusty green clip) and now he kept poking his head out of the snow and pursing his lips to whistle very much like a frightened marmot.

'A-a-hew-ew!..' he would pipe up, scanning the line with goggling eyes.

Stepan Astakhov rolled about, weeping with laughter, but Antip, the Braggart's son, swore angrily.

'Stoppit, you bastard! You've found a fine time to fool about!'

'A-a-hew-ew!' Anikei repeated, turning in his direction with bulging eyes.

The Red battery was evidently short of shells and, after firing about thirty rounds, it fell silent. Petro glanced impatienly over his shoulder towards the brow of the hill. He had sent two messengers to the village with an order that the whole adult population was to come out armed with forks and scythes. He wanted to scare the Reds and deploy his forces in three lines as well.

Soon a large crowd appeared on the skyline, pouring down hill.

'Look at that—like a lot of jackdaws!'

'The whole village has turned out!'

'And the women too, by the look of it!'

The Cossacks shouted across to each other, grinning widely. They stopped shooting altogether. On the Red side only two machine-guns were firing, with an occasional volley from the infantry.

'It's a pity their battery's quietened down. If they'd drop a shell in that women's army, there'd be a fine how-d'ye-do! They'd be running back to their village with wet skirts!' one-armed Alexei said with relish, as though seriously regretting that the Reds had not lobbed a shell among the women.

The crowd spread out. Soon it was drawn up in two long lines and came to a halt.

Petro would not allow the village folk to come anywhere near the Cossack positions. But their mere appearance on the scene produced a noticeable impression on the Reds, whose lines began to fall back to the lower end of the meadows. After a brief consultation with the squadron commanders Petro exposed his right flank by pulling two squadrons of Yelanskaya men out of the line and ordering them to ride northwards to the Don, to back up Grigory's attack. In full view of the Reds the squadrons formed up on the edge of Red Ravine and rode down towards the Don.

The Cossacks opened fire again at the retreating Red lines.

Meanwhile several of the more adventurous women and a flock of children had scampered out of the 'reserve' and found their way into the firing line. Darya, Petro's wife, was with them.

'Petro, let me have a shot at a Red! I know how to handle a rifle.'

Suiting action to words, she took Petro's carbine, went down on one knee and with manly assurance pressed the butt to her breast and narrow shoulder and fired twice.

But the 'reserve' was feeling the cold. They began to stamp their feet, jump about and blow their noses. Both lines swayed, as if stirred by the wind. The women's cheeks and lips turned blue; the frost began to play havoc under their wide skirts. Many of the more doddery old men, including Old Grishaka, were very cold by the time they had been half carried up the steep hill from the village. But here, on the windy summit, the chill air and the distant firing brought them back to life, and they talked endlessly of past wars and battles, and of the misery of the present war, in which brother was fighting against brother, and father against son, and the cannon fired from so far away that they could not be seen by the naked eye.

XXXIII

Grigory and his men gave the Reds' first-line transports a good trouncing. Eight Red Army men were cut down. Four sledgeloads of ammunition and two cavalry mounts were captured. The Cossacks got away with the loss of one horse and a mere scratch on the body of one of their men.

But while Grigory was making off along the Don with the captured sledges, unpursued and greatly heartened by his success, the battle on the hill was unexpectedly decided. A squadron of the Trans-Amur Regiment had set out before the fighting started on a ten-verst out-flanking movement and now it suddenly appeared from behind the hill and struck at the horse-minders. Confusion followed. The minders dashed out of the mouth of Red Ravine, and managed to hand over horses to some of the fighting Cossacks, but the rest were already threatened by the gleaming swords of the Trans-Amur cavalry. Many of the unarmed horse-minders let their charges go and galloped away in all directions. The infantry, unable to open fire for fear of hitting their own men, poured into the ravine, like peas out of a sack, scrambled up the other side and scattered in disorder. The mounted Cossacks who managed to catch their horses (and these were the majority) set out in a mad race for the village, as though vying to see who had the best horse.

As soon as he turned his head and saw the avalanche of cavalry sweeping down on the horse-minders, Petro had commanded, 'To horse! Infantry! Latyshev! Across the ravine!'

But he never reached his own horse-minder. His mount

was in the charge of young Andryushka Beskhlebnov. Andryushka came galloping up the hill towards Petro with two horses, Petro's and Fedot Bodovskov's on his right. But a Red Army man with his yellow sheepskin flapping open charged him from the other side and with a shout of 'Call yourself a fighter, you—!' dealt him a mighty blow from the shoulder.

Luckily for Andryushka his rifle was slung over his back and the sabre, instead of cutting through the lad's neck in its warm white scarf, scraped up the rifle barrel, leapt out of the Red Army man's hand with a shriek and spun away into the air. Andryushka's startled horse swung aside and bolted. Petro and Bodovskov's mounts followed it.

Petro gasped and stood white-faced for a moment as the sweat broke out on his cheeks and forehead. When he glanced round a dozen Cossacks were running towards him.

'We're done for!' Bodovskov screamed, his face distorted with fear.

'Slip into the ravine, Cossacks! Down into the ravine, brothers!'

Petro took a grip on himself and was the first to run to the edge and start slithering down the steep two-hundred-foot slope. His coat caught on something and was ripped open from the breast pocket to the hem, but he leapt to his feet and shook himself like a dog. The other Cossacks came rolling and somersaulting down behind him.

In the space of a minute ten men reached the bottom. Petro was the eleventh. Shots were still crackling overhead, shouts and the rumble of hooves could be heard. But at the bottom of the ravine the Cossacks stood foolishly shaking the snow and sand off their caps, while some rubbed bruised shoulders and sides. Martin Shamil removed the bolt from his rifle and started blowing the snow out of the barrel. Manytskov, son of the late village ataman, was weeping openly and his tear-stained cheeks were shaking in terror.

'What shall we do? Tell us, Petro! This is death... Where can we go? They're sure to kill us!'

Fedot's teeth began to chatter and he darted away down the frozen streambed towards the Don.

The others lurched after him, like sheep.

Petro only just managed to stop them. 'Hold on there! Let's think it over... Don't run! You'll get shot!'

He led them all up a gully in the red-clay side of the ravine and proposed his plan, stammering but trying to appear calm.

'We mustn't go down. They'll be chasing our lads all over the place. The best thing's to stay here. Split up and take cover... Three on that side... We can shoot it out. We could hold off any attack here.'

'We're done for! Fathers! Dear fathers! Let me go from here! I don't—I don't want to die!' young Manytskov's sobbing rose to a moan.

Fedot's Kalmyk eyes blazed and without warning he hit the lad full in the face with his fist.

Blood spurted from the lad's nose. He staggered back against the side of the ravine, bringing down a shower of dry clay, but stopped moaning.

'How can we shoot it out?' Shamil asked, gripping Petro's arms. 'How much ammo have we got? None!'

'If they toss a grenade, it'll be all up with us.'

'Well, what else can we do?' Petro suddenly turned blue in the face and foam appeared at the corners of his lips. 'Get down! Who's in command here? I'll kill you!'

And he actually did brandish his revolver over the Cossacks' heads.

His hissing whisper seemed to breathe new life into them. Bodovskov, Shamil and two other Cossacks ran across the ravine and took up their position along another gully; the rest stayed with Petro.

In spring the reddish flood of water pouring down the hillside loosened boulders, hollowed out the bed of the ravine, crumbled the layers of red clay and washed crevices and gullies in its sides. And it was in these that the Cossacks took cover.

Beside Petro crouched Antip, son of the Braggart, with his rifle at the ready, whispering in a frenzy, 'Stepan Astakhov caught his horse by the tail and got away, but I wasn't so lucky... And the infantry left us in the lurch... We're done for, lads! Sure to God, we've had it!'

The crunch of running feet sounded from above. Snow and clay sprinkled down into the ravine.

'That's 'em!' Petro whispered, snatching at Antip's sleeve, but Antip tore his arm free and looked up, keeping his finger on the trigger.

No one came close to the edge of the ravine.

Voices could be heard. Someone was shouting at the horses.

'They're talking it over,' Petro thought to himself,

and again sweat broke out on his face, on his back, and in the hollow of his chest, as though all the pores in his body were opening.

'Hi, you there! Come out of it! We'll finish you off all the same!' came a shout from above.

A milky-white stream of snow gushed down into the ravine. Someone must have stepped on the edge.

Another voice up there said confidently, 'Here's where they jumped, look at the marks. Anyway I saw 'em myself!'

'Petro Melekhov! Come out of there!'

For a second Petro was overcome by a blind rush of joy. 'Who would know me among the Reds?' he thought. 'These are our men! They've driven them off!' But then the same voice sent shivers through his body.

'It's Mikhail Koshevoi speaking! We offer you surrender. You can't escape!'

Petro wiped his wet forehead and streaks of pinkish sweat appeared on his hand.

A strange feeling of indifference came over him; it was like being in a trance.

Bodovskov's answering shout seemed unbelievable. 'We'll come out if you promise to let us go. If not, we'll shoot it out! Take your choice!'

'We'll let you go,' came the reply from above, after a pause.

With a desperate effort Petro shook off his torpor. He felt as if he had seen the invisible sneer, behind that 'we'll let you go.'

'Back!' he shouted huskily, but no one obeyed him.

Petro was the last to start climbing. Life was struggling within him like an unborn child in its mother's womb. Guided by the urge to survive, he threw away his cartridges and tackled the steep slope. His head was swimming, his heart seemed to swell and fill his chest. He felt stifled, trapped, as in a childhood nightmare. He tore open the collar of his tunic and his dirty undervest. Sweat streamed into his eyes, his hands slipped on the frozen ledges of the ravine. Wheezing and gasping for breath, he climbed out on to the trampled snowy edge, dropped his rifle and raised his hands. The Cossacks who had climbed out before him were gathered in a tight bunch nearby. Mishka Koshevoi had stepped out of a crowd of mounted and foot soldiers of the Trans-Amur Regiment and was walking towards them. More Red cavalrymen were approaching.

Mishka came right up to Petro and asked quietly, without raising his eyes, 'Had enough fighting?' He paused, waiting for an answer, then, still staring at Petro's feet, he asked, 'Were you in command?'

Petro's lips twitched. With a gesture of great weariness he lifted his hand to his wet forehead. Mishka's long, curling eyelashes fluttered and his full upper lip with its rash of cold sores rose tremulously. He began to shake violently, as if he were about to fall. But he raised his eyes and met Petro's, eyeball to eyeball, thrusting into them with an estranged stare, and muttered hastily, 'Take off your clothes!'

Petro deftly discarded his sheepskin, folded it carefully and put it down on the snow; then he took off his tall lambskin busby, his belt and tunic, and sat down on his coat to pull off his boots, growing paler every moment.

Ivan Kotlyarov dismounted, came up to them and, at the sight of Petro, clenched his teeth for fear of bursting into tears.

'Never mind your underclothes,' Mishka whispered and with a shudder suddenly cried out, 'Hurry up!'

Petro crumpled the woollen socks he had just taken off, stuffed them into his boots, straightened up and stepped off the coat; his bare feet looked saffron yellow against the snow.

'Kinsman!' he appealed to Ivan, his lips scarcely moving. The latter silently watched the snow melting under Petro's bare feet. 'Ivan, you were my child's godfather... Don't put me to death, kinsman!' Petro said and, noticing that Mishka had already levelled a revolver at his chest, opened his eyes wide as if expecting to see some blinding vision, quickly bunched his fingers to make the sign of the cross, and drew his head into his shoulders like a man about to jump.

He did not hear the shot when he fell backwards as though from a great push.

Koshevoi's outstretched hand had suddenly grabbed his heart and squeezed all the blood out of it. With a last effort Petro ripped open his vest, revealing the bullet hole under his left nipple. The blood seeped from it slowly at first, then, finding an outlet, gushed forth in a whistling pitch-black stream.

XXXIV

At first light the patrol that had been sent out to Red Ravine returned with the news that no Red troops were in sight as far as the Yelanskaya border, and that Petro Melekhov and a dozen other Cossacks were lying at the top of the ravine, cut to pieces.

Grigory arranged for sledges to fetch the dead and, driven from the house by the women's, particularly Darya's, piercing shrieks, went off to spend the rest of the night at Khristonya's. He sat by the stove-bench in Khristonya's little house until dawn. He would smoke a cigarette greedily, as though afraid of being left alone with his thoughts, with his grief for Petro, then snatch up his pouch to make another and, filling his lungs with the pungent smoke, start talking about other things with the nodding guardsman.

The sun rose and the snow at once began to thaw. By ten o'clock puddles appeared on the dung-strewn road. The roofs began to drip. The cocks crowed with springlike vigour and somewhere a hen broke into a lonely clucking, as though in the heat of a sultry noon.

On the sunny side of the farmyards the bullocks rubbed up against the fences. The moulting fur was brushed off their greyish brown backs by the wind. The air was full of the fresh, spicy scent of thawing snow and a yellow-chested tomtit chirped and swung to and fro on a bare branch of the apple-tree beside Khristonya's gate.

Grigory stood by the gate, waiting for the sledges to come in from the hill and found himself involuntarily translating the bird's chirping into words he had known since childhood. 'Sharpen plough! Sharpen plough!' the tomtit was calling joyfully on this unusually warm day; but if a frost were on the way, Grigory knew, its voice would change and it would sound like, 'Thick shoes! Thick shoes!'

Grigory switched his glance from the road to the little bird bouncing on its branchy saddle. 'Sharpen plough! Sharpen plough!' it chirped. And Grigory recalled how he and Petro, as children, had been minding some turkeys in the steppe and how Petro, with hair as white as straw and a little snub nose that was always peeling, had skilfully imitated the turkey-cock's gobbling and likewise translated it into his childish fun language. He would mimic the squeal of an offended young turkey and cry out in a high-pitched voice, 'Everyone's got boots but me! Everyone's got boots but me!' And then he would roll his eyes, stick out his elbows and sidle along like an old turkey-cock muttering, 'Gobble! Gobble! Gobble! We'll buy boots for the ragamuffin at market!' Grigory would laugh happily and ask him to talk some more turkey language and beg to be shown what a flurry the young turkeys would get into if they found some unusual object like a tin or a bit of cloth in the grass.

The first sledge appeared at the end of the street. A Cossack was walking beside it. After the first came a second and a third. Grigory brushed away a tear and the quiet smile that these unbidden memories had evoked, and hurried off to his own gate. He wanted to be able to hold back his grief-stricken mother in the first terrible moment and keep her away from the sledge that bore Petro's body. It was Alexei Shamil who was walking beside the first sledge, his cap tucked under the stump of his left arm, while his right held the horse-hair halter. Grigory's glance went straight from Alexei's face to the sledge. Martin Shamil was lying on his back on a litter of straw. His face, the green tunic covering his chest and his sunken belly were caked with frozen blood. The second sledge was carrying Manytskov. His slashed face was half buried in the straw. His head was huddled into his shoulders and the back of it had been sliced off by a skilful sabre stroke; black icicles of hair hung in a fringe over the bared cranium. Grigory looked at the third sledge. He could not recognise the face, but he noticed the hand with its wax-like nicotine-stained fingers. It was hanging from the sledge and the two fingers and a thumb that before the moment of death had been held together to make the sign of the cross were trailing in the wet snow. The dead man was wearing boots and a greatcoat; even his cap was there, lying on his chest. Grigory seized the horse of the fourth sledge by its bridle and led it into the yard at a trot. The neighbours, children and women ran in after it and gathered in a crowd round the porch.

'Here he is, our dear Petro Panteleyevich! His feet will tread this earth no more!' someone said quietly.

Stepan Astakhov entered the gate bareheaded. Grandad Grishaka and three other old men appeared as if from nowhere. Grigory looked round in embarrassment.

'Let's carry him into the house.'

The driver of the sledge was about to grasp Petro's

legs, but the crowd parted silently and respectfully to make way for Ilyinichna as she came down the steps.

She glanced at the sledge. A deathly pallor spread across her forehead, covered her cheeks, her nose and crept over her chin. Pantelei, himself shaking, seized her elbows to hold her up. Dunyashka was the first to give tongue, and her wail was taken up in a dozen other places all over the village. Darya, face swollen, hair dishevelled, ran down from the porch, slamming the door behind her, and flung herself on to the sledge.

'Petro, dearest! Oh, my darling! Get up! Get up!'

Grigory saw black.

'Go away, Darya!' he shouted wildly, not knowing what he was doing and, underrating his strength, pushed her in the chest.

She fell into a snowdrift. Grigory seized Petro under his arms and the driver grasped his bare ankles, but Darya crawled after them on to the porch, snatching at and kissing her husband's stiff, frozen hands. Grigory pushed her away with his foot, feeling that in another second he would lose control of himself. Dunyashka tore Darya's hands away by main force and pressed the grief-stunned head to her chest.

* * *

There was a deathly silence in the kitchen. Petro lay on the floor, looking strangely small, as though he had shrunk. His nose had tapered, his wheaten moustache had darkened, his whole face was longer and better looking. His bare hairy legs protruded from the ties of his baggy trousers. He was slowly thawing out and a puddle of pinkish water was forming beneath him. And the softer the night-frozen body became, the more pungent was the salty smell of blood and the sickly-sweet minty odour of decaying flesh.

Under the overhang of the shed Pantelei was planing boards for a coffin. The women were fussing about round the still unconscious Darya in the front room. Now and then a sharp, hysterical sob broke out and was followed by a soothing brooklike burble from Auntie Vasilissa, who had come round to share the family's grief. Grigory was sitting on a bench opposite his brother, rolling a cigarette and staring at Petro's face as it yellowed round the edges, at his hands with their rounded bluish fingernails. He was already separated from his brother by the great coldness of estrangement. Petro was not one of them any more; he was but a passing guest with whom it was time to part. Here he lay, as if expecting something, his cheek lolling indifferently against the earthen floor and a resigned and mysterious half-smile frozen under his wheaten moustache. Tomorrow his wife and mother would prepare him for his last journey.

Overnight their mother had heated three cauldrons of water and his wife had prepared clean linen and his best trousers and tunic. Grigory, his blood brother, and his father would wash the body, which no longer belonged to him, which was not ashamed of its nakedness. They would dress it in his best clothes and place it on the table. And then Darya would come and set between those broad, icy hands that only yesterday had embraced her the candle which had shone for both of them at their wedding as they walked round the lectern, and then Cossack Petro Melekhov would be ready for his send-off to the place whence none return for even a day or two at home.

'You should have got killed somewhere in Prussia, not here, in front of Mother!' Grigory thought reproachfully as he stared at the corpse, and suddenly he turned pale: a tear was crawling down Petro's cheek towards the drooping tip of his moustache. Grigory leapt to his feet, but then looked more closely and gave a sigh of relief. It was not a tear but a drop from Petro's thawing curly forelock that had fallen on his forehead and rolled slowly down his cheek.

XXXV

By order of the commander of the combined insurgent forces of the Upper Don Grigory Melekhov was given command of the Vyoshenskaya Regiment. He led ten squadrons of Cossacks against Karginskaya. His orders were to smash Likhachov's detachment at all costs and drive it out of the district, so that all the villages around Karginskaya and Bokovskaya and along the River Chir could be stirred to rebellion.

On March 7th Grigory set out with his men. On the thawed crest of the hill, where the earth showed in black patches, he halted by the roadside and sat hunched in the saddle, keeping his restless horse on a tight rein while

8—1108

the ten squadrons rode past each from one of the Don-side villages—Bazki, Byelogorka, Olshansky, Merkulov, Gromkovsky, Semyonovsky, Rybinsky, Vodyansky, Lebyazhy and Yerik.

Grigory stroked his black moustache with his glove; his hawklike nose twitched and his gaze from under his winged brows was sombre and peremptory. Hundreds of bedraggled horses' legs pounded the brown mush of snow. The men who knew Grigory smiled at him as they rode past. Tobacco smoke hovered and melted over their lambskin busbies. Steam rose from the horses.

Grigory attached himself to the last squadron. About three versts farther on they were met by a patrol. The sergeant in command of it rode up to Grigory.

'The Reds are retreating along the road to Chukarin!'

Likhachov's detachment refused battle but Grigory sent out three of his squadrons to turn its flank and pursued so hotly with the rest that by the time they reached Chukarin the Red troops were abandoning sledges and caissons. On the road out of Chukarin a Red battery had got stuck in a stream by a dilapidated little church. The drivers slashed the traces and galloped away through the poplar groves towards Karginskaya.

The fifteen versts from Chukarin to Karginskaya yielded no opposition. More to the right, beyond Yasenovka an enemy patrol opened fire on one of the Vyoshenskaya patrols, but that was the end of it and the Cossacks soon began to joke among themselves— 'It'll be like this all the way to Novocherkassk!'

Grigory was delighted with the captured battery. They didn't even manage to smash the breech-locks, he thought contemptuously. Bullocks were used to pull out the guns, and crews to man them were found at once among the squadrons. Six pairs of horses were harnessed to each gun, while a half-squadron provided an escort and covering force for the battery.

At dusk they swooped on Karginskaya. Part of Likhachov's detachment with its remaining three guns and nine machine-guns were captured. The rest of the Red Army men and the Karginskaya revolutionary committee got away through the villages in the direction of Bokovskaya.

It rained all night. By morning the gulleys and ravines were in spate. The roads became impassable and every little dell was a trap. The moisture-soaked snow was treacherously soft. Horses were helpless and the men ready to drop with fatigue.

Two squadrons commanded by Cornet Kharlampy Yermakov, of Bazki, which had been sent out by Grigory to pursue the retreating enemy, caught about thirty Red Army men who had fallen behind in the adjoining villages of Latyshevsky and Visloguzovsky; in the morning they were herded back to Karginskaya.

Grigory had taken up his quarters in the huge house of a rich local man named Kargin. The prisoners were driven into his yard. Yermakov came in and wished him good morning.

'I've taken twenty-seven Reds. Your orderly is ready with your horse. Will you be riding out now or what?'

Grigory fastened his belt over his greatcoat and went to the mirror to comb his hair, which had matted under his lambskin busby, and only after that did he turn to Yermakov.

'Let's go. It's time we got moving. We'll hold a meeting on the square, then we march.'

'What do we need a meeting for?' Yermakov shrugged one shoulder and smiled. 'Everyone's in the saddle already without any meeting. But look at that! They aren't Vyoshenskaya men!'

Grigory looked out of the window. Several squadrons were riding down the street four abreast, in splendid order. The Cossacks looked like picked troops and the horses were fine enough for a review.

'Where're they from? Where the hell?' Grigory muttered joyfully, buckling on his sabre as he ran out of the house.

Yermakov caught up with him at the gate.

The commander of the first squadron was already coming over to report. He raised his hand respectfully to his cap, not daring to offer it to Grigory.

'Are you Comrade Melekhov?'

'Yes. Where are you from?'

'Enroll us in your unit. We're joining you. Our squadron was formed last night. We're from the village of Likhovidov, and the other two squadrons are from Grachov, Arkhipovka and Vasilevka.'

'Take your Cossacks out on to the square. We're just going to hold a meeting.'

Grigory's orderly (it was Prokhor Zykov) gave him his horse and even held his stirrup. With great agility Yermakov threw his lean, iron-hard body into the saddle, scarcely touching the pommel or the horse's mane. He rode up to Grigory and, as he straightened the slit of his greatcoat over the saddle with a habitual gesture, asked, 'What do we do about the prisoners?'

Grigory bent forward and took him by the button of his coat. Reddish sparks glinted in his eyes, but his lips under his moustache were smiling, though rather brutally.

'Order them to be driven to Vyoshenskaya. Get me? And mind they don't go any farther than that mound over there!' He waved his whip in the direction of a sandy mound rising above the stanitsa, and rode off.

'That'll be their first payment for Petro,' he thought, breaking into a trot, and for no apparent reason raised a white weal on his horse's croupe with a cut of the whip.

XXXVI

Grigory left Karginskaya for Bokovskaya with a force of three and a half thousand sabres. Messengers from headquarters and the District Executive Committee pursued him with orders and instructions. One of the headquarters staff sent him a personal message with the following ornate request:

Much esteemed Comrade Grigory Panteleyevich,

Wicked rumours are reaching our ears that you are allegedly meting out brutal treatment to captured Red Army men. It is said that on your orders thirty Red prisoners captured by Kharlampy Yermakov at Bokovskaya were destroyed, that is to say, cut to pieces. According to these rumours, there was among the aforementioned prisoners a commissar fellow who might have been of great use to us in the matter of obtaining information about their forces. So kindly rescind the order not to take prisoners, dear comrade. Such an order does us great harm and the Cossacks are said to be grumbling about such cruelty and fear that the Reds, too, will cut down their prisoners and destroy our villages. Provide an escort and send their commanders back to us alive as well. We'll get rid of them quietly in Vyoshenskaya or Kazanskaya, but you are riding with your squadrons like Taras Bulba, in the historical novel by the writer Pushkin, laying everything waste with fire and sword, and alarming the Cossacks. Steady up, please, and stop putting prisoners to death; send them to us instead. This will be of advantage to us, as stated above. Hereby we wish you all the best. We send you our deepest respects and await further successes.

Grigory tore up the letter and threw it away without

reading it to the end. In reply to Kudinov's order 'Develop the offensive immediately southwards, in the Krutenky-Astakhovo-Grekovo sector. Headquarters considers it necessary to link up with the Cadets' front. Otherwise we shall be surrounded and defeated', he wrote without dismounting, 'I am attacking Bokovskaya in pursuit of the retreating enemy. I won't go to Krutenky as I think your order is foolish. Who'd I be attacking at Astakhovo? Nothing there but winds and Ukrainians.'

That was the end of his official correspondence with insurgent headquarters. The squadrons, now organised into two regiments, were approaching the village of Konkovo not far from Bokovskaya. For another three days fortune favoured Grigory on the field of battle. Having stormed Bokovskaya, he advanced at his own risk on Krasnokutskaya. A small detachment that barred his path was soon dealt with, but he refrained from ordering the cutting down of prisoners and sent them into the rear.

On March 9th he was bringing his squadrons up to the settlement of Chistyakovka. By this time the Red command felt the threat to its rear and threw several regiments and batteries against the rebels. At Chistyakovka the Red regiments clashed with Grigory's in a battle that lasted some three hours. Afraid of being encircled, Grigory pulled back his units towards Krasnokutskaya. But in a morning battle on March 10th the Vyoshenskaya men were well trounced by Red Cossacks from the Khopyor. It was a straight fight between Cossacks with charges and counter-charges. They sabered each other well and truly, and Grigory, after losing his horse and having his cheek slashed, withdrew his regiments and retired to Bokovskaya.

That evening he interrogated a prisoner. The man was a Cossack from Tepikinskaya on the Khopyor, and by no means young. He stood before Grigory, tow-haired, narrow-chested, with a ragged red bow on the lapel of his greatcoat, answering questions readily, but with a strained and rather crooked smile.

'What regiments were in action yesterday?'

'Our 3rd Cossack, all Cossacks of the Khopyor District. The 5th Trans-Amur, the 12th Cavalry and the 6th Mtsensk.'

'Who was in command? They say it was Kikvidze*?'

---

*Kikvidze, Vasily Isidorovich (1894—1919), revolutionary, communist, hero of the Civil War (1918—1920) in which he commanded a division. Killed in action February 11, 1919.

'No, it was Comrade Domnich. He had command of the whole detachment.'

'How're you off for supplies? Plenty?'

'A hell of a lot!'

'What about guns?'

'Eight, at least.'

'Where was your regiment before it came here?'

'The Kamenskaya villages.'

'Did they tell you where you were going?'

The Cossack hesitated but replied. Grigory wanted to know what kind of mood the Khopyor men were in.

'What did the Cossacks talk about amongst themselves?'

'They wasn't very keen on going.'

'Do they know in the regiment what we've rebelled against?'

'How could they know?'

'Then why didn't they want to go?'

'You're Cossacks, aren't you! We're fed up with war anyway. We was with the Reds and now look where it's landed us.'

'Maybe you'll serve with us?'

The Cossack shrugged his narrow shoulders.

'That's up to you. I'm not too keen.'

'Well, get out then. We'll let you go back to your wife... You're missing her, I reckon?'

With eyes narrowed Grigory watched the Cossack go, then called for Prokhor. He stood for a while smoking in silence, went over to the window and, standing with his back to Prokhor, calmly ordered him, 'Tell the lads to walk that one I just questioned off into the orchards. I don't take Red Cossacks prisoner!' Grigory swung round on his worn-down heels. 'They can deal with him right away... Go!'

Prokhor went out. Grigory stood for a minute, breaking the brittle shoots of a geranium on the windowsill, then walked quickly out on to the porch. Prokhor was talking quietly to some Cossacks seated by the sunlit wall of a barn.

'Let the prisoner go. Get a pass made out for him,' Grigory said without looking at the men he was talking to and returned to his room. As he entered, he halted in front of the shabby mirror and spread his arms in bewilderment.

He could not explain to himself why he had gone out and ordered the prisoner's release. He had felt a gloating satisfaction when with an inward sneer he had said, 'We'll let you go back to your wife', knowing that he was about to call in Prokhor and order him to finish off the prisoner in the orchards.

He was slightly annoyed at this feeling of pity. For what else but an unaccountable pity had prompted him to free an enemy? And at the same time he felt refreshed, almost joyful. How had it happened? He could find no explanation. What made it all the stranger was that only yesterday he had been saying to his Cossacks, 'The muzhik is an enemy, but the Cossack who goes along with the Reds is twice as bad! We treat such Cossacks as spies. One, two— and off they go to heaven.'

Grigory left his quarters with this unresolved and nagging contradiction, this feeling that he was in the wrong, still in his mind. The commander of the Chir Regiment, a tall guardsman with an undistinguished, easily forgotten face, and two squadron commanders, had come to report to him.

'We've got a fresh lot of reinforcements!' the regimental commander informed him, smiling. 'Three thousand horses from Napolov, from Yablonyeva Rechka, and Gusyanka, and a couple of squadrons of infantry besides. What are you going to do with 'em?'

Grigory hitched on the Mauser pistol and fine-looking field-bag he had taken off Likhachov, and strode out into the yard. The sun was warm. The sky was as lofty and blue as in summer and fleecy white clouds were drifting southwards. Grigory assembled all the commanders in a sidelane for a conference. There were about thirty in all. They squatted down on a fallen fence and someone's tobacco pouch was passed round.

'What plans are we going to make? How're we going to smash the regiments that pushed us back from Chistyakovka? And where do we head for then?' Grigory asked and, in passing, mentioned Kudinov's order.

'How many against us? Did you find out from the prisoner?' one of the squadron commanders asked after a pause.

Grigory enumerated the regiments opposing them and gave a rough estimate of the enemy's strength in bayonets and sabres. The Cossacks were silent. A council of war was not the place for hasty, ill-considered opinions. The Grachovo squadron's commander said as much.

'Wait a bit, Melekhov! Give us time to think. You can't decide a thing like that at a stroke. We'll be off on the wrong track, if we don't look out.'

And he was the first to have his say.

Grigory listened to them all. The general view was not to range far afield and, even in the event of success, to wage a defensive war. But one of the men from Chir warmly supported the order from the commander of the rebel forces.

'There's no need for us to stick around here. Let Melekhov lead us to the Donets. Are you all mad? We're only a handful and we've got all Russia ready to jump on us. How can we stand up to that? They'll clout us and we'll be finished! We've got to break through! We haven't much ammunition, but we can get more. We must carry out a raid! Make up your minds!'

'What do we do with our own folk? The women, the old people, the kids?'

'They can stay behind!'

'Clever head you've got, but it's on a fool's shoulders!'

The commanders on the fringe of the group had been talking in whispers about the approaching spring ploughing, and what would become of their farms if they had to attempt a breakthrough in the direction of the Don Army, but after the Chir man's speech they all raised an outcry. The conference became as riotous as a village meeting. An old Cossack from Napolovo outshouted the rest.

'We won't go far from our farms! I'll be the first to take my squadron back to the village! If we must fight, we'll fight for our own homes, but we're not going off to save other people's lives!'

'Don't jump down my throat! I'm trying to argue and you just shout!'

'What's there to argue about!'

'Let Kudinov go to the Donets himself!'

Grigory waited for silence, then put his decisive vote on the scales.

'We'll hold the front here! If the Krasnokutskaya men join us, we'll defend their land as well! There's nowhere for us to go. The council is over. Back to you squadrons! We'll be taking the field right away.'

Half an hour later, when the close-ranked columns of cavalry were flowing endlessly along the streets, Grigory felt a surge of proud jubilation; never before had he commanded such a huge number of men. But alarm and a caustic bitterness stirred ominously beneath his pride. Would he be able to provide the leadership that was needed? Had he the skill to command thousands of Cossacks? It was not a squadron but a division that was to obey him. Was it for him, an uneducated Cossack, to govern thousands of lives and bear the sacred responsibility for them? 'But the real question is, who am I leading them against? Against the people... Who is right?'

Gritting his teeth, Grigory stood watching the squadrons as they marched past. And even as he watched, the intoxicating sense of power drooped and faded. Anxiety and bitterness remained, leaning on him with a weight that bowed his shoulders.

XXXVII

Spring opened the veins of the rivers. There was more heart in the days, more sound in the green hillside torrents. The sun grew ruddier and shed its feeble yellow hue. Its rays bushed out and their heat made the skin tingle. At noon the bare ploughland steamed and the porous, scaly snow shone unbearably bright. The air, saturated with fresh moisture, was rich and scented.

The sun warmed Grigory's back, and all the other backs in the regiment. Their saddle seats were pleasantly hot. The wet lips of the wind moistened their weather-beaten cheeks. Sometimes it also brought a breath of cold air from a snow-banked hill. But the warmth was overcoming winter. The horses frisked and reared with all the lusty vigour of spring, their moulting fur flew from their flanks, and their sweat stung the nostrils with a fresh pungency.

The Cossacks had tied up their horses' lank, bushy tails. Their camel-hair hoods now hung uselessly down their backs, their foreheads sweated under their busbies, and it was too hot for them in their sheepskins and warm uniforms...

Grigory was leading his regiment along a track that was already clear of snow. Fighting had begun around the village of Sviridovo and in the distance, beyond the gaunt cross formed by a windmill's sails, the Red squadrons were wheeling into line for a charge.

Grigory had not yet learned the art of commanding his forces from a distance. He led the Vyoshenskaya squadrons into action himself, throwing them into the most dangerous gaps, while the battle developed without any general control. Each regiment, breaking the plan agreed on beforehand, acted as circumstances dictated.

The absence of a continuous front allowed both sides a wide range of manoeuvre.

The abundance of cavalry (most of Grigory's force were mounted) was an important advantage. And making use of this advantage, Grigory decided to fight the war in Cossack style, by turning the enemy's flanks, striking from the rear, destroying transports, and harassing and demoralising the Reds by nocturnal raids.

But at Sviridovo he resolved on a different line of action. At a fast trot he led the Vyoshenskaya squadrons into position, having left one of them in the village with orders to dismount, hide their horses and lay an ambush in the poplar groves. With the other two he rode out on to a hillock about half a verst from the windmill and set about engaging the enemy.

Against him were more than two squadrons of Red cavalry. They were not Cossacks from the Khopyor. Through his field glasses Grigory could see that their horses' tails had been docked. Cossacks never spoiled a horse's looks by shortening its tail. So it must be the 13th Cavalry or some newly arrived units that were advancing upon them.

Grigory scanned the terrain through his field glasses. From the saddle the world always seemed wider and he felt surer of himself with his feet in the stirrups.

On the other side of the River Chir he could see the long brown column of three and a half thousand Cossacks under his command. It was weaving slowly up a hill northwards, in the direction of the border between the Yelanskaya and Ust-Khopyor districts, to meet the enemy advancing from Ust-Medveditskaya and help the hard-pressed Yelanskaya Cossacks.

There was about a verst and a half between Grigory and the Red forces that were preparing to charge. Hurriedly Grigory swung his squadrons into the traditional attack formation. Not all the Cossacks had lances, but those who did moved up into the front line, some twenty paces ahead of the rest. Grigory rode out in front of them and, half-turning, drew his sabre.

'At a slow trot—forward!'

In the very first minute his horse caught its foot in a snow-covered marmot-hole and stumbled. Grigory recovered his balance, turned pale with anger and struck the animal hard with the flat of his sabre. He was riding a fine army charger, taken from one of the Vyoshenskaya Cossacks, but inwardly he mistrusted the animal. He knew that it could not have got used to him in two days, that he himself had not studied its ways and character, and he was afraid that this new horse would not respond to the slightest touch of the reins with the instant understanding of his former mount, killed under him at Chistyakovka. Excited by the blow, the horse broke into a canter. Grigory felt a shiver of alarm. 'He'll let me down!' came the stabbing thought. But as the horse's canter levelled out into a long-striding gallop and it became increasingly responsive to the barely perceptible movements of the hands guiding its progress, Grigory recovered his confidence. For a second he tore his eyes from the scattered enemy formation moving towards him and glanced at the horse's neck. Its chestnut ears were flattened fiercely against its head, its neck, outstretched as if on an executioner's block, was pulsing rhythmically. Grigory straightened up in the saddle, drew air hungrily into his lungs, thrust his boots deep into the stirrups, and looked round. How many times had he seen behind him that thundering avalanche of men and horses and always his heart had contracted with fear of what was to come and an inexplicable feeling of savage, brutal animal excitement. Between the point when he gave the horse its head and that of reaching the enemy he experienced an instantaneous inner transformation. In that one terrible instant reason, cool-headedness, and calculation deserted Grigory and his will was guided powerfully and indivisibly by brute instinct alone. And yet, could anyone have observed Grigory from the side during a charge, he would surely have concluded that his actions were guided by a cool and imperturbable mind. So confident, practised and calculated was the impression they produced.

The distance between the two sides was shrinking mercifully fast. The figures of riders and horses grew larger. The short stretch of scrubby snow-sprinkled village common between the two masses of cavalry disappeared under the horses' hooves. Grigory noticed one rider galloping about three lengths ahead of his squadron. The big dark bay horse under him was bounding along with short wolf-like strides. The rider was brandishing an officer's sabre and the silver sheath was flapping against his stirrup, glittering fierily in the sun. A second later Grigory recognised him. It was Pyotr Semiglazov, a Communist from among the non-Cossack population of Karginskaya. In 1917 he had been the first to return from the German war. Then a lad of twenty-four, wearing a kind of leg wrappings no one had ever seen, he brought back with him Bolshevik convictions and all the drive and assurance he had learned at the front. And a Bolshevik he had remained. He had served in the Red Army and before the rebellion had come from his unit to set up Soviet rule in his home district. This was the man who was galloping towards Grigory, riding his horse with picturesque assurance and waving an officer's sabre, confiscated during a search and of no use for anything but parades.

Grigory bared his clenched teeth and, as he lifted the reins a little, the horse obediently put on speed.

Grigory had a trick of his own that he used in the attack when he saw or sensed the approach of a powerful adversary or when he wanted to make certain of a kill at one stroke. In childhood Grigory had been left-handed. He would pick up a spoon with his left hand and even make the sign of the cross with it. His father had tried to knock the habit out of him and his playmates had nicknamed him 'Lefty Grishka'. The beatings and scoldings had their effect. At the age of ten he lost both his nickname and the habit of substituting left hand for right. But he could still do with his left everything that he could do with his right hand. And his left was actually the stronger of the two. In attack Grigory used this advantage with unfailing success. He steered his horse at his chosen adversary like everyone else, approaching on the left to slash with the right; the man who was about to clash with Grigory did the same. But when there were only about ten lengths to go and his adversary was already leaning over with his sabre raised to strike, Grigory would swerve sharply but smoothly and come in from the right, tossing his sabre into his left hand. His disconcerted opponent would change position but it was difficult to lunge from right to left, over the horse's head, and as he felt death breathing in his face he would lose his nerve. Then came the terrible slashing stroke that Grigory delivered with all the strength of his left arm.

Much time had passed since 'curly' Uryupin had taught Grigory the 'Baklanov' stroke. In the course of two wars Grigory had got his hand in. There was more in swordsmanship than in following the plough and he had learned a great deal about the technique of using a sabre.

He never put his wrist through the sword-knot, so that he was always free to toss the sabre instantly from one hand to the other. He knew that if his sabre was at the wrong angle, a powerful blow would tear it out of his hand or even dislocate his wrist. And another trick he knew, which few could master, was that of suddenly knocking an opponent's weapon out of his hand or paralysing his arm with a quick light prick. Well versed was Grigory in the art of killing his fellow creatures with cold steel.

When willow rods are trimmed, a fierce slash sends the severed twig to the ground without even shaking the trestle. Its sharp end plunges softly into the sand beside the rod from which it was cut by the Cossack sabre. And thus did the handsome, Kalmyk-looking Semiglazov fall from his rearing horse. Sliding quietly from the saddle, his hands clasped to his diagonally slashed chest, his body already wrapped in the chill of death...

At the same moment Grigory straightened up and rose in his stirrups. Another attacker was coming at him blindly, unable to rein in his horse. Grigory could not see the rider behind the horse's upflung, foaming head, but he could see the curving descent of the sabre, its dark blade. With all his might Grigory dragged on the reins and parried the blow, then, holding the reins in his right hand, slashed at the red clean-shaven neck bowed before him.

He was the first to gallop out of the milling mob. Before his eyes there was nothing but a swarm of horsemen. His hand was itching with a nervous quiver. He drove the sabre into its sheath, snatched out his pistol, and sent his horse back towards the village at full gallop. The Cossacks broke away and flocked after him. Here and there a Cossack cap or busby with a white ribbon was to be seen drooping over a horse's neck. A sergeant Grigory knew was galloping beside him in a fox-fur cap and cloth riding coat. His ear and cheek had been slashed to the chin. His chest looked as if a basket of ripe cherries had been squashed against it. His teeth were bared in a slobbering red snarl.

The Red cavalry, which had faltered and were about to retire, turned their horses. The Cossack retreat had spurred them to pursuit. One of Grigory's Cossacks who had fallen behind was swept off his horse as if by the wind and trampled into the snow. The village loomed into view with the black clusters of its orchards, the shrine on the outskirts, and the broad road leading through it. It was not more than two hundred paces to the fence where the squadron lay in ambush. The horses' backs were wet with foam and blood. Grigory, who had been firing furiously over his shoulder, thrust the jammed pistol into its holster, and shouted fiercely, 'Divide!'

The flood of Cossack squadrons broke smoothly into two streams, like a river thrusting against a cliff, and exposed the Red cavalry riding in pursuit. The squadron in ambush behind the fence fired a volley, then another, then a third... There was a scream as a horse and its rider somersaulted. Another horse buckled at the knees and its muzzle ploughed into the snow. Three or four other Red Army men were snatched out of the saddle by bullets. While the rest tried to turn at full gallop, the ambushers emptied their rifles once again and then stopped firing. Grigory had only time to bawl in a cracked voice, 'Squadrons!..' as thousands of hooves churned the snow and swung round to pursue the pursuers. But the Cossacks responded half-heartedly; their horses were tired, and after about a verst and a half they turned back. They stripped the dead Red cavalrymen and unsaddled their dead horses. One-armed Alexei Shamil finished off three wounded. He stood them with their faces to the fence and cut them down one by one. For some time afterwards the Cossacks crowded round the spot, smoking and examining the bodies. All three bore the same mark: the trunk cleft diagonally from collar bone to waist.

'I've made six out of three,' Alexei boasted, with a wink and twitch of his cheek.

The other Cossacks fawningly treated him to tobacco and gazed with unconcealed respect at Alexei's fist, which was not very big, about the size of a wild pumpkin, and his stove-door chest bulging under his uniform coat.

The sweating horses stood beside the fences shivering under the men's greatcoats. The Cossacks tightened their saddle girths and queued up for water at the well in the lane. Many led their weary, stumbling mounts by their halters.

Grigory rode on ahead with Prokhor and five other Cossacks. It was as if a blindfold had been taken from his eyes. Again, as before the charge, he saw the sun shining upon the world, the snow melting round the straw ricks, heard the chirping of the village sparrows, and felt the subtle scents of awakening spring. Life returned to him in no way faded or aged by the recent bloodshed, but even more alluring with its meagre, deceptive joys. Against the blackness of the thawed earth a surviving patch of snow always looks brighter and more beguiling.

XXXVIII

The uprising swelled and spread like the waters of the spring thaw, flooding all Donside and the surrounding steppes for four hundred versts. 25,000 Cossacks took to horse. The villages of the Upper Don district alone, mustered 10,000 foot soldiers.

The conflict was assuming unprecedented proportions. The Don Army was holding a line somewhere near the Donets, covering Novocherkassk and preparing for the decisive clash. And in the rear of the 8th and 9th Red armies ranged against it there raged a rebellion that made infinitely more complex the already difficult task of securing the Don.

In April the Revolutionary Military Council of the Soviet Republic was clearly faced with the threat of a link-up between the insurgents and the Whiteguard armies. The revolt had to be suppressed at all costs, before it eroded the Red front from the rear and broke through to link up with the Don Army. The best troops available were sent in for this purpose. The expeditionary force was stiffened with sailors from the Baltic and Black Sea fleets, the most reliable regiments, the crews of armoured trains and the most daring cavalry units. Five regiments of the militant Boguchar Division were withdrawn from the front. Altogether they fielded eight thousand bayonets, several batteries and five hundred machine-guns. In April the Ryazan and Tambov military schools were already fighting with unstinting courage on the Kazanskaya sector; later a unit from the Kremlin military school arrived, and at Shumilinskaya the insurgents were engaged by units of the Latvian Red infantry.

The Cossacks were desperately short of arms. At first there were not enough rifles, and ammunition was running out. They could only be obtained at the cost of blood, by cavalry charges or nocturnal raids. But obtained they were. By April the insurgents had a full quota of rifles, six batteries and about a hundred and fifty machine-guns.

At the beginning of the revolt there were five million empty cartridge cases at the armoury in Vyoshenskaya. The insurgents' District Soviet mobilised the best blacksmiths, locksmiths and armourers and a workshop for casting bullets was set up. But lead was in short supply and there was nothing to make bullets with. The District Soviet then appealed to all villages to make a collection of lead and copper. All stocks of these metals were taken from the steam mills. Messengers were sent out to the villages with the following brief appeal:

Your husbands, sons and brothers have nothing to shoot with. Their only ammunition is what they can capture from the accursed enemy. Contribute everything you have on your farms that can be used for making bullets. Take off the lead screens from your winnowing machines.

Within a week there was not a screen left on any winnowing machine in the district.

'Your husbands, sons and brothers have nothing to shoot with...' And the women took everything, useful or useless, to the village Soviets; the children in the villages where fighting had taken place dug canister shot out of the walls and scoured the earth for shell splinters. But even on this point there was not always unanimity. Some of the women of the poorer families who had refused to give up their last kitchen utensils, were arrested and sent to district headquarters for showing 'sympathy for the Reds'. In Tatarsky the old men from among the well-to-do administered a savage beating to Anvil Semyon, when he came home on leave from his unit and let fall just one careless remark, 'Let the rich break up their winnowers. I bet they're more afraid of the Reds than being ruined.'

The lead was melted down in the Vyoshenskaya workshop, but the bullets that were made from it without a coating of nickel also melted. The home-made bullet came out of the barrel as a lump of molten lead and made a frightening sizzling noise but was effective at no more than two hundred or two hundred and fifty paces. On the other hand, the wounds inflicted by such bullets were terrible. When the Red Army men found out about them, their patrols would ride up close to those of the Cossacks and shout, 'Firing beatles instead of bullets, are you! Give in! We'll wipe you out anyway!'

The thirty-five thousand rebels were divided into five divisions and one brigade, known as the 6th Separate Brigade. The 3rd Division, under Yegorov, was in action on the Meshkovskaya-Setrakov-Vezhe sector. The 4th Division was manning the Kazanskaya-Donetskoye-Shumilinskaya sector under the command of Kondrat Medvedev, a sullen-looking Junior Cornet, who was a terror in battle. The 5th Division was fighting on the Slashchovskaya-Bukanovskaya sector and was commanded by Ushakov. Sergeant-major Merkulov and his 2nd Division were in action on a line running through the Yelanskaya villages, Ust-Khopyor and Gorbatov, where the 6th Separate Brigade was also fighting. The latter was a close-knit unit, which had sustained scarcely any losses because it was commanded by Junior Cornet Bogatiryov, a Maksayevskaya Cossack. Bogatiryov was cautious and shrewd, never took any risks and wasted none of his men. The 1st Division was spread out along the River Chir and commanded by Grigory Melekhov. His was a key sector and came under attack from the south by the Red units that had been transferred from the main front, but he managed not only to repulse their onslaughts but also to help the less reliable 2nd Division with his infantry and squadrons of cavalry.

The rebellion had not succeeded in spreading to the Khopyor and Ust-Medveditskaya districts. They, too, were in a state of ferment and messengers arrived with appeals that forces should be sent to the Buzuluk and the upper reaches of the Khopyor, but the insurgent command dared not venture beyond the boundaries of the Upper Don district, knowing that the great majority of the Khopyor Cossacks supported the Soviet Government and would not take up arms. Even the messengers made no promise of success and said outright that there were not so many Cossacks in the villages who had a grudge against the Reds, that the officers who had remained in the remote corners of the Khopyor district were in hiding and could not rally enough forces to support the rebellion because the frontline men were either at home or with Mironov's Reds and the old men had been told where to go and now had none of their former power and influence.

In the south, in the areas settled by Ukrainians the Reds were mobilising the young men, who joined the regiments of the militant Boguchar Division and were only too glad to fight the rebels. The rebellion was thus confined to the borders of the Upper Don District. And it was becoming increasingly clear to everyone, including the insurgent command, that their homes could not be defended for long. Sooner or later the Red Army would swing round from the Donets and crush them.

On March 18th Grigory Melekhov was summoned by Kudinov to a conference in Vyoshenskaya. Grigory handed over his division to his second-in-command Ryabchikov and set out early in the morning with his orderly for district headquarters.

He arrived there just at the moment when Kudinov, in Safonov's presence, was talking to a messenger from Alexeyevskaya. Kudinov was sitting hunched at his desk, twisting the end of his Caucasian belt in his lean brown fingers. He questioned the Cossack seated opposite him without raising his eyes, which were puffy and inflamed from lack of sleep.

'What about yourselves? What do you think about it?'

'We'd join you, o'course... But on our own it's a bit awkward... How can you tell what the others might do. The folk up there, you know what they're like? They're scared. They're mighty keen really, but they're scared all the same...'

' "Mighty keen"! "Scared"!' Kudinov shouted, turning pale with anger, and squirmed in his chair as if someone had thrown hot coals on the seat. 'You're like a lot of blushing virgins. You would and you wouldn't and Mummy says you mustn't. Go back to your village and tell your old men we won't send you as much as a platoon till you start something yourselves. The Reds can hang every one of you for all I care!'

The big Cossack's purple hand eased the round sparkling fox-fur cap on to the back of his head. Sweat streamed down the creases in his forehead like spring torrents, and his whitish eyelashes blinked rapidly, but his eyes were smiling and apologetic.

'O'course, there's not a cat in hell's chance of your coming our way. We've got to spark it off. But it's that there spark that takes so much striking.'

Grigory, who had been listening attentively to this exchange, stepped aside to make way for a shortish black-moustached individual in a short sheepskin, who had come in from the corridor without knocking. He greeted Kudinov with a nod, and sat down at the desk, resting his cheek on a white hand. Grigory, who knew all the staff officers by sight, had never seen him before and watched him closely. The finely chiseled face, brown but not weatherbeaten, the soft whiteness of the hands, the good manners, all clearly indicated that he was not a person of local origin.

With his eyes on the stranger, Kudinov addressed Grigory.

'Let me introduce you, Melekhov. This is Comrade Georgidze. He...' And he broke off, toyed with the nielloed silverwork on his belt, and said, rising and addressing the messenger from Alexeyevskaya, 'Well, off you go, Cossack. We have business on hand. Go home and tell the right people what I said.'

The Cossack rose from his chair. The fiery red fox-fur cap with its black top-hair almost reached the ceiling. His burly shoulders blocked out so much light that the room at once seemed small and cramped.

'Did you come for help?' Grigory asked, still unpleasantly aware of the feel of the Caucasian's handshake.

'That's it! For help. But you see how it works out...' The Cossack turned gladly to Grigory, seeking support with his eyes. His ruddy face, which matched his cap, was so dismayed and the sweat was running down it so abundantly that even his beard and drooping ginger moustache were beaded.

'So you don't fancy Soviet power either?' Grigory went on, pretending not to notice Kudinov's impatient gestures.

'It wouldn't be so bad, chum,' the big Cossack boomed reasonably. 'Only we're worried it might get worse.'

'Have there been any shootings up your way?'

'No, God forbid! I've not heard of that. In a word, as you might say, they took our horses and some grain and, o'course, they arrested the ones who spoke up agin' that. In a word, we're scared.'

'And if the Vyoshenskaya men came, would you rise up? Would you all rise up?'

The Cossack's small, sun-gilded eyes darted cunningly away from Grigory's, and the fox-fur cap slipped down over the creases and bumps in the thoughtful brow.

'How can I speak for all?.. Well, the good farmers, the ones who care about property would have a go.'

'What about the poor ones, the ones who don't care?'

Grigory, who had vainly tried to catch the Cossack's eye, now encountered a direct stare of childlike astonishment.

'Huh!... The lazy lot? Why the devil should they back

us? With this government they'll have the time of their lives!'

'Then what are you here for, you great blockhead!' Kudinov shouted, no longer bothering to hide his irritation, and the chair under him gave a mournful creak. 'Why did you come egging us on? Or are they all rich in your village? What sort of uprising will it be if only two or three households take part? Get to hell out of here! The hot cockerel hasn't pecked you in the arse yet, but when it does, you'll start fighting without any help from us! You, sons-of-bitches, have got used to ploughing a quiet furrow while other people bear the brunt! All you care about is your own comfort. Go on, get out! It makes me sick to look at you!'

Grigory frowned and turned away. Red blotches were appearing on Kudinov's cheeks. Georgidze twirled his moustache and the nostrils of his hooked nose quivered.

'Well, beg pardon then, if that's how it is. And you, Your Honour, you needn't try to bully me, we're all in this voluntary like. I've passed on to you the request from our elders and I'm taking your answer back to 'em, but there's no cause for you to bawl at me! How much longer will they go on bawling at us, true Christians? The Whites did it, the Reds did it, and now you're bawling too. Everyone wants to show his power and give you a rough ride besides. Ay, it's a stinking rotten life on the land these days, like being licked by a dirty bitch!'

The Cossack clamped his big fur cap furiously on his head, heaved himself out into the corridor, and closed the door quietly behind him; but in the corridor he gave free rein to his anger and slammed the front door so hard that plaster sprinkled down on to the floor and windowsills for the next five minutes.

'That's what people are like nowadays!' Kudinov declared with a smile, toying with his belt and growing more cheerful every minute. 'Back in the spring of 'seventeen I was driving to the station and it was ploughing time, round about Easter. And there were our free Cossacks ploughing away and they'd got so dizzy with this new-found freedom of theirs they were even ploughing up the roads—as if they hadn't got enough land already! Beyond Tokin village I called over one of these ploughmen and he came up to the carriage. "Here, you so-and-so, what have you ploughed up the road for?" That scared him all right. "I won't do it any more," he says, "I'm very sorry, I can stamp it flat again if you like." And I scared two or three more in the same way. But when we left Grachov, the road was ploughed up again and there was another of these bumpkins with his plough. "Hi you! Come over here!" I shouted. So up he comes. "What right have you got to plough up the road?" And what a look he gave me! Handsome Cossack he was, with very bright, clear eyes. He turns round without a word and trots back to his oxen. When he gets there, he pulls the iron bolt out of their yoke and back he comes to me, at the double, grabs the mudguard and climbs on to the step. "Who are you?" he says. "And how much longer are you going to suck our blood? D'you want me," he says, "to bust your head to bits?" And he makes a swing at me with his bolt. "Certainly not, Ivan, I was only joking!" I says. "And I'm not Ivan to you any more, but Ivan Osipich, and I'm going to smash your face in for your rudeness!" And believe it or not, I only just managed to get away from him. And that one's the same. He snivelled and bowed, but in the end he showed his real feelings. The people's pride has been awakened.'

'Not pride but the lout in them, that's what has awakened and is coming out. Loutishness has been legitimised,' the Caucasian officer said calmly, with a slight accent and, before anyone could object, put an end to further discussion. 'Kindly let us begin our conference. I should like to get back to my regiment today.'

Kudinov banged on the wall and shouted for Safonov, then turned to Grigory. 'You stay here, we'll all talk this over together. You know the saying, "Two heads are even worse than one"? To our great good fortune, Comrade Georgidze stayed behind in Vyoshenskaya, and now he's helping us out. He's a lieutenant-colonel and a graduate of the General Staff academy.'

'How was it you stayed in Vyoshenskaya?' Grigory asked, for some reason inwardly chilled and on his guard.

'I went down with typhus and was left behind in the village of Dudarevsky when the retreat from the Northern Front began.'

'What unit were you in?'

'No, I'm not an officer of the line. I was with the staff of a special group.'

'What group? General Sitnikov's?'

'No.'

Grigory was about to ask something else, but the

expression on the lieutenant-colonel's face, a kind of tense alertness, restrained him from further questioning, and he broke off.

Presently they were joined by Safonov, the chief of staff, Kondrat Medvedev, the commander of the 4th Division, and Grigory Bogatiryov, a ruddy-faced, white-toothed junior cornet, who was commanding the 6th Separate Brigade. The conference began. Kudinov informed the assembled commanders about the situation on the fronts. The lieutenant-colonel was the first to speak. He slowly spread out a large-scale map on the table and started talking in a smooth, self-assured way, with a slight accent.

'First of all, I regard it as absolutely necessary to transfer some of the reserve units of the 3rd and 4th divisions to the sector held by Melekhov's division and Junior Cornet Bogatiryov's special brigade. According to information of a secret nature that has come into our possession and from the interrogation of prisoners it is becoming quite clear that the Red command is preparing to hit us very hard on the Kamenka-Karginskaya-Bokovskaya sector. From what we have been told by deserters and prisoners it may be assumed that the command of the 9th Red Army has despatched from Oblivy and Morozovskaya two cavalry regiments taken from the 12th Division, and five security detachments with the three batteries and machine-gun platoons attached to them. At a rough estimate these reinforcements will give the enemy five and a half thousand men. They will thus have a clear numerical advantage, not to mention their superiority in armaments.'

Criss-crossed by the window frame, a sun as yellow as a sunflower, peered into the room from the south. A light-blue cloud of cigarette smoke hung motionless under the ceiling. The bitterish smell of homegrown tobacco mingled with the stench of sodden boots. Somewhere near the ceiling a fly, intoxicated by the smoke, was buzzing desperately. Grigory stared drowsily at the window. He had not slept for two nights running. His eyelids were lead heavy and sleep was invading his body along with the warmth of the overheated room. A drunken weariness was draining him of will and awareness. But outdoors the blustering spring winds were buffeting the window, the last snow was shining pinkly on the hill above Bazki, and crowns of the poplars on the other side of the Don were swaying so violently that at the sight of them Grigory imagined he could hear their deep unceasing roar.

But the lieutenant-colonel's clear and persistent voice captured his attention. He made an effort to listen and the mussiness seemed to melt away.

'...The slackening of enemy activity on the 1st Division's front and their persistent attempts to take the offensive on the Migulinskaya-Meshkovskaya line have put us on our guard. I believe...' the lieutenant-colonel coughed as the word 'comrades' stuck in his throat and, with an angry sweep of that womanishly white, almost transparent hand, raised his voice, 'that your commander Kudinov with Safonov's support is making a great mistake in taking the Reds' manoeuvres at their face value and weakening the sector held by Melekhov. Forgive me, gentlemen, but it's only elementary strategy to induce the enemy to remove some of his forces when one is preparing to strike...'

'But Melekhov doesn't need a reserve regiment,' Kudinov interrupted.

'On the contrary! We must keep some of the reserves of the 3rd Division in readiness, so that we shall have enough to block any breakthrough.'

'It looks as if Kudinov doesn't want to ask me whether I'll give him my reserves or not,' Grigory burst out angrily. 'I won't give him any! Not a single squadron!'

'Come off it, chum, that's...' Safonov drawled, smiling and smoothing down the yellowish fringe of his moustache.

'Don't "chum" me! I won't give any, that's all there is to it!'

'From the operational point of view...'

'Don't talk to me about operational points of view. I'm responsible for my sector and my men.'

The unexpected argument was cut short by Lieutenant-Colonel Georgidze. The red pencil in his hand traced a dotted line round the threatened sector and, when all heads bent over the map, everyone saw clearly enough that the thrust the Red command was preparing could only be delivered at the southern sector, the nearest to the Donets and with better communications.

The conference ended an hour later. The sullen-faced Kondrat Medvedev, wolf-like in his appearance and his ways, who was almost illiterate and had kept silent all through the conference, ended up by saying with a scowl at everyone, 'We'll give Melekhov a hand if it comes to

231

that. We've got more men than we need. But there's an idea in the back of my mind that's got me worried, drat it! What if they start closing in on us from all sides--what do we do then? They'll scrape us up into a heap and we'll be marooned like snakes in the spring floods.'

'Snakes can swim but there'll be nowhere for us to swim to!' Bogatiryov chuckled.

'We've considered that,' Kudinov responded thoughtfully. 'Well, if we're in a tight spot, we'll leave behind anyone who can't carry arms, abandon our families and fight our way through to the Donets. We're quite a force, thirty thousand of us.'

'But will the Cadets take us? They've got a grudge against the Cossacks from the Upper Don.'

'Counting your chickens before... What's the use of talking about it!' Grigory pulled on his cap and went out into the corridor. Through the door he heard the rustle of the map being folded and Georgidze's voice saying, 'The Vyoshenskaya Cossacks, and all the insurgents in general, will redeem their guilt in the eyes of the Don and Russia if they go on fighting bravely against the Bolsheviks...'

'He talks like that but he's laughing up his sleeve, the snake!' Grigory thought as he strained to catch the officer's tone of voice. And once again, as before, when he had unexpectedly met this officer in Vyoshenskaya, Grigory felt a mixture of alarm and inexplicable anger.

At the gate he was overtaken by Kudinov. For a time they walked on in silence. The wind was rippling the puddles on the dung-strewn square. Evening was approaching. White clouds, round and heavy, were gliding across the sky like swans. The damp smell of thawed earth was refreshing and fragrant. The grass, now free of snow, was sprouting greenly by the fences and the exciting rustle of the poplars could indeed be heard in the wind from across the Don.

'The Don will be breaking up soon,' Kudinov said, coughing.

'Yes, it will.'

'What the hell... We'll be done for without something to smoke. A glass of home-grown costs forty Kerensky roubles.

'Now you tell me this,' Grigory asked abruptly, turning in his stride. 'That Caucasian officer, what's he doing here?'

'Georgidze? He's the chief of the operations department. He's a brainy devil! He works out the plans. He's a jump ahead of all of us on strategy.'

'Is he permanent in Vyoshenskaya?'

'No... We got him transferred. Officially he's attached to the support section of Chernov's regiment.'

'How does he know what's going on then?'

'Well, you see, he often visits us. Nearly every day.'

'Why don't you keep him here?' Grigory asked, trying to get to the bottom of the matter.

Kudinov answered unwillingly, coughing and covering his mouth with his hand.

'It's a bit awkward in front of the Cossacks. You know what they're like? They'll say the officers are taking over and forcing their line on us, the old days are back, and all that.'

'Any more like him in our forces?'

'There's two in Kazanskaya, or mebbe three... Now don't start griping, Grisha, I can see what you're driving at. We've no one else to turn to except the Cadets, lad. Isn't that so? Or d'you reckon to organise a republic out of ten stanitsas? It's no good splitting hairs... We'll get together and go to Krasnov and ask for pardon. Don't be too hard on us, we'll say, we made a bit of a mistake when we abandoned the front.'

'A mistake?' Grigory repeated questioningly.

'Well, didn't we?' Kudinov replied in sincere surprise as he stepped carefully round a puddle.

'But I've got another idea...' Grigory's face darkened and he forced himself to smile. 'I reckon we made a mistake when we started the uprising... You heard what that man from the Khopyor said, didn't you?'

Kudinov glanced at him searchingly and made no reply.

At the crossroads on the other side of the square they parted company. Kudinov set off past the school to his billet. Grigory returned to headquarters and signed to an orderly to bring the horses. In the saddle, as he slowly gathered up the reins and straightened the shoulder strap under the sling of his rifle, he was still trying to account for the strange feeling of dislike and distrust he had conceived for the lieutenant-colonel who had turned up at headquarters. And suddenly, with a sense of horror, he thought, 'What if the Cadets purposely left these trained officers on our territory, to stir us to rebel in the Reds' rear and then run things in their own way, the way they've been trained in their military academies?' And with gleeful readiness his mind suggested further surmises and arguments. 'He didn't say what unit he was from ... he dodged that... Calls himself a staff officer, but there's no proper headquarters around here... What the hell brought him to Dudarevsky, to such an out-of-the-way place? That wasn't for nothing! We've landed ourselves in trouble, that we have.' And as his mind grappled with the truth, he thought huntedly, desperately, 'These clever people have got us tied up... The gentry have trapped us. They've put a hobbling thong on our life and they're making us do their dirty work for them. You can't trust anyone an inch.'

On the other side of the Don he put his horse into a brisk canter. Behind him, on a creaking saddle was his orderly, a valiant Cossack from the village of Olshansky. He was typical of the men Grigory chose to have around him, a man who would follow him anywhere, a veteran of the German war. A former reconnaissance scout, he kept silent all the way and even contrived to light himself a smoke with the aid of a flint and a large handful of pungent tinder primed with sunflower ash. As they rode down towards the village of Tokin he advised Grigory, 'If there's no hurry, let's put up for the night here. The horses are dead-beat, let 'em have a rest.'

They rode on and spent the night in Chukarin. After the frosty wind it was cosy and warm in the little hut with its two rooms joined by a porch. The earthen floor gave off a salty smell of calf and kid's urine, and from the stove came the fragrance of unleavened slightly burnt loaves, baked on cabbage leaves. Grigory replied reluctantly to the questions of the mistress of the house, an old Cossack woman, who had seen off her three sons and aged husband to take part in the uprising. She spoke in a deep voice, patronisingly stressing her superiority in age and, almost before Grigory could open his mouth, told him rather roughly, 'You may be the head man over our Cossack fools but you've no power over an old woman like me because you're young enough to be my son. Then be so kind, my young hawk, and talk to me. You sit there yawning as if you don't want to please a woman with your conversation. But you'd better! For this war of yours—a plague on it!—I've given up three sons and my old man, more's the pity. You may be in command of them, but I gave birth to those sons of mine, I fed them and looked after them, and carried them with me in my skirt to the melon patches and vegetable beds, where I worked. I went through a lot for their sakes.

There was nothing easy about that! So don't turn up your nose, don't show off, just you talk sense to me. Will they make peace soon?'

'Yes, pretty soon... You'd better go to bed, Mother!'

'Soon, you say! But how soon? Don't you send me off to bed, I'm the mistress here, not you. I've still to go out and tend to the goats and lambs. We bring 'em indoors for the night, they're not big enough yet to stay outside. Will you make peace by Easter?'

'We'll drive out the Reds and then we'll make peace.'

'Now just listen to that!' the old woman clasped the sharp corners of her withered knees with her overworked, rheumaticky fingers and sorrowfully munched her withered lips that were as dry and brown as cherry bark. 'What in the devil's name do you need to be fighting them for? You must have all got the rabies... It's all very well for you wretches to go around shooting off your guns and showing off on your horses, but what about the mothers? It's their sons that are being killed, isn't it? What's the sense of all your wars?'

'We're mothers' sons too, aren't we? Or d'you think we're sons of bitches?' Grigory's orderly, stung by the old woman's talk, grunted furiously. 'We're getting killed and you go on with your "showing off on your horses"! Sounds as if it's worse for the mothers than for the ones that get killed! You've lived all this time, you old curmudgeon, and you can talk like that... You go on and on, and you won't let a man sleep.'

'You'll get all the sleep you need, you snarler! What are you staring at? You've been lying low like a wolf, and now you're angry. Listen to him! He's made himself hoarse he's so cross.'

'She won't let us sleep, Grigory Panteleyevich!' the orderly croaked desperately and, as he lit his cigarette, struck the flint so hard that a shower of sparks flew from the iron.

While the tinder smouldered acridly and caught fire, the orderly had a final malicious dig at the garrulous old woman.

'You're as bitter as boot polish, woman! If your old man gets killed at the front, I reckon he'll be glad to die. "Thank the Lord," he'll say. "At last I'm free of my old biddy, may the earth be like swan's down for her!"'

'And may you get warts on your tongue, you unclean spirit!'

'Go to sleep, Granny, for Christ's sake. We haven't

slept for three nights. Go to sleep! People have died for such things without the sacrament.'

Grigory only just managed to make it up between them. As he dozed off he was pleasantly aware of the sour warmth of the sheepskin covering him and through his drowsiness heard the door bang and a steamy chill creep over his feet. Then a lamb bleated just by his ear. The little hooves of the young goats pattered on the floor and a fresh, joyful smell of hay, sheep's milk, frost and all the other odours of the cattle shed spread through the room.

Sleep left him at midnight. He lay with his eyes open. The embers glowed red under the whitish ash in the well covered lower grate of the stove. The lambs were hubbling together in the heat, by the stove guard. In the sweet midnight stillness he could hear the clicking of their small teeth and an occasional snort or sneeze. A full and very distant moon was looking in through the window. In the yellow square of light on the earthen floor a restless black kid kept jumping up and kicking. Pearly dust hung slantwise in the moonlight. The bluish-yellow light was almost as bright as day. A scrap of mirror embedded in the face of the stove sparkled and only the silvered mounting of the icon in the front corner reflected a dull dark gleam... Grigory's mind went back to thoughts of the conference in Vyoshenskaya, the messenger from the Khopyor and once again, at the memory of the lieutenant-colonel, with his refined manners and way of talking that were so alien to him, he felt a nagging anxiety. By this time the kid had perched itself on the sheepskin covering his stomach. It stared at him foolishly for a while twitching its ears, then, growing bolder, jumped once or twice and suddenly parted its curly legs. A thin jet pattered off the sheepskin and trickled on to the outstretched hand of Grigory's orderly, who was sleeping beside him. The orderly moaned and woke up, wiped his hand on his trouser leg and shook his head vexedly.

'It's pissed on me, the bastard... Shoo!' and with some relish gave the kid a flick on the forehead.

The kid gave a piercing little cry and jumped off the sheepskin, then came up and for a long time licked Grigory's hand with its tiny rough, warm tongue.

XXXIX

After their flight from Tatarsky Stokman, Koshevoi, Ivan Kotlyarov, and several other Cossacks who had served as militiamen, attached themselves to the 4th Trans-Amur Regiment. At the beginning of 1918 during its march back from the German front the whole regiment had merged with a detachment of the Red Army and after a year and a half's fighting on the fronts of the Civil War still retained its hard-core personnel. The Trans-Amur men were splendidly equipped, their horses were well fed and trained, and the regiment was noted for its combat ability, high morale, and dashing cavalry skill.

In the early days of the rebellion the Trans-Amur men with only the support of the 1st Moscow Infantry Regiment had held up the insurgents' drive on Ust-Medveditskaya. When reinforcements arrived, the regiment, instead of scattering its forces, had gained a firm hold on the sector from Ust-Khopyorskaya along the River Krivaya.

At the end of March the insurgents forced the Red units out of the Yelanskaya district and captured some of the villages in the Ust-Khopyorskaya area. A stalemate developed that kept the front immobile for nearly two months. Covering Ust-Khopyorskaya in the west, a battalion of the 1st Moscow Regiment, supported by a battery, was holding the village of Krutovsky, which stood high above the Don. From the steep spur of the Donside hills south of the village the Red battery concealed in a field threshing barn, launched daily bombardments of rebel groups that had assembled on the right-bank hills and gave covering fire to the Moscow Regiment's infantry, then it would transfer its fire to the village of Yelansky on the other side of the Don. Puffs of smoke from bursting shrapnel shells melted high and low over the clustered farmsteads. Mortar bombs landed either in the village, sending the panic-stricken cattle stampeding through fences and making villagers bend double as they ran for cover, or on the deserted sandy ridges beyond the Old Believer cemetery by the windmills, where they raised spouts of chunky, still frozen earth.

On March 15th Stokman, Mishka and Ivan drove out of the village of Chebotaryov in the direction of Ust-Khopyorskaya. They had heard that a company of Communists and Soviet functionaries who had fled from the rebel areas was being organised there. Their driver was a

Cossack Old Believer with such a childishly pink complexion that even Stokman felt his lips twitch into a smile as he looked at him. Despite his youth the Cossack had a thick curly golden beard, in which his fresh rosy mouth showed up like a slice of water melon; the golden fluff curled up under his eyes and either this beard or the full-blooded colouring of his face made them look very blue.

Mishka hummed songs to himself all the way. Ivan sat in the back of the wagon with his rifle across his knees, hunching his shoulders glumly, and Stokman struck up a conversation with the driver almost out of nothing.

'Your health gives you no cause for complaint, comrade, I should say?' he asked.

The lusty young adherent of the Old Faith threw open his short sheepskin coat and smiled warmly.

"No, God has spared me my sins so far. Why should I be unhealthy? We've never smoked from time immemorial, we drink only natural vodka and eat only wheat bread. Where could any illness come from?'

'Have you served in the army?'

'Ay, for a bit. The Cadets got hold of me.'

'Why didn't you go with them across the Donets?'

'You've a strange way of talking, comrade!' The Cossack dropped the horse-hair reins, took off his gauntlet and wiped his mouth, frowning offendedly. 'Why should I go there? To look for new songs? I wouldn't have served with the Cadets either if they hadn't forced me. Your government is just, only there's a few things you don't do right.'

'What exactly?'

Stokman rolled a cigarette, lighted up and waited for the answer.

'Why d'you burn that poison?' the Cossack said, turning his face away. 'Look how pure the air is all around and you foul your chest with that stinking smoke... I've no respect for that! And as for what you've been doing wrong—well, I'll tell you. You've come down too hard on the Cossacks and spoiled it all, otherwise your power would have lasted for ever. You've got too many crazy fellows on your side, that's why there was an uprising.'

'Spoiled it all? You mean we've done a lot of foolish things? What things?'

'You must know that... You've been shooting people. First one, then another... Who's going to wait for his turn to come up? Even a bull shakes its head when it's

being led to the slaughter. Look what happened in Bukanovskaya, for instance... There it is over there—see the
church? Where I'm pointing with my whip, see it?.. Well,
this is what folk say. A commissar, name of Malkin, is
stationed there with his detachment. And is he treating
the people there justly? Now I'll tell you. He rounds
up the old men from the villages, marches them off into
the bushes, tortures them, puts them to death, strips
them naked and won't even let their families come and
bury them. And what landed 'em in this trouble was
that they had at one time been elected honorary judges.
But d'you know what kind of judges they were? Some
of 'em could hardly write their names and others either
dipped their fingers in the ink or put a cross. Old men
like them are only in court for appearance's sake. Their
only merit is their long beards and they're so old they
forget to button up their flies. What can you expect of
them? They're like little children. But this Malkin, he
goes about disposing of other people's lives like God
Almighty, and one day an old man called Linyok—
that was his nickname—was crossing the square with a
bridle over his shoulder to go to his threshing floor and
fetch his mare. And just for a joke some of the kids say,
"Malkin wants to see you." Well, Linyok made his he-
retical sign of the cross—they're all of the new faith
there, and even took off his cap while he was still on the
square. In a real tizzy he was when he came in. "Did you
want to see me?" he says. And this Malkin, he guffaws
till he has to hold his sides. "Aha," he says, "so you're
asking for it. No one summoned you but we might as
well have you now you've come. Take him, comrades.
Third category for him!" So, of course, they grabbed him
and marched him out into the bushes. His old woman
waited and waited, but he never came back. He'd just
disappeared, had Grandad. Gone off to heaven with his
bridle. And another old man, Mitrofan, from Andreya-
novsky village, ran into Malkin in the street and gets
called in. "Where're you from? What's your name?"
he asks with a big laugh. "What a beard you've grown,
like a fox's tail! You look just like St. Nicholas with that
beard. We'll make soap out of you, you fat hog! Third
category for him." And that old fellow, unluckily for
him, did have a beard like a besom. So they shot him
just for growing himself a fine beard and happening to
meet Malkin at the wrong moment. Isn't that an outrage
against the people?'

Mishka had stopped singing when the story began, and at the end of it he snapped angrily, 'You're not much good at telling lies, feller!'

'Tell a better one, then! Before you call it a lie, you ought to find out first. Then you can talk!'

'But do you know this for a fact?'

'That's what folk say.'

'Folk! Folk will say you can milk a hen, but it hasn't got any teats. You've listened to a pack of lies and now you gossip like a woman!'

'Those old men wouldn't harm a fly.'

'Wouldn't harm a fly! That's what you say!' Mishka mimicked him bitterly. 'It was those harmless old men of yours, I reckon, that stirred up this revolt. Mebbe those honorary judges had machine-guns buried in their yards, and you say it was for their beards or just for a joke they got shot... Why didn't they shoot you for your beard? It's as big as an old he-goat's.'

'I'm only telling you what I heard. I'll be plagued if I know. Mebbe somebody made it up and they did do something against the government...' the Old Believer muttered in some confusion.

He jumped off the driver's seat and for a long time squelched along in the melting snow, his feet sliding about in the bluish, yielding mush. The sun shone tenderly over the steppe. The light-blue sky encompassed the distant hills and passes in its mighty embrace. The fragrant breath of approaching spring could be felt in the faint stirrings of the wind. In the east, beyond the whitish zigzag of the Donside ridges the jutting summit of the hill above Ust-Medveditskaya loomed faintly through a lilac haze. The distant horizon was shrouded in a huge undulating canopy of fluffy white clouds.

The driver jumped back on to the sledge and his face looked coarser as he turned to Stokman and spoke again.

'My grandfather is still alive, he'll be a hundred and eight this year. He told me, and his grandfather told him that he could remember the day—that is, his grandfather could—when Tsar Peter sent a prince—what did they call him—Long Arm or Strong Arm—to our upper part of the Don. And this prince came from Voronezh with his soldiers and sacked the Cossack settlements here because they wouldn't accept Nikon's rotten faith and obey the tsar. The soldiers rounded up the Cossacks, cut off their noses, hanged some of 'em and floated the gallows down the Don on rafts.'

'What are you driving at?' Mishka asked on a stern note of caution.

'What I'm driving at is this. His name may have been Long Arm, but the tsar never gave him any such rights. And this commissar in Bukanovskaya, for example, went about it like this. "I'll de-Cossack you, you bastards, so you won't forget it for the rest of your life!" That's how he carried on in front of everyone at Bukanovskaya. But had the Soviet government given him such rights? That's the question! There couldn't be any mandate for such action, for such wholesale slaughter. The Cossacks are not all the same, you know.'

The skin on Stokman's cheeks had bunched up lumpily.

'Well, I've listened to what you had to say, now you listen to me.'

'I may have got something wrong, of course, in my foolishness. If so, I beg pardon.'

'Wait a minute... Now listen. What you've been telling us about this commissar doesn't sound like the truth. I'll check up on that. But if it is, if he did ill-treat the Cossacks and play the tyrant, we won't forgive him.'

'I wonder!'

'No need to wonder, it's a fact! When the front was running through your village, didn't the Red Army men shoot one of their own soldiers for robbing a Cossack woman? I was told about that in your village.'

'That's right! He had a go at Perfilovna's chest. That's true. Ay, of course, that was strict. You're right there— they shot him behind the threshing barns. Afterwards we had a long argument about where he ought to be buried. Some said in the graveyard, but others said it would defile the spot. So they dug a hole for him right there, by the threshing floor.'

'So such a thing did happen?' Stokman flicked his cigarette impatiently.

'Ay, I won't deny that,' the Cossack agreed readily.

'Then why d'you think we won't punish a commissar if we find him guilty?'

'My good comrade! You mayn't have anyone with authority over him. After all, he's not just a soldier, he's a commissar.'

'That only makes it worse! Don't you see? The Soviet government takes reprisals only against its enemies and any representative of the Soviets that treats the working population unjustly must be severely punished.'

241

The stillness of the March noon, disturbed only by the hiss of sledge runners and the squelching of hooves, was shattered by a great rumble of gunfire. The first shot was followed at regular intervals by three others as the battery at Krutovsky resumed its shelling of the left bank.

The conversation on the sledge broke off. The crashing chords of gunfire destroyed the pale enchantment of the steppe, which approaching spring had wrapped in a drowsy languor. Even the horses quickened their pace, picking up their feet as if they were weightless and briskly twitching their ears.

They drove out on to the Hetman's highway and the broad expanse beyond the Don spread out before their eyes, a huge patchwork of thawed-out yellow sands, headlands and blue-grey islands of willow and alder.

In Ust-Khopyorskaya the Cossack drove the sledge up to the Revolutionary Committee building, next to which was the headquarters of the Moscow Regiment.

Stokman rummaged in his pocket, found a forty-rouble Kerensky note in his pouch and handed it to the driver. The Cossack's face broke into a delighted smile, revealing a row of yellowish teeth under his damp moustache, but he hesitated in embarrassment.

'God bless you, comrade! It wasn't worth all that!'

'Take it—for your horses' labour. And you need have no doubts about our government. Remember this: we're fighting for the power of the workers and peasants. You were tempted into rebelling by our enemies—the kulaks, atamans and officers. They're the ones behind the uprising. And if any of our people did mistreat a working Cossack who sympathised with us and was helping the revolution, the culprit could have been dealt with.'

'You know the saying, comrade: God's too high and the tsar's too far away... And it's still a long way to your tsar... The strong can't be fought nor the rich taken to court. And you're both strong and rich.' He smiled craftily. 'What a man you are! Giving me forty of the best! And the whole trip wasn't worth five at the most. Well, God bless you!'

'He slipped you the extra for your talk,' Mishka Koshevoi said grinning as he jumped off the sledge hitching up his trousers. 'And for your lovely beard. Don't you know who you were driving, you chuckle-headed chump? A Red general.'

'Oho!'

'Never mind the "ohos"! You're a fine lot! Tip you too little and you'll tell the world, "I gave some of them comrades a lift and they only paid me a fiver, the so-and-sos!" And you'll be grumbling the rest of the winter. Tip 'em too much and it's "Look how rich they are! Gave me forty roubles! They've got more money than they can count..." I wouldn't have given you a penny! And you could grumble your head off. You'll never be satisfied. Well, let's go... Goodbye, big beard!'

Even the gloomy-faced Ivan smiled at the end of Mishka's sally.

At that moment a Red Army cavalry scout rode out of the headquarters yard on a shaggy Siberian pony.

'Where's the sledge from?' he shouted, wheeling his mount on a tight rein.

'How does that concern you?' Stokman asked.

'There's some ammunition here to be taken to Krutovsky. Drive in!'

'No, comrade, we'll let this sledge go.'

'Who are you then?'

The Red Army man, a handsome young lad, rode down on them.

'We're from the Trans-Amur Regiment. Don't detain the sledge.'

'Ah, I see... All right then, he can go. Off you go, chum.'

XL

In the event it turned out that no company of irregulars was being organised in Ust-Khopyorskaya. One such company had been mustered, not in Ust-Khopyorskaya but in Bukanovskaya. The organiser was that very same commissar Malkin. He had been sent by the command of the 9th Red Army to the stanitsas on the lower reaches of the Khopyor that the Old Believer Cossack had talked about on the road. The irregulars, mostly local Communists and Soviet functionaries, with a sprinkling of Red Army men, made up a fairly impressive force, fielding some two hundred bayonets and several dozen sabres of the mounted reconnaissance attached to them. They were stationed temporarily in Bukanovskaya and with the help of a company of the

243

Moscow Regiment were holding up the insurgent forces that were trying to advance from the upper reaches of the rivers Yelanka and Zimovnaya.

After talking to the chief of staff, a gloomy and harassed former regular officer, and the political commissar, a worker from the Mikhelson factory in Moscow, Stokman decided to stay in Ust-Khopyorskaya and join the Moscow Regiment's 2nd Battalion. He had a long discussion with the political commissar in a clean little room stacked with resistance coils, spools of telephone wire and other bits of equipment.

'You see, comrade,' the stocky yellow-faced commissar, who had a rumbling appendix, told him, 'this is a tricky bit of machinery. My lads are mostly from Moscow and Ryazan with a few from Nizhny Novgorod. They're steady lads, most of 'em workers. But we had a squadron of Mironov's men here from his 14th Division and they were no good. We had to pack 'em off to Ust-Medveditskaya... You stay here, there's plenty of work to be done. We've got to talk to the local people, explain things to them. You know what the Cossacks are... Round here you've got to keep your ear to the ground.'

'Yes, I know all that as well as you do,' Stokman said, smiling at the commissar's patronising tone and looking at the yellowish whites of his suffering eyes. 'But you tell me this. What kind of a commissar is he that you have in Bukanovskaya?'

The commissar stroked the grey stubble of his clipped moustache and replied lethargically, only occasionally raising his bluish transparent eyelids.

'He did make things too hot for them over there at one time. He's a good lad but he hasn't much idea of the political situation. Still, you can't chop down a tree without making the chips fly, can you? At the moment he's evacuating the male Cossack population into the depths of Russia... Go and see the quartermaster, he'll put you down for rations,' he concluded, grimacing with pain and pressing his hand to his greasy wadded trousers.

The next morning the 2nd Battalion was tumbled out in response to an alert and the roll was called. In an hour it was marching towards the village of Krutovsky.

Stokman, Koshevoi and Ivan marched together in one rank.

From Krutovsky a cavalry patrol was sent to reconnoitre the other side of the Don, then the whole column crossed the river. There were puddles on the slushy dung-stained road. The river ice was honeycombed with faint bluish bubbles. They crossed the thawings along the bank by means of fences thrown down in the water. The battery on the hill behind them sent round after round into the poplar groves behind Yelansky. The battalion was to bypass the village, which the Cossacks had abandoned, advance in the direction of Yelanskaya stanitsa and, having linked up with a company of the 1st Battalion advancing from Bukanovskaya, capture the village of Antonov. The battalion commander's orders were to head for the village of Bezborodov. The mounted patrol soon reported that no enemy forces had been discovered at Bezborodov but that heavy rifle fire could be heard some four versts to the right of the village.

Shells flew high overhead with a grating roar and not far away the earth shuddered under the explosions. Behind the column the river ice burst with a loud crack. Ivan glanced round.

'The water must be rising.'

'It's daft crossing the Don at this time. It'll be breaking up any moment now,' Mishka grunted resentfully. He could not get used to being a foot soldier and marching in step.

Stokman looked at the backs of the men marching in front, their belts, the rhythmical swaying of their rifles and the damp bluish-grey bayonets fixed to them. When he looked round, he saw the men's serious and impassive faces, all of them so different and yet infinitely alike, the grey caps with their five-pointed red stars, the grey greatcoats, some yellowed with age, others that were newer, a prickly lightish grey, all swaying with the rhythm of the march; he heard the squelch and clump of their marching feet, the muffled talk, the discordant coughing, and the clank of their mess tins; and all the time he was aware of the pungent smells of sodden boots, coarse tobacco, and leather belts. With his eyes half closed, trying not to get out of step and feeling a great affection for all these men who had been utter strangers to him a few days ago, he thought, 'But why do I feel so fond of them, and so sorry for them right now? What is it that binds us? Well, there's the common idea... No, it's not just the idea, but the cause. And what else? Perhaps, the nearness of danger and death? Yes, somehow they're specially dear to me...' And a mocking light came into his eyes. 'Surely I'm not getting old?'

With an almost paternal feeling of satisfaction Stokman eyed the powerful back of the Red Army man in front of him, the fresh ruddy skin of the youthfully smooth neck between collar and cap, and then switched his glance to his neighbour. A dark clean-shaven face with firm blood-red cheeks, a fine, courageous mouth. Tall but well built, he was marching along scarcely swinging his free arm and frowning as if in pain, and at the corner of his eye there was a web of wrinkles. Stokman felt an urge to talk to him.

'Have you been in the army long, comrade?'

His neighbour's light-brown eyes gave him a cold, searching glance.

'Since 'eighteen,' came the tight-lipped reply.

But Stokman was not put off.

'Where are you from?'

'Looking for somebody from home, Dad?'

'I'd be glad to find one.'

'I'm a Muscovite.'

'Worker?'

'Uh-huh.'

Stokman glanced quickly at the man's hand. The ingrained traces of metal work were still there.

'Metalworker?'

And again the brown eyes scanned Stokman's face and his greying unkempt beard.

'Yes, a metal-turner. Were you in that too?' And a warmer light came into the stern brown eyes.

'I was a mechanic... Why are you always wincing, comrade?'

'My boots are too tight, they've shrunk. I got my feet wet on outpost duty during the night.'

'Maybe you're a bit scared?' Stokman smiled understandingly.

'What of?'

'Well, we're going into action...'

'I'm a Communist.'

'Aren't Communists afraid of death then? They're human like anyone else, aren't they?' Mishka broke in.

The man next to Stokman deftly hitched his rifle a little higher on his shoulder and, without looking at Mishka, thought for a moment, then replied, 'You've not yet found your depth in such matters, mate. I'm not allowed to be scared. I've told myself not to be— understand? And don't come groping for my thoughts unless you've got clean hands. I know what I'm fight-

246

ing for and who I'm fighting, and I know we'll win. That's the main thing. The rest don't matter.' Smiling at some memory and watching Stokman from the side, he told him, 'Last year I was in action with Krasavtsev's detachment in the Ukraine. We were being pushed back all the time and losing men. We even had to abandon our wounded. And then not far from Zhmerinka we got surrounded. That meant that someone would have to slip through the Whites' line at night and blow up the railway bridge across the river in their rear, so their armoured train couldn't reach them, then we'd be able to break out across the railway. Well, volunteers were called for. But no one came forward. So the Communists—there weren't many of us—said, "Let's draw lots and it'll be one of us." Well, I thought it over and volunteered. I took the sticks of dynamite, the fuse and the matches, said goodbye to my comrades and started off. It was a dark night and misty. I walked about two hundred paces, then started crawling. I crawled through some unreaped rye, then along a ravine. And as I was crawling out of that ravine, I remember a bird fluttering up right in front of my nose. Well... I crawled past their outpost, only about twenty paces away from it and got to the bridge. There was a machine-gun post guarding it. I lay low for about two hours, waiting for a good moment. Then I primed the charge and started striking matches under the hem of my coat, but they were damp and wouldn't burn. I'd been crawling, you see, and I was all wet from the dew—soaking wet, and so were the matches. And then, Dad, I did feel scared! It would soon be daybreak and my hands were shaking and the sweat was streaming into my eyes. It's a washout, I thought. If I don't blow up that bridge now, I'll shoot myself. But I went on struggling with those matches, and at last I did manage to light the fuse, and crawled away. When the bridge went up in flames behind me—I was lying under some snow screens on the embankment—there was a real hullabaloo. They raised the alarm. Two machine-guns opened up. A lot of horsemen galloped past me but how can you find anyone at night? I crawled out from under those screens and into the rye. But then, you know, my arms and legs just went numb and I couldn't move. All I could do was lie still. I'd felt brave enough on the way there but on the way back—I was as sick as a dog. Everything came up! Nothing inside, but I was still retching. Well, of course, I got back to my own side in the end.' He livened up and an unusual warmth made his gleaming brown eyes more handsome. 'In the morning after we'd been in action I told the lads what a fix I'd been in with those matches and a chum of mine says, "What about your lighter, Sergei, have you lost it?" I clapped my hand to my breast pocket—and there it was! And when I snapped it—just imagine—it lighted at once.'

From a distant island of poplars two ravens flew high overhead, swept along by the wind. They were not far from the column when the guns on Krutovsky hill opened up again after an hour's break. The first, ranging shell, came screaming over and when the sound reached what seemed to be its highest pitch one of the ravens that had been flying higher than the other suddenly twisted madly like a straw caught in a whirlwind and with its wings all awry, spiralling but still trying to stay up, began to fall like a great black leaf.

'It flew into its own death!' a Red Army man behind Stokman burst out excitedly. 'What a spin, eh!'

The company commander came galloping down from the head of the column on a tall dark bay mare.

'Keep in line!'

Three sledges armed with machine-guns went past at the gallop, spattering the silently marching Ivan with slush. One of the machine-gunners fell out of the speeding rear sledge and guffaws rose from the column until the cursing driver swung his horses round and the gunner jumped back on to the moving sledge.

XLI

Karginskaya stanitsa had become the main stronghold for the 1st Insurgent Division. Grigory Melekhov, fully realising the strategic advantages of the Karginskaya position, had decided to hold it at all costs. The hills running along the left bank of the Chir with their command of the surrounding country were ideal for defence. Beneath them, on the other side of the river lay Karginskaya and beyond it the gently rolling steppe stretched for many versts to the south, gashed in places by ravines and gulleys. On one of the hills Grigory himself chose the position for his three-gun battery. Not far away an ancient mound covered with oak woods and dominating the locality provided an excellent observation post.

There was fighting around Karginskaya every day. The Reds usually attacked from two sides: across the southern steppe from the Ukrainian settlement of Asta- khovo, and from Bokovskaya in the east, forcing their way from village to village along the Chir. The Cossacks would take up positions on the outskirts of Karginskaya loosing off a few rounds now and then. The fierce fire from the Reds nearly always forced them to retreat into the stanitsa, and then up the steep gulleys on to the overlooking hills. But the Reds lacked sufficient forces to drive them any further. Their attacking operations were severely hampered by a lack of cavalry for out- flanking movements that would have forced the Cossacks into further retreat, created a diversion and given free- dom of action to their own infantry, which hung back irresolutely on the outskirts. The infantry could not be used for such movements because they were too slow and unmanoeuvrable and because most of the Cossack forces were mounted and could at any moment attack them on the march and divert them from their main objective.

The insurgents also had the advantage of a perfect knowledge of the terrain and seldom missed a chance of moving their squadrons quietly along ravines to threat- en the enemy's flanks or rear and thus paralyse his further advance.

By this time Grigory had decided on a plan for rout- ing the Red forces. He wanted to lure them into Kargin- skaya by staging a mock withdrawal and then close in on their flanks by way of the eastern and western ravines, using Ryabchikov's regiment of cavalry to surround and destroy them. The plan was carefully worked out. At a conference on the eve of the operation all the com- manders of independent units were given exact instruc- tions and orders. It was Grigory's idea that the outflank- ing movement should begin at dawn, when it could be more easily concealed. It was all as simple as a game of draughts. And when Grigory had checked and gone over in his mind all the possible accidents that might upset his plan, he drank two glasses of home-brew and flung himself on his bed without undressing; almost as soon as he covered his head with the damp skirt of his greatcoat, he fell into a dead sleep.

At about four in the morning the Red forces took possession of Karginskaya. Part of the Cossack infantry made a show of fleeing on to the hills behind the stanitsa and were sprayed by two machine-guns on carts, which swerved wildly to a halt on the road into the stanitsa. Meanwhile the Red infantry spread slowly through the streets and lanes.

Grigory was on the observation mound near the battery. He saw the Reds occupying Karginskaya and mustering near the river. It had been agreed that after the first shot from the battery two squadrons of Cossacks concealed in the orchards at the foot of the hills would attack, while the cavalry regiment on the flanks would begin its encircling movement. The commander of the battery was about to try a direct shot at the machine-gun cart racing down from Klimov's Knoll into Karginskaya when a spotter reported that Red artillery had appeared on a bridge in the village of Lower-Latyshevsky about three and a half versts away; the Reds were simultaneously attacking from the direction of Bokovskaya.

'Give 'em a blast from the mortar,' Grigory advised, keeping his eyes to his Zeiss field glasses.

The gun-layer exchanged a few words with the sergeant-major acting as battery commander and took quick aim. The crew went into action and the four-and-a-half-inch mortar gave a throaty bark and ploughed the ground with its tail. The first shell hit the end of the bridge, just when the Red battery's second gun was driving on to it. The shell scattered the team of horses that was pulling the gun. It was later discovered that only one of the six survived, and the driver who had been riding it had his head cut clean off by a shell fragment. Grigory saw a yellow-grey wad of smoke burst into flames in front of the gun, there was a sickening crash and the horses reared on their hindlegs amid the smoke, then fell as if pole-axed; men ran, crouching and falling. A mounted Red Army man who had been near the limber when the shell landed was thrown out on to the ice together with his horse and the bridge rails.

The Cossack gunners had not expected such a lucky shot. For a minute there was silence round the gun; only the spotter on the mound rose to his knees, shouting and waving his arms.

But at that moment from the densely overgrown cherry orchards and poplar groves below there came a ragged cheer and a rattle of rifle fire. Forgetting caution, Grigory ran up on to the mound. Red Army men were running down the streets; scattered shouting, sharp words of command, and heavy volleys of fire could be heard. One of the machine-gun carts made a dash for the knoll, but almost at once, near the cemetery, swung round and opened fire over the heads of the running and ducking Red soldiers at the Cossacks galloping after them out of the orchards.

Grigory scanned the horizon in vain for signs of the Cossack cavalry. Ryabchikov's outflanking force still did not appear. The Red soldiers who had been on the left flank were already making for the bridge across Zaburunny Ravine that linked Karginskaya with the adjoining village of Arkhipovsky, while those on the right flank were still running through Karginskaya and being shot down by the Cossacks who had captured the two streets nearest the river.

At last Ryabchikov's first squadron appeared on the hill, followed by the second, third and fourth. Spreading out in attack formation, they swung sharply to the left to cut off the crowd of Red Army men fleeing across the slope towards Klimovka. Crushing his gloves in his hands, Grigory watched excitedly, without field glasses, as the charging Cossacks bore down on the Klimovka road and the Reds turned in confusion and ran back singly and in bunches towards Arkhipovsky and then, as they came under fire from the Cossacks developing the pursuit up the river were again forced back towards the road. Only a few of them succeeded in breaking through to Klimovka.

The terrible silent slaughter began. Ryabchikov's squadrons wheeled again, this time towards Karginskaya, and drove the Red infantry back like leaves before the wind. Near the bridge across Zaburunny Ravine about thirty Red Army men, seeing that they were cut off and could not escape, tried to shoot their way out. They had a heavy machine-gun and a fair supply of ammunition belts. As soon as the insurgent infantry appeared from the orchards, the machine-gun burst into action. Cossacks fell and crawled away under cover of the barns and stone fences. From the hill Grigory saw some of his men dragging their machine-gun through the stanitsa. They stopped for a minute by one of the barnyards on the outskirts of Arkhipovsky, then ran inside. Soon a lively rat-a-tat came from the roof of a barn. Through his field glasses Grigory spotted the machine-gunners. One was lying on the roof behind the gun shield with his white-stockinged legs spread out behind him; another was climbing a ladder with a machine-gun belt over his shoulder. The Cossack gunners decided to help their infantry. One shrapnel shell burst over the spot where the Red infantry were making their stand and the last round exploded far away on the outskirts.

After a quarter of an hour the Reds' machine-gun suddenly fell silent. Immediately a brief cheer went up and mounted Cossacks appeared among the bare trunks of the willows.

It was all over.

* * *

On Grigory's orders the villagers dragged the one hundred and forty-seven sabred Red Army men with boat-hooks and poles into a shallow pit by Zaburunny Ravine and covered them with a thin layer of earth. Ryabchikov captured six ammunition carts with their horses and cartridges and one machine-gun cart with its gun but no breach. In Klimovka he seized forty-two wagons loaded with military equipment. The Cossacks lost four men killed and fifteen wounded.

After the battle Karginskaya was quiet for a week. The enemy turned his attention to the 2nd Insurgent Division and, after driving them out of a number of villages around Migulinskaya, approached the village of Upper-Chirsky.

Every day the rumble of their guns could be heard at dawn, but news of the fighting was long delayed and gave no clear picture of the situation on the 2nd Division's front.

During these days, in an attempt to escape black thoughts and dull his mind to the events which were going on around him and in which he was playing so prominent a part, Grigory started drinking heavily. If the insurgents, though possessing huge stocks of grain, were badly short of flour (the mills could not cope with the army's demands and the men often had to eat boiled wheat grain) there was no lack of home-brewed vodka. The home-brew flowed in rivers. In an action on the far side of the Don a squadron of Dudarevsky Cossacks, all of them drunk to the wide, charged several machine-guns head on and half of them were wiped out. Cases of drunkenness in the fighting line were a common occurrence. Grigory was always obligingly supplied with liquor, particularly by Prokhor Zykov. After the Karginskaya battle at Grigory's request he brought three huge jugs of home-brew and invited the best singers in the division, and Grigory with a joyful sense of release and freedom from reality and his own thoughts drank with the Cossacks until dawn. In the morning he had another drink to clear his head, and then a few more, and by evening he was again in need of singers, the merry roar of voices, hubbub and dancing—anything to create the illusion of true jollity and conceal the sober and painful reality.

The need to get drunk quickly became a habit. As soon as he sat down at table in the morning, Grigory felt an irresistible desire for a gulp of vodka. He drank heavily but not beyond all measure and was always firm on his feet. Even in the early hours of the morning, when all the others had thrown up and were sprawling over the tables or sleeping on the floor under greatcoats and saddle-cloths, he still managed to look sober, though much paler and more sombre-eyed, and with a way of clutching his head in his hands and letting his curly forelock fall forward.

After four days of constant carousing, his face grew bloated and his shoulders sagged; baggy bluish folds appeared under his eyes and more and more often they gleamed with insensate cruelty.

On the fifth day Prokhor Zykov suggested with a promising smile, 'Let's go and see a good woman I know, in Likhovidov? Well, what do you say? Only don't miss your chance, Grigory Panteleyevich. That woman's as sweet as a ripe water melon! I haven't tried her myself but I know. Only she's an untamed fury, that she is! Real wild. You won't get what you want out of her rightaway, she won't even let you pat her. But the home-brew she makes—there's nothing better. She's the best moonshine-maker on the Chir. Her husband went with the retreat, across the Donets,' he concluded casually.

They rode off to Likhovidov that evening. Grigory was accompanied by Ryabchikov, Kharlampy Yermakov, one-armed Alexei Shamil and Kondrat Medvedev, commander of the 4th Division, who had come over from his sector. Prokhor led the way. In the village he reined in his horse to a walk, turned down a side-lane and opened a gate leading to a threshing floor. Grigory rode after him. His horse jumped over a huge half-melted snowdrift by the gate, sank its forelegs in the snow, but snorted, pulled itself out and stumbled on through the drifts that were as high as the fence and gate. Ryabchikov dismounted and led his horse by the bridle. For about five minutes Grigory rode behind Prokhor past ricks of straw and hay, then through a bare glassily ringing cherry orchard. The golden cup of the young moon hung tilted in the blue-flooded sky, the stars were quivering, a bewitching stillness was being woven and the distant bark of a dog and the crunch of hooves only added to its spell. A yellow light shone through the fine tracery of cherry branches and spreading apple boughs and the outlines of a big rush-thatched Cossack house showed up clearly against the backdrop of the starry sky. Prokhor bent forward in his saddle and obligingly opened the creaking gate. Near the porch a reflected moon swayed in a frozen puddle. Grigory's horse cracked the edge of the puddle with its hoof and stopped, taking one deep breath. Grigory sprang to the ground, looped the reins round the rail, and entered the dark porch. A murmur of voices rose behind him as the Cossacks dismounted and broke quietly into song.

Grigory groped for the door-latch, found it and stepped into a large kitchen. A young Cossack woman, short but shapely as a partridge, with a dark complexion and black beautifully moulded brows was standing with her back to the stove, knitting a stocking. A fair-haired little girl of about nine was lying asleep on the stove-bed, arms outspread.

Grigory sat down at the table without taking off his coat.

'Got any vodka?'

'Don't you think you should say good evening first?' the woman asked without looking up, still flicking her knitting needles as rapidly as ever.

'Good evening, if that's what you want! Got any vodka?'

She raised her eyelashes and smiled at him with round brown eyes, listening to the hubbub and clatter of boots in the porch.

'Yes, there's vodka. But are there many of you night birds come here to roost?'

'Plenty. The whole division.'

Ryabchikov burst into the room in a dance, squatting on his haunches dragging his sabre behind him and slapping the tops of his boots with his lambskin busby. The Cossacks crowded round the door, one of them beating out a wild dance rhythm with a pair of wooden spoons.

Greatcoats were heaped on the bed and weapons piled on the benches. Prokhor busily helped the mistress of the house to lay the table. One-armed Alexei went to the cellar for salted cabbage, slipped on the ladder and climbed out carrying bits of a broken plate and a bunch of wet cabbage in the skirt of his long tunic.

By midnight, when they had drunk about five buckets of home-brew and eaten any amount of cabbage, they decided to slaughter a sheep. Prokhor groped in the darkness of the pen, caught a ewe, and Kharlampy Yermakov—as good a swordsman as any—cut off its head and skinned it there and then by the shed. The mistress of the house stoked up the stove and started cooking a large cauldron of mutton.

Again they danced to the beat of spoons and Ryabchikov went round in circle, kicking out his feet, slapping the tops of his boots fiercely and singing in a sharp but pleasant tenor voice:

> Now's the time to dance and drink hard,
> When there's nowt to chase in the farmyard.

'I want a good time!' Yermakov roared and kept trying to test the strength of the window frames with his sabre.

Grigory, who liked Yermakov for his exceptional bravery and Cossack daring, thumped on the table with a copper mug to restrain him.

'Don't play the fool, Kharlampy!'

Yermakov obediently sheathed his sabre and gulped down a glass of vodka.

'In good company like this I wouldn't be afraid to die, Grigory Panteleyevich,' Alexei declared, sitting down beside Grigory. 'You're our pride and joy! We wouldn't be here but for you. Let's drink another one together, eh?.. Prokhor, bring us some liquor!'

The unsaddled horses had been allowed to gather freely round a hay rick and the Cossacks took it in turns to go out and attend to them.

Not until first light did Grigory feel he was drunk. The Cossacks' voices seemed to come to him from afar, the bloodshot whites of his eyes rolled heavily and it cost him a great effort of will to remain conscious.

'The gold epaulettes are getting their hands on us again! They've grabbed all the power!' Yermakov bellowed, throwing his arm round Grigory.

'What epaulettes?' Grigory asked, removing Yermakov's arm.

'In Vyoshenskaya. Didn't you know? There's a Caucasian prince there, he's cock o' the walk now. A colonel!.. I'll cut him down! Melekhov! I'd lay down my life for you but don't give us up! The Cossacks are worried. Lead us to Vyoshenskaya—we'll smash the lot of 'em and send the place up in smoke! Sofonov, Kudinov, the colonel—we'll smash 'em all! Enough of their oppression! Let's fight the Reds and the Cadets as well. That's what I want!'

'We'll kill that colonel. He stayed behind on purpose... Kharlampy! Let's go and beg pardon of the Soviets; we're in the wrong...' But then, as his head cleared for a minute, Grigory smiled crookedly and added. 'I'm joking, Kharlampy—drink!'

'Why are you joking, Melekhov? Don't joke, this is a serious matter,' Medvedev intervened sternly. 'We want to shake up this government. We'll throw 'em all out and put you there instead. I've talked to the Cossacks about it and they agree. We'll put it fair and square to Kudinov and his lot, "Give up your power," we'll say. "You don't suit us." And if they give it up, all well and good. But if not, we'll march a regiment against Vyoshenskaya and send 'em all to hell!'

'No more of that talk!' Grigory shouted furiously.

Medvedev left the table with a shrug and stopped drinking. In a corner of the room Ryabchikov lay with his tousled head on a bench, scratching the dirty floor with his hand and singing plaintively:

> Oh, my poor laddie, my poor little laddie,
> Come, lean your noddle, your dear little noddle,
> Oh! Now to the right side,
> And now to the left,
> And then let it rest
> Upon my white breast.

And blending with his womanishly sweet and plaintive tenor, Alexei Shamil intoned in his husky bass:

> On her breast as I did lie,
> Oh, so sadly did I sigh,
> Oh, so sadly did I sigh,
> And many a time did cry:

> *'Farewell, forgive, my past love,*
> *'My lousy rotten past love!'*

A violet dawn was showing at the window when the mistress of the house took Grigory into the front room.

'You've forced enough drink down him! Keep off, you devil! Can't you see he's no good for anything,' she said, trying to hold Grigory up with one hand and with her other pushing away Yermakov, who had followed them with a mug of liquor.

'Going to have the morning in bed?' Yermakov said with a wink, spilling his drink.

'Yes—sleeping.'

'Don't go to bed with him, you won't get any joy there!'

'It's nothing to do with you! You're not my father-in-law.'

'Better take a spoon with you!' Yermakov roared, falling over in a fit of drunken laughter.

'You shameless devil! Got yourself blind drunk and saying such things!'

She pushed Grigory into the room, put him to bed, and in the half light gazed with revulsion and pity at his deathly pale face and unseeing open eyes.

'Would you like some stewed fruit?'

'Get me some.'

She brought a glass of cold stewed cherries, then sat down on the bed, untangling and stroking Grigory's matted hair until he fell asleep. She made a bed for herself next to her daughter on the ledge above the stove, but Shamil gave her no chance to sleep. With his head resting on his elbow he kept snorting like a frightened horse, then suddenly waking up and bawling confusedly:

> *From the war we came marching home!*
> *Medals on our shoulder,*
> *Pips on our chests...*

His head sank on to his arms but a few minutes later he started up again, staring wildly round the room:

> *From t' war we came...*

XLII

When he awoke the next morning, Grigory remembered the talk with Yermakov and Medvedev. He had not been so hopelessly drunk and without much difficulty recalled what had been said about replacing the government. Obviously the carousal in Likhovidov had been organised for a purpose: to get him to support a coup. The leftward-leaning Cossacks, who secretly dreamed of complete secession from the Don and setting up a kind of Soviet government without Communists, were weaving a plot against Kudinov, who made no secret of his desire to march to the Donets and link up with the Don Army. They wanted to win Grigory over to their side, not realising how disastrous it would be for the insurgent camp to be torn by dissension when at any moment the Red front, which had been shaken on the Donets, might turn and sweep them and all their squabbles off the face of the earth. 'It's a kid's game,' Grigory told himself and jumped lightly out of bed. When he had dressed, he wakened Yermakov and Medvedev, called them into the front room, and closed the door firmly behind him.

'Now, look here, lads. Forget everything that was said yesterday and stop arguing, or you'll be in a mess! It's not who's in command that matters. It's not a matter of Kudinov, it's the fact that we're hemmed in. They've got us over a barrel. And sooner or later that barrel's going to roll and crush us. It's not Vyoshenskaya, but Migulinskaya and Krasnokutskaya that we ought to be marching against,' he said significantly, keeping his eyes on Medvedev's sombrely impassive face. 'That's how it is, Kondrat, it's not good stirring up trouble. Use your brains and you'll see that if we start ditching the command and holding all kinds of discussion, we'll be done for. We've got to side with the Whites or with the Reds. We can't stay in the middle—we'll get crushed.'

'Mind you say nothing of this,' Yermakov suggested, turning away.

'It'll go no further, but only on the condition you stop stirring up the Cossacks. As for Kudinov and his advisers, they haven't got all the power—I lead my division as best I can. They're a poor lot, that's for sure, and they want to get us wedded to the Cadets again. But where else can we turn? There's no way out for us—we're hamstrung!'

'That's true enough...' Medvedev agreed unwillingly, and for the first time since the conversation began raised his small spiteful bearlike eyes to look at Grigory.

Grigory spent another two days and nights drinking in the villages around Karginskaya, turning his life into a drunken whirl. Even his saddle cloth began to smell of home-brew. Women and girls that had lost the flower of maidenhood passed through his hands and shared a brief time of love with him. But in the morning, sated by the ardours of a passing passion, he would think soberly and indifferently, as he might of a stranger, 'I've lived and been through everything in my time on earth. I've had women and girls in plenty, I've ridden the steppe on some fine horses, I've delighted in fatherhood and I've killed my fellow men, I've faced death myself and loved to look up at the blue sky. What more has life to offer me? Nothing new! So now it won't be so terrible to die. And I can play at war without risk, like a rich man. There'll be nothing much to lose!'

Haphazard memories of childhood floated by like a blue sunny day: starlings nesting in a quarry, his own bare feet in the hot dust, the Don majestically still between its green fringes of reflected forest, the boyish faces of friends, his mother, young and slender... Grigory would cover his eyes with his hand and in his mind's eye see familiar faces, events, sometimes quite trivial but for some reason firmly lodged in his memory; forgotten voices, snatches of talk, mingled laughter would sound in his ears. Memory would guide the ray of recall to a long-forgotten scene and suddenly he would be dazzlingly confronted by a wide expanse of steppe, the summer track across it, a wagon, his father on the driver's seat, the oxen, a wheatfield bristling with golden stubble, a black scattering of rooks on the road... Amidst thoughts tangled like a fish-net Grigory would rummage through his past, and in this life that was gone for ever he would suddenly come across Aksinya and think: 'Ah, my dearest love! I'll never forget you!' With a sigh of disgust he would turn away from the woman sleeping beside him and wait impatiently for the dawn. And as soon as the sun began to weave its patterns of purple and gold in the east he would spring up, wash and hurry out to his horse.

XLIII

The uprising raged like an all-consuming steppe fire. A steel ring of fronts closed round the rebellious stanitsas. The shadow of doom was burned into men's faces as if with a branding iron. The Cossacks played with life, as if spinning a coin, and many of them lost the toss. The young men loved lustily, the older ones drank themselves stupid and gambled at cards for money and bullets (valued above all), and rode home on leave so that just for a minute they could prop the rifles they were sick of against the wall, take up an axe or plane and enjoy the heart's ease of weaving sweet-smelling willow branches into a fence or mending a harrow or a wagon for the spring work in the fields. And many, after a taste of the peaceful life, came back to their units full of drink and, on sobering up, in their bitterness against this 'rotten life', charged straight at the enemy machine-guns on foot or, if mounted, rode out wildly on nocturnal raids, took prisoners and with a barbarous cruelty and savagery desecrated their captives' bodies and then, grudging a bullet, finished the victim with the sabre.

The spring of that year blazed with colour as never before. The April days were fine and clear as glass. The flocks of wild duck and trumpeting cranes flew on and on, overtaking the clouds, across the inaccessible blue flood of the heavens. Swans that had settled to feed in the ponds glowed like scattered pearls on the pale-green carpet of the steppe. A ceaseless chatter and crying of birds sounded over the water-meadows by the Don. On the field balks and ridges of unflooded land the geese called to one another as they prepared to fly northward; among the willows the drakes hissed tirelessly in the ecstasy of love. The catkins greened out on the willows, the poplars burgeoned with sticky fragrant buds. Enchanting beyond words was the steppe as it grew green and was filled with the primeval smell of thawed black soil and the eternally youthful fragrance of sprouting grass.

The one good thing about the insurgent war was that every Cossack had a home near by. When he grew tired of outpost duty or riding on patrol over hill and dale, he could ask permission of his squadron commander and go home, sending out his aged grandfather or under-age son to replace him. Despite the coming and going, the squadrons were always up to strength. But some managed it another way. A Cossack would ride out of camp as the sun began to set, throw his horse into a gallop and with thirty or forty versts behind him be home before the afterglow had died. After a night with his wife or sweetheart he would saddle his horse at second cockcrow and, before the Pleiades grew dim, he was back in his squadron.

Many of the happy-go-lucky ones were only too glad to be fighting a war on their own doorsteps. 'Life's too good to leave!' the Cossacks who saw a lot of their wives would joke.

Desertion was a real problem for the insurgent command when the spring season began. Kudinov made a special tour of the units and declared with, for him, unusual firmness, 'I don't care if the winds graze over our fields and we don't sow a single seed, but I'm not going to let any Cossacks leave their units! Anyone who leaves without permission will be flogged and shot!'

XLIV

And there was yet another battle, at Klimovka, that Grigory took part in. At noon one day firing broke out on the outskirts and Red infantry began to close in on the village. On the left flank black-jacketed sailors—a ships's crew from the Baltic Fleet—were advancing steadily. With a fearless charge they drove two squadrons of the Karginskaya insurgent regiment out of the village and forced them back along the ravine towards Vasilyovsky.

When the Red Army units began to gain the upper hand, Grigory, who had been watching the action from a low hill, waved with his glove to Prokhor Zykov, who was holding his horse by an ammunition cart, and sprang into the saddle as his mount was led towards him; he rounded the ravine and cantered swiftly towards the slope into Gusinka, where he knew the 2nd Regiment's reserve mounted squadron was concealed among the poplar groves. Through orchards and across fences he made his way to the squadron's hide-out. He spotted the dismounted Cossacks and their tethered horses from a distance and, drawing his sabre, shouted, 'To horse!'

In one minute two hundred riders sorted out their horses. The squadron commander came galloping towards Grigory.

'Into action?'

'Yes, and high time! You're late!' Grigory snapped with a glint in his eyes.

He reined in his horse and dismounted but, as luck would have it, when he began tightening the saddle girths the sweating overexcited horse snorted and swelled its belly, preventing him from tightening the girth, and, baring its teeth fiercely, tried to knock him over. When he had eventually made the saddle firm, Grigory put his foot in the stirrup and without looking at the squadron commander, who had been listening nervously to the mounting roar of firing, shouted, 'I'll lead the squadron. In troop order till we get out of the village, at the trot, forward!'

Outside the village Grigory swung the squadron into attack formation. Testing his sabre to make sure it came easily out of its sheath, he rode out some fifty paces ahead of the squadron and led them at a gallop towards Klimovka. On the crest of the hill that sloped southwards into the village, he reined in his horse for a second to scan the scene. Red Army men, mounted and on foot, were retreating out of the village, ammunition carts and wagons were fleeing at a gallop. Grigory turned towards the squadron.

'Sabres out! Into the attack! Follow me, lads!' He snatched out his sabre and was the first to raise the 'Hurrah!' Then with a cold shiver and a familiar lightness in his body, he urged the horse forward. He felt the taut reins quivering between the fingers of his left hand and heard the swish of the upraised sabre as it cut the resisting air.

A huge white cloud, foaming in the spring wind, covered the sun for a minute and a grey shadow overtook Grigory as it spread with apparent slowness over the hill. Grigory switched his gaze from the approaching farmsteads of Klimovka to this shadow gliding over the brown, still damp earth, and then to the joyous yellow strip of light racing away before it. And as he did so he felt a sudden inexplicable and instinctive desire to catch that fleeing strip of light. Pressing his heels into the horse's flanks, he gave it its head and, as he urged it on, began to approach the fluid line separating light from shadow. A few more seconds of desperate galloping and the horse's head and outstretched neck were sprinkled with lucent, dazzling rays. But just at the moment when Grigory crossed the edge of the cloud shadow, shots crackled fiercely from a side-lane in the village. The wind

262

carried the sounds swiftly towards him, amplifying them. Another brief second passed and Grigory, through the drumming of his own horse's hooves, through the whistle of bullets and the roar of the wind in his ears ceased to hear the thunder of the squadron behind him. The heavy, earth-shaking hoofbeat of the great mass of horses seemed to break off, then grow distant and die away. At that moment the firing ahead flared up like dry twigs tossed on to a blaze and whining bullets swarmed around him. Grigory looked back in confusion and fear. His face was contorted with bewildered anger. The squadron had turned and was galloping back, leaving him behind. Not far away, the squadron commander was wheeling his horse brandishing his sabre absurdly, and weeping and shouting in a hoarse, broken voice. Only two Cossacks were still following Grigory. Prokhor Zykov had swung his horse round and was galloping toward the squadron commander. The rest were riding away in scattered formation, their sabres sheathed and whips working.

Only for a second had Grigory checked his horse, trying to understand what had happened behind him and why the squadron had suddenly turned tail before losing a single man. But in that brief second something told him not to turn back and flee, but to go forward! Behind a fence in a lane some two hundred paces away from him about seven Red Army men were struggling with a machine-gun cart, trying to point the gun at the attacking Cossacks. But evidently the lane was too narrow; the machine-gun was silent and fewer and fewer shots whined about Grigory's ears. Turning his horse, he rode to reach the lane by jumping a broken fence that had once bordered a poplar grove. Taking his eyes off the fence for a moment, with sudden clarity, as if through field glasses, he saw the sailors close up, in their black, mud-spattered pea-jackets and their tight peakless caps that made their faces look strangely round, hastily unharnessing the horses. Two were slashing the traces, a third, his head drawn into his shoulders, was struggling with the gun; the others, standing or kneeling, were shooting at Grigory with their rifles. As he rode down on them, he saw their hands working the bolts and heard the sharp crack of the shots at point-blank range. The shots came so rapidly, the rifle butts rose and were pressed into shoulders so quickly that, although he was in a muck sweat of fear, Grigory realised with a joyful certainty: 'They won't hit me!'

The fence crunched under his horse's hooves and dropped behind. Grigory raised his sabre and with narrowed eyes chose the leading sailor. Another surge of fear tore through him like lightning: 'They'll hit me point-blank... The horse will rear... fall backwards... they'll kill me!..' Two shots sounded very close and then a shout, as if from afar: 'We'll take him alive!' Straight in front of him he saw the bared teeth in a brave bare-browed face, the fluttering ribbons of the peakless cap, the tarnished gold of the ship's name on the band... Up in the stirrups, a slash, and Grigory felt the sabre bite into the sailor's softly yeilding body. A second sailor, thick-necked and burly, managed to wound Grigory in the fleshy part of his left shoulder and was at once felled by Prokhor, his head slashed in two. Grigory turned at the click of a rifle bolt close by. The black muzzle of a rifle barrel was pointing straight at his face from behind the cart. He flung himself to the left so violently that the saddle shifted and his panting half-crazed horse staggered. Death whined over his head, and as the horse jumped the shaft of the cart he cut down the man who had fired before his hand could send another bullet into the breech.

In an inconceivably brief instant of time (afterwards it spread out to immense dimensions in his mind) Grigory had sabred four sailors and, oblivious of Prokhor's shouts, was galloping in pursuit of a fifth who had disappeared round a bend in the lane. But the squadron commander rode across ahead of him and seized Grigory's bridle.

'Whoa! They'll kill you!.. They've got another machine-gun there, behind the shed!'

Two other Cossacks and Prokhor dismounted, ran up and pulled Grigory off his horse by main force. He struggled in their grip, shouting, 'Lemme go, swine!.. Sailor crap!.. I'll... I'll kill 'em all!..'

'Grigory Panteleyevich! Comrade Melekhov! Come to your senses!' Prokhor urged him.

'Let go, brothers!' Grigory said in a different, quieter voice.

They released him. The squadron commander whispered to Prokhor, 'Put him on his horse and take him to Gusinka. He must be ill.'

He turned to his horse and commanded his men to mount.

But Grigory threw his busby down in the snow, stood for a moment swaying, then suddenly gnashing his teeth, gave a terrible groan and with his face convulsed began to tear at the fastenings of his greatcoat. Before the commander could step up to him, Grigory fell flat with his chest bared to the snow. Sobbing until his whole body began to shake, he plunged his mouth, like a dog, into an unmelted snow drift by the fence. Then in a moment of terrible clarity he tried to rise but it was no use and, turning his tearful pain-twisted face to the Cossacks crowding round him, he shouted in a broken unrecognisable voice, 'Who have I killed!..' And for the first time in his life he writhed in a fit, screaming and spitting out words with the froth on his lips, 'I can never be forgiven, brothers!.. Kill me, for God's sake... Bloody hell ... I want to die ... put me to death!'

The squadron commander and a troop leader threw themselves upon him, ripped off his sword belt and field bag, stopped his mouth and held his legs. But for a long time he heaved and arched his back under them, dug the grainy snow with his convulsively kicking legs and groaned, and beat his head on the hoof-churned, richly glistening black earth of the land where he had been born and lived, taking in full measure from a life, rich in sorrows, poor in joys, all that had been apportioned to him.

Only grass grows on earth, carelessly accepting sun and rain, feeding on the soil's life-giving juices, and humbly bowing before the storm's destructive breath. And then, having scattered its seed to the winds, just as carelessly dies, welcoming with the rustle of its withered leaves the death-dealing rays of the autumn sun.

XLV

The next day Grigory handed over command of the division to one of his regimental commanders and with Prokhor Zykov as his escort rode off to Vyoshenskaya.

In Rogozhkinsky pond beyond Karginskaya, which lay at the bottom of a deep hollow, a flock of wild geese had settled. Prokhor pointed in the direction of the pond with his whip and said with a laugh, 'If only we could bring down a wild goose, we could have a fine drink-up around it!'

'Let's get a bit closer and I'll try with a rifle. I used to be not a bad shot.'

They rode down into the hollow. While Prokhor held

the horses in a fold of the hill, Grigory took off his greatcoat, put his rifle on the safety catch and crawled down a shallow ravine bristling with last year's scrub. He crawled for a long time, barely raising his head, he crawled as if he were stalking an enemy outpost, as he had done on the German front, near the Stokhod, when he had captured a German sentry. His faded tunic merged with the greenish-brown of the soil; the ravine hid him from the vigilant eye of the guard goose, which was standing on one leg near the water, on a brown clump of driftage. Grigory crawled until he was within close range and lifted his head a little; the guard goose turned its stone-grey snakelike head and looked round suspiciously. Behind it the geese were scattered over the pond like a greyish black shroud, interspersed with mallards and pochards. A quiet hissing, quacking and splashing rose from the pond. No need to raise the sights, Grigory thought excitedly as he hugged the rifle butt into his shoulder and took aim at the guard goose.

After the shot Grigory jumped to his feet, deafened by the flapping of wings and the cries of the whole flock. The goose he had aimed at was flapping desperately in an effort to gain height, the others were flying over the pond in a dense cloud. Disappointedly Grigory fired a couple more shots at the soaring birds, watched to see if anything would fall and walked back towards Prokhor.

'Look! Look!' Prokhor had jumped into his saddle and was standing up at full height, pointing with his whip at the flock receding into the blue distance.

Grigory turned and felt a quiver of joy and hunting zest. One goose had broken away from the wedge formation and was coming down, its wings working slowly and jerkily. Grigory stood on tip-toe and watched with his hand shielding his eyes. The goose drifted away from the worriedly crying flock, losing height and speed, and suddenly dropped like a stone with one dazzling flash from the white underside of its wing.

'Into your saddle!'

Grinning from ear to ear, Prokhor tossed Grigory the reins. They galloped up on to the hill and then cantered for about a hundred and fifty paces.

'There it is!'

The goose was lying with its neck extended and wings outspread, as though holding the unfriendly earth in one last embrace. Grigory leaned over and picked up his prey without dismounting.

'Where did it get him?' Prokhor wanted to know. The bullet had pierced the lower half of the bird's beak and dislodged a bone near the eye. Death had come in flight, plucking its victim out of the flock and hurling it to the ground.

Prokhor lashed the bird to his saddle and they rode on.

They rowed across the Don, leaving their horses behind in Bazki.

In Vyoshenskaya Grigory lodged with an old man he knew, ordered the goose to be roasted at once and, instead of reporting to headquarters, sent Prokhor for some home-brew. They drank until evening. In the course of the conversation the old man let fall a complaint.

'The chiefs here in Vyoshenskaya have been throwing their weight about a bit too much, Grigory Panteleyevich.'

'What chiefs?'

'The self-made ones... Kudinov and the others.'

'What have they done?'

'They've got their knife into the non-Cossacks. The families of anyone who went off with the Reds are being put in prison—women, children, old men. They've gaoled my son-in-law's mother because of her son. It's all wrong! Now just suppose you, for instance, went off with the Cadets across the Donets and the Reds came and locked up your dad, Pantelei Prokofyevich—that would be wrong, wouldn't it?'

'Of course!'

'But that's what the authorities here are doing. When the Reds came through they didn't harm anyone, but this lot are like mad dogs, there's no holding 'em!'

Grigory stood up, swayed a little and reached for his greatcoat that was hanging over the bed. He was only slightly drunk.

'Prokhor! My sabre! Pistol!'

'Where're you going, Grigory Panteleyevich?'

'That's none of your business! Give 'em to me, d'you hear?'

Grigory buckled on his sabre and pistol, fastened and belted his greatcoat and strode straight across the square to the prison. The sentry at the gate, a reservist, barred his way.

'Got a pass?'

'Let me in! Stand back, I tell you.'

'I can't let anyone in without a pass. I'm not allowed to.'

Before Grigory had bared half his sabre, the sentry disappeared through the door. Grigory followed him into the corridor, his hand still on the hilt of his sabre.

'Bring me the prison governor!' he shouted.

His face was white, his hooked nose twitching rapaciously, and one eyebrow had risen crookedly.

A lame and weedy-looking Cossack, who was performing the duties of warder, ran into the corridor, a boy clerk peeped out of the office. Presently the governor appeared, sleepy-faced and annoyed.

'Coming in here without a pass? You know what you can get for that!' he boomed, but then he recognised Grigory and after one look at his face broke into a frightened babble, 'Is it you, Your ... Comrade Melekhov? Is anything wrong?'

'The keys of the cells!'

'Of the cells?'

'Have I got to tell you forty times? Now then! Give me the keys, dog face!'

Grigory stepped towards the governor, who backed away but said firmly enough, 'I won't give you any keys. You have no right...'

'No right?!..'

Grigory ground his teeth and snatched out his sabre. In his hand it described a glittering circle under the low ceiling. The clerk and warders scattered like frightened sparrows. The governor recoiled against the wall, his face whiter than the whitewash, and hissed through clenched teeth, 'Making trouble, eh! Here're the keys then. But I'm going to complain.'

'I'll trouble you! You've got used to skulking here in the rear!.. You're very brave when it comes to gaoling women and old men!.. I'll shake the lot of you out of here! Get going to the front right now, you swine, or I'll cut you down!'

Grigory thrust his sabre into its sheath, cuffed the terrified governor on the neck, then propelled him towards the door with his fists and knees, shouting, 'To the front!.. Get moving! Go to... You rear rat!'

When he had turned out the governor, noises from inside the prison led him to the inner yard. Three warders were standing by the kitchen door; one was tugging at the rusty bolt of a Japanese rifle and jabbering, 'He's attacked the prison!.. We must stop him... What do the old regulations say?'

Grigory snatched out his pistol and the warders

tumbled over each other up the steps into the kitchen.

'Come out! Home you go!' Grigory bellowed as he flung open the doors of the crowded cells, shaking the bundle of keys.

He released every prisoner in the gaol (about a hundred in all), pushing out those who were afraid to leave, and then locking the doors of the empty cells.

A crowd gathered round the prison gate. The prisoners poured out into the square and with bowed backs and furtive looks made their way home. The Cossacks of the guard platoon came running down from headquarters, holding their sabres to their sides. Kudinov himself followed them, stumbling.

Grigory was the last to leave the deserted prison. As he strode through the crowd that had fallen back to make way for him he hurled curses at the whispering, curious women and, hunching his shoulders, walked slowly towards Kudinov. To the Cossacks of the guard platoon, who had recognised him as they ran up and greeted him, he shouted 'Back to your quarters, you stallions! What are you galloping for, seen a mare? Off you go, quick march!'

'We thought there was mutiny in the prison, Comrade Melekhov!'

'The clerk came running in and says there's a swarthy fellow smashing the locks!'

'It was a false alarm!'

The Cossacks turned back, laughing and talking. Kudinov hurried up to Grigory, pushing back the long hair that had slipped out from under his cap.

'Hullo, Melekhov. What's up?'

'Hullo there, Kudinov! I've just busted up your prison.'

'On what grounds? What's this all about?'

'I've let 'em all go, and that's it. What are you goggling at? What grounds had you for putting non-Cossack women and old men into gaol? What d'you call that? You watch out, Kudinov!'

'How dare you take these liberties! This is sheer high-handedness!'

'I'll high-hand you into your coffin! I'll call my regiment in from Karginskaya and give you hell!'

Grigory suddenly seized Kudinov by his raw-hide Caucasian belt and, jerking him to and fro, hissed with cold fury, 'Do you want me to throw open the front? Want me to have your blood right now? You..!' Grigory gnashed his teeth and released the quietly smiling Kudinov. 'What are you grinning at?'

Kudinov straightened his belt and took Grigory by the arm.

'Come back to my place. What's got you on the boil like this? You ought to see your face now. You look like the devil himself... We've been missing you here, brother. And as for the prison, that's a piddling thing... So you let 'em go, did you? What's the harm?.. I'll tell the lads to ease off a bit. They've been pulling in all the non-Cossack women with husbands that went off with the Reds... But why undermine our authority? Huh, Grigory! What a madman you are! Why didn't you come and say, "The prison's overcrowded, release so and so." We'd have gone through the lists and let some of 'em out. But you barge in and set the whole lot free! It's a good thing that we've got the important criminals locked up separate. Suppose you'd let them out? You're a hothead!' Kudinov slapped Grigory's shoulder and laughed. 'But if someone goes against you when you're in a state like this, you'll kill him. And—you never know—you might stir up the Cossacks...'

Grigory jerked his arm free and stopped outside the headquarters building.

'You've all got very brave with us to shield you! Packed a whole prison full of people... Why don't you show what you can do in the fighting line!'

'I've shown that no worse than you, Grisha, in my time. And I would now if you'd take my place and give me your division.'

'No, thanks!'

'That's just the point!'

'Well, I haven't got all day to talk to you. I'm on my way home for a week's rest. I'm out of sorts, it seems. And now I've had a bit of a wound in the shoulder.'

'What made you out of sorts?'

'Sheer misery,' Grigory smiled wryly. 'I'm sick at heart.'

'No, joking apart, what's wrong with you? We've got a doctor here, he may even be a professor. He's a prisoner. Our lads captured him near Shumilinskaya, he was with some sailors. Looks important, in black spectacles. Mebbe he could have a look at you?'

'To hell with him!'

'All right then, go and have a rest. Who did you leave in charge of the division?'

'Ryabchikov.'

'Now wait a bit. Where are you hurrying off to? Tell me how things are going. I hear you've been using your sabre. A message came through last night that at Klimovka you'd cut down I don't know how many. Is it true?'

'Goodbye!'

Grigory walked away but after a few paces he half turned and called out to Kudinov, 'Heh! If I get word you've started locking people up again...'

'No, don't worry! Have a good rest!'

The day was following the sun into the west. A cold breeze began to blow from the Don, from the flooded banks. A flock of teal whirred over Grigory's head. He was about to enter the yard of his lodgings when from further up the Don, somewhere near Kazanskaya the resounding octave of an artillery salvo floated across the water.

Prokhor saddled the horses quickly and, as he led them out, asked, 'Are we making for home? To Tatarsky?'

Grigory took the reins in silence and gave a silent nod.

XLVI

Tatarsky without its Cossacks was deserted and dreary. The last of its menfolk had been formed into an unmounted squadron, attached to one of the regiments of the 5th Division, and sent across to the left bank of the Don.

At one time the Red forces, supported by reinforcements from Balashov and Povorino, had made a big push from the northeast, captured several villages around Yelanskaya and closed in on the stanitsa itself. In the fierce engagement on the approaches, the insurgents had won the day. This was because the Yelanskaya and Bukanovskaya regiments, retreating under the onslaught of the Moscow Regiment and two squadrons of Red cavalry, had been massively reinforced. The 4th Insurgent Regiment of the 1st Division (it included a squadron of Tatarsky men), a three-gun battery and two reserve mounted squadrons had marched from Vyoshenskaya along the left bank of the Don to Yelanskaya. In addition substantial reinforcements were moved up along the right bank to the villages of Pleshakov and Matveyevsky, which were about three or five versts from Yelanskaya across the Don. An artillery troop was stationed on Krivsky hill. One of the gun-layers, a Cossack from Krivsky village, who was renowned for his marksmanship, destroyed a Red Army machine-gun nest with his first shot and with a few rounds of shrapnel scattered a Red Army skirmish line that had taken cover in some willow thickets, forcing them to rise and abandon their position. The battle ended in the insurgents' favour. They drove the retreating Red units across the little river Yelanka and launched a pursuit with eleven mounted squadrons, which on a hill not far from Zatalovsky caught and cut down a whole squadron of Red Army cavalry.

Ever since then the Tatarsky 'footsloggers' had been tramping about among the sand hills on the left bank of the Don. Hardly any of the squadron managed to get home on leave. Only at Easter, as if by some secret agreement, nearly half the squadron turned up in the village. They spent a day at home, broke their fast, changed their linen and with a fresh supply of fatback, dried bread and other provisions crossed the Don and, like a crowd of pilgrims (only they carried rifles instead of staves), set out for Yelanskaya. From the hills round Tatarsky their wives, mothers and sisters watched them go. The women wept and wiped their eyes with the corners of their kerchiefs and shawls and blew their noses into the hems of their underskirts. And on the other side of the Don the Cossacks—Khristonya, Anikei, Pantelei, Stepan Astakhov and others—plodded away across the sand hills beyond the flooded riverside woodland. Homespun foodbags hung from their fixed bayonets, a few songs, sad as the scent of wild thyme, lingered on the wind, and the talk flowed feebly. There was no cheerfulness on the march but at least their bellies were full and their shirts clean. Before Easter their women had heated the water, scrubbed the grime off their bodies and combed the bloodthirsty army lice out of their hair. Why couldn't they stay at home and bask in its delights? But no, they must march out to face death—and march they did. Young lads of sixteen or seventeen, only just called to the insurgent colours, padded along over the warm sand, carrying their boots and rough leather slippers. They could not have said why they were cheerful but merriment flared up among them and their breaking immature voices struck up a song. War was a novelty to them, a new game. For the first few days they would even lift their heads from the grey earthwork protecting the trench to listen to the whine of bullets. 'Bulrushes!'

the veterans called them scornfully, while they trained them on the spot to dig trenches, to shoot, to carry their equipment on the march, to choose the best cover, and even the knack of smoking out lice over a fire and winding footcloths so that their feet never grew tired and had 'room to move' in their boots; yes, there was plenty that senseless youth had to learn. And a 'bulrush' would go on looking at the surrounding world of war with his startled birdlike eyes and lifting his head and staring out of the trench, burning with curiosity to see the 'Reds' until—until a Red Army bullet hit him. If it was death, the sixteen-year-old 'soldier' would fall and lie still, and then you'd never give him his brief sixteen years. He would lie there like a big child with big boyish hands, protruding ears and the makings of an Adam's apple in his thin, unmanly neck. They would carry him home to be buried in the same plot where his grandfather and great-grandfather had turned to dust, his mother would come out to meet him and spread her arms in grief, and for long would she weep for her dead son and tear her grey hair. And afterwards, when they had buried him and the clay was dry on the grave, she would go to church, aged and bent by a mother's unsleeping sorrow, to pray for her 'lost' Vanyushka or Syomushka.

But sometimes the bullet does not sting to death, and that's when Vanyushka or Syomushka gets to know the ruthlessness of war. His lips tremble under their thin brown fluff and the 'soldier' yelps like a hare and cries out for his mummy. The tears sprinkle like beads from his eyes. And then the ambulance wagon shakes him up on the rutty tracks and aggravates the wound. And a veteran surgeon's assistant will wash the hole made by the bullet or shell splinter and humorously comfort the sufferer as he might a child, 'It's the cat it's hurting, not you, Vanyushka!' While 'soldier' Vanyushka cries and begs to go home and calls for his mother. But if the wound heals and he comes back to the squadron, then he really grasps the full meaning of war. After a fortnight or so in action, in battle or skirmishes, his heart is properly hardened, and then watch him standing in front of a Red Army prisoner. Leaning back on one foot and spitting sideways in imitation of some brute of a sergeant-major, he snarls in his wobbly little bass, 'Well, you peasant, you rotten bastard, so you're caught, eh? Aha! Wanted land, did you? Equality? I bet you're a commie, aren't you? Own up, you swine!' And in his desire to demonstrate his audacity, his 'Cossack dash and daring' he raises his rifle and kills a man who lived and faced death on Donland soil, fighting for the power of the Soviets, for communism, for a world without war.

And somewhere in Moscow or Vyatka province, in some out-of-the-way village in the vast land of Soviet Russia the mother of that Red Army man receives a notification that her son has 'died in the struggle against the Whiteguards, for the emancipation of the working people from the yoke of the landowners and capitalists...' And she bursts into tears and lamentations. A burning grief closes around the mother's heart, tears gush from her dim eyes, and every day, forever, until the hour of death itself she remembers the child she once carried in her womb, the baby boy she bore in blood and labour, and who died by an enemy's hand somewhere in that unknown country called the Don...

The returning deserters marched on over the rolling sand hills, past the gleaming purple willow shrubs. The young were cheerful and carefree, the old men tramped on with sighs and a secretively hidden tear; for it was time to plough, to harrow and to sow; the land was beckoning, calling tirelessly day and night, but they had to go off to war, pine away in strange villages from enforced idleness, fear, hardship and boredom. That was what made the bearded ones weep, that was why they looked so sombre. Every one of them was thinking of his abandoned farm, his animals and tools. Men's hands were needed everywhere, all things wept without a master to attend to them. What could you expect of the women? The soil would dry out, they wouldn't manage the sowing, and next year would threaten famine. Not for nothing do folk say 'an old gaffer's better than a young flapper on a farm'.

The old men tramped across the sands in silence. They livened up only when one of the youngsters took a pot-shot at a hare. For wasting a bullet (this was strictly forbidden by the insurgent command) the old men decided to punish the culprit. It made them feel better to give someone a thrashing.

'Forty of the best!' Pantelei proposed.

'That's a bit too much!'

'He won't finish the march after that!'

'Sixteen then!' Khristonya barked.

Sixteen was agreed upon as a nice round figure. The culprit was laid out on the sand with his trousers down.

Khristonya cut the fluffy yellow twigs with a penknife, humming a tune, and Anikei laid on. The others sat around smoking. Then they set off again. The lad who had been punished followed behind all the rest, wiping his tears and pulling the seat of his trousers as tight as he could.

As soon as they had passed the sandy stretch and came out on to the grey loam, the talk took a peaceful turn.

'There she is, lovely soil that is, just waiting for her master, but he's got no time for her. The devils have sent him off over hill and dale to fight their war,' sighed one of the old men, pointing to an empty drying stretch of land that had been ploughed in autumn.

They marched on past the ploughland and each man stooped to pick up a dry lump of earth that smelled of spring sunshine, rub it between his hands and suppress a sigh.

'The soil's ready!'

'And, just the time now to take the plough to it.'

'Wait another three days and it'll be too late to sow.'

'Spring's a bit early on our side.'

'Early! Look, the snow's still lying atop the ravines on that side of the Don.'

When they halted for their noonday meal, Pantelei treated the sufferer to some skimmed milk. (He had been carrying it in a bag tied to his rifle barrel and at the sight of the whey dripping out all along the road, the chuckling Anikei had remarked, 'Anyone could get on your tracks, Prokofievich. You've got a wet trail behind you like a bull.') Pantelei served up the milk with some dignified advice.

'Don't you be offended with the old men, you young ninny. Yes, you got a thrashing, but what's the harm! One lad whacked is worth two unwhacked.'

'If they'd done it to you, Grandad Pantelei, you'd be singing a different tune, I reckon!'

'I've had a lot worse done to me than that, my lad.'

'Worse!'

'Ay, a lot worse. Surely you know they laid it on harder in the old days?'

'Did they?'

'O' course, they did. One day, lad, my father hit me across the back with a wagon shaft, but I recovered.'

'A wagon shaft!'

'That's what I said—a wagon shaft. And that's what I meant. Huh, you ninny! Don't stare at me, finish up your milk! What's this, his spoon's got no handle. Broke it, did you, stupid? They didn't give you enough just now!'

After the meal they decided to take a nap in the light and winy spring air. They lay down with their backs to the sun, snored for a bit, then trecked on across the brownish-grey steppe, over the stubble of the previous year, avoiding the road and heading straight for the front. They were dressed in frock coats, greatcoats, homespun coats and tanned sheepskins; on their feet they wore top boots or rough leather slippers with their trousers tucked into white socks, and some went barefoot. Their food bags dangled from their bayonets.

The appearance of the deserters returning to their unit was so unbellicose that even the larks, when they had warbled their song in the blue flood of the heavens, dropped into the grass within a few paces of the passing troops.

* * *

There was not a Cossack in the village when Grigory Melekhov arrived. In the morning he lifted his Mishatka, who was getting bigger now, on to his horse and told him to ride it down to the river to drink. Meanwhile he and Natalya went to see his mother-in-law and Grandad Grishaka.

Lukinichna met him with tears.

'Grisha dear, dearest boy! We're lost without our Miron Grigorievich, God rest his soul!.. Who is there to work on our fields now? The barns are full of grain but there's no one to sow it. Oh, my poor dear boy! We're orphans, no one wants us, we're strangers to everyone!.. Just look what a state the farm's in! We can't get anything done...'

The farm was indeed rapidly decaying. The oxen had smashed or pushed over the fences of the yards; ploughshares had fallen from the hooks; the clay and dung wall of one of the sheds had been eaten away by the spring torrents and collapsed; the fences of the threshing floor were down; the yard was unswept; under the overhang of a shed stood a rusty reaper with a broken crankshaft lying beside it. There were signs of neglect and decay everywhere.

'How soon the place has gone to bits without its master,' Grigory thought indifferently as he walked round the Korshunovs' farmyard.

He returned to the house.

Natalya had been talking to her mother in a whisper, but at the sight of Grigory she broke off and a wheedling smile appeared on her face.

'Mummy has something to ask of you, Grisha... As you were going to be working in the fields like... Could you sow a couple of acres for them perhaps?'

'But why sow anything, Mother?' Grigory asked. 'Your bins are full of wheat as it is.'

Lukinichna clasped her hands.

'But Grisha, dear! What about the land? Why, my late husband ploughed twelve acres last autumn.'

'What'll happen to the land then? It won't be lying fallow all that long, will it? We'll sow it some time this year, if we're still alive.'

'But how can we let the land be wasted?'

Grigory tried to dissuade his mother-in-law. 'When the fronts move away, then you can sow.'

But she stuck to her guns, grew offended with him and in the end pursed her quivering lips.

'Well, if you can't spare the time, or perhaps you don't want to help us...'

'All right then! I'll go out to sow tomorrow and I'll do five acres for you as well. That'll be plenty for your needs... Is Grandad Grishaka still alive?'

'Oh, thank you, what a good provider you are!' Lukinichna cheered up at once. 'I'll tell Agripina to bring the seeds over right away... Our grandad? The Lord still don't take him. Yes, he's alive, but he seems to have gone a bit funny in the head like. He sits all day and night, reading the Scriptures. Sometimes he starts off a-talking, but you can't understand a thing he says because it's all church language... You ought to go in and see him. He's in the front room.'

A tear-drop crept down Natalya's plump cheek.

Smiling through her tears, she said, 'I've just been in there and he says, "You bad girl! Why don't you ever come to see me now? I'll soon be dead, my dear... And when I face the Lord I'll put in a word for you, my little granddaughter. I long for the earth, Natalya... The earth is calling me. It's time!"'

Grigory went into the front room. The smells of incense, must and decay, and of an unkempt old man, struck his nostrils: Grandad Grishaka, still in the same grey army tunic with red tabs on the collar, was seated on the couch. His baggy trousers were neatly patched, his woollen socks darned. He was now in the care of Agripina, who had grown up and was looking after him with the same love and attention that Natalya had given him as a girl.

The old man was holding a Bible in his lap. He peered from under the tarnished metal frames of his spectacles and opened his white-toothed mouth in a smile.

'Is that you, soldier? Still alive? So the Lord has preserved you from a cruel bullet? Praise be to God. Sit down, my boy.'

'How's your health, Grandad?'

'Eh?'

'How's your health, I said.'

'You're a queer fellow, that you are! What kind of health could I have at my age? I'm getting on for a hundred, you know. Ay, a hundred... It's gone by without my noticing it. Only yesterday it seems I was walking around with a fine head of hair, hale and hearty. And today I wake up, just an old ruin... Life's gone in a flash, like summer lightning... My flesh has grown feeble. For many a year now my coffin's been standing in the barn, but God seems to have forgotten me. Sometimes, sinner that I am, I pray to him, "Turn thy merciful gaze upon me, thy servant Grigory! For I am as much a burden to the earth as it is to me..." '

'You'll live a while longer yet, Grandad. Your mouth's full of teeth.'

'Eh?'

'You've still got a lot of teeth!'

'Teeth? Now that's a fool!' the old man declared crossly. 'Teeth won't keep your soul in your body once it chooses to leave... Are you still fighting, you wayward fellow?'

'Yes, still fighting.'

'Our Mitka also left in the retreat. Trouble will strike him one day, you'll see, real hot trouble.'

'It will.'

'That's what I say. What are you fighting for? You don't know yourselves! Everything happens according to God's will. Why did our Miron meet his death? Because he went against God, because he roused the people against the government. All authority is from God. Even if it's an anti-Christ government, it's still given by God. I told him at the time, "Miron! Don't stir up the

Cossacks, don't set them against the government, don't lead them into temptation!" And he says to me, "No, Father, I can't stand any more of it! We've got to rebel and destroy this government; it'll be the ruin of us. We lived like people once but we'll end up beggars." No, he couldn't bear it. He who liveth by the sword shall perish by the sword. And it's true. I've heard tell, Grisha, that you hold the rank of general, that you command a division now. Is that true or not?'

'Yes, it is.'

'You're in command of a division?'

'Yes, what about it?'

'Where are your epaulettes then?'

'We've abolished them.'

'Oh, you crazy fellows! Abolished them! What kind of a general will you make? You'll be a sorry sight! The generals in the old days—it was a pleasure to look at 'em with their big bellies and grand airs! But just look at you now... It makes me want to spit! Your great-coat's all stained and muddy, you haven't any epaulettes on your shoulders or braid on your chest. The seams are full of lice, I'll be bound.'

Grigory burst out laughing. But Grandad Grishaka went on heatedly, 'You needn't laugh, you rascal! You're leading men to their death, you've turned them against the government. You're committing a great sin, so don't stand there grinning! What's that? Eh... All the same they'll destroy you, and us as well. God shows us the way himself. Look what the Bible says—isn't this about our troubled times? Now then, listen, and I'll read to you from Jeremiah the Prophet.'

With a yellowed finger the old man turned the yellowed pages and, slowly, syllable by syllable, began to read:

' "Declare ye among the nations, and publish, and set up a standard; publish, and conceal not; say, Babylon is taken, Bel is confounded, Merodach is broken in pieces; her idols are confounded, her images are broken in pieces. For out of the north there cometh up a nation against her, which shall make her land desolate, and none shall dwell therein; they shall remove, they shall depart, both man and beast..." Do you understand, Grishka? They'll come from the north and wring your necks for you, Babylonians. And listen to this, "In those days, and in that time, saith the Lord, the children of Israel shall come, they and the children of Judah together, going

and weeping: they shall go and seek the Lord their God...
My people hath been lost sheep; their shepherds have
caused them to go astray, they have turned them away
on the mountains: they have gone from mountain to
hill..." '

'What's it all about? What does it mean?' asked Grigory, who found it hard to understand Church Slavonic.

'It means, scoundrel, that you trouble-makers will
have to take to the hills. Because you're not shepherds to
the Cossacks, but the worst and stupidest kind of rams!
You don't know what you're doing... Listen further:
"They have forgotten their resting place. All that found
them have devoured them." And that's right on the
mark! Aren't the lice devouring you right now?'

'There's no getting away from the lice,' Grigory confessed.

'That just shows you then. And further: "And their
adversaries said, We offend not, because they have sinned
against the Lord... Remove out of the midst of Babylon,
and go forth out of the land of the Chaldeans, and be
as the he-goats before the flocks. For, lo, I will raise and
cause to come up against Babylon an assembly of great
nations from the north country: and they shall set themselves in array against her, from thence she shall be taken;
their arrows shall be of a mighty expert man; none
shall return in vain. And Chaldea shall be a spoil: all
that spoil her shall be satisfied, saith the Lord. Because
ye were glad, because ye rejoiced, O ye destroyers of
mine heritage." '

'Grandad! Couldn't you tell it to me in ordinary Russian, because I don't understand it,' Grigory interrupted.

But the old man munched his lips, stared at him
absently and said, 'I'm just coming to the end. Listen.
"Because ye are grown fat as the heifer at grass, and bellow as bulls. Your mother shall be sore confounded;
she that bare you shall be ashamed: behold the hinder-
most of the nations shall be a wilderness, a dry land,
and a desert. Because of the wrath of the Lord it shall
not be inhabited, but it shall be wholly desolate; every
one that goeth by Babylon shall be astonished, and hiss
at all her plagues." '

'But what does it mean?' Grigory asked again, beginning to feel irritated.

Old Grishaka made no reply, closed the Bible and lay
back on the couch.

'People are always like that,' Grigory thought as he

walked out of the room. 'When they're young, they guzzle vodka and sin like the devil, and the worse they were when they were young, the more they try to hide behind God in their old age. And Grandad Grishaka, he's the same. He's got teeth like a wolf. When he was young, they say, after he came out of the army, all the women in the village, high and low, were in trouble because of him. They all fell for him. But now... Well, if I ever live to old age, I won't read that crap! I'm no lover of Bibles.'

Grigory walked back from his mother-in-law's, thinking of the old man's talk and the mysterious and incomprehensible utterances from the Bible. Natalya also walked in silence. On this homecoming her welcome had been unusually cool. Evidently rumours of his drinking and sleeping around with women in the Karginskaya villages had reached her ears too. In the evening on the day of his arrival she had made up a bed for him in the front room and herself spent the night on a chest in the corner, covering herself with her fur coat. But not a word of reproach had she uttered, nor had she asked any questions. Grigory also kept silent the whole night long, having decided that it would be better for the time being not to go into the reasons for so unusual a coldness in their relationship.

They walked silently along the deserted street, more estranged than ever before. A warm caressing breeze was blowing from the south and thick, vernally white clouds were piling up in the west. Their sugary blue-tinged crests foamed and reshaped themselves and billowed over the greening Donside hills. The first thunder rumbled and the whole village was filled with the blissful, reviving scent of bursting tree buds and thawed black earth. Whitecaps were skimming across the blue flood of the Don and with the lower wind came an invigorating dampness and the astringent smell of rotting leaves and wet wood. A strip of ploughed land sewn on to a hillside like a patch of black velvet was steaming, and the hilltops were wrapped in a quivering haze; a lark was singing exultantly right over the road and susliks were running across it, uttering their thin, high-pitched whistles. And above this world with all its great fertility and abundance of lifegiving strength rode a proud and lofty sun.

In the middle of the village, by a bridge over a gully, where spring torrents from the hills were still babbling merrily, Natalya halted. Bending down as if to fasten the strap of her shoe but actually to hide her face from Grigory, she asked, 'Why are you silent?'

'What is there to talk about with you?'

'There is something... Why don't you tell me about your carrying on around Karginskaya, about your drinking and whoring?'

'So you know already?' Grigory took out his pouch and made himself a cigarette. The mixture of clover and homegrown tobacco gave off a fragrant scent. Grigory took his first pull at the cigarette and asked again, 'So you know, do you? Who from?'

'I know if I say I do. The whole village knows, so I had plenty of people to hear it from.'

'Well, if you know, why should I tell you?'

Grigory walked off with long strides. The crisp beat of his footsteps on the wooden planks of the bridge and the echoing patter of Natalya's as she hurried after him resounded in the stillness of the clear spring air. For a time Natalya walked on without speaking, wiping her now rapidly flowing tears, then she choked back her sobs and asked, 'So you're going back to your old ways, are you?'

'Drop it, Natalya!'

'You great greedy dog! Will you never be satisfied? Why are you torturing me again, damn you?'

'You shouldn't listen to so much gossip.'

'But you admitted it yourself!'

'They must have told you more than really happened. Well, I may be a bit in the wrong with you... But it's this life, it makes you like that... When you're risking death all the time, you can't help stepping out of the furrow sometimes.'

'Think of your children, they're growing up! Where's your conscience? How can you look them in the face!'

'Conscience! Pah!' Grigory showed his dazzling teeth in a smile and laughed. 'I've forgotten what the word means. What conscience can you have when life's all out of joint... You go about killing people... And you don't know what the whole bloody mix-up is all about... But how can I tell you? You wouldn't understand! Nothing ever burns in you but a woman's fury. You'll never understand what's eating at my heart, sucking my blood. Now I've taken to vodka. The other day I had a fit. My heart stopped beating altogether for a minute, my body went cold...' Grigory's face darkened and he forced out the words, 'I'm having a bad time. That's why I look for something to make me forget—vodka, women... No, wait a minute! Let me speak! There's something nagging at my guts, gnawing me... Our life's taken a wrong turn and maybe I'm to blame... We ought to be making peace now with the Reds and joining up with them against the Cadets. But how can we? Who can bring us and the Reds together? How can we write off the wrongs on both sides? Half the Cossacks over there, across the Donets, and the ones that have stayed behind are so bitter they'd bite the land they walk on... My head's all fuzzed, Natalya... Even your Grandad Grishaka reads to me from the Bible and says we didn't do right, we shouldn't have rebelled. He blamed your father.'

'Grandad's out of his mind by now! It'll be your turn next.'

'That's the only way you can argue, your mind can't rise to anything else.'

'Don't try to talk me round! You've done wrong, you've done a rotten mean thing, and now you try to blame it all on the war.You're all the same! Haven't I had enough pain to bear because of you, you devil? It's a pity I didn't stab myself to death when I tried.'

'It's no use talking to you. If you're so upset, have a cry—tears always soften a woman's grief. But I can't be any comfort to you. I'm so stained with the blood of others that I haven't a grain of pity left for anyone. I hardly feel anything for the children, let alone myself. The war's sucked it all out of me. And I'm afraid of what I've become... If you looked into my heart, you'd see it's as black as an empty well.'

They had almost reached home when the rain came lashing down from a small grey cloud that had drifted over. It laid the light sun-scented dust on the road, pattered on the roofs, and made the air fresh and vibrantly cool. Grigory unbuttoned his greatcoat, covered the now violently weeping Natalya and put his arm round her. And so they walked into the yard in the pelting spring rain, covered by one greatcoat and holding each other tight.

That evening Grigory put the ridger in order and checked the hoses of the seeder. Anvil Semyon's fifteen-year-old son, who had learned his father's trade and since the uprising become the only blacksmith in the village, fitted the share on the Melekhovs' old plough as best he could. Everything was ready for the spring work. The oxen, well fed with the hay Pantelei had laid by, looked sleek and fit after the winter.

The next morning Grigory intended going out to the steppe. When it was almost bedtime, his mother and Dunyashka decided to light the stove and cook some food for the ploughman to take with him to the fields. Grigory planned to work there for about five days, sow enough grain for himself and his mother-in-law, plough up another five acres or so for melon and sunflowers, and then send for his father and let the old man finish off the sowing.

A lilac wisp of smoke spiralled up from the chimney and Dunyashka, who was by now every inch a woman though not yet married, darted about the yard collecting dry twigs for the fire. Grigory glanced now and then at her shapely figure, the steep rise of her breasts, and thought with sad vexation, 'What a fine wench she's grown up to be! Life's flying by like a racehorse. A short while ago she was only a snotty little girl; her plaits used to dance from side to side when she ran about, but now look at her—she'd be ripe for marriage any day. And here I am with my hair going grey already. Life's slipping away from me... Grandad Grishaka was right, "Life has gone by in a flash like summer lightning." A man's time on earth is short enough as it is and we're not going to get even that... Oh, to hell with it all! If I'm going to be killed, let it be soon.'

Darya came over to him. Her recovery since Petro's death had been remarkably rapid. She had missed him badly at first, her face had sallowed with grief and she had looked older. But as soon as the spring breezes began to blow and the sun grew a little warmer, Darya's sorrows had vanished with the melting snow. Her oval cheeks had a fine bloom on them, her eyes had acquired a new sparkle and the hip-swaying lightness had come back into her walk. Her old habits had also returned. Once more the slender arches of her brows were pencilled in black and her cheeks glistened with face cream; she had recovered her desire to banter and embarrass Natalya with a lewd jest, and more and more often her lips curved in a smile of mysterious expectation. Life had triumphed.

She came up to Grigory and halted, smiling. Her handsome face gave off the intoxicating scent of cucumber pomade.

'Couldn't I help you in some way, Grisha, love?'

'There's no way.'

'Oh, Grigory Panteleyevich! How sternly you treat

me, and me a widow! I never get a smile or even a sign of attention from you!'

'Why don't you go and get on with your cooking, glad eyes?'

'And why should I?'

'You might give Natalya a hand. Look at Mishatka, he's up to his ears in dirt.'

'As if I had nothing better to do! So you'll have the children and I'm to run around keeping them clean? Not likely! Your Natalya breeds like a rabbit. She'll bear you another dozen or so. Why, my arms will drop off while I'm washing them all for you.'

'That's enough! Off you go now!'

'Grigory Panteleyevich! You're the only Cossack in the whole village. Don't drive me away, let me look at your lovely black moustache from a distance at least.'

Grigory burst into a laugh and tossed the hair back from his sweating forehead.

'What a hussy you are! How did Petro ever manage to live with you... You'll always get what you're after, I reckon.'

'Indeed I will!' Darya affirmed proudly and with half-closed eyes sent a playful look at Grigory, then glanced in feigned alarm towards the house. 'Ooh! I thought Natalya had come out... She's so jealous, something awful! When we were having our lunch the other day, I took one little look at you and her face went as long as a fiddle. But only yesterday the young women around here were saying to me, "This isn't fair! There's not a man in the whole village and your Grisha comes home on leave and doesn't stir from his wife's side. How are we supposed to get along? Maybe there's only half of him left after all his wounds, but we'd be glad to get our hands on that half even. Tell him he'd better not go about the village at night or we'll catch him and he'll be in trouble!" So I told them, "It's no good, girls, our Grisha only lets himself go in other villages, but while he's at home he clings to Natalya's skirts. Of late he's got quite saintly..."'

'What a bitch you are!' Grigory said unoffendedly, laughing. 'You've got a tongue as long as a broomstick!'

'I'm what I am. But your dear Natalya, the pure and undefiled, gave you short shrift last night, didn't she? Serves you right, you randy dog, you won't misbehave in future!'

'Now look here, I'll... Go away, Darya, and mind your own business.'

'That's what I am doing. What I mean is your Natalya's a fool. Her husband comes home for once in a while and she gives herself airs. Went to bed on the chest... I wouldn't refuse a Cossack right now! So look out! I'd scare even a brave man like you if I got hold of you!'

Darya snapped her teeth, burst into a laugh and walked off to the house, looking back at the laughing and embarrassed Grigory, her gold ear-rings glinting in the sunshine.

'You were lucky to die, brother Petro,' Grigory thought to himself more cheerfully. 'That's not Darya, it's the devil incarnate! She'd have scragged the life out of you anyway!'

XLVII

The last lights were going out in the village of Bakhmutkin. A mild frost was spreading a thin crust of ice over the puddles. A flock of belatedly migrating cranes had alighted for their night's rest in the stubble on the fringe of the village. A breeze from the north-east carried the sound of their weary trumpeting to the village. It blended with and brought out the placid stillness of the April night. Deep shadows gathered in the orchards; somewhere a cow mooed; then all was silent. For half an hour the stillness was broken only by the mournful calls of the sandpipers, still on the wing even at night, and the whirring of the countless wild duck as they sped on towards the abundant waters of the flooded Don. After a while voices sounded in one of the streets on the outskirts, cigarettes glowed in the darkness, a horse snorted and frozen mud crackled under hooves. A patrol was returning to the village where two insurgent Cossack squadrons of the 6th Separate Brigade were stationed. The Cossacks rode into the yard of the last house in the village, and there was a murmur of talk as they tethered their horses to some sledges that had been left lying in the middle of the yard and tossed them some fodder. A rather husky voice started up a ditty, uttering the words clearly but in a tired, slow way:

> One day when I was walking,
> With a lassie I got talking,
> And just for old time's sake
> A joke I chanced to make...

And then a lively tenor soared like a bird over the husky bass and with a cheerful flourish continued:

> *The lass, she didn't take the joke*
> *And—wham! my head she nearly broke,*
> *My Cossack heart it burned*
> *To feel itself so spurned...*

Several other deep voices joined in the song, the pace quickened and the tenor descant, showing off on the high notes, burst into a rollicking tirade:

> *So I rolled up my right sleeve,*
> *And on her ear a mark did leave.*
> *That lassie, there she stood,*
> *Red as raspberries, ripe and good,*
> *Red as raspberries, ripe and good,*
> *And through her tears she said,*
> *What kind of friend are you,*
> *You've had seven girls I knew,*
> *A widow was number eight,*
> *Your wife was number nine,*
> *And I'm the tenth, you swine...*

The trumpeting of the cranes in the bare stubble, the Cossack song and the swish of ducks' wings in the impenetrable darkness reached the ears of the Cossacks on guard at an outpost by the mill. They were fed up with spending the night on the cold, frosty ground, not allowed to smoke or talk or warm themselves with a walk or a tussle. All they could do was lie amongst those dry sunflower stalks and stare into the yawning darkness and listen with their ears to the ground. There was nothing visible at ten paces and the April night was so full of rustlings, so many suspicious sounds came from the darkness that any could rouse alarm. Was that a Red Army patrol making its stealthy way towards the post? Might that be the crackle of someone breaking through the scrub in the distance, the hiss of restrained breathing?.. Vypryazhkin, a young Cossack, who had been straining his eyes in the darkness, wiped away a tear with his glove and nudged his neighbour. The latter had curled up into a ball and was dozing with his head on his leather field bag; his Japanese cartridge belt was sticking into his ribs but he could not be bothered to find a more comfortable position and did not want to let the cold night air in through the tight folds of his greatcoat. The rustle of brushwood and the hiss of suppressed breathing grew louder and suddenly sounded quite close by. Vypryazhkin raised himself on his elbow, stared through the tangled scrub and with an effort made out the shape of a large hedgehog. The hedgehog was hurrying along on the trail of a mouse with its small piggy nose close to the ground and its spiky back scratching the dry sunflower stalks. Suddenly it sensed the presence of an enemy a few paces away and looked up to see the man examining it. The man breathed a sigh of relief and whispered, 'You rotten devil! How you scared me...'

The hedgehog hastily hid its head, drew in its feet and lay in a prickly ball for a minute, then slowly unrolled, put its feet to the cold ground and scurried away, butting the sunflower stalks and crushing the withered bindweed. And once again the silence wove its spell and the night was like a fairy-tale...

Second cock-crow echoed over the village. The sky was clearer. The first stars were showing through a curtain of thin clouds. Then a wind sprang up and scattered them and the sky looked down with countless golden eyes.

And it was just at this time that Vypryazhkin heard the steady beat of horse's hooves, the crackle of brushwood, the clank of metal and a little later, the creaking of a saddle. The other Cossacks heard it too. Fingers curled round rifle triggers.

'Ready!' the section commander whispered.

The black shape of a horseman stood out against the background of the starry sky. Someone was walking his horse in the direction of the village.

'Halt!.. Who goes there?.. Where's your pass?'

The Cossacks jumped up, ready to shoot. The rider halted and raised his hands.

'Comrades, don't shoot!'

'Where's your pass?'

'Comrades!'

'Where's your pass? Troop...'

'Stop!.. I'm alone... I surrender!'

'Wait, lads! Don't shoot! We'll take him alive!'

The section commander ran up to the rider. Vypryazhkin seized the reins. The horseman lifted his leg over the saddle and dismounted.

'Who are you? A Red? That's it, lads! See the star on his cap. Caught you, eh!'

The horseman stretched his legs and replied calmly.

'Take me to your commander. I have a message of great importance for him. I am the commander of the Serdobsk Regiment and have come here to parley.'

'The commander? Kill the swine, lads! Here, Luka, lemme...'

'Comrades! You'll always have time to kill me, but first let me deliver the message I have for your commander. I repeat, it's a matter of the greatest urgency. You are at liberty to take my weapons if you're afraid I shall attempt to escape.'

The Red commander unbuckled his sword-belt.

'Go on! Off with it!' one of the Cossacks urged him.

The sabre and revolver were passed to the section commander.

'Search the commander of the Serdobsk Regiment!' he ordered, mounting his prisoner's horse.

The prisoner was searched. The section commander and Vypryazhkin escorted him to the village. The latter walked at his side, holding an Austrian carbine at the ready. The section commander rode behind them, well satisfied with himself.

For about ten minutes they went on in silence. The prisoner often stopped to light a cigarette, shielding the fluttering match flame with the hem of his greatcoat. The scent of good cigarettes was too much for Vypryazhkin.

'Give me one,' he said.

'Certainly!'

Vypryazhkin took the well filled leather cigarette case, helped himself, and put the case into his pocket. The Red commander raised no protest, but a little later, when they entered the village, he asked, 'Where are you taking me?'

'You'll find out when you get there.'

'But where?'

'To the squadron commander.'

'Take me to brigade commander Bogatiryov.'

'There isn't anyone of that name.'

'Isn't there? I know that he arrived here with his staff yesterday.'

'We don't know about that.'

'Come now, comrades! How is it I know if you don't. It's not a military secret, particularly if it has come to the ears of your enemies.'

'Keep moving.'

'I am moving. So you must take me to Bogatiryov.'

'Stuff it! I'm not even allowed to talk to you, according to army regulations!'

'Do army regulations permit you to take my cigarette case?'

'Huh! Keep moving and hold your tongue or I'll have your greatcoat off your back. Touchy, isn't he!'

It took time to wake the squadron commander. He sat rubbing his eyes with his fists, yawning and frowning, unable to grasp what the joyfully grinning section commander was telling him.

'Who is he? Commander of the Serdobsk Regiment? You're not having me on? Show me his papers.'

A few minutes later he and the Red commander were on their way to the brigade commander's quarters. Bogatiryov jumped out of bed like a madman as soon as he heard that the commander of the Serdobsk Regiment had been captured. He buttoned his trousers, slung the braces over his broad shoulders, lighted the oil lamp and turned to the Red commander standing at attention in the doorway.

'Are you the commander of the Serdobsk Regiment?'

'Yes and my name is Voronovsky.'

'Please, sit down.'

'Thank you.'

'How was it you... What were the circumstances of your capture?'

'I came here deliberately. I must speak to you in private. Tell the others to leave the room.'

Bogatiryov waved his hand. The squadron commander and the master of the house, a red-bearded Old Believer who had been standing open-mouthed beside him, withdrew. Bogatiryov sat at the table in his dirty undervest, rubbing his shaven head, which was as dark and round as a watermelon. His face with its bloated cheeks creased red by sleep, expressed restrained curiosity.

Voronovsky, a stockily built man in a well-fitting greatcoat criss-crossed by the straps of an officer's sword belt, straightened his square shoulders; a smile slipped from under his black clipped moustache.

'I hope I have the honour of speaking to an officer? Allow me to say a word or two about myself, then I shall tell you about the mission that has brought me here... I was a nobleman by birth and a Captain in the service of the tsar. During the war with Germany I served in the 117th Lyubomir Rifle Regiment. In 1918 as a regular officer, I was mobilised under a decree of the

Soviet Government. At present, as you know, I command the Serdobsk Regiment of the Red Army. While serving in the Red Army I have for long sought an opportunity of going over to your ... to the side of those who are fighting the Bolsheviks...'

'You were a long time about it, captain.'

'Yes, but I wanted to redeem my guilt towards Russia and not only change sides myself (I could have done that long ago) but also bring with me a Red Army unit, the soundest elements of it, of course, those who were deluded by the Communists and drawn into this fratricidal war.'

Former Captain Voronovsky glanced with his close-set grey eyes at Bogatiryov and, noticing his unbelieving smile, flushed like a girl and continued hurriedly. 'You may naturally feel a certain distrust of me and what I am telling you. In your place I should probably feel the same. But allow me to offer you factual proof ... irrefutable proof.'

He turned back the skirt of his greatcoat, took a penknife out of his trouser pocket, bent down with a creak of the straps over his shoulders, and carefully unpicked the hem. A minute later he extracted some yellowed papers and a small photograph.

Bogatiryov examined the papers carefully. One of them certified that 'the bearer is Lieutenant Voronovsky of the 117th Lyubomir Rifle Regiment travelling on convalescent leave for two weeks to the Smolensk Province'. The warrant bore the stamp and signature of the Chief Surgeon of No. 8. Field Hospital of the 14th Siberian Rifle Division. The other papers in Voronovsky's name testified indisputably to the fact that Voronovsky was an officer and the eyes that looked at Bogatiryov from the photograph were the merry close-set eyes of the young Second Lieutenant Voronovsky. An officer's Cross of St. George glittered on the splendidly cut field tunic, and the virgin whiteness of the shoulder straps threw into relief the second lieutenant's brown cheeks and dark moustache.

'Well?' Bogatiryov asked.

'I am here to tell you that I and my assistant, former Lieutenant Volkov, have won over the Red soldiers, and that the whole Serdobsk Regiment, with the exception of the Communists, of course, is prepared at any minute to come over to your side. They are practically all peasants of the Saratov and Samara provinces. They have agreed to fight the Bolsheviks. Now we must at once come to terms about the surrender. The regiment is at present in Ust-Khopyorskaya. Its strength is about one thousand two hundred men; it has a Communist group of thirty-eight, plus a platoon of thirty local Communists. We'll take over the battery attached to the regiment. The crews will probably have to be destroyed because most of them are Communists. My Red Army men's discontent arises from the hardships suffered by their fathers on account of the food requisitioning campaign. We have taken advantage of this fact and talked them into going over to the Cossacks, that is, to you. My soldiers have misgivings that if the regiment surrenders, they may be subjected to ill-treatment... And on this point—it's a minor one, of course, but—you and I must come to some agreement.'

'What kind of ill-treatment could there be?'

'Well, killings, robbery...'

'No, we shan't allow that!'

'And another thing: the men insist that the Serdobsk Regiment be kept intact and fight with you against the Bolsheviks, but as an independent combat unit.'

'It's not in my power to tell you that...'

'Yes, I quite understand! You'll get in touch with higher authority and inform us later.'

'Yes, I'll have to report this to Vyoshenskaya.'

'Forgive me but I have very little time. If I'm as much as an hour late my absence will be noticed by the regimental commissar. I think we shall agree about the terms of surrender. Don't be long in telling me the decision of your command. The regiment may be transferred to the Donets or given reinforcements, and that will mean...'

'Yes, I'll send a despatch rider to Vyoshenskaya right away.'

'And another thing. Tell your Cossacks to return my weapons. I was not only disarmed,' Voronovsky interrupted his smooth recital and smiled in some embarrassment, 'They also took ... my cigarette case. It's only a small thing, of course, but I value it as a family heirloom...'

'You'll get everything back. How can I inform you when we get the answer from Vyoshenskaya?'

'Here, in Bakhmutkin. In two days' time a woman will come from Ust-Khopyorskaya. Let's say the password will be "union". You will tell her. And only verbally, of course.'

* * *

Half an hour later a Cossack of the Maksayevskaya squadron galloped westward to Vyoshenskaya.

The next day Kudinov's personal orderly arrived in Bakhmutkin, found the brigade commander's quarters and without even bothering to tether his horse strode into the house and handed Grigory Bogatiryov a packet marked, 'Very Urgent. Top Secret'. Bogatiryov broke the seal with the greatest impatience. On the headed note-paper of the Upper Don District Soviet there was a message in Kudinov's own bold hand:

Good health to you, Bogatiryov! This is joyful news. We authorise you to conduct negotiations with the Serdobsk men and persuade them to surrender at all costs. I advise you to make concessions and promise that we'll keep the regiment intact and not even disarm it. Absolutely insist on the arrest and surrender of the Communists, the regimental commissar and, above all, our Vyoshenskaya, Yelanskaya and Ust-Khopyorskaya Communists. Make sure the battery, transports and equipment are seized. And get on with it as fast as you can! Concentrate your forces at the point of arrival, then quietly surround the regiment and disarm it at once. If they make any fuss, wipe out the lot, to the last man. Act cautiously but resolutely. As soon as you've disarmed them, herd the whole regiment to Vyoshenskaya. Drive them along the right bank. That'll make it easier for you because the front will be further away and it's open steppe—they won't get far if they do come to their senses and decide to make a break for it. Send them through the villages along the Don with two mounted squadrons to keep an eye on them. In Vyoshenskaya we'll sort them out, two or three men to a squadron, and see how they go about fighting their own lot. After that it won't be our worry. When we link up with our own lads across the Donets, they can try them and do what they like with them. They can hang the lot for all I care. I shan't be sorry. I rejoice in your success. Keep me informed daily by despatch rider.

Kudinov.

A postscript read:

If the Serdobsk Regiment surrenders any of our local Communists, send them to Vyoshenskaya under a strong escort, also through the villages. But let the regiment go through first. For the escort choose the most reliable Cossacks (the fiercer and older ones) and let them spread the word among the people in advance.

293

There's no need for us to stain our hands with them. The women will beat the life out of them if the thing is properly organised. Get me? It's the best policy for us; if we shoot them, the rumour will reach the Reds that prisoners are being shot; but this is simpler; set the people against them, release the people's anger, like a dog off its chain. Mob law and have done with it. No questions asked and no answers given!

XLVIII

On April 12th the 1st Moscow Regiment was badly mauled in an engagement with the insurgents at Antonov, a village of the Yelanskaya stanitsa.

The Reds fought their way into the village without knowing the terrain. The farmsteads lay far apart, islanded on small patches of firm loamy ground, while the brushwood-covered streets and lanes ran through almost impassable marshy ground. The village was buried in dense alder thickets in a wet low-lying locality. Along its edge flowed the River Yelanka, which, though shallow, had a muddy, treacherous bottom.

The Moscow Regiment tried to make a sweep through the village, but as soon as they had passed the first farmsteads and entered the alder thickets they found they could make no further progress in line. The commander of the 2nd Battalion, a stubborn Latvian, ignored the arguments of one of the company commanders, who had only just managed to pull his horse out of a deep slough, and gave the order to advance, leading the way boldly over the quaking ground. His men hesitated and then followed him, carrying their machine-guns. They had advanced for about a hundred paces, sinking knee-deep in the mud, when warning shouts came from the right flank and echoed along the line, 'They're outflanking us!' 'Cossacks!' 'We're surrounded!'

Two insurgent squadrons had in fact turned the battalion's flank and were attacking from the rear.

In the alder thickets the 1st and 2nd battalions lost nearly a third of their men and retreated.

During the battle Ivan was wounded in the leg by a home-made insurgent bullet. Mishka Koshevoi carried him out of the line, stopped a Red Army ammunition cart galloping across the dike, and forced the driver at sabre point to take the wounded man.

The regiment was routed and thrown back to the

village of Yelansky. The defeat had a disastrous effect on the offensive of all the Red Army units advancing along the left bank of the Don. Malkin's force was obliged to leave Bukanovskaya and march twenty versts northward to Slashchevskaya; it was then pushed back by insurgent forces attacking furiously in greatly superior numbers and, the day before the ice broke up, crossed the Khopyor, drowning several of its horses, and made for Kumylzhenskaya.

The 1st Moscow Regiment, cut off by floating ice in the mouth of the Khopyor, crossed to the right bank of the Don and halted in Ust-Khopyorskaya, awaiting replacements. Soon the Serdobsk Regiment arrived. There was a vast difference between the two regiments. The workers, from Moscow, Tula and Nizhny Novgorod, who formed the core of the Moscow Regiment, fought valiantly and stubbornly, taking on the insurgents in hand-to-hand combat and losing scores of men in killed and wounded every day. Only the trap in Antonov had temporarily put the regiment out of action, but even in retreat it did not leave behind a single cart or crate of ammunition for the enemy to make use of. But in its first engagement at the village of Yagodinsky a company of Serdobsk men failed to stand up to an insurgent cavalry attack; at the sight of the charging Cossack cavalry they left their trenches and would undoubtedly have been cut to pieces if the Communist machine-gunners had not repelled the attack with a barrage of machine-gun fire.

The Serdobsk Regiment had been hastily mustered in the town of Serdobsk. They were all Saratov peasants of the older age groups, and obviously in no mood for fighting. The depressing thing was that most of them were illiterate or came from well-to-do kulak families. Half of the regiment's command were former officers of the old army; the commissar, an uninspiring, weak-willed individual, enjoyed no authority among the men, and the traitors—the regimental commander, his chief of staff, and two of the company commanders—who intended to surrender the regiment, carried on their criminal work of demoralising the rank and file before the very eyes of the oblivious Communist group. With the help of the counter-revolutionary kulak elements, they agitated skilfully against the Communists and spread disbelief in the possibility of suppressing the uprising.

Stokman, who was billeted with three men of the Serdobsk Regiment, observed developments in the regiment worriedly and was finally convinced of the grave danger that threatened it after a clash between himself and the men with whom he was sharing quarters.

On the 27th of April, when it was growing dark, two of the Serdobsk men came into the house. One of them, named Gorigasov, gave Stokman and Ivan, who was lying on the bed, an unpleasant smile and instead of a greeting said, 'So this is what we've come to! Back home they're confiscating our folk's grain while here we have to fight for no one knows what.'

'Don't you know what you're fighting for?' Stokman asked sharply.

'No, I don't! The Cossacks are farmers like us! We know what they're rebelling against! That we do know!'

Stokman's usual restraint deserted him. 'And do you know, you swine, what language you're talking? It's Whiteguard language!'

'Don't you "swine" me! Or you'll get one on your fine moustache!.. Did you hear that, lads? What d'ye think of him!'

'Calm down, big beard! We've seen plenty of your kind before now!' the other, a short thick-set man, solid as a sack of flour, intervened. 'You think that if you're a Communist you can stop our gob? You'd better watch out, or we'll knock your cockiness out of you!'

He stepped in front of the puny Gorigasov and advanced on Stokman, keeping his strong, stumpy arms behind his back and rolling his eyes.

'What's this? Are you all infected with the Whiteguard spirit?' Stokman asked, breathing heavily, and pushed the man away with some force.

The man staggered and, scowling angrily, was about to seize Stokman's arm, but Gorigasov stopped him.

'Don't muck with him!'

'This is counter-revolutionary talk! We shall try you as traitors to the Soviet government!'

'You can't put the whole regiment on trial!' one of the men quartered with Stokman remarked.

He was supported.

'The Communists get sugar and cigarettes, but there's none for us!'

'That's a lie!' Ivan shouted from his bed, raising himself on his elbow. 'We get just the same as you!'

Stokman put on his coat and left without another word. No one attempted to stop him but he was followed by jeers.

Stokman found the regimental commissar at headquarters. He called him into another room, agitatedly reported the clash with the Serdobsk men, and said they should be arrested. The commissar listened, scratching his fiery red beard and irresolutely fingering his black horn-rimmed spectacles.

'Tomorrow we'll get the group together and discuss the situation. As things stand at the moment I don't think we can arrest these lads.'

'Why not?' Stokman asked bluntly.

'Well, you know, Comrade Stokman.. I've noticed myself that things are not too good in the regiment. There's some kind of counter-revolutionary organisation at work, but we can't put our finger on it. But most of the regiment's under its influence. It's the peasant element—what can you do! I've reported the situation and suggested withdrawing the regiment and disbanding it.'

'But why do you consider it impossible to arrest these Whiteguard agents here and now and have them up before the division's Revolutionary Tribunal? After all, such talk is sheer treachery!'

'Yes, but this might lead to some undesirable excesses and even a mutiny.'

'So that's it? Then why, if you noticed this mood of the majority, didn't you inform the political department long ago?'

'I've just told you I did inform them. For some reason the answer from Ust-Medveditskaya has been delayed. As soon as the regiment is taken out of line we'll crack down on all infringers of discipline and particularly those who said what you've just reported.' The commissar frowned and added in a whisper, 'I have suspicions of Voronovsky and... the chief of staff Volkov. After the meeting tomorrow I'll go to Ust-Medveditskaya myself. Urgent measures must be taken to localise this danger. Please, keep our conversation secret.'

'But why not get the Communists together now? There's no time to lose, comrade!'

'I understand. But at the moment it's impossible. Most of the Communists are on guard or outpost duty. I insisted on that because it would have been unwise to trust anyone but Communists in this situation. And the battery, which is manned mainly by Communists, won't get here from Krutovsky until tonight. I summoned it because of the trouble in the regiment.'

Stokman returned from headquarters and gave Ivan and Mishka Koshevoi a brief account of what the commissar had told him.

'Can you walk yet?' he asked Ivan.

'With a limp. I was afraid of making it worse, but I'll have to walk now, whether I like it or not.'

Stokman wrote a detailed report on the state of the regiment and at midnight wakened Koshevoi. Tucking the packet into the front of Mishka's shirt, he said, 'Get yourself a horse and ride at once to Ust-Medveditskaya. Deliver this letter to the political department of the 14th Division at all costs. How many hours will it take you to get there? Where d'you think you can find a horse?'

Mishka grunted as he stamped his feet into his stiff, rusty-looking boots, and answered between pauses:

'I'll steal a horse ... from one of the mounted patrols. To get to Ust-Medveditskaya?.. Two hours at the most. The patrol horses aren't much good or I'd make it ... in an hour and a half. I served on the range as a herdsman... I know how to squeeze the last drop of speed out of a horse.'

He transferred the packet to the pocket of his greatcoat.

'Why put it there?' Stokman asked.

'So it'll be handy if the Serdobsk men grab me.'

'And then what?' Stokman was still puzzled.

'I'll put it in my mouth and swallow it.'

'Good for you!' Stokman smiled bleakly and, as though seized by foreboding, hugged Mishka and kissed him hard with cold trembling lips. 'Off you go.'

Mishka managed to untie one of the reconnaissance patrol's best horses, walked it quietly past the guard post, keeping his finger on the trigger of his new cavalry carbine, and made his way across country to the highway. Only there did he sling his carbine over his shoulder and start 'squeezing' out of the docktailed Saratov nag a speed that nature had never intended for it.

XLIX

At dawn it began to drizzle. The wind rose and a black stormcloud approached from the east. The Serdobsk men quartered with Stokman and Ivan got up and left at first light. Half an hour later Tolkachov, a Communist from Yelanskaya, who, like Stokman and his comrades, had been attached to the Serdobsk Regiment, burst breathlessly into the room.

'Stokman, Koshevoi, are you home? Come at once!'

'What's the matter? Come in here!' Stokman went out into the front room, pulling on his greatcoat.

'Trouble!' Tolkachov whispered, following Stokman into the room. 'The infantry has just been trying to disarm ... to disarm the battery that arrived from Krutovsky. There was shooting... The gunners fought off the attack, took out the breech-blocks and got away to the other side by boat.'

'Go on!' Ivan urged him, groaning as he pulled his boot on over his wounded leg.

'And now they're holding a meeting by the church... The whole regiment.'

'Get a move on!' Stokman ordered Ivan and, gripping Tolkachov's sleeve, asked, 'Where's the commissar? Where are all the other Communists?'

'I don't know... Some have cleared out. I came here. The telegraph's occupied, they won't let anyone in... We've got to get away! But how can we?' Tolkachov slumped down on a chest and let his hands dangle between his knees.

At that moment there was a clatter of footsteps in the porch and half a dozen men of the Serdobsk Regiment crowded into the house, their faces flushed with angry determination.

'Communists, out to the meeting! Hurry up!'

Stokman exchanged glances with Ivan and compressed his lips sternly.

'We're coming!'

'Leave your weapons behind. You're not going into battle!' one of the Serdobsk men suggested, but Stokman, seeming not to hear, slung his rifle over his shoulder and was the first to leave.

One thousand one hundred throats were roaring discordantly on the square. There was no sign of the local people, who were staying indoors in fear of what might happen (the day before there had been persistent rumours that the regiment was going over to the insurgents and there might be fighting with the Communists). Stokman was the first to approach the seething crowd. He looked round, searching for members of the command. The commissar of the regiment was marched past them with two men holding his arms. Pale-faced, he was pushed through the milling crowd of Red Army men. For a few minutes Stokman lost sight of him, then he appeared in their midst, standing on a card-table that someone had dragged out of a neighbouring house. Stokman glanced back. Ivan had limped up behind him and was standing leaning on his rifle with the men who had come for them beside him.

'Comrades, men of the Red Army!' the commissar's voice rose faintly above the crowd. 'Holding meetings at a time like this, when the enemy is within shooting distance... Comrades!'

He was not allowed to continue. The grey Red Army caps swirled round the table, the grey-blue stubble of bayonets swayed, fists were brandished, and short, wickedly angry cries cracked out across the square like pistol shots.

'So we're comrades now!'

'Take your leather jacket off!'

'You tricked us!'

'Who're you making us fight?!'

'Pull him down!'

'Hit him!'

'Stick a bayonet in him!'

'His commissar days are over!'

Stokman saw a huge elderly Red Army man scramble on to the table and grab the commissar's short red beard with his left hand. The table lurched and both the soldier and the commissar fell into the outstretched arms of the assembly. The place where the card-table had been became a seething mass of grey greatcoats; the commissar's lone desperate cry was drowned in a great roar of voices.

Stokman leapt forward and made for the spot where the commissar had spoken, relentlessly pushing and levering apart the unyielding grey-greatcoated backs. No one stopped him but fists and rifle butts rained on his back and neck, the rifle was ripped off his shoulder, and the big red-topped fur hat from his head.

'Where're you going, you devil?' one of the Red Army men whose foot Stokman had trodden on bawled indignantly.

By the overturned table a stocky platoon commander barred Stokman's path. His grey lambskin cap had slipped to the back of his head, his greatcoat hung wide open, sweat was streaming down his brick-red face and his burning, spiteful eyes were squinting savagely.

'Where're you barging to?'

'Let me speak! Let one of the rank and file speak!' Stokman croaked, scarcely able to catch his breath, and in one swift movement turned the table on to its legs. He was even helped to climb on to it. But the furious yelling was still rolling in waves across the square and Stokman had to shout at the top of his voice, 'Silence!' Half a minute later, when the noise had abated, he began in a strained voice, suppressing a cough, 'Men of the Red Army! Shame on you! You are betraying the people's government in its gravest hour! You are wavering when you should be striking the enemy to the heart! You hold meetings when the land of Soviets is being throttled by its enemies! You stand on the brink of downright betrayal! Why has this happened? You have been sold to the Cossack generals by your traitor commanders! These former officers of the old army have betrayed the trust of the Soviet government and, taking advantage of your ignorance, intend to surrender the regiment to the Cossacks. Come to your senses! They want to use you to strangle the power of the workers and peasants!'

The commander of the 2nd Company, Veistminster, a former ensign, lifted his rifle, but Stokman noticed his movement and shouted, 'Don't you dare! You'll have time to kill me later on. Listen to what a soldier Communist has to say! We Communists have given our whole lives ... all our blood ... drop by drop...' Stokman's voice rose to a frighteningly high pitch, his face grew deathly pale and convulsed, '...to the cause of serving the working class ... the oppressed peasantry. We are used to looking death fearlessly in the face. You can kill me...'

'We've heard that once!'

'That's enough of your yarns!'

'Let him speak!'

'Shut up!'

'...you can kill me, but I repeat: come to your senses! You shouldn't be holding meetings, you should be attacking the Whites!' Stokman scanned the hushed crowd with narrowed eyes and caught sight of the regimental commander not far away from him. Voronovsky was standing next to a Red Army man, whispering to him with a forced smile on his face. 'The commander of your regiment...'

Stokman stretched his arm and pointed at Voronov-sky, but the regimental commander put his hand to his mouth and whispered something anxiously to the Red Army man beside him, and before Stokman could utter the phrase, a shot sounded dully in the damp April air, charged with the moisture of young rain. The sound was slack and muffled, like the flick of a whip's end, but Stokman clutched his chest and sank to his knees, dropping his bare grizzled head... The next moment he jumped swaying to his feet.

'Osip Davydovich!' Ivan groaned as he saw Stokman rise, and he tried to reach him but his elbows were seized and someone whispered, 'Keep quiet and don't move! Give us your rifle, your bastard!'

Ivan was disarmed, his pockets searched, and he was led away from the square. On all sides Communists were being seized and disarmed. A burst of five or six shots sounded in a lane near a solidly built merchant's house and a Communist machine-gunner who had refused to surrender his Lewis gun was killed.

Meanwhile Stokman with pink blood foaming on his lips and hiccoughing violently, his face deathly white, stood for a minute swaying on the card-table and with a last great effort of will managed to shout, '...You have been misled!.. These traitors ... they are winning their pardon, new officer's rank... But communism will live!.. Comrades!.. Come to your senses!..' Once again the Red Army man standing beside Voronovsky brought his rifle to his shoulder. The second shot flung Stokman face downwards at the feet of the crowd. One of the Ser-dobsk men, with a long mouth, flat teeth and a face deeply scarred by smallpox, sprang youthfully on to the table and bellowed, 'We've heard all kinds of promises, but it's all a pack of lies and threats, dear comrades. This big-bearded speaker here has fizzled out—a dog's death for a dog! Death to the Communists, the enemies of the toiling peasantry! I'm telling you, comrades, dear soldiers, that our eyes have been opened. We know who we ought to be fighting! For example, now, what was it they said in our Volsk district? Equality, frater-nity of the peoples! That's what they said, these com-munists tricksters... But what has happened in practice? Sheer cannibalism! Take my own father, he's just sent us a message, a letter stained with tears. He writes: this is unheard-of outright robbery! They've swept all the grain out of my dad's barn and confiscated his little mill, but their decree proclaims they're for the toiling peasantry, don't it? If that mill was earned by my parents' sweat, then I ask you —isn't this sheer robbery by the Communists? Beat 'em up, beat 'em to pulp!'

The speaker never finished his oration. Two mounted insurgent squadrons trotted into Ust-Khopyorskaya from the west while Cossack infantry approached from the southern slopes of the Donside hills; escorted by a half-squadron, Cornet Bogatiryov, commander of the 6th Insurgent Separate Brigade, rode in with his staff.

And at that moment rain deluged from a cloud that had approached from the east and there was a long muffled rumble of thunder from the other side of the Don, above the Khopyor.

The Serdobsk Regiment hastily reassembled and formed fours and, as Bogatiryov's mounted staff group appeared, former captain Voronovsky raised his voice in a growling roar of command, unheard-of in the Red Army, 'Re-gi-ment! Atten-shun!'

L

Grigory Melekhov spent five days in Tatarsky, during which time he sowed several acres of wheat for himself and his mother-in-law, but as soon as his father Pantelei, eaten up by lice and a yearning to be at work on his farm, arrived home, he started making ready to rejoin his unit, which was still stationed on the Chir. In a confidential letter Kudinov informed him of the negotiations that had begun with the command of the Serdobsk Regiment and asked him to go and take over command of his division.

Grigory had decided he would try to reach Karginskaya that day. At noon he led his horse down to the Don to drink before leaving and as he went down the slope to the river, which had risen right up to the wattle fences of the vegetable patches, he saw Aksinya. It may have just seemed so to him, or perhaps she really did linger expectantly as she drew water, but Grigory involuntarily quickened his pace and in the brief moment that passed while he was approaching her, a flock of sad memories passed through his head.

Aksinya turned at the sound of his footsteps and her face expressed what was undoubtedly feigned surprise, but her joy at the meeting and the old pain betrayed her.

She gave him such a smile, so pitiful and confused, and so out of keeping with her proud features, that Grigory's heart quivered with pity and love. Stung by regret and overcome by a sudden flood of memories, he checked his horse and said, 'Hullo, Aksinya dear!'

'Hullo.'

Aksinya's quiet voice suggested widely differing shades of feeling—surprise, affection, bitterness...

'It's a long time since we talked.'

'Yes, it is.'

'I'd forgotten the sound of your voice.'

'So soon!'

'But was it soon?'

The horse strained forward and Grigory held it back by the bridle. Aksinya bent her head and tried to hook her pail on to her yoke but missed the handle. For a minute they stood in silence. A duck swished over their heads, as if thrown by a bowstring. The surf broke against the cliff, insatiably licking the slabs of light-blue chalk. White-fleeced waves flocked among the flooded forest. The wind carried a fine spray and the vapid smell of the Don as it rolled in a mighty flood towards its lower reaches.

Grigory turned his gaze from Aksinya's face to the Don. The pale waterlogged poplars rocked their bare branches and the flowering willows draped with catkins billowed proudly over the water like strange, very light green clouds. With a slight vexation and bitterness in his voice Grigory asked, 'Haven't we anything to say to each other these days? Why are you silent?'

But Aksinya had regained her composure; her face was cold and not a muscle stirred there when she replied, 'It looks as if we've said it all.'

'Are you sure?'

'It must be so. A tree only blooms once a year.'

'You think ours has bloomed and faded?'

'Hasn't it?'

'It's a funny thing...' Grigory let the horse go to the water and looked at Aksinya with a sad smile. 'But I still can't tear you out of my heart, love. My children are growing up and I'm half grey, we've been parted for so many years now... But I still think of you. I see you in my dreams and love you still. And sometimes, when I think of you, I remember the way we used to live at Listnitsky's ... how we loved each other ... and those memories... Sometimes, when your whole life comes back, you look at it and it's like an empty pocket, turned inside out.'

'Yes, it's the same with me... I must go now... We've been talking too long.'

Aksinya lifted her pails resolutely, rested her arms, already touched by the spring sun, on the arched beam of the yoke and was about to set off up the hill, but suddenly she turned to face Grigory and a barely perceptible youthful flush coloured her cheeks.

'This was where our love began, by this pier, Grigory. Don't you remember? We were seeing the Cossacks off to camp that day,' she said, smiling, and an almost merry note sounded in her voice.

'I remember every bit of it!'

Grigory led his horse into the yard and stabled it. Pantelei, who had not gone out to harrow that morning so that he could see Grigory off, came out from under the overhang of the shed and asked, 'Well, ye'll soon be on your way, will ye? Shall I give your horse some grain?'

'On my way? Where?' Grigory stared absently at his father.

'God bless ye! Why, to Karginskaya.'

'I won't be going today!'

'How so?'

'I've ... I've changed my mind.' Grigory licked his dry lips and looked up at the sky. 'The clouds are gathering, it's going to rain. What's the use of getting myself soaked?'

'No use at all,' the old man agreed but without believing him because only a few minutes ago from the cattle yard he had spotted Grigory and Aksinya talking by the pier. 'He's up to his old tricks,' the old man thought worriedly. 'I hope it's not going to upset things again between him and Natalya... That Grishka of mine, may the devil strike him! Who does he take after, the young hell-hound? Surely not me?' Pantelei turned away from the birch-tree trunk he had been stripping with his axe, stared at his son's slouched back and, pondering memories of what he had been like in his youth, decided, 'Yes, he takes after me, the devil! And he's gone one better than his father, the skirt-chaser! He needs a good thrashing to stop him from putting ideas into Aksinya's head again and starting trouble between our families. But how can you thrash him now?'

In other times, if Pantelei had seen Grigory chatting

305

to Aksinya in a back-lane, he would have laid into him with the first thing that came to hand, but now, at a loss, he said nothing and gave not so much as a hint that he had guessed the true reason for Grigory's delayed departure. And all because Grigory was no longer 'Grishka', a wild young Cossack, but the commander of a division, a 'general', who even without epaulettes was obeyed by thousands of Cossacks, and never addressed as anything but 'Grigory Panteleyevich'. How could he, Pantelei, who had never ranked higher than a sergeant, lift a hand against a general, even if that general was his own son? Respect for rank would not allow Pantelei even to contemplate such a thing, and for this reason he felt inhibited and somehow estranged from Grigory. It was his son's astonishing promotion that was to blame. Even when they were out ploughing the day before yesterday and Grigory had bawled at him, 'Hi, mind where you're going! Watch your plough!' Pantelei had borne it without a word. Lately their roles seemed to have been reversed. Grigory would shout at his ageing father now and then and Pantelei, hearing the rasp of command in his voice, would hurry about on his lame leg, doing his best to please.

'Afraid of the rain! There won't be any rain! How could there be when the wind's in the east and there's only one little cloud in the sky! Should I tell Natalya?'

At this enlightening thought Pantelei was about to go into the house, but changed his mind; fearing the row that might follow, he returned to his unfinished birch pole.

But as soon as Aksinya got home, she emptied her pails and went to the mirror embedded in the stove wall and made a long and anxious examination of her slightly aged but still lovely face. The wanton, alluring beauty was still there, but life's autumn had already cast its faded colours on the cheeks, yellowed the eyelids, woven fine threads of grey into the black hair, and dulled the eyes. There was a mournful weariness in them now.

Aksinya stood looking at herself for a while, then went to the bed, flung herself face downwards and gave way to tears more abundant and more sweetly relieving than she had known for many a long day.

In winter the freezing winds howl and whirl over the steep slopes of the Donside hills and, wherever there's a ridge, they carry snow from the bare ground and pile it in drifts, then pack it down in slabs. Sugar-white in the sunshine, light-blue in the twilight, pale violet in the morning and pink at sunrise, the snow monster hangs poised over the precipice. And hang it will, terrifying in its silence, until a thaw eats it away from beneath or a gust of wind adds to the burden of its own weight. And then, drawn irresistibly downwards, it will plunge with a soft and muffled roar, sweeping away the stunted thorn bushes, breaking the hawthorn that clings shyly to the slope, and dragging after it a seething, swirling train of snow dust.

The snowdrift of Aksinya's love needed only the smallest push. And that push had been given by her meeting with Grigory, by his tender 'Hullo, Aksinya dear!' And he? Wasn't he dear to her? Wasn't he the one she had remembered all these years, every day, every hour, forever going back to him in unrelenting thoughts, always to him? No matter what she was thinking or doing, always in her thoughts she was with Grigory. So does the blind horse plod in a circle, turning the water-wheel.

Aksinya lay on the bed till evening, then rose puffy-eyed, washed her face, combed her hair and with feverish haste, like a girl before betrothing, began to dress. She put on a clean blouse, a dark cherry-red woolen skirt, and tied her kerchief, and after another glance in the mirror left the house.

Tatarsky was wrapped in blue-grey twilight. Wild geese were calling anxiously from somewhere on the flooded banks. A pallid moon was rising feebly from behind the riverside poplars and a rippling greenish moonway lay across the water. The herd had come in from the steppe before dark. The cows had not eaten their fill on the young grass and were lowing in the yards. Aksinya left hers unmilked. She let a white-muzzled calf out of its pen and put it in with its mother; the calf greedily seized the scraggy udder between its lips and strained with its hind legs, swinging its little tail.

Darya Melekhova had just milked her cow and was going back to the house with a pail and a strainer in her hand, when she heard a call from over the fence.

'Darya!'

'Who's that?'

'It's me, Aksinya... Come in for a minute.'

'What d'you need me for all of a sudden?'

'I do, badly! Do come, please! For love of Christ!'

'I'll come when I've strained the milk.'

'I'll be waiting for you in the yard.'

'All right.'

Darya came out a little later. Aksinya was waiting for her at her own gate. Darya still had about her the warm smell of fresh milk and the cow-shed. She was surprised to see Aksinya not with her skirt tucked up but clean and dressed.

'You've finished your work early today, neighbour.'

'There's not much to do without Stepan. Only one cow and I hardly bother with cooking... I make do with a bite here and there.'

'What did you call me for?'

'Come into the house for a minute. There's something I want to tell you.'

There was a quiver in Aksinya's voice. Vaguely suspecting the reason, Darya followed her in silence.

Without lighting the lamp Aksinya began rummaging in the chest as soon as she entered the front room, then took Darya's hand in her dry hot hands and hurriedly pushed a ring on to her finger.

'What are you doing? A ring? For me?'

'Yes, for you! From me, as a keepsake.'

'Is it gold?' Darya inquired practically, going to the window and examining the ring on her finger by the dull light of the moon.

'Yes, it's gold. Keep it!'

'Well, God bless you!.. What do you want? Why did you give it me?'

'Call out ... call out your Grigory for me.'

'What, again?' Darya smiled knowingly.

'Oh, no! Nothing like that!' Aksinya flushed in fright and tears came to her eyes. 'I've got to talk to him about Stepan... He might be able to get him some leave.'

'Why didn't you come to our place then? You could have talked to him there, if that's what you wanted,' Darya said slyly.

'I couldn't do that... Natalya might think... It would have been awkward.'

'All right, then. I'll call him. You can have him for all I care!'

* * *

Grigory was finishing his supper. He had just put down his spoon and licked and wiped the traces of stewed fruit off his moustache, when he felt someone's foot touching his under the table and noticed Darya give him a quick wink.

'If she wants me to take Petro's place and says so now, I'll hit her. I'll take her to the threshing floor, tie her skirt up over her head and thrash her like a bitch!' Grigory told himself angrily. His response to all Darya's advances so far had been surly. But when he had risen from the table and lighted a cigarette, he walked unhurriedly to the door. Darya followed almost at once.

As she passed Grigory in the porch, she pressed close up against him and whispered, 'Oh, you devil! Go to her—she wants you.'

'Who?' Grigory breathed.

'You know.'

About an hour after Natalya and the children had gone to sleep, Grigory with his greatcoat buttoned to the neck walked out of the Astakhovs' yard with Aksinya. They stood silently in the dark lane for a moment, then just as silently walked out into the steppe, drawn by its stealth, its darkness and the intoxicating scents of the young grass. Grigory opened his greatcoat and, as he pressed Aksinya to his side, felt her body tremble and her heart throb violently under her blouse.

LI

Next day, before leaving, Grigory had a few brief words with Natalya. She called him aside and asked in a whisper, 'Where were you last night? Why were you so late back?'

'Was it so late?'

'Well, wasn't it? I woke up at first cock-crow and you were still out.'

'Kudinov came over. I went to see him about military matters. It's not something a woman would understand.'

'But why didn't he spend the night with us?'

'He was in a hurry to get to Vyoshenskaya.'

'Who did he stay with then?'

'The Aboshchenkovs. They're distant relatives of his.'

Natalya asked no more questions. She seemed to hesitate but there was a secretive gleam in her eyes and Grigory could not decide whether she had believed him or not.

He ate a hasty breakfast. Pantelei went out to saddle his horse and Ilyinichna made the sign of the cross over him, kissed him and whispered, 'Don't forget God, son, don't forget God! We heard a rumour that you cut down some sailors... Lord above! Come to your senses, Grisha dear! Look at the children you've got growing up. The men you killed must have had some too, I'm sure... How can you do such things? As a little one you were so affectionate and lovable, but now you live with a frown on your face. Your heart has grown like a wolf's... Listen to your mother, Grisha dear! Your life isn't charmed, you know; some bad man has a sword waiting for your head too.'

Grigory smiled cheerlessly, kissed his mother's lean hand, and went up to Natalya. She embraced him coldly and turned away, and it was not tears that Grigory saw in her eyes but bitterness and pent-up anger. He said goodbye to the children and left.

With his foot in the stirrup, holding the horse's harsh mane, he paused for a moment and thought to himself, 'Well, life's taken a new turn, but my heart's as cold and empty as before... I reckon even Aksinya won't be able to fill the gap now.'

Without looking back at his family gathered round the gate, he rode away down the street and, as he passed the Astakhovs' house, glanced sideways and in the last window of the front room caught sight of Aksinya. She smiled and waved an embroidered handkerchief, then crushed it to her mouth, to eyes darkened by the sleepless night.

Grigory rode away at a swift trot, reached the hill, and from there spotted two horsemen and an ox-drawn wagon slowly approaching along the summer track. He recognised the riders as Antip, son of the Braggart, and Stremyannikov, a young lively black-haired Cossack from the upper end of the village. 'They're bringing back the dead, Grigory surmised, looking at the wagon. Before he drew level with the Cossacks, he asked, 'Who've you got there?'

'Alexei Shamil, Ivan Tomilin and Horseshoe Yakov.'

'Dead?'

'Dead as can be.'

'When?'

'Yesterday, just before sunset.'

'Is the battery all right?'

'Sure it is. The Reds caught our gunners in their billets

in Kalinov Ugol. And Shamil was cut down—just daft like!'

Grigory took off his cap and dismounted. The driver, an elderly Cossack woman from the Chir, halted the oxen. The sabred Cossacks lay side by side in the wagon. Even before he approached, Grigory felt the sickly sweet smell on the breeze. Alexei Shamil was lying in the middle. His tattered blue tunic was unbuttoned, the empty sleeve had been folded under the slashed head, and the rag-wrapped stump of the arm he had lost long ago, always so mobile, was now pressed rigidly to the bulging breathless chest. Violent fury was frozen for ever in the death snarl of Alexei's white-toothed mouth, but his glazed eyes were staring up with a calm and seemingly sad thoughtfulness at the blue sky, at a small cloud floating over the steppe.

Tomilin's face was unrecognisable; in fact, there was no face left, just something red and shapeless, sheared by a slanting stroke of the sabre. Horseshoe Yakov was lying on his side; he was saffron yellow and wry-necked because his head had been almost severed from his body. One white collar bone was sticking out of the unbuttoned tunic and in the forehead, just above the eyes, a bullet had gouged a dark and bloody star-shaped hole. Evidently one of the Reds had taken pity on the Cossack in his death agony and shot him almost point-blank, so that even the gun-flash had left its speckled mark on Horseshoe's face.

'Well, brothers, let's remember our lads, let's have a smoke for the peace of their souls,' Grigory suggested. He led his horse off the road, slackened the saddle girths, took out the snaffle, tied the halter to the horse's left foreleg and let it crop the silken shoots of the young grass.

Antip and Stremyannikov gladly dismounted, hobbled their horses and let them graze. They stretched out on the ground and lighted up. Grigory watched the shaggy, not yet moulted bullock reaching down for the small roadside plantains and asked, 'How was Shamil killed?'

'You wouldn't believe it, but it was all his own stupid fault!'

'But how?'

'Well, it happened like this,' Stremyannikov began. 'Yesterday, at high noon we went out on patrol. Platon Ryabchikov himself sent us out under the command of a sergeant-major... Antip, where was he from, that sergeant-major we rode with yesterday?'

'Damned if I know!'

'To hell with him then! He wasn't one of ours. Hum... So there we were, jogging along, fourteen of us Cossacks, and Shamil was there. Yesterday he was in a good mood, real jolly he was, so I reckon his heart never told him anything. There he was with his reins on the pommel, shaking his stump and saying, "Ah, when will our Grigory Panteleyevich come back! I'd like to have just one more drink with him and sing a few more songs!" And all the time till we reached Latyshevsky hill, he was singing away:

> Across the hills we came aflying
> Like locusts in a swarm,
> With our Berdan rifles firing,
> All Cossacks of the Don.

'Ay, that's how we rode along and then, near Boggy Ravine, we went down into a gully and the sergeant-major, he says, "I don't see any Reds around here, lads. I reckon they haven't left that Ukrainian settlement yet. These muzhiks, they're lazy when it comes to getting up early. I'll bet they're still having their second breakfast, cooking up the Tufties' chickens. So let's have a rest too, our horses have got themselves into a lather." "All right, then," we say. So we dismount and lie down in the grass with just one look-out up atop. And then I see our Alexei, God rest his soul, fiddling about with his horse, letting out the surcingle. And I says to him, "Alexei, you'd better not loosen the girth. You never know, you might have to go into action urgent like, and when would you get it tight again with your stump of an arm?" But he just gives me a grin, "I'll manage a lot quicker than you! Who d'you think you're teaching, you bulrush?" And with that he loosened the surcingle and took the snaffle out of his horse's mouth. So we lay there smoking, someone telling a tale, some dozing. And our look-out, he dozed off too. He got his head down—curse his guts!—and started having sweet dreams. Then I thought I heard a horse give a snort in the distance. I felt too lazy to get up, but I did get up and climb out of the gully on to the hillock. And there, only about a hundred paces away the Reds were riding up the gully towards us. In front was their commander on a bay. His horse was like a lion. And they had a disk-fed machine-gun with 'em. Down I tumbled into the gully. "Reds! To horse!" I shouted. And they must have seen me because I heard their commander giving the order. We flung ourselves on our horses, the sergeant-major, he wants to draw his sword and go into the attack. But what kind of a charge could we make when there was only fourteen of us and half a squadron of them, with a machine-gun into the bargain! So we rode to get away up the gully. They tried their machine-gun on us, but it was no good because we had cover. Then they came after us, but our horses were faster and we got a good stage ahead of 'em, then dropped out of the saddle and started shooting back. And only then we noticed that Alexei Shamil's not with us. Ye see, when the scramble began, he ran to his horse and reached for the pommel with his sound arm, put his foot in the stirrup, and down the saddle went under the horse's belly. So Shamil never managed to mount his horse and was left face to face with the Reds; the horse came careering after us with its nostrils well nigh flaming and the saddle swinging under its belly. It's got so scary since then, it won't let anyone near it and snorts like the devil! That was how Alexei met his end! If he hand't loosened the surcingle, he'd be alive to this day, but ye see how it was...' Stremyannikov smiled into his black moustache and concluded, 'Only the other day he was singing,

> Oh, big grandad bear,
> My cow would you tear,
> And rip my head bare...

'Well, they ripped his head bare all right... You wouldn't know his face now! The blood that came out of him, like from a slaughtered bull... Afterwards, when we'd driven off the Reds we went down into that gully and we saw him lying there. And under him there was a great pool of blood—floating in it he was!'

'Shall we be going soon?' the wagon driver asked impatiently, freeing her lips of the kerchief that she was using to keep the sunburn off her face.

'Don't hurry, woman. We'll be going in a minute.'

'Don't hurry? The stink from these bodies is enough to knock you down!'

'Well, you wouldn't expect it to be a good smell, would you?' Antip observed thoughtfully. 'They ate meat and pawed women. And anyone who does that begins to stink even before he's dead. I've heard tell that only the saints give off a light vapour after they're dead, but I reckon that's a lot of cock. No matter how saintly he was, it's nature's law that a man must stink like a shithouse after he's dead. The saints take food through their bellies like anyone else, and their gut is the same length that God made for all men.'

But for no apparent reason Stremyannikov flared up and shouted, 'What the hell! Why talk about saints! Come on, let's get going!'

Grigory said goodbye to the Cossacks and went over to the wagon to take his leave of the dead men from his village and only then did he notice that all three were barefooted and three pairs of boots were lying with the tops under their feet.

'Why did you take the boots from the dead?'

'That was the work of our Cossacks, Grigory Panteleyevich. The dead men all had good boots, so we talked it over in the squadron and decided to take 'em for the men whose boots were worn out, and bring the worn-out ones back to the village. These men had families, ye know. Their kids will wear out even the bad stuff... Anikei put it this way, "The dead won't have to walk," he says, "or ride either. Give me Alexei's boots, they've got fine soles on 'em still. Otherwise, I may catch my death of cold while I'm waiting to capture a pair from a Red."'

As Grigory rode off, he heard an argument flare up between the two Cossacks. Stremyannikov cried in his ringing tenor voice, 'You're lying, Son of the Braggart. That's what your Dad got his nickname for! There never were any saints from among the Cossacks. They all came from the muzhiks!'

'Yes, there were!'

'You're lying your head off!'

'But there were!'

'Who?'

'What about St. George?'

'Pah! Wake up, you plague-struck bastard! He wasn't a Cossack!'

'Yes, he was. A pure Don Cossack, from one of the lower stanitsas—Semikarakovskaya.'

'The things you cook up. You ought to have steamed it first. He was no Cossack!'

'No? Then why is he always shown with a lance?'

Grigory heard no more. He went into a trot, dropped down into a ravine and, as he crossed the Hetman's highway, saw the wagon and the horsemen slowly going down the hill into the village.

Grigory trotted nearly all the way to Karginskaya. A light breeze played in the horse's mane and not once did it break into a sweat. Long-bodied brownish-grey susliks ran across the road, whistling anxiously. Their sharp warning cries blended strangely with the vast silence that reigned over the steppe. On the hillside and ridges away from the road the cock bustards would take wing from time to time. Glittering like snow in the sunshine one climbed with rapid vigorous sweeps of its wings and at the zenith of its flight seemed to float in the fading blue expanse, stretching its neck in its black velvet marriage ruff as it sped away into the distance. But after two or three hundred yards it came lower and, flapping its wings even faster, appeared to hover over one spot. Close to the earth, to the green sward of the steppe the blazing plumage of the wings gleamed once more like a flash of lightning and then died as the bird disappeared into the deep grass.

Everywhere the cock birds' passionate, vibrant call could be heard. At the very top of a hill overlooking the Chir, only a few paces from the road Grigory noticed a bustards' mating ground. A little round patch had been trampled smooth by the feet of the male birds fighting for the hen. Not a blade of grass had survived in the patch; there was only a layer of grey dust, criss-crossed with foot-marks, while round the edges, among the dry stalks and wormwood, the pale but colourful, pink-tinged feathers torn in battle from the plumage of the contesting males hung fluttering in the wind. Not far away a dowdy grey hen bustard jumped out of her nest. Hunched like an old woman, she ran nimbly under a clump of broom and hid there, not daring to take wing.

The invisible life begotten by spring, strong and throbbing with energy, was astir in the steppe. Grass and plants were growing riotously; in refuges hidden from man's rapacious eye bird and beast were mating; the fields were bristling with the spikes of countless shoots. Only last year's withered scrub and tumbleweed drooped despondently on the slopes of the look-out mounds scattered over the steppe, clinging to the earth for protection, but the fresh, invigorating wind tore them ruthlessly from their withered roots and drove them hither and thither across the radiant, sun-drenched steppe that had risen to new life.

Grigory rode into Karginskaya in the early evening. He forded the Chir and soon found Ryabchikov at the garrison paddock by the river.

The next morning he took over the command of the units of the 1st Division that were scattered among the surrounding villages and, after reading the latest reports from headquarters, and consulting with Mikhail Kopylov, his chief of staff, decided to advance southwards to the Ukrainian settlement of Astakhovo.

His troops were starved of ammunition and the only way to replenish supplies was to capture them from the enemy.

This was the main objective of the offensive Grigory had decided to launch.

By evening one foot and three mounted regiments had been assembled in Karginskaya. Of the twenty-two light and heavy machine-guns in the division's possession they decided to take with them only six, since there were not enough ammunition belts for the rest.

The following morning the division began its offensive. Grigory abandoned his headquarters while it was on the move, took command of the 3rd Cavalry Regiment, sent out mounted patrols and marched southwards in the direction of Ponomaryovka, where his reconnaissance had reported concentrations of the Red Army's 101st and 103rd infantry regiments, which in their turn were preparing to advance on Karginskaya.

He had ridden only about three versts from Karginskaya when he was overtaken by a dispatch rider, who handed him a letter from Kudinov.

The Serdobsk Regiment has surrendered to us! All their men have been disarmed; about twenty of them who tried to cause trouble were disposed of by Bogatiryov; he had them all sabred. Four guns were surrendered to us (but those damn Communist gunners managed to remove the breech-blocks); we also got 200 shells and 9 machine-guns. There is great jubilation here! We are putting the Red Army men in the infantry squadrons and making them fight their own lot. How are things with you? Yes, and I nearly forgot—some Communists from your locality were captured. Kotlyarov, Koshevoi and a good many from Yelanskaya. They'll all be done away with on the road to Vyoshenskaya. If you're badly in need of cartridges, tell the bearer of this letter and we'll send you about 500.

Kudinov.

'Orderly!' Grigory shouted.

Prokhor Zykov rode up at once and was so alarmed by the change in Grigory's face that he actually saluted.

'What's the order?'

'Ryabchikov! Where's Ryabchikov?'

'Bringing up the rear.'

'Off you go and get him! Hurry up!'

Platon Ryabchikov cantered along the column and rode up level with Grigory. The skin on his face was peeling and his fair moustache and eyebrows, scorched by the spring sun, had a foxy reddish tinge. He was smiling and smoking a large home-made cigarette. His dark bay ambler, as sleek as ever despite the rigours of spring, kept up a lively pace, its breast plate gleaming.

'Is it a letter from Vyoshenskaya?' he asked, noticing the messenger at Grigory's side.

'Yes, it is,' Grigory replied curtly. 'Take over the regiment and the division. I'm leaving.'

'All right then. But what's the hurry? What's the letter say? Is it from Kudinov?'

'The Serdobsk Regiment has surrendered in Ust-Khopyorskaya.'

'So that's it! We still stand a chance then? Are you going now?'

'Right now.'

'God be with you then. We'll be in Astakhovo by the time you're back!'

As he lashed his horse wildly and galloped down the hill, Grigory told himself, 'I must get hold of Mishka and Ivan while they're still alive... Find out who killed Petro... Save Ivan and Mishka from death! I must save them... There's blood between us but we're not strangers?!'

LII

As soon as the insurgent squadrons entered Ust-Khopyorskaya and surrounded the Serdobsk men at their meeting, Bogatiryov, the commander of the 6th Insurgent Brigade, went off to confer with Voronovsky and Volkov. The conference took place in a wealthy merchant's house quite near the square, and did not last long. Bogatiryov greeted Voronovsky without removing the whip that dangled from his wrist, and said, 'Everything's going well. You'll get the credit for it.

But how come you couldn't save the guns?'

'It was an accident! A pure accident, Cornet! Nearly all the gunners were Communists and they put up a desperate resistance when we started disarming them; they killed two men of the regiment and got away with the breech-blocks.'

'That was a pity!' Bogatiryov threw down on the table his peaked cap, which still showed the mark where the officer's cockade had been torn out of the band, wiped the sweat from his shaven head and weathered face with a dirty handkerchief, and smiled grudgingly, 'Still, never mind that. Now go and tell your soldiers... Talk to 'em properly, so they don't start ... so they don't... So they lay down all their arms.'

Affronted by the Cossack officer's peremptory tone, Voronovsky repeated questioningly, 'All their arms?'

'Do I have to say everything twice? When I say all I mean all—the lot!'

'But you, Cornet, and your command accepted the condition that the regiment should not be disarmed, did you not?.. Of course, I understand that machine-guns, artillery, hand grenades, all that kind of thing, must be surrendered, but as for the weapons carried by the Red Army men themselves...'

'They're not Red Army men any more!' Bogatiryov's shaven upper lip went back in a snarl and he thwacked the muddied top of his boot with the plaited whiplash. 'They're not Red Army men, they're soldiers, who are going to defend the Don lands. Get me?.. And if they don't do what they're told, we'll make 'em! I won't beat about the bush! You've done a lot of harm here on our land, and now you start thinking up your own conditions! There aren't any conditions between us! Do you understand that?'

Young Lieutenant Volkov, the Serdobsk Regiment's chief of staff, took offence. Nervously fingering the buttons on the high collar of his worsted black shirt and ruffling his dark curly hair, he asked sharply, 'So you regard us as prisoners? Is that it?'

'I didn't say that. You needn't pester me, putting words into my mouth!' the Cossack brigade commander interrupted rudely, demonstrating quite plainly that the men he was talking to were directly and utterly dependent on him.

For a minute there was silence in the room. A muffled clamour could be heard from the square. Voronovsky paced the room several times, pulling at his fingers till the joints cracked, then buttoned up his warm field-service tunic and, blinking nervously, said to Bogatiryov, 'Your tone is insulting to us and unworthy of you as a Russian officer! I put that to you straight. And we shall consider, since you have challenged us... we shall consider how to act in future... Lieutenant Volkov! This is an order! Go to the square and tell the sergeants-major not to surrender their weapons to the Cossacks on any account! Order the regiment to keep their arms at the ready. I shall finish my conversation with this—with this gentleman Bogatiryov, and come to the square myself.'

Bogatiryov's face went black with anger. He was about to say something but, realising that he had gone much too far, restrained himself and immediately changed his manner of address. He clamped his cap on his head and, still toying fiercely with the tasseled whip, began to speak, but in an unexpectedly soft and considerate voice.

'Gentlemen, you didn't quite understand me. Of course, I haven't had any special education in these cadet colleges, I've never been trained in the sciences, and mebbe I didn't explain things properly, but nothing's perfect. We're all in this together, aren't we! So we mustn't start getting offended with each other. Now what did I say? I only said that your Red Army men have got to be disarmed at once, specially the ones that neither we nor you can trust... That's the ones I was talking about!'

'But, come now! You should have explained yourself more clearly, Cornet! And you must agree that your provocative tone, your whole behaviour...' Voronovsky gave a shrug and in a more conciliatory voice but still with a shade of unplaced indignation went on, 'We ourselves have always maintained that the waverers and unreliable elements should be disarmed and put at your disposal...'

'That's right! That's just what I meant!'

'And I, too, say that we had ourselves decided to disarm them. But as for our action group, that we shall keep! We shall keep it at all costs! I myself or Lieutenant Volkov, whom you permitted yourself to address in such familiar terms just now—we shall take command of it and honourably redeem the shame of our service in the Red Army. You must grant us that opportunity.'

'How many bayonets will there be in your group?'

'About two hundred.'

'All right then,' Bogatiryov agreed reluctantly. He rose, opened the door and bawled for the mistress of the house. And when an elderly woman with a woolen shawl round her head appeared in the doorway, he snapped, 'Bring me some fresh milk! And quick about it!'

'We haven't any milk. Please, excuse us.'

Bogatiryov smiled sourly. 'I expect you've got plenty for the Reds, but none when it's for us.'

Once again an awkward silence filled the room.

It was broken by Lieutenant Volkov.

'May I go?'

'Yes,' Voronovsky replied with a sigh. 'Go and give orders that those we listed for disarming are to be disarmed. Gorigasov and Veistminster have the lists.'

It was only the affront to his officer's self-esteem that had made him say, 'We shall consider how to act in future.' Captain Voronovsky knew perfectly well that the game was up and there was no turning back. He had information that forces sent by the command of the Red Army to disarm the Serdobsk mutineers were advancing from Ust-Medveditskaya and might appear at any moment. But Bogatiryov had also realised that Voronovsky was a perfectly safe and reliable man, who could not possibly go back on his word. On his own responsibility the brigade commander agreed to the formation of an independent fighting force out of the reliable elements in the regiment, and on that note the conference ended.

Meanwhile in the square the Cossack insurgents were already taking energetic steps to disarm the Serdobsk men. Greedy Cossack eyes and hands were going through the regimental baggage trains; the insurgents were taking not only cartridges but the thick-soled Red Army boots, rolls of footcloths, padded jackets and trousers, and provisions. About twenty of the Serdobsk men, when they saw for themselves what kind of treatment was to be expected from the Cossacks, tried to offer resistance. One of them lashed out with the butt of his rifle at an insurgent who had searched him and calmly transferred his purse to his own pocket.

'What's the idea, you bandit?! Give it back or I'll use my bayonet on you!'

He was supported by his friends and a roar of protest went up.

'Comrades, to arms!'

'We've been tricked!'

'Don't give 'em your rifles!'

In the ensuing brawl the Red Army men were forced back to a fence and mounted insurgents, with the encouragement of the commander of the 3rd Mounted Squadron, cut them down in two minutes.

The disarming made even better progress when Lieutenant Volkov arrived in the square. The Red Army men were formed up and searched in the pouring rain. Rifles, hand grenades, field telephone equipment, crates of rifle and machine-gun ammunition were piled all along the line.

Bogatiryov galloped on to the square and, wheeling his excited caracoling horse this way and that in front of the Serdobsk men, waved his heavy plaited whip and shouted, 'Now listen to me! As from today you'll be fighting those scoundrel Communists and their troops. All of you who go along with us will be forgiven, but anyone who kicks over the traces will get the same reward as them!' and he pointed his whip at the slaughtered Red Army men, whom the Cossacks had already stripped to their underclothes and left in a shapeless white heap that was steadily getting soaked in the rain.

A whisper rippled along the line, but no one broke ranks or uttered any audible protest.

Foot and mounted Cossacks were on the prowl everywhere. They had formed a tight cordon round the square. From a vantage point by the churchyard the Serdobsk Regiment's green-painted machine-guns had been trained on the Red Army ranks, and behind their shields the drenched Cossack machine-gunners were crouching at the ready.

It took Voronovsky and Volkov an hour to select the 'reliable' elements they had listed. There turned out to be one hundred and ninety-four. The newly formed unit was designated the 1st Separate Insurgent Battalion; on the same day it was sent into the line opposite the village of Belavinsky, from which regiments of Mironov's 23rd Cavalry Division, lately transferred from the Donets, were attacking. It was rumoured that the regiments were the 15th, under the command of Bykadorov, and the 32nd, led by the renowned Mishka Blinov. They had been rolling over the insurgent Cossack squadrons, and one squadron that had been hastily mustered by a village in the Ust-Khopyorskaya district had been cut to pieces.

So Bogatiryov had decided to use Voronovsky's battalion against Blinov and test its reliability with a baptism of fire.

The remaining Serdobsk men, over eight hundred of them, were marched on foot along the Don to Vyoshenskaya, just as the commander of the insurgent forces Kudinov had ordered in his letter to Bogatiryov. They were watched from the overlooking hills by three mounted squadrons, armed with the Serdobsk men's own machine-guns.

Before quitting Ust-Khopyorskaya, Bogatiryov attended church service but left hurriedly as soon as the priest had uttered the prayer for victory for the 'Christ-loving Cossack Host'. When his horse was brought for him he mounted and beckoned to one of the commanders of the squadrons left to defend Ust-Khopyorskaya. Leaning over from his saddle, he whispered in his ear, 'Guard the Communists closer than you would a powder magazine! Tomorrow morning drive them to Vyoshenskaya with a trustworthy escort. But today send messengers round the villages to say who's coming. The people will find their own punishment for them!'

And he rode off.

LIII

At noon one day in April an aeroplane appeared over the village of Singin, near Vyoshenskaya. Alerted by the drone of the engine, children, women and old men ran out of their houses and, shading their eyes with their hands, watched the plane circling like a bird of prey in the hazy overcast sky. The drone rose to a roar as the plane came in to land, choosing a level stretch of common outside the village as a landing ground.

'Now it'll start dropping its bombs! Watch out!' a quick-witted old fellow cried in dismay.

The crowd that had gathered in the lane scattered in all directions. The women dragged their howling children away, the old men jumped fences with the nimbleness of goats and disappeared into the poplar groves. Only one old woman was left in the lane. She too would have run, but either her legs had collapsed under her in her fright or she had tripped over a rut, but she fell down and lay kicking her bare skinny legs shamelessly in the air and wailing for help in a feeble voice, 'Help! Save me! I'm dying!'

No one came to the old soul's rescue. With a terrible thunder and roar the aeroplane swept just over the top of the barn and for a second its winged shadow hid the world from her mortally frightened eyes, then it touched down softly on the damp soil of the village common and ran out into the steppe. The effect on the old woman was to make her commit one of the sins of childhood, after which she lay half dead, feeling nothing and hearing nothing around her or under her. Naturally she was too far gone to notice two men in black leather emerge from the fearsome bird that had just alighted, and after a moment's hesitation, make their way cautiously towards the village.

But the old woman's husband, who had hidden in a poplar grove amidst a dry clump of brambles, was a brave old man. Although his heart was fluttering like a trapped sparrow's, he had the courage to peep out, and it was he who recognised one of the men approaching his yard as Petro Bogatiryov, an officer and the son of a man who had been in his regiment. Petro Bogatiryov, who was a cousin of Grigory Bogatiryov, the commander of the 6th Separate Insurgent Brigade, had retreated across the Donets with the Whites. But it was undoubtedly he.

For a minute the old fellow peered inquisitively, squatting like a hare with his arms dangling in front of him. When he was finally convinced that the man's rolling gait was indeed that of Petro Bogatiryov, who was just as blue-eyed as he had been the previous year but not so well shaven, the old man rose to his feet and tested his legs to see if they would still carry him. They trembled slightly but held him up well and the old fellow trotted out of the poplar grove with an ambler's gait.

Ignoring his spouse, who was still lying prostrate in the dust, he made straight for Petro and his companion and while still at a distance removed his faded Cossack cap from his bald head. Petro recognised him and greeted him with a wave and a smile.

'Allow me to inquire, is it really you, Petro Bogatiryov?'

'Yes, it is, Grandad.'

'So the Lord willed that I should see a flying machine in my old age! What a scare you gave us!'

'Are there any Reds about, Grandad?'

'No, none of 'em around here, my boy! They've been driven off way beyond the Chir, to the Tufties.'

'Have your Cossacks also risen?'

'Ay, they rose all right, but a lot of 'em were put down again.'

'How d'you mean?'

'I mean, killed.'

'Ah!.. How about my family, my father—are they all alive?'

'Safe and sound, all of 'em. Are you from across the Donets? You didn't see my son Tikhon there, did you?'

'Yes, I'm from there. I have greetings from Tikhon for you. Now go and mind our machine for us, Grandad, keep the kids away from it. I'm going home.'

Petro Bogatiryov and his companion walked on. Meanwhile the scared populace crept out of the poplar groves, out of sheds and cellars and various other nooks where they had taken cover. A crowd gathered round the aeroplane, which was still breathing the heat of its warm engine and the fumes of oil and petrol. Its cloth-covered wings had been holed in many places by bullets and shell splinters. The astonishing machine stood silent and hot, like an overridden horse.

The old man who had been the first to meet Bogatiryov trotted into the lane to tell his terror-stricken wife the good news about their son Tikhon, who had retreated in December with the district administration. But the old woman was not there. She had hurried back to the house, taken refuge in a storeroom and was hastily changing her blouse and skirt. The old man found her after searching for some time and shouted, 'It was Petro Bogatiryov came in that aeroplane! He brought us greetings from Tikhon!' But the sight of his wife changing her clothes made him deeply indignant. 'What's the idea of dressing yourself up, ye old hag? A pox on your mother! Who needs ye, ye moulting old pixy? Think you're a youngster, do ye!'

Soon the old men came knocking at the door of the Bogatiryovs' house to pay their respects. Each one took off his cap as he entered, crossed himself before the icons and sat down sedately on a bench, leaning on his stick. They began to talk. Petro, sipping cool unskimmed milk from a glass, told them that he had flown in on orders from the Don Government, that his mission was to make contact with the insurgent Cossacks of the Upper Don and help them fight the Reds by flying in ammunition and officers. He also told them that the Don Army would soon launch an offensive along the whole front and link up with the insurgent army. In passing he chided the old men for having so little influence over the young Cossacks, who had abandoned the front and allowed the Reds to invade their land. In conclusion he said, 'But since you have come to your senses and cleared the Soviet authorities out of the stanitsas, the Don Government forgives you.'

'But we've still got a Soviet government here, only without the Communists. Our flag isn't a three-colour one, ye know; it's red and white,' one of the old men told him irresolutely.

'Even in the way they talk our young scamps will call each other "comrade"!' another old man added.

Petro Bogatiryov smiled into his clipped reddish moustache, screwed up his round light-blue eyes derisively, and said, 'Your Soviet government is like ice in early spring. It'll break up as soon as the sun gets a bit warmer. But as for the ringleaders, the ones that deserted the front at Kalach, as soon as we return from the Donets they shall be flogged.'

'Flog 'em, the young bastards, till they bleed!'

'That's the way!'

'Ay, a right good flogging!'

'Flog 'em in public till they wet their pants!' the old men clamoured joyfully.

* * *

That evening, Kudinov and his chief of staff, who had been informed of the news by despatch rider, drove into Singin in a tarantass drawn by three foaming horses.

They were so delighted by Bogatiryov's arrival that they almost ran into the house, without stopping to scrape the mud off their boots and tarpaulin coats.

LIV

Twenty-five Communists, surrendered to the insurgents by the Serdobsk Regiment, marched out of Ust-Khopyorskaya under a strong escort. Escape was out of the question. As he limped along in the middle of the crowd of prisoners, Ivan looked with misery and hatred at the stony faces of the Cossack guards and thought,

325

'They'll finish us off! If there's no trial, we're done for!'

Most of the escorts were bearded. Their commander was an elderly sergeant-major of the Ataman's Regiment, an Old Believer. As soon as they left Ust-Khopyorskaya, he ordered the prisoners not to talk or smoke or ask the escorts any questions.

'Say your prayers, you servants of the devil! You're going to your death, so there's no need to sin in the little time you've got left! Pah! You've forgotten God! Sold yourselves to the evil one! Branded yourselves with the mark of the devil!' he thundered, now waving his revolver, now toying with its cord that hung round his neck.

Among the prisoners there were only two Communists from the command of the Serdobsk Regiment, the rest, except for Ivan, were all non-Cossacks from Yelanskaya, big burly lads who had joined the Communist Party the moment Soviet forces had entered the stanitsa and had served as militiamen or chairmen of village revolutionary committees and, after the uprising, had fled to Ust-Khopyorskaya and attached themselves to the Serdobsk Regiment.

In the past nearly all of them had been craftsmen— carpenters, cabinet-makers, coopers, stone-masons, stove-makers, cobblers, tailors. The oldest was not more than thirty-five, the youngest about twenty. Strapping, handsome young fellows with big work-scarred hands, they presented a striking contrast to the hunch-backed old men who were guarding them.

'D'you think they'll try us?' one of the Yelanskaya Communists walking beside Ivan asked in a whisper.

'Not much chance of that.'

'Will they kill us?'

'I expect so.'

'But they don't shoot people any more? Don't you remember what the Cossacks told us?'

Ivan said nothing but hope flared in him, too, for an instant, like a spark in the wind. 'It's true,' he thought. 'They won't be able to shoot us. The bastards did put out that slogan, "Down with the Communists, robbery and shootings!" It's rumoured they've only been handing out sentences of hard labour. They'll sentence us to a flogging and hard labour. That's not so terrible! We'll be doing hard labour till winter and in winter, as soon as the Don freezes, our lot will crack down on them again.'

But hope flared like a spark in the wind and died like one. 'No, they'll kill us! They're as sore as hell! Goodbye, life! But it shouldn't have been like this. All the time I was fighting them I felt sorry for them. But I shouldn't have been, I should have cut 'em down, torn 'em out with their roots.'

He clenched his fists and gave a shrug of helpless fury. The next moment a blow on the head from behind sent him reeling and he nearly fell.

'What are ye clenching your fists for, whelp of a wolf! What are ye clenching your fists for, I asked?!' the sergeant-major in charge of the escort bellowed, riding down on him.

He struck Ivan again with his whip, slashing his face from the eyebrow to the tip of his firm, dimpled chin.

'Who're you knocking about! Hit me, dad! Hit me! He's wounded, why treat him like that?' one of the Yelanskaya men shouted with a pleading smile and a quiver in his voice and, stepping out of the bunch, he shielded Ivan with his big carpenter's chest.

'There's enough for you too! Beat 'em up, Cossacks! Beat up the commies!'

The whip tore into the Yelanskaya man's summer tunic with such force that the cloth curled up like a scorched leaf. It was quickly washed with black blood from the weal that swelled up on his shoulder.

Panting with fury the sergeant-major rode in among the prisoners and set to work ruthlessly with his whip.

Another blow landed on Ivan. Purple flashes blazed before his eyes, the ground heaved and the green forest fringing the sandy left bank seemed to lean over.

Ivan grabbed a stirrup in his gnarled hand and tried to jerk the raging sergeant-major out of his saddle, but a blow with the flat of a sabre threw him to the ground, choking velvet dust filled his mouth and blood spurted from his ears and nose.

The escorts drove them into a tight bunch like sheep and gave them a long cruel beating. Lying on his face in the road, Ivan heard, as if in a dream, the muffled cries, the thud of feet around him and the wild snorting of the horses. A fleck of warm froth from a horse's mouth fell on his bare head and almost at the same time came the frightening sound of a man sobbing and shouting just above his head.

'Bastards! Beating defenceless... Oo-o-oh!'

A horse trod on Ivan's wounded leg and the blunt tips of the horse-shoe bit into the flesh of the calf, a rain of blows sounded from above and the next minute a heavy wet body, reeking of sweat and the salty smell of blood, fell at his side and, before he finally lost consciousness, he heard blood gurgling from the man's throat, as if from an upturned bottle.

Later they were herded down to the Don and forced to wash off the blood. Standing knee-deep in the water, Ivan splashed his burning wounds and swollen bruises, scooped up water mixed with his own blood and drank greedily, afraid that he would not have time to quench his blazing thirst.

Back on the road they were overtaken by a mounted Cossack. His dark bay horse, vernally sleek and gleaming with sweat, went by at a swift playful canter. The horseman disappeared into the next village and before the prisoners reached the first houses they saw a mob of men and women running towards them.

At the sight of those Cossacks and their womenfolk coming at him, Ivan realised that this was death. The others realised it too.

'Comrades! Let's say goodbye!' one of the Serdobsk Communists shouted.

Armed with pitchforks, hoes, stakes and iron wagon ribs, the crowd bore down on them.

The rest was a nightmare. For thirty versts they trudged from village to village and at every village they were met by mobs of tormentors. The old men, the women and the youngsters beat them and spat in the bruised and bleeding faces of the Communist prisoners, threw stones and chunks of dried earth and scattered dust and ash into their bruised and battered eyes. The women excelled in savagery and the cruellest tortures. The twenty-five doomed men had to run the gauntlet. Towards the end they were unrecognisable even as human beings, so monstrously disfigured were their bodies and faces, beaten to a bleeding black and blue pulp and coated with a mixture of dirt and blood.

At first they tried to avoid the blows by bunching together; each man tried to stay as far away as possible from the guards. But they were constantly separated, dragged apart. And soon they lost all hope of protecting themselves in any way and staggered along separately, possessed only by one agonising urge to keep themselves from falling, for once down they would never be able to rise again. Gradually apathy overcame them. At first each man had covered his face with his hands, helplessly shielded his eyes when the iron prongs of hay-forks glared into his very pupils or the blunt whitish end of a stake gleamed over his head, and pleas for mercy, groans, curses, and animal-like cries drawn from the guts by unbearable pain had risen over the crowd. But by noon they were all silent, except for one Yelanskaya man, the youngest, once a jester and the favourite of his company; he still yelped when hit on the head. He even walked as if on hot coals, jigging and twitching, and dragging the leg that had been smashed by a pole.

After the washing in the Don Ivan had recovered some of his spirit. At the sight of the villagers running towards them he took a hasty farewell of his closest comrades and said in a low voice, 'Well, lads, we showed we could fight, now we must show that we can die proudly... There's one thing we must remember to the last gasp. We've only one ray of comfort: they may club us to death but they can't smash the power of the Soviets with a club! Communists! Brothers! Die bravely, don't let the enemy have the laugh on us!'

One of the Yelanskaya Communists cracked when the old men of Bobrovsky village started beating him with vicious skill. He broke into mad, child-like cries, tore open the front of his tunic and showed the Cossacks and their women the small crucifix hanging from his neck on a dirty sweat-stained string.

'Comrades! I only joined the party recently!.. Have mercy! I believe in God!.. I've got two children!.. Take pity! You've got children too!..'

'We're no comrades of yours! Shut up!'

'Remembered your children, have ye, ye viper? Show us your cross, would ye? Come to your senses? But did ye remember God when ye shot our men, put 'em to death?' a button-nosed old man with an ear-ring, who had already struck him twice, snarled the questions and, without waiting for an answer, aimed again at his head.

Fragments of what his eyes and ears perceived passed through Ivan's mind without registering. His heart seemed to be enclosed in a wall of stone and it faltered only once. At noon they entered the village of Tyukovnovsky and walked down the street under a hail of curses and blows. Ivan happened to see a little boy of about seven with tears pouring down his face clinging to his mother's skirts and crying out at the top of his voice, 'Mummy! Don't hit him! Oh, don't hit him any more!.. I'm sorry for him! I'm frightened! He's all bleeding!..'

The woman, who had been brandishing a fence stake at one of the Yelanskaya men, suddenly shrieked, threw down the weapon, and, snatching up her child in her arms, ran away down a lane. Ivan was so touched by the boy's tears, by his spontaneous childish sympathy that an unbidden tear welled from his eye and salted his battered blood-encrusted lips. He gave a brief sob at the thought of his own son and wife, and this sudden lightning flash of recall evoked a desperate desire that they should not see him killed. Let death come soon, he thought.

They staggered on, swaying with exhaustion and the pain that racked every joint. At the sight of a steppeland well on the common outside the village they begged the commander of the escort to let them drink.

'No drinking! We're late already! Get going!' the sergeant-major bawled.

But one of the escorts, an old man, stood up for the prisoners.

'Have a little heart, Akim Sazonovich! They're human beings, you know.'

'Human beings? Communists aren't human! Don't try to teach me! Who's the chief here—you or me?'

'There're too many chiefs like you! Go and have a drink, lads!'

The old fellow dismounted and drew a bucket of water from the well. The prisoners crowded round him and twenty-five pairs of hands reached for the bucket; charred, bruised eyes glowed and a gasping, husky whisper broke out.

'Gimme some, Grandad!'

'A mouthful.'

'Just a drop!'

'Comrades, not everyone at once!'

The old man did not know who to give the first drink. After a few agonising seconds, he poured the water into the wooden cattle trough embedded in the ground, then stepped back and shouted, 'What are you pushing for, like a lot of bullocks! Drink properly, in turn!'

The water flowed over the mossy green musty bottom of the trough into one corner where a smell of damp wood was rising in the hot sun. With what was left of their strength, the prisoners threw themselves on it.

The old man drew eleven buckets and filled the trough, frowning with pity as he surveyed the prisoners.

Ivan drank on his knees and, when he looked up, a little refreshed, he saw everything vividly, almost palpably: the frosty white layer of limestone dust on the Donside road, the spurs of the chalky hills rising like a blue vision in the distance, and above them, over the flowing stream of the ruffled Don, in the unattainable majestic azure of the heavens, far beyond the reach of man—a small cloud. Winged by the wind, with a sparkling white crest, like a sail, it was gliding swiftly northward and only its opal shadow was reflected in a distant curve of the Don.

LV

At a secret conference of the high command of the insurgent forces the decision was taken to ask the Don Government, Ataman Bogayevsky, for assistance.

Kudinov was entrusted with the task of writing a letter expressing repentance and regret that at the end of 1918 the Cossacks of the Upper Don had entered into negotiations with the Reds and abandoned the front. He wrote it. In the name of all insurgent Cossacks of the Upper Don, he promised to fight the war against the Bolsheviks staunchly, to a victorious conclusion and asked for assistance in the shape of regular officers to command the insurgent units, and rifle ammunition, all of which were to be flown in across the front by aeroplane.

Petro Bogatiryov stayed for a time in Singin, then moved on to Vyoshenskaya. The pilot flew back to Novocherkassk with Kudinov's letter.

From that day on close contact was established between the Don Government and the insurgent command. Nearly every day smart new aeroplanes, manufactured in France, arrived with officers, rifle ammunition and even small quantities of shells for the three-inch guns. The pilots brought letters from the Upper Don Cossacks who had retreated with the Don Army and returned from Vyoshenskaya with answers from their families.

With an eye to the situation on both fronts and his own strategic plans, General Sidorin, the new commander of the Don Army, started sending Kudinov operational plans drawn up by his staff, orders, communiqués and intelligence reports about the Red Army units that were being transferred to the insurgent front.

Kudinov initiated only a chosen few into his correspondence with Sidorin; from everyone else it was kept a strict secret.

LVI

The prisoners were driven into Tatarsky at about five in the afternoon. The fleeting spring twilight was near and already the flaming disc of the setting sun had touched the edge of a ragged dove-grey cloud that lay prone in the west.

A squadron of Tatarsky infantry were sitting or standing about in the shade of the huge barn where the village grain was stored. They had been transferred to the right bank of the Don to help the Yelanskaya squadrons, who were hard pressed by Mironov's thrusting Red cavalry, and on the way to their positions the Tatarsky men had by common consent stopped off in the village to see their families and stock up with food.

They should have continued their march that day but they had heard that some Communist prisoners were being driven to Vyoshenskaya, that among them were Mishka Koshevoi and Ivan Kotlyarov, and that they would soon be arriving in Tatarsky; so they had decided to wait. The Cossacks who had relatives that had been killed along with Petro Melekhov in the first battle of the uprising were particularly insistent on waiting for Koshevoi and Ivan.

The Tatarsky men lounged about by the barn, their rifles propped against the wall, chatting, smoking and spitting out the husks of sunflower seeds; a crowd of women, children and old men had gathered round them. The whole village was out of doors and from the roofs the little boys kept a constant watch to see if they were coming.

'There they are! That's 'em!' a boy's voice rang out.

The soldiers rose hurriedly, the crowd surged, the talk grew to a muffled roar, and there was a patter of feet as the children dashed off to meet the prisoners. Alexei Shamil's widow, her grief still unassuaged, burst into a wailing lament.

'It's our enemies they're bringing!' one of the old men boomed.

'Beat 'em up, the rotten devils! What are you standing there for, Cossacks?'

'We'll try 'em ourselves!'

'Just think how many of our folk they executed!'

'We'll string up Koshevoi and his pal!'

Darya Melekhova was standing beside Anikei's wife. She was the first to recognise Ivan in the approaching crowd of battered, bleeding prisoners.

'We've brought you a man from your village! Look at him, the son-of-a-bitch! Kiss him—for love of Christ!' the sergeant-major in charge of the escort bawled hoarsely, drowning the fierce babble of talk and the shrieks and weeping of the women, and flung out his arm to point at Ivan.

'Where's the other one? Where's Mishka Koshevoi?'

Antip, son of the Braggart, pushed his way through the crowd, unbuttoning the shoulder strap that held the sling of his rifle and knocking people with its butt and bayonet.

'Only one from your village, no one else. But there'll be enough to go round if you each tear off a chunk,' the sergeant-major replied, mopping the sweat off his brow with a red handkerchief and lifting his leg laboriously over the saddle.

The women's shrieking and shouting rose to breaking-point. Darya pushed her way through to the escorts and just beyond the wet crupper of an escort's horse, only a few paces away, she saw Ivan's battered immobile face. His horribly swollen head with its crust of blood-caked hair looked like an upturned bucket and was almost as big. The skin on his forehead had bulged and cracked, his cheeks were a glistening purple, and on the very top of his jellied pate lay a pair of woollen gloves, which he must have put there to protect the lacerated scalp from the stinging rays of the sun, and the swarms of flies and midges. The gloves had dried on to the wound and stayed there.

He looked round huntedly, his eyes seeking and yet fearing to find his wife and little son. He wanted to ask someone to take them away if they were there. He knew now beyond a doubt that he would go no further than Tatarsky, that here he was to die, and he did not want his family to see his death, although for death itself he yearned with intense and ever growing impatience. With drooping shoulders, turning his head slowly and with difficulty, he scanned the familiar faces and not in one an-

swering glance did he see a trace of regret or sympathy—
the looks of both men and women were fierce and scowling.

His faded army shirt rustled and rucked up whenever
he turned. It was covered in brownish streaks of blood,
and there was also blood on his wadded Red Army
trousers, and his big bare feet with their fallen arches and
twisted toes.

Darya stood facing him. Choking with the hatred
that had risen to her throat, with pity and a foreboding
that something terrible was about to happen, she stared
into his face and could not tell whether he had seen her
and recognised her.

But Ivan went on anxiously scanning the crowd with
one wildly gleaming eye (the other was closed by a swelling) and suddenly, as his glance came to rest on Darya a
few paces away from him, he stepped forward unsteadily,
as if he were drunk. He was dizzy from loss of blood and
on the verge of fainting, but this intermediate state,
when everything seemed unreal and a sickening bemuse-
ment made the world spin and go dark before his eyes,
agitated him, and with a great effort he was still able to
stay on his feet.

When he saw and recognised Darya, he lurched forward.
A faint and distant semblance of a smile touched his
once firm but now disfigured lips. The smiling grimace
made Darya's heart beat fast and loud; it seemed to be
throbbing almost in her throat.

She came close up to Ivan, breathing heavily, and
growing paler every second.

'Well, hullo, cousin!'

The intense brittle voice, its extraordinary intonations,
cast a hush on the crowd.

The answer came huskily but firmly through the silence.

'Hullo, cousin Darya.'

'Now then, cousin dear, tell us how you treated your
own kinsman, my husband, how you—' Darya choked
and clasped her breast as her voice failed her.

The silence was complete and in this strained menacing
hush the barely audible continuation of Darya's question was heard right at the back of the crowd.

'—how you killed, how you put to death my husband,
Petro Panteleyevich?'

'No, cousin, I didn't put him to death!'

'You didn't put him to death?' Darya's vibrating voice

rose to an even higher pitch. 'It was you and Mishka Koshevoi who killed our Cossacks, wasn't it?'

'No, cousin... We... I didn't kill him.'

'Then who did? Who? Tell us!'

'The Trans-Amur Regiment was—'

'It was you! You killed him! The Cossacks said they saw you on the hill! You were on a white horse! Do you deny that, you bastard?'

'No, I was in that battle...' Ivan's left hand rose with an effort to the level of his head and straightened the woollen gloves that were stuck to it. There was an obvious note of uncertainty in his voice when he said, 'I was in that battle but I didn't kill your husband; it was Mishka Koshevoi. He shot him. I'm not to blame for Petro.'

'Then who of our folk did you kill? Whose children did you turn into orphans and send a-begging?' Horseshoe Yakov's widow screamed piercingly from the crowd.

The already tense atmosphere was further charged with hysterical sobbing, screams and funereal wailing.

Later Darya said she could not remember how the cavalry carbine came to be in her hands, who put it there. But when the women began to wail, she felt a strange object there and realised by the feel of it that it was a gun. At first she seized it by the barrel to strike Ivan with the butt, but the foresight dug painfully into her hand and she changed her grip on the stock, then turned it, threw the gun to her shoulder and took aim at the left side of Ivan's chest.

She saw the Cossacks behind him rush aside, exposing the grey log wall of the barn, and heard their frightened shouts, 'Look out! You're mad! You'll kill your own folk! Wait, don't shoot!' And incited by the animal-like alertness and expectancy of the crowd, the glances focussed upon her, the desire to avenge her husband's death and also, in part, by a vanity that had suddenly possessed her because at this moment she was not like all the other women, because even the men were staring at her and waiting in astonishment and fear, and because for this reason she had to do something unusual, out of the ordinary, that would strike terror into all hearts—driven simultaneously by all these different feelings and moving at frightening speed towards something which had already been decided in the depths of her consciousness, and about which she would not and could not think at that moment, she paused for a second, cautiously feeling for the trigger, and suddenly, to her own complete surprise, squeezed it hard.

The recoil knocked her backwards and the sound of the shot deafened her, but through the narrowed slits of her eyes she saw Ivan's startled face change at once, terribly and irrevocably, saw him spread his arms, then bring them together, as if about to dive from a great height into water, and then fall flat on his back, and saw his head jerk feverishly and the fingers of his outspread hands begin assiduously scratching at the ground.

Darya threw down the gun and, still not clearly aware of what she had done, turned her back on the fallen man and with a gesture that now looked quite unnatural in its everyday simplicity straightened her kerchief and tucked in the hair that had fallen loose.

'He's still breathing...' said one of the Cossacks as with far too much deference he made way for Darya to pass.

She looked back without knowing who or what was meant and heard a deep long drawn-out groan all on one note that seemed to come not from the throat but from the very guts and broke off in a death rattle. And only then did she realise that the groan had come from Ivan, who had met his death at her hands. She strode quickly and lightly past the barn towards the square; only a few people watched her go.

Their attention had switched to Antip. As if taking part in an assault at arms, he ran on tiptoe towards Ivan, for some reason hiding behind his back the bared knife-edge bayonet of a Japanese rifle. His movements were perfectly timed and accurate. He squatted on his haunches and as he drove the point of the bayonet into Ivan's chest he said quietly, 'Breathe your last, Kotlyarov!' and pressed with all his strength on the hilt.

Death came slowly and painfully to Ivan. Life was unwilling to quit his strong, muscular body. Even after the third thrust of the bayonet he still opened his mouth and a gasping groan came from under his bared and bloodied teeth.

'A-a-a-ah!'

'Get to hell out of it, you horse butcher!' the sergeant-major in charge of the escort said, pushing Antip away, and lifted his pistol, closing his left eye in a business-like manner.

The shot served as a signal for the Cossacks who had been accosting the other prisoners to start beating them up. They scattered and ran. Rifle shots mingled with shouts rang out harshly and briefly.

An hour later Grigory Melekhov galloped into Tatarsky.
He had ridden his horse to death. It had collapsed under
him on the road from Ust-Khopyorskaya. Grigory had
carried his saddle to the next village, borrowed a non-
descript nag—and arrived too late. The Tatarsky infantry
had taken the hill road out of the village towards the
Ust-Khopyorskaya border, where fighting was going on
against a Red Cavalry division. Tatarsky was quiet and
deserted. Night had draped a thick blanket over the
surrounding hills, the far bank, and the groves of murmuring poplar and ash.

Grigory rode into his yard and entered the house.
The lamp was not lit. Mosquitoes were buzzing in the intense darkness, only the icons in their corner showed a
gleam of tarnished gold. Breathing in the familiar, heart-
catching smell of home that he had known since childhood, Grigory asked, 'Anyone here? Mother! Dunyashka!'

'Grisha! Is it you?' came his sister's voice from the
front room. There was a slapping of bare feet and the
white figure of Dunyashka loomed in the doorway,
hurriedly tying the strings of her petticoat.

'Why're you in bed so early? Where's mother?'

'Something happened—'

Dunyashka broke off. Grigory heard her agitated
breathing.

'What's been happening here? When did the prisoners
come through? Long ago?'

'They've all been killed.'

'Wh-a-at?'

'The Cossacks killed them... Oh, Grisha! Our Darya,
the vicious creature...' Indignant tears sounded in Dunyashka's voice, '...she killed Ivan Alexeyevich herself ...
she shot him.'

'What are you blathering about?' Grigory cried, seizing
the collar of her embroidered petticoat in fright.

The whites of her eyes were glistening with tears
and by the fear that lurked in the pupils Grigory realised that he had not misheard.

'And Mishka Koshevoi? Stokman?'

'They weren't with the prisoners.'

His sister gave a brief, faltering account of the massacre
and Darya's part in it.

'...Mummy was scared to sleep in the same house with
her, she's gone next door, and Darya came in from some-

337

where drunk ... filthy drunk she was. Now she's asleep—'

'Where?'

'In the barn.'

Grigory strode into the barn and flung the door wide open. Darya was sleeping on the floor, her legs shamelessly exposed. Her slender arms were thrown apart, her right cheek was glistening with spit, and a stench of home-made liquor rose from her gaping mouth. She lay with her head turned awkwardly and her left cheek pressed to the floor, breathing laboriously.

Never before had Grigory felt such a frenzied desire to use his sabre. For a few seconds he stood over Darya, moaning and swaying, gritting his teeth, and surveying the prostrate body with a feeling of utter disgust and revulsion. Then he stepped forward and pressed the iron-tipped heel of his boot on to Darya's face, on to its dark arched eyebrows and gasped, 'You rotten snake!'

Darya broke into a moan and mumbled drunkenly, but Grigory had already clutched his head in his hands and run out into the yard, the sheath of his sabre clattering on the barndoor steps.

He rode off to the front the same night without seeing his mother.

LVII

Having failed to break the Don Army's resistance and cross the Donets before the spring floods, the 8th and 9th Red armies continued their efforts to develop their offensive on some sectors of the front. Most of these attempts came to nothing and the initiative passed into the hands of the Don Army command.

By the middle of May there had still been no perceptible changes on the Southern Front. But there soon would be. According to a plan drawn up by General Denisov, the former commander of the Don Army, and his chief of staff General Polyakov, units of the so-called strike force were being concentrated in the Kamenskaya and Ust-Byelokalitvenskaya areas and the process was almost complete. The best units of trained regulars in the young army, the well-tested regiments from the lower reaches of the Don, the Gundorovsky, Georgievsky, and others, had been brought up to this sector of the front. At a rough estimate this strike force numbered sixteen thousand bayonets and sabres and could field twenty-four artillery pieces and a hundred and fifty machine-guns.

General Polyakov's plan was that this force, combined with the units commanded by General Fitzhelaurov, should thrust in the direction of Makeyevka, dislodge the 12th Red Division and, operating on the flanks and in the rear of the 13th and the Ural divisions, break through into the Upper Don district to link up with the insurgent army and then drive into the Khopyor district to 'sanitate' the Cossacks infected by Bolshevism.

Intensive preparations for the offensive and breakthrough were in progress on the Donets. The command of the strike force had been entrusted to General Sekretev. Clearly the Don Army was beginning to gain the upper hand. Its new commander General Sidorin, who had replaced Krasnov's protégé, the retired General Denisov, and the newly elected Ataman of the Don Army, General Afrikan Bogayevsky, were oriented towards the Allies. In collaboration with representatives of the British and French military missions grandiose plans were being worked out for a march on Moscow and clearing all Russian territory of Bolsheviks.

Cargoes of arms were brought in through the Black Sea ports. Ocean-going ships delivered not only British and French aircraft, tanks, artillery, machine-guns and rifles, but even mule teams and supplies of food and uniforms devalued by the peace with Germany. Bales of dark-green English riding breeches and tunics with the British lion rampant on their brass buttons filled the warehouses of Novorossiisk. The stores were bursting with American flour, sugar, chocolate, and wines. Capitalist Europe, alarmed by the Bolsheviks' persistent vitality, generously supplied the south of Russia with shells and bullets, the very same shells and bullets that the Allied forces had not used up on the Germans. International reaction was on the march to strangle Soviet Russia, which had already been drained of much of its life-blood. British and French officers who had arrived on the Don and the Kuban to teach the Cossack officers and the officers of the Volunteer Army how to drive tanks and use British artillery were already looking forward to a triumphant entry into Moscow.

Meanwhile the events that were to decide the success of the Red Army's offensive in 1919 were taking place on the Donets.

There can be no doubt that the main reason for the failure of the Red Army's offensive was the Cossack uprising on the Upper Don. For three months it had gnawed at the rear of the Red front like an ulcer, demanding constant transfers of troops, interrupting the flow of food and ammunition to the front and hindering the dispatch of sick and wounded to the rear. To suppress the uprising some 20,000 infantrymen had been sent in from the 8th and 9th Red armies alone.

The Revolutionary Military Council of the Soviet Republic, lacking information about the true dimensions of the uprising*, was slow in taking sufficiently energetic measures to suppress it. At first, separate detachments, some of them quite small (the Kremlin military school, for instance, assigned a detachment of 200 men to the task), understrength units and weak security detachments were sent to the area. It was like trying to put out a huge fire with a few glasses of water. Scattered Red Army units were strung out round the insurgent territory, which had by now attained a diameter of one hundred and ninety kilometres. They acted independently, outside

---

*Characteristically, the true dimensions of the Upper Don rebellion have to this day not been established by our historians working on the history of the Civil War. For example, in N. Kakurin's very thorough and valuable work (*How the Revolution Fought*, Gosizdat, 1925, vol.1), the Upper Don uprising is described as follows:

'The most widespread and organised movements, with a definite counter-revolutionary character, in the sphere of the Red fronts in Great Russia and the Urals were the Izhevsk-Votkino uprising in August 1918 and the uprising of the Don Cossacks in the northern part of the Don Region in March 1919.

'...The Don uprising flared most fiercely in March 1919 in the rear of the 9th Army of our Southern Front, in the very period when both sides had concentrated their greatest attention on this front. In contrast to the first uprising (the Izhevsk-Votkino, M.Sh.), which broke out when the fronts of both sides had only just begun to take shape, the Don Cossack uprising began in the rear of a front that was already sufficiently manned and clearly delineated, in its direct vicinity, and at a time when decisive operations were developing. It thus had a much more substantial effect and compelled the Red command to expend considerable forces and time in combating it. The centre of the uprising was Vyoshenskaya stanitsa; the area affected covered nearly 10,000 sq.km., extending from Ust-Medveditskaya stanitsa to the town of Boguchar; the number of Cossacks involved is estimated at 15,000 whose arms included several machine-guns. A few secondary revolts involving only deserters took place around this main nucleus in Novokhopyorsk, Buturlinovka, and other areas. The need to suppress the uprising as soon as possible, before it undermined from the rear the

the general operational plan and, despite the fact that the forces deployed against the insurgents had as many as 25,000 bayonets, there were no effective results.

One after another, 14 reserve companies and dozens of security detachments were sent to localise the uprising; units made up of party members trained for posts of command arrived from Tambov, Voronezh and Ryazan. Only when the uprising had gained ground and the insurgents had armed themselves with machine-guns and artillery captured from the Red forces did the 8th and 9th Red armies each assign one expeditionary division with artillery and machine-gun companies to the task. The insurgents sustained heavy losses but were not broken.

Sparks from the conflagration on the Upper Don flew into the neighbouring Khopyor district, where several minor Cossack groups commanded by officers attempted to rise. In Uryupinskaya Lieutenant-Colonel Alimov had got together a fairly large number of Cossacks and officers who had been in hiding. Their rising was timed to begin on the eve of May Day, but the plot was uncove-

---

section of the front opposing the White armies, called for the transfer of substantial forces and weakened the front. During April, the 8th and 9th Red Armies both assigned expeditionary divisions totalling as many as 14,000 men with artillery and machine-guns. These forces were dispersed along a cordon of 400 km around the insurgent area and acted uncoordinatedly. Like the Izhevsk uprising, this outbreak tended to be Socialist-Revolutionary in character: the insurgents tried to retain the power of the Soviets, but without Communists. With the appointment of Comrade Khvesin, the former commander of the 8th Army, as commander of all the expeditionary forces operating against the insurgents, the suppression of the uprising proceeded more successfully. In the week from 24 May to 1 June, 1919, the uprising on the right bank of the Don was put down.'

In actual fact, the insurgents numbered not 15,000 but between 30 and 35 thousand, and their armaments consisted not of 'several machine-guns', but of 25 guns (including mortars) and about 100 machine-guns, and rifles for practically every man. Moreover, at the end of the section characterising the Upper Don uprising there is a substantial error: the uprising was not, as Kakurin writes, put down in May on the right bank of the Don. The Red expeditionary forces cleared the right bank of insurgents but armed insurgent forces and the whole population withdrew to the left bank. Trenches were dug along the river for two hundred versts, where the insurgents defended themselves for two weeks, until the breakthrough by Sekretev and the link-up with the main forces of the Don Army.

(M.Sh.)

341

red in time. Alimov and some of his accomplices were captured at one of the villages near Preobrazhenskaya and shot by order of the Revolutionary Tribunal; deprived of its leaders, the uprising misfired and the counter-revolutionary elements in the Khopyor district were unable to link up with the insurgents of the Upper Don.

In the early days of May Trotsky, the Chairman of the Military Revolutionary Council of the Republic, left Moscow to deal with the uprising. From Liski he travelled in a special carriage with its own locomotive as far as Chertkovo, where the detachment from the Kremlin military school was detraining, and where several scratch Red Army regiments were stationed. Chertkovo was one of the last stations on the South-Eastern Railway, which ran along the edge of the western sector of the insurgent front. At that time the Cossacks of Migulinskaya, Meshkovskaya and Kazanskaya had built up huge masses of cavalry in this area and were engaged in desperate fighting against the attacking Red Army units.

In the square outside the station Trotsky made a speech to the assembled Red Army men and military school trainees. The latter were formed up on the left side of the square, leaving their rifles neatly piled. The Red Army men fell in with their rifles, in full combat readiness. As soon as the speech had been delivered they were to march off to the front.

In the middle of the speech, in which Trotsky called for rapid and ruthless suppression of the uprising, for courageous struggle against the enemies of the revolution, a machine-gun somewhere on a hill above the town fired two short bursts and fell silent.

Rumours reached the station that Cossacks had surrounded Chertkovo and were about to attack. And despite the fact that the front was not less than fifty versts away and there were Red Army units ahead that would have reported any Cossack breakthrough, panic broke out at the station. The ranks of the assembled Red Army units began to waver. Somewhere behind the church a raucous commanding voice bellowed, 'To arms!' and people in the streets took to their heels.

Trotsky sent one of his staff to the telegraph office while he himself steered what had been an enthusiastic oration to a hasty conclusion and proceeded to the station. Five minutes later the locomotive that had brought the chairman of the Revolutionary Military Council of the Republic gave a piercing whistle and rumbled away, putting on speed, towards Liski.

The alarm turned out to be false. A squadron of Red Army cavalry approaching the station from Mankovo had been mistaken for Cossacks. The military school men and two of the scratch regiments marched out in the direction of Kazanskaya.

The next day a regiment that had recently arrived from Kronstadt was nearly wiped out by Cossacks in a night attack.

After the first clash with the Cossacks, the regiment had camped for the night in the open steppe rather than risk occupying a village abandoned by the insurgents. It had mounted the usual outposts and ambushes but at midnight several Cossack mounted squadrons surrounded the regiment and opened fire with all their guns, making wide use of a terror weapon someone had invented— huge wooden rattles, which at night served the insurgents as machine-guns because the sound they made was almost indistinguishable from that of the real thing.

When the surrounded Kronstadt men heard the chatter of scores of 'machine-guns' in the impenetrable darkness, the scattered firing from their own outposts, the Cossacks' whooping, and the roar and thunder of their attack formations, they made a rush for the Don. They broke through the encirclement, but were then routed by cavalry. Out of the whole regiment only a few men who had managed to swim the great flooded expanse of the Don survived.

In May more and more Red reinforcements arrived from the Donets. The 33rd Kuban Division appeared on the insurgent front and for the first time Grigory Melekhov felt the full impact of a real attack. The Kuban division pursued his 1st Division relentlessly. Grigory yeilded one village after another, retreating northwards to the Don. Near Karginskaya on the Chir he held out for a day, but then under pressure from the enemy's superior forces was compelled not only to give up Karginskaya but to send out an urgent request for reinforcements.

Kondrat Medvedev sent him eight mounted squadrons from his own division. His Cossacks were splendidly equipped. They had plenty of ammunition and their clothing and footwear, all taken from captured Red Army men, were in excelllent condition. Despite the heat many of them sported leather jackets and nearly all had revolvers or field glasses. For a time the new squadrons checked the onslaught of the 33rd Kuban Division. Grigory took the opportunity to pay a routine visit to Vyoshenskaya, responding at last to Kudinov's incessant requests that he should come and talk things over.

LVIII

He arrived in Vyoshenskaya early in the morning.

The Don flood waters had begun to recede. The air was drenched in the cloyingly sweet scent of poplars. Down by the river the sappy dark-green leaves of the oak-trees were rustling drowsily. The bare hills were steaming. Sharp-bladed young grass had sprouted on the hill tops, but in the hollows stagnant water still gleamed, the bitterns were booming, and, although the sun had risen, the dank, fusty-smelling shade was swarming with midges.

At headquarters an ancient typewriter was rattling and the rooms were full of people and tobacco smoke.

Grigory found Kudinov engaged in a curious pastime. When Grigory quietly entered the room, Kudinov did not look up. He was busy pulling off the legs of a big emerald-green fly that he had caught. He would pull off a leg, enclose the fly in his lean fist, hold it to his ear and listen with his head cocked intently to one side while the fly buzzed now on a low, now on a high note.

At the sight of Grigory he tossed the fly disgustedly and with some impatience under the desk, wiped his hand on his trousers, and leaned wearily on the shiny back of his chair.

'Take a seat, Grigory Panteleyevich.'

'Hullo, chief! How are you?'

'Not so bad, and not so good either. How are you getting on? Hard-pressed?'

'Very hard!'

'Did you hold out on the Chir?'

'The thing is how long? Medvedev's Cossacks saved the day.'

'There's something I want to tell you, Melekhov.' Kudinov wound the tassel of his rawhide Caucasian belt round his finger and studied the tarnished silver with affected curiosity. 'It looks as if there's worse to come for us. Something's going on around the Donets. Either our lot are giving the Reds a real rough time and ripping up their front or the Reds have realised we're the root of all evil and are trying to get a lock on us.'

'What've you heard about the Cadets? What news did you get with the last aeroplane?'

'Oh, nothing special. They won't tell us much about their strategies, chum. Sidorin, he knows his business! You won't get it all out of him at once. They've got a plan to break through the Red front and give us a helping hand. They promised to help. But these promises, they don't always come off. And it's not so easy to break through a front. I know that because I tried it once, with General Brusilov. How do we know what forces the Reds have got on the Donets? Maybe they've taken a few army corps that were fighting Kolchak and brought them down here, eh? We're living in the dark! We can't see any further than our own noses!'

'Then what did you want to talk about? What was the conference you had in mind?' Grigory asked with a yawn.

His heart was not in the uprising. He hardly cared now how it ended. He had pondered the question day after day, like a horse plodding round a threshing floor and eventually he had put it out of his mind. ' We can't make it up with the Soviet authorities. We've spilled too much of each other's blood for that. Right now the Cadet government is stroking us gently, but later they'll be stroking us up the wrong way. To hell with it all! We'll have to put up with it whatever way it ends.'

Kudinov unfolded a map and, still avoiding Grigory's eyes, said, 'While you were away, we had a conference here and decided—'

'Who with—with that prince?' Grigory interrupted him, recalling the conference that had been held in this very room in winter, and the Caucasian Lieutenant-Colonel who had been there.

Kudinov frowned and looked uncomfortable.

'He's no longer among the living.'

'How come?' Grigory asked, with revived interest.

'Didn't I tell you? They killed Comrade Georgidze.'

'How could he be a comrade of yours or mine... While he went about in a sheepskin, he was a comrade. But if we'd linked up with the Cadets—which God forbid—and he'd come through alive, he'd have dolled himself up the very next day and wouldn't deign to shake hands with you. He'd just offer you his little finger—like that.' Grigory stuck out his dark grimy finger and his teeth flashed in a laugh.

Kudinov's frown deepened. There was annoyance, even suppressed anger in his eyes and voice.

'You needn't laugh. No one laughs over another man's death. You're getting like Ivan the Simple. A man's been killed and it sounds as if you're saying, "The more the merrier!"'

Though slightly offended, Grigory showed no sign of resentment at Kudinov's comparison; he replied with a chuckle, 'Well, it is the more the merrier with the likes of him. I've got no sympathy for that lot with their white faces and white hands.'

'Anyway, they've killed him.'

'In battle?'

'Hard to say... It's a bit of a mystery and you can't get at the truth. My orders were that he should be with the transport company. But it seems he didn't get on with the Cossacks. There was some fighting at Dudarevka and the wagon he was riding on was standing about two versts from the firing line. He was sitting on the shaft (so the Cossacks told me) and a stray bullet happened to hit him in the temple. He went out like a light. Our Cossacks must have done it, the bastards!'

'And a good thing they did!'

'Oh, give over! Don't stick your oar in.'

'All right, you needn't get cross. I was only joking.'

'You make silly jokes sometimes... You're like a bull in a field. You drop dung on the grass you've eaten from. So you think it's right to kill officers, do you? The same old cry— "Down with epaulettes!"? Isn't it about time you started using your brains, Grigory? If you must limp, you'd better limp on the same leg all the time!'

'Stop jawing and tell me what happened!'

'There's nothing to tell! I guessed the Cossacks had killed him and decided to have it out with 'em. "So you're up to your old tricks, you devils?" I said. "Isn't it a bit too soon to start shooting the officers again? You shot a few last autumn, but when we got into a tight corner, you found out that the officers were needed. You yourselves," I told 'em, "came crawling on your knees. 'Take over command, lead us!' But now you're at it again?" Well, I went on at 'em for a bit, tried to put them to shame. They denied it, said they'd never done such a thing, God forbid! But I could tell by their eyes— they had given him the works! What can you do with 'em? It you pissed in their eyes, they'd say it was the dew of heaven!' Kudinov crushed the tassel of his belt irritably and flushed. 'They killed a man who knew what he was talking about. Real stuck I am without him.

Who's to draw up a plan? Who'll give you advice? We can talk like this together, but when it comes to strategy and tactics, we're all at sixes and sevens. Thank goodness, Petro Bogatiryov came over in his aeroplane, or there'd be no one at all to have a word with... Still, drat all that! This is what I have to say: if our lot from the Donets don't break through the front, we won't be able to hold out here. We've decided, as we said before, that we've got to try to break through with the whole army of thirty thousand. If you're defeated, you retreat back to the Don. We'll leave them the whole right bank from Ust-Khopyorskaya to Kazanskaya, dig trenches along this side of the Don and defend ourselves.'

There was a sharp knock on the door.

'Come in! Who is it?' Kudinov called.

Grigory Bogatiryov, commander of the 6th Brigade, entered the room. His burly red face was glistening with sweat, his bleached ginger eyebrows were knitted angrily. He sat down at the desk without removing his sweat-dampened cap.

'What brings you here?' Kudinov asked, looking at Bogatiryov with a restrained smile.

'Give us ammunition.'

'We've given you some already. How much more do you want? What d'you think I've got here—a munitions factory?'

'What did you give us? One bullet apiece? There they are, bashing away at me with their machine-guns and all I can do is duck and keep my head down. Call that war? It's a bloody farce! That's what it is!'

'Just a minute, Bogatiryov, we're discussing something serious.' But when Bogatiryov got up to go, Kudinov added, 'Hold on, don't go away. We've no secrets from you... Now listen, Melekhov, if we can't hold out on this side, we'll try again to make a breakthrough. We'll leave behind everyone that's not in the army, abandon all our baggage, put the infantry in wagons, take our three batteries with us and fight our way to the Donets. We want to put you in front, as the spearhead. Any objections?'

'It's all the same to me. But what about our families? It'll be all up with our wives and sisters, our old men.'

'That's a fact. But it's better than for all of us to get the chopper.'

Bogatiryov smiled and shook his head. 'This year our women will be having such a crop of babies, you'll

347

never count 'em! The Reds are right hungry for women just now. The other day we were retreating from Belavino, and the local people came with us, but one young wench got left behind. We saw her in the morning and she could only crawl. The comrades had been having such a go at her she couldn't even walk...'

Kudinov sat silently for a moment with drooping lips, then pulled a newspaper out of his drawer.

'And here's another bit of news. Their commander-in-chief Trotsky has come to take over. We've had word he's in Millerovo, or Kantemirovka. See how they're getting after us!'

'But is it true?' Grigory said doubtfully.

'It's true all right! Here, read this. The Kazanskaya men sent it. Yesterday morning one of our patrols caught two of their horsemen on the other side of Shumilinskaya. Both of 'em Reds, from the Party school. The Cossacks cut 'em down and on one of 'em, not so young by the look of him, they said, maybe a commissar or something, they found in his map case this newspaper, called *On the Road*, dated 12th of this month. There's a lovely description of us here!' Kudinov held out the newspaper, the corner of which had been torn off to make a cigarette.

Grigory glanced at the heading of the article, which had been marked with indelible pencil, and began to read.

UPRISING IN THE REAR

An uprising of some of the Don Cossacks has now lasted several weeks. Instigated by agents of Denikin—counter-revolutionary officers—it has found support among the Cossack kulaks, and the kulaks have dragged a considerable number of the middle Cossacks after them. It is quite possible that in either case the Cossacks suffered injustice at the hands of individual representatives of Soviet power. This has been skilfully exploited by Denikin's agents to spread the flames of revolt. In the area of the uprising the White-guard scoundrels pretend to be supporters of Soviet power so as to worm their way into the confidence of the middle Cossack. In this way counter-revolutionary scheming, kulak interests, and the ignorance of the mass of the Cossacks have temporarily merged in a senseless and criminal revolt in the rear of our armies of the Southern Front. For a soldier a rebellion behind his own lines is the same thing as a sore shoulder is for a workman. To be able to fight, to defend the Land of the Soviets, to finish off Denikin's landowner gangs, we must have a reliable, calm and united worker-peasant and working-Cossack rear. It is, therefore, a task of the greatest importance to clear the Don of rebellion and the rebels.

The central Soviet government has given orders for this task to be accomplished in the shortest possible time. Splendid reinforcements have arrived and are still arriving to help the expeditionary forces operating against the treacherous counter-revolutionary revolt. The best worker organisers are being sent to deal with this urgent task.

The revolt must be put down. Our Red Army men must be inspired with a clear awareness of the fact that the insurgents of Vyoshenskaya or Yelanskaya or Bukanovskaya are the direct accomplices of the Whiteguard generals Denikin and Kolchak. The longer the uprising drags on, the more losses there will be on both sides. There is only one way to curtail the bloodshed, and that is by delivering a swift, severe and crushing blow.

The revolt must be put down. The sore on our shoulder must be opened and cleansed with hot steel. The arm of the Southern Front will then be freed to inflict a mortal blow on the enemy.

Grigory finished reading and smiled grimly. The article had filled him with bitterness and anger. 'Making me an accomplice of Denikin, just like that, with a stroke of the pen,' he thought.

'Well, how do you like that? So they're going to cleanse us with hot steel. We'll see who does the cleansing. Won't we, Melekhov?' Kudinov waited for a reply, then turned to Bogatiryov. 'You want ammunition? We'll give you some! Thirty bullets per horseman, for the whole brigade. Will that do?.. Go and draw 'em from the stores. The chief of the supply department will write out the warrant for you. But you rely on your sabres a bit more, on cunning, Bogatiryov. They're the thing!'

'Think yourself lucky to get a handful of wool off a mangy sheep,' the gratified Bogatiryov said with a grin of pleasure and took his leave.

Melekhov also left when he and Kudinov had decided on the plan for the expected retreat to the Don. But before going, he asked, 'Suppose I bring the whole division to Bazki, what can we use for crossing the Don?'

'Any more bright ideas? All the cavalry will swim across. Who ever heard of cavalry being ferried?'

'I haven't got many men from the Don, you know. The Cossacks from the Chir are no swimmers. They've spent their lives in the steppe, how can you expect them to swim? Most of 'em would sink like a stone.'

'They'll swim with their horses. They've done it on manoeuvres and they had to do it in the German war.'

'I'm talking about the infantry.'

'There's a ferry. We'll have some boats ready, don't worry.'

'The local people will want to cross too.'

'I know.'

'Mind there's enough room on the ferry for everyone or I'll have your guts! It'll be no joke for anyone that's left behind.'

'I'll fix everything!'

'What about the guns?'

'Blow up the mortars and bring the three-inch guns over here. We'll knock together some big boats and bring the battery over to this side.'

Grigory left the insurgent headquarters with the words of the article ringing in his head.

'They call us accomplices of Denikin... And what are we? That's just what we are. So why get huffy about it. It stings because it's true.' He remembered something Horseshoe Yakov had told him before he was killed. One evening in Karginskaya, when he returned late to his quarters, Grigory had dropped in to see the gunners who were quartered in one of the houses in the square. As he had knocked the snow off his boots in the porch he had heard Yakov arguing with someone and saying, 'You say we're separate? And won't be under anyone's authority? Huh! You've got a pumpkin for a head! Right now, if you want to know, we're like a homeless dog. If a dog has upset its master or done something wrong, it'll sometimes leave home. But where can it go? It can't join the wolves because it's afraid and it knows they're wild animals, and it can't go back to its master because it'll get beaten for its mischief. And we're the same. Mark my words, we'll tuck our tails between our legs and come wriggling on our bellies to the Cadets. "Take us back, dear brothers, have mercy on us!" That's how it'll be!'

Ever since the battle when he had cut down the sailors near Klimovka, Grigory had lived in a state of cold, stupefied indifference. He went about with his head sunk on his chest, dispirited and unsmiling. For a day or so he had felt pain and pity over the killing of Ivan Alexeyevich, then even that had passed. All that was left to him in life (or so he thought) was his passion for Aksinya, which had now revived with such relentless force. Only she attracted him, as the quivering light of a campfire in the steppe beckons the traveller on a dark and freezing autumn night.

And now too, as he was returning from headquarters, he remembered Aksinya and thought, 'What'll happen to her if we try to break through?' And without hesitation or reflection he decided, 'Natalya will stay with the children and Mother, and I'll take Aksinya with me. I'll give her a horse and let her ride with my staff.'

He crossed the Don at Bazki, went to his quarters, tore a sheet from his notebook and wrote, 'Aksinya, love! We may have to retreat to the left bank. If we do, leave all your stuff behind and go to Vyoshenskaya. You'll find me there and be with me.'

He sealed the note with thin cherry glue, handed it to Prokhor Zykov and, flushing purple as he tried to hide his embarrassment under a mask of severity, said, 'Go to Tatarsky, and give this note to Aksinya Astakhova. And do it ... well, mind none of my family sees you. Get me? You'd better do it at night. There's no need for an answer. And then you can take two days' leave. Off you go!'

Prokhor went to his horse, but Grigory called him back.

'Look up my family and tell Mother or Natalya to send our clothes and anything of value over to this side in good time. They can bury the grain and swim the animals across the Don.'

LIX

On May 22nd the insurgent forces began a retreat all along the right bank. It was a fighting retreat, with each unit putting up stiff resistance on every line. The population of the villages in the steppeland zone made a panic-stricken rush for the Don. The women and old men harnessed all the draught animals they could find and piled their wagons high with chests, pots and pans, sacks of grain and children. Cows and sheep were taken out of the village herds and driven along the roads. Huge baggage trains rolled in advance of the army towards the Donside villages.

The infantry had been ordered to retreat a day earlier than the rest of the army. On May 21st the Tatarsky foot and the Vyoshenskaya non-Cossack recruits left the village of Chebotaryov near Ust-Khopyorskaya, marched over forty versts, and stopped for the night in the village of Rybinsky, near Vyoshenskaya.

At daybreak on May 22nd the sky was wrapped in a pallid haze. There was not a cloud in the murky expanse, save for a small dazzling pink puff of vapour that appeared in the south over a gap in the Donside hills before sunrise. Its eastern edge was flooded with purple light and seemed to bleed. The sun rose from behind the dew-cooled sand hills of the left bank and the cloud disappeared. The cries of the corncrakes in the meadow grew harsher, the sharp-winged fisher gulls dropped like blue flakes into the wide waters, then soared with silvery glittering fish in their rapacious beaks.

By noon it was unusually hot for May. The air was very close, as though there would be rain. Even before sunrise waves of refugee wagons had been rolling towards Vyoshenskaya along the right bank of the Don from the east. Wagon wheels clattered incessantly along the Hetman's highway, and the snorting of horses, the bellowing of oxen and human talk could be heard all along the bank from the hilltops to the water meadows.

The Vyoshenskaya non-Cossack company, numbering about two hundred men, was still in Rybinsky. At about ten in the morning it received orders to proceed to the village of Bolshoi Gromok, set up outposts along the highway and in the village, and stop all Cossacks of service age heading for Vyoshenskaya.

A wave of refugee wagons bound for Vyoshenskaya rolled up to Gromok. The cattle were being driven by women, their faces dusty and dark with sunburn, while the men rode along the shoulder of the road on horseback. The creak of wheels, the snorting of horses and sheep, the lowing of cows, the wailing of children, and the groans of the typhus-stricken, who were also being taken in the retreat, shattered the customary stillness of the village, hidden away among its cherry orchards. So remarkable was this multitudinous roar that the village dogs grew utterly hoarse from barking, no longer pounced on every passer-by as they had at first, and gave up following the wagons along the streets and far out into the steppe for want of anything better to do.

Prokhor Zykov spent two days at home, passed Grigory's note on to Aksinya, and his verbal message to Ilyinichna and Natalya, and on the 22nd set out for Vyoshenskaya.

He had been counting on meeting his squadron in Bazki, but the sound of muffled gunfire that reached the banks of the Don still seemed to come from somewhere on the Chir. Since he had no desire to turn off in the direction of the fighting, Prokhor decided to push on to Bazki and wait there until Grigory and his 1st Division reached the Don.

He jogged along, nearly all the time at a walk with refugee wagons overtaking him. He was in no hurry. After the village of Rubezhin he attached himself to the staff of the recently formed Ust-Khopyorskaya Regiment.

The regiment's staff was travelling in a sprung droshky and two wagons. They had six saddled horses tethered behind them. One of the wagons was carrying various staff documents and telephones, and in the droshky sat an elderly wounded Cossack and another man in a grey officer's lambskin cap, terribly thin, with a hooked nose, who never raised his head from the saddle pad on which it rested. Evidently he was just recovering from typhus. He had drawn his greatcoat up to his chin; his pale prominent forehead and thin high-bridged nose were gleaming with perspiration and grimed with dust, but he kept asking to have his feet wrapped up in something warmer, wiping his forehead with a lean bony hand and scolding. 'Lazy swine! Bastards! Damn you! There's a draught on my feet, d'you hear? Polikarp, do you hear me? Put a rug over them! When I was well, you needed me, but now...' and he looked away with the sternly aloof gaze of one who had endured a severe illness.

The man whom he had addressed as Polikarp—a tall jaunty-looking Old Believer—sprang off his horse and came up to the droshky.

'You'll catch your death of cold, Samoilo Ivanovich, if you go on like this.'

'Cover me, I tell you!'

Polikarp complied obediently with the order and returned to his horse.

'Who's that?' Prokhor asked him, indicating the sick man with his eyes.

'An officer from Ust-Medveditskaya. He was at our headquarters.'

There were refugees from Tyukovny, Bobrovsky, Krutovsky, Zimovny and other villages travelling with the staff.

'Where's the devil taking you?' Prokhor asked an old

man perched on a hay wain stacked with various belongings.

'We want to get to Vyoshenskaya.'

'Do they want you there so badly?'

'No one said they wanted us, lad, but who wants to stay and meet his death? We're going because we're scared.'

'That's why I'm asking you! You could cross over at Yelanskaya and it wouldn't be half so far.'

'But what on? Folk say they've no ferry there.'

'What is there at Vyoshenskaya then? D'ye think they'll give you a special ferry? Will they leave troops behind and take you and your wagons? You're a daft lot, I must say, Grandad! Wandering about like lost sheep. What have you got here on this wagon of yours?' Prokhor demanded crossly, pointing at the bundles with his whip.

'All kinds of things! Clothes and horse-collars, flour, and plenty more you need on a farm. We couldn't leave it all behind. We'd have come back to an empty house. So I harnessed a couple of horses, three pairs of oxen, loaded 'em as heavy as I could, put the women on top and off we went. I earned it all by the sweat of my brow, lad, by tears and sweat—who wouldn't be sorry to leave it? I'd have brought the house as well if I could, so the Reds wouldn't get it—devil take 'em!'

'What about that great sieve? Why're you humping that along? Or the chairs—what's the good of them? The Reds won't want 'em!'

'But could I leave 'em behind! You're a queer fellow... If I didn't take 'em along, they'd either be burnt or broken. No, they won't get anything out of me. May they burn in hell! I've cleared the place out and brought it with me!'

The old man waved his whip at the plodding well-fed horses, then turned round and jabbed his whipstock at the third wagon, drawn by oxen.

'That lass with her head wrapped up that's driving the bullocks is my daughter. She's got a sow and its litter in that wagon. The creature was expecting and when we tied her up we must have squeezed her. And there you are—in the middle of the night she brings forth on the wagon! Hear those piglets squealing? No, the Reds won't make 'emselves very rich out of me, may the fever shake 'em!'

'You'd better not come my way near that ferry, granfer!' said Prokhor, eyeing the old man's broad perspiring face with some malice. 'Because if you do, your pigs and piglets and all the rest of your property will go crashing into the Don!'

'Whatever for?' the old fellow asked astoundedly.

'Because people are getting killed, losing everything, and you, you old devil, drag everything along with you like a spider!' the usually quiet and docile Prokhor shouted. 'I can't stick these muck-grubbers. Hate 'em like poison!'

'Go along. Go along with you!' the old man turned away huffily. 'Someone's got too big for his boots, wanting to throw other people's property into the Don... And I talked to him as if he was a good sort... My own son, a sergeant-major, and his squadron are holding up the Reds' advance at this very moment... So go along with you now! There's no need to envy other people's goods! Set to work and get some for yourself, then it won't trouble you so much to see other people's!'

Prokhor went off at a trot. From behind him came the piercing squeal of a young pig and the worried grunting of the mother. The pig's squealing bored into his eardrums like a gimlet.

'What the devil? Where did that pig come from? Polikarp!..' the officer in the droshky burst out, frowning painfully and almost weeping.

'A little pig fell off its wagon and the wheel made a mess of its leg,' Polikarp replied, riding closer.

'Tell him... Go and tell the owner to cut its throat quickly. Say there are sick men here... It's hard enough to bear without that squealing. Hurry up!'

As Prokhor drew level with the droshky, he saw the hook-nosed officer listening with a fixed frown on his face to the piglet's lament and trying in vain to stop his ears with the grey lambskin cap... Polikarp came cantering back.

'He doesn't want to kill it, Samoilo Ivanovich. He says it'll recover. But if it doesn't, they'll have it for supper this evening.'

The officer's face paled and with an effort he sat up on the droshky and let his legs dangle over the side.

'Where's the Browning? Stop the horses! Where's the owner of that pig? I'll show him... Which wagon is it?'

The thrifty old man was obliged to put the pig out of its misery, after all.

Chuckling to himself, Prokhor trotted on past the line of Ust-Khopyorskaya wagons. A verst further on another string of wagons and horsemen came into view. No less than two hundred wagons, and about forty horsemen, riding in loose order.

'It'll be like the end of the world at the ferry!' Prokhor thought to himself.

As he caught up with the wagons, a woman came galloping towards him from the head of the column on a splendid dark-bay horse. On reaching Prokhor she drew rein. Her horse was richly saddled, the breast-band and bridle gleamed with silver, the flaps were hardly rubbed, and the girths and seat had the sheen of fine leather. The woman sat her horse well and her grip on the reins was correct, but the big charger seemed to scorn its rider; it kept rolling its bloodshot eyes, arching its neck and, baring its massive yellow teeth, tried to snap at the shapely knee that showed from under the woman's skirt.

Her face was muffled to the eyes in a freshly washed and blue-bagged kerchief. Drawing it away from her lips, she asked, 'Have you passed a wagon carrying wounded?'

'More than one. What about it?'

'I'm trying to find my husband,' the woman said with a slight drawl in her voice. 'He's with a field hospital coming from Ust-Khopyorskaya. He was wounded in the leg and it started festering. So he wanted me to bring him his horse. This is it,' the woman thwacked the sweat-beaded animal's neck with her whip. 'I saddled it up and rode to Ust-Khopyorskaya, but the hospital had already left. I've been all over the place but I can't find him.'

Gazing in admiration at the Cossack woman's handsome oval face and delighting in the soft low-pitched tones of her voice, Prokhor cleared his throat.

'Ah, lady! Why the devil should you look for your husband! Let him ride with his hospital. Why, anyone would marry a beauty like you and with such a fine horse for a dowry! I'd risk it myself.'

The woman smiled reluctantly and bent her buxom figure to pull the skirt over her knee.

'Tell me without the sweet nothings whether you passed a field hospital.'

'In that bunch back there they've got both sick and wounded,' Prokhor replied with a sigh.

The woman swung her whip, the horse wheeled on its hind legs, showed a flash of foam on its loins and broke abruptly from a trot into an all-out gallop.

The wagons rolled on slowly. The bullocks swung their

tails lazily to drive away the buzzing cattle flies. The heat was so intense, the thundery air so close and exhausted that even the young leaves of the sunflowers by the roadside had begun to droop.

Prokhor once again rode beside the wagons. He was surprised to see so many young Cossacks. They had either lost their own squadrons or simply deserted, joined up with their families and were riding with them to the crossing. Some had hitched their army mounts to the wagons and were lying back, chatting to the women or nursing the children, while others stayed on horseback without taking off their rifles or sabres. 'They've left their units and run for it,' Prokhor decided as he watched them out of the corner of his eye.

The air was full of the stench of horse and bullock's sweat, the smell of hot wagon wood, pots and pans, and wheel greese. The bullocks plodded on despondently, their flanks heaving. Braids of spit hung down to the dusty road from their lolling tongues. The line was moving at not more than four or five versts an hour, the horse-drawn wagons not bothering to overtake those drawn by oxen. But as soon as the boom of a gun spread softly from far away in the south, everything stirred into action. The two-horse and one-horse wagons broke out of the long line, the horses trotted, whips were brandished, and there was a flurry of shouts, 'Come on, there!' 'Now, then, you devils! Get moving!' Switches and whips thwacked the bullocks' backs and the wheels set up a livelier clatter. Fear hastened every movement. The hot dust rose in heavy grey streamers and billowed away behind, settling on the shoots of grain and grass.

Prokhor's sturdy little horse reached down as it went along, pulling now a sprig of sweet clover, now a stalk of cress or a clump of quitch, and munched with its alert ears twitching, its tongue working to dislodge the snaffle, which had begun to rub its gums. But after the gunshot Prokhor dug in his heels and the horse, apparently realising this was no time for grazing, obediently broke into a jerky trot.

The rumble of gunfire increased. The heavy, jarring shots merged into one and a thunderous roar played its jangling octaves in the stifling air.

'Lord Jesus!' a young woman on a wagon made the sign of the cross, then snatched her milky brown-pink nipple from her child's mouth and tucked the taut yellowish breast into her blouse.

357

'Who's shooting? Ours or theirs? Hi, soldier!' an old man stumping along beside his oxen hailed Prokhor.

'The Reds, Grandad! Our lot haven't got any shells.'

'Queen of Heavens, save them!'

The old man dropped the rope he had round the bullocks' horns, took off his old and battered Cossack cap and, without stopping, turned his face to the east and crossed himself.

In the south, from behind a ridge spiky with the shoots of late-sown maize there rose a ragged black cloud. Soon it had spread like a fog across half the horizon.

'Look! That's a big fire!' someone shouted from a wagon.

'What's burning?'

'Where's the fire?' voices sounded above the chatter of wagon wheels.

'Along the Chir somewhere.'

'The Reds are burning the villages along the Chir!'

'God forbid!'

'Look what a great black cloud it's making!'

'That's not just one village burning!'

'It's further down the Chir from Karginskaya, that's where the fighting is right now.'

'Mebbe it's down along the Chornaya? Get a move on, Ivan!'

'That's some fire!'

The black murk reached out across the sky. The rumble of artillery grew louder. After half an hour a breeze from the south brought to the Hetman's highway the acrid and alarming smell of the fires that were raging thirty-five versts away in the villages along the Chir.

LX

The road through Bolshoi Gromok passed along a wall made of grey stone slabs, then turned sharply and ran down to the Don, dipping into a shallow ravine spanned by a log bridge.

In dry weather the bottom of the ravine reflected the glow of yellow sand and multi-coloured pebbles. But after a summer storm muddy streams of rain water swept down from the hill above, merged into a solid wall and charged on down the ravine, overturning and dislodging stones, and roaring into the Don.

358

At such times the bridge was flooded, but not for long; after two or three hours of ruining vegetable patches and tearing up posts and fences the wild hill water abated, and the damp freshly washed pebbles, smelling of chalk and moisture, glowed anew on the bed of the ravine and the brown silt gleamed along its edges.

The sides of the ravine were thickly wooded with poplar and willow, which offered a cool refuge at even the hottest time of a summer day.

Tempted by the shade, the Vyoshenskaya non-Cossack platoon, numbering eleven men, had set up their check post by the bridge. When there were no refugee wagons coming through the village, the men lounged about under the bridge, playing cards and smoking. Some stripped down and cleaned the seams of their shirts and underwear of the insatiable army lice; two of them got permission from their commander and went down to the Don for a swim.

But they had little time to rest. The wagons soon began rolling down to the bridge. They came in a steady stream and the shady, sleepy lane at once grew crowded, noisy and stuffy, as though the acrid sultriness of the steppe had entered the village with the wagons.

The commander of the post, who was also commander of the 3rd non-Cossack platoon, a tall, lean warrant officer with a clipped brownish beard and large boyishly protruding ears, stood by the bridge with his hand on the battered holster of his revolver. He let through about a score of wagons but, on noticing one driven by a young Cossack of about twenty-five, he abruptly ordered it to halt.

The Cossack heaved on the reins, frowning sullenly.

'What unit?' the platoon commander asked sternly, stepping up to the wagon.

'What's that to you?'

'What unit are you from, I asked. Now then?'

'The Rubezhin squadron. But who are you?'

'Get down!'

'Who are you then?'

'Get down, I said!'

The platoon commander's round ears turned a fiery red. He unbuttoned his holster, pulled out the revolver and transferred it to his left hand. The Cossack passed the reins to his wife and jumped down from the wagon.

'Why aren't you with your unit? Where are you heading for?' the platoon commander questioned him.

'I've been ill. I'm on my way to Bazki and I'm—taking the family with me.'

'Got any papers to show you were ill?'

'Where from? There wasn't a doctor in our squadron...'

'Oh, wasn't there?.. Karpenko, take him to the school!'

'Now, look here, who are you?'

'We'll show you who we are when we get there!'

'I've got to get back to my unit! You've no right to arrest me!'

'We'll send you back to your unit ourselves. Have you got any weapons?'

'Just a rifle.'

'Take it, and be quick or I'll plug you! A young man like you hiding behind a woman's skirts, you bastard! D'you expect us to defend you?' And scornfully, as the Cossack turned away, 'A fine Cossack!'

The Cossack pulled his rifle out from under a rug, took his wife's arm and, hesitating to kiss her in public, only held her rough hand for a minute and whispered something, then followed the guard to the village school.

The wagons jammed in the lane started off again and rumbled over the bridge.

In the course of an hour the post arrested about fifty deserters. Some of them resisted. A Cossack with a long moustache, gallant-looking but by no means young, from the village of Lower-Krivsky, gave a lot of trouble. In reply to the post commander's order to leave his wagon he whipped on his horses. Two guards grabbed the bridles and managed to stop them only on the other side of the bridge. The Cossack promptly snatched up an American Winchester from the floor of the wagon and threw it to his shoulder.

'Out of the road!.. I'll shoot you, you swine!'

'Get down! Our orders are to shoot anyone who doesn't come quietly. You don't stand a chance!'

'Muzhiks!.. Only yesterday you were Reds and now you think you can order Cossacks about? You stinking bastards! Stand back or I'll drill you!'

One of the guards, his legs wrapped in new winter puttees, stepped on to the front wheel of the wagon and after a brief struggle wrenched the rifle out of the Cossack's hands. The Cossack then crouched with the agility of a cat and, reaching under a cover, snatched his sabre out of its sheath; kneeling down, he stretched across the painted seat and would have reached the guard's head with the point of his sabre if the latter had not jumped aside.

'Timosha, stoppit! Oh, Timosha!.. You mustn't! Don't!

They'll kill you!' the raging Cossack's thin, plain-faced wife cried, weeping and wringing her hands.

But he rose to his full height on the wagon and swung his bluishly glittering sabre this way and that, keeping the guards at bay, swearing hoarsely and rolling his eyes in a frenzy. 'I'll cut you down! Back!' His dark, almost black face twitched convulsively, foam bubbled from under his long yellowish moustache, and the bluish whites of his eyes grew more and more bloodshot.

Eventually he was overpowered and tied up, and then a simple explanation was found for the dashing Cossack's aggression. When the wagon was searched they found a large, already opened jug of home-distilled double-strength vodka among the chattels.

The lane was by this time so tightly packed with transports that the oxen and horses had to be unharnessed and the wagons wheeled down to the bridge by hand. Shafts cracked and broke, horses neighed fiercely, the oxen, tormented by the flies, ignored their masters' shouts and pawed at the fences. Shouts and swearing, the crack of whips, and women's lamentations resounded over the bridge for a long time. The wagons in the rear, if they were able to turn round, drove back on to the highway and headed for the Don through Bazki.

The arrested deserters were sent to Bazki under guard, but since they were all armed the escort could not control them. As soon as they crossed the bridge a fight broke out between the prisoners and their escorts. After a while the escorts returned and the deserters marched off to Vyoshenskaya on their own.

Prokhor Zykov was also stopped at Gromok, but he showed the leave permit Grigory had given him and was allowed to go his way without hindrance.

That evening he rode into Bazki. Thousands of wagons of all kinds from the villages along the Chir had blocked all the streets and side-lanes. The scene by the Don was indescribable. The whole bank for about two versts was jammed with refugee wagons. About fifty thousand people on the bank and in the surrounding woods were waiting to be ferried across.

Batteries, command staffs and military equipment were being taken aboard the Vyoshenskaya ferry. The infantry rowed across in small boats. Scores of them were scurrying to and fro across the river, carrying three or four passengers. People were almost fighting each other in the crush at the water's edge, by the pier. But the cavalry, which had stayed behind to guard the rear, had not yet arrived. The rumble of artillery fire was still coming from the Chir and the bitter stench of burning was even more pungent.

Ferrying continued until dawn. At about midnight the first mounted squadrons began to appear. At daybreak they were to make the crossing.

On learning that the mounted units of the 1st Division had not yet arrived, Prokhor decided to wait for his squadron at Bazki. With difficulty he led his horse past the wagons ranged solidly along the wall of Bazki Hospital, then he tethered it to the side of someone's stationary wagon, removed the snaffle but left the saddle on, and went to look for familiar faces among the crowd.

Near a small dike he caught sight of Aksinya Astakhova. She was coming down to the Don with a warm jacket over her shoulders, clasping a small bundle. Her striking beauty attracted the attention of the infantry crowding the bank. Lewd remarks showered on her from all sides, grinning teeth showed white in the sweating, dust-grimed faces, and bawdy laughter and whistles rose in her wake. A big blond Cossack with his shirt unbelted and his cap on the back of his head seized her from behind and pressed his lips to her dark, sculptured neck. Prokhor saw Aksinya push the Cossack away and say something to him, baring her teeth. There was a roar of laughter and the Cossack doffed his cap, booming hoarsely, 'Oh, missy! Give us a go!'

Aksinya quickened her pace and walked past Prokhor. Her full lips were quivering in a scornful smile. Prokhor did not hail her. His eyes roved over the crowd in search of men from his village. As he moved slowly among the wagons with their shafts pointing impotently skywards, he heard drunken voices and laughter. Three old men were sitting beside a wagon on a strip of sackcloth. One of them had a pail of home-brew between his legs. The old tipplers were taking turns to scoop liquor from the pail with a bronze mug made from a shell case, and helping the drink down with dried fish. The pungent odour of the home-distilled vodka and the salty tang of the fish brought the hungry Prokhor to a halt.

'Hi, soldier! Have a drink with us for all the good things in life!' one of the old men called out to him.

Prokhor did not need much persuading. He sat down, crossed himself and smilingly accepted from the hands of the hospitable old man a mugful of the fragrant home-brew.

'Drink while you're still alive! Here's a bit of bream to go with it. You mayn't turn up your nose at the old men, lad. Old men are wise men! You young fellers have a lot to learn from us about how to live and—well, how to drink vodka,' another old fellow, with no nose left and his upper lip eaten down to the gums, declared with a nasal twang in his voice.

Prokhor drank the mug, glancing apprehensively at the noseless old man. Between the second and third mugfuls he could not help asking, 'Did you lech your nose away, Grandad?'

'No, laddie! I caught cold. I was always catching cold in my young days and that's what done it.'

'And I was in a way to think badly of you. Was it some evil disease that gave him a nose like that, I wondered. I wouldn't like to pick up any of that rubbish!' Prokhor confessed frankly.

Reassured by the old man's statement, he put his lips thirstily to the mug and without further misgivings emptied it.

'Life's going to the dogs! How can ye help taking to drink?' the owner of the home-brew, a strong, thick-set old man bellowed. 'I've brought two hundred poods of wheat with me but I left a thousand behind. I'm driving five pair of oxen, but it'll all have to be left here. You can't carry it across the Don on your own back! All I worked for and saved for is going to be lost. So let's sing up and drink up, Cossacks!' the old man grew purple in the face and his eyes glistened with tears.

'Don't cry, Trofim Ivanich. Moscow don't believe in tears. We'll get some more one day, if we stay alive,' the nasal-voiced old man soothed his friend.

'O' course, I'm crying!' the other shouted in a voice choking with tears. 'The grain's wasted! The oxen will die! The Reds will burn my house down! They killed my son last autumn! O' course, I'm crying! Who did I do all that work for? Why, in one summer I'd rot ten shirts with my sweat, and now I'll be left with nothing to show for it all, naked and barefoot... Drink!'

While they were talking, Prokhor ate a bream as big as a stove-door, drank seven mugfuls of home-brew and began to feel so loaded that he could rise only with the greatest effort.

'Soldier! Our defender! Want me to give ye some grain for your horse? How much d'ye want?'

'Sackful!' Prokhor mumbled, by now quite indifferent to his surroundings.

The old man filled a big five-pood sack with the finest oats and helped him to heave it on to his shoulder.

'Bring the sack back! Don't forget, for Christ's sake!' he begged, embracing Prokhor and weeping drunken tears.

'No, I won't bring it back. I've said I won't and I won't,' Prokhor insisted stubbornly for some unknown reason.

He staggered away from the wagon. The sack weighed him down and swung him from side to side. He seemed to be walking over bare icy ground, his legs trembling and sliding apart like those of an unshod horse cautiously stepping on to ice. After taking a few more uncertain steps, he halted. He just couldn't remember whether he had been wearing a cap or not. A white-browed bay gelding tethered to a wagon, scenting oats, reached out to the sack and bit off the corner. The oats spilled out with a soft rustle. Prokhor felt lighter and staggered on.

He might even have carried what was left of the oats as far as his horse, but a huge bullock that he happened to be passing suddenly lashed out sideways at him as bullock sometimes do. Tormented beyond endurance by the flies and midges and enraged by the heat, the beast would not let anyone come near it. Prokhor, who was not the first victim of its fury, was knocked flying, hit his head on the hub of a wheel, and immediately fell asleep.

He woke up at midnight. In the greyish-blue sky above him leaden clouds were tumbling westwards. A young tilted moon appeared for a brief moment in the rifts between them, then the sky was again shrouded in a blanket of cloud and the rough cool wind seemed to grow stronger in the darkness.

Cavalry was passing close to the wagon beside which Prokhor was lying. The earth groaned under the multitude of iron-shod hooves. The horses snorted in expectation of rain; sabres clattered on stirrups, cigarettes flared red. From the passing squadron spread a stench of horse sweat and the sour smell of leather harness.

Like any serving Cossack, Prokhor had acquired a liking for this blend of smells peculiar to the cavalry. The Cossacks had carried it along all the roads from Prussia and Bukovina to the Don steppes and its indestructible tang was as familiar to them as the smell of their own home. His nostrils twitching, Prokhor raised his heavy head.

'What unit are you, lads?'

'Mounted...' a deep voice answered playfully in the darkness.

'Which unit are you, I asked?'

'Petlyura's!' the same voice replied.

'There's a bastard for you!' Prokhor waited a bit, then repeated his question. 'What regiment is this, comrades?'

'Bokovskaya.'

Prokhor tried to get up but the blood rushed to his head and he felt a wave of sickness rising in his throat. He lay back and fell asleep again. Towards dawn the damp and cold began drifting up from the Don.

'Is he dead?' the question came to him in his sleep.

'No, he's still warm—and drunk!' someone replied right at Prokhor's ear.

'Pull him away, damn him! Lying about like dead cattle! Give him a dig in the ribs!'

The wooden end of a lance gave the drowsy Prokhor a painful jab in the side and a pair of hands gripped his feet and dragged him along on his back.

'Now clear those wagons out of the way! Are you all dead, blast you! This is a fine time to be sleeping! The Reds are right on our heels and they lie here dead to the wide, as if they're at home! Move those wagons, there's a battery coming through right now! Look lively!.. You've blocked the whole road!.. These people!' a commanding voice boomed impatiently.

The refugees sleeping on the wagons and under them stirred into action. Prokhor jumped to his feet. He had neither a rifle nor sabre, and his right leg was short of a boot—all lost since the carousal of the night before. Staring round in astonishment, he was about to start looking for them under the wagon, but the drivers and crews of the approaching battery ruthlessly overturned the wagon and all the chattels with which it was loaded, instantly clearing a path for the guns.

'Move!'

The drivers sprang on to their horses. The broad traces jerked and tautened. The big wheels of a tarpaulin-covered gun clattered over a rut. The axle of a caisson caught on the shaft of the wagon and broke it.

'Abandoning the front, are you? Fine soldiers you

are, curse your guts!' the noseless old man Prokhor had been drinking with the night before shouted from his wagon.

The gunners rode past in silence, hurrying to reach the crossing. In the dim light of approaching dawn Prokhor searched in vain for his rifle and horse. Down by the boats he took off his other boot, threw it into the river and stood pouring water over his head, which was gripped in a vise of pain.

The cavalry began to cross at sunrise. A hundred and fifty unsaddled horses of the first squadron were driven down to the Don at a point just above the bend where the river turns due east. The ferocious-looking squadron commander with a hooked nose and a bristling ginger beard that came up to his eyes bore a striking resemblance to a wild boar. His left arm was hanging in a dirty blood-stained sling, his right played tirelessly with his whip.

'Don't let the horses drink! Keep 'em going! What the bloody hell... Are you afraid of the water?! Wade, man!.. That horse ain't made of sugar, it won't melt!' he bawled at the Cossacks herding the horses into the water, and a pair of fang-like white teeth showed from under his moustache.

The horses huddled together and hung back from the chilly water. The Cossacks shouted at them and lashed them on. The first to swim was a black stallion with a white muzzle and a broad pinkish blaze on its forehead. Evidently this was not its first experience of swimming. The waves lapped over its sloping crupper, its long, bushy tail was swept sideways by the current, but its neck and back stayed above water. It was followed by the other horses. Snorting and neighing, they churned into the foaming waves and breasted the current. The Cossacks followed them in six boats, each with a man in the bows, holding a lasso at the ready.

'Don't go in front! Head 'em off. Don't let 'em get carried away.'

The whip in the squadron commander's hand came to life again, swung in a circle, gave a loud crack, then thwacked the leg of his chalk-stained boot.

The swift current carried the horses downstream. The black stallion swam strongly, about two lengths ahead of the others, and was the first to reach the sandbar along the left bank. At that moment the sun peeped through the bushy branches of a poplar, a pink ray fell on the stallion's flank, and for an instant its glistening coat flared with black inextinguishable flame.

'Watch Mrykhin's filly! Give her a hand!.. She's got her bridle on still... Hurry! Come on, row!' the boarlike squadron commander bellowed hoarsely.

The horses made the crossing safely. On the other side, Cossacks were waiting to sort them out and put on their bridles. Then the saddles were brought across in boats.

'Where was the fire yesterday?' Prokhor asked a Cossack who was carrying saddles to the boat.

'Along the Chir.'

'Was it started by a shell?'

'Not by a shell!' the Cossack answered grimly. 'The Reds are setting fire—'

'To everything?' Prokhor asked in surprise.

'No, not everything... They burn the rich houses, the ones with iron roofs, or anyone's with a good yard and sheds.'

'What villages were burning then?'

'From Visloguzov to Grachov.'

'D'you know where the headquarters of the 1st Division is right now?'

'At Chukarinsky.'

Prokhor returned to the refugee wagons. All over the huge camp the wind was catching the smoke of fires made of driftwood, broken fences and dry cattle dung; the women were cooking breakfast.

During the night several more thousand refugees had arrived from the steppes of the right bank.

From the campfires and the wagons and other means of transport there rose a buzz of talk.

'When will our turn come to get across? It'll be too late, I reckon!'

'May God punish 'em. I'll throw the grain into the Don rather than let the Reds get it!'

'What a mob there is round the ferry!'

'But how can we leave our chests on this side, my dear?'

'After all the work and trouble we had getting it, and now... Lord Jesus, our provider!'

'We should've crossed at our own village...'

'What the devil did we have to come to this Vyoshenskaya place for!'

'They say Kalinov Ugol has been burnt to the ground.'

'And we were so keen to get to that ferry...'

'You think they'll show any mercy?'

'Their orders are that all Cossacks from the age of six

to the oldest ones living are to be cut to pieces.'

'They'll catch us on t'other side, and then what'll become of us?'

'It'll be wholesale slaughter!'

By a gaily painted Ukrainian wagon a dignified grey-browed old man, by his appearance and air of authority a village ataman, who had been carrying his brass-topped staff of office for many a year, was holding forth.

'...So I asked him, "Are we all going to perish on this bank? When shall we be able to get over there with all our stuff? The Reds are going to cut us down, root and branch, you know!" And their officer, he says to me, "Don't worry, Father! We shall hold out until all the people have got across. We'll lay down our lives but we won't let the women, children and old folk come to any harm!" '

The grey-browed ataman was surrounded by old men and women. They listened to what he had to say with strained attention, then a wild clamour arose.

'Why has the battery made off like that then?'

'It nearly trampled us underfoot the way it galloped down to the ferry!'

'And the cavalry's here...'

'They say Grigory Melekhov has abandoned the front.'

'What a way to do things? They leave folk to fend for themselves, while they—'

'Ay, the troops trot on ahead!'

'Who's going to defend us?'

'There goes the cavalry, they're swimming for it!'

'Save your own skin, eh?'

'That's just it!'

'We've been let down all round!'

'The end is near, I reckon!'

'We ought to send out the elders to greet the Reds as guests. Mebbe they'd show some mercy and not put us to death.'

A horseman appeared at the top of the lane, near the large brick building of the hospital. His rifle was strapped to the pommel of his saddle and a green-painted lance was swaying at his side.

'Why, that's my Mikishka!' An elderly woman with her kerchief draped loosely over her shoulders cried joyfully.

She ran towards the horseman, jumping over shafts and squeezing her way between wagons and horses. Meanwhile hands had grabbed the rider's stirrups and dragged him to a halt. He lifted a grey sealed packet above his head and shouted, 'It's a message for head-quarters! Let me pass!'

'Mikishka! My son!' the woman cried excitedly. Her untidy greying black hair fell over her radiant face. With a tremulous smile she pressed her body to the stirrup, to the horse's sweating flank and asked, 'Have you been in our village?'

'Yes, I was. The Reds are there now.'

'And our house, is it—? '

'It's still standing. They burned down Fedot's. Our shed caught fire but they put it out themselves. Fetiska got away and she tells us the top man among the Reds said, "Not a single poor man's house is to be burnt, but burn all the rich places down".'

'Well, thank the Lord! May Christ save them!' the woman exclaimed, crossing herself.

A stern-faced old man protested, 'What's all this, my good woman! They burnt down your neighbour's house and you say, "Thank the Lord"?'

'The devil won't take him!' the woman burst out hotly. 'He'll build himself another, but how in the world could I have got another home if they'd burnt that one! Fedot's got a pot of gold hidden away, but what have I got... I've been working for other folk all my life with poverty hanging round my neck!'

'Let me go now, Mum! I've got to hurry with this packet,' the horseman urged her, leaning over from his saddle.

The mother walked along beside the horse, kissing her son's dark sunburnt hand as she went, then ran to her wagon and the horseman shouted in a youthful tenor voice, 'Make way! Message for the commander-in-chief! Stand back!'

His horse danced and twisted its hindquarters restively. The crowd made way reluctantly, the messenger rode on and, though he seemed to linger, soon disappeared behind the wagons, the oxen and horses, until only his swaying lance could be seen steadily approaching the Don.

LXI

In one day all the insurgent units and refugees were brought across the Don. The last to cross were the mounted squadrons of the Vyoshenskaya Regiment of Grigory Melekhov's 1st Division.

369

Until evening Grigory and twelve crack squadrons held up the advance of the Reds' 33rd Kuban Division. At about five in the afternoon he had received Kudinov's report that all the military units and the refugees had been taken across, and only then did he give the order to retreat.

According to the plan that had been worked out beforehand the insurgent squadrons of the Donside area were to cross the river and deploy opposite their home villages. At noon the reports from the squadrons started coming in to headquarters. Most of them had taken up their positions on the left bank facing their villages. Where there were gaps between the villages the command sent in Cossack squadrons from the steppeland zone. The Kruzhilinskaya, Maksayevo-Singinskaya, the Karginskaya infantry, the Latyshevskaya, Likhovidovskaya and Grachovskaya squadrons filled the gaps between Pegarevka, Vyoshenskaya, Lebyazhyinsky, and Krasnoyarsky, while the rest withdrew to the rear, to the villages beyond the Don—Dubrovka, Chorny and Gorokhovka. It was Safonov's idea that they would form the reserves that the command would need for a breakout.

On the left bank of the Don, from the westernmost villages of the Kazanskaya stanitsa to Ust-Khopyorskaya in the east the insurgent front stretched for a distance of one hundred and fifty versts.

The units that had crossed the Don prepared for positional warfare, hastily digging trenches and felling poplars, willows and oaks for shelters and machine-gun emplacements. All the empty sacks found among the refugees were filled with sand and piled to form a breastwork in front of the long line of trenches.

By evening all the trenches had been dug. In the pine plantations behind Vyoshenskaya the 1st and 3rd insurgent batteries were mounted and camouflaged. For eight guns there were only five shells. Rifle ammunition was also running out. Kudinov sent round a mounted messenger with strict orders that there was to be no routine answering fire. One or two of the best marksmen were to be chosen from each squadron, supplied with sufficient ammunition and given the task of picking off Red machine-gunners and any of the Reds that showed themselves in the streets of the right-bank villages. The other Cossacks were allowed to shoot only if the Reds attempted a crossing.

At dusk Grigory Melekhov rode round to inspect the units of his division scattered along the Don and returned to Vyoshenskaya for the night.

No fires were allowed along the bank. And there were no lights in Vyoshenskaya either. The whole left bank lay in violet darkness.

The first Red patrols appeared early the next morning on the hill above Bazki. Soon they were to be seen on every hill and mound of the right bank, from Ust-Khopyorskaya to Kazanskaya. The Red front was rolling massively towards the Don. Then the patrols disappeared and until noon the hills lay in a deathly deserted hush.

The wind whirled white columns of dust along the Hetman's highway. The purple-black murk of fires still hung over the southern horizon. The clouds scattered by the wind began to gather again. The winged shadow of a thundercloud settled on the hill. Lightning flashed white in the daylight. In a single instant it edged the blue thundercloud with silver, then plunged like a shining spear into the bulging chest of a look-out mound. The thunder seemed to split the great bellying cloud and rain gushed out of it. The wind drove it in whitish dancing waves over the chalky slopes of the Don headlands, the wilting sunflowers, and drooping fields of corn.

The rain revived the young but already dust-grizzled foliage. The spring wheat glistened sappily, the yellow sunflowers raised their round heads, and the honey scent of flowering pumpkins rose from the vegetable patches. Its thirst slaked, the earth breathed steamily.

In the afternoon the Red patrols again appeared on the lookout mounds that stretched in a thin line all the way along the Don to the Sea of Azov.

From the mounds the flat sandy yellow expanse of the lands beyond the Don, dotted with dells and marshy hollows, could be seen for dozens of versts. Cautiously the Red Army patrols rode down into the villages. Lines of infantry followed them from the hills. Behind the look-out mounds, where the sentinels of the Polovtsians and Brodniks had once watched for signs of an approaching enemy, the Red batteries took up their positions.

The battery stationed on Byelogorskaya hill started shelling Vyoshenskaya. The first shell burst on the square, and soon the stanitsa was covered with the grey puffs of high-explosive bursts and the milk-white bursts of shrapnel melting in the wind. Three more batteries opened fire on Vyoshenskaya and the Cossack trenches along the Don.

At Bolshoi Gromok machine-guns broke into a furious chatter. Two Hotchkiss guns fired in short bursts, and a baritone Maxim kept up a ceaseless iron tattoo when it had got the range of the insurgent infantry moving about on the opposite bank. The baggage trains came up and trenches were dug on the thorny slopes. Carts and troop transports clattered along the Hetman's highway, leaving long billowing trains of dust.

The gunfire resounded all along the front. From the commanding heights of the right bank the Red batteries bombarded the far side till late evening. The insurgents' riverside trenches remained silent all the way from Kazanskaya to Ust-Khopyorskaya. The horse-minders took shelter with their charges in thickets overgrown with reeds and rushes, where the horses were not troubled by the midges and the wild hops offered a cool shade. The surrounding trees and tall willow shrubs provided good cover from the Red Army's spotters.

Not a soul was to be seen on the green water meadows. Only now and then a few refugees, crouching in fear, showed themselves as they worked their way further from the Don. A Red Army machine-gun would spit a few bursts at them and the whine of bullets would throw the terrified fugitives to the ground, where they would lie in the thick grass till dusk, and only then make a dash for the forest, hurrying northwards towards the dells with their dense thickets of alder and birch.

*   *   *

For two days Vyoshenskaya was under heavy artillery bombardment. The inhabitants kept to their cellars and basements, and the shell-torn streets came to life only at night.

At headquarters it was suggested that such an intensive bombardment could only be the prelude to an offensive, an attempt to force a crossing. It was feared that the Reds would make their thrust at Vyoshenskaya with the object of capturing the stanitsa, driving a wedge into the extended line of the front, dividing it into two, and then launching a crushing flank attack from Kalach and Ust-Medveditskaya.

On Kudinov's orders more than twenty machine-guns

with adequate supplies of ammunition were concentrated in Vyoshenskaya. The battery commanders were ordered to use their remaining shells only if the Reds tried to cross the river. The ferry and all boats were towed away to a backwater above Vyoshenskaya and kept under heavy guard.

To Grigory Melekhov the command's apprehensions seemed unjustified and at a conference on May 24th he ridiculed the conjectures of Ilya Safonov and his supporters.

'What can they get to cross the Don on at Vyoshenskaya?' he said. 'Is this the place for a crossing? Just take a look. On that side there's just a bare bank and a flat stretch of sand. There's nothing at the water's edge, not a bush or a scrap of forest. What fool would try to cross at this point? Only Ilya Safonov with his abilities would stick his nose into such a trap... On that bare bank the machine-guns would mow down every man! And you, Kudinov, needn't think that the Red commanders are any stupider than we are. Some are a lot smarter! They won't try a head-on attack on Vyoshenskaya, so we'd better be expecting a crossing where it's shallow, where there's a fold, or plenty of cover, from the ravines and the forest. We'll have to watch such places, specially at night, and warn the Cossacks not to get caught napping. We'll have to bring up our reserves to the danger spots, so we'll have something to throw in in case of trouble.'

'You say they won't attack Vyoshenskaya? Then why have they been shelling the place till midnight?' Safonov's assistant asked him.

'You'd better ask them that. Is this the only place they're shelling? What about Kazanskaya and Yerinsky? They're even blasting away from Semyonovskaya hill. They're keeping it up all along the line. They've got a few more shells than we have. It's our poor bloody artillery that's got only five shells to bless itself with—and the shell-cases are made of wood.'

Kudinov burst out laughing.

'You're right on the mark there!' he said.

'It's no good just criticising!' the commander of the 3rd Battery protested offendedly, 'We ought to be talking seriously.'

'Well, talk on, who's stopping you?' Kudinov frowned, and toyed with his belt. 'You were told time and again not to waste shells! But you used 'em up right and left, even on baggage trains. And now you're stuck, you've got nothing to hit back with. Why get huffy when you're criticised? Melekhov's quite right to laugh at your wooden artillery. Your equipment deserves to be laughed at!'

Kudinov took Grigory's side and firmly supported his proposal to keep a close watch on suitable crossing places and concentrate the reserve units near the threatened sectors. It was decided to take some of Vyoshenskaya's machine-guns and assign them to the Byelogorskaya, Merkulovskaya and Gromok squadrons, whose sectors were most vulnerable.

Grigory's idea that the Reds would not attempt to force the river at Vyoshenskaya but look for a more convenient place was confirmed the very next day. That morning the commander of the Gromok squadron reported that the Reds were preparing to attack across the river. All night the squadron had heard voices, the banging of hammers and a creak of wheels on the other side. Wagon after wagon had arrived in Gromok. First there was a sound of planks being unloaded, then saws began to rasp, followed by the tap of axes and hammers. Clearly the Reds were building something. At first the Cossacks thought it must be a pontoon bridge. During the night two daredevils went about half a verst upstream of the place where the sounds were coming from, undressed, and with branches tied to their heads to look like bushes, swam quietly downstream towards the other bank. Lurking in the shallow, they heard the crew of a machine-gun post talking close by; they also heard voices and the tapping of axes from the village, but there was no sign of anything on the water. If the Reds were building anything, it was not a bridge.

The Gromok squadron commander intensified his watch on the enemy. At dawn the observers staring through their field glasses were unable to spot anything. But presently, in the dim light, one of them, who during the war against Germany had been considered the best marksman in the regiment, noticed a Red Army man coming down to the Don with two saddled horses.

'There's a Red going down to the water,' the Cossack whispered to his comrade and put down his glasses.

The horses waded in up to their knees and began to drink.

The Cossack let out the sling of his rifle, wound it

round his left elbow, raised the back sight and took long and careful aim.

After the shot one of the horses rolled over gently on to its side and the other galloped away up the hill. The Red Army man bent down to take the saddle off the dead horse. The Cossack fired again and laughed softly; the Red Army man straightened up suddenly and tried to run away from the Don, then fell on his face and lay still.

As soon as he heard the news that the Reds were preparing to cross the river, Grigory Melekhov saddled his horse and rode to the Gromok squadron's sector. He forded the narrow channel that branched off the Don and ran to the end of the stanitsa, then cantered through the woods.

The road crossed a meadow but to take it would have been dangerous and Grigory decided to go by a roundabout route—through the wood to the end of Rassokhov Lake, and then through the tussocky willow scrub to the Kalmyk Ford (a narrow channel overgrown with water-lilies, sedge and rushes, which linked one of the meadow ponds with Lake Podstoilitsa). Only when he had crossed the boggy Kalmyk Ford, did he stop his horse and give it a few minutes' rest.

It was now two versts to the Don as the crow flies, but again across meadowland and that could mean coming under fire. He could have waited till dusk, but Grigory, who had always said, 'the worst thing in the world is waiting or making up for lost time,' decided to go at once. They won't hit me if I ride flat out, he thought as he emerged from the bushes.

He aimed for a green spur of willow jutting out of the Donside woods and raised his whip. The stinging blow on the crupper and Grigory's wild whoop sent a shudder through the horse's body, flattened its ears and started it off at a flying gallop towards the Don. But before Grigory had galloped a hundred paces, a machinegun opened up with long bursts from the hill on the other side. Bullets whistled overhead like marmots crying in the steppe. 'You're too high, chum!' Grigory muttered, squeezing his horse's sides, letting out the reins and pressing his cheek to the windswept mane. And as though guessing his thoughts, the Red machine-gunner crouching behind the green shield of his heavy machine-gun somewhere on the white-browed hill, aimed ahead of him, brought the cutting edge of his fire lower, and the hot lead smacked juicily into the ground right under the horse's hooves, hissing like a snake and spattering warm mud from soil that had not yet dried out after the spring floods. Then again they were flying overhead and by the horse's flanks.

Grigory rose in his stirrups and lay almost flat along the horse's neck. The green ridge of willows was rushing towards him. When he had covered half the distance a gun boomed from Semyonovskaya hill. The air shook with the shell's grinding roar and the blast of the explosion close by almost flung Grigory out of the saddle. Before the whine and scream of the splinters had died out of hearing, before the flattened rushes in a nearby pond could rise, the gun on the hill boomed again. The roar of the approaching shell bore down on Grigory and crushed him into his saddle.

The oppressive roar seemed to reach its peak and break off for a fraction of a second, and in this fleeting instant a black cloud reared up before his eyes, the earth shook, and the horse's forelegs seemed to plunge into nowhere.

Grigory opened his eyes as he fell. He hit the ground so hard that his worsted army trousers split at the knees and the straps under the instep snapped off. The powerful wave of air displaced by the explosion flung him far away from his horse and, when he landed, he slid some distance on the grass, burning his hands and cheek.

Grigory rose to his feet in a daze. Chunks and crumbs of earth and clumps of uprooted grass pattered down like black rain. The horse was lying about twenty paces from the shell hole. Its head was motionless but its mud-spattered hindlegs, sweating crupper and sloping back were shivering convulsively.

The machine-gun on the other side of the Don had fallen silent. For about five minutes there was a hush. The blue fisher gulls cried anxiously over the pond. Grigory walked to his horse, fighting dizziness. His legs were shaking and strangely heavy. He felt as though he had been sitting for a long time in a cramped position, his legs no longer obeyed him and every step vibrated through his whole body.

Grigory removed the saddle from the dead horse and had only just entered the splinter-torn rushes of the nearest pond when the machine-gun started again, firing at regular intervals. But there was no sound of flying bullets, so the gunner on the hill must have found a new target.

An hour later he reached the squadron leader's dug-out.

'They've just stopped their carpentry,' the squadron commander told him. 'They'll be at it again tonight. Couldn't you give us a few cartridges. It's enough to make you howl—only one or two clips a man!'

'They'll bring some this evening. Keep your eyes on that bank!'

'We're watching it. Tonight I'm going to ask for volunteers to swim over and have a look at what they're building.'

'Why didn't you send some last night?'

'I did, Grigory Panteleyevich—two. But they were scared to go into the village. They swam along by the bank but they were scared of the village... Who can you force nowadays? It's a big risk. If you run into one of their outposts, they'll have the guts out of you. The Cossacks don't show much daring somehow on their home ground... In the German war there used to be any number of daredevils out to win crosses, but now you can't even get 'em to tackle an outpost, let alone go in deep. And now we're in trouble with the women. They've found their husbands. They spend the night in the trenches and I can't chase 'em out. I tried it yesterday but the Cossacks cut up rough, "Tell him to behave himself," they says, "or we'll soon settle his hash!" '

From the dug-out Grigory went to the trenches, which zigzagged along the edge of the forest, about forty paces from the Don. Young oaks, clumps of wormwood and a dense scrub of poplars hid the yellow breastwork from the Red Army's watchers on the other bank. The trenches were linked by communication passages with shelters where the Cossacks rested. The ground round these shelters was strewn with bluish offal from dried fish, mutton bones, sunflower seed husks, cigarette butts and bits of rag; washed stockings, underpants, footcloths, women's underwear and skirts were hanging from nearby branches.

A sleepy-eyed young woman showed her bare tousled head from the first dug-out. She stared indifferently at Grigory, rubbing her eyes, then disappeared into the darkness of the shelter like a suslik into its hole. Quiet singing was coming from the next shelter. A woman's voice, muted but high and clear, merged with those of the men. By the entrance to the third shelter a Cossack woman, no longer young but tidily dressed, was sitting with a Cossack's grizzled curly head in her lap. He was lying comfortably on his side and dozing, while his wife cleaned his head of lice, squashed the black-backed vermin on the wooden comb and brushed away the flies that settled on the face of her aged 'chum'. But for the vicious chatter of a machine-gun on the other side of the river and the hollow rumble of guns floating down-stream from Migulinskaya or Kazanskaya, one might have taken the squadron's position for a mowers' camp.

It was the first time in five years of war that Grigory had observed such a scene on the frontline. Unable to restrain a smile, he walked on past the dug-outs and every-where found women attending to their menfolk, mend-ing and darning, washing their clothes, cooking and clean-ing up after their simple meals.

'You don't have such a bad life here! Everything laid on!' he said to the squadron commander on returning to his dug-out.

The commander grinned, 'Couldn't be better, I'm sure.'

'But it's a bit too comfortable!' Grigory frowned. 'Get those women out of here at once! This kind of thing at war! What have you got here—a market or a fairground? If you go on like this, the Reds will cross the Don without your even hearing 'em. You'll all be too busy busting yourselves on your women... Turn the lot out of here as soon as it gets dark! If I see a single skirt when I come back tomorrow, yours'll be the first neck for the chopper.'

'Ay, that's how it is...' the squadron commander agreed readily. 'I'm agin the women being here myself, but what can you do with the Cossacks? Discipline's gone to the dogs... The women are aching for their hus-bands, we've been away fighting for three months now!'

Suddenly going purple in the face, he sat down on an earthen couch to hide a red apron that was lying there and, avoiding Grigory's glance, squinted menacingly at a curtain across a corner of the dug-out, from behind which a pair of laughing brown eyes (his own wife's) was peeping.

LXII

Aksinya Astakhova stayed in Vyoshenskaya with a cousin of her mother's, who lived on the outskirts, near the new church. She spent the first day looking for Grigory but he had not arrived yet, and on the second day bullets were flying and shells bursting in the streets and lanes until late at night and she did not venture out.

'He asked me to come here himself, promised we'd be together, and now where's he got to?' she thought bitterly as she lay on the chest in the front room, biting her still bright and yet fading lips. Her elderly relative sat by the window, knitting a stocking and crossing herself after every gun shot.

'Oh, Lord Jesus! What a terrible thing! Why are they fighting like this? What's put them at loggerheads?'

A shell burst in the street about a hundred paces from the little house and several small windowpanes fell out with a plaintive tinkle.

'Do go away from the window, Auntie! You may get hit!' Aksinya begged her.

The old woman stared quizzically from under her spectacles and replied vexedly, 'Oh, Aksinya! A right stupid lass you are, I see. What am I, the enemy? Why should they shoot at me?'

'They may kill you by accident! They can't see where their bullets are going.'

'Kill me! They can see all right! They're shooting at the Cossacks, the Cossacks are the enemy of the Reds. But I'm an old woman, a widow, what do I matter to them? They must know who to aim at with their rifles and cannon!'

At noon Grigory galloped past, crouching over his horse's neck, towards the lower bend of the river. Aksinya saw him from the window, rushed out on to the creeper-covered porch and called to him. But Grigory had already vanished round a corner and all that remained was the dust kicked up by his horse's hooves slowly settling on the road. It was no use trying to chase him. Aksinya stood for a while on the porch and burst into angry tears.

'That wasn't Stepan who galloped by just now, was it? What did you rush out like mad for?' her aunt wanted to know.

'No, it was just someone from our village,' Aksinya replied through her tears.

'What are you crying about then?' the inquisitive old woman persisted.

'Don't bother me, Auntie! You wouldn't understand!'

'Oh, wouldn't I... So it was a sweetheart of yours that went by. Of course, it was! Otherwise, you wouldn't have cried out like that. I've lived a long life, my girl, and I know!'

That evening Prokhor Zykov came.

'Good evening to you! Is there anyone here from Tatarsky, good woman?'

'Prokhor!' Aksinya gasped delightedly as she ran out of the front room.

'Well, girl, you've given me a real chase around! I've worn my feet out looking for you! You know what he's like, don't you? Just as mad as his father. Here they are blazing away at us, every living thing's taken cover, but he keeps on at me, "Find her or I'll send you to your grave!"'

Aksinya seized Prokhor's sleeve and pulled him into the porch.

'Where is he, the wretch?'

'Humph... Where d'you think he is? He's just walked back from the trenches. His horse was killed under him. He came back as fierce as a dog on a chain. "Have you found her?" he asks. "How d'you expect me to find her?" I says. And he says to me, "She's a woman, not a needle in a haystack!" And he gives me such a look—a wolf in human clothing, that's what he is!'

'What did he ask you to tell me?'

'Get yourself ready and come with me, that's all!'

Aksinya tied up her bundle in no time and hurriedly said goodbye to her aunt.

'Has Stepan sent for you?'

'Yes, Auntie!'

'Well, give him my regards. Why didn't he call himself? He could have had some milk and some of these dumplings that are left over...'

Aksinya ran out of the house without listening.

She walked so fast that long before she reached Grigory's quarters she was pale and out of breath. In the end Prokhor had to restrain her, 'Now just you listen to me! When I was a young feller I used to run after the girls, but I never in my life ran as fast as you do. Can't you wait? Is his house on fire? I'm out of breath! Nobody walks over sand at this pace! You never act like ordinary human beings...'

And to himself he thought, 'They're at it again... Well, this time even the devil won't pull 'em apart! A fine time they'll be having, but I had to look for her, the bitch, with bullets flying round my head... God forbid, if Natalya gets to know, she'll skin me alive... She's the Korshunov breed, she is! No, if I hadn't lost my horse and my rifle on account of my weakness for drink,

I wouldn't have gone looking for you all over the place, I'll be damned if I would! You got yourselves into this, so get yourselves out of it!'

In Grigory's closely shuttered room an oil lamp was burning smokily. Grigory was sitting at the table. He had just cleaned his rifle and was still wiping the barrel of his pistol when the door creaked. Aksinya was standing on the threshold. Her narrow white forehead was damp and her dilated angry eyes were burning in her pale face with such frenzied passion that Grigory's heart leapt joyfully at the sight of her.

'You got me here, you promised ... and then you disappear!' she panted.

Just as it had been long ago, in the first days of their love, nothing existed for her but Grigory. Again the world simply died when Grigory was absent and came to life only when he was at her side. Disregarding Prokhor, she flung herself at Grigory, twined herself round him like wild hops and, weeping and kissing her beloved's stubbly cheeks, covering his nose, eyes, lips with brief kisses, and whispered between little sobs, 'It was such torture... It's made me ill! Grisha darling! Oh, my love, my blood!'

'Now, not so much... You can see... Wait, Aksinya, don't go on so,' Grigory muttered in embarrassment, turning his face away and avoiding Prokhor's glance.

He made her sit down on a bench, took off the shawl that had slipped to the back of her head, and stroked her dishevelled hair.

'You're like a—'

'I'm like I've always been! But you—'

'No, honestly, you're kind of crazy!'

Aksinya let her arms rest on Grigory's shoulders, laughed through her tears and said in a rapid whisper, 'But how could you? You asked me to come... I walked all the way, left everything, and then you're not here... Then you galloped past, I ran out and called, but you'd vanished round the corner... They might have killed you and I'd never have seen you, not even once...'

She went on saying the sweet, loving foolish things that only a woman can say, all the time fondling Grigory's bowed shoulders and meeting his gaze with forever devoted eyes.

There was something pathetic and at the same time desperate in her eyes, like a hunted animal's, something that made it painful and embarrassing for Grigory to look at her.

He let his sun-scorched lashes droop, forced himself to smile, and said nothing, but a more and more feverish flush burned in her cheeks and her pupils seemed to be veiled in a blue mist.

Prokhor went out without saying goodbye. In the porch he spat and trod the spit into the floor with his boot.

'It's a mess-up!' he said bitterly as he walked down the steps, having pointedly banged the door behind him.

LXIII

For two days they lived in a dream, mixing day and night and forgetting the world around them. Sometimes Grigory would awake after a brief bemusing sleep and see Aksinya's attentive gaze fixed upon him in the semi-darkness, as though she were studying him. Usually she lay with her cheek resting on her hand, gazing steadily.

'What are you looking at?' Grigory would ask.

'I want to see all I can of you... They'll kill you soon, my heart tells me so.'

'Well, if that's what it tells you, you'd better have a good look,' he said, smiling.

He went out for the first time on the third day. Kudinov had been sending messengers for him since morning, asking him to come to a conference. 'I won't be there. Let them confer without me,' Grigory had replied.

Prokhor brought him a new horse from headquarters and during the night rode out to the Gromok squadron's sector for the saddle Grigory had left there.

'Where are you going?' Aksinya asked in fright, when she saw Grigory preparing to leave.

'I want to go down river as far as Tatarsky to see how our lads are manning the defences opposite the village, and to find out where my family is while I'm about it.'

'Missing your little ones?' Aksinya gave a shiver as she pulled her shawl round her brown sloping shoulders.

'Yes.'

'Must you go?'

'Yes, I must.'

'Don't go!' Aksinya begged and her eyes caught fire in their dark charred sockets. 'So your family is dearer to you than I am? Is it? You feel pulled both ways? Then you'd better take me into the family, I suppose. Natalya and me, we'll get on together somehow... Oh, all right, go then! Go! But don't come back to me any more! I won't have you. I don't want it like that... I don't want that!'

Grigory went out without a word and mounted his horse.

* * *

The Tatarsky infantry squadron had been too lazy to dig proper trenches.

'It's a daft idea,' Khristonya boomed. 'Do they think we're at the German front? Just make the usual slits, lads, about knee deep. Who would ever think of digging seven feet down in hard cake like this? You can't shift it with a crowbar, let alone a spade.'

His advice was taken and in the stubborn soil of the left-bank ravines they dug trenches that they could only lie in, and built a few shelters in the forest.

'So this is what we've come to—living like marmots,' the undesponding Anikei jested. 'We'll live in our burrows and have grass for grub. You can't go on walloping pancakes and cream all the time, all that meat and noodles, and sterlet... Why not try a bit of clover for a change?'

The Tatarsky men were not much troubled by the Reds. There was no battery near the village. Only occasionally a machine-gun would chatter on the right bank, sending short bursts at an observer who had shown himself, then a long silence would ensue.

The Red Army's trenches were on the hill above the village. Sometimes a few shots came from there too, but the Red troops visited the village only at night, and not for long.

* * *

Grigory rode on to his home ground in the early evening.

Everything was familiar, every tree awakened memories... The road took him across Maiden's Clearing, where every year on St. Peter's day, after sharing out the meadowland the Cossacks would come to drink vodka. A spur of forest jutted into the meadow like a headland. It was known as Alexei's Coppice. Many years ago in that, then nameless coppice, the wolves had killed a cow belonging to a certain Alexei, who lived in Tatarsky. Alexei himself had died, and the memory of him had faded as an epitaph fades on a gravestone, even his second name had been forgotten by neighbours and relatives, but the coppice named after him still lived, rearing the dark-green crowns of its oaks and elms to the sky. Now and then they were felled by the Tatarsky folk for their household needs, but in spring lusty young shoots would rise from the sturdy stumps and after a year or two of imperceptible growth Alexei's Coppice in summer would once again be clad in the malachite green of branching boughs, and in autumn in the golden chain mail of flaming oak leaves ignited by the morning frosts.

In summer prickly brambles covered the damp soil of the coppice and fine-feathered rollers and magpies nested in the tops of the old elms; in autumn, when the coppice smelled of the bitter invigorating odour of acorns and fallen oak leaves, migrating woodcocks rested there, but in winter only the clear circling trail of a fox would lie like a pearl necklace on the white canopy of snow. In his youth Grigory had often gone to Alexei's Coppice to set traps for foxes.

He rode in the cool shade of the overhanging branches along the overgrown ruts of a track that had not been used since the previous year. As he crossed Maiden's Clearing and came out at Black Ravine, memories rushed to his head like strong drink. By those three poplars as a boy he had chased a brood of wild ducklings around the pond, and in Round Pool he had stood from dawn till dusk fishing for tench... And not far away there was a branching guelder-rose tree. It stood by itself, lonely and old. It could be seen from the Melekhovs' farm and every autumn Grigory would admire it when he came out on the porch of his house. From a distance it seemed to be wrapped in long tongues of flame. How his brother Petro had loved pies filled with the tart guelder-rose berries.

In silent sadness Grigory surveyed the familiar scene of his childhood. His horse jogged along, waving the midges and vicious brown mosquitoes away with its tail. The quitch and meadow grass bowed gently with the wind, and green ripples flowed across the meadow.

When he reached the Tatarsky infantry's trenches, Grigory sent for his father. Somewhere on the left flank Khristonya shouted, 'Prokofievich! Come on, hurry up, Grigory's here!'

Grigory dismounted, passed the reins to Anikei and from a distance caught sight of his father limping hastily towards him.

'Well, hullo there, chief!'

'Hullo, Father!'

'So you've arrived?'

'It was a job getting away! How's the family? How's Mother? Where's Natalya?'

Pantelei cut the air hopelessly with his hand and frowned. A tear ran down his dark cheek.

'What is it? What's happened to them?' Grigory asked sharply.

'They didn't get across.'

'But why not?!'

'Two days before it started, Natalya was struck down. It must be typhus. And the old woman didn't want to leave her... But don't be scared, son, they're getting on all right over there.'

'What about the children? Mishatka? Polyushka?'

'They're there too. But Dunyashka came across. She was afraid to stay. She's still a girl, you know. She's gone off with Anikei's wife to Volokhov. And I've been home twice. I rowed over quietly in the middle of the night and had a look at 'em. Natalya's in a bad way, but the little ones, praise the Lord... Natalya's unconscious and she's got such a fever her lips are all cracked and parched.'

'Why didn't you bring them over here?' Grigory asked indignantly.

The old man lost his temper. Resentment and reproach made his voice shake.

'And what have ye been doing? Couldn't ye have come here earlier to bring them over?'

'I've got the division on my hands! I had to get that across!' Grigory retorted explosively.

'We've heard about what ye've been so busy at in Vyoshenskaya... You've got no use for your family, have ye? Ah, Grigory! It's time to think of God if ye won't think of other people... I didn't cross here during the retreat or I'd have brought them over with me. My platoon was at Yelanskaya and while we were getting here, the Reds took the village.'

'What I've been doing in Vyoshenskaya! That's none of your business... So don't you...' Grigory's voice was hoarse and choking.

'Oh, never mind then!' the old man took fright and

glanced round with displeasure at a bunch of Cossacks not far away. 'I don't mean that... You talk a bit quieter because people are listening over there...' And his own voice dropped to a whisper. 'Ye're not a little child, ye ought to know how to behave by now. And don't worry about your family. God willing, Natalya'll come through and the Reds aren't doing 'em any harm. They did kill a yearling calf, and that's about all. They've been merciful and don't touch our folk... They've taken about forty measures of grain... Still you can't help losing something in a war!'

'Maybe we could get them across now?'

'I don't reckon there's any need. How can you bring a sick woman across? And it'd be risky anyway. It's not so bad for them there. The old woman is looking after the farm. That sets my mind at rest because there've been some fires in the village!'

'Whose house was burnt?'

'The whole square was burnt down. Merchants' houses mostly. They razed our relatives the Korshunovs' place to the ground. Our kinswoman Lukinichna is in Andropovo just now, but Grandad Grishaka, he stayed behind to look after the house too. "I'm not leaving my own home," he said, "and the anti-Christs won't come in here, they'll be afraid of the sign of the cross." By that time he was really off his head. But it seems the Reds didn't take fright at his cross, the house and the farm were all wrapped in smoke and nothing more's been heard of him since... It was time for him to die. Made himself a coffin twenty years ago and still alive and kicking... But the one that's burning the village down is that friend of yours, may he drop down dead!'

'Who?'

'Mishka Koshevoi, damn his eyes!'

'It couldn't be?!'

'Sure as God! He was at our place and asking about you. This is what he said to Mother, "As soon as we get across on that side, your Grigory will be the first one we string up. He's going to hang from the highest oak. I won't even soil my sabre on him," he says. And he asked about me, too, with a snarl on his face. "That lame devil of yours," he says, "where's he got to? He ought to be at home, lying up on the stove bunk. If I catch him, I won't kill him, but I'll give him the thrashing of his life!" That's the kind of devil incarnate he's turned out to be! He goes about the village, setting fire

to the merchants' and priests' houses and saying, "That's
for Ivan Alexeyevich, and that's for Stokman, I'll burn
the whole of Vyoshenskaya down!" How do you like
the sound of that?'

Grigory talked for another half an hour with his father, then went back to his horse. The old man had not
said another word in allusion to Aksinya, but Grigory
felt depressed enough as it was. Everyone must have
heard about it, if his father knew. Who could have told
them? Who besides Prokhor had seen them together?
Surely Stepan didn't know? Grigory gritted his teeth
in shame and a fury of self-reproach.

He spoke briefly with the Cossacks. Anikei, jesting
as usual, wanted him to send the squadron a few pails
of home-brew.

'We can do without the bullets, as long as we've got
some vodka!' he said, chortling and winking and flicking
the collar of his tunic expressively.

Grigory treated Khristonya and all the other men of
his village to the tobacco he had saved up and, before
leaving, saw Stepan Astakhov. Stepan came up and
uttered an unhurried greeting, but did not offer his hand.

It was the first time Grigory had met him since the
day of the uprising. He eyed him closely and in some
alarm. Did he know? But Stepan's lean handsome face
was calm, almost cheerful, and Grigory gave a sigh of
relief, 'No, he doesn't know!'

LXIV

Two days later Grigory returned from his tour of his
division's sector of the front. Command headquarters
had moved to the village of Chorny, so Grigory halted,
let his horse rest for half an hour, watered it and rode
straight on to the village.

Kudinov met him cheerfully and eyed him with an
expectant grin.

'Well, Grigory, what have you seen? Tell us all about
it.'

'I've seen Cossacks and I've seen Reds on the hills.'

'A fat lot you've seen then! We've had three aeroplanes fly in here. They brought us cartridges and some
letters.'

'What does your old pal General Sidorin write to you?'

'My old mate?' the unusually cheerful Kudinov continued the conversation in the same joking tone. 'He writes that we've got to hold out for all we're worth and not let the Reds force the river. And he also writes that the Don Army is just about to launch a decisive offensive.'

'Sounds good.'

Kudinov looked more serious.

'They're going to try for a breakthrough. You're the only one I'm telling and it's top secret! In a week they'll crack the front of the 8th Red Army. We must hold out.'

'We are holding out.'

'At Gromok the Reds are preparing to force the river.'

'Are they still tapping away with their axes?' Grigory asked in surprise.

'Yes, they are... Well, and what did you see? Where have you been? Or did you have your feet up in Vyoshenskaya all the time? Perhaps you didn't go anywhere! The day before yesterday I scoured the place for you, and one of my messengers comes in and says, "Melekhov wasn't in his quarters, but a beautiful bit of goods comes out to me from the front room and says, 'Grigory Panteleyevich has left', and her eyes were all swollen". So I thought to myself, "Maybe our division commander is having fun and games with his sweetheart and keeping out of our way?"'

Grigory frowned. Kudinov's joke was not to his liking.

'You should listen to fewer tales and choose orderlies with shorter tongues! And if you send any more long-tongued ones I'll shorten their tongues with my sabre—to stop them yapping over nothing.'

Kudinov burst out laughing and slapped Grigory on the shoulder.

'Sometimes you just can't take a joke, can you? Well, let's drop it. I've got something serious I want to talk to you about. We've got to snatch an information prisoner—that's one thing. And the other is this. Somewhere not farther than the Kazanskaya border we ought to send a couple of squadrons across at night to shake the Reds up a bit. We could even send 'em over at Gromok, so as to start a panic there. What d'you think?'

Grigory was silent for a minute, then replied, 'It's not a bad idea.'

'What about yourself,' Kudinov stressed the last word, 'would you lead them?'

'Why myself?'

'They'll need a commander with some guts, that's why! He's got to be a real fighter because this will be no joking matter. It could be bungled and not a single man would get back alive!'

Grigory was flattered and agreed unhesitatingly. 'Of course, I'll lead them!'

'We've been planning the thing and our idea is this,' Kudinov rose from his stool, speaking excitedly and pacing about the creaking floor of the room. 'There's no need to go in deep. You've just got to swoop on two or three villages along the Don and knock 'em silly, grab all the shells and cartridges you can, take a few prisoners and come back the same way. You'll have to do it all in one night and be back at the ford by dawn, won't you? So, think it over and tomorrow pick any Cossacks you want and go to it. We decided: Melekhov is the only man for this job! And if you succeed, the Don Army will never forget it. As soon as we link up, I'll write a glowing report to the Ataman himself. I'll recount all your exploits, and your promotion will be—'

Kudinov glanced at Grigory and broke off in midsentence. Grigory's hitherto calm face had darkened and was twisted with anger.

'Who d'you take me for?' Grigory quickly put his hands behind his back and stood up. 'You think I'll be doing this for the sake of promotion? Are you hiring me? Promising me promotion? Why I—'

'Now just wait a minute!'

'I spit on your ranks!'

'Wait! You didn't understand—'

'I spit on them!'

'You didn't understand, Melekhov!'

'Oh, yes I did!' Grigory took a deep breath and sat down again on the stool. 'Look for someone else. I won't lead any Cossacks across the Don!'

'You're getting steamed up over nothing!'

'I've said I won't lead them and I won't. That's the end of it.'

'But I'm not forcing you or begging you. It's just up to you. We're in a tight corner at the moment, so we decided we'd put the wind up them and stop them from preparing to cross. As for the promotion, I was just joking! You just can't take a joke, can you! And I was joking when I mentioned that woman. I saw you were in a stew over something, so I thought I'll stir him up a bit more! You see, I know you're a half-baked Bolshevik and don't approve of ranks or anything of that kind. Did you think I was serious?' Kudinov sidetracked and laughed so naturally that for a moment Grigory wondered whether he was really a bit queer in the head. 'You were a bit too hasty there, chum!' Kudinov went on. 'Honestly, I meant it as a joke! I was teasing you.'

'I still refuse to cross the Don, I've changed my mind.'

Kudinov sat toying with the tassel of his belt and fell into a long, indifferent silence, then he said, 'Well, whether you changed your mind or got scared, it doesn't matter. What does matter is that you're ruining our plan! But, of course, we'll send someone else. You're not our one and only... But as for the position being serious, you can judge for yourself. Only today Kondrat Medvedev sent us a new order issued by their commander-in-chief Trotsky. He himself lives in Boguchar at the moment, as you can see from the order, and he'll be here any day now. He's throwing in more forces against us... Here, read it yourself or you'll be saying you don't believe me...' Kudinov took out of his field case a yellow sheet of paper stained with spots of dried blood and gave it to Grigory. 'It was found on the commissar of some International Company or other. He was a Latvian. He used up his last cartridge, then charged a whole troop of Cossacks with an empty rifle... Some of them, the dedicated ones, are real fighters too, you know... Kondrat cut down that commissar himself and in his breast pocket he found this.'

The order on the yellow blood-spattered sheet was in close black print:

ORDER OF THE CHAIRMAN OF THE REVOLUTIONARY
MILITARY COUNCIL OF THE REPUBLIC TO THE
EXPEDITIONARY FORCES
8 No. 100

Boguchar   25 May 1919

To be read out to all companies, squadrons, batteries and commands.

This is the end of the treacherous Don uprising!
Its last hour has struck!
All the necessary preparations have been made. Enough forces

have been concentrated to crush the turncoats and traitors. The hour of retribution has come for these Cains who for over two months have been stabbing in the back our armies operating on the Southern Front. All worker-peasant Russia views with disgust and hatred the Migulinskaya, Vyoshenskaya, Yelanskaya, and Shumilinskaya bands, who under a false Red flag are helping the Black Hundred landowners: Denikin and Kolchak.

Soldiers, commanders, commissars of the punitive forces! The preparatory work has been done. All the necessary forces and means have been concentrated. Your units are poised.

Now when the signal is given—forward!

The nests of these dishonourable turncoats and traitors must be destroyed. The Cains must be wiped out. No mercy for the stanitsas that offer resistance. Pardon only for those who voluntarily surrender their arms and come over to our side. Against the accomplices of Kolchak and Denikin—lead, steel and fire!

Soviet Russia is relying on you, comrade soldiers!

In the next few days we must cleanse the Don of the black stains of treachery. The final hour has struck.

All of you, as one man-forward!

LXV

On May 19th Mishka Koshevoi was sent by Gumanovsky—the chief of staff of the 9th Army's Expeditionary Brigade—with an urgent dispatch to the headquarters of the 32nd Regiment, which according to Gumanovsky's information was in the village of Gorbatovsky.

Koshevoi galloped into Gorbatovsky on the same day, but the headquarters of the 32nd Regiment was not there. The village was jammed with second-line transports of the 23rd Division commanded by Mironov. They were on their way from the River Donets to Ust-Medveditskaya on the Don with a covering force of two infantry companies.

Mishka roamed about the village for a few hours, asking the whereabouts of the regimental command. Eventually a Red Army man on horseback told him that the day before the headquarters of the 32nd had been in the village of Yevlantyevsky, near Bokovskaya.

Mishka fed his horse and set out for Yevlantyevsky after nightfall, but the headquarters was not there either. Some time after midnight, on his way back to Gorbatovsky Koshevoi met a Red Army patrol in the steppe.

'Who goes there?' Mishka was challenged.

'Friend.'

'Now then, let's have a look at you, friend—' the patrol commander in a white Kuban hat and long blue tunic drawled in a husky bass. 'What unit?'

'Expeditionary Brigade of the 9th Army.'

'Any papers?'

Mishka showed his papers.

The commander looked them over by the light of the moon and asked suspiciously, 'Who's your brigade commander?'

'Comrade Lozovsky.'

'Where's the brigade now?' the commander asked.

'On the other side of the Don. What unit are you, comrade? Not the 32nd Regiment by any chance?'

'No, we're in the 33rd Kuban Division. Where are you coming from?'

'From Yevlantyevsky.'

'And where are you going?'

'Gorbatovsky.'

'Are you though? Right now the Cossacks are in Gorbatovsky.'

'You don't mean it!' Mishka exclaimed.

'I'm telling you the Cossack insurgents are there. We've just seen 'em.'

'How can I get to Bobrovsky then?' Mishka asked worriedly.

'That's up to you.'

The commander of the patrol rode off on his black sloping heavily-built stallion, then turned in his saddle and advised, 'You'd better come with us or you might get your head chopped off.'

Mishka gladly joined the patrol and that night rode into the village of Kruzhilin, where the 294th Taganrog Regiment was stationed, handed the dispatch to the regiment's commander, explained why he had been unable to deliver it according to his instructions, and asked for permission to stay with the regiment in the mounted reconnaissance.

The 33rd Kuban Division, recently formed out of units of the Taman Army and volunteers from the Kuban, had been transferred from somewhere near Astrakhan to the Voronezh-Liski area. One of its brigades, which included the Taganrog, Derbent and Vasilkov regiments, had been sent to suppress the uprising. And it was this brigade that had swooped on Melekhov's 1st Division and driven it across the Don.

The brigade had proceeded by forced marches along the right bank of the Don from Kazanskaya to the westernmost villages of the Ust-Khopyorskaya stanitsa, struck at the villages along the Chir with its right wing, and then turned back, spending about two weeks altogether in the Don country.

Mishka took part in the fighting for Karginskaya and a number of the Chir villages. On the morning of the 27th, in the steppe outside the village of Nizhne-Grushinsky, the commander of the 3rd Company of the 294th Taganrog Regiment formed up his men along the road and read out an order that had just been received. And Mishka Koshevoi was to remember for long afterwards the words, '...The nests of the dishonourable turncoats and traitors must be destroyed. The Cains must be wiped out...' And also, 'Against the accomplices of Kolchak and Denikin—lead, steel and fire!'

After the murder of Stokman, after word of the death of Ivan Alexeyevich and the Yelanskaya Communists had reached his ears, Mishka's heart had filled with burning hatred of the Cossacks. He no longer stopped to think or listen to the faint voice of pity when a captured Cossack insurgent fell into his hands. He had no compassion for any of them. With eyes as blue and cold as ice he would look at the man and ask, 'Did you fight against the Soviets?' and without waiting for an answer, without looking at the prisoner's death-shadowed face, he wielded his sabre. He wielded it ruthlessly. And not only did he wield the sabre, he also sent the 'red cock' under the roofs of houses in the villages abandoned by the insurgents. And when the fear-maddened bullocks and cows broke through the fences of the burning farmyards and charged out into the street, Mishka shot them down point-blank with his rifle.

He waged an implacable, ruthless war upon Cossack affluence, Cossack treachery, upon the whole inviolable and stagnant way of life that had endured for centuries beneath the roofs of the solid Cossack houses. His hatred was fed by the death of Stokman and Ivan Alexeyevich and the words of the order were no more than a vivid expression of what Mishka felt but did not know how to tell. That day he and three of his comrades burned about a hundred and fifty farmsteads in Karginskaya. Somewhere in the storeroom of a merchant's shop he found a can of kerosene and went round the square with a box of matches in his grimy fist, and behind him acrid smoke and flame rose from the smart weather boarded and painted merchants' and priests' houses, the roomy dwellings of well-to-do Cossacks, and all those 'whose scheming instigated the ignorant Cossack masses to rebel'.

The mounted reconnaissance patrols were always the first to enter villages abandoned by the enemy and, while the infantry were still on the way, Koshevoi sent the richest houses up in smoke. Above all, he wanted to get to Tatarsky to take revenge on the Tatarsky folk for the death of Ivan Alexeyevich and the Yelanskaya Communists, to burn down half the village. He had already compiled in his mind a list of those who were for burning and if it so happened that his unit headed further to the left after leaving the Chir he had decided to make off during the night and spend some time in his own village.

There was yet another reason spurring him on to Tatarsky. In the past two years, in the brief meetings he had managed to snatch with Dunyashka Melekhova there had grown up between them a feeling that had not yet been put into words. It was Dunyashka's brown fingers that had sewn the bright embroidery on Mishka's tobacco pouch, it was she who without telling her family had in winter brought him a pair of grey goat-hair gloves, and it was Dunyashka's embroidered handkerchief that Koshevoi kept carefully in the breast pocket of his soldier's tunic. And the tiny handkerchief, which after three months still retained the faint hay-like smell of the girl's body, was dear to him beyond all words! When he was alone and took that handkerchief out of his pocket, a poignant memory always came unbidden to his mind: a frost-rimed poplar by a well, flurries of snow swooping out of a dark sky, and Dunyashka's firm quivering lips, the crystal gleam of snowflakes melting on her curling eyelashes...

He made careful preparations for his homecoming. From a wall in a Karginskaya merchant's house he tore down a colourful rug and fitted it under his saddle. And what a splendid saddle-cloth it made, delighting the eye from afar with its vivid array of colours and patterns. From a Cossack family chest he obtained an almost new pair of trousers with side stripes. He cut up half a dozen women's shawls to make three pairs of footcloths, and kept a pair of women's gloves in his saddle bag, so that he could put them on not now, while he was engaged in the everyday business of war, but on the hill before his entry into Tatarsky.

For centuries it had been the custom that a soldier returning to his native village should look smart. And Mishka, who had still not shaken off all Cossack traditions, intended to sacredly observe the old custom.

The horse he was riding was a fine dark bay with a white muzzle. Its former owner—a Cossack from Ust-Khopyorskaya—had been cut down by Koshevoi in a charge. The horse was a trophy and was something to show off; its height, speed, gait and military bearing were all admirable. But Koshevoi's saddle was not much to write home about. The seat was worn and patched, the rear girth was a strip of rawhide, and the stirrups had a stubborn coating of rust that would not come off. The bridle was the same, without a scrap of ornament. He had to find some way of smartening up his bridle at least. Mishka worried over this problem until at last a splendid idea dawned on him. On the square in front of a burnt-out merchant's house he noticed a nickel-plated bedstead that had been pulled out of the flames by the merchant's servants. The four silvery knobs on its corner posts shone dazzlingly bright in the sunshine. All he had to do was to take or break them off and, fix them to the bridle and it would make quite a different impression. So Mishka unscrewed the hollow knobs and, attached them with silk cords to the bridle, two to the snaffle and two to the cheek-straps, and the horse's head glowed in the white-hot noonday sun. The glitter of the knobs was unbearably bright. So bright that the horse rode into the sun with its eyes closed, frequently stumbling and stepping uncertainly. But despite the damage to the horse's vision, despite the tears streaming from its eyes, Mishka did not remove a single knob from the bridle. And soon the time came to leave half-gutted Karginskaya with its stench of burnt bricks and ashes.

The regiment had been ordered to proceed to the Don in the direction of Vyoshenskaya. So Mishka had no difficulty in obtaining permission from his patrol commander to absent himself for a day and see his family.

Not only did his commander grant him a short leave; he went even further.

'Are you married?' he asked Mishka.

'No.'

'You've got a lay, though, I reckon?'

'A what?... What's that?' Mishka asked in surprise.

'Well, a mistress!'

'Oh, I see... No, my sweetheart's a decent girl.'

'Have you got a watch and chain?'

'No, comrade.'

'You're a fine one!' And the reconnaissance commander, a man from Stavropol, formerly a long-service
warrant officer who had been home on leave many a
time from the old army, and knew from experience how
miserable it was to turn up in one's home village looking
like a tramp, took off his chest a watch with an unbelievably heavy chain and said, 'You're a fine soldier!
Here you are, wear it at home, cut a dash in front of the
girls, and when you're well in remember me. I was
young myself once, I laid plenty of girls and rolled the
women over and over, so I know... The chain is made of
new American gold. If anyone starts asking questions,
that's what you can tell him. But if some nosey bugger
turns up and wants to see the hallmark, give him a
punch on the kisser! There are some nosey blighters
around and the only thing to do is to let 'em have it
without wasting words. Sometimes in a tavern or some
public place, in other words, a brothel, one of those
drapers' shop assistants or clerks would come up to me
and try to put me to shame, "Showing off with a
chain on your big belly, as if it was real gold... But
where's the hallmark, may I ask?" And I never used to
give 'em time to take a second look, "Want to see the hallmark? Here it is!" ' And Mishka's good-natured commander clenched his huge brown hand into a fist as big as a
baby's head, and jabbed it forward with frightening
force.

Mishka put on the watch, shaved himself at night by
the light of the campfire, saddled his horse, and galloped
off. At daybreak he was in Tatarsky.

The village was just the same as ever. The squat bell-
tower of the brick-built church still raised its faded gilt
cross to the pale-blue sky, the square was still hemmed in
by the solid houses of the priests and merchants and
the poplar still whispered as of old beside the Koshevoi's
crumbling little hut...

The only surprising thing was the great silence, so
unlike the village of former days; it lay like a web of
gossamer over every lane. There was not a soul in the
streets. Every window was shuttered and some of the
doors were padlocked, but more had been left wide

open. It was as though a plague had visited the village and filled it with desolation and neglect.

Not a voice was to be heard, no lowing of cattle, not even the cheerful crowing of a cock. Only a few sparrows were chirping excitedly under the eaves of the sheds and in the stacks of firewood.

Mishka rode into his own yard. None of the family came out to greet him. The door into the porch was wide open, by the doorstep lay a torn Red Army leg-wrapping, a crumpled bandage, black with congealed blood, some chickens' heads coated with flies and already decaying, and a few feathers. Evidently some Red Army men had eaten a meal a few days ago in the house. On the floor there were fragments of broken bowls, picked chicken bones, fag-ends, and trampled scraps of newspapers... Suppressing a sigh, Mishka went into the front room. Everything there was untouched, except that one half of the trap-door leading to the cellar, where the water melons used to be kept, looked as if it had been slightly raised.

Mishka's mother had also stored dried apples there, out of reach of the children.

Remembering this, Mishka went to the cellar door. 'Mum must have been expecting me? Perhaps she put something away for me here?' he thought. He drew his sabre, inserted the point into the chink, and prised open the trap. A whiff of damp and mildew rose from the cellar. Mishka knelt down and for a long time his unaccustomed eyes could make out nothing in the darkness. But at last they did see: on an old tablecloth stood half a bottle of home-brew, a frying-pan with a mouldy egg on it, and a hunk of bread, half of which had been eaten by mice; there was also an earthenware pot, firmly covered with a wooden lid. The old woman had been expecting her son. She had waited for him as the dearest of all guests! Mishka's heart leapt with love and joy as he went down into the cellar. A few days ago his mother's loving hands had touched all these things that were carefully arranged on the old but clean tablecloth! A canvas bag was hanging from a beam. Mishka hurriedly took it down and found in it a pair of his old but skilfully patched, washed and pressed underpants.

The mice had ruined the food. Only the milk and the home-brew were untouched. Mishka drank the spirits and ate the milk, which had set beautifully in the cool cellar, took the clean underwear and climbed out.

'Mother must be on the other side of the Don. She

was afraid to stay behind. And it's a good thing she didn't, or the Cossacks would have killed her. I reckon they pretty near shook the life out of her as it was,' he mused, pausing as he went out. He untied his horse but changed his mind about going to the Melekhovs'. Their farm was right on the edge of the Don and from the other side a skilled marksman could easily have picked him off with a soft-nosed insurgent bullet. So Mishka decided to ride first to the Korshunovs', and then at dusk return to the square and under cover of darkness set fire to Mokhov's and the other merchants' and priests' houses.

By backways he cantered up to the Korshunovs' spacious yard, rode in through the open gate, tethered his horse to the porch rail and was just about to enter the house when Old Grishaka appeared on the porch. His snow-white head was shaking and his faded eyes blinked short-sightedly. His everlasting grey Cossack uniform with its red tabs on the greasy collar was neatly buttoned, but his trousers were baggy and falling down, and the old man had to hold them up.

'Hullo, Grandad!' Mishka stood in front of the porch, flicking his whip.

Old Grishaka made no reply. His sombre gaze was one of mingled hatred and disgust.

'Hullo, I said!' Mishka raised his voice.

'Praise the Lord,' the old man replied unwillingly.

He continued to study Mishka with malevolent attention. Mishka stood easily, feet apart, toying with his whip, frowning and pursing his girlishly full lips.

'Why didn't you retreat across the Don, Grandad Grigory?'

'How do you know what my name is?'

'I was born here, that's how.'

'Who are you then?'

'Koshevoi.'

'Akim's son? The one who used to live here as a farmhand?'

'That's right.'

'So you're the one, young sir? You were named Mishka at your christening? A fine fellow! Takes after his father! That one sometimes used to bite the hand that fed him, and you, I see, are the same?'

Koshevoi pulled one of the gloves off his hand and his frown deepened.

'What I'm called or what I am is none of your business. Why didn't you retreat across the Don, I said?'

'I didn't want to go, so I didn't. And what are you doing here? Have you become a servant of the anti-Christ? Put a red star on your cap? So you're against our Cossacks, are you, you son-of-a-bitch? Against your own folk?'

Old Grishaka tottered down the steps of the porch. Evidently he had not had much to eat since the Korshunovs had crossed the Don. Abandoned by his family, haggard and unkempt, he stood facing Mishka, staring at him in surprise and anger.

'Yes, I'm against them,' Mishka replied, 'and soon we'll put an end to 'em!'

'Don't you know what is written in the Holy Scriptures? "With what measure ye measure it shall be meted out unto you." How about that?'

'Don't you try to muddle me, Grandad, with any Holy Scriptures. I didn't come here for that. Now then, clear out of this house,' Mishka's face suddenly became sterner.

'What d'you mean by that?'

'What I said.'

'But how can you?'

'Never mind that! Clear out, I said!'

'I'm not going to leave my own home, I know what's right... You're a servant of the anti-Christ, you've got his brand on your cap! It's about you that 'tis said in the book of the Prophet Jeremiah, "Behold, I will feed them with wormwood and give them water of gall to drink, and from them there shall come filth upon all the land." So it has come to pass that son has risen against father and brother against brother...'

'Don't try to get me mixed up, Grandad! It's nothing to do with brothers, it's simple arithmetic. My Dad worked for you till his dying day, and before the war I used to thresh your wheat for you, straining my young guts out with your sacks of grain. But now the time has come to settle accounts. Get out of the house because I'm going to set fire to it! You've lived in a good house but now you'll live like we lived, in a mud-walled hut. Now d'you understand, old man?'

'That's it! That's how it is! For in the book of the Prophet Isaiah it is written, "And they shall go forth and look upon the carcasses of the men that have transgressed against me: for their worm shall not die, neither shall their fire be quenched; and they shall be an abhorring unto all flesh."'

'Well, I've no time to dilly-dally with you here!' Mishka said in a cold fury. 'Will you get out of the house?'

'No! Go forth, enemy of Christ!'

'It's because of diehards like you that this war is going on! You stir up the people and set 'em against the revolution...' Mishka hurriedly slung the carbine off his shoulder.

After the shot Grandad Grishaka fell flat on his back and said quite audibly, 'So ... have I died ... not for mine own good but by the will of our Lord... Lord take thy servant ... and ... may he go in peace...' his voice changed to a croak, and a trickle of blood flowed from under his white whiskers.

'He'll take you! It was high time someone sent you there, you old devil!'

Mishka disgustedly walked round the old man's body and ran up the steps on to the porch.

Some dry shavings carried into the entrance by the wind burst into pink flame, the thin partition separating the storeroom from the inner porch caught quickly. Smoke rose to the ceiling and was swept by the draught into the rooms.

Koshevoi walked out of the house and, while he was setting light to the shed and barn, the fire in the house broke out through the windows and flames started licking the deal window facings and reached up eagerly to the roof.

Until dusk Mishka slept in a nearby poplar grove, in the shade of some thorn bushes tangled with wild hops. His unsaddled and hobbled horse grazed beside him, lazily pulling at some juicy stalks of timothy. Toward evening, growing thirsty, it gave a loud snort and wakened its master.

Mishka rose, rolled his greatcoat, watered his horse from a well in the grove, then saddled it and rode out into the lane.

A few black charred ploughs were still smoking in the Korshunovs' burnt-out yard and the air was full of acrid fumes. All that was left of the big Cossack house was the high brick foundation and the gutted stove, which still pointed its blackened chimney to the sky.

Koshevoi set out straight for the Melekhovs' farm.

As he rode into the yard without dismounting, he saw Ilyinichna gathering some wood chips for kindling in her apron.

'Hullo, Auntie!' he greeted her affectionately.

The old woman was so frightened that she could make
no reply and, dropping her hands, let the chips fall to
the ground.

'Good health to you, Auntie!'

'Praise ... praise the Lord!' Ilyinichna stammered in
reply.

'Are you still alive and well?'

'I'm still alive, but you'd better not ask about my
health.'

'Where are your Cossacks?'

Mishka dismounted and walked up to the barn.

'Across the Don.'

'Waiting for the Cadets, eh?'

'I'm only a woman... I don't know anything about
such things...'

'Is Dunyashka ... Yevdokia Panteleyevna at home?'

'She's over the other side too.'

'The devil took her there!' Mishka's voice shook,
then hardened with anger. 'I'll tell you this, good woman,
your son Grigory has turned out to be the very worst
enemy of Soviet power. When we cross over to that side,
he'll be the first to get a rope round his neck. But Pantelei Prokofievich needn't have run away. He's old and
lame, he ought to have stayed at home...'

'And waited to be killed?' Ilyinichna asked grimly,
and began gathering up the chips in her apron.

'He's a long way from being killed yet. He might have
earned himself a few lashes, but no one would have
killed him. But that's not what I came here about.' Mishka
straightened the watch chain on his chest. 'I came to see
Yevdokia Panteleyevna. And I'm right sorry she's away
in the retreat, but I'll tell you, Auntie, as you're her
mother. I'll tell you this: I've been in love with her a
long time now but just at the moment we haven't much
time for courting the girls, we're fighting the counter-
revolutionaries and killing them off ruthlessly. But as
soon as we're through with them and the peaceful power
of the Soviets is established all over the world, then I'll
be sending you the matchmakers for your Yevdokia.'

'It's not the time to talk about that!'

'Yes, it is!' Mishka frowned, and a stubborn crease
appeared between his brows. 'It's not the time for match-
making but we can still talk about it. I can't choose
another time. I'm here today and gone tomorrow. I may
be sent off across the Donets. So I'm warning you. Don't
be so foolish as to marry Yevdokia off to anyone else

401

or you'll be in trouble. If you get a letter from my unit saying I've been killed, then you can marry her off, but not now, because there's love between us. I haven't brought her a present, there was nowhere to get one, but if you need anything from a bourgeois or merchant's property just say the word and I'll go and get it for you!'

'God forbid! We've never taken what doesn't belong to us!'

'Well, that's up to you. Pass my deepest regards to Yevdokia Panteleyevna if you see her before I do, and now goodbye and, please, don't forget what I've said, Auntie.'

Ilyinichna walked into the house without answering and Mishka mounted his horse and rode off to the village square.

That night some Red Army men came down from the hill into the village. Their excited voices could be heard in the lanes. Three of them, who were carrying a light machine-gun to the outpost overlooking the Don, questioned Mishka and checked his papers. Near Anvil Semyon's little hut he met four more. Two of them were carting some oats on a big army transport while the other two, accompanied by Semyon's consumptive wife, were carrying a treadle sewing-machine and a sack of flour.

She recognised Mishka and greeted him.

'What have you got there?' Mishka inquired.

'We're putting this woman of the poor-labourer class on her feet. We're setting her up with a bourgeois sewing-machine and some flour,' one of the Red Army men answered promptly.

Mishka set fire to seven houses belonging to the merchant Mokhov and his partner Lispy Atyopin, to the priest Vissarion, to the sanctimonious Father Pankraty, and to three other well-to-do Cossacks, all of whom had fled across the Donets with the Whites, and only then did he ride out of the village.

He trotted up on to the hill and wheeled his horse. Below him in Tatarsky a sparkling ruddy foxtail of flame was flaring against the slate-black sky. Now the fire blazed up so high that its reflections quivered in the flowing waters of the Don, now it dropped and veered to the west, hungrily devouring the buildings in its path.

A light steppeland breeze raided in from the east. It fanned the flames and carried the glittering coal-black ashes from the fire far away.

BOOK FOUR

PART SEVEN

I

The rising on the Upper Don, by diverting considerable Red forces from the Southern Front, allowed the
command of the Don Army not only to freely regroup
its forces on the front covering Novocherkassk, but
also to concentrate in the Kamenskaya and Ust-Belokalitvenskaya area a powerful strike force composed
of the staunchest and most reliable regiments, mainly
from the lower reaches and the Kalmyks. Its task was
to cooperate with General Fitzhelaurov's units in knocking out the 12th Division of the 8th Red Army and
then, operating in the rear and on the flank of the 13th
and Urals divisions, break through to the north and link
up with the insurgent forces on the Upper Don.

The plan for concentrating the strike force, which
had initially been drawn up by the former commander
of the Don Army General Denisov, and his chief of
staff, General Polyakov, had by the end of May been
almost completely executed. Nearly 16,000 infantry
and cavalry with 36 field guns and 140 machine-guns
had been transferred to Kamenskaya; a few remaining cavalry units and the crack regiments of the so-
called Young Army, formed in the summer of 1918
out of young Cossacks who had just reached call-up
age, were still moving into position.

Meanwhile the surrounded insurgents continued to
repel the attacks of the Red forces that had been sent to

put down the rebellion. In the south, two insurgent divisions were firmly entrenched along the left bank of the Don and preventing the enemy from crossing the river, despite the almost continual fierce shelling by numerous Red Army batteries all along the front; the remaining three divisions were defending insurgent territory in the west, north and east and suffering enormous losses, particularly in the north-east sector; but they did not retreat and the line held firm all along the borders of the Khopyor district.

The Tatarsky squadron, which was holding the line opposite its own village, grew tired of its enforced idleness and on one occasion caused some alarm among the Red troops. One dark night a party of volunteers rowed silently across to the right bank of the Don, took the Red Army outpost by surprise, killed four of the defenders and captured a machine-gun. The next day the Reds brought up a battery from near Vyoshenskaya, and began to pound the Cossack trenches. As soon as the shrapnel started clip-clopping among the trees, the squadron hastily left its positions along the bank and withdrew deep into the woods. A day later the battery was withdrawn and the Tatarsky men went back to the positions they had abandoned. The squadron had suffered losses from the shelling; two 19-year-olds from the replacements who had recently arrived had been killed and the squadron commander's messenger, who had just ridden in from Vyoshenskaya, had been wounded.

The incident was followed by a comparative lull, and life in the trenches resumed its former course. The women put in frequent appearances, bringing bread and homebrew at night. But the Cossacks were by no means short of provisions. They had killed two stray heifers and every day they went fishing in the nearby lakes. Khristonya was accounted the chief fisherman. He had taken charge of a seventy-foot drag-net which someone had left behind on the bank, and which was now the property of the squadron. He was always carrying out a 'broad sweep' and boasting that there was not a lake in the vicinity that he could not wade. After a week of tireless effort, his shirt and trousers were so steeped in slime that Anikei refused to spend another night with him in the same dug-out.

'You stink like a dead pike! If I have another day here with you, I'll never be able to look at a fish again...'

Despite the mosquitoes, Anikei took to sleeping outside. Before turning in, he would gather a bunch of twigs and, frowning in disgust, sweep away the fish scales and evil-smelling entrails scattered around on the sand, but the next morning Khristonya would return from his expedition, seat himself with calm dignity by the entrance to the dug-out, and again start scraping and gutting his catch of crucians. Emerald bluebottles swarmed around him and fierce yellow ants flocked to the scene. Then a breathless Anikei would appear and bellow while still at a distance, 'Can't you find another spot? I wish you'd choke on a fishbone, you lousy devil! For Christ's sake go away from here! This is where I sleep and you've fouled it up with fish guts, drawn all the ants in the district, and made the place stink like the wharves of Astrakhan!'

Khristonya would wipe his home-made knife on his trouser leg, study Anikei's beardless indignant face, and say calmly, 'You must be suffering from worms, my boy, if you don't like the smell of fish. Ever tried garlic, on an empty stomach?'

Whereupon Anikei would take himself off, spitting and swearing.

The quarrels continued day after day. But on the whole the squadron passed the time peaceably enough. The plentiful cooking kept all the Cossacks cheerful except Stepan Astakhov.

Either a fellow villager or his own heart had whispered to him that Aksinya was seeing Grigory in Vyoshenskaya, but he suddenly grew moody, picked a quarrel with the troop commander, and flatly refused to do sentry duty.

He sulked in his dug-out for two days, lying on a black felt blanket, sighing to himself and smoking greedily and showed himself only when he heard that the squadron commander was sending Anikei to Vyoshenskaya for ammunition. Bleary-eyed from lack of sleep, he stared suspiciously at the fluttering vivid leaves of the swaying trees and the white-maned clouds rearing in the wind, listened for a while to the murmur of the forest, and then set off along by the dug-outs to find Anikei. When he found him, not wishing to speak in the other men's presence, he took Anikei aside.

'Find Aksinya in Vyoshenskaya and tell her I want to see her. Say I've got lice all over me, my shirts and pants need washing, and, what's more, tell her...' Stepan paused for a moment, burying an embarrassed leer under

407

his moustache, and concluded, 'Tell her I'm missing her right bad and expecting to see her soon.'

Anikei arrived in Vyoshenskaya that night and soon found Aksinya's lodgings. After the tiff with Grigory she had gone back to her aunt's. Anikei conscientiously repeated Stepan's message but, to drive the point home, added on his own behalf that Stepan had threatened to come to Vyoshenskaya himself if she did not respond to his wishes.

She listened patiently and began to get ready. Her aunt hastily set some dough and baked buns, and two hours later Aksinya, the dutiful wife, was driving with Anikei to the Tatarsky squadron's trenches.

Stepan met his wife with an anxiety he tried hard to conceal. He scanned her gaunt face, and questioned her cautiously but let fall no word of inquiry as to whether she had seen Grigory or not. Once, however, lowering his eyes and turning away, he did ask, 'Why did you cross over at Vyoshenskaya? Couldn't you have crossed from the village?'

Aksinya answered drily that there had been no strangers willing to take her across and she had not wanted to ask the Melekhovs. The next moment she realised that this meant the Melekhovs were not strangers but their own folk. Her heart sank at the thought that Stepan might have taken it so. And probably that was how he had taken it. Something twitched under his eyebrows, and a shadow seemed to pass over his face.

He looked up at Aksinya questioningly and she, understanding his mute query, suddenly blushed in confusion and self-reproach.

Stepan tactfully pretended not to have noticed anything and changed the subject to domestic matters, asking her what belongings she had managed to hide before leaving and how safely she had hidden them.

Aksinya noted her husband's magnanimity and answered his questions but could not shake off an inward sense of constraint. To convince him that everything between them was above board and to hide her own agitation, she affected a deliberate, matter-of-fact manner of speaking.

They talked sitting in the dug-out. All the time they were interrupted. Khristonya came in and lay down for a nap. Stepan, seeing that there was no hope of their being left alone together, reluctantly abandoned the conversation.

Aksinya rose gladly, hurriedly untied her bundle and gave her husband the buns she had brought, then she took Stepan's dirty linen out of his pack and went out to wash it in a nearby pool.

Stillness and the blue mist of early morning hung over the forest. The dew-burdened grass was bowing to the earth. Frogs were croaking discordantly in the pools, and somewhere, not far from the dug-out, behind a branching maple bush a corncrake was uttering its harsh cries.

Aksinya walked past the bush. From its very crown to the base hidden amid the dense grass it was all webbed in gossamer. Beaded with tiny drops of dew, the threads glistened like strings of pearls. The corncrake fell silent for a moment, but before the grass rose from under Aksinya's bare feet, spoke up again and was answered sadly by a lapwing that had risen from the pool.

Aksinya threw off her blouse and the constricting bodice, waded knee-deep into the warm steamy water and set about her washing. Midges and whining mosquitoes swarmed above her. She crooked her brown shapely arm to brush them away from her face. All the time she was thinking of Grigory, of that last quarrel before he had gone off to visit the squadron.

'Perhaps he's looking for me right now? I must go back tonight!' Aksinya decided irrevocably, and smiled at the thought of their meeting and reconciliation.

And how strange! When thinking of Grigory of late, for some reason she never pictured him the way he really looked now. It was not the present Grigory who rose before her eyes, a big, tough Cossack, who had been through so much, a man with a weary shrewdness in his eyes, with rusty ginger tips to his black moustache, a premature greyness at the temples and deep harsh lines in his forehead—the indelible marks of the hardships he had endured through the long years of war—but the former Grisha Melekhov, youthfully awkward and unskilled in his caresses, with a boyishly smooth and slim neck and lips always ready to break into a carefree smile.

And this made Aksinya love him more than ever, with an almost motherly tenderness.

And now too, as she recalled with perfect clarity the features of that infinitely dear face, she caught her breath and smiled, then straightened her back, threw down her husband's half-washed shirt and, feeling the hot sweet spasm rising in her throat, whispered, 'You've got into me for life, damn you!'

Her tears brought some relief, but all the colour seemed to have gone out of the blissful blue morning world around her. She wiped her cheeks with the back of her hand, tossed the hair back off her damp forehead and with dulled eyes stared vacantly at a small grey gull darting over the water and disappearing into the pink lace-work of the mist that had begun to stir in the wind.

Having done her washing, she hung it out to dry on the bushes and returned to the dug-out.

Khristonya was awake and sitting by the entrance, twitching his gnarled, twisted toes and pestering Stepan with conversation. The latter was lying on his felt blanket, smoking in silence and stubbornly refusing to answer Khristonya's questions.

'So you reckon the Reds won't try to cross over to this side? You won't talk, eh? Well, keep quiet then. But, if you ask me, they're bound to have a try at the ford... Ay, they'll try the ford, that's for sure! There's nowhere else. Or d'you reckon they'll make their cavalry swim across? Have you lost your tongue, Stepan? Things are coming to a head like and you just lie there like a log of wood!'

At this Stepan jumped up and replied irately, 'What're you pestering me for? You're a fine lot! My wife comes to see me and there's no getting rid of you... Bothering me with your stupid talk and won't let me have a word with my own woman.'

'What can you talk to her about?' The disgruntled Khristonya stood up, pulled on his battered down-at-heel shoes, and went out, bumping his head painfully on the door beam.

'They'll never let us talk here, let's go into the woods,' Stepan suggested and, without waiting for an answer, made for the door. Aksinya followed him obediently.

They returned to the dug-out at noon. At the sight of them some Cossacks of the second troop who had been lying in the shade of an alder clump, put aside their playing cards, winked at one another, and started smirking and heaving feigned sighs.

Aksinya walked past them with scornfully curled lips, straightening her white lace kerchief as she went. They allowed her to pass in silence but as soon as Stepan came up, Anikei rose and stepped out of the group. With mock respect he bowed to Stepan and said loudly, 'Gratulations, sir... On breaking your fast!'

410

Stepan smiled willingly. He was glad the Cossacks had seen him returning from the woods with his wife. It might help to quell the rumours that they did not get on. He even gave a debonair twitch of his shoulders to show off the still damp patch of sweat on the back of his shirt.

Only after this encouragement did the Cossacks break into banter and guffaws.

'She's a wild rider, that woman, eh, lads! Old Stepan's shirt is soaked through... It's sticking to his shoulders!'

'She rode him into the ground. The foam's dripping off him.'

And a young fellow, whose mistily admiring eyes had followed Aksinya all the way to the dug-out, exclaimed dazedly, 'You won't find such a beauty anywhere in the whole wide world, may God be my judge!'

To which Anikei remarked reasonably enough, 'How far have you looked?'

Aksinya paled a little at the crude jests, and she stepped into the dug-out, frowning in disgust both at the memory of her recent intimacy with her husband and at the lewd remarks of his comrades. Stepan sensed her mood at once and said appeasingly, 'Don't be angry with them stud-horses, Aksinya, love. They're just a bit restive, that's all.'

'There's no one to be angry with,' Aksinya answered huskily, rummaging in her homespun bag and turning out everything she had brought her husband. And on an even lower note she muttered, 'I ought to be angry with myself, but I haven't the heart...'

Their conversation quickly flagged. After about ten minutes Aksinya stood up. 'Now I'll tell him I'm going back to Vyoshenskaya,' she thought, and suddenly remembered that she had not yet brought in the washing she had done for Stepan.

She spent a long time mending her husband's sweat-rotted shirts and pants, sitting by the entrance to the dug-out and glancing frequently at the declining sun.

Aksinya did not leave that day. She lacked the resolve. But the next morning, as soon as the sun was up, she began to get ready. Stepan pleaded with her to stay on another day, but she was so firm in her determination to go that he made no further attempt to dissuade her.

Before they parted he asked, 'Will ye be living in Vyoshenskaya?'

'I will, for the time being.'

'Mebbe you'll stay here with me?'

'It won't do for me to be here ... with the Cossacks.'

'You're right there,' Stepan agreed, but said goodbye coldly.

The wind was blowing hard from the south-east. After its long journey, it had flagged a little during the night, but by morning it brought the fierce heat of the Transcaspian deserts and, pouncing on the water meadows of the left bank, dried up the dew, scattered the mists and wrapped the chalky spurs of the Donside hills in a pink sultry haze.

Aksinya took off her shoes and, gathering the hem of her skirt in her left hand (there was still some dew on the grass in the wood), walked lightly along the deserted forest path. Her feet were pleasantly cooled by the damp earth and the dry wind kissed her bare shapely calves and neck with hot searching lips.

In a clearing, by a flowering bush of sweet briar she sat down for a rest. Not far away wild duck were churping among the bulrushes of a half dried-up lake, a drake was calling its mate. From across the Don came the scattered but almost continuous rattle of machine-guns and an occasional boom of gunfire. The shells burst on this side with a rolling echo.

After a while the firing moved away and the world revealed itself to Aksinya in its own secret harmonies: the green white-flecked foliage of the ash-trees and the intricately carved leaves of the oaks rustled vibrantly in the wind; a steady drone came from the thickets of young aspen; far, far away a cuckoo was faintly and sadly counting out someone's unspent years; a crested lapwing flying over the little lake called persistently 'Peewit, peewit'; a tiny grey bird only two steps away from Aksinya was drinking from a rut in the road, throwing its head back and closing one small eye blissfully; dusty velvet bumblebees were buzzing; dark-coated wild bees swayed to and fro in the heart petals of wild flowers, then dived away and carried their fragrant "taking" into the cool shady hollow of a tree. Sap was dripping from the poplar branches, and from under a hawthorn bush seeped the dry, yeasty smell of last year's leaves.

Aksinya sat quite still and drank in the manifold scents of the forest. All around her the forest lived its mighty primeval life, full of wondrous and many-voiced sound. The water-meadow soil, plentifully charged with

412

spring moisture, had thrown up such an abundance of herbage that Aksinya was dazzled by the miraculous blending of flowers and grass.

Smiling and moving her lips soundlessly, she carefully separated the stems of nameless light-blue flowers, then bent her now rather full waist to smell them and suddenly caught the sweet overpowering smell of a lily-of-the-valley.

She found it growing just beside her, in the deep shade of the bush. Its broad, once green leaves were still jealously guarding from the sun the short curved flower-stem with its drooping snow-white bells. But the leaves, covered with dew and yellow rust were dying, and the flower itself was already touched by mortal decay. Two of the lower bells had withered and turned black and only the top ones—all in sparkling tears of dew— suddenly caught the sunlight and burst into dazzling, captivating whiteness.

And for some reason in that brief moment, while she was looking at the flower through her tears and breathing in its sad scent, Aksinya recalled her youth and all the long years of her life that had been so poor in joys. Ah, Aksinya, you must be getting old. Would a young woman cry just because a chance memory gripped her heart?

She fell asleep, lying with her tear-stained face buried in her hands, her wet swollen cheek pressed into her crumpled kerchief.

The wind strengthened, bowing the crowns of poplars and willows towards the west. The pale trunk of an ash-tree swayed in a foaming white whirlpool of fluttering leaves. The wind swept lower and fell upon the fading bush of sweet briar under which Aksinya was lying, and its leaves fluttered with an anxious rustle like a flock of magical green birds, scattering pink featherlike petals all around. Sprinkled with wilting wild-rose petals, Aksinya slept on and heard neither the sullen murmur of the forest nor the firing that had begun again on the other side of the Don; nor did she feel the high sun blazing down on her unprotected head. She awoke at the sound of human speech and the snorting of a horse above her and hastily sat up.

Beside her stood a young white-moustached and white-toothed Cossack, holding the bridle of a saddled horse with a white muzzle. He was smiling broadly, jerking his shoulders and jigging about, and uttering the words of a merry ditty in a rather hoarse but pleasant tenor voice:

> Down I fell and there I lay,
> Looking round me every way.
> Looking here,
> Looking there—
> No one to help me anywhere.
> Then I gave just one look back,
> Right behind me—there's a Cossack...

'I'll get up myself!' Aksinya smiled and jumped lightly to her feet, straightening her crumpled skirt.

'Good health to you, my dear! Won't your legs take you any further or are you feeling lazy?' the cheery Cossack greeted her.

'I suddenly felt so sleepy,' Aksinya confessed blushing.

'On your way to Vyoshki?'

'That't right.'

'Want a lift?'

'But what on?'

'You get on my horse and I'll walk. For a consideration... Is it a deal?' The Cossack winked to illustrate his meaning.

'No, thanks. Go along and God be with you. I'll make my own way.'

But the Cossack revealed both experience in matters of love, and persistence. Seizing his chance while Aksinya was covering her head, he put his short but strong arm round her waist, and tried to kiss her.

'Don't be a fool!' Aksinya cried, and struck him hard with her elbow between the eyes.

'Now, my little love-bird, don't get rough! Look how beautiful it is all round... All God's creatures are pairing up... Why not do a little pairing ourselves?...' the Cossack whispered, tickling Aksinya's neck with his moustache and narrowing his laughing eyes.

Aksinya pressed her hands unmaliciously but with some strength against the Cossack's ruddy brown face and tried to free herself, but he held her tight.

'You fool! I'm sick, I've got the disease... Let me go!' she panted, imagining this innocent trick would relieve her of his attentions.

'Oho... But who's had it longer?' the Cossack muttered, now with a snarl, and all of a sudden swept her off her feet.

414

Realising that the joke was over and she was in trouble, Aksinya punched him as hard as she could on his sunburnt nose and broke out of his imprisoning arms.

'I'm the wife of Grigory Melekhov! Just you come near me, you rotten bastard!... If I tell him, he'll...'

Not sure of the effect of her words, Aksinya picked up a thick stick. But the Cossack cooled off at once. Wiping the blood of his moustache with the sleeve of his tunic, he exclaimed disappointedly, 'There's a stupid woman for you! Why didn't you tell me before? Look how you've made me bleed... As if we didn't shed enough blood fighting the enemy, our own women start letting it out of us...'

His face suddenly grew grey and sullen. While he was washing his face with water from a roadside puddle, Aksinya hurriedly left the track and made off across the clearing. Five minutes later the Cossack caught up with her. He gave her a sidelong glance, smiling silently, straightened the shoulder strap holding his rifle sling in place, and rode on at a fast trot.

II

That night near the village of Maly Gromchonok a Red Army regiment crossed the Don on makeshift rafts.

The Gromchonok squadron was taken by surprise because most of its men that night were celebrating. Their wives had come out to the trenches in the evening, bringing food and drink in jugs and pails. By midnight they were all drunk to the wide. From the dug-outs came the sound of singing, the tipsy shrieks of the women, and the men's guffaws and wolf-whistles. Twenty Cossacks who were supposed to be on outpost duty also took part in the drinking, leaving only two men and a horse-bucket of homebrew by the machine-gun.

The rafts loaded with Red Army men cast off from the right bank in total silence. When they reached the other side, the Red troops formed into line and advanced silently towards the dugouts about a hundred paces from the Don.

The engineers who had built the rafts paddled quickly back for the fresh batch of Red Army men waiting on the right bank.

For about five minutes the incoherent Cossack singing went on uninterrupted on the left bank, then the roar of hand grenades shattered the stillness, a machine-gun chattered, rifle fire flared up, and intermittent cheering floated away into the distance.

The Gromchonok squadron was knocked out of its positions and escaped total destruction only because pursuit was impossible in the impenetrable darkness.

Suffering insignificant losses, the Cossacks and their women stampeded across the water-meadow in the direction of Vyoshenskaya. Meanwhile the rafts had brought over reinforcements and a half-company of the first battalion of the 111th Regiment with two light machine-guns was attacking the flank of the Bazki insurgent squadron.

The reinforcements poured into the breach, but their advance was severely hampered by their ignorance of the locality. The units had no guides and, as they pushed on blindly in the darkness, they kept running into lakes and channels still so deep in floodwaters that they could not be forded.

The brigade commander in charge of the attack decided to halt the pursuit until dawn, so that by morning he would be able to bring up his reserves, concentrate on the approaches to Vyoshenskaya and, after an artillery softening-up, continue his offensive.

But in Vyoshenskaya urgent measures were already being taken to close the breach. As soon as the messenger galloped in with news of the Red assault, the headquarters duty officer sent for Kudinov and Melekhov. Cavalry squadrons of the Karginskaya Regiment were summoned from the villages of Chorny, Gorokhovka and Dubrovka. Grigory Melekhov undertook to direct the operation. He sent three hundred horse to the village of Yerinsky to strengthen the left flank and help the Tatarsky and Lebyazhy squadrons to block any attempt by the enemy to outflank Vyoshenskaya in the east; he also sent the Vyoshenskaya non-Cossack company and one of the Chir dismounted squadrons downstream to help the Bazki squadron; he strengthened threatened sectors with eight machine-guns, then at about two in the morning he himself with two mounted squadrons rode to the edge of Gorely Forest and waited for the dawn to launch a cavalry attack on the Red troops.

The Pleiades had not yet burned out when the Vyoshenskaya non-Cossacks, who had been making their way through the woods towards the Bazki bend in the river, encountered the retreating Bazki Cossacks, mistook them for the enemy, and after a brief skirmish beat a hasty retreat. The company swam the broad lake dividing Vyoshenskaya from the bend and in their haste left their clothes and boots on the shore. The mistake was soon discovered, but the rumour that the Reds were approaching Vyoshenskaya spread at astonishing speed. Refugees who had been living in basements and cellars streamed northward out of the stanitsa, taking the rumour everywhere that the Reds had crossed the Don, breached the front and were advancing on Vyoshenskaya.

Day was just beginning to glimmer on the horizon when Grigory received the report of the non-Cossack company's flight and galloped down to the Don. The company had sorted out the misunderstanding and were returning to the trenches, talking loudly amongst themselves. Grigory rode up to one group and asked derisively, 'Did many of you drown when you were swimming the lake?'

A soaking wet rifleman, squeezing out his shirt as he walked, replied sheepishly, 'We swam like fish! How could we drown...'

'Everyone gets into a muddle sometimes,' another in only his underpants argued reasonably, 'But our platoon commander nearly went to the bottom. He didn't want to bother unwinding his puttees, so he waded in as he was and one of them puttees came undone in the water and tangled round his legs... Did he yell! I reckon they could hear him in Yelanskaya!'

When he had found Kramskov, the company commander, Grigory ordered him to bring his men out on to the edge of the forest and position them so that, if need be, they could open fire on the Red lines from the flank. Then he rode off to his squadrons.

Half way there he met a headquarters messenger, who reined in his badly winded horse with an audible sigh of relief.

'Found you at last!'

'What's the matter?'

'Orders from headquarters to tell you the Tatarsky squadron have left their trenches. They're scared of being surrounded, so they're retreating... Kudinov said you'd better get there quick.'

With a half-troop of Cossacks on the fastest mounts Grigory rode through the forest on to the road. After twenty minutes' galloping they reached Lake Goly Ilmen. Infected by the general panic, the Tatarsky men were fleeing across a meadow to their left. The old hands were taking their time and keeping to the edge of the lake, where there was cover among the rushes; but the majority, evidently guided by only one desire—to reach the forest as soon as possible—ignored the occasional bursts of machine-gun fire and made straight across the meadow.

'After 'em! And use your whips!' Grigory shouted, squinting with fury, and was the first off in pursuit of his fellow villagers.

Behind all the rest, limping along with a weird ambling gait, was Khristonya. While fishing the day before, he had cut his heel badly on some rushes and could not run as fast as his long legs usually carried him. Grigory overtook him with his whip poised high above his head. At the sound of hooves behind him, Khristonya glanced back and increased his speed perceptibly.

'Where're you off to?! Stop!... Stop, I tell you!' Grigory roared vainly.

But Khristonya had no intention of stopping. He put on even more speed, until he was loping along like a runaway camel.

The enraged Grigory then let out a terrible oath, urged on his horse and as he drew level brought down his whip on Khristonya's sweating back with real gusto. Khristonya whirled into the air, swerved like a hare, then sat down on the ground and started feeling his back with cautious thoroughness.

Grigory's Cossacks rode ahead of the runaways and halted them, but refrained from using the lash.

'Thrash 'em! Thrash 'em!' Grigory bawled hoarsely, brandishing his whip.

His horse wheeled and reared, refusing to go on. With an effort Grigory brought it under control and galloped ahead. As he rode he caught a glimpse of Stepan Astakhov standing beside a bush and smiling silently, and of Anikei doubled up with laughter, cupping his hands round his mouth and squealing in a womanish voice, 'Run for it, lads! It's the Reds!... After 'em!... Grab 'em!'

Grigory overtook another of the village Cossacks, in a wadded jacket and running tirelessly. His bowed figure was strangely familiar but there was no time for identification, and while still at a distance Grigory shouted, 'Stop, you son-of-a-bitch!... I'll cut you down!'

Suddenly the man in the wadded jacket broke into a

walk, then stopped and turned round, and the astonished Grigory was able to recognise by a gesture of extreme agitation that he had known since childhood—his own father.

Pantelei's cheeks were twitching convulsively.

'Your own father—a son-of-a-bitch? Threatening to cut down your own father?' he screeched in a cracked falsetto.

His eyes smoked with such familiar ungovernable fury that Grigory's indignation cooled at once and, reining his horse to a halt, he shouted, 'Couldn't recognise you from the back! What are you bawling for, Dad?'

'Didn't recognise me? Didn't recognise your own father?'

The old man's touchiness was so absurd and out of place that Grigory began to laugh and, as he drew level with his father, said appeasingly, 'Don't be angry, Dad! That jacket you've got on, I've never seen it before and, besides, you were galloping like a prize race-horse! What happened to your limp! How could I have recognised you?'

And once again, as always in the old days at home, Pantelei calmed down and, still panting but composed, agreed resignedly, 'It's a new jacket I'm wearing. You're right there, I swapped it for my topcoat—a topcoat's far too heavy. And as for limping... How could I limp? This is no time to be limping, my lad!... Death was staring me in the face and you talk about my leg...'

'You're a long way from death yet. About turn, Dad! Haven't thrown your ammo away, have you?'

'About turn? Where to?' the old man protested.

But Grigory raised his voice and rapped out, 'I order you to go back! Don't you know the penalty for disobeying orders on the battlefield?'

His words had their effect. Pantelei straightened the rifle on his back and reluctantly retraced his steps. When he came up with another old man who was plodding back even more slowly, he said with a sigh, 'That's what our sons are like nowadays, eh! Instead of showing respect for his parent, or mebbe letting him off combat duty, he tries to push him right into the thick of it... Petro, now—God rest his soul!—he was far better! Always quiet and easy-going, but this queer fish Grigory, though he's a division commander and been decorated for his services, he's different. He's got corns all over him and you mustn't tread on one of 'em. I shouldn't wonder if all the help I get from him in my old age is kick on the arse.

The Tatarsky men were brought to their senses without much difficulty.

A little later Grigory assembled the whole squadron and marched it to a sheltered spot, then, without dismounting, briefly explained the situation.

'The Reds have crossed over and are trying to capture Vyoshenskaya. They're fighting on this bank now. And it's no laughing matter. I wouldn't advise anyone to run away. If you do it again, I'll order the cavalry stationed at Yerinsky to cut you down as traitors!' Grigory surveyed the motley crowd and concluded with unconcealed contempt, 'There's a lot of scum in your squadron and they're the ones that're spreading panic. Fine fighters! Running away, shitting your pants! Call yourselves Cossacks! And you old gaffers, too, you'd better watch your step! If you're going to fight, it's no good ducking out of danger! Now then, by troops, at the double to that line of bushes, and from there down to the Don. There you link up with the Semyonovsky squadron and with them strike at the Reds' flank. March! And quick about it!'

The Tatarsky men listened in silence and silently headed for the bushes. The old men grunted despondently as they watched Grigory and his escort set off at a swift canter. But old Obnizov, who was marching beside Pantelei, burst out admiringly, 'That's a real hero of a son God granted you! A true eagle! How he took the lash to Khristonya's back! Restored order right away!'

And with his paternal feelings thus flattered Pantelei readily agreed, 'You can say that again! You'd go a long way to find such a son anywhere in the world! A whole chestful of medals—that's something, that is! Now my other boy, Petro, the one that got killed—God rest his soul!—though he was my own son and my first one, he was different! A bit too obedient like, half-baked somehow. Underneath he had the heart of a woman! But this one—he takes after me! Even goes one better!'

* * *

Grigory and his half-troop made their way to the Kalmyk Ford. When they reached the woods, they thought they were safe, but they had been spotted by an observers' post on the other side of the Don. A battery opened up. The first shell flew over the willows and ploughed into the swampy thickets without exploding. The second landed near the road, among the bare roots of an old black poplar, sent up a spout of fire and showered the Cossacks with clods of greasy mud and rotted wood splinters.

Momentarily stunned, Grigory instinctively shielded his eyes with his hand and ducked down over his saddle bow as he felt a dull wet slap on the horse's crupper.

As if by command, the Cossack horses responded to the explosion by falling back on their haunches then straining forward, but Grigory's mount reared heavily on its hindlegs, staggered back and lurched sideways. Grigory leapt out of the saddle and grasped the bridle. Two more shells flew overhead, and then a pleasant stillness descended on the fringe of the forest. The smoke settled on the grass and there arose a smell of freshly exposed soil and half-rotten wood. From a distant thicket came the anxious chatter of magpies.

Grigory's horse snorted as its trembling hindlegs gave way. Its yellow teeth were bared in agony, its neck outstretched. Pink foam bubbled on its velvety grey muzzle. It began to shiver violently and great shudders ran in waves under the reddish fur.

'Done for, is he, our provider?' a Cossack asked as he galloped up.

Grigory looked into the horse's dimming eyes without answering. He did not even glance at the wound, and only stepped back a little when the horse bestirred itself uncertainly, straightened its back, and then suddenly fell forward on its knees, bowing its head low as if begging its master's forgiveness. With a hollow groan it rolled over on to its side and tried to raise its head, but its last strength was ebbing; the shivering began to subside, the eyes became glazed with death and patches of sweat glistened on the neck.

A few last ripples of life still pulsed in the fetlock just above the hooves. The worn saddle flap vibrated slightly.

Grigory glanced at the left groin, saw the deeply gouged wound and the warm black blood spurting out of it, and said to the Cossack, stammering and not bothering to wipe away his tears, 'Shoot him with one bullet!' and gave him his Mauser.

Remounted on the Cossack's horse, he rode to the place where he had left his own squadron. There the fighting had flared up.

The Red forces attacked at dawn. Their skirmish lines rose in the layered mist and silently advanced towards Vyoshenskaya. On the right flank there was a moment's hesitation when they came to a water-filled hollow, then they went in up to their chests, holding their ammunition bags and rifles high over their heads. A little later four batteries on the Donside hills spoke in majestic harmony. As the shells fanned out over the forest, the insurgents opened fire. By this time the Red Army men were no longer walking but running, with their rifles at the ready. Half a verst ahead of them shrapnel was bursting harshly over the forest, shell-torn trees were falling, and smoke was rising in white puffs. Two Cossack machine-guns opened up in short bursts. Men in the first line began to fall. The Red Army soldiers with their rolled greatcoats slung across their shoulders were whipped out of the line by bullets and flung down on their faces or backs, but no one dived for cover and the distance separating them from the forest steadily diminished.

In front of the second line the commander was running with a light swinging stride, the hem of his greatcoat tucked up and his head bare. The line slowed down for a second but the commander turned as he ran and shouted something, and his men made a fresh spurt and once again the terrible, husky cheering swelled to a new pitch of fury.

Then all the Cossack machine-guns spoke at once, rifle shots cracked feverishly and continuously on the forest edge... From somewhere behind where Grigory and his squadrons were stationed on the road leading out of the forest, the Bazki squadron's heavy machine-gun opened up in long bursts. The attackers wavered, dropped to the ground and started to return the fire. For about an hour and a half the fighting continued, but the insurgents had got the range and their fire was so intense that the second line broke cover and fell back amidst the third line, which had been coming up from behind in short dashes... Soon the meadow was scattered with Red Army men running back in disorder, and it was then that Grigory led his squadrons out of the forest, swung them into attack formation and charged in pursuit. The Chir squadron swept forward in a flat-out gallop and cut off the way of retreat to the river. Hand-to-hand fighting broke out in the riverside woods. Only some of the Red Army men reached the rafts, crowded aboard and cast off. Those who were left fought with their backs to the Don.

Grigory dismounted his squadrons, ordered the horse-minders not to leave the forest, and led the Cossacks towards the bank. Darting from tree to tree, they approached the river. The hundred and fifty or so Red Army men who had been left behind stopped the insurgents with hand grenades and machine-gun fire. The rafts set out again for the left bank, but the Bazki Cossacks picked off nearly all the rowers with rifle fire. The fate of those left behind was sealed. The weaker-spirited dropped their rifles and tried to swim the river. They were caught by the fire of insurgents who had taken cover along the bank. Many drowned in midstream, swept away by the strong current. Only two crossed safely. One wearing a sailor's striped vest—evidently a strong swimmer—dived in head first from a steep part of the bank and did not reappear until he reached midstream.

Sheltering behind a massive willow Grigory watched the sailor striking out powerfully until he reached the other bank. And yet another got away safely. He fired off the rest of his ammunition standing up to his chest in water, shouted something, and shook his fist at the Cossacks, then struck out for the other bank. Bullets splashed all round him but not one hit the lucky soldier. Where there had once been a cattle pen on the far bank he climbed out of the water, shook himself and un-hurriedly made his way up the ravine to the farm-steads.

Those who were left behind took refuge behind a sandy hillock. Their machine-gun rattled continuously until the water boiled in the cooling chamber.

'Follow me!' Grigory commanded quietly as soon as the gun fell silent, and made for the hillock with his sabre drawn. Laboured breathing and the thud of running feet sounded behind him.

The Reds were only about a hundred paces away. After three volleys from behind the hillock, their swarthy black-moustached commander rose to his full height. He was supported by a woman wearing a leather jacket. Dragging his wounded leg, he came down the slope, took a firm grip on his rifle with its fixed bayonet and ordered huskily, 'Comrades! Forward! Smash the Whites!'

Singing the *Internationale*, the little bunch of brave men counterattacked—to the death.

The one hundred and sixteen who were the last to fall on the bank of the Don were all Communists of an International Company.

III

Late that night Grigory returned from headquarters to his billet. Prokhor Zykov was waiting for him at the gate.

'Any news of Aksinya?' Grigory asked in a deliberately casual tone.

'Not a thing, dunno what's become of her,' Prokhor replied yawning, and was immediately struck by a worrying thought, 'I hope to God he don't send me out looking for her again... I'm paying a pretty price for this hanky-panky of theirs!'

'Bring me something to wash with. I'm all sweaty. And jump to it!' Grigory added irritably.

Prokhor went into the house for water and poured mug after mug into Grigory's cupped hands. Grigory washed himself with evident pleasure, then pulled off his stinking shirt and asked for a dousing.

The cold water on his sweating back made him gasp. He snorted and took a long time rubbing his strap-chaffed shoulders and hairy chest. As he wiped himself dry with a clean horse blanket, he ordered Prokhor in a more cheerful voice, 'They'll bring me a horse in the morning. Take it, groom it and find some oats for it. Don't wake me. Unless it's a call from headquarters. Got that?'

He walked away to the shed, lay down in a wagon parked under the overhang and was immediately engulfed in sleep. At daybreak, feeling cold, he bunched up his legs and drew his dew-sprinkled greatcoat more tightly round him, but when the sun came up, fell sound asleep again and did not awake until about seven, when he was disturbed by a loud gunshot. A dully gleaming aeroplane was circling in the clear blue sky over the stanitsa. Machine-guns and artillery were shooting at it from the other side of the Don.

'They may hit him, y'know!' Prokhor remarked, furiously brushing down a tall chestnut stallion tethered to a post in the yard. 'Just look at the devil they've sent for you to ride!'

Grigory looked the stallion over quickly and, well satisfied, said, 'I didn't see how old he was. Five, isn't he?'

'That's right.'

'Fine animal! Clean legs and all stockinged. A real good-looker, eh! Well, saddle him up and I'll ride over and find out who's just flown in.'

'Ay, he looks grand. And what will he be like on the go? Real fast by all the signs,' Prokhor muttered, tightening the saddle girths.

Yet another smoky white puff from a shrapnel burst appeared near the plane.

Having chosen a place to land, the pilot went into a dive. Grigory rode out of the gate and cantered towards the Vyoshenskaya stables, beyond which the plane had landed.

The stables—a long brick building on the edge of the stanitsa—were crammed with more than eight hundred Red Army prisoners. The guards would not let them out to relieve themselves and there were no latrines in the building. The nauseating stench of human excrement surrounded it like a wall. Stinking streams of urine flowed from under the doors and emerald-green flies hovered over them.

Day and night muffled moans rose from this prison for the doomed. Hundreds died of starvation, and typhus and dysentery were raging among the others. Sometimes the bodies were not removed for days.

Grigory rode round the stables and was about to dismount when a gun boomed on the other side of the river. The scream of the approaching shell rose until it merged with the crash of the explosion.

The pilot and the officer who had arrived with him climbed out of the cabin and were surrounded by Cossacks, but then all the guns of the battery on the hill opened up. Shells landed in a neat pattern round the stables.

The pilot climbed back into the cabin but the engine would not start.

'Push it!' the officer ordered the Cossacks brusquely, and was the first to grip a wing.

The aeroplane swayed and rolled lightly towards the pines. The battery followed it with rapid fire. One of the shells hit the crowded stables. A corner collapsed amid dense smoke and clouds of whitewash dust, and the whole building rocked with the animal-like cries of the panic-stricken prisoners. Three Red Army men rushed out through the shattered wall and were gunned down point-blank by Cossacks who had run to the scene.

Grigory rode clear.

'You'll get killed! Ride into the pines!' a Cossack shouted as he ran past with a scared face and bulging whitish eyes.

'I might too! The devil will play any trick,' Grigory thought and unhurriedly made for home.

That day Kudinov held a top-secret conference at headquarters, to which Grigory Melekhov was not invited. The officer who had flown in from the Don Army stated briefly that any day now the Red front would be pierced by units of the strike force concentrated near Kamenskaya, and a cavalry division of the Don Army commanded by General Sekretev would march to link up with the insurgents. The officer proposed that the means for crossing the river should be prepared at once so that the insurgent cavalry regiments could be transferred to the right bank of the Don as soon as the link-up with Sekretev took place; he advised bringing up the reserve units closer to the Don and at the end of the conference, after the plan for the crossing and pursuit had been drawn up, asked, 'Why are you holding prisoners in Vyoshenskaya?'

'There's nowhere else, the villages have no room for them,' one of the staff commanders replied.

The officer wiped his perspiring shaven head carefully with a handkerchief, unbuttoned his tunic collar, and said with a sigh, 'Send them to Kazanskaya.'

Kudinov raised his eyebrows in surprise.

'But why?'

'And from there, back to Vyoshenskaya,' the officer explained condescendingly, narrowing his cold blue eyes. His lips tightened and he ended harshly, 'I don't know why you stand on ceremony with them, gentlemen. It's hardly the time for that. This scum, a hotbed of all kinds of infection, both physical and social, must be exterminated. In your place I would do just that!'

The next day the first batch of two hundred prisoners was marched out into the sands. Scarcely able to lift their feet, the emaciated Red Army men moved like pale blue shadows. A mounted escort hemmed in the straggling crowd... Over the ten versts between Vyoshenskaya and Dubrovka the whole two hundred were cut down to the last man. The next batch was marched out towards evening. The escort was given strict orders that all stragglers should be sabred; there should be no shooting except in an emergency. Of the one hundred and fifty

426

only eighteen reached Kazanskaya... One of them, a young soldier of Gypsyish appearance, went mad on the road. He sang, danced and wept, pressing to his heart a bunch of sweet-scented thyme that he had picked by the wayside. He frequently fell face downwards in the scorching sand, the wind ruffled the dirty tatters of his calico shirt and the escorts could see the taut skin on his bony back and the black fissured soles of his feet. He was picked up, water was splashed in his face and he would open dark madly gleaming eyes, laugh quietly, and totter forward.

Some kind-hearted women in one of the villages surrounded the escorting Cossacks and a majestic, buxom old soul said sternly to their commander, 'Let that dark one go free. He's gone out of his mind and come nearer to God. It'll be a great sin if ye kill such a creature.'

The commander of the escort—a dashing ginger-moustached junior cornet—gave a smirk, 'We're not afraid to take a few more sins on our conscience, Granny. We'll never be saints anyway!'

'Let him go, don't be stubborn,' the old woman persisted. 'Death's hovering over all of you, you know.'

The women rallied to her support and the junior cornet agreed.

'I don't mind, take him if you want him. He can't do any harm now. And for our kindness bring us some unskimmed milk, a bowl each.'

The old woman led the madman away to her house, fed him and made up a bed for him in the front room. He slept round the clock and, when he awoke, got up and stood with his back to the window, singing softly. The old woman came in, sat down on the chest, rested her cheek on her hand, and stared hard at the lad's gaunt face, then said in a rather deep voice, 'Your people are not far away, so I've heard.'

For a second perhaps the madman stopped singing, then began again, but more quietly.

Then the old woman said severely, 'Now, my dear, that's enough of your singing. Stop pretending and don't try that hocus-pocus on me. I've lived a long time and I'm not easily fooled! I know ye're in your right mind... I heard the way ye talked in your sleep, very sensible it was too!'

The Red Army man went on singing, but more and more quietly. The old woman continued, 'Don't be afraid of me, I wish ye no harm, lad. I had two sons killed in the German war, and in this one my youngest died at Cherkassk. But I'd carried them all 'neath my heart, hadn't I? I'd fed them and clothed them, and didn't sleep at nights when they were young... So I'm sorry for all the young lads that have to serve in the army and go to war...' She paused briefly.

The Red Army man, too, stopped singing. He closed his eyes and a slight flush showed on his dark cheekbones; a blue vein pulsed tensely in his thin neck.

For a minute he stood in expectant silence, then opened his dark eyes a little. There was comprehension in them and they burned with such impatient expectation that the old woman gave a faint smile.

'Do ye know the road to Shumilinskaya?'

'No, Granny,' the Red Army man replied, barely moving his lips.

'Then how will ye get there?'

'I don't know.'

'That's the trouble! What am I to do with ye now?'

The old woman waited some time for an answer, then asked, 'Can ye walk?'

'I'll manage somehow.'

'Somehow won't do. Ye've got to walk at night and look slippy—real slippy! Spend the day here, then I'll give ye some food and my grandson as a guide to show ye the way—and good luck to ye! Your lot, the Reds, are t'other side of Shumilinskaya, I know that for sure. Ye'll find them there all right. But ye mustn't take the road—only across the steppe, by wood and dell, or the Cossacks will catch ye again and ye'll come to grief. That's how it is, lovey!'

The next day, as soon as it grew dusk, the old woman made the sign of the cross over the two of them, her twelve-year-old grandson and the Red Army man, now dressed in a Cossack homespun coat, and said sternly, 'Well, God be with ye! And mind ye don't run into any of our men!... Don't thank me, lovey, thank holy God! I'm not the only one. We're all kind, all mothers are... And we're sorry to see you poor wretches done to death! Now go and the Lord protect ye!' and she slammed the sagging clay-washed door of her tiny cottage.

IV

Every day Ilyinichna awoke at first light, milked the cow and started cooking. Rather than kindle the stove in the house, she made a fire in the outdoor kitchen, cooked the dinner on it, and then went back to the house to look after the children.

Natalya was slowly recovering from the typhus. On Whit Monday she rose from her bed for the first time and walked from room to room, barely able to drag herself along on her emaciated legs. She spent a long time searching the children's heads for lice and, sitting on a stool, even tried to wash some of their clothes.

There was a constant smile on her thin face, her hollow cheeks had a pink flush, and her eyes, made large by illness, glowed with the kind of radiant warmth that comes after childbirth.

'Polyushka, my lovely, my little darling! Mishatka wasn't rough with you while I was ill, was he?' she asked in a weak voice, uttering each word uncertainly, with an effort, and stroking her daughter's black hair.

'No, Mummy! Mishatka only hit me once and all the rest of the time we had good games together,' the little girl whispered, and pressed her face into her mother's lap.

'Was Granny kind to you?' Natalya went on, smiling.

'Ever so kind!'

'What about strangers? Did the Red soldiers trouble you at all?'

'They killed our calf, the damned devils!' Mishatka, who was astonishingly like his father, answered in a deep little voice.

'You mustn't swear, Mishatka, dear! You think you're master of the house, eh! You mustn't use bad words about grown-ups!' Natalya said in an edifying tone, hiding a smile.

'It was Granny who called them that, you can ask Polyushka,' the little Melekhov replied somberly.

'It's true, Mummy, and they killed all our chickens too!'

Polyushka livened up and her dark eyes shone as she recounted how the Red Army men had come into the yard, how they had caught the chickens and ducks, how Ilyinichna had begged them to leave them the yellow cockerel with the frost-bitten comb for breeding, and a jolly Red Army man had replied, shaking the cockerel in the air, 'This cock, Gran, has been crowing against Soviet power and for that we have condemned him to death! It's no good pleading, we're going to make a chicken soup out of him with noodles, and in exchange we'll leave you an old pair of felt boots.'

And Polyushka spread her arms to demonstrate. 'Great big felt boots they were! Like this!... And all in holes!'

Laughing and crying at the same time, Natalya fondled the children and, unable to take her admiring eyes off her daughter, whispered joyfully, 'Ah, you're Grigory's daughter, that you are! The very image! Just like your father from top to toe!'

'And me? Ain't I like him?' Mishatka asked jealously, and leaned shyly against his mother.

'Yes, you are too. But mind you aren't so wayward as your father, when you grow up.'

'Is he wayward? Why is he wayward?' Polyushka wanted to know.

A shadow passed over Natalya's face. She said nothing and rose with an effort.

Ilyinichna, who had been present while they were talking, turned away in displeasure. Natalya, no longer listening to the children's prattle, stood at the window, staring at the closed shutters of the Astakhovs' house, sighing and toying agitatedly with the frill of her faded blouse.

The next day she awoke at the first gleam of light, rose quietly so as not to waken the children, washed herself, and took out of the chest a clean skirt and blouse and a big white shawl. She was noticeably agitated and by the way she dressed in sorrowful and austere silence Ilyinichna guessed that she was going to visit Grandad Grishaka's grave.

'Where are you off to?' she asked to confirm her conjecture.

'I'm going to see Grandad,' Natalya murmured without raising her head, afraid of bursting into tears.

She knew how her grandfather had died and how Koshevoi had burned down their house and farm.

'You're not strong enough yet.'

'I'll get there if I rest on the way. Give the children their breakfast, Mother, I may be a long time.'

'Well, I don't know! Why should you stay there so long? You might be unlucky and run into some of those devils, God forgive me. Don't go, Natalya dear!'

'No, I must,' Natalya said with a frown and grasped the door handle.

'But do wait a little. You can't go off hungry like this! Let me bring you some milk?'

'No, Mother, God bless you. I don't want any... I'll eat when I come back.'

Seeing that her daughter-in-law was determined to go, Ilyinichna advised her to take the lower road. 'Keep to the edge of the Don, along by the kitchen gardens. You won't be so much in view.'

The Don was blanketed in mist. The sun had not yet risen, but the poplar-fringed skyline to the east was blazing with a purple dawn and a chilly morning breeze was blowing from under the banked-up clouds.

Natalya stepped over the derelict creeper-covered fence into her home orchard and with her hand pressed to her heart halted beside a fresh mound of earth.

The orchard was overgrown with weeds and stinging nettles. The air smelled of dew-sprinkled burdock, damp soil and mist. A starling with its feathers all ruffled was perched on an old appletree that had withered after the fire. The grave-mound had settled. Blades of grass were shooting up here and there among the bits of dry clay.

Overwhelmed by a flood of memories, Natalya sank silently to her knees and pressed her face to this unfriendly earth that would for ever smell of mortal decay...

An hour later she crept out of the orchard, looked back in anguish for the last time at the place where her youth had bloomed and faded—the charred timbers of the sheds, the fire-scorched ruins of stoves and foundations stood black and sombre in the deserted yard—and walked away quietly down the lane.

* * *

Every day Natalya recovered a little more of her health and strength. Her legs grew stronger, her shoulders plumped out, her figure acquired a healthy fullness. Soon she began helping her mother-in-law with the cooking. While busy over the stove, they had long talks.

One morning Natalya said vexedly, 'When will it all end? I'm sick to death of it!'

'Our men'll soon be back from across the Don, you'll see!' Ilyinichna said confidently.

'What makes you so sure, Mother?'

'I feel it in my heart.'

'I only hope they'll get across safe. God forbid any of them get killed or wounded. Grisha, he's so reckless,' Natalya said with a sigh.

'They'll be all right, I reckon. God is merciful. Our old man promised to come over again and see us, but he must have changed his mind. If he came, you could go back with him, out of harm's way. They're all men from our village on the other side, in the trenches. The other day, when you were still wandering, I went down to the Don at dawn and, as I was drawing water, I heard Anikei's voice booming across the water, "Hullo there, Granny! Greetings from the old man!" '

'Where's Grigory?' Natalya asked guardedly.

'He commands 'em all from his headquarters,' Ilyinichna replied simply.

'Where's that?'

'Vyoshenskaya, I suppose. There's nowhere else.'

Natalya lapsed into a long silence. Ilyinichna glanced up at her and asked anxiously, 'What is it, dear? Why are you crying?'

Natalya pressed her dirty apron to her face and sobbed quietly without replying.

'Don't cry, Natalya, dearie. Tears won't help. God grant we'll see them all again safe and sound. You take care of yourself, don't go out too much or these anti-Christs will see you and get fresh...'

The kitchen grew suddenly darker as a figure at the window blocked the light. Ilyinichna turned with a gasp.

'It's them! The Reds! Natalya! Get into bed quick and pretend you're ill... You never know... Here's some sacking to cover yourself with!'

No sooner had Natalya, trembling with fear, thrown herself on the bed than the latch clicked and a Red Army man, too tall to pass through the doorway without lowering his head, entered the kitchen. The children clung to Ilyinichna's skirt and the old woman, pale-faced, flopped down on a bench by the stove, upsetting a bowl of baked milk.

The Red Army man glanced quickly round the kitchen and said loudly, 'Don't be scared, I won't eat you. Good morning to you!'

Natalya groaned and covered her head with the sack-cloth, Mishatka scowled at the visitor, and then announced joyfully, 'Granny! That's the one who killed our cock! Don't you remember?'

The Red Army man took off his army cap, clicked his tongue, and smiled.

'Spotted me, eh, you young rascal? And still can't forget that cock? Well, missus, this is what I've come

432

about. Could you bake us some bread? We've got the flour.'

'Oh, yes, I could... Why not, I can do that...' Ilyinichna answered hastily, not looking at the visitor and wiping the spilt milk off the bench.

The Red Army man sat down by the door, pulled a pouch out of his pocket and, as he made himself a cigarette, struck up a conversation.

'Will you manage it by tonight?'

'I can do, if you're in a hurry.'

'We're always in a hurry in wartime, Gran. And you mustn't be sore about the cock.'

'Oh, we don't mind!' Ilyinichna responded in fright. 'That's just the child's foolishness... He's bound to say the wrong thing!'

'You're a miserly feller, you are,' the talkative visitor said, smiling at Mishatka good-naturedly. 'Now what are you scowling at me for, like a wolf-cub? Come over here and we'll talk to our heart's content about your cock-a-doodle.'

'Go on, dear!' Ilyinichna whispered, pushing her grandson forward with her knee.

But Mishatka broke away from his grandmother's skirt and tried to escape from the kitchen by sidling towards the door. The Red Army man reached out with a long arm and pulled him back.

'Are you cross with me?'

'No,' Mishatka responded in a whisper.

'Well, that's good! A cock don't mean all that much. Where's your father? Across the Don?'

'Yes.'

'So he's fighting against us, is he?'

Won over by the man's friendly manner, Mishatka spoke out willingly, 'He's in command of all the Cossacks!'

'Oh, that's a whopper, lad!'

'Ask Granny!'

His grandmother, reduced to despair by her grandson's loquacity, could only spread her arms and groan.

'In command of 'em all?' the Red Army man asked again in surprise.

'Well, maybe not all...' Mishatka said with less assurance, discouraged by the desperate looks his grandmother was giving him.

The Red Army man was silent for a time, then with a sidelong glance at Natalya asked, 'Is the young woman ill then?'

433

'She's got typhus,' Ilyinichna replied shortly.

Two other Red Army men carried a sack of flour into the kitchen and set it down by the threshold.

'Get your stove going, missus!' said one of them. 'We'll come for the loaves this evening. And mind you give us our full score or you'll be in trouble!'

'I'll do what I can,' Ilyinichna replied, overjoyed that the newcomers had cut short this dangerous line of talk, and that Mishatka had run out of the kitchen.

One of them asked with a nod at Natalya, 'She got typhus?'

'Yes.'

The Reds chatted quietly among themselves and left the kitchen. Before the last of them turned the corner of the lane, rifle shots rang out from across the Don.

The Red Army men ducked down and ran to a tumbledown stone wall, and took cover behind it, slamming their rifle bolts home as they returned the fire.

Scared out of her wits, Ilyinichna ran into the yard to look for Mishatka. From the wall one of the men shouted, 'Go indoors, Granny! You'll get killed!'

'Our little boy's out in the yard! Mishatka, dear! Where are you, lovey!' the old woman cried with tears in her voice.

She ran out into the middle of the yard and the firing from across the river stopped at once. Evidently the Cossacks on the other side had seen her. As soon as she had gathered Mishatka up in her arms and carried him off into the kitchen, the firing began again and went on until the Red Army men had quitted the Melekhovs' yard.

Talking in whispers to Natalya, Ilyinichna set the dough, but she did not have to bake any loaves.

At noon the crews of the Red machine-gun posts hurriedly abandoned the yards and made their way up the ravines on to the hill, hauling their guns behind them.

The company that had been entrenched on the hill formed up and marched off at a rapid pace along the Hetman's Highway.

A great stillness seemed to spread over the whole Donside. Artillery and machine-guns fell silent. Transports and batteries started moving in endless procession along the roads and grassy tracks from the villages to the highway; infantry and cavalry marched away in columns.

Ilyinichna, who had been watching from the window as a few stragglers climbed the chalky slopes of the hill, wiped her hands on her apron and crossed herself with great feeling.

'God has been merciful, Natalya dear! The Reds are retreating!'

'It couldn't be, Mother! They're only leaving the village to go to their trenches on the hill. They'll be back this evening.'

'What are they running for then? Our men have sent 'em packing! They're retreating, the wretches. They're on the run, the heathens!' Ilyinichna exulted, and started kneading her dough again.

Natalya went out on to the porch and, shielding her eyes with her hand, gazed at the sunlit chalky hill and the scorched brownish slopes running down to the river. Billowing white cloud crests were rising from behind it in the majestic stillness of an approaching storm. The noonday sun was beating down. Susliks were whistling on the common and their quiet sad calls combined strangely with the joyous trilling of the larks. So dear to Natalya's heart was the hush after the roar of gunfire that she stood quite still, drinking in the artless song of the lark, the creak of the well sweep, and the rustle of the wind charged with the bitter scent of wormwood.

It was both bitter and fragrant, this winged steppeland wind from the east. It breathed out the heat of warm black earth, and the intoxicating scents of the grasses wilting under the fierce sun, but already the approach of rain could be felt: a vapid dampness was drifting up from the Don, the swallows were swooping low, nearly touching the ground with their wings, and far away, just beneath the clouds a young steppe eagle was gliding away from the approaching storm.

Natalya walked across the yard. On the crumpled grass by the wall lay glittering piles of spent cartridges. The windows and whitewashed walls of the house had been holed by bullets. At the sight of Natalya one of the surviving chickens squawked and flew up on to the barn.

The caressing stillness did not linger long over the village. The wind sprang up, the open shutters and doors of abandoned houses clattered. A snow-white thunder cloud imperiously covered the sun and floated westward.

Catching her hair as it streamed out in the wind, Natalya went to the outdoor kitchen and again scanned the hill. On the horizon carts and lone riders were trotting away in a lilac haze of dust. 'So it's true: they are leaving!' she decided with relief.

Before she could step into the porch a muffled boom of artillery rolled over from afar and, as if in response, the joyous ringing of bells from the two Vyoshenskaya churches floated across the Don.

Crowds of Cossacks had emerged from the woods on the other side. They were carrying and dragging boats down to the bank and launching them. The oarsmen in the stern paddled skilfully. Some three dozen boats joined in a race for the village.

'Natalya darling! Our men are coming!' Ilyinichna sobbed as she ran out of the kitchen.

Natalya picked up Mishatka and held him high in the air. Her eyes were shining ardently and her voice broke as she panted, 'Look, dear! Look! Your eyes are sharp... Maybe your father's with the Cossacks... Can't you see him? Isn't that him in the first boat? No, no! You're not looking the right way!'

At the pier they met only a much thinner Pantelei. The old man first inquired about the bullocks, the farm and the grain, then shed a tear as he embraced his grandchildren. But when he limped hurriedly into his own yard, his face paled and he went down on his knees, swept his arm across his chest in the sign of the cross, bowed to the east, and for a long time did not raise his grey head from the hot sun-scorched earth.

V

On June 10th the Don Army's three-thousand-strong cavalry group under the command of General Sekretev broke through the Red front with a devastating thrust near Ust-Belokalitvenskaya and advanced along the railway in the direction of Kazanskaya.

Early in the morning two days later, an officers' patrol of the 9th Don Regiment encountered an insurgent outpost near the Don. At the sight of the mounted detachment the insurgents took to the ravines, but the Cossack major in command of the patrol recognised them by their uniforms and, waving a handkerchief tied to his sabre, bellowed, 'Friends!... Don't run, Cossacks!'

The patrol rode up fearlessly to the flank of the ravine. The commander of the insurgent outpost, an elderly grey-haired sergeant-major, stepped out, buttoning up his dew-drenched greatcoat as he walked. Eight officers dismounted and the major went up to the sergeant-major, took off his army cap with its brightly gleaming white cockade, and said, 'Greetings, Cossacks! Let's kiss in accordance with the old Cossack custom!'

He kissed the sergeant-major on both cheeks, wiped his lips and moustache with a handkerchief and, sensing the expectant glances of his companions, asked with a meaningful smile and deliberately stressing each word, 'Well, have you come to your senses? So your own people turned out to be better than the Bolsheviks, did they not?'

'Yes, they did, Your Honour! We've paid for our sins... We've been fighting for three months, waiting and hoping to see you here!'

'Well, it's a good thing you got your ideas straight in the end, late though it was. It's all over now, so let bygones be bygones. What stanitsa are you from?'

'Kazanskaya, Your Honour!'

'Is your unit on the other side of the Don?'

'That's right, Your Honour!'

'Where did the Reds make for?'

'Upstream, I reckon, towards Donetsky.'

'Has your cavalry not crossed over yet?'

'Not yet.'

'Why not?'

'I dunno, Your Honour. We were the first to be sent across.'

'Did they have any artillery here?'

'Two batteries.'

'When did they leave?'

'Last night.'

'You ought to have pursued them! You lackadaisical lot!' the major said reproachfully and went over to his horse for his field bag, notebook and map.

The sergeant-major stood stiffly at attention. A couple of paces away the other Cossacks had gathered in a bunch, staring with feelings of mingled joy and vague anxiety at the officers, their saddles and the thoroughbred but march-thin horses.

The officers, dressed in neat-fitting English tunics with shoulder straps, and broad riding breeches, were stretching their legs beside their horses, glancing sideways at the Cossacks. Not one of them was wearing the makeshift shoulder-straps marked in indelible pencil that had been used in the autumn of 1918. Their boots, saddles, ammunition pouches, field glasses, and the carbines strapped to their saddles were all new and not of Russian manufacture. Only the oldest of them was wearing a long Circassian tunic of fine blue cloth, a Kuban hat made of gold-tinted Bukhara lambskin, and heelless highlanders' boots. He was the first, treading softly, to approach the Cossacks. From his map case he took out a smart-looking packet of cigarettes with a portrait of the King of the Belgians on the lid and offered it round.

'Have a smoke, lads!'

The Cossacks reached greedily for the cigarettes. The other officers came over to them.

'Well, how did you fare under the Bolsheviks?' a cornet with a large head and massive shoulders asked.

'Not so good,' a Cossack dressed in an old homespun coat replied with restraint, pulling greedily at his cigarette and staring at the tall gaiters laced up to the knee encasing the cornet's plump calves.

The Cossack's battered leather slippers barely held together on his feet. The white much-darned woollen stockings into which his wide trousers were tucked were torn and ragged. No wonder he could not take his enchanted gaze off the British boots with their indestructibly thick soles and gleaming brass eyelets. Unable to restrain himself, he innocently expressed his admiration.

'That's a fine pair of boots you've got there!'

But the cornet was in no mood for peaceable conversation. With a malicious challenge in his voice he said, 'You decided to change your foreign equipment for Moscow's bast shoes, so you needn't envy other people's goods now.'

'Ay, we tripped up there. We were in the wrong,' the Cossack replied in some confusion, looking round at his friends for support.

The cornet went on with his mocking rebuke.

'You had as much brains as an ox. An ox always acts like that. First it takes a step, then it stops to think about it. Tripped up, did you! What were you thinking about last autumn, when you left the front undefended! Thought you'd become commissars! Fine defenders of the Fatherland, I must say!'

A young lieutenant whispered quietly in the ear of the irate cornet, 'Now then, that's enough!' The cornet stamped out his cigarette on the ground, spat and swaggered away to the horses.

The major gave him a scribbled note and said something in a low voice.

With surprising agility the burly cornet jumped on to

his horse, swung it round and galloped away westwards.

The Cossacks stood in subdued silence. The major came up to them and, playing on the lower notes of his fruity baritone, asked cheerfully, 'How many versts is it to the village of Varvarinsky?'

'Thirty-five,' several different voices answered.

'Good. Now listen to me, Cossacks. Go and tell your commanders that the mounted units must be sent across without delay. Our officer will go as far as the crossing with you. He will take command of the cavalry. The infantry had better march to Kazanskaya. Do I make myself clear? Well then, as they say, about turn, God be with you, and quick march!'

The Cossacks set off down the hill in a crowd. For about two hundred paces, as if by common consent, they marched in silence, but then the bedraggled Cossack in a homespun coat, the one who had been taunted by the belligerent cornet, shook his head and heaved a regretful sigh.

'So that's our reunion, lads...'

Another Cossack promptly capped the remark.

'Out of the frying pan into the fire,' he commented, and swore with gusto.

VI

As soon as the news of the Red units' hurried retreat became known in Vyoshenskaya, Grigory Melekhov and two mounted regiments swam across the Don, sent out strong patrols, and marched south.

Fighting was going on beyond the Donside hills. The muffled roar of continuous artillery fire seemed to come from underground.

'The Cadets don't grudge their shells, by the sound of it. They're giving 'em rapid fire!' one of the commanders said delightedly as he rode up to Grigory.

Grigory made no reply. He was riding at the head of the column, looking round him attentively. Over the three versts from the Don to the village of Bazki thousands of wagons were still standing where they had been left behind by the insurgents. The forest was strewn with abandoned property—broken chests, chairs, clothes, harness, crockery, sewing-machines, sacks of grain, everything that had been picked up and carted away with all the grudging possessiveness of the husbandman during the retreat to the Don. In places the road was knee-deep in golden wheat. By the roadside lay the swollen stinking carcasses of oxen and horses, horribly disfigured by decay.

'That's how they looked after their things!' Grigory, badly shaken, exclaimed as he bared his head and, trying not to breathe, rode round a mound of rotting grain on which lay the spread-eagled body of an old man in a Cossack cap and a homespun coat stained with blood.

'Grandad looked after his goods a bit too well! The devil must have tempted him to stay on this side,'one of the Cossacks said regretfully.

'Didn't want to leave his wheat behind, I reckon...'

'Get a move on there! What a stink! Hi, there! Get moving,' came indignant shouts from the rear of the column.

The squadron broke into a trot. The talk died away. Only the clatter of hundreds of hooves and the clinking of well-fitting Cossack equipment sounded harmoniously through the forest.

...The fighting was raging not far from the Listnitsky estate. Bunches of Red Army men were running down the dry valley away from Yagodnoye. Shrapnel was bursting over their heads and machine-guns were hammering at their backs, and from the flank a Kalmyk Regiment in attack formation was sweeping down the hill to cut off their retreat.

Grigory arrived with his regiments when the battle was over. The two Red Army companies covering the withdrawal over the Vyoshenskaya Pass of miscellaneous units and transports of the 14th Division were routed and destroyed by the 3rd Kalmyk Regiment. On the hill above Yagodnoye Grigory handed over command to Yermakov and said, 'They've managed here without us. Go and link up with them and I'll drop in at the estate for a minute.'

'Why do you have to do that?' Yermakov asked.

'Well, how shall I put it? I worked here as a young man. I just feel like looking round the old places...'

Grigory called Prokhor and turned his horse towards Yagodnoye. After riding about half a verst he saw a white flag that one of the Cossacks had had the forethought to bring along break over the leading squadron and flap in the wind.

'Looks as if they were surrendering!' Grigory thought with a stab of anxiety and unconscious regret as he watched the column riding slowly, almost unwillingly into the valley, and a mounted group of Sekretev's men riding to meet them straight across the young green corn.

Sadness and desolation breathed over Grigory when he rode through the broken gate into the overgrown yard of the estate. Yagodnoye was unrecognisable. Everything bore the grim mark of neglect and decay. The house had lost all its former smartness and seemed to have sunk into the ground. The long-unpainted roof was spotted with yellow rust, broken drainpipes were lying by the porch. Shutters hung crookedly, the wind whistled through the broken windowpanes, and from inside came the dank, fusty smell of unlived-in rooms.

The eastern corner of the house and the porch had been demolished by a shell from a three-inch gun. The crown of a maple that had been knocked down by the shell was poking through the Venetian window of the corridor. It had been left to lie there with its trunk resting on a pile of bricks that had tumbled out of the foundation. Wild hops were creeping and curling over its withered branches, whimsically tangling round the surviving panes and reaching up to the eaves.

Time and rough weather had done their work. The outbuildings were derelict and looked as though they had not felt the touch of human hands for many years. One of the stone walls of the stable had been undermined by the spring floods and collapsed, the roof of the coachhouse had been ripped off by a storm and only a few wisps of half-rotten thatch remained on the deathly white joists and rafters.

Three borzoi hounds that had run wild were lying on the steps. At the sight of human beings they sprang up and with low growls took refuge in the porch. Grigory rode up to the open window of the servants' quarters, leaned out of his saddle and asked loudly, 'Is there anyone alive in there?'

For some time the lodge was silent, but then a quavering voice answered, 'Wait a minute, for love of Christ! I'll be out in a minute.'

A much aged Lukerya padded out on to the steps barefooted. Screwing up her eyes in the sunshine, she stared at Grigory.

'Don't you recognise me, Auntie Lukerya?' Grigory asked dismounting.

Only then did something stir in Lukerya's pock-marked face and stolid indifference gave way to great emotion. She burst into tears and for a long time could not utter a word.

Grigory tethered his horse and waited patiently.

'The terrors I've been through! May you never know the like...' Lukerya began to whimper, wiping her cheeks with a dirty linen apron. 'I thought it was them had come back again... Oh, Grisha dear, the things that happened here... You couldn't describe it!... I'm the only one left...'

'What about Grandad Sashka, where's he? Did he retreat with the masters?'

'If he had, he might have been alive still.'

'Don't say he's dead?'

'They killed him... He's been lying in the cellar for three days... He ought to be buried, but I'm not well myself... I only just managed to get up... And besides I'm scared to death of going down there, with him a corpse...'

'Why did they kill him?' Grigory asked huskily, not raising his eyes.

'Because of the mare... Our masters went off in a hurry, you see. They only took their capital and left nearly all the property for me to look after.' Lukerya's voice dropped to a whisper. 'And I've kept it all safe, to the last bit of thread. It's all buried still. And as for the horses, they only took three Orlov stallions and left the rest behind with Grandad Sashka. When the uprising started, though, both the Cossacks and the Reds came and took what they liked. Mebbe you remember the black stallion Whirlwind. The Reds took him in early spring. They could hardly get a saddle on him. He'd never been a saddle horse before, you see. But they didn't get much riding out of him. The Karginskaya Cossacks rode by a week later and told us. Up on the hill there they'd run into the Reds and started shooting. But just then a daft young filly the Cossacks had with 'em happened to give the call. Off Whirlwind went, hot speed to the mare, and the rider that had taken him couldn't hold him back. He saw his horse had got the better of him, so he tried to jump off at full gallop. But his foot caught in the stirrup. And Whirlwind dragged him right into the Cossacks' arms.'

'Clever horse!' Prokhor exclaimed admiringly.

'Now there's a Karginskaya cornet riding that stallion,' Lukerya went on steadily with her tale. 'He's promised to bring Whirlwind straight back to the stable as soon as the master returns. By and by they took all the rest of our horses. All we had left was the mare Strelka, the one by Primer out of Suzhenaya. A racer she was, and in foal, so no one had touched her. Not long ago she foaled and Grandad Sashka was that fond of the foal, that fond of it he was—I just can't tell you! He nursed it in his arms and fed it with milk from a horn, and gave it some special drink of herbs to make its legs stronger. And that's how the trouble came about... The day before yesterday three horsemen rode up just before evening. Grandad was out in the orchard, mowing some grass. They start shouting at him, "Come over here, you old so-and-so!" He dropped his scythe, came up and greeted them. But they didn't even look at him, just drank their milk and asked, "Got any horses?" So he says, "There's one but she's no use for your fighting job; she's a mare and what's more she's got a sucking foal." And the fiercest one, how he shouts, "That's none of your business! Bring out this mare, you old devil! My horse has back sores, I've got to change it." Grandad Sashka, he ought to have done as he was told and not stuck out for that mare, but you know yourself, a real character he was... You remember, I'm sure?'

'You mean he didn't let 'em take her?' Prokhor interrupted.

'How could he stop them? All he said was, "We had a lot o' horsemen here, took all our horses, they did, but they all showed pity for this one. And now you come here..." And that did it. "Ah, you lackey," they shouted, "so you're keeping it for your master, are you!" And they pushed him away... One of 'em led out the mare and started saddling it and the foal runs up to its mother to suck. Grandad began to plead, "Have mercy, don't take her! What'll we do with the foal?" And one of 'em says, "I'll show you what!" And he drove it away from its mother, slung his gun off his shoulder and shot the poor thing. All in tears I was then, but I ran over and begged them and tried to get Grandad out of harm's way. But he took one look at the foal and his beard started shaking and he went as white as a sheet and says, "If that's how it is, then shoot me, too, you son-of-a-bitch!" And he threw himself at them and hung on to the mare, wouldn't let 'em saddle her. So they got angry and shot him too. I just went out of my mind when they did it... And now I can't think what to do with him. He ought to have a coffin, but is that a woman's work?'

'Give me two spades and a cloth,' Grigory said.

'Are you going to do it?' Prokhor asked.

'Yes.'

'You don't want to go to all that trouble, Grigory Panteleyevich! Let me go and get some Cossacks. They'll make a coffin for him and dig him a proper grave...'

Obviously Prokhor didn't want to bother with burying an old man he had never known, but Grigóry flatly declined his suggestion.

'We'll dig the grave ourselves and bury him. He was a good old man. Go into the orchard and wait by the pond while I have a look at him.'

Under the old branchy poplar beside the weed-covered pond, where he had buried Grigory and Aksinya's little daughter, Grandad Sashka found his own last refuge. They laid to rest his lean body wrapped in a clean piece of sacking that smelled of hops, and covered it with earth. Beside the little grave mound there rose another, neatly stamped down and gleaming festively with fresh, damp loam.

Saddened by memories, Grigory lay down on the grass not far from this small cemetery that was so dear to his heart and gazed up at the majestic blue sky above him. Somewhere up there, in those boundless upper regions, the winds roamed free and the cold sunlit clouds floated by, but on this earth, which had just taken unto itself Grandad Sashka, the merry horseman and drunkard, life was still seething furiously. In the steppe, which had surged in a green flood to the very edge of the orchard, and in the tangle of wild hemp along the fences of the old threshing floor, the sonorous mating cries of the quails sounded ceaselessly, the susliks whistled, the bumble-bees buzzed, the wind-fondled grass rustled, the larks sang in the shimmering haze and, asserting the majesty of man in nature, from somewhere far away down the valley came the persistent angry mutter of a machine-gun.

VII

General Sekretev, who arrived in Vyoshenskaya with his staff and a squadron of Cossacks as his personal escort, was given a civic welcome with the traditional gifts of bread and salt and ringing of church bells. All day the bells of both churches resounded as if at Easter. Cossacks from the Lower Don rode through the streets on Don stallions, lean to the bone after their long march. Their blue shoulder-straps gleamed challengingly on their shoulders. The square outside the merchant's house where the general had his quarters was crowded with orderlies. They stood around, chewing sunflower seeds and spitting out the husks, and chatting to the local girls who came strolling by in their best dresses.

At noon three mounted Kalmyks marched about fifteen Red Army prisoners up to the general's quarters. They were followed by two horses pulling a wagon loaded with wind instruments. The Red Army men were unusually dressed, in grey cloth trousers and tunics of the same material with red piping on the cuffs. One of the Kalmyks, an elderly man, rode up to the orderlies lounging by the gate and tucked his clay pipe into his pocket.

'Our men Red trumpeters brought to you. You understand?'

'Why shouldn't I understand?' a fat-faced orderly responded lazily, spitting out a husk on to the Kalmyk's dusty boots.

'Then go see about prisoners. Fat face from big eating talk stupid!'

'Now then! I'll give you "talk stupid", you sheep's tail!' the orderly retorted offendedly, but went in to report the prisoners' arrival.

A corpulent major in a brown tightly belted beshmet emerged from the gate. Planting his plump legs wide apart and his hands on his hips in a picturesque pose, he surveyed the bunch of prisoners and boomed, 'So you entertained the commissars with music, did you, you Tambov trash! Where did those grey uniforms come from? Off the Germans?'

'No, sir,' a Red Army man standing in front of the others replied blinking rapidly. 'This uniform was made for our bandsmen's company back in the time of Kerensky, before the June offensive... We've been wearing it ever since.'

'Have you, though? Talk back, would you, you scum?' The major pushed back his flat round cap, exposing a still unhealed purple scar on his shaven head, and swung round on his high but worn-down heels to face the Kalmyk. 'What did you bring 'em here for, you squinting heathen? What the devil for? Couldn't you have rubbed them out on the way?'

The Kalmyk imperceptibly drew himself up, brought his bandy legs together smartly and, without dropping his hand from the peak of his army cap, replied, 'Squadron commander, he order must drive them here.'

'Order must drive them here, did he?' the dandified major mimicked, curling his thin lips, and with his broad buttocks wobbling waddled forward to inspect the prisoners with the care and thoroughness of a dealer about to buy horses.

The orderlies sniggered. The faces of the Kalmyk escort remained as impassive as ever.

'Open the gate! March 'em into the yard!' the major commanded.

The Red Army men and the wagonload of carelessly piled instruments halted in front of the porch.

'Who's the bandmaster?' the major asked, lighting a cigarette.

'We haven't got one', several voices replied.

'Where is he? Did he get away?'

'No, he was killed.'

'Good riddance then. We'll manage without him. Now, then sort out those instruments!'

The Red Army men went to the wagon. Amid the incessant clanging of bells, the brassy tones of trumpets sounded in the yard.

'Get ready! Now let's have "God Save the Tsar".'

The musicians exchanged silent glances. No one played. For a minute there was an awkward silence, then one of them, with no boots but with his feet and legs neatly wrapped in puttees, said, staring at the ground, 'None of us know the old anthem...'

'None of you? How interesting... Hi there! Half a platoon of orderlies, with rifles!'

The major tapped his foot, as though beating time to inaudible music. From the corridor of the house came the clatter of the orderlies forming up with their carbines. Sparrows were twittering in the dense locust bushes by the fence. The yard smelled oppressively of hot iron roofs and pungent human sweat. The major stepped back into the shade and then the bootless musician looked wistfully at his comrades and said quietly, 'Your Excellency! All of us here are young bandsmen. We've never had to play the old pieces... It's been mostly revolutionary marches... Your Excellency...'

The major toyed absently with the tip of his silver-embossed belt and said nothing.

446

The orderlies formed up by the porch and waited for orders. From the rear an elderly bandsman with a wall eye pushed his way hastily through the bunch of prisoners and, clearing his throat, requested, 'Allow me? I can play it.' And without waiting for permission, put his sun-heated bassoon to his trembling lips.

The nasal dreary sounds that floated up over the big yard of the merchant's house brought an angry frown to the major's face. He cut the air with his hand and shouted, 'Stop that caterwauling! You sound as if you're pulling a beggar by his balls! D'you call that music?'

The smiling faces of staff officers and adjutants appeared at the windows.

'Tell them to play a funeral march!' a young lieutenant, leaning head and shoulders out of the window, called in a youthful tenor voice.

The overpowering clangour of the bells ceased for a minute and, twitching his eyebrows, the major asked insidiously, 'You can play the *Internationale*, can't you? Come on then! Don't be scared! I give you the order!'

And in the sudden stillness of that sultry noon the protesting notes of the *Internationale* blared forth in majestic harmony, like a battle call.

The major stood like a bull at a fence, head lowered, feet planted wide apart. He stood and listened. His muscular neck and the bluish whites of his eyes gradually swelled with blood.

'Stop!' he bawled furiously.

The band stopped playing at once, all except a belated French horn, and its passionate unfinished plea lingered long in the sultry air.

The bandsmen licked their parched lips and wiped them with sleeves and dirty hands. Their faces were tired and indifferent. Only one let a treacherous tear run down his dusty cheek, leaving a damp trail.

Meanwhile General Sekretev had been dining with the family of a fellow officer he had known since the days of the Russo-Japanese war. Supported by a tipsy adjutant, he appeared on the square. The heat and the home-distilled liquor had gone to his head. At the corner opposite the brick building of the grammar school, the befuddled general tripped and fell on his face on the hot sand. The embarrassed adjutant tried in vain to lift him. Helpers from the nearby crowd hastened to his assistance. With the greatest respect two aged Cossacks lifted the general a little by the arms, and he was at once sick in public. But between his vomitings he went on shouting and shaking his fists. Somehow he was placated and escorted to his quarters.

The Cossacks who had witnessed the scene from a distance watched him go, muttering amongst themselves.

'He's cooked! Can't hold his liquor, though he is a general.'

'Liquor don't have no regard for ranks and medals.'

'He shouldn't have downed everything that was set before him.'

'Ah, kinsman, not everyone can stand the temptation! A drunkard will get sloshed and swear never to touch it again... But you know the saying: the pig promised never to eat another scrap, and the next thing it sees is two scraps lying about.'

'That's just it! Send those kids away. Look at the young brats staring as if they'd never seen a drunk before.'

...The bell-ringing and the drinking went on till nightfall. And that evening, in a house that had been converted into an officers' club the insurgent command gave a banquet for the new arrivals.

The tall, well set-up Sekretev—a Cossack of ancient lineage, born in one of the villages of Krasnokutskaya stanitsa—was a devoted connoisseur of horses, a superb rider, and a daring cavalry general. But he was no orator. The speech he made at the banquet was full of drunken bragging and ended with some unambiguous reproaches and threats addressed to the Cossacks of the Upper Don.

Grigory, who was present at the banquet, listened to Sekretev's speech with concentrated and angry attention. The general had not had time to sober up and leaned on the table, supporting himself with the fingers of one hand and spilling the strong-smelling home-brew from the glass he held in the other; he also leaned too heavily on every phrase.

'...No, it's not we who ought to thank you, but you who must thank us for our help! Yes, you! And that must be stated with the utmost firmness. But for us, the Reds would have annihilated you. You know that perfectly well yourselves. And we would have smashed those swine even without you. We are smashing 'em and we shall go on smashing 'em until we've cleaned up the whole of Russia. Last autumn you abandoned the front and let the Bolsheviks on to Cossack soil... You wanted to live in peace with them, but it didn't work!

448

So then you rebelled to save your property and your lives. To put it bluntly—to save your own and your bullocks' hides. Today I recall the past not in order to reproach you for your past sins... I don't want to offend you. But it never does any harm to establish the truth. We have forgiven your betrayal. As brothers, we came to your assistance in your hour of need. But your shameful past must be redeemed in the future. Is that clear, gentlemen? You must redeem it by your exploits and irreproachable service to the quiet Don! Is that clear?'

'Well, here's to redemption!' addressing no one in particular and smiling faintly said an elderly Cossack lieutenant-colonel who was sitting opposite Grigory and, without waiting for anyone to join him, drank first.

He had a courageous, slightly pockmarked face and mocking brown eyes. During Sekretev's speech, his lips had more than once curled into a vaguely derisive smile and his eyes had darkened until they seemed quite black. Grigory had noticed that he was on familiar terms with Sekretev and talked freely to him, while remaining deliberately cold and aloof with the other officers. He was the only guest at the banquet who wore khaki-coloured shoulder straps sewn into the shoulders of his khaki tunic and a Kornilov chevron on his sleeve. He must be an instructor of some kind, probably one of the Volunteers, Grigory surmised. The lieutenant-colonel drank like a fish without eating, but showed no sign of getting drunk, except that he occasionally let out his broad English leather belt.

'Who's that one opposite me, with the pockmarks on his face?' Grigory whispered to Bogatiryov, who was sitting beside him.

'The devil knows,' Bogatiryov shrugged tipsily.

Kudinov had not spared the home-brew for his guests. Some pure alcohol had also appeared on the table. Sekretev finished his speech with an effort, unbuttoned his field tunic, and sat down heavily. A young lieutenant with a distinctly Mongolian face leaned over and whispered something.

'To the devil!' Sekretev responded, turning purple, and gulped down a glass of pure alcohol that Kudinov had obligingly poured for him.

'And who's that one with the squinting eyes? His adjutant?' Grigory asked Bogatiryov.

Covering his mouth with his hand, the latter replied, 'No, that's his adopted son. During the Japanese war he brought him back from Manchuria when he was still a boy. He brought him up and sent him to the military college. The little Chink seems to have made good. He's a daring devil! Yesterday at Makeyevka he captured the Reds' treasury box. Walked off with a couple of million. Look, he's got wads of it sticking out of all his pockets. Lucky bastard! What a haul! Here, have something to drink! What are you staring at them for?'

The answering speech was made by Kudinov, but by now hardly anyone was listening. The banquet was turning into a carousal. Sekretev had thrown off his tunic and was sitting in nothing but a vest. His close-shaven head was gleaming with sweat and the immaculately clean vest showed up his purple face and olive-brown sunburnt neck. Kudinov said something to him in a low voice, but without looking at him Sekretev went on stubbornly repeating, 'Oh no, pardon me! Pardon me! We trust you, but only so far... Your treachery will not soon be forgotten. And those who went over to the Reds last autumn had better get that into their heads!'

'Then we'll serve you only so far,' Grigory reflected with cold fury as the drink went to his head, and he rose to his feet.

Without putting on his cap, he went out on to the porch and with a feeling of relief gulped the fresh night air into his lungs.

Down by the Don frogs were croaking and water beetles humming sullenly, as if before rain. Water-hens were calling mournfully to one another on the sandbar. Far away in the watermeadows a foal that had lost its mother was whinnying piteously. 'It was bitter need that brought us together or we wouldn't have touched you with a barge pole. The rotten bastard! Showing off like a toy soldier, poking his reproaches at us, and in a week or two he'll be riding roughshod over us... That's what we've come to. We're stuck whichever way we turn. And I knew it all along... It was bound to work out this way. The Cossacks will soon jib at this! They've got out of the habit of saluting and standing to attention in front of "Your Honours",' Grigory thought as he walked down the steps and groped his way to the sidegate.

The drink had affected him too. His head was spinning and he moved ponderously. As he left the gate, he swayed and clamped his cap on his head, then staggered off along the street.

Outside the house of Aksinya's aunt he stopped and thought for a minute, then strode resolutely towards the porch. The door was not locked. Grigory entered the front room without knocking and found himself face to face with Stepan Astakhov, who was sitting at the table. Aksinya's aunt was pottering at the stove. An unfinished bottle of home-brew stood on the clean tablecloth beside a plate of smoked fish, cut into pink slices.

Stepan had just emptied a glass and was apparently about to take a snack, but at the sight of Grigory he pushed his plate away and leaned back against the wall.

Drunk though he was, Grigory noticed the deathly pallor that spread over Stepan's face and the wolfish glare in his eyes. He overcame his astonishment sufficiently to utter a husky greeting.

'Praise be,' the mistress of the house responded in fright. Obviously she knew about her niece's relationship with Grigory and dreaded the outcome of this chance encounter between husband and lover.

Stepan silently stroked his moustache with his left hand, his burning eyes fixed on Grigory.

Grigory stood with his feet planted wide apart on the threshold and, smiling wryly, said, 'Well, I just dropped in to see you... Excuse me.'

Stepan said nothing. The awkward silence lasted until the mistress of the house ventured to invite Grigory in.

'Come in and sit down.'

Now Grigory had nothing to hide. His appearance at Aksinya's lodgings had told Stepan everything. Grigory came straight to the point, 'Where's your wife?'

'So you ... came to see her?' Stepan asked quietly but distinctly and his eyelashes trembled slightly as he closed his eyes.

'Yes,' Grigory confessed.

Anything could be expected from Stepan at that moment and, growing suddenly sober, Grigory prepared to defend himself. But Stepan opened his eyes (the fire that had blazed there so recently had died) and said, 'I sent her for some vodka. She'll be back in a minute. Sit down and wait.'

He even rose, tall and well built, and offered Grigory a chair; without looking at the mistress of the house, he asked her to bring them a clean glass and said to Grigory, 'Will you have a drink?'

'All right, a small one.'

'Well, sit down then.'

451

Grigory seated himself at the table... Stepan filled their glasses evenly with what was left in the bottle and raised his strangely misted eyes.

'To all that's good!'

'Your good health!'

They clinked glasses and drank. For a time neither of them spoke. The mistress, as nimble as a mouse, gave the guest a plate and a fork with a chipped handle.

'Take some fish! It's only a little salted.'

'Thank you kindly.'

'Put some on your plate, tuck in!' the woman insisted more cheerfully.

She was delighted that the whole thing had passed off so well, without a fight, without broken crockery, without anything coming out in public. The kind of talk that had promised trouble was over. The husband was sitting peacefully at table with his wife's boy-friend. Now they were eating in silence and not looking at each other. With some forethought she took a clean towel out of the chest and brought Grigory and Stepan together, as it were, by spreading it so that the ends were in both their laps.

'Why aren't you in the squadron?' Grigory asked, picking the bones of a small bream.

'I came to see her too,' Stepan replied after a pause, and it was hard to tell by his tone whether he was serious or ironic.

'The squadron's all at home, I suppose?'

'They're all having a good time in the village. Well, shall we finish it?'

'All right then.'

'Good health!'

'For all the best!'

The latch of the front door clicked. Now quite sober, Grigory glanced up at Stepan and noticed a fresh wave of pallor sweep over his face.

Aksinya with her head muffled in a shawl came up to the table without recognising Grigory but a sidelong glance brought horror flooding into her dark dilated eyes. She gasped for breath and just managed to say, 'Hullo, Grigory Panteleyevich!'

Stepan's big knotted hands, which had been lying on the table, suddenly began to shake. Grigory noticed them and bowed to Aksinya without saying a word.

As she placed two bottles of liquor on the table, Aksinya gave Grigory another quick glance, full of alarm and hidden joy, then turned and withdrew to a dark corner of the room, sat down on the chest and adjusted her hair with trembling hands. Overcoming his agitation, Stepan unbuttoned the collar of his shirt, filled the glasses and turned to face his wife.

'Take a glass and sit down at the table.'

'I don't want any.'

'Come and sit down!'

'But I don't drink, Stepan!'

'How many times do I have to ask you?' Stepan's voice shook.

'Come and sit down, neighbour!' Grigory smiled encouragingly.

She glanced at him imploringly and walked quickly to the cupboard. A saucer fell off the shelf and broke with a clatter.

'Oh, what a pity!' her aunt spread her arms in dismay.

Aksinya silently picked up the pieces.

Stepan poured her a full glass and again his eyes blazed with misery and hatred.

'Well, let's drink...' he began and broke off.

In the silence that followed as Aksinya sat down at the table her laboured breathing could be heard quite distinctly.

'...Let's drink, wife, to a long parting. What is it, don't you want to? Won't you drink?'

'But you know...'

'Now I know everything... Well, not to a parting then! To the health of our dear guest, Grigory Panteleyevich.'

'I'll drink to his health,' Aksinya said in a ringing voice and drank the glass in one breath.

'Oh, you headstrong creature!' her aunt whispered and ran out into the kitchen.

She crouched in a corner with her hands to her chest, expecting at any moment to hear the crash of an overturned table, the deafening roar of a gun... But dead silence reigned in the front room. The only sound was of the flies disturbed by the light buzzing under the ceiling and, from outside, the midnight crowing of the local roosters.

VIII

June nights on the Don are dark. In the oppressive stillness golden flashes of summer lighting flare across

453

the slate-black sky and falling stars are reflected in the fast-flowing waters. From the steppe a dry, warm wind carries the honey scents of flowering thyme into the villages, but in the water-meadows the air is dank with the smells of lush grass and silt, the corncrakes cry ceaselessly, and the riverside woods are all veiled in a silver brocade of mist.

Prokhor awoke at midnight.

'Hasn't my boss come back yet?' he asked his host.

'No. He's celebrating with the generals.'

'They're knocking back the vodka there, I bet,' Prokhor sighed enviously and with a yawn began to pull on his clothes.

'Where're you off to?'

'I'll go and tend the horses. Grigory Panteleyevich said we'd be leaving for Tatarsky at dawn. We'll spend the day there, then we'll have to catch up with our unit.'

'It's a long time yet till dawn. Why don't you sleep on?'

'I can see you were never in the army, grandad!' Prokhor replied disapprovingly. 'In our job, if you don't look after your horses and keep 'em fed and watered proper, you may not stay alive. You can't gallop far on a skinny nag, can you? The better the animal under you, the faster you can get away from the enemy. As for me, I've no taste for chasing them, but if we're in a tight corner I'm the first to make a dash for it! How many years now have I been ducking bullets—I'm fed up with it! Light the lamp, grandad, I can't find my footcloths. Ah, thank ye kindly! Ay, it's our Grigory Panteleyevich who's been collecting medals and ranks, sticking his neck out, but I'm not such a fool, I don't need none of that... What's that now? Here he comes and I bet he's sloshed.'

There was a quiet knock at the door.

'Come in!' Prokhor shouted.

A strange Cossack with a junior sergeant's stripes and a cockade in his cap opened the door.

'I'm an orderly from General Sekretev's headquarters. May I see His Honour *Gospodin* Melekhov?' he asked, saluting and standing at attention on the threshold.

'He's not here,' Prokhor replied, astonished by the orderly's splendid bearing and manner of address. 'Don't stand so stiff, man. When I was young I was a fool like you. I'm his orderly. What's your business here?'

'General Sekretev ordered me to fetch *Gospodin*

Melekhov. His presence is urgently requested at the officers' assembly rooms.'

'He was heading that way this evening.'

'Yes, he was there, but later on he left and went home.'

Prokhor gave a long whistle and winked at his host, who was sitting on the bed.

'Hear that, grandad? So he's slipped away to his lady friend... Well, you'd better go, soldier, and I'll scout around and dish him up for you, all warm and ready.'

Having instructed the old man to water and feed the horses, Prokhor set off to the house of Aksinya's aunt.

Impenetrable darkness wrapped the sleeping stanitsa. Nightingales were jugging with all their might in the woods on the other side of the Don. Unhurriedly Prokhor walked up to the little house, entered the porch and had just grasped the door handle, when he heard Stepan's deep voice. 'Now I'm in a nice mess,' Prokhor told himself. 'They'll ask me why I came. And I won't know what to say. Still, never mind, worse things have happened to me! I'll tell 'em I came to buy some homebrew. I'll say the neighbours sent me here.'

Plucking up courage, he entered the front room—and his jaw dropped in astonishment. Grigory and Astakhov were sitting together at the same table, sipping a cloudy green liquor like the best of pals.

Stepan glanced at Prokhor and, forcing a smile, said, 'What are you standing there for with your mouth open? Can't you say hullo? Or have you seen a ghost?'

'Feels like it...' the dumbfounded Prokhor mumbled, shifting from one foot to another.

'Well, don't be scared, come in and sit down,' Stepan invited him.

'I've no time for sitting down... I've come for you, Grigory Panteleyevich. Orders are General Sekretev wants to see you right now.'

Even before Prokhor's arrival, Grigory had made several attempts to leave. He had pushed his glass away and stood up, then sat down again, fearing that Stepan would take his departure as an open admission of cowardice. Pride would not allow him to leave the field to Stepan. He went on drinking but the liquor no longer had any effect on him. Soberly assessing the ambiguity of his position, he waited for something to cut the knot. For a second, when Aksinya had drunk his health, he had thought Stepan was going to hit his wife. But he was mistaken. Stepan raised his hand, drew his calloused palm over his sunburnt forehead, and after a short silence, looking at Aksinya with admiration, said, 'Good for you, wife! That's the spirit!'

Then Prokhor came in.

After a moment's thought, Grigory decided not to go, so that Stepan would have a chance to speak his mind.

'Go and tell 'em you couldn't find me. Understand?' he said to Prokhor.

'I understood all right. But you ought to go yourself, Grigory Panteleyevich.'

'That's none of your business! Off with you!'

Prokhor turned towards the door, but unexpectedly Aksinya intervened. Without looking at Grigory, she said drily, 'You'd better go too, Grigory Panteleyevich! Thank you for calling, for spending your time with us... But it's getting late, past second cockcrow. It'll soon be light and Stepan and me, we've got to start for home at dawn... You've had enough to drink. Have done now!'

Stepan made no effort to detain him, and Grigory rose. When he said goodbye, Stepan kept Grigory's hand in his own cold rough hand, as if he wanted to say something at the last moment; but he said nothing, followed Grigory silently to the door with his eyes, then reached unhurriedly for the unfinished bottle.

As soon as he stepped outside, Grigory was overcome by a terrible weariness. He dragged himself as far as the first crossroads, then turned to Prokhor, who was following close behind him.

'Go saddle up the horses and bring them here. I can't walk any further.'

'Should I report that you're on your way?'

'No.'

'Well, wait here, I won't be a minute!'

And Prokhor, who always believed in taking things easy, set off at the double.

Grigory sat down by the fence and lighted a cigarette. As he went over the encounter with Stepan in his mind, he thought indifferently, 'Well, now he knows. What's it matter as long as he doesn't get rough with Aksinya?' Then overcome by fatigue and the tension he had endured, he lay down and dozed off.

Prokhor soon rode up with the horses.

They crossed the Don on the ferry, then set off at a brisk trot.

They rode into Tatarsky at dawn. At the gate of his

yard Grigory dismounted and tossed the reins to Prokhor. With a sudden burning impatience he strode towards the house.

Natalya had for some reason come out into the porch. She was only half dressed. At the sight of Grigory her eyes blazed with such joy that his heart leapt and his eyes grew instantly and unexpectedly moist. Silently Natalya embraced her one and only beloved, cleaving to him with her whole body, and by the quivering of her shoulders Grigory could tell that she was crying.

He went into the house, kissed the old folk and the children sleeping in the front room, and stood still in the middle of the kitchen.

'Well, how did you get on under the Reds? Are you all safe and well?' he asked, breathless with emotion.

'Praise the Lord, son. We've been real frightened, but they didn't treat us too bad,' Ilyinichna hastened to reply, and with a sidelong glance at the weeping Natalya rebuked her sternly, 'You ought to be overjoyed and you're bawling, you fool! Don't stand there doing nothing! Bring in some wood to get the stove going.'

While she and Natalya hurriedly cooked breakfast, Pantelei brought his son a clean towel and offered to pour the water for him. 'I'll pour and you have a wash. It'll freshen you up. You do reek of vodka. Had a good drink yesterday, did you, to celebrate the joyful event?'

'Something like that. Only we don't know yet whether it's joyful or sad.'

'How do you mean?' the old man was surprised beyond belief.

'Sekretev's mighty sore with us.'

'Well, there's no harm in that. D'you mean you were drinking together?'

'Yes, of course.'

'Just think of that! What an honour for you, Grigory! Sitting at the same table with a real general! Just think!' And gazing rapturously at his son, he clicked his tongue in admiration.

Grigory smiled. He certainly did not share the old man's innocent enthusiasm.

As he asked staidly about their property and animals and how much grain had been lost, Grigory noticed that his father was not as interested in talk of the farm as he had been of old. There was something more important weighing on the old man's mind.

He was not long in coming out with it.

'How'll it be now, Grisha? Have we got to serve again?'

'Who's "we"?'

'I mean us, old men. Me, for example.'

'No one knows that yet.'

'So we'll have to be ready?'

'You can stay at home.'

'You don't say so!' Pantelei burst out joyfully, and went stomping about the kitchen in his excitement.

'Sit down, you lame devil! Don't spread dirt all over the house with your clodhoppers! Look at him, capering about like a silly puppy!' Ilyinichna scolded.

But the old man took no notice of the rebuke. He limped to and fro several times between the table and the stove, smiling and rubbing his hands. But then he was struck by doubt.

'Can ye give me my release?'

'Of course, I can.'

'Will you put it on paper?'

'Sure I will.'

The old man hesitated, then asked 'What kind of paper though?... It won't have a stamp on it, will it? Or mebbe you've got a stamp handy?'

'It'll do all right without a stamp!' Grigory said smiling.

'Well, then, there's no more to be said!' the old man cheered up again. 'Thank you, son. When do you expect to start out yourself?'

'Tomorrow.'

'Have your troops gone on ahead? To Ust-Medveditsa?'

'Yes. And you needn't worry, Dad. All the old men will soon be allowed to go home. You've done your bit.'

'God grant it!' Pantelei crossed himself, and seemed to be finally reassured.

By this time the children were awake. Grigory picked them up in his arms and sat them on his knees and smiling and kissing them in turn, listened for a long time to their merry chatter.

How wonderful their hair smelled! Of sun, grass, a warm pillow and something else infinitely dear. And they themselves—this flesh of his flesh—were like tiny steppe-land birds. How clumsy their father's big dark hands looked as he held them close. And how alien to this peaceful scene was he himself, a horseman parted from his horse for a mere day, still steeped in the stench of soldiery and horse sweat, the bitter odour of long marches and leather equipment.

Tears clouded Grigory's eyes and his lips trembled under his moustache... Two or three times he failed to answer his father's questions, and came to the table only when Natalya touched the sleeve of his tunic.

No, Grigory was by no means the man he once had been! Never particularly sensitive he had seldom cried even as a child. But here he was in tears, with his heart beating hard and fast, and the feeling that a little soundless bell was ringing in his throat. But perhaps it was all because he had drunk a lot the night before and not slept at all.

Darya came in after driving the cows out to pasture. She presented her smiling lips to Grigory and closed her eyes as he jokingly twirled his moustache and brought his face nearer to hers. Grigory saw her lashes quivering as if from the wind and for a moment felt the spicy scent of pomade from her unfadingly fresh cheeks.

Yes, Darya was the same as ever. No grief, it seemed, had the power to break her or even bow her spirit. She lived on earth like a willow wand—supple, beautiful, always available.

'Still blooming?' Grigory asked.

'Like the roadside henbane!' Darya narrowed her radiant eyes, gave him a dazzling smile, and at once went over to the mirror to pat the hair that had fallen out from under her kerchief.

That was Darya and nothing, it seemed, would change her. Petro's death had only spurred her on. As soon as she recovered from her grief, she had grown even more greedy for life and attentive to her appearance.

Dunyashka, who had been sleeping in the barn, was also awakened. After saying their prayers, the whole family sat down to table.

'How you've aged, brother!' Dunyashka said regretfully. 'You're as grey as a wolf.'

Grigory looked at her across the table silently and without smiling, then said, 'That's as it should be... Time for me to grow old and for you to find a husband... But I'll tell you this: forget Mishka Koshevoi and never think of him again. If I ever hear you're still pining for him—I'll pull you apart like a frog! Understand?'

Dunyashka blazed poppy red and stared at Grigory through tears.

He kept his angry gaze upon her, and everything in that embittered face—in the bared teeth under the moustache, in the narrowed eyes—revealed the innate animal-like ferocity of the Melekhovs.

But Dunyashka, too, was of the same breed and, when she had recovered from her confusion and disappointment, she said quietly but resolutely, 'Surely you should know, brother? We can't tell our hearts what to feel!'

'Tear out a heart that won't obey you,' Grigory advised coldly.

You're not the one to talk, my son, Ilyinichna thought to herself.

But at that moment Pantelei intervened. Crashing his fist down on the table, he said, 'Hold your tongue, you little bitch! Or I'll give you such a heart, you won't have a hair left on your head! There's a slut for you! Just let me fetch a pair of reins...'

'Father, dear! We haven't got a single pair left. They took them all!' Darya interrupted him with a humble air.

Pantelei flashed a frenzied glance at her and went on with unabated fury.

'I'll take a saddle girth then. And by all the devils I'll...'

'The Reds took all the saddle girths too!' Darya said more loudly, but still looking at her father-in-law with innocent eyes.

That was too much for Pantelei. For a second he stared at his daughter-in-law, growing purple in his dumb fury and opening his mouth wide (at that moment he looked like a freshly caught pike), and then roared hoarsely, 'Silence, you hussy! May a hundred devils take you! Can't I speak a word! But remember this, Dunyashka, my girl: that is never to be! You have your father's word on it! And Grigory was right. If you go on thinking about that scoundrel, death will be too good for you! A fine boy-friend you've found! Pining for a gallows-bird like him! Why, he's not human! Have a Judas like him for my son-in-law! If he came my way at this moment, I'd put him to death with my own hands! If I hear one more squeak out of you, I'll take some bark strippings and I'll...'

'You won't find any bark strippings in the yard either, not even with a lamp in broad daylight,' Ilyinichna said with a sigh. 'The yard's as bare as a bone, there's not even a twig to light a fire with. That's what we've come to!'

Even in this innocent remark Pantelei espied some malicious intent. He gave his wife a fixed stare, then sprang up like a madman and ran out into the yard.

Grigory dropped his spoon, covered his face with a towel and shook with silent laughter. His anger had passed and he laughed as he had not done for many a day. Everyone laughed, except Dunyashka. For a moment good cheer reigned at table. But as soon as Pantelei came stomping on to the porch all faces grew serious. The old man burst in like a hurricane, dragging a long alder branch.

'Here! This'll do for all of you, you yapping hussies! You long-tailed witches!... No bark strippings?! What's this then? And you'll get some too, you old devil! You'll have a taste all right!'

The branch was too long for the kitchen and, after knocking over an iron cooking-pot, the old man heaved it into the porch and sat down at table, breathing heavily.

Obviously his good mood was spoilt. He snorted and ate in silence. No one else spoke either. Darya kept her eyes on the table, afraid of breaking into laughter. Ilyinichna sighed and whispered under her breath, 'Oh, lord, lord! Grievous are our sins!' Only Dunyashka did not feel like laughing, and Natalya, who had forced a smile while the old man was out of the room, again became thoughtful and sad.

'Pass the salt!... Bread!' Pantelei barked menacingly from time to time, surveying his family with glittering eyes.

The quarrel ended rather unexpectedly. Amid the general silence young Mishatka treated his grandfather to a fresh insult. More than once he had heard his grandmother cursing the old man up hill and down dale and now, childishly upset by his grandfather's outburst and threats, he piped up shrilly, nostrils quivering, 'Shut up, you lame devil! You need a good box on the ears to stop you frightening me and Granny!'

'What?! Would you talk to me ... your grandfather ... like that?'

'Yes, you!' Mishatka affirmed boldly.

'How can you say such things to your own grandfather?'

'What are you shouting for then?'

'Listen to the little imp!' Stroking his beard, Pantelei surveyed the family in astonishment. 'And it all comes from you, you old harridan, he picked it up from you! You teach him!'

'Who teaches him! He takes straight after you and his unbridled father!' Ilyinichna protested crossly.

Natalya got up and gave Mishatka a slapping, and repeated as she did so, 'Don't talk like that to your grandad! Don't talk like that!'

Mishatka howled and buried his face in Grigory's lap. Pantelei, whose grandchildren were the apple of his eye, jumped up from the table and, wiping the tears that streamed down his beard, shouted joyfully, 'Grigory! My son! By all the devils, the old woman speaks true! He's one of us. He's the Melekhov breed!... That's when the blood tells!... This one won't be afraid to speak out to anyone... Little grandson! My own dear boy. Here, give the old fool a knock with anything you like!... Pull his beard!' And snatching Mishatka out of Grigory's arms, the old man lifted him high above his head.

They finished breakfast and rose from the table. The women started on the washing-up, Pantelei lit a cigarette and said to Grigory, 'It seems a bit awkward to ask you, you're our guest, but what else can I do... Can you help me to put the fence up round the threshing floor? It's right down, and I can't ask others to help me. We're all in the same boat.'

Grigory gladly consented and the two of them toiled till dinner-time in the yard, putting the fences in order.

As he dug holes for the posts the old man asked, 'It'll be mowing-time soon and I don't know whether to buy grass or not. What would you say? Is it worth the trouble? The Reds may be back in a month and everything will go to the devil again.'

'I don't know, Father,' Grigory confessed frankly. 'I don't know how things will turn out and who's going to win. Live so there's nothing much to spare in the yard or in the bins. The way things are now, it's not worth the effort. Take my father-in-law, all his life he toiled away making his fortune, strained his own guts and other peoples', but what's left? Just a few charred stumps in a yard!'

'Ay, lad, that's the way I look at it myself,' the old man agreed, suppressing a sigh.

He returned no more to the subject of the farm. Only in the afternoon, when he noticed Grigory fixing the threshing-floor gate with special care, he said with vexation and unconcealed bitterness, 'It'll do the way it is. What are you trying so hard for? It hasn't got to last a lifetime!'

Only now, it seemed, had the old man realised the futility of his efforts to pick up the threads of the old life...

Just before sunset Grigory downed tools and went indoors. Natalya was alone in the front room. She had dressed herself up as if for some occasion. Her dark-blue woollen skirt and light blue poplin blouse with stitching down the front and lace cuffs were quite becoming. Her face was a delicate pink and a little shiny because she had recently washed it with soap. She was looking for something in the chest, but at the sight of Grigory lowered the lid and straightened up with a smile.

Grigory sat down on the chest and said, 'Sit down with me a while. Otherwise I'll be leaving tomorrow and we won't have had a word together.'

She sat down meekly and glanced at him sideways with slightly frightened eyes. But he surprised her by taking her hand and saying affectionately, 'Why, you're as plump as if you'd never been ill.'

'I've got my weight back... We women have as many lives as a cat,' she said, smiling shyly and lowering her head.

Grigory noticed the tenderly flushed lobe of her ear covered with soft down, and the yellowish skin showing through the hair on the back of her head.

'Is your hair falling out?' he asked.

'Nearly all of it has. I'm moulting, I'll soon be bald.'

'Let me shave your head for you now?' Grigory proposed suddenly.

'Shave me?' she exclaimed in fright. 'Whatever should I look like then?'

'You must shave it or your hair won't grow again.'

'Mother promised to cut my hair with scissors,' she said, smiling in confusion and deftly covered her head with a well-blued white kerchief.

She was at his side, his wife and the mother of his children, Mishatka and Polyushka. It was for him she had dressed up and washed so carefully. In the kerchief she had hastily donned so that he should not see how unsightly her head had become since her illness, she sat there looking so wretched, so ugly and yet beautiful, radiant with a kind of pure, intrinsic beauty. She always wore high collars to hide the scar that had disfigured her neck. And it was all for him... A great wave of tenderness surged through Grigory's heart. He wanted to say something warm and affectionate but could not find the words and, drawing her silently towards him, he kissed her white sloping forehead and sorrowful eyes.

Never in the past had he shown her much affection. All her life she had been overshadowed by Aksinya. Shaken by her husband's display of feeling and all afire with her own emotion, she took his hand and pressed it to her lips.

For a minute they sat in silence. The setting sun cast purple rays into the room. Out on the porch the children were playing noisily. Darya could be heard taking out the bowls that had been baking in the stove and saying grumpily to her mother-in-law, 'You didn't even milk the cows every day, I dare say. The old one isn't yielding so well as she used to...'

The herd came in from pasture. The cow mooed and the herdboys cracked their horsehair whips. The village bull bellowed hoarsely. Its silky dewlap and solid sloping back were bleeding from the bites of the gadflies. It shook its head angrily, butted the Astakhovs' fence with its short, widely spaced horns, toppled it and stamped on down the lane. Natalya looked out of the window and said, 'The bull was in the retreat too. Mother told us that as soon as the shooting started in the village, he broke out of his pen, swam straight across the Don and kept out of the way all the time.'

Grigory was lost in thought and said nothing. Why did she have such sad eyes? And there was something else, something secret and illusive that showed from time to time and then disappeared. Even in her joy she was sad and somehow distant... Perhaps she had heard of his meetings with Aksinya in Vyoshenskaya?

Finally he asked, 'Why are you so down in the mouth today? What's troubling you, Natalya? Why don't you tell me?'

He was expecting tears, reproaches. But Natalya answered with alarm in her voice, 'Oh no, you imagined it, I'm all right... It's just that I'm not quite well yet. My head gets dizzy and if I bend down or lift something, everything goes dark before my eyes.'

Grigory looked at her keenly and was still not satisfied.

'Did anything happen to you while I was away?... Did anyone harm you?'

'Oh no, don't think that! I was lying in bed ill all the time.' She looked Grigory straight in the eye and even gave him a faint smile. Then, after a pause, she asked, 'Will you be off early tomorrow?'

'At dawn.'

464

'Couldn't you stay another day?' There was a shy, timid note of hope in her voice.

But Grigory shook his head and Natalya said with a sigh, 'How will you dress now... Will you wear your shoulder straps?'

'I'll have to.'

'Then take off your tunic. I'll sew them on while it's still light.'

With a dissatisfied grunt Grigory pulled off his tunic. It was still damp with sweat. There were dark patches on the back and shoulders, which bore the shiny marks left by the straps of his equipment. Natalya took a pair of faded field-service shoulder straps out of the chest.

'Are these the ones?'

'That's 'em. So you kept them, did you?'

'We buried the chest,' Natalya muttered as she threaded her needle, and furtively putting the dusty tunic to her face, drank in the beloved brackish smell of his sweat.

'What are you doing?' Grigory asked in surprise.

'It smells of you,' Natalya said with shining eyes, and, inclining her head to hide the flush in her cheeks, set to work nimbly with her needle. Grigory put on the tunic, frowned and jiggled his shoulders.

'You look better with them on!' Natalya said, gazing at her husband with unconcealed admiration.

But he squinted sideways at his left shoulder and sighed.

'I'd be glad never to see 'em again. But you wouldn't understand!'

They sat on the chest for a long time, hand in hand, each thinking his own thoughts in silence.

Later, when dusk was falling and the violet shadows from the outbuildings had spread over the cooling earth, they went into the kitchen for supper.

And so the night passed. Flashes of summer lightning blazed across the sky until dawn, and the nightingales sang in the cherry orchard until day break. Grigory awoke and lay for a long time with closed eyes, listening to the sweet bursts of song, then quietly, trying not to wake Natalya, rose, dressed and went out into the yard.

Pantelei was feeding his horse and wished to oblige him further.

'Shall I take him for a wash and a rub-down before you set off?'

'It doesn't matter,' Grigory replied, shivering in the damp morning air.

465

'Did you have a good sleep?' the old man inquired.

'Like a log! But the nightingales woke me. They're a pest the way they go on all night!'

Pantelei took off the horse's nosebag and smiled.

'That's all they have to do, lad. Sometimes it makes you envy God's creatures... No wars for them, no ruin...'

Prokhor rode up to the gate. He was freshly shaven and as cheerful and talkative as ever. He tied the halter to a plough and walked up to Grigory. His shirt was well ironed and there were new shoulder straps on the shoulders.

'So you've put yours on, too, Grigory Panteleyevich?' he called as he approached. 'The darn things got back on us at last. We'll never wear 'em out now! "They'll last till we take our last tumble," I told the wife, "Don't sew 'em on so tight, you fool. Just tack 'em on so the wind won't blow 'em away." In our job that's how it is, eh? If I get taken prisoner they'll see by my stripes I've got a rank, not an officer's may be, but still I'm a senior sergeant. And when they see that they'll say, "Ah, so you knew how to get promoted, now know how to put your head on the block!" Look how mine are tacked on! You'll die of laughing!'

Prokhor's shoulder straps were indeed attached by a mere thread and would barely stay in place.

Pantelei burst into a guffaw. His white teeth, untouched by time, gleamed amid his grizzled beard.

'That's a soldier for you! So as soon as things go wrong, off come the shoulder straps, eh?'

'What did you think?' Prokhor said with a grin.

Grigory smiled and said to his father, 'See what an orderly I've got myself? He'll always get me out of trouble!'

'But the way I see it, Grigory Panteleyevich... I'm in no hurry to die even if you are,' Prokhor said apologetically and without difficulty tore off his shoulder straps and stuffed them into his pocket. 'When we get near the front, I can sew 'em on again.'

Grigory made a hasty breakfast and said goodbye to his family.

'May the Mother of God watch over you!' Ilyinichna whispered frenziedly as she kissed her son. 'You're the only one we have left now.'

'Well, long partings mean too many tears. Goodbye!' Grigory said with a quiver in his voice, and walked to his horse.

Natalya put on her mother-in-law's black kerchief and followed Grigory out of the gate. The children clung to her skirts. Polyushka wept inconsolably and, choking with tears, begged her mother, 'Don't let him go! Don't let him go, Mummy! People get killed at the war. Don't go there, Daddy!'

Mishatka's lips were trembling, but no, he was not crying. He kept a brave face and rebuked his sister crossly.

'Shut up, silly fool! Not everyone gets killed there!'

He had taken to heart his grandfather's injunction that Cossacks never cry, that it was a great disgrace for a Cossack to cry. But when his father reached down, lifted him on to the saddle and kissed him, he noticed in wonder that his father's eyelashes were wet. Such an ordeal was too much even for Mishatka and the tears poured out of his eyes. He buried his face on his father's strapped and belted chest and cried out, 'Let Grandad go and fight! What do we need him for!... I don't want you to...'

Grigory lowered his little son carefully to the ground, wiped his eyes with the back of his hand and rode off in silence.

How many times had a cavalry horse wheeled sharply and, scattering the earth beside the home porch, carried him off along the roads and over roadless steppe to a front line, where blackwinged death lay in wait for Cossacks, where in the words of the Cossack song 'every day and hour brings fear and grief', but never had Grigory left the village with such a heavy heart as he did on that gentle summer morning.

Oppressed with vague forebodings, nagging anxiety and regret, he rode with his reins resting on the saddle pommel and did not look back until he was on the hill. At the fork where the dusty track turned off towards the windmill, he turned his head. Only Natalya was standing at the gate, and the fresh breeze of early morning was tugging the funereally black kerchief from her hands.

* * *

On and on in the bottomless blue depths floated the clouds foaming in the wind. A shimmering haze hovered over the undulating horizon. The horses were walking. Prokhor was swaying in the saddle, dozing. Grigory, gritting his teeth, often looked back. At first he saw the green clumps of willows, the silver whimsically meandering ribbon of the Don, and the slowly turning sails of the mill. Then the road curved away to the south. The water-meadows, the Don and the mill dropped out of sight beyond the trampled cornfields. Grigory started to whistle a tune, keeping his eyes fixed on the horse's golden chestnut neck all covered in tiny beads of sweat, and no longer turned in the saddle... To hell with the war! The fighting had been on the Chir, then it had passed along the Don, and later it would roar on the Khopyor, the Medveditsa and the Buzuluk. And, in the long run, what did it matter where an enemy bullet finally laid him low?

IX

A battle was being fought on the approaches to Ust-Medveditskaya. Grigory heard the muffled roar of artillery as he turned off the cart track on to the Hetman's Highway.

All along the highway there were traces of the Red units' hasty retreat. Abandoned carts and wagons were scattered everywhere. In a gully on the other side of Matveyevka village a gun lay with its axle smashed by a shell and its cradle buckled. The traces on the limber had been slashed. In the salt marshes half a verst further on, the bodies of soldiers in field-service tunics and trousers, puttees and heavy nailed boots lay thick on the stunted sun-scorched grass. They were Red Army men who had been overtaken and cut down by the Cossack cavalry.

As he rode past, Grigory had no difficulty in ascertaining this by the abundant blood that had dried on the rucked up tunics and by the positions of the bodies. They lay like mown grass. In the heat of the pursuit the Cossacks had not had time to strip them.

Beside a hawthorn bush lay a dead Cossack. The trouser stripes glowed red on his sprawling legs. Not far away lay his dead horse, a light bay, with an old and battered saddle, its frame daubed with ochre.

Both Grigory's and Prokhor's horses were tired and needed feeding, but Grigory had no desire to stop at a place that had been the scene of recent fighting. He rode on for another verst or so, dropped down into a ravine and reined in his horse. Not far away was a pond with a dam that had been all but washed away. Prokhor rode as far as the caked mud at the edge, then turned back.

'What's up?' Grigory asked.

'Go and look.'

Grigory rode up to the dam. In the crumbling gap lay the body of a dead woman. Her face had been covered by the hem of her blue skirt. Her shapely white legs with their sunburnt calves and dimples on the knees were shamelessly and horribly splayed. Her left arm was twisted under her back.

Grigory hurriedly dismounted, took off his cap, bent down and straightened the murdered woman's skirt. Her brown youthful face was beautiful even in death. The half-closed eyes gleamed dully under the painfully arched black brows. The clenched close-set teeth glowed like mother-of-pearl in the softly shaped mouth. A fine lock of hair had fallen over the cheek that was pressed to the grass. And on that cheek, which death had already tinged with its saffron-yellow shades, the busy ants were crawling.

'What beauty those bastards ruined!' Prokhor muttered in a low voice.

For a minute he was silent, then spat bitterly.

'I'd have 'em... I'd have them high-riders up against a wall! Let's get out of here for God's sake! I can't look at her. It fair wrings my heart!'

'Mebbe we'll bury her?' Grigory suggested.

'What, have we taken on the job of burying all the dead we come across?' Prokhor protested. 'In Yagodnoye we dug in some old grandad, and here's this woman... If we start burying everyone, we'll need hooves instead of hands! What could we dig a grave with? You couldn't do it with a sabre, mate. The ground's baked hard for about two feet down with this heat.'

Prokhor was in such a hurry to get away that he could scarcely find the stirrup with his toe.

They rode out on the hill again, and Prokhor, who had been pondering something intently, asked, 'What d'you think, Panteleyevich, haven't we soaked the earth with enough blood yet?'

'Just about.'

'D'you reckon it'll soon end?'

'It'll end when they've smashed us.'

'Well, it's a cheerful life that's come our way for the devil's pleasure! I wish they'd get on and smash us, eh? In the German war a selfwounder would shoot off his finger and they'd send him off home with a clean record, but nowadays you could chop your whole hand off and they'd still keep you in the line. They recruit the one-armed, the lame, the cross-eyed, the ruptured, and any old scum, as long as he can totter along on two legs. Will the war ever end that way? Not a chance in hell!' Prokhor said despairingly. He turned off the road, dismounted, muttering something under his breath, and started loosening his horse's saddle girths.

* * *

It was night when Grigory rode into the village of Khovansky, not far from Ust-Medveditskaya. The guard post of the 3rd Regiment stopped him but, on recognising the voice of their division commander, the Cossacks told him that the divisional headquarters was in this village and the chief of staff, Lieutenant Kopylov, was eagerly awaiting him. The communicative guard commander detailed a Cossack to escort Grigory to headquarters and said in parting, 'They're darn well dug in, Grigory Panteleyevich. I don't reckon we'll take Ust-Medveditskaya in a hurry. But who knows... We've got a good bit of muscle here too. They say there's some British troops coming up from Morozovskaya. Have you heard anything?'

'No,' Grigory replied as he rode off.

The house that had been taken over for headquarters had its windows tightly shuttered. Grigory thought at first the rooms were deserted but, as he entered the corridor, he heard muffled but lively conversation. After the darkness the light of a big oil-lamp hanging from the ceiling in the best room blinded him; the pungent scent of tobacco smoke stung his nostrils.

'Here you are at last!' Kopylov exclaimed joyfully, appearing from the wreaths of smoke over the table. 'We thought you'd never come!'

Grigory greeted the assembled company, took off his greatcoat and cap, and strode up to the table.

'What a fug you've made in here! There's nothing to breathe. Open a window! Why've you boxed yourself up like this!' he said frowning.

Kharlampy Yermakov, who was sitting beside Kopylov, smiled.

'We've got used to it,' he said and pressed out a pane of glass with his elbow, then threw open the shutter.

The fresh night air poured into the room. The lamp flame flared and went out.

'That's good management for you! Why did you break the window?' Kopylov grumbled, groping about the table. 'Who's got some matches? Be careful, there's a bottle of ink just by the map.'

They lit the lamp and closed one shutter, and Kopylov began a hurried report.

'The situation at the front, Comrade Melekhov, as of today's date is as follows. The Reds are holding Ust-Medveditskaya. It's covered on three sides by a force of approximately four thousand bayonets. They have a fair amount of artillery and machine-guns. By the monastery and in several other places they've dug trenches. They command the high ground along the Don. Not that their positions are impregnable but they're going to be rather difficult to capture. On our side, beside General Fitzhelaurov's division and two officers' assault detachments, the whole of Bogatiryov's Sixth Brigade has arrived and also our First Division. But this division is not up to full strength; its infantry regiment is still somewhere near Ust-Khopyorskaya and though the cavalry are all here, the squadrons are by no means fully manned.'

'In the 3rd Squadron of my regiment, for instance, we have only thirty-eight Cossacks,' said Junior-Cornet Dudarev, commander of the 2nd Regiment.

'How many were there before?' Yermakov asked.

'Ninety-one.'

'How come you let the squadron fall apart like this? What kind of a commander are you?' Grigory asked, frowning and drumming his fingers on the table.

'The devil alone knows how to keep 'em! While we were passing through the villages, they went off to see the folk at home. But they're catching up. Three rode in today.'

Kopylov moved the map towards Grigory, pointed out the positions of the various units with his little finger, and went on.

'We haven't got on to the offensive yet. Only the 2nd Regiment made an infantry attack yesterday, in this sector here, and it was unsuccessful.'

'Heavy losses?'

'According to the regimental commander's report, in the course of yesterday he lost twenty-six men killed and wounded. Now about the balance of forces. We have a numerical advantage, but to keep up an offensive

471

there're not enough machine-guns for the infantry, and we're also short of shells. Their munitions chief has promised us 400 shells and 1,500 cartridges as soon as he gets them. But when will that be?! And we've got to attack tomorrow—General Fitzhelaurov's orders. He wants us to detail a regiment to support the assault troops. Yesterday they attacked four times and sustained tremendous losses. They fought like the devil! So now Fitzhelaurov wants to strengthen the right flank and concentrate the blow at this point, d'you see? Here the terrain makes it possible to approach to within two or three hundred paces of the enemy trenches. Incidentally, his adjutant has only just left. He brought us oral instructions to report tomorrow at six in the morning for a conference to coordinate our operations. General Fitzhelaurov and his divisional staff are at present in the village of Bolshoi Senin. Generally speaking, the object of the operation is to crush the enemy at once, before any reinforcements reach them from Sebryakovo Station. On the other side of the Don our troops are not very active... The Fourth Division has crossed the Khopyor, but the Reds have put out strong covering forces and have a firm hold on the roads leading to the railway. Right now they've floated a pontoon bridge across the Don and are hurriedly evacuating equipment and ammunition from Ust-Medveditskaya.'

'The Cossacks say the Allies are on their way here. Is that so?'

'There's a rumour that a few British batteries and tanks are coming up from Chernyshevskaya. But the question is how will they get those tanks across the Don? If you ask me, the talk about tanks is just hot air! They've been talking about 'em for ages.'

A long silence ensued.

Kopylov unbuttoned his brown high-collared officer's tunic, propped his hands under his chubby unshaven cheeks covered with a scrub of chestnut bristles, and sat thoughtfully chewing the cardboard holder of his burnt-out cigarette. His round widespaced dark eyes gazed wearily from under drooping lids, and his handsome face was crumpled from sleepless nights.

At one time he had been a teacher at a parish school. On Sundays he visited the stanitsa merchants, played rummy with their womenfolk and 'préférence' for small stakes with the men; a skilled performer on the guitar, he was a cheerful, sociable young man. In due course he married a young school-mistress and would have gone on living his habitual life in the stanitsa until he earned a pension, but war came and he was called up. After finishing at a cadet training school, he was sent to serve in a Cossack regiment on the Western front. The war changed neither his appearance nor his character. There was something inoffensive and profoundly civilian in his squat tubby figure, in his good-natured face, in the way he wore his sabre, and in his manner of addressing his subordinates. His voice lacked the rasp of command, there was none of the soldier's laconic brevity of expression in his conversation, his officer's uniform was loose and baggy. In his three years at the front he had acquired neither smartness nor bearing; everything about him suggested the civilian. He was more like an overweight townsman disguised as an officer than a genuine officer, but notwithstanding all this the Cossacks treated him with respect, his opinion was listened to at staff conferences, and the insurgent command fully appreciated his sober intelligence, obliging disposition and a bravery that was by no means affected and had been proved more than once on the battlefield.

Before Kopylov, Grigory's chief of staff had been the illiterate and unintelligent Cornet Krushilin. He had been killed on the Chir, and Kopylov, who had taken charge of the staff had managed its affairs skilfully, coolly and to good effect. He had worked as conscientiously at headquarters, planning operations, as he had once sat correcting his pupils' exercise books, but in an emergency a word from Grigory was enough to make him abandon headquarters, mount his horse and, taking command of a regiment, lead it into battle.

Grigory's attitude to his new chief of staff had at first been somewhat prejudiced, but in two months he had got to know him better and one day after battle he had said straight out, 'I didn't think much of you to start with, Kopylov, but now I see I was wrong, so you'll have to forgive me somehow.' Kopylov smiled and said nothing but was obviously flattered by this gruff acknowledgement.

Devoid of ambition or any strong political convictions, Kopylov treated the war as an unavoidable evil and only longed for it to be over. At this present juncture he was not thinking how to develop the operation for the capture of Ust-Medveditskaya, but of his own home and family. He was even considering the possibility of going home on leave for a month or six weeks.

Grigory looked hard at Kopylov, then rose to his feet. 'Well, guardsmen, let's call it a day and go to bed. We needn't worry our heads about how to take Ust-Medveditskaya. From now on the generals are going to do our thinking and deciding for us. We'll report to Fitzhelaurov tomorrow and let him teach us, poor beggars, in the way we should go... But as regards the 2nd Regiment, I reckon that, while we've still got the power, we'd better give regimental commander Dudarev the sack and strip him of all his ranks and medals...'

'And his plate of porridge,' Yermakov put in.

'No, joking apart,' Grigory went on. 'We'll put him in charge of a squadron and make Kharlampy the commander of the regiment. Off you go rightaway, Yermakov, take over the regiment and wait for our instructions in the morning. Kopylov will write out the order replacing Dudarev straightaway and you can take it with you. The way I see it, Dudarev won't get us anywhere. He hasn't got a clue what he's doing and he might easily get a lot more Cossacks mown down. Fighting on foot is like that... It's easy enough to get men killed, if the commander's a blockhead.'

'Quite right. I'm in favour of replacing Dudarev,' Kopylov supported him.

'And you, Yermakov, are you against?' Grigory asked, noting a certain dissatisfaction on Yermakov's face.

'Why, not at all! Can't I even lift an eyebrow?'

'So much the better. Yermakov isn't against it. His cavalry regiment will be taken over for the time being by Ryabchikov. So write the order, Kopylov, then go to bed and get your beauty sleep. You've got to be up at six. We'll be going to see this general and I'm taking four orderlies with me.'

Kopylov raised his eyebrows in surprise.

'Why so many?'

'To show off! To let 'em know I'm not just a country bumpkin, but a division commander.' Grigory laughed, flung his greatcoat onto his shoulders and strode to the door.

He bedded down on a horse blanket under the overhang of a shed without even taking off his boots or greatcoat. In the yard the orderlies talked long into the night and from somewhere nearby came the occasional snort of a horse and a steady munching. The air smelled of dried dung and earth that had not yet cooled from the heat of the day. As he dozed off, Grigory heard the voices and laughter of the orderlies. One of them, a young man judging by his voice, said with a sigh as he saddled his horse, 'Ah, lads, I'm right fed up with all this. Here we are in the middle of the night and I've got to deliver this packet. Never a minute's peace or sleep... Steady there, you devil!'

And another, a thick, husky bass, began to sing quietly, 'Oh, we're right fed up with soldiering, fed right up to here...' and then broke into businesslike wheedling, 'Give us a pinch of 'baccy, Proshka! What a miser you are! Forgotten the Red Army boots I gave you at Belavin? You rotten pig! Other folk would remember a pair of boots like that for the rest of their lives and you won't even spare a pinch of 'baccy.'

The snaffles clanked against the horse's teeth. The horse took a great gulping breath and trotted off, its hooves clip-clopping on the dry, flint-hard ground.

'That's what they're all saying... Oh, we're right fed up with soldiering, fed right up up to here,' Grigory repeated to himself, smiled and at once dropped off to sleep. But as soon as he was asleep he had a dream that had come to him before. Lines of Red Army men were advancing across a brownish field, covered with high stubble. The first line extended right across his field of vision. Behind it came another six or seven lines. The attackers were approaching in oppressive silence. The black figures loomed ever larger and now he could make out their rapid stumbling strides as they came within shooting distance and began to run with their rifles at the ready—men in hats with long earflaps, their mouths open, gaping silently. Grigory was lying in a shallow trench, jerking the bolt of his rifle and firing rapidly; with every shot a Red Army man would reel and fall; as he punched another clip into magazine he glanced round and saw Cossacks jumping up and running from the nearby trenches, their faces contorted with fear. Grigory felt his heart beating wildly and shouted, 'Shoot! You, swine! Where're you going? Stop, don't run away!...' He shouted at the top of his voice but it sounded strangely weak, barely audible. Terror gripped him. He, too, sprang to his feet and, standing, fired a last shot at an elderly brown-faced Red Army man, who was running straight towards him, and saw that he had missed. The Red Army man had a fearless, excitedly serious face. He was running lightly, barely touching the ground with his feet, his brows knitted, his hat pushed back, the skirts of his greatcoat tucked up. For an instant Grigory scanned the enemy soldier bearing down on him, saw his shining eyes and pale cheeks with its fresh curly beard, saw the short wide tops of his boots, the black muzzle of the slightly lowered rifle barrel and the tip of the dark bayonet above it, rising and falling with the motion of the runner. Grigory was seized by inexplicable fear. He jerked the bolt of his rifle, but it had jammed. In desperation he battered it on his knee—no use! And the Red Army man was now only five paces away. Grigory turned and ran. The whole bare brown field before him was dotted with fleeing Cossacks. Behind him Grigory could hear the laboured breathing of his pursuer, the clumping of his boots, but he could run no faster. A terrible effort was needed to force his weakly sagging legs to move quicker. In the end he reached a gloomy derelict graveyard, jumped over the broken fence and ran among the sunken grave-mounds with their skewed crosses and shrines. Just one more effort and he would be safe. But then the thunder of footsteps behind him grew louder still. He felt his pursuer's hot breath on his neck, a pair of hands seizing the back-belt and skirts of his greatcoat. Grigory uttered a choking scream and woke up. He was lying on his back. His feet in their tight boots had gone numb, his forehead was damp with cold sweat, his whole body ached as if he had been beaten. 'Ugh! What the devil!' he gasped, and listened with joyous relief to his own voice, still not quite believing that it had all been a dream. Then he turned over, pulled his greatcoat over his head, and said to himself, 'I ought to have let him get nearer, parried the blow, knocked him down with the butt of my rifle, and then run.' For a minute he thought about this recurrent dream, revelling in the knowledge that it had been nothing but a nightmare, and that in reality he was in no danger, at least for the time being. 'Why is it ten times worse in a dream than in real life? With all the fighting I've been in, I've never known such fear!' he thought as he fell asleep, blissfully stretching his cramped legs.

X

At dawn he was woken by Kopylov.

'Up you get, it's time we were moving! We were ordered to be there at six!'

The chief of staff had just shaved, cleaned his boots and put on a crumpled but clean tunic. Evidently he had shaved in a hurry, for both chubby cheeks had been snicked by the razor. Nevertheless he was looking quite uncharacteristically trim.

Grigory surveyed him critically from head to foot and thought. 'Aren't we smart! Can't look sloppy in front of a general!'

As though picking up his train of thought, Kopylov said, 'I can't go there looking slovenly. I advise you to make yourself tidy too.'

'I'll do as I am,' Grigory muttered, stretching himself. 'So we've been ordered to report at six, you say? Now they've started giving us orders, have they?'

Kopylov gave a little laugh and shrugged.

'New times, new tunes. We have to obey our superiors in rank. Fitzhelaurov's a general, you can't expect him to come to us.'

'That's right! We've got just where we were heading for,' Grigory replied, and walked away to the well to wash.

The mistress of the house darted indoors, brought out a clean embroidered towel, and handed it to Grigory with a bow of respect. He rubbed his face until it was brick red after the dousing with cold water, and said to Kopylov, 'Ay, you may be right, but there's something their excellencies the generals ought to remember. The people are different since the revolution, it's like they'd been born again! But these generals, they still measure everything by the old yardstick. And that stick, if they don't look out, is going to break... They're a bit slow on the uptake. They need a bit of cart grease in their brains, to stop 'em creaking!'

'What do you mean by that?' Kopylov asked absently, blowing a speck of dust off his sleeve.

'What I mean is that they're all hankering after the old ways. Take me, I've had officer's rank since the German war. I earned it with my own blood! But as soon as I find myself in officers' company, it's like going out into the frost in my underpants. The cold shoulder they give me sends shivers down my back!' Grigory's eyes glinted with fury and, without noticing it, he raised his voice.

Kopylov gave him a look of disapproval and glanced over his shoulder.

'Not so loud, the orderlies are listening!' he whispered.

'But why is it, I ask you?' Grigory went on, lowering his voice. 'Because for them I'm an outsider. They've got hands, but my hands are so horny they're more like hooves! They know how to bow and scrape, but whenever I turn round in a room I knock something over. They smell of face soap and all kinds of women's creams and I stink of horse piss and sweat. They're all educated, but I only just managed to get through a parish school. To them I'm the wrong sort, from head to foot. That's the long and the short of it! After I've been with them, I feel as if I'd got a spider's web over my face. It gives me the creeps, and I want to wipe it off.' Grigory threw the towel down on the well frame and clawed his hair into place with a broken comb. His white forehead, untouched by the sun, contrasted sharply with his swarthy face. 'They won't understand that all the old life has gone right down the bloody drain!' Grigory's voice was quieter now. 'They think we're made of some different stuff, that any unlearned man, from the common folk, is just an animal. They think that I, or anyone like me, can't understand the art of war like they can. But who commands the Reds? Budyonny—is he an officer? He was a sergeant-major in the old army but he gave the generals of the general staff a pretty good beating, didn't he? Wasn't he the one that sent the officers' regiments packing? Or take even Guselshchikov, he's the best of the Cossack generals, but didn't he have to gallop out of Ust-Khopyorskaya in his underpants last winter? And do you know who tumbled him out on to the ice? A Moscow mechanic, in command of a Red regiment. The prisoners were talking about him later. That's something you've got to understand! And what about us, unlearned officers, did we lead the Cossacks so badly in the uprising? Did the generals help us all that much?'

'They helped quite a bit,' Kopylov replied significantly.

'Well, mebbe they helped Kudinov, but I went in and beat the Reds without any help or advice from anyone.'

'You mean you deny the importance of learning in war?'

'No, I don't deny that. But it's not the main thing, brother.'

'What is then, Panteleyevich?'

'The cause you're fighting for.'

'Well, that's a different matter,' Kopylov said, smiling guardedly. 'That stands to reason... In this business, the idea is the main thing. Only the man who really knows what he's fighting for and believes in his cause can win. That truth is as old as the hills so it's no good your pretending you made the discovery. I'm for the old, for the good old days. If things were different, I wouldn't have budged an inch to go anywhere and fight for something. Our side is made up of people who've taken up arms to defend their old privileges and suppress the rebel masses. And you and I are among the suppressors. But I've been watching you for some time now, Grigory Panteleyevich, and I can't understand you...'

'You'll understand later. Let's get going,' Grigory snapped, and strode towards the shed.

The mistress of the house, who was watching Grigory's every movement, in her efforts to please him suggested, 'Won't you have some milk?'

'No, thanks, ma, we haven't got time to drink milk. Some other time.'

* * *

Prokhor Zykov was standing by the shed, zealously spooning soured milk out of a bowl. He didn't bat an eyelid when he saw Grigory untethering his horse. He merely wiped his lips on his sleeve and asked, 'Going far? Should I come with you?'

Grigory boiled over and said with cold fury, 'You bloody loafing bastard! Don't you know your duties, damn you? Why was the horse standing tethered? Who ought to have my horse ready for me? You damn guzzler! You never stop eating! Drop that spoon this minute! Don't you know what discipline is! Seed of the devil!'

'What are you carrying on about?' Prokhor muttered in aggrieved tones, perching himself in the saddle. 'No need to bawl at me! You're not such a big shot yourself! Aren't I allowed to have a bite before we go? What's all the shouting about?'

'Because you're letting me down, you pig's gut! How do you address me? We're going to report to a general, so watch your step!... You've got used to being all free-and-easy with me... Remember who I am! Stay five paces behind me!' Grigory ordered as he rode out of the gate.

Prokhor and the other three orderlies fell behind,

and Grigory resumed his conversation with Kopylov, who was riding beside him.

'Well what is it you don't understand?' he asked mockingly. 'Mebbe I can explain it to you?'

Kopylov ignored the mockery in his tone and in the way the question was put.

'I can't understand your position, that's what! On the one hand, you're a fighter for the old ways, and on the other, you're—forgive me for putting it so bluntly—you're a kind of Bolshevik.'

'In what way am I a Bolshevik?' Grigory frowned, and swung round in the saddle.

'Not a Bolshevik but something like a Bolshevik.'

'It's all the same. In what way, I asked you.'

'Well, take even the way you talk about the officers and their attitude towards you. What do you expect of these people? What do you expect of life in general?' Kopylov persisted, smiling good-naturedly and toying with his whip. He glanced back at the orderlies talking animatedly in the rear, and raised his voice. 'You resent the fact that they don't accept you in their circle as an equal, that they look down on you. But from their point of view they're right, and that's something you should understand. Admittedly, you're an officer, but it's a pure accident as far as they're concerned. Even though you wear officer's insignia, you have remained—forgive my saying so—an uncouth, unpolished Cossack. You have no decent manners, you express yourself incorrectly and rudely, you lack all the qualities that are essential in a cultivated person. For example, instead of using a handkerchief like anybody with some manners, you blow your nose with the help of two fingers. While eating you wipe your hands either on your boot-tops or on your hair, and after washing your face you have no qualms about wiping it on a horse cloth. You either bite your nails to keep them short or cut them with the tip of your sabre. Or here's an even better instance. Remember, last winter in Karginskaya, in my presence, while you were talking to an educated woman whose husband had been arrested by the Cossacks, you buttoned your trousers in front of her...'

'So I'd better have left 'em undone, had I?' Grigory said, smiling grimly.

They were riding abreast. Grigory glanced sideways at Kopylov's good-natured face and, not without resentment, went on listening.

'That's not the point!' Kopylov exclaimed, frowning irritably. 'How in any case could you receive a lady in nothing but your trousers and barefooted? You didn't even pull your tunic over your shoulders, as I very well remember! These are all small things, of course, but they typify you as a person—well, how shall I put it...'

'Come on, spit it out!'

'As an extremely ignorant person. And the way you speak? It's appalling! And like any half-literate person, you have an inexplicable love of foreign words and use them in and out of season with the most incredible distortions. At staff conferences, when you hear someone using such special military terms as deployment, dispositions, concentration, and so on, you gaze at the speaker in admiration, I would almost say—envy.'

'Laying it on a bit thick, aren't you!' Grigory exclaimed, and sparks of merriment flashed in his eyes. Stroking his horse's head between the ears and scratching the warm silky skin under its mane, he said, 'All right, go on then. Skin your commander alive!'

'Why should I skin you? You must see perfectly well that you are deficient in these things. And yet you take offence because the officers don't treat you as their equal. In matters of politeness and literacy you're just a blockhead!' Kopylov uttered the offensive word that had come accidentally to his lips, and then lost his nerve. He knew how unrestrained Grigory could be in anger and feared an explosion, but a quick sideways glance reassured him. Grigory was leaning back in his saddle, laughing soundlessly, his teeth gleaming white under his moustache. This was such an unexpected result of what he had been saying, and Grigory's laughter was so infectious, that Kopylov himself burst out laughing and said, 'There you are! Any reasonable man would be reduced to tears by such a dressing-down, and you roar with laughter... You are a strange fellow, aren't you?'

'So you say I'm a blockhead, eh? Well, go to the devil then!' Grigory said when he had done laughing. 'I don't want to learn your good manners and polite ways. They won't be any good to me while I'm driving my oxen. And if, God willing, I get out of this alive—I'll have my oxen to look after and it won't be any use me bowing and scraping in front of them. "Do move up a little, Baldy! I beg your pardon, Humpy! Allow me to adjust your yoke for you? My dear sir, m'lord ox, I humbly request you not to muck up the furrow!" All they need is something short and snappy like Giddy-up! That's enough to get a bullock depositioned.'

'Dispositioned, not depositioned,' Kopylov corrected him.

'All right, dispositioned then. But there's one thing I don't agree with you about.'

'What is it?'

"That I'm a blockhead, I may be one while I'm with you, but just you wait. One day I'll go over to the Reds, and then I'll be sharp as steel. Then you'd better not fall into my hands, you good-mannered, educated parasites! I'll rip the guts out of you, heart and all!' Grigory said half-joking, half-serious, and with a flick of his whip put his horse into a swift canter.

The Donside morning came amidst such a fine-spun stillness that every sound, even the mildest, broke through it and awakened the echoes. The larks and quails reigned supreme in the steppe but over the almost adjoining villages there hung the unceasing rumble that usually accompanies the movements of large troop units. The wheels of guns and caissons clattered over the road ruts, horses whinnied by the wells, dismounted squadrons padded along softly in the dust, commandeered wagons and carts rattled along with ammunition and equipment for the front line; over the field kitchens rose the sweet scents of boiled millet, stewed meat flavoured with bay leaves, and freshly baked bread.

From around Ust-Medveditskaya itself came the fierce crackle of small-arms fire and the occasional sonorous thud of an artillery shot. The day's fighting had just begun.

General Fitzhelaurov was at breakfast when his rather elderly and debauched-looking adjutant reported, 'The commander of the First Insurgent Division, Melekhov, and the division's chief of staff, Kopylov, to see you.'

'Ask them into my room.' With a big, veined hand Fitzhelaurov pushed away a plate littered with egg shells, unhurriedly drank a glass of fresh milk and, after neatly folding his napkin, got up from the table.

Tall, paunchy and ageing, he seemed unbelievably huge in this tiny Cossack front room with its sagging door lintels and squat dim windows. Straightening the high collar of his perfectly cut tunic and coughing loudly, the general walked into the next room, bowed curtly to Kopylov and Grigory, who had risen as he entered, and without offering them his hand, motioned them to the table.

Holding his sabre to his side, Grigory sat down carefully on the edge of a stool and shot a sidelong glance at Kopylov.

Fitzhelaurov sat down ponderously on a creaking bentwood chair, tucked his long thin legs under it, placed his large hands on his knees, and began to speak in a deep, fruity bass.

'I invited you here, gentlemen, to settle certain questions... The insurgent partisan free-for-all is over! Your units have ceased to exist as an independent entity. In fact, they never were an entity. That was mere fiction. They are now being incorporated in the Don Army. We are launching a planned offensive, and it's time you became fully aware of the fact and gave unconditional obedience to the orders of the supreme command. Why, will you kindly tell me, did your infantry regiment fail to support the attack of the assault battalion yesterday? Why in defiance of my order did the regiment refuse to attack? Who is in command of your so-called division?'

'I am,' Grigory replied quietly.

'Then take the trouble to answer my question!'

'I only arrived in the division yesterday.'

'Where had you been?'

'I stopped off at home.'

'At a time of combat operations in the field the commander of a division allows himself to go visiting his family! The division's a shambles! No discipline whatever! Monstrous!' The general's bass thundered in the cramped little room; outside the door the adjutants tiptoed about, whispering and chuckling; Kopylov's cheeks went pale, then white, but Grigory looked at the general's purple face and clenched swollen fists and felt his own uncontrollable fury begin to rise.

Fitzhelaurov sprang to his feet with unexpected agility and stood gripping the back of his chair.

'Yours is not a cavalry unit but a Red Guard rabble!' he barked. 'They're riff-raff, not Cossacks! And you, Melekhov, have no business to be commanding a division! You'd do better as a batman—cleaning boots! Do you hear?! Why was my order not carried out? Hadn't you had a meeting about it? Hadn't you debated the subject? Well, get this into your head. You'll find no comrades here and we shall not allow you to institute your Bolshevik ways here! Most certainly not!'

'I will not have you shouting at me!' Grigory said in a low voice and stood up, pushing the stool aside with his foot.

'What did you say?!' Fitzhelaurov wheezed breathlessly, leaning forward over the table.

'I will not have you shouting at me!' Grigory repeated louder. 'You got us here to decide...' he broke off for a second and dropped his eyes then, fixing his gaze on Fitzhelaurov's hands, he lowered his voice almost to a whisper. 'If you, Your Excellency, lift so much as a finger against me, I'll cut you down on the spot!'

It grew so quiet in the room that Fitzhelaurov's laboured breathing was distinctly audible. For about a minute there was silence. The door creaked faintly. A frightened-looking adjutant peeped in. The door closed again as quietly as before. Grigory stood with his hand on the hilt of his sabre. Kopylov's knees were trembling and he was staring vacantly at the wall. Fitzhelaurov lowered himself ponderously on to his chair, cleared his throat wheezily, and grunted, 'A fine thing indeed!' And then quite calmly, but not looking at Grigory, he said, 'Now sit down. We both lost our tempers and that'll do. Kindly listen to me. I order you to transfer all cavalry units at once... Do sit down, man!'

Grigory sat down and wiped away with his sleeve the abundant sweat that had broken out on his face.

'...Now then, you will immediately transfer all the cavalry units to the south-east sector and attack at once. Your right flank will be in contact with Lieutenant-Colonel Chumakov's second battalion...'

'I won't take my division there,' Grigory said wearily and groped in his trouser pocket for a handkerchief. With one of Natalya's lace-edged handkerchiefs he again wiped the sweat off his forehead. 'I won't take the division there.'

'And why not?'

'Regrouping will take too long.'

'That doesn't concern you. I am responsible for the outcome of the operation.'

'Yes, it does. You're not the only one who's responsible...'

'Do you refuse to obey my order?' Fitzhelaurov asked hoarsely, restraining himself with an obvious effort.

'Yes.'

'In that case kindly hand over command of the division! Now I see why my order of yesterday was not carried out...'

'You can see what you like but I won't hand over the division!'

'How do you expect me to take that?'

'The way I said,' Grigory smiled faintly.

'I dismiss you from your command!' Fitzhelaurov raised his voice and Grigory stood up at once.

'I don't take orders from you, Your Excellency!'

'Do you take orders from anyone?'

'Yes, from Kudinov, the commander of the insurgent forces. And it's mighty strange for me to hear all this from you... At present you'd better not shout at me... Just as soon as they make me a squadron commander, then go ahead—shout all you want. But as for using your fists...' Grigory lifted a grimy forefinger, smiling but at the same time flashing his eyes murderously, and concluded, 'even then I won't let you do that!'

Fitzhelaurov rose, eased down the tight collar of his tunic, and with a slight bow said, 'There is nothing more to be said between us. Do as you like. I shall at once inform army headquarters of your conduct and, I can assure you, the results will be quick to take effect. Our court-martial has so far functioned with great efficiency.'

Ignoring Kopylov's desperate glances, Grigory pulled on his cap and walked to the door. At the threshold he stopped and said, 'Inform anyone you're supposed to, but don't try to scare me, I'm not the scary kind... And in the meantime keep your hands off me.' He thought for a moment, then added, 'Otherwise I'm afraid my Cossacks might rough you up a bit...' He kicked the door open and strode into the porch with his sword clattering.

On the porch steps he was overtaken by a badly shaken Kopylov.

'You're out of your mind, Panteleyevich!' he whispered, clasping his hands in despair.

'Horses!' Grigory bellowed, twisting his whip in his hands.

Prokhor darted up to the porch with astonishing alacrity.

When they were out of the gate, Grigory looked back. Three orderlies were fussing round General Fitzhelaurov, helping him to mount a tall splendidly saddled stallion.

For half a verst they rode in silence. Kopylov said nothing because he realised that Grigory was in no mood to talk, and that to argue with him might not be very safe. At length Grigory could contain himself no longer.

485

'Why're you so quiet?' he asked sharply. 'What did you come with me for? Just as a witness? Playing mum?'

'Well, that was a fine way to carry on!'

'How did *he* carry on then?'

'He was in the wrong too, I'll admit. The tone he took in talking to us was appalling!'

'D'you call that talking? He was bawling from the start, as if someone had stuck a needle in his arse!'

'But the things you said! Insubordination to a superior ... in the field. That amounts to...'

'Damn all! That's what it amounts to! Pity he didn't take a swipe at me! I'd have cracked his skull open with my sabre!'

'You'll be in trouble enough without that,' Kopylov said disapprovingly, and reined his horse to a walk. 'Obviously now they'll start trying to tighten up discipline, so look out!'

Their horses loped along side by side, snorting and flicking off the gadflies with their tails. Grigory looked at Kopylov derisively.

'What did you doll yourself up for? Thought they'd invite you to tea, did you? Escort you to table, eh? Shaved himself, cleaned his tunic, polished his boots... I saw you, spitting on your hanky and rubbing the spots off your knees!'

'Oh, please, drop that!' Kopylov protested, blushing.

'And all your work was in vain!' Grigory mocked. 'He didn't even let you kiss his hand, did he? Let alone anything else.'

'That was only to be expected with you around,' Kopylov muttered, then, peering into the distance, exclaimed, 'Look! They're not our troops. That's the Allies!'

A team of six mules was approaching along the narrow lane, hauling a British gun. It was accompanied by a British officer riding a short-tailed chestnut horse. The driver of the leading pair of mules was also in British uniform, but with a Russian officer's cockade in his cap and a lieutenant's insignia on his shoulder straps.

When he was still several paces from Grigory the British officer put two fingers to the brim of his pith helmet and with a movement of his head requested the right of way. The lane was so narrow that the riders could pass only by keeping their horses right up against the stone wall.

The muscles tensed in Grigory's cheeks. Gritting his teeth, he rode straight at the officer. The Britisher raised his eyebrows in surprise and gave way a little but they were able to pass only when he lifted his right leg in its tight leather gaiter on to the glossy well-groomed croup of his thoroughbred mare.

One of the gun crew, a Russian officer judging by his appearance, surveyed Grigory angrily.

'Surely you could have given way! Must you show your disgusting manners on an occasion like this?'

'Ride on and shut up, you bitch's udder, or I'll give you "give way"!' Grigory growled.

The officer stood up on the limber and, turning his head, shouted, 'Gentlemen! Arrest this arrogant lout!'

Twirling his whip expressively, Grigory rode on at a walk down the lane. The tired dusty gun crews, all of them beardless young officers, gave him hostile looks, but no one attempted to detain him. The six-gun battery disappeared round the bend and Kopylov, biting his lips, rode up to Grigory.

'You're playing the fool, Grigory Panteleyevich! You're behaving like a little boy!'

'You been sent here to teach me manners?' Grigory snapped back.

'I understand why you lost your temper with Fitzhelaurov,' Kopylov said, shrugging his shoulders. 'But why take it out on this Englishman? Or didn't you like his helmet?'

'I didn't like him here, around Ust-Medveditskaya... Let him wear it somewhere else... When two dogs are fighting there's no need for a third to butt in, don't you know that?'

'Ha! So you're against foreign intervention? But in my view, when someone's got you by the throat you should be glad of any help you can get.'

'Well, be glad then, but I wouldn't let 'em set foot on our soil!'

'You saw the Chinese in the Red Army, didn't you?'

'What of it?'

'Is that not the same thing? That's also foreign help.'

'Don't give me that! The Chinese joined the Reds as volunteers.'

'And you think these people were brought here by force?'

Grigory could find no answer to this and rode on for some time, racking his brains. When he spoke, there was a clear note of chagrin in his voice.

'You learned folk are always like that... You twist

and turn like a hare on the snow! I feel you're telling me wrong, but I can't pin you down... Let's pack it in. Don't muddle me, I'm muddled enough as it is!'

Kopylov lapsed into an offended silence and nothing further passed between them all the way back to their quarters. Itching with curiosity, Prokhor rode up behind them and asked, 'Grigory Panteleyevich, Your Honour, would you kindly tell us what breed of animal that was the Cadets had pulling their guns? It had ears like a donkey's and all the rest was horse. It's shockin' to look at such an animal... What devil's breed is it? Could you explain, please, because we've got a bet on it...'

For about five minutes he rode behind them but, receiving no answer, he dropped back and, when the other orderlies came up with him, informed them in a whisper, 'They're keeping mum, lads, looks as if it's got 'em guessing too. They don't know where such a monster could have sprung from...'

XI

For the fourth time the Cossack squadrons rose from their shallow trenches and under the withering fire of the Red machine-guns dropped flat again. Since daybreak the Red Army batteries concealed in the woods along the left bank had been continuously bombarding the Cossack positions and their reserves stationed in the ravines.

Shrapnel burst over the Donside hills in melting milk-white puffs. Bullets were kicking up the brownish dust behind and in front of the jagged line of the Cossack trenches.

By noon the action grew more intense and a westerly wind carried the rumble of artillery fire far away along the Don.

Grigory was watching the course of the battle through field glasses from an insurgent battery's observation post. He could see the officers' companies stubbornly attacking despite their losses. When the fire grew too heavy, they hit the ground and dug in, then moved forward again in quick dashes to a new line; but to the left, in the direction of the monastery, the insurgent infantry would not leave its trenches. Grigory scribbled a note to Yermakov and sent it by messenger.

Half an hour later Yermakov rode up in a white-hot fury. He dismounted at the battery picketing post and, breathing heavily, climbed the hill to the observation trench.

'I can't get the Cossacks up! They won't budge!' he roared from a distance, waving his arms. 'We've lost twenty-three already. Don't you see the way the Reds are mowing us down with their machine-guns?'

"The officers are attacking and you can't get your lot moving?' Grigory ground out through clenched teeth.

'But look, every platoon of theirs has got a light machine-gun and all the ammo they want—and what have we got?'

'Don't argue with me! Get 'em moving at once, or we'll have your head!'

Yermakov swore and ran down the hill. Grigory followed him. He had decided to lead the 2nd Infantry Regiment into the attack himself.

By the battery's last gun, skilfully camouflaged with hawthorn branches, the battery commander button-holed him.

'Grigory Panteleyevich, just take a look at the English at work. In a minute they'll be shelling the bridge. Let's go up on the hill, eh?'

Through their binoculars they could see the thin line of the pontoon bridge that the Red engineers had thrown across the Don. Wagons were moving across it in a steady stream.

About ten minutes later the British battery emplaced on the stony side of a dell opened fire. The fourth shell smashed the bridge almost in the middle. The flow of wagons halted. Red Army men could be seen darting about, heaving shattered wagons and dead horses into the river.

Four boats carrying engineers immediately put out from the left bank, but before they could make good the damage, the British battery sent over another packet. One of the shells churned up the approach dam on the left bank, a second sent up a green spout of water right by the bridge itself and the renewed movement along it was once again halted.

'That's sharp shooting, eh! The sons-of-bitches!' the battery commander exclaimed admiringly. 'Now they won't let 'em cross till nightfall. That bridge can't live!'

Keeping his eyes to the glasses, Grigory asked, 'Why don't I hear a sound from you? You could support your infantry. Can't you see the machine-gun nests over there?'

'I'd be only too glad but I haven't got a single round

left! I fired my last shell half an hour ago and haven't had any since.'

'Then why're you standing here? Get going and drive to hell out of here!'

'I've sent to the Cadets for shells.'

'They won't give you any,' Grigory said with conviction.

'They've refused once already, so I sent again. Mebbe they'll take pity. A couple of dozen would do to silence those machine-guns. It's no joke—twenty-three of our men knocked out already. And how many more will be yet? Look at 'em bashing away!'

Grigory switched his eyes to the Cossack trenches— bullets were still hacking the dry ground on the slope. Every burst raised a strip of dust, as if an invisible hand had instantly pencilled a grey line along the trenches. The puffs of dust extended along the whole length of the Cossack trenches.

Grigory stopped watching the fire of the British battery. For a minute he listened to the unceasing artillery and machine-gun fire, then strode down the hill and caught up with Yermakov.

'Don't attack until you get the order from me. We won't knock 'em out of there till we have artillery support.'

'Isn't that what I told you?' Yermakov said reproachfully as he mounted his horse, which the hard riding and shooting had whipped into a lather.

Grigory watched Yermakov galloping away fearlessly under fire and thought worriedly, 'Why the hell does he have to go straight? The machine-guns will get him! He could have gone down into the dell, then along it and up behind the hill and he'd be home and dry.' Going at a wild gallop, Yermakov reached the dell, plunged into it and did not reappear on the other side. 'Ah, so he guessed! Now he'll make it,' Grigory thought with relief, and lay down on the slope for a smoke. A strange feeling of indifference had taken possession of him. No, he was not going to lead his Cossacks into attack under machine-gun fire. There was no point. Let the officers' assault companies do the attacking. Let them take Ust-Medveditskaya. Grigory lay there on the slope overlooking the battlefield, and for the first time in his life evaded taking direct part in a battle. No, it was not cowardice, not fear of death or pointless sacrifice that guided him at that moment. Only recently he had fought without spar-

490

ing his own life or the lives of the Cossacks under his command. But now something seemed to have snapped... Never before had he felt so clearly the utter futility of what was taking place around him. Whether it was the talk with Kopylov or the clash with Fitzhelaurov, or perhaps the two taken together, that had triggered the mood that had suddenly come over him, but he had decided not to face any more fire. He told himself vaguely that it was not for him to make peace between the Cossacks and Bolsheviks and he himself remained inwardly unreconciled, but he could not and would not defend people who were alien and hostile to him, people like Fitzhelaurov, who had the deepest contempt for him and whom he despised no less profoundly. And once again the former contradictions faced him as ruthlessly as before. 'Let 'em fight. I'll look on. As soon as they relieve me of the division, I'll ask to be sent to the rear. I've had enough!' he thought and, as his mind went back to the argument with Kopylov, he caught himself seeking excuses for the Reds. 'The Chinese come to the Reds empty-handed and risk their lives every day for next to nothing. Not that the pay counts for much! What the hell can you buy with it anyway? Play cards mebbe... So it's not for gain, there's something else... But the Allies are sending officers, tanks, guns, even mules! And then they'll be wanting a pile of rubles for it all. There's the difference! Yes, that's what we'll argue about this evening! As soon as I get back to headquarters, I'll get him in a corner and say, "There is a difference, Kopylov, so don't try to pull the wool over my eyes!" '

But the argument did not take place. In the afternoon Kopylov rode out to the positions of the 4th Regiment, which was being kept in reserve, and was killed on the way by a stray bullet. Grigory heard about it two hours later.

The next morning Ust-Medveditskaya was stormed and captured by units of General Fitzhelaurov's Fifth Division.

XII

Mitka Korshunov appeared in Tatarsky about three days after Grigory had left. He did not come alone. With him were two other members of his punitive detachment. One of them was an elderly Kalmyk from somewhere near Manych, the other a seedy-looking Cossack from Raspopinskaya. Mitka referred contemptuously to the Kalmyk as 'the blink', but honoured the Raspopinskaya drunkard and rogue with his full name, Silanty Petrovich.

Evidently Mitka had performed some by no means trivial services for the Don Army in the punitive troops. During the past winter he had been promoted to sergeant-major, then to the rank of junior-cornet, and now he rode into the village in all the glory of his officer's uniform. Life, it seemed, had been not unkind to Mitka in the retreat across the Donets; his light field-service tunic was stretched taut across his massively broad shoulders, the pink skin of his neck bulged in greasy folds over the high collar, his close-fitting whipcord trousers with side stripes looked as if they were about to split at the back... With his imposing presence Mitka would have been an Ataman's Life Guard living at the palace and guarding the sacred person of his Imperial Majesty, if it had not been for this accursed revolution. But even so Mitka had no complaints about life. He, too, had acquired officer's rank, and not like Grigory Melekhov, by risking his neck in reckless exploits. Meritorious service in a punitive detachment required other qualities... And Mitka had enough and to spare of such qualities. Having no great faith in his Cossacks' efficiency, Mitka himself dispatched any Bolshevik suspects and was not averse to using a whip or cleaning rod for dealing with deserters, and when it came to interrogating prisoners there was no one in the whole detachment to equal him. Even Lieutenant-Colonel Pryanishnikov himself shrugged his shoulders and said, 'No, gentlemen, say what you like, but Korshunov is unbeatable! He's not a man but a dragon!' And Mitka was distinguished by yet another splendid quality. When the punitive troops had no right to shoot an arrested person but did not want to let him go alive, he would be sentenced to corporal punishment and the administration of it would be entrusted to Mitka. He would perform the task with such zeal that after fifty strokes the victim would begin to vomit blood and after a hundred could safely be wrapped in sackcloth without even listening for his heartbeat... No man thus sentenced had yet been known to survive Mitka's ministrations. He himself would say with a chuckle, 'If I took all the trousers and skirts off the Reds I've got rid of, I could clothe the whole village of Tatarsky!'

The cruelty that had been a part of Mitka's nature

since childhood had not only found a worthy application in the punitives but, with nothing to restrain it, had grown to monstrous proportions. Brought into contact by the nature of his duties with all the dregs of the officer class—cocaine addicts, rapists, looters and other educated scoundrels—Mitka gladly, with peasant thoroughness assimilated everything they in their hatred of the Reds could teach him, and had little difficulty in surpassing his mentors. Where a neurotic officer, weary of blood and others' suffering, would give up, Mitka would merely narrow his yellow, glittering eyes and pursue the matter to its conclusion.

Such was the Mitka that had left his Cossack unit and qualified for easy pickings in Lieutenant-Colonel Pryanishnikov's punitive detachment.

On his arrival in the village Mitka rode homeward at a walk, with a great display of his own importance and scarcely acknowledging the bows of the women he passed. At the charred, half-demolished gate he dismounted and handed his reins to the Kalmyk, then swaggered into the yard. Accompanied by Silanty, he walked silently round the foundations of the house, touched a turquoise lump of glass that had congealed during the fire with the tip of his whipstock, and said in a husky voice, 'They burnt it down... And it was a fine house! The best in the village. A man from our village did it—Mishka Koshevoi. And he killed my grandfather too. Well, I've come back to the ashes of my own home, Silanty Petrovich.'

'Any of these Koshevois in the village now?' Silanty asked eagerly.

'There should be. We'll see them later... Let's go and visit our in-laws.'

On the way to the Melekhovs Mitka asked the Bogatiryovs' daughter-in-law, who happened to be passing, 'Is my mother back from across the Don?'

'Not yet, I'd say, 'Mitry Mironovich.'

'What about Melekhov?'

'The old man?'

'Yes.'

'The old man's at home. So's the whole family but for Grigory. Petro was killed back in winter, did ye hear?'

Mitka nodded and put his horse into a trot.

As he rode down the deserted lane his yellow catlike eyes, cold and sated, showed not a trace of his recent emotion. On reaching the Melekhovs' yard, he said quietly, without addressing either of his companions in particular, 'That's how my home village greets me! I even have to turn to relatives for my dinner... Never mind, we'll have it out with 'em yet!'

Pantelei was in the shed, mending a reaper. At the sight of the horsemen and recognising Korshunov among them, he came out to the gate.

'Welcome back,' he said hospitably as he opened the wicket. 'Be our guests! Glad to see you!'

'Hullo there, kinsman! Safe and well?'

'Praise the Lord, not doing badly so far. Are you an officer then now?'

'Did you think only your sons were fit to wear golden shoulder straps,' Mitka said complacently, offering the old man his long sinewy hand.

'Mine weren't all that keen on 'em,' Pantelei answered with a smile, and walked on ahead to show them where to put their horses.

The hospitable Ilyinichna gave the guests a good meal, and then the talk began. Mitka wanted to know everything about his family but was reticent himself and showed neither anger nor sorrow. In a casual way he asked whether any of the Koshevois were still in the village and, on learning that Mishka's mother and the children were at home, gave Silanty a quick, barely perceptible wink.

The guests soon took their leave. As he saw them off Pantelei asked, 'D'you think to be long in the village?'

'Two or three days.'

'Will you see your mother?'

'Depends how things work out.'

'Going far just now?'

'Not far... Just got to see one or two folk in the village. We'll soon be back.'

Before Mitka and his companions returned to the Melekhovs' house the news was all over the village, 'Korshunov and the Kalmyks have butchered the whole Koshevoi family!'

Pantelei had heard nothing when he brought back a mower from the blacksmith's and was about to busy himself again with the reaper, but Ilyinichna called him into the house.

'Come in, Prokofievich! And be quick, do!'

There was a note of unconcealed alarm in the old woman's voice and in some surprise Pantelei at once made for the house.

Natalya was standing by the stove, pale and with traces of tears on her cheeks. Ilyinichna shot a glance at Anikei's wife and asked in a low voice, 'Have you heard the news, husband?'

'Something must have happened to Grigory, God forbid!' the thought burned into Pantelei's brain. His face paled and in a frenzy of fear because no one was saying anything, he exclaimed, 'Out with it, damn you!.. What's happened? Is it Grigory?' And, as though exhausted by the shout, he sank down on a bench, stroking his shaking legs.

Dunyashka was the first to guess the reason for her father's consternation, and hastened to say, 'No, Father, it's not about Grigory. Mitka's slaughtered the Koshevois.'

'Slaughtered what? Who?' the weight fell from Pantelei's heart at once and, still unable to grasp his daughter's meaning, asked again, 'The Koshevois? Mitka?'

Anikei's wife, who had run in with the news, began to stammer out her story.

'I was going out past the Koshevoi's place to look for the calf, and just then Mitka and two other soldiers rode up and went into the house. And I was thinking that the calf won't go further than the windmill, it was my turn to graze the calves...'

'To the devil with your calf, woman!' Pantelei interrupted her wrathfully.

'...Well, they went into the house,' she went on, panting with excitement. 'And there I was, standing waiting. That bodes no good, I thought, them coming here. And then what a screaming there was and I could hear—blows. I was frightened to death and wanted to run away, but I'd just turned away from the fence when I heard a tramp of feet behind me and it was Mitka. He'd got a rope round the old woman's neck and was dragging her along the ground, just like a dog, for God's sake! He got her to the shed and the poor thing wasn't making a sound, she must have fainted; and that Kalmyk that was with him climbed up on a rafter... And as I watched, that Mitka, he throws him the rope and shouts to pull it up and tie it tight. Oh, was I frightened! Before my very eyes they strangled the poor old woman, then jumped on their horses and rode off down the lane, to the ataman's office, I reckon. I was afraid to go into the house... But I could see the blood running out from under the door and down the steps. God grant I never see such a sight again!'

'Fine guests the Lord sent us!' Ilyinichna said, looking expectantly at the old man.

Pantelei had listened to the story in terrible agitation and, without saying a word, he went out into the porch.

Presently Mitka and his two henchmen appeared at the gate. Pantelei limped out quickly to meet them. 'Wait!' he shouted while still at a distance. 'Don't bring your horses in here!'

'What's the matter, kinsman?' Mitka asked in surprise.

'Back you go!' Pantelei came up to them and, looking into Mitka's yellow glittering eyes, said firmly, 'Don't be angry, kinsman, but I don't want you in my house. You'd better go away from here while the going's good.'

'Ah...' Mitka drawled comprehendingly, and his face paled. 'So you're turning us out?'

'I don't want you to foul my house!' the old man repeated resolutely. 'And may you never set foot in it again. We Melekhovs are no kinsmen of executioners!'

'So that's it! You're very tender-hearted, kinsman!'

'Well, you haven't got any mercy left, if you've started putting women and children to death! It's a rotten trade you're following, Mitka... Your late father wouldn't have been glad to see you now, that he wouldn't!'

'And you, you old fool, did you expect me to coddle them? They killed my father and my grandfather, and I'm supposed to kiss 'em and say Christ is risen, am I? Go to hell!' Mitka jerked the halter furiously and led his horse out of the gate.

'Don't talk like that, Mitka, you're young enough to be my son. There's nothing for us to quarrel over, so go and God be with you!'

Growing even paler, Mitka brandished his whip and shouted huskily, 'Don't tempt me into sin, don't tempt me! I'm sorry for Natalya, or I'd have given it to you, you merciful man... I know you! I can see just what's in your mind! You didn't retreat with us across the Donets, did you? Gave yourselves up to the Reds? Don't forget that!.. You all ought to be done away with, you bastards, like the Koshevois! Come on, lads! So mind out, you mangy cripple, don't cross my path again! You won't slip through my fingers! And I'll remind you of the hospitality you showed me! Bugger such kinsmen!'

Pantelei bolted the gate with shaking hands and limped back to the house.

'I've turned out that brother of yours,' he said, not looking at Natalya.

Natalya said nothing, although in her heart she agreed with her father-in-law's action. Ilyinichna quickly made the sign of the cross and said with joyful relief, 'Thank the Lord for that! That's something we've been spared. Forgive my saying such a thing, Natalya dear, but your Mitka has turned out a real bad lot! And what a service to be in. He couldn't serve like the other Cossacks in the loyal units but has to go with them punitives! Is that the work for a Cossack—to be an executioner, hanging old women and cutting innocent children to pieces?! Were they to blame for their Mishka? If that's how it is, the Reds could have killed both of us and Mishatka and Polyushka as well because of Grisha. But they didn't, did they? They had mercy. No, God protect us, but I don't hold with that kind of thing!'

'Don't think I defend him, Mother,' was all Natalya said, wiping her tears with the corner of her kerchief.

Mitka left the village the same day. It was rumoured that he had joined up with his punitive detachment somewhere near Karginskaya and gone off with them to impose order on the Ukrainian settlements of the Donets District, the population of which had been guilty of taking part in suppression of the Upper Don rebellion.

For a week after his departure the village buzzed with talk. The majority condemned the killing of the Koshevoi family. The victims were buried out of public funds; an attempt was made to sell the little house, but there were no buyers. On the orders of the village ataman the windows were boarded up and for long afterwards the village children were afraid to play near that terrible spot. The old folk crossed themselves as they passed by and prayed for the souls of those who had been murdered.

Then it was time to go out mowing in the steppe and even such recent happenings were forgotten.

The village again became absorbed in work and rumours of what was going on at the front. The Cossacks who still had some draught animals left grunted and grumbled when they had to be put in the shafts of commandeered wagons. Nearly every day horses and oxen had to be taken off work and sent to the stanitsa. As they unharnessed the horses from the reapers the old men had many a harsh word to say about this never-ending war. But the shells, bullets, rolls of barbed wire and food supplies had to be carted to the front. And carted they were. Although, as luck would have it, the

17–1108

weather had turned so fine that now was just the time to mow and rake the unusually rich ripe grass.

Pantelei, who had been making ready for the mowing, was very much annoyed with Darya. She had taken a pair of oxen to cart some ammunition and should have been back from the staging point, but a week had passed and still there was no sign of her; without that pair of his oldest and most reliable oxen it would be no use going out into the steppe.

The fact was that he should never have sent Darya in the first place. Pantelei had grudgingly entrusted her with the oxen, knowing how happy she always was to spend her time in frivolous pursuits and how lazy about caring for the animals, but there had been no one else to send. Dunyashka could not be sent because it was not proper for a girl to go off on a long journey with strange Cossacks; Natalya had small children, and how could the old man himself take those damn cartridges? But Darya had been only too willing. Even in the old days she had enjoyed any kind of trip—to the windmill or the millet mill or on any other errand—only because away from home she felt free to do as she liked. Every trip provided diversion and amusement. Once she had escaped her mother-in-law's supervision, she could gossip with other women to her heart's content and, as she was fond of saying, 'have a spot of love' with some handy Cossack who caught her ever roving eye. But at home, even after Petro's death, the strait-laced Ilyinichna never let her off the leash, as though Darya, who had many a time deceived her living husband, were obliged to remain true for ever to a dead one.

Pantelei had known the oxen would not be properly cared for but he had no choice, so he had sent his eldest daughter-in-law. And having sent her, he lived the whole week in the greatest anxiety and self-reproach. 'My oxen are done for,' he told himself more than once, awakening in the middle of the night and sighing despondently.

Darya arrived home in the morning of the eleventh day. Pantelei had just come in from the fields. He had done his mowing by pairing up with Anikei's wife and, having left her and Dunyashka out in the steppe, had returned to the village for water and food. The old couple and Natalya were having breakfast when a wagon drove past the windows with a familiar rumble. Natalya darted to the window and saw Darya, her face swathed to the eyes in her kerchief, leading in the weary, emaciated oxen.

'Is it her?' the old man asked, choking on a piece of bread.

'Yes, it's Darya.'

'I never thought I'd see the oxen again! The Lord be praised! That wretched hussy! It's a wonder she ever got home at all,' the old man muttered, crossing himself and belching contentedly.

After unyoking the oxen, Darya came into the kitchen, put down a folded sacking by the threshold and greeted the family.

'Well, m'dear, why didn't you take another week about it!' Pantelei exclaimed vexedly, scowling at Darya and not responding to her greeting.

'You should've gone yourself then,' Darya snapped back, taking off her dusty kerchief.

'What kept you away so long?' Ilyinichna stepped in to pour oil on troubled waters.

'They wouldn't let me go, that's why.'

Pantelei shook his head unbelievingly.

'They let Khristonya's wife back from the staging post. Why should they keep you?'

'Because they didn't!' Darya flashed her eyes angrily and added, 'If you don't believe me, go and ask the man in charge.'

'I'm in no mind to go finding out about you, but next time you'll stay at home. I won't send you anywhere.'

'Oh, what a threat! You have frightened me now! Why, I wouldn't go myself! I won't go even if you send me!'

'What about the oxen—are they all right?' the old man asked more peaceably.

'They're all right. Nothing's happened to your oxen...' Darya answered unwillingly, looking as black as thunder.

'She's just parted with some sweetheart on the road, that's why she's in such a mood,' Natalya guessed.

She always treated Darya and her dubious love affairs with mixed feelings of sympathy and distaste.

After breakfast Pantelei was about to set off for the fields again, but the village ataman appeared.

'I was going to wish you a good journey, Pantelei Prokofievich, but wait a bit, don't go yet.'

'It wouldn't be more transport you're wanting?' the old man asked with affected humility, although fury was choking him.

'No, it's a different tune this time. The Commander of

the whole Don Army, General Sidorin himself, is on his way here. Understand? I've just had a special message from the stanitsa ataman, ordering all the women and old men to assemble for a village meeting.'

'Are they in their right mind?' Pantelei cried. 'Who arranges such things at a busy time like this? Will your General Sidorin stack the hay to keep me alive this winter?'

'He's just as much yours as mine,' the ataman replied calmly. 'I do what I'm told. Off with that yoke! We've got to give him a royal welcome. They say he's bringing some Allied generals with him.'

Pantelei stood silently by the hay wagon, pondered for a while, and then began to unyoke the oxen. Seeing that his words had taken effect, the ataman looked more cheerful and asked, 'Mebbe I could have the use of your mare?'

'What d'you want her for?'

'The orders are—may they sit on hedgehogs—to send out two troikas as far as Bad Ravine to meet 'em. But where am I to find the tarantasses and horses—I'm at my wits' end! I've been on the run since daybreak, made five of my shirts wet through, and only got hold of four horses. People are all up to their eyes in work—it's enough to make you howl!'

The resigned Pantelei agreed to supply his mare and even his little sprung tarantass. After all, it was the commander-in-chief that was to be met, and there were foreign generals with him, and Pantelei had always experienced a feeling of tremulous respect for generals.

Thanks to the ataman's efforts, two troikas were somehow assembled and sent out to Bad Ravine to meet the honoured guests. A crowd gathered on the square. Many had abandoned the mowing and hurried in from the steppe.

Pantelei let the work go hang, smartened himself up, putting on a clean shirt, his best cloth trousers with side-stripes, and the peaked cap Grigory had brought him many years before as a present, and limped off to the square at a dignified pace, having instructed his wife to send Darya out to the steppe with food and water for Dunyashka.

Soon a dense cloud of dust billowed over the Hetman's Highway and streamed towards the village. A gleam of metal showed through the murk and the melodious voice of a motor horn could be heard in the distance. The visitors were driving in two shiny new dark-blue motor-cars; far behind them, overtaking the mowers coming in from the fields, the troikas were galloping along empty, with the postman's bells that the ataman had obtained specially for this solemn occasion jingling dolefully under the shaft-bows. The crowd stirred, a murmur of talk arose, and cheerful shouts came from the children. The harassed ataman darted about among the crowd, looking for respected old men to whom he could entrust the task of presenting the traditional gifts of bread and salt. He spotted Pantelei, and buttonholed him joyfully.

'Help us out, for Christ's sake! You're an old hand at this kind of thing... You know how to shake hands with 'em and all that... Why, you've been a member of the Council, and with a son like yours... Please, now, take the bread and salt. I feel a bit shy, you know, and my knees are shaking.'

Flattered beyond measure by the honour that had befallen him, Pantelei at first refused for form's sake, but then tucked his head into his shoulders, crossed himself deftly, and accepted the dish with its loaf covered with an embroidered towel, and elbowed his way out to the front.

The cars drove swiftly towards the square accompanied by a pack of dogs that had barked themselves hoarse.

'How d'you feel? Not scared?' the pale-faced ataman inquired anxiously. This was the first time he had seen such important personages. Pantelei showed him the bluish whites of his eyes and said in a voice that gurgled with excitement, 'Here, hold this for a minute while I comb my beard. Hold it!'

The ataman obligingly took the dish and Pantelei smoothed down his moustache and beard, puffed out his chest bravely and, keeping his game leg on tip-toe, so that his lameness would not be noticed, resumed his grip on the dish. But it began to shake so violently in his hands that the ataman asked in fright, 'You won't drop it, will you? Oh, do be careful!'

Pantelei twitched his shoulder scornfully. Him do a thing like that! How could the man say anything so foolish! He, who had been a member of the Council and had shaken hands with everyone in the Vice Ataman's palace—would he suddenly be scared of a general? This wretched creature must have lost his head altogether!

'When I was in the Army Council, my lad, I drank tea with sugar in it with the Vice Ataman himself...'

Pantelei began, but then his voice broke off.

The leading motor-car had stopped no more than ten paces away from him. A clean-shaven chauffeur in a cap with a broad peak and narrow, un-Russian shoulder straps on his tunic, jumped out smartly and opened the rear door. Two army officers in field-service uniforms stepped out in a dignified manner and headed towards the crowd. They were walking straight towards Pantelei, who drew himself up to attention and froze in that position. He realised that these modestly dressed individuals were, in fact, the generals, while those behind them, who looked smarter, were merely their accompanying suite. The old man stared unblinkingly at the approaching visitors and his gaze expressed increasing astonishment. Where were the fringed general's epaulettes? Where were the shoulder-knots and medals? What kind of generals were these, if there was nothing in their appearance to distinguish them from rank-and-file army clerks? Pantelei was instantly and bitterly disillusioned. He felt ashamed both of his own solemn preparations for the meeting and of these generals who were a disgrace to the rank of general. By the devil, if he'd known what kind of generals were going to appear he wouldn't have dressed up so carefully or have waited in such fear and trembling. In fact, he wouldn't have been standing here at all with a dish in his hands and a loaf badly baked by some snotty old woman. No, Pantelei Melekhov had never yet been a laughing-stock, but now that moment had come; only a minute ago he had heard the kids tittering behind him, and one little devil had even shouted at the top of his voice, 'Look, lads! Look how that old cripple Melekhov is puffing his chest out! Like he'd swallowed a hedgehog!' If only there had been something to make it worthwhile putting up with these jibes and straining his lame leg. Inwardly Pantelei was boiling with indignation. And the one to blame for it all was that blasted coward of an ataman! Came round telling the tale, took the mare and the tarantass, ran all over the village with his tongue hanging out, looking for bells and other baubles to put on the troikas. Truly 'tis said, a man who's never had anything better is glad of any old rag. But Pantelei had seen far finer generals than these in his time! Take the imperial review, for instance, the generals they had there– chests all covered in crosses and medals and gold braid. It warmed your heart to look at 'em—not a general but an ikon! But this lot—all in green like so

502

many jays... One of them didn't even have a proper cap, but a kind of pot with cheesecloth hanging down from it, and his face all shaven bare, not a single hair on it... Pantelei frowned and nearly spat in disgust, but someone gave him a powerful shove from behind and whispered loudly, 'Go on, offer it to them!'

Pantelei stepped forward. General Sidorin looked over his head, quickly scanned the crowd and boomed, 'Greetings to you, elders!'

'We wish you good health, Your Excellency!' the villagers responded raggedly.

The general graciously accepted the bread and salt from Pantelei's hands, said thank-you, and passed it back to his adjutant.

A tall lean English colonel standing next to Sidorin surveyed the Cossacks with cold curiosity from under the brim of the helmet that was tilted low over his eyes. On the orders of General Briggs, the head of the British military mission in the Caucasus, he was accompanying Sidorin on his tour of inspection of the Don Army's territory that had been cleared of the Bolsheviks, and with the help of an interpreter was conscientiously studying Cossack morale and also acquainting himself with the situation on the fronts.

The colonel had been wearied by the hardships of travel, the monotonous steppe scenery, the tedious conversation and all the other complex duties of a representative of a great power, but he set the interests of His Majesty's service above all else. He listened attentively to the speech made by the spokesman from the stanitsa and understood nearly everything because he actually knew the Russian language, though he concealed the fact from strangers. With true British aloofness he surveyed the diverse faces of these warlike sons of the steppes and marvelled at the mingling of races that always strikes the eye when one is confronted by a crowd of Cossacks; beside a blond Slav Cossack stood a typical Mongol, while next to him a young Cossack, as dark as a raven's wing, with his arm supported by a dirty bandage was chatting quietly with a grey-haired patriarch of biblical appearance. And that old fellow leaning on his staff and wearing an old-fashioned Cossack chekmen— the colonel was prepared to bet—had the blood of Caucasian highlanders in his veins.

The colonel knew a little history, and as he surveyed the Cossacks he was thinking that neither these barbarians nor their grandchildren would ever be marching to India under the command of some new Platov. After victory over the Bolsheviks, a Russia, bled white by civil war, would for long cease to exist as a great power and for the next few decades there would be no threat to Britain's eastern possessions. That the Bolsheviks would be defeated the colonel was firmly convinced. He was a sober-minded person, had lived in Russia for a long time before the war and could not, of course, believe for a moment that in such a semi-barbaric country the Utopian ideas of communism would triumph.

The colonel's attention was diverted for a moment by some women nearby who were whispering loudly among themselves. Without turning his head he scanned their weathered high-cheekboned faces, and a barely perceptible smile of contempt hovered on his firmly compressed lips.

Having presented the bread and salt, Pantelei withdrew into the crowd. Instead of listening to the Vyoshenskaya orator welcoming the newcomers on behalf of the stanitsa, he made his way round the back of the crowd to where the troikas had halted.

The horses were covered with foam and their flanks were still heaving. The old man went up to his mare, which was harnessed in the leading position, wiped her nostrils with his hand and sighed. He wanted to fire off a volley of oaths, unhitch the mare and take her home, so great was his disappointment.

Meanwhile General Sidorin was making a speech to the people of Tatarsky. After expressing approval of their military operations in the rear of the Red forces, he said, 'You have fought courageously against our common enemies. Your services will not be forgotten by the motherland, which is gradually freeing itself from the Bolsheviks, from their terrible oppression. I should like to make an award to the women of your village who, so we have been informed, earned special distinction in the armed struggle against the Reds. I ask our Cossack heroines to step forward as their names are read out!'

One of the officers read out a short list. The first name was that of Darya Melekhova, the others were the widows of Cossacks who had been killed when the uprising began and who, like Darya, had taken part in the slaughter of the Communist prisoners that had been brought to Tatarsky after the surrender of the Serdobsk Regiment.

Darya had not obeyed her father-in-law's order to drive out to the fields. She was right there among the village women and dressed up in her Sunday best.

As soon as she heard her name called, she pushed her way through the crowd of women and stepped boldly forward, adjusting her white lace-edged kerchief, screwing up her eyes, and smiling with a touch of embarrassment. Though tired after the journey and her amorous adventures, she was still devilishly beautiful. Her pale cheeks, untouched by the sun, set off the hot glow of her narrowed, seeking eyes, and in the wilful curve of the pencilled eyebrows and the corners of the smiling lips there lurked something defiant and impure.

Finding her way barred by an officer standing with his back to the crowd, she gave him a gentle push and said, 'Make way for the bridegroom's family!' and walked up to Sidorin.

He took the medal with the St. George ribbon that the adjutant handed him, pinned it clumsily to Darya's blouse over her left breast, and looked into her eyes with a smile.

'Are you the widow of Cornet Melekhov, who was killed in March?'

'I am.'

'You will now receive the sum of five hundred rubles. They will be paid to you by this officer. The Ataman of the Don Army, Afrikan Petrovich Bogayevsky, and the Don Government thank you for the noble courage that you displayed and beg you to accept their sympathy... They sympathise with you in your grief.'

Darya did not take in everything the general was saying. She thanked him with a nod, accepted the money from the adjutant and, smiling silently, also looked straight into the eyes of the by no means elderly general. They were nearly the same height and Darya scanned his lean face without much embarrassment. 'You didn't put much of a price on my Petro, no more than for a pair of bullocks... Still, the general's not so bad, looks as if he might do,' she was thinking at that moment with characteristic cynicism. Sidorin waited for her to step back but for some reason Darya tarried. The adjutant and the other officers standing behind Sidorin twitched their eyebrows in the direction of the sprightly widow; sparks of merriment glowed in their eyes; even the British colonel stirred into life, straightened his belt, shifted from one foot to the other, and something remotely resembling a smile appeared on his impassive face.

'Can I go now?' Darya asked.

'Er, yes ... by all means!' Sidorin hastily assented.

With an ungraceful gesture Darya tucked the money into the front of her blouse and walked off into the crowd. All the officers, by now thoroughly tired of speeches and ceremonies, watched her as she tripped lightly away.

The widow of the late Martin Shamil approached Sidorin timidly. When the medal had been pinned to her shabby blouse, she suddenly burst into tears, and so helplessly and with such womanly bitterness that the officers' faces at once lost all their joviality and became serious and sympathetically sour.

'Was your husband also killed?' Sidorin asked, frowning.

The weeping woman covered her face with her hands and nodded silently.

'She's got enough children to fill a wagon!' one of the Cossacks boomed in a deep voice.

Sidorin turned towards the Englishman and said loudly, 'We are rewarding women who displayed exceptional bravery in fighting the Bolsheviks. The husbands of most of them were killed at the beginning of the rebellion against the Bolsheviks and these widows, in revenge for their husbands' deaths, destroyed a large force of local Communists. The first woman I decorated dispatched a notoriously cruel Communist commissar with her own hands.'

The interpreting officer rattled off something in English. The colonel listened, bowed his head, and said, 'I greatly admire the bravery of these women. Tell me, general, did they take part in the fighting on an equal footing with the men?'

'Yes,' Sidorin answered shortly, and with an impatient gesture invited the third widow to come forward.

The visitors departed soon after the ceremony. The crowd broke up, people hurried away to the mowing, and a few minutes after the cars, accompanied by a chorus of barking, had disappeared from view, there were only three old men left by the churchyard wall.

'Queer times have come upon us!' said one, spreading his arms wide. 'They used to give the George cross or medal for something big, for valour! And who did they give 'em to? The real dare-devils! There weren't so many who'd take such risks. "A cross on your chest or a cross in the ground!" — that's what they used to say. But now they hand out medals to women... It wouldn't be so bad if it was for something, but this... The Cossacks herded prisoners, unarmed men, into the village and they laid 'em out with cudgels. What kind of heroism is that? Strike me dead, but I don't understand it!'

Another old man, feeble and half blind, moved a foot to steady himself, and pulled out of his pocket a cloth tobacco pouch tied in a roll.

'The ones up top there, in Cherkassk, know best. I reckon they saw it like this. Women need a bait, too, to get 'em fighting mad. A medal here, five hundred in cash there—what woman would resist such an honour? There might be a few Cossacks around don't want to go to the front, want to keep away from the war, but how could they? Their women will be buzzing at them, not give 'em a minute's peace! The cuckoo that sings at night, y'know, beats all the others! Every woman now will be thinking, "Mebbe I'll get a medal too?"'

'That's the wrong way to look at it, Fyodor!' a third remonstrated. 'They deserved some reward and they've got it. The women are widows, the cash will be a big help at home, and they got their medals for daring. That Darya Melekhova, she was first to bring Kotlyarov to justice, and she was right too! God will judge 'em all, you can't just blame the women. Blood's thicker than water, y'know.'

The old men argued and wrangled until the churchbell rang for evensong. But as soon as the bell-ringer sounded the first note, they all three stood up, took off their caps, crossed themselves and walked off staidly towards the church.

XIII

It was surprising how life had changed in the Melekhov family! But a short while ago, Pantelei had been master in his own house. All the family had obeyed him implicitly, the work followed its seasonal course, joy and grief were shared in common, and the whole daily round bore the stamp of a great and lasting harmony. It had been a close-knit family, but since spring everything had changed. Dunyashka was the first to break away. She showed no direct disobedience to her father, but any work that she was called upon to do she performed with

507

obvious unwillingness and as though she were doing it not for herself but for hire; outwardly, too, she had become more reserved, estranged; seldom now was her carefree laughter heard about the house.

After Grigory had left for the front Natalya also kept at a distance from the old folk, spending nearly all her time with the children; she would willingly talk and have to do only with them. She seemed to be nursing some secret grief, but not a word would she say about it to anyone. Far from complaining, she made every effort to hide her unhappiness.

As for Darya, she had never been the same since her trip with the commandeered wagons. More and more often she would contradict her father-in-law, and she took no notice at all of Ilyinichna; for no apparent reason she was cross with everyone, excused herself from the mowing on grounds of ill health and behaved as though she were living her last days in the Melekhov home.

Pantelei's family was falling apart before his very eyes. He and his old wife were left on their own. The ties of kinship were swiftly and unexpectedly disintegrating, the warmth had gone out of family relationships, and more and more frequently notes of irritability and estrangement crept into the conversation. They sat down to table no longer as a united family but as individuals thrown together by chance.

The war was to blame for it all—of that Pantelei was perfectly well aware. Dunyashka was angry with her parents for dashing her hopes of ever marrying Mishka Koshevoi—the only man she loved with the devoted strength of virgin passion; Natalya was silently and deeply, with characteristic secretiveness, grieving over Grigory's fresh desertion to Aksinya. Pantelei saw all this but could do nothing to restore order to his house. How could he, after all that had happened, consent to his daughter's marriage to an out-and-out Bolshevik? And what was the use of consenting when that devil of a suitor was sloping around at the front, and in a Red Army unit at that? And it was the same with Grigory. But for his officer's rank, Pantelei would have dealt with his son promptly enough. So drastically would he have dealt with him that Grigory would never again have let his eye wander in the direction of Astakhov's yard. But the war had thrown everything into confusion and robbed the old man of any opportunity of managing his own home as he saw fit. The war had ruined him, stifled his former love of toil, taken away his elder son, and sown dissension and rebellion in his family. It had swept through his life like a storm over a field of wheat; but wheat, even after a storm, rises and flaunts its beauty in the sunshine, and the old man could not rise. Mentally he had thrown in his hand—let things take their course!

After the award she had received from General Sidorin, Darya grew more cheerful. That day she returned from the square in an animated, happy frame of mind. With shining eyes she showed Natalya the medal.

'What did they give you that for?' Natalya asked in surprise.

'That's for our kinsman, Ivan Alexeyevich, may his soul rest in peace, the rotten bastard! And this is for Petro.' Boastfully she unwrapped the packet of crisp Don bank notes.

Darya did not go out to the fields after all. Pantelei wanted to send her with food for the mowers but she firmly refused.

'Leave me alone, Dad, I'm dead tired after my journey.'

The old man frowned, whereupon Darya softened her rough answer by saying half jokingly, 'It'd be a sin to send me out into the fields at a time like this. This is my big day!'

'All right, I'll take it myself,' the old man consented. 'Well, and what about the money?'

'What about it?' Darya raised her eyebrows.

'I'm asking ye what ye'll do with the money?'

'That's my business! I'll do what I like with it!'

'But how can you? They gave you the money for Petro, didn't they?'

'They gave it to me and it's not for you to say how I spend it.'

'You're one of the family, aren't ye?'

'And what do you expect of one of the family, Father dear? To have the money for yourself?'

'I don't mean all of it, but Petro was our son, wasn't he? Or don't ye think so? The old woman and me, aren't we entitled to our share?'

Her father-in-law's claim obviously lacked confidence, and Darya drove her advantage home. Mockingly calm, she said, 'I won't give you any, not even a ruble! None of it's for you, otherwise they'd have said so. What makes you think there's a share for you here? There was never any talk of it and you won't get any of mine!'

Pantelei then made his last attempt.

'You live in the family, you eat our bread, so everything ought to be in common. How can we carry on with each of us managing his own lot separate? I won't allow that!' he said.

But Darya parried even this attempt to take possession of the money that belonged to her. Smiling shamelessly, she declared, 'I'm not wedded to you, Father. I'm here today, but tomorrow I may get married again and you won't see my heels for dust! I'm not bound to pay you for my keep. I've worked ten years for your family without a break.'

'You worked for yourself, you randy bitch!' Pantelei let fly indignantly. He shouted something else but Darya refused to listen, turned her back on him and flounced away into her room. 'You've picked the wrong one for bullying!' she whispered, smiling derisively.

No more was said on the subject. Darya was certainly not the kind to give up what belonged to her for fear of an old man's wrath.

Pantelei made ready to drive out to the fields and, before leaving, had a brief word with Ilyinichna.

'Keep an eye on Darya,' he said.

'Why should I?' his wife asked in surpise.

'Because she may march out of the house any minute and take some of our belongings with her. She's not flapping her wings for nothing, I reckon... Looks as if she's found herself a man and may run off tomorrow or the day after to get married.'

'That's as like as not,' Ilyinichna agreed with a sigh. 'She's turned her back on us. Nothing pleases her, nothing suits her... She's like a slice cut off the loaf, you can't stick it on again!'

'And there's no need for us to try! Don't you hang on to her, you old fool, if she says anything on that score. I've had enough bother with her.' Pantelei climbed on the hay wagon and, lashing the oxen, concluded, 'She's always dodging work, the lazy slut. All she thinks about is eating well and gadding about in the evenings. Now that Petro's gone, rest his soul, we don't need a creature like her in the family. She's just a pest, not a woman!'

The old people's conjectures were mistaken. Darya was not thinking of marriage. She had other matters on her mind.

All that day Darya was sociable and cheerful. Even

the tiff over the money had not spoiled her mood. She flounced about in front of the mirror looking at the medal from all angles, changed about five blouses to see which went best with the striped ribbon of St. George. 'I must get myself some crosses now!' she jested. Then she called Ilyinichna into the side room, pushed two twenty-ruble bank notes into her sleeve and, clasping the older woman's knotted hand to her breast, whispered, 'That's to pay for a mass for Petro... Order a grand mass for him, Mother, make some wheaten porridge...' And she burst into tears. But the next minute, with eyes still glistening, she was playing with Mishatka, throwing her best silk shawl over his head and laughing as if she had never known the salty taste of tears.

Her high spirits rose to a fresh pitch when Dunyashka came in from the fields. She related how she had been presented with the medal and then gave an imitation of the general's solemn speech and the way the Englishman had stood staring at her like a stuffed dummy, and then with a conspiratorial wink at Natalya went on in serious tones to claim that she, Darya, the widow of an officer, decorated with the medal of St. George, would also be elevated to officer's rank and appointed to command a squadron of old Cossacks.

Natalya sat mending the children's shirts and listened to Darya with a suppressed smile, while the confused Dunyashka clasped her hands imploringly and begged, 'Darya darling! Don't tell such stories for goodness sake! I don't know whether you're making it up or telling the truth. Be serious!'

'Don't you believe me? Then you're a silly girl! I'm telling you the honest truth. All the officers are at the front, so who's going to drill the old men and lick 'em into shape? They'll be put under my command and I'll handle 'em, the old devils!' Darya closed the door into the kitchen, so that her father-in-law would not see, swiftly tucked the hem of her skirt between her legs and, holding it from behind, marched about the front room displaying her gleaming bare calves, halted in front of Dunyashka, and in a deep voice commanded, 'Grandads and grandpas, atten-shun! Up with those beards— higher now! By the left, left wheel, quick march!'

Dunyashka burst into giggles, covering her face with her hands. Through her laughter Natalya said, 'You'll come to no good! You'll be laughing on the other side of your face one day!'

'No good, huh! Have you ever seen anything good! If I didn't brighten you up, you'd all get the mildew from misery!'

But Darya's burst of high spirits ended as suddenly as it had begun. Half an hour later she went off into her little room, vexedly tore off the ill-fated medal and tossed it into the chest, then sat by the window with her cheeks propped in her hands. That night she took herself off somewhere and returned only after first cock-crow.

For the next four days she worked diligently in the fields.

The mowing was not making much headway. With so few hands they could not mow more than five acres a day. The swathes of mown grass were soaked by rain and had to be pulled apart and dried in the sun. No sooner had they built the haycocks than there was more heavy rain, pouring down from dusk till dawn with steady autumnal persistence. After that the weather improved, an east wind sprang up, the mowers again began to clatter across the steppe, the sweet tang of mildew rose from the blackened haycocks, the steppe was wrapped in steam, and the bluish haze all but obscured the outlines of the look-out mounds, the purple gashes of the ravines, and the green crowns of the willows above the distant ponds.

On the fourth day Darya got her things together with the intention of going to the stanitsa straight from the fields. She announced this when they gathered for the midday meal.

Pantelei was displeased and asked sarcastically, 'What's the great hurry? Couldn't you wait till Sunday?'

'I wouldn't be in a hurry if there wasn't a reason.'

'And you can't even wait another day?'

'No!' Darya snapped out the answer.

'Well, if you're so keen you can't wait for a little while, you'd better go. But what's bitten you all of a sudden? Can't we know?'

'If you know everything you'll die before your time.'

As usual Darya had a ready answer and Pantelei could only splutter with annoyance and give up his inquiries.

Darya returned the next day. Only Ilyinichna and the children were at home. Mishatka ran up to his aunt, but she pushed him aside coldly and asked her mother-in-law, 'Where's Natalya, Mother?'

'She's out hoeing the potatoes. What do you want

her for? Or did the old man send for her? He must be mad! Tell him that!'

'No one's sent for her, I wanted to tell her something myself.'

'Did you come on foot?'

'Yes.'

'Do our people expect to finish soon?'

'Tomorrow, I reckon.'

'Stand still for a minute, where're you off to now? The hay must have been spoiled right bad by the rain?' the old woman persisted with her questions, following Darya down from the porch.

'Not that bad. Well, I'm going, there's not much time...'

'Call in on your way back and take a shirt for the old man. D'ye hear?'

Darya pretended not to hear and hurried off through the cattle yard. By the pier she stopped and scanned the greenish moistly breathing expanse of the Don, then walked on slowly towards the vegetable patches.

The wind was frolicking across the Don, gulls' wings were flashing. Waves lapped the low bank idly. The chalky hills gleamed dully in the sunlight through a veil of violet haze, but the woods on the other side of the Don, newly washed by the rain, shone with the youthful freshness of early spring.

Darya took off her leather slippers, washed her sore feet and sat for a long time on the hot pebbles of the beach, shading her eyes with her hand and listening to the sad cries of the gulls and the steady splash of the waves. She was moved to tears by this stillness, by the heart-wringing call of the gulls, and the misfortune that had so suddenly descended on her seemed even more bitter and unbearable.

Natalya straightened her back with an effort, propped the hoe against the fence and, catching sight of Darya, went to meet her.

'Have you come for me, Darya?'

'I've come to tell you my troubles.'

They sat down together. Natalya took off her kerchief, patted her hair into place, and looked at Darya. She was struck by the change that had come over Darya's face in these past few days. Her cheeks had become gaunt and dark, a deep furrow had cut across her brow, and a feverish gleam of anxiety had appeared in her eyes.

'What's the matter, dear? You've gone all dark in the face,' Natalya asked sympathetically.

'It's enough to make anyone dark...' Darya forced a smile and paused for a moment. 'Have you got a lot more hoeing to do?'

'I'll manage by evening. What's wrong?'

Darya swallowed convulsively and came out with her story in quick husky tones.

'I'll tell you what. I'm ill... I've got the pox... I must have picked it up on this last trip... One of those officer bastards landed me with it.'

'So that's where your gallivanting has got you!' Natalya clasped her hands in fright and dismay.

'Yes, that's where... I've only got myself to blame... It's my weakness... He got round me, the devil, with his soft talk. Such lovely white teeth, but he was rotten inside... And now I'm done for.'

'Oh, you poor thing! How awful! What shall you do now?' Natalya stared wide-eyed at Darya and she, mastering her feelings and keeping her eyes on the ground, went on more calmly, 'I noticed even on the way back. At first I thought it might be just... You know yourself all kinds of things can happen to a woman... Last spring I lifted a big sack of wheat and my period went on for three weeks. And this time I could see something was wrong... There were signs... So yesterday I went to the doctor. I felt like falling through the earth from shame... And now it's all up, the little girl's had her fun.'

'You must get it treated, but it's such a disgrace! They say these diseases can be cured.'

'Not mine, girl,' Darya smiled wryly, and for the first time since they had been speaking she raised her burning eyes. 'I've got syphilis. There's no cure for that. That's the kind that makes your nose fall in... Like old Andronikha's—you've seen her, haven't you?'

'What will you do now?' Natalya asked tearfully.

Darya lapsed into a long silence. She plucked a flower from a creeper that had tangled itself round a maize stalk. The tender pink-edged cup, so transparently light, almost weightless, gave off the pungent, fleshy scent of sun-warmed earth. Darya stared at it eagerly and with astonishment, as though it were the first time she had ever seen this plain and humble flower; she smelled it with wide quivering nostrils, then placed it carefully on the loose, wind-dried soil and said, 'What'll I do now, you ask? All the way home I was wondering, trying to work it out... I'll do away with myself, that's what! It's a pity, but it looks as if I've got no choice. Even if

I did go for treatment, the whole village would know. They'd point at me, then turn away and laugh... Who'll want me in such a state? All my good looks will go, I'll dry up, I'll rot while I'm still alive... No, I won't have that!' She spoke as though arguing with herself and ignored Natalya's gesture of protest. 'I thought before I went to the doctor that if it was that, I'd try and get cured. That's why I didn't give Father the money—I'd need it to pay the doctors... But now I've changed my mind. To hell with it all, stuff it!'

Darya swore obscenely, like a man, spat on the ground and wiped a tear from her long lashes with the back of her hand.

'How can you talk like this... Have you no fear of God!' Natalya said quietly.

'God's no good to me right now. He's been a drag on me all my life anyway.' Darya smiled, and in that mischievously winning smile Natalya caught a glimpse of the old Darya. 'I couldn't do this, couldn't do that, they kept scaring me with Judgement Day... Well, you couldn't think of anything more scary than the judgement I'm going to make on myself. I'm sick of it all, Natalya! People make me sick... It'll be easy for me to put an end to myself. I've got no one behind me or ahead of me. And no one to cast out of my heart... So that's it!'

Natalya broke into fierce remonstrances, begging her to change her mind and not think of suicide but, after listening inattentively at first, Darya stiffened and interrupted her angrily.

'Oh, stop it, Natalya! I didn't come here to have you begging and persuading me! I came to tell you my trouble and warn you not to let the children come near me from now on. My disease is catching, the doctor says, and I've heard the same myself. So mind they don't pick it up from me! Understand, silly? And tell the old woman, too. I haven't got the face. But I ... I won't be stringing myself up right away, don't think that, there's plenty of time yet. I'll stay on for a while, take a delight in the world, say goodbye to it. You know how it is? Until your heart gives you a twinge you go around without noticing a thing... The way I've lived all this time, as if I was blind! But as I was coming back along the Don and thought of how I'd soon be leaving it all, it was like my eyes had been opened! I looked across the water and it had waves on it and the sun had made it all silver, all gleaming and rippling, so it hurt to look at it. Then I looked around me and I thought, Lord, how lovely it all is! But I'd never noticed it before...' Darya smiled shyly, fell silent and, overcoming the grief that had seized her throat, began to speak again; her voice grew tense and rose to a higher pitch. 'I had a good few cries on the way here... When I got near the village I saw the kids swimming in the Don... And one look at them was enough to set me bawling like a donkey. I lay there on the sand for about two hours. It's not going to be easy for me, come to think of it...' She stood up and dusted her skirt and adjusted her kerchief with her usual flourish. 'My only joy when I think of death is that I'll be seeing Petro in the other world... "Here I am, Petro love," I'll say, "take your wayward wife!"' And with her usual cynical jocularity she added, 'He won't be able to wallop me in that world, will he? They don't let the quarrelsome kind into heaven, do they? Well, bye for now, Natalya! Don't forget to tell our mother-in-law about my trouble.'

Natalya sat with her face buried in her narrow grimy hands. The tears shone through her fingers like resin on pine splinters. Darya walked as far as the wattle gate, then came back and said in a businesslike fashion, 'From now on I'll be eating off a separate plate. Tell Mother that. And there's another thing. She'd better not tell Father about this or the old feller will get mad and turn me out of the house. As if I hadn't enough to bear without that. I'll go straight on to the mowing from here. Goodbye!'

XIV

The next day the mowers came in from the fields. Pantelei had decided to start carting the hay after the midday meal. Dunyashka drove the oxen down to the Don while Ilyinichna and Natalya busied themselves laying the table.

Darya was the last to sit down, at the far end of the table. Ilyinichna set before her a not very large bowl of cabbage soup with a spoon and a slice of bread and for the others as usual filled the big common bowl.

Pantelei looked in surprise at his wife and with a glance at Darya's bowl asked, 'What's that for? Why d'you feed her separate? Or is she no longer of our faith?'

'It's none of your business! Eat your food!'

The old man gave Darya a quizzical look and smiled.

'Ah, I've got it! Since she was given that medal, she doesn't want to eat with us. What is it, Darya, are you chary of eating from the same bowl as us?'

'I'm not chary, but I mustn't,' Darya replied hoarsely.

'Why's that?'

'I've got a sore throat.'

'What of it?'

'I went to the stanitsa and the doctor said I was to eat separate.'

'When I had a sore throat, I didn't set myself apart and, thank the Lord, no one else caught it. What kind of a cold have you got then?'

Darya paled, wiped her lips with her hand and put down her spoon. Indignant at the old man's questioning, Ilyinichna snapped at him, 'What are ye pestering the woman for? Even at table he gives us no peace! He sticks to you like a burr and there's no getting him off!'

'Don't matter to me!' Pantelei grunted irritably. 'For all I care she can sup straight from the bowl.'

In his annoyance he swallowed a whole spoonful of hot soup and, spitting the cabbage out on to his beard, burst out at the top of his voice, 'Can't you serve soup properly, you bitches! Who brings boiling soup to the table?!'

'If you didn't talk so much at table, it wouldn't have burnt you,' Ilyinichna assured him.

Dunyashka was about to giggle at the sight of her purple-faced father picking cabbage and bits of potato out of his beard, but the faces of the others were so grave that she restrained herself and averted her gaze for fear of giving offence.

After the meal the old man and his two daughters-in-law drove out for the hay on two wagons. Pantelei loaded with a long fork while Natalya spread the mildewy smelling hay on the wagon and stamped it down. She and Darya returned from the fields together. Pantelei with his wagon and two sturdy old oxen had driven far ahead.

The sun was setting behind a mound. The bitter wormwood-scented air from the mown steppe had acquired a new, softer aroma and lost its choking noonday tang. The heat had abated. The oxen were plodding along willingly and the vapid dust kicked up by their hooves rose and settled on the roadside clumps of thistle. The full-blown thistle tops were a blazing crimson and bumble-bees were circling over them. Lapwings called to one another as they flew to a distant steppeland pond.

Darya lay on the swaying load, resting on her elbows and glancing now and then at Natalya, who was gazing pensively at the sunset; her calm face was radiant in the bronze-red glow. 'Yes, Natalya's a lucky woman, she has a husband and children. She lacks for nothing and the family's fond of her. But I'm finished. When I die, no one will give so much as a sigh,' Darya thought to herself and she suddenly felt an inward desire to upset Natalya, to cause her pain. Why should Darya alone feel the pangs of despair, think of nothing but her ruined life, and suffer so cruelly? She glanced again at Natalya and, trying to sound affectionate and sincere, said, 'I've got a confession to make to you, Natalya.'

Natalya did not respond at once. As she watched the sunset, she had been recalling how Grigory had ridden over to see her when she was still only his betrothed, and how she had gone out of the gate to see him off. There had been just such a blazing sunset then, with a crimson afterglow spreading across the western sky and the rooks cawing in the willows... Grigory had ridden off, turning and looking back, and she had watched him go with tears of rapturous joy and, as she pressed her hands to her sharp young breasts, had felt the swift pulsing of her heart... Darya's voice was an unpleasant interruption of the reminiscences and she asked unwillingly, 'What have you to confess?'

'A sin I committed... Remember when Grigory was here in spring, on leave from the front? That evening, I remember, I was milking the cow. I was just going back to the house and I heard Aksinya calling me. Well, she called me in and gave me this ring, just forced it on me,' Darya twisted the gold ring on her third finger, 'and begged me to tell Grigory to come and see her... Well, it was none of my affair... So I told him. And all that night... Remember, he said it was Kudinov had arrived and he'd been with him? That was all lies! He was with Aksinya!'

Stunned and pale, Natalya silently broke a dry thistle stem into pieces.

'Don't be cross with me, Natalya. I wish I hadn't confessed it now...' Darya said ingratiatingly, trying to catch her sister-in-law's eye.

Natalya swallowed her tears in silence. The blow had been so powerful and unexpected that she could find no

518

response but to turn away to hide her suffering face.

By the time they reached the village, Darya was thinking to herself, 'The devil must have tempted me to knock the stuffing out of her like that. Now she'll be weeping for a whole month! She'd better not have known. Cows like her are happier when they live blind.' Wishing to soften the impression produced by her words, she said, 'Don't get so upset. Call that trouble! I'm in a far worse fix, but I'm keeping my pecker up. Who knows, maybe he didn't go and see her after all? Maybe he really was with Kudinov; I didn't keep watch on him. A thief's not a thief till he's caught, you know.'

'I guessed it,' Natalya said quietly, wiping her eyes with the corner of her kerchief.

'Then why didn't you have it out with him? You're a fine one! He wouldn't have wriggled out of it with me! I'd have had his guts for garters!'

'I was afraid to hear the truth... You think it's easy?' Natalya's eyes flashed, and in her agitation she began to stammer. 'You and Petro ... you could live like that... But when I ... when I remember ... everything I've been through ... I'm, I'm scared!'

'Then forget all about it,' Darya advised artlessly.

'As if I could!' Natalya whispered in a husky voice, unlike her own.

'I'd forget it. What's it matter!'

'You forget about your disease then!'

Darya burst out laughing.

'I'd be only too glad, but it keeps reminding me, the poxy thing! Listen, Natalya, if you want me to, I'll find out all about it from Aksinya. She'll tell me! God punish me, if there's a woman in the world can keep from telling who loves her and how much. I know that from myself!'

'I don't want your help. You've helped me enough as it is,' Natalya replied drily. 'I'm not blind. I know why you told me this. It wasn't pity made you confess your part in it. You wanted me to suffer.'

'That's right,' Darya agreed with a sigh. 'Why should I suffer alone?'

She got off the wagon, grasped the halter, and led the weary oxen down the hill. At the beginning of the lane she came back to the wagon.

'Natalya! There's something I want to ask you... Do you really love your man so much?'

'The best I can,' Natalya responded faintly.

'That must be a lot then,' Darya sighed again. 'But I've never loved anyone all that much in my life. I've just picked up what I could find... If only I could start life over again, perhaps I might be different.'

Black night succeeded the brief summer twilight. They unloaded the hay in darkness. The women worked in silence and for once Darya turned a deaf ear to her father-in-law's gruff shouts.

XV

In rapid pursuit of the enemy forces retreating from Ust-Medveditskaya the combined units of the Don Army and insurgent Cossacks of the Upper Don advanced northwards. At the village of Shashkin on the Medveditsa the shattered regiments of the 9th Red Army attempted to stop the Cossacks but were again driven from their positions and retreated almost as far as the Gryazi-Tsaritsyn railway without offering any serious resistance.

Grigory and his division took part in the action at Shashkin and gave great assistance to General Sutulov's infantry brigade, which had been caught by a thrust from the flank. Attacking on Grigory's orders, Yermakov's cavalry regiment captured about two hundred Red Army men, four heavy machine-guns and eleven ammunition carts.

Towards evening Grigory rode into Shashkin with a group of Cossacks from the 1st Regiment. Near the house that had been taken over by Division Headquarters stood a mob of prisoners, guarded by half a squadron of Cossacks. The prisoners' calico vests and underpants showed up whitely in the dusk. Most of them had been stripped of their boots and uniforms and only a few dirty green tunics were to be seen among the pallid crowd.

'Oho, aren't they white—like geese!' Prokhor Zykov exclaimed, pointing to the prisoners.

Grigory reined in, turned his horse sideways and beckoned to Yermakov whom he had spotted among the Cossacks.

'Come here. What are you hiding behind other men's backs for?'

Yermakov rode up coughing into his fist. There was congealed blood on his torn lips under his sparse moustache and his right cheek was swollen and dark with fresh scratches. During the charge his horse had stumbled at full gallop and catapulted him out of the saddle. Yermakov had slithered for about five paces on his belly over the rough and rutty common. Both he and his horse had jumped to their feet at the same time and a minute or two later, capless and with a fearsome bloodied face, but sabre in hand, Yermakov was again with the charging Cossacks as they swept down the slope.

'Why'd I be hiding?' he asked in apparent surprise as he drew level with Grigory, but averted his frenzied bloodshot eyes, that were still smouldering with the fire of battle.

'The cat knows whose meat it's eaten! Why're you riding behind?' Grigory snapped angrily.

Yermakov forced his swollen lips into a grin and glanced at the prisoners.

'What meat d'you mean? Don't ask me riddles because I won't be able to answer 'em. I took a header off my horse today...'

'Is that your work?' Grigory pointed his whip at the Red Army men.

Yermakov opened his eyes wide, as though he had never seen the prisoners before and made a show of indescribable astonishment.

'Look at that, the sons-of-bitches! They've stripped 'em, the devils! When did they manage it?... Well, I'll be damned! I told them they weren't to lay a finger on the prisoners, and look what they've done—stripped 'em naked, the poor things!'

'Don't try your games on me! What's the fooling for? Did you give orders to strip them?'

'God forbid! Are you in your right mind, Grigory Panteleyevich?'

'D'you remember the order?'

'You mean about...'

'Yes, I mean about that very thing!'

'Of course, I remember it. By heart! Like one o'them poems we used to learn at school.'

Grigory smiled in spite of himself and, leaning out of his saddle, grabbed Yermakov by his sword belt. He was fond of this daring, recklessly brave commander.

'Kharlampy! No joking now, why did you allow it? The new colonel they've got at headquarters instead of Kopylov will report this, and you'll have to answer for it. You won't like it when they get you up on the carpet.'

'I couldn't help it, Panteleyevich!' Yermakov replied

seriously and simply. 'Fitted out fine they were, all new stuff, just issued in Ust-Medveditskaya. My lads were going about in rags, and they hadn't got much left to wear at home either. What did it matter about this bunch, they'd all have been stripped anyway in the rear! Why should we do the capturing while the rear rats grab the clothes off their backs? No fear! I'd rather let our lot have the use of it! If I have to answer, they won't get much out of me! And don't you pick on me, please! I don't know nothing about it, and I've seen nothing, even in my dreams!'

They rode up to the crowd of prisoners. The mutter of talk ceased. The men on the fringe of the crowd backed away from the horsemen and eyed the Cossacks with sullen wariness and guarded expectation. One of the Red Army men, recognising Grigory as a commander, stepped forward and touched his stirrup.

'Comrade chief! Tell your Cossacks to at least give us back our greatcoats. Do us that favour! It's cold at night and we're as good as naked, you can see that for yourself.'

'You won't freeze, it's midsummer, you suslik!' Yermakov said grimly and drove the man back with his horse, then he turned to Grigory and said, 'Don't worry, I'll see to it they get some of the old stuff. Stand back there, you warriors! You ought to be chasing the lice in your pants, not fighting Cossacks!'

At headquarters a captured company commander was being interrogated. At a desk covered with shabby oilcloth sat the new chief of staff, Colonel Andreyanov, an elderly snub-nosed officer with a lot of grey at the temples and big boyishly protruding ears. The Red Army commander stood facing him, two paces from the desk. The prisoner's statements were being taken down by one of the staff officer, Lieutenant Sulin, who had come to the division with Andreyanov.

The Red commander—a tall ginger-moustached man with a short crop of ashy-white hair—stood shifting his bare feet awkwardly on the ochre-painted floor and shooting an occasional glance at the colonel. The Cossacks had left the prisoner only an army vest of yellow unbleached calico and, in exchange for the trousers they had taken, a pair of tattered Cossack breeches with faded stripes and clumsily sewn patches. As he walked to the desk, Grigory noticed the prisoner's embarrassed attempt to adjust the rags that barely covered his buttocks.

'The Orel Province military commissariat, you say?' the colonel asked, glancing briefly at the prisoner over his spectacles, then lowered his eyes and began to examine and toy with a sheet of paper, evidently some kind of credential.

'Yes.'

'Last autumn?'

'At the end of autumn.'

'You are lying.'

'I'm telling the truth.'

'I maintain that you are lying!'

The prisoner shrugged. The colonel glanced at Grigory and with a contemptuous nod in the direction of the prisoner said, 'Just look at this specimen. A former officer of the Imperial Army and now, as you see, a Bolshevik. Caught red-handed and pretends he's with the Reds by accident, because they mobilised him. He comes out with a pack of lies, like a high-school girl, and thinks we shall believe him. He simply hasn't the civic courage to admit that he betrayed his country... He's afraid, the scoundrel!'

Swallowing hard, the prisoner said, 'I see that you, Colonel, have the civic courage to insult a prisoner.'

'I don't speak to scoundrels!'

'But I can't avoid doing so.'

'Be careful! Don't compel me to make the insult physical!'

'In your position that would not be difficult and also quite safe!'

Without a word Grigory sat down at the desk and smiled sympathetically at the prisoner, who had grown pale with indignation, as he snapped back his fearless replies. He took the colonel down a peg very nicely, Grigory thought with pleasure, and not without malice watched Andreyanov's fleshy, purple cheeks twitching nervously.

Grigory had taken a dislike to his chief of staff at their first encounter. Andreyanov was one of those officers who during the world war had used their service and family connections to keep themselves safely in the rear. Even during the civil war Colonel Andreyanov had managed to stay on defence work in Novocherkassk and only after the removal of Ataman Krasnov had been compelled to go to the front.

In the two nights he had been quartered with Andreyanov Grigory had learned that the colonel was very devout, that he could not speak of the great church festivals without tears, that his wife was the most exemplary of wives that could be imagined, that her name was Sofya Alexandrovna and that she had once been unsuccessfully courted by the Vice Ataman himself, Baron von Grabbe. In addition, the colonel volunteered a detailed account of the estate of his late father, the stages in his promotion to the rank of colonel, and all the highly placed personages he had hunted with in 1916; he also informed Grigory that he considered whist the best card game, caraway brandy the healthiest of beverages, and the quartermaster's corps the most profitable branch of the service.

Gunshots in the vicinity made Colonel Andreyanov jump; he avoided riding on horseback because of a liver complaint, was constantly at pains to increase the headquarters guard company, and treated the Cossacks with barely concealed dislike because, as he put it, they had all been traitors in 1917, and since that year he had begun to hate all 'lower ranks' indiscriminately. 'Only the nobility will save Russia!' he insisted, hinting that he himself was of noble descent and that the Andreyanov family was one of the oldest and most honoured on the Don.

Undoubtedly Andreyanov's main fault was his garrulity, the frightening, uncontrollable garrulity of old age that afflicts in their later years some talkative and unintelligent individuals who have been accustomed to speak of everything lightly and carelessly in their youth.

Grigory had met such twitterers before and had always found them deeply repellent. After one day's acquaintance he began avoiding the colonel, and in the daytime he was successful, but as soon as they halted for the night Andreyanov would seek him out and without waiting for an answer to his hasty 'Shall we spend the night together?' launch into conversation. 'My dear fellow, you say the Cossacks are not to be relied on when fighting on foot, but when I was A. D. C. to his Excellency... Hey there, someone, bring me my suitcase and bedding!' Grigory would lie in bed, eyes closed and gritting his teeth, and then turn his back on the indefatigable talker, pull his greatcoat over his head and think, 'As soon as I get a transfer I'll clobber the bastard; maybe that'll shut him up for a week!' 'Are you asleep, Lieutenant?' Andreyanov would ask. 'Yes, I am!' Grigory would mutter. 'Oh, but I haven't finished telling you...' And the tale would continue. Half asleep, Grigory would think, 'They've landed me with this blatherer on purpose. It must be Fitzhelaurov's work. What can I do with such a half-wit?' And as he fell asleep, the colonel's penetrating, high-pitched voice pattered on his eardrums like rain on an iron roof.

So Grigory now took a malicious pleasure in seeing the captured Red commander making circles round his garrulous chief of staff.

For a minute Andreyanov sat with his eyes half closed and said nothing. The long lobes of his prominent ears glowed a vivid purple; his white, plump hand with a heavy gold ring on the forefinger was shaking.

'Listen, you bastard!' he said in a strained voice. 'I didn't have you brought here to bandy words with me and don't you forget it! Don't you realise you can't wriggle out of this?'

'I realise that perfectly well.'

'So much the better for you. I don't really care whether you volunteered for the Reds or they called you up. That's not the point. The point is that because of a misconceived sense of honour you refuse to say...'

'Apparently we have different conceptions of honour.'

'That's because you haven't one little bit of it left!'

'Judging by the way you're treating me, Colonel, I doubt if you ever had any!'

'I see you want to hasten the outcome.'

'Do you see any reason for me to delay it? You needn't try to scare me.'

Andreyanov opened his cigarette case with trembling hands, lighted a cigarette, took a couple of hungry pulls, and addressed the prisoner again.

'So you refuse to answer questions?'

'I've told you about myself.'

'To hell with that! I couldn't be less interested in your horrible little person. Will you kindly answer the question. What units came to reinforce you from Sebryakovo?'

'I've told you, I don't know.'

'But you do!'

'All right, just to make you happy, I do know but I won't tell you.'

'I'll have you flogged with ramrods and then you will talk!'

'I doubt it!' the prisoner touched his moustache with his left hand and smiled confidently.

'Did the Kamyshinsky Regiment take part in this action?'

'No.'

'But your left flank was covered by a cavalry unit. What unit was it?'

'Oh, drop all that! I repeat, I refuse to answer such questions.'

'You have the choice. Either you come clean, you dog, or in ten minutes from now we'll have you up against a wall! Now then?'

At this juncture the prisoner replied in an unexpectedly high-pitched, youthfully resonant voice, 'I'm fed up with you, you old fool! You nitwit! If you'd fallen into my hands, I'd have dealt with you differently!'

Andreyanov turned pale and snatched at his revolver holster, but a this point Grigory rose unhurriedly and raised a warning hand.

'Oho! That's enough! You've had your little chat. You're both firebrands, by the look of it... If you can't agree, never mind. What's the good of quarrelling? He's right not to give his own side away. Honestly! That was great! I never expected it of him!'

'I must protest!' Andreyanov blustered, trying vainly to unbutton his holster.

'No, we can't have this.' Grigory interposed cheerfully, putting himself between the captive and his interrogator. 'It's a daft business killing prisoners. Aren't you ashamed to go for an unarmed man, a prisoner? First you take his clothes, and now you want to slap a bullet into him...'

'Stand back! This scoundrel has insulted me!' Andreyanov pushed Grigory roughly aside and drew his revolver.

The prisoner turned quickly to face the window, his shoulders twitching as if from cold. Grigory watched Andreyanov with a smile. But even with the ribbed butt of the revolver in his hand, the colonel could do no more than flourish it absurdly, then lower the barrel and turn away.

'I won't soil my hands,' he said hoarsely when he had recovered his breath, and licked his dry lips.

Making no attempt to hide the laughter that gleamed forth in a dazzling white grin from under his moustache, Grigory said, 'You wouldn't have had the chance! Look at your gun—it isn't even loaded. I woke up early this morning and saw it laying on the chair... There wasn't a single round in it and it hadn't been cleaned for a month, I reckon! You don't take much care of your personal weapon!'

Andreyanov lowered his eyes, span the drum of the revolver with his thumb, and smiled.

'Well, I'm damned! It isn't either.'

Lieutenant Sulin, who had been watching the scene in contemptuous silence, folded the interrogation sheet and said with a pleasant burr in his voice, 'I've told you before, Colonel, that you keep your personal weapon in a disgusting state. Today's incident only proves it once again.'

Andreyanov frowned and shouted into the doorway, 'Hullo! Anyone there? Come here!'

Two orderlies and the commander of the guard appeared from the anteroom.

'Take him away!' Andreyanov indicated the prisoner with a nod.

The man turned to face Grigory, bowed silently and walked to the door. Under the prisoner's reddish moustache Grigory thought he saw the lips move in a barely perceptible smile of gratitude.

When the footsteps had died away, Andreyanov wearily removed his spectacles, wiped them carefully with a bit of suede leather and said acrimoniously, 'Your defence of that swine was brilliant. Presumably you were guided by convictions, but how could you discuss my revolver in his presence? How could you put me in such an awkward position?'

'No great harm done, I reckon,' Grigory said appeasingly.

'You were wrong. But I might have killed him, you know. Preposterous fellow! I had been wrestling with him for half an hour before you came. The lies he told, tried to throw me off the scent, gave me false information—appalling! And when I finally cornered him, he simply refused to speak. Said his honour as an officer would not permit him to disclose military secrets to the enemy. But he didn't think about his honour when he hired himself out to the Bolsheviks, the son-of-a-bitch... I think he and two other members of the command will have to be quietly shot. There's not a hope of their providing the kind of information we're interested in. They're errant and incorrigible scoundrels, so why spare them? What do you think?'

'How did you find out he was the company commander?' Grigory countered.

'One of his own men gave him away.'

'I think that man ought to be shot and the commanders left alive!' Grigory glanced expectantly at Andreyanov.

The colonel shrugged and smiled as someone might smile at the feeble joke.

'You can't mean it seriously.'

'I do.'

'But, look here, for what purpose?'

'What purpose? To maintain discipline and subordination in the Russian army! Last night, when we went to bed, Colonel, you had a whole lot to say about the way we ought to run the army after we've smashed the Bolsheviks—to get the Red infection out of the young fellows. And I agreed with you all along the line, remember?' Grigory stroked his moustache and, watching the changing expression of the colonel's face, went on argumentatively, 'But now what are you proposing? This way you'll only spread corruption! Let the soldiers betray their commanders? Is that what you want to teach 'em? Suppose you and me were in such a position? No, you'll have to excuse me, but I'm digging my heels in! I'm against it.'

'Just as you like,' Andreyanov replied coldly and gave Grigory a keen look. He had heard that the insurgent division commander was headstrong and rather eccentric, but he had never expected anything like this. All he could say was, 'That was how we used to deal with captured Red commanders in the past, particularly former officers. Yours is a new idea... And I don't quite understand your attitude to what would appear to be a perfectly simple question.'

'In the past we used to kill them in battle if we could, but we didn't shoot prisoners unless we had to!' Grigory replied, flushing purple.

'Very well then, we'll send them into the rear,' Andreyanov agreed. 'Now here's something else. Some of the prisoners are mobilised peasants from the Saratov Province and have expressed the desire to fight in our ranks. Our 3rd Infantry Regiment can scarcely muster three hundred bayonets. Do you think it possible to reinforce it with volunteers after they have been carefully screened. We have certain instructions on that score from the Army Command.'

'I won't take a single peasant in any of my units. I want Cossacks to make good my losses,' Grigory declared categorically.

Andreyanov tried to persuade him.

'Now don't let us argue. I understand your desire to have your division manned entirely by Cossacks, but we can't afford to spurn prisoners. Even the Volunteer Army uses them to bring some regiments up to strength.'

'They can do what they like, but no peasants for me. That's final,' Grigory retorted sharply.

A little later he went out to see about sending off the prisoners.

Over dinner Andreyanov said worriedly, 'I feel we won't be able to work together.'

'That's how I feel too,' Grigory replied indifferently. He fished a lump of mutton out of his plate with his fingers and, not noticing Sulin's smile, chewed the gristle with such a wolf-like grinding of teeth that the lieutenant winced as if in pain and momentarily closed his eyes.

* * *

Two days later General Salnikov's group took over the pursuit of the retreating Red units and Grigory was summoned urgently to headquarters, where the chief of staff, an elderly, benevolent-looking general showed him the order from the Commander of the Don Army on the disbanding of the insurgent army and said without more ado, 'In the guerilla war against the Reds you successfully commanded a division. But in our army we can't trust you with a regiment, let alone a division. You have no staff training and are not competent to command a large formation on a broad front in the conditions of modern warfare. Do you agree with that?'

'Yes,' Grigory replied. 'I myself wanted to give up command of the division.'

'It's a very good thing that you don't overrate your abilities. That's a quality one seldom finds among young officers today. Now then, front headquarters had put you in command of the fourth squadron of the 19th Regiment. The regiment is at present on the march, about twenty versts from here, somewhere near the village of Vyaznikov. You should set out today or tomorrow at the latest. I think you wanted to say something?'

'I'd like to be posted to a supply unit.'

'That's impossible. You can't be spared from the front.'

'In two wars I've been shell-shocked and wounded fourteen times.'

'Never mind that. You're young, you look splendid, and you can still fight. As for your wounds, all our officers have them. You may go. And good luck to you.'

Probably to avert the discontent that was bound to arise among the Upper Don Cossacks when the insurgent army was disbanded, immediately after the capture of Ust-Medveditskaya many of the rank-and-file who had distinguished themselves during the uprising were given promotion. Nearly all the sergeants-major were promoted to the rank of junior cornet, and the officers who had taken part in the uprising were also promoted and decorated.

Grigory was no exception. He had been made a lieutenant, his outstanding services in the struggle against the Reds were mentioned in an army order of the day and he received an official message of thanks.

The disbanding took only a few days. The illiterate commanders of divisions and regiments were replaced by generals and colonels, and experienced officers were put in command of the squadrons; the commanders of batteries and the staff commanders were replaced to a man, and the rank-and-file Cossacks were set to reinforce the regular regiments of the Don Army, which had been badly mauled in the fighting on the Donets.

Towards evening Grigory assembled the Cossacks and announced the disbanding of the division.

In farewell he said, 'Remember me kindly, Cossacks! We served together because we had to, but from now on we'll be busting trouble each on our own. The main thing is to keep your head out of the line of fire, so the Reds don't make a hole in it. They—our heads, I mean—may be muddled, but there's no need to stop bullets with 'em. We'll still need 'em to think with, and think hard, how we're to live now...'

The Cossacks listened in depressed silence, then a general murmuring and muttering broke out.

'So it's the old times coming back?'

'Where do we go now?'

'They kick us around just how they like, the bastards!'

'We don't want to be disbanded! What's this new set-up?!'

'Looks as if we let ourselves in for it, lads, when we joined armies!'

'Their lordships will start pitching into us all over again!'

'Watch out! They'll shake us up now!'

Grigory waited for silence and said, 'It's no use yelling. The good old days when you could discuss orders and go against the higher-ups are over. Go back to your quarters and don't wag your tongues too much, or the way things are now your tongue won't get you to Kiev, but it will get you to a court-martial and a punishment squadron.'

The Cossacks came up in troops to shake hands with Grigory.

'Goodbye, Panteleyevich! And you remember us kindly too.'

'We're in for a rough time, serving with strangers—real rough!'

'You didn't ought to have given us up like this. Why didn't you hang on to the division?'

'We're real sorry to see you go, Melekhov. Other commanders may have more education, but that won't make it any easier for us, only harder—that's the trouble!'

But one Cossack, from the village of Napolovsky, the wit of his squadron, said, 'Don't you believe 'em, Grigory Panteleyevich! It's as bad working with your own folk as it is with strangers, if the work goes against the grain!'

* * *

Grigory spent the night drinking with Yermakov and the other commanders, and the next morning he rode off with Prokhor Zykov to catch up with the 19th Regiment.

Before he could take over the squadron and get to know his men, he was told to report to the regimental commander. The order came early in the morning. Grigory took his time inspecting the horses and did not report until half an hour had passed. He was expecting to be severely reprimanded by the commander, who had a reputation for demanding a lot from his officers, but he received a friendly welcome. 'Well, how do you find the squadron? Are they any good?' the commander asked and then, without waiting for a reply, looked past Grigory and said, 'My dear fellow, I have some bad news for you... A great misfortune has befallen your family. We had a telegram last night from Vyoshenskaya. I give you a month's leave to arrange your affairs. Go when you wish.'

'Give me the telegram,' Grigory said, turning pale.

He unfolded the message slip, read it and crushed it in his hand, which had suddenly grown clammy. It took him only a slight effort to regain possession of himself and there was no more than a quiver in his voice when he said, 'No, I never expected that. I'd better be going. Goodbye.'

'Don't forget to take your leave warrant.'

'Thanks, I won't forget.'

He strode out firmly and confidently, steadying his sabre as usual, but as he walked down from the high porch he suddenly ceased to hear his own footsteps and felt a fierce, bayonet-like thrust of pain in the heart.

On the bottom step he lurched sideways and grabbed the flimsy rail with his left hand, unbuttoning his collar with his right. For no more than a minute he stood breathing in short deep gasps, but in that minute seemed to grow drunk with grief, and when he dragged himself away from the rail and made for the gate, where his horse was tethered, he was staggering.

XVI

For a few days after her conversation with Darya Natalya lived as if in the grip of a nightmare, suffering agonies but unable to open her eyes. She tried to think of a plausible excuse for going to Prokhor Zykov's wife and finding out from her how Grigory had spent his time in Vyoshenskaya during the retreat and whether he had seen Aksinya there. She wanted to be quite sure of her husband's guilt, for she believed and yet disbelieved what Darya had told her.

Late one evening she walked up to the Zykov's yard, carelessly waving a willow twig. Prokhor's wife had finished her chores and was sitting by the gate.

'Hullo there, lonesome! You haven't seen our calf, have you?'

'Praise the Lord, love. No, I haven't.'

'It's such a wanderer, the wretch! It just won't stay at home. I don't know where to look for it, honestly I don't.'

'Well, sit down and take a rest. He'll come home. Want some sunflower seeds to chew?'

Natalya sat down and the two women began to talk.

'Have you heard anything of your soldier?' Natalya inquired.

'Not a word. He seems to have vanished, the devil! Heard anything from your man?'

'No, Grigory promised to write but there's been no sign of a letter. Folk say our men have gone beyond Ust-Medveditskaya and that's all I've heard.' Natalya changed the subject to the recent retreat across the Don and probed cautiously to find out how the men had lived in Vyoshenskaya and who else from the village had been with them. Prokhor's sharp-witted wife guessed at once the reason for Natalya's visit and answered with dry restraint.

From what her husband had told her she knew all about Grigory but, although she was itching to speak, she was afraid, remembering Prokhor's warning, 'Mark my words. If you so much as breathe a word to anyone about it, I'll put your head on the chopping block, pull your tongue out till it's a yard long, and cut it off. If Grigory ever hears you've been talking, he'll kill me on the spot! I'm fed up with you, but not with life—yet! Get me? So keep quiet as the grave!'

'Your Prokhor didn't happen to see Aksinya Astakhova in Vyoshenskaya, did he?' Natalya asked straight out, losing patience.

'How could he have done! What time did they have for that kind of thing? Honest to God, I don't know, and don't try to pump me. I can't get any sense out of my tow-headed devil. He never has a word to say except "give me this" or "take that".'

So Natalya left with nothing for her pains and even more angry and upset. But unable to bear the suspense any longer, she decided to call on Aksinya.

As neighbours over the past few years they had met and bowed silently to each other, occasionally passing a few remarks. Gone were the days when they had cut each other and exchanged only hate-filled glances; time had blunted the edge of their mutual dislike, so Natalya could hope not to have the door shut in her face. If Aksinya was willing to talk of anyone, surely it would be Grigory. She was not mistaken in her conjectures.

With unconcealed astonishment Aksinya invited her into the front room, drew the curtains, lit the lamp and asked, 'What brings you here? Anything good?'

'There's nothing good that would bring me to you.'

'Tell me the bad news then. Has something happened to Grigory Panteleyevich?'

The anxiety in Aksinya's voice told Natalya everything. One phrase had been enough to reveal Aksinya, all that she lived for, all that she feared. After that there really was no point in asking her about her feelings for Grigory, but still Natalya lingered.

After a pause she said, 'No, my husband is alive and well, so don't be frightened.'

'I'm not frightened. What makes you think that? His health is your worry, I've got plenty of worries of my own.' Aksinya spoke freely but, feeling the blood rush to her face, she turned quickly away from her guest and spent some time needlessly adjusting the lamp, which was burning quite well enough already.

'Have you heard anything of your Stepan?'

'He sent me his love not so long ago.'

'Is he well?'

'I expect so,' Aksinya shrugged.

Once again honesty got the better of her and betrayed her feelings. Her indifference to her husband showed so plainly in her reply that Natalya was forced to smile.

'I see you're not all that sorry to be without him... But that's your business. Now this is what I came to see you about. There's a rumour going around the village that Grigory is chasing you again, that you saw him when he came home. Is it true?'

'You've picked the right person to ask!' Aksinya said mockingly. 'Suppose I ask you whether it's true or not?'

'Are you afraid to tell the truth?'

'No, I'm not.'

'Then tell me, so that I'll know and not torment myself. Why should I eat my heart out for nothing?'

Aksinya narrowed her eyes and her dark brows quivered.

'Don't think I'm sorry for you,' she said sharply. 'That's how it is with you and me. When I'm suffering you're happy, and when you suffer, life is good for me... We're sharing one man, aren't we? Well, I'll tell you the truth then, so you'll know in good time. It's all true, no one's making anything up. I've got Grigory again and I mean to hold him. So what are you going to do about it? Break all my windows or stick a knife in me?'

Natalya rose, twisted the slender willow twig into a knot, tossed it behind the stove and answered with unexpected firmness.

'Right now I won't do you any harm. I'll wait a bit and, when Grigory comes home, I'll talk it over with him. Then I'll see what to do about the pair of you. I've got two children and I mean to stand up for them and myself!'

Aksinya smiled.

'So for the time being I'm safe?'

Not noticing the mockery in her voice, Natalya went up to Aksinya and plucked at her sleeve.

'Aksinya! You've been a thorn in my flesh all my life. But I'm not going to plead with you now as I did then, remember? When I was younger and sillier, I thought, I'll move her, she'll take pity on me and give up Grisha. Not now! But there's one thing I do know. You don't love him, you're just clinging to him out of habit. And did your ever love him as I do? Not likely. You got mixed up with Listnitsky and how many others did you have, you loose creature? When a woman loves a man she doesn't carry on like that.'

Aksinya turned pale and, shaking off Natalya's hand, rose from the chest where she had been sitting.

'He doesn't hold it against me, so why should you? What business is it of yours? Never mind then! You're a good woman and I'm a bad one, so now what?'

'That's all. Don't get angry. I'm going now. Thanks for telling me the truth.'

'You needn't thank me, you'd have found out anyway. Wait a minute, I'll come out and close the shutters.' On the porch Aksinya paused for a moment and said, 'I'm glad we're parting without a fight, but these are my parting words to you, good neighbour. Take him if you can. But if not, don't blame others. I won't give him up of my own free will. I'm not all that young and, though you called me a loose creature, I'm not a one like your Darya. I've never played that game in my life... You, at least, have got children, but I—' Aksinya's voice broke and sank to a lower, husky note, 'I have only him in the whole wide world! He's my first and last love. But don't let's talk about it any more. If he comes through alive—and may the Holy Mother of God protect him—if he comes back, he'll choose for himself.'

Natalya had no sleep that night and in the morning she went out with Ilyinichna to weed the melon patch. In her work she found some relief. She thought less as she dunked steadily with her hoe at the crumbling clods of sandy loam, now and then straightening her back to rest, wipe the sweat from her face, and drink some water.

Wind-frayed white clouds floated and dissolved in the deep-blue sky. The sun beat down on the scorching earth. But rain was coming up from the east. Even without raising her head Natalya felt the momentary cool on her back as the passing clouds covered the sun;

for a moment a grey shadow would flit across the brown-ish heat-breathing earth, the tangled stems of the water-melons, the tall stalks of the sunflowers. It would cover the melon patches spread over the slope, the wilted grass, the sloe and hawthorn bushes, whose drooping leaves were bespattered with bird droppings. The persistent piping of the quails would grow more sonorous, the sweet song of the larks would come through more clearly, and even the wind stirring the warm grass would seem less sultry. But then the sun would cleave the blindingly white edge of a westward floating cloud and, breaking free, once again pour its golden, brilliant rays on earth. Somewhere far away, over the blue spurs of the Donside hills the cloud shadow would be darkening the earth, but on the melon patches the amber-yellow noon was again in full command, a fluid haze was shimmering and quivering on the horizon and the smell of the earth and the grasses it fed was even more stifling.

At midday Natalya went down to a well in a nearby ravine and brought back a jug of ice-cold spring water. She and Ilyinichna quenched their thirst, washed their hands and sat down to eat. On an apron that she had spread on the ground Ilyinichna cut neat slices of bread, took two spoons and a bowl out of her bag, and from under her jacket produced a narrow-necked jug of milk that she had been hiding from the sun.

Noticing Natalya's lack of appetite, Ilyinichna asked her, 'I've noticed for some time now that you're not yourself... Has something happened between you and Grisha?'

Natalya's wind-parched lips trembled pitifully.

'Oh, Mother, he's living with Aksinya again.'

'How ... how do you know that?'

'I went to see Aksinya yesterday.'

'And she admitted it, the hussy?'

'Yes.'

Ilyinichna mused silently. Stern folds appeared amid the wrinkles at the corners of her mouth.

'Maybe she's only boasting, the pest?'

'No, Mother, it's true. What's the use of pretending?'

'You haven't been keeping an eye on him as you should...' the old woman said cautiously. 'With a husband like that you mustn't take your eyes off him for a minute.'

'But how can I?... I counted on his conscience... Surely I didn't have to tie him to my apron strings?' Natalya smiled bitterly and added in barely a whisper, 'He's not

Mishatka to be kept in tow. His hair's half grey, but still he won't forget what's past.'

Ilyinichna washed and wiped the spoons, rinsed the bowl and put them all away in her bag, and only then did she ask, 'Is that all the trouble?'

'But Mother! It's trouble enough to make life not worth living!'

'What d'you think to do about it?'

'I've no choice. I'll take the children and go back to my own folk. I won't live with him any more. Let him take her in and live with her. I've had enough.'

'I thought the same when I was young,' Ilyinichna said with a sigh. 'Mine was a randy dog too. I can't tell you what I went through on his account. But it's not easy to leave your own husband and it's no good either. Just think it over and you'll see. And how can you take the children away from their father? No, girl, that won't do, it's no use talking like that! I won't allow you to do it.'

'Mother, I'm not going to live with him. So don't waste your breath.'

'Don't waste my breath?' Ilyinichna burst out indignantly. 'Aren't you one of my own kin? Am I sorry for you, you poor wretches, or not? And you can say such things to me, and old woman, his mother? I've told you to put the whole thing out of your head, and that's all there is to it. The idea! "I'm going to leave home!" Where will you go? Who of your own folk needs you? Your father's dead, your house was burnt down, your mother's living under a strange roof for mercy's sake. How can you go there and take my grandchildren with you? No, my dear, you won't have it your way. When Grisha comes home, we'll decide what to do about him, but now I don't want to hear any more about it! I won't listen!'

All that had for so long been pent up in Natalya's heart suddenly broke out in a great fit of sobbing. With a groan she tore the kerchief from her head, flung herself face downward on the dry, comfortless earth and clung to it, sobbing without tears.

Ilyinichna—wise and brave old soul that she was—did not move an inch. She carefully wrapped the jug in her jacket and placed it in the cool, then poured some water into a bowl and sat down beside Natalya. She knew that no words could help in such grief, and she also knew that tears were better than dry eyes and tight lips. When

Natalya had shed her tears, Ilyinichna placed her rough hand on her head, and, stroking the dark glossy hair, said sternly, 'Now, that's enough! You can't weep out all your tears, leave some for next time. Here, have a drink of water.'

Natalya grew quieter. Only occasionally did her shoulders heave and a shiver run through her body. All of a sudden she sprang up, pushed aside Ilyinichna and the bowl of water she was holding and, turning her face to the east, folded her tear-stained hands as if in prayer, and let out a choking rush of words.

'Lord! Lord! He's wrung the heart out of me! I can't go on living like this! Punish him, Lord God! Strike him dead! May he live no more and stop torturing me!'

A foaming black cloud crawled up from the east. Thunder rumbled in the distance. A searingly white shaft of lightning shot across the sky and jagged into the rounded cloud crests. The wind bowed the muttering grass towards the west, carried bitter dust from the highway, and bent the seed-laden sunflower tops almost to the ground.

For a few seconds Ilyinichna stared at her daughter-in-law in superstitious horror. Against the towering black stormcloud she was a strange and terrifying figure.

The rain was approaching swiftly. In the short-lived stillness before the storm a sideway swooping falcon screeched anxiously and a suslik gave a last whistle before darting into its hole. The wind flung fine sandy dust in Ilyinichna's face and howled away over the steppe. With an effort the old woman got to her feet. Her face was deathly pale when, through the roar of the approaching storm, she cried hoarsely, 'Come to your senses! God in heaven! Whose death are you asking for?'

'Oh God, punish him! Punish him, Lord!' Natalya continued to shout, fixing her crazed eyes on the heaped, rearing clouds shot through by blinding flashes of lightning.

Thunder broke over the steppe with a dry crack. Overcome by fear, Ilyinichna crossed herself, staggered towards Natalya and seized her by the shoulder.

'Down on your knees! Do you hear, Natalya?!'

Natalya stared at her mother-in-law with unseeing eyes and dropped limply to her knees.

'Beg the Lord's forgiveness!' Ilyinichna commanded. 'Beg him not to heed your prayer. Whose death did you ask for? The father of your own children. It's a great sin... Cross yourself! Bow down to the earth. Say, "Lord, forgive me, sinner that I am, for my grave offence." '

Natalya made the sign of the cross, whispered something with palid lips and, clenching her teeth, slumped awkwardly on to her side.

* * *

The rain-washed steppe glowed a wondrous green. A humpbacked rainbow stretched from the far pond to the Don. Thunder rumbled faintly in the west. Muddy water coursed down the ravine screeching like an eagle. Foaming torrents swirled over the melon patches into the Don, carrying rain-slashed leaves, uprooted grass, and broken stalks of rye. Greasy sand banks piled up over the tangled melon and watermelon stalks; the rebellious waters dug deep ruts in the summer tracks. At the end of a wooded dell a hayrick that had been fired by the lightning was slowly burning out, and the column of violet smoke rose .high until it almost reached the top of the rainbow.

Ilyinichna and Natalya walked down to the village, picking their way carefully with their bare feet over the slippery muddy road and holding their skirts high.

Ilyinichna was saying, 'You young folk have far too much temper, God knows! The slightest little thing and you're up in arms. How would you have fared if you'd been in my shoes in my young days? Grisha has never hurt a hair on your head and you're offended. What a state you got yourself into! You were going to leave him, you fell down in a faint, and what else! You even had to bring God into your sinful dealings... Now tell me, dear, what's the good of it all? Why, that lame monster of mine beat me nearly to death when I was young, and for no reason at all; there was nothing he could blame me for. He'd kicked over the traces himself and was taking it out on me. When he came in at dawn, I'd start crying and reproaching him, and he'd fly at me with his fists... Black and blue I'd be for a month afterwards, but I survived and brought up the children, and never once thought of leaving home. I'm not praising Grisha, but he's a man you can live with. If it wasn't for that snake of a woman, he'd be the best Cossack in the village. She's bewitched him, I'm sure.'

Natalya walked on in silence, lost in thought, and then

539

she said, 'Mother dear, I don't want to talk about it any more. When Grigory comes home, we'll see what I am to do... Maybe I'll leave him myself, maybe he'll turn me out, as things are now I won't leave your house.'

'That's what you should have said long ago!' Ilyinichna exclaimed gladly. 'God willing, everything will come right. He would never turn you out, don't think that! He loves you and the children. How could such a thing ever enter his head? No, never! He won't change you for Aksinya, he never could! But all kinds of things can happen in the family, can't they? If only he comes home alive...'

'I don't want him to be killed... I said that in anger... You mustn't hold it against me... I can't get him out of my heart, but it's so hard to go on like this!'

'Dear child! D'you think I don't know? But never do things in a rush. You're right, don't let's talk about it any more! And don't you say anything to the old man, for the Lord's sake. It's nothing to do with him.'

'There's one thing I want to tell you... Whether I'll be living with Grigory is not yet decided, but I don't want to bear him any more children. I don't even know what I'm going to do with the ones I've got. And right now, Mother, I'm pregnant.'

'Since when?'

'I'm in my third month.'

'Then what can you do about it? You'll have to have it whether you like it or not.'

'I won't,' Natalya said decidedly. 'I'll go to the leach-woman Kapitonovna. She'll get rid of it for me... She's done it for others.'

'You would kill your own baby? How can your tongue move to say such a thing, you shameless creature?' Ilyinichna halted indignantly in the middle of the road. She was about to say something else, but from behind her came the clatter of wagon wheels, the squelching of hooves in the mud and a man's urging voice.

Ilyinichna and Natalya stepped off the road, lowering their skirts as they did so. Old Beskhlebnov drew level with them and reined in his spirited mare.

'Get in, women, I'll take you home. Why should you churn up the mud.'

'Well, thank you, Agevich, we're right tired of slipping and sliding about,' Ilyinichna responded gladly and was the first to climb on to the big wagon.

* * *

After dinner Ilyinichna made up her mind to talk to
Natalya and persuade her not to rid herself of her child;
while she did the washing-up she searched for what
seemed to her the best arguments and even thought of
telling her husband of Natalya's decision to enlist his aid
in dissuading her grief-maddened daughter-in-law, but
before she had finished her chores Natalya quietly put
some of her things together and left the house.

'Where's Natalya?' she asked Dunyashka.

'She went off somewhere with a bundle.'

'Where to? What did she say? What bundle?'

'How should I know, Mother? She wrapped up a clean
skirt and a few other things and went without saying
anything.'

'Oh, the poor dear thing!' And to Dunyashka's surprise her mother broke into helpless tears and sank down
on a bench.

'What is it, Mother? For Lord's sake, why are you
crying?'

'Oh, leave me alone, you pest! It's nothing to do with
you! What did she say? And why didn't you tell me as
soon as she started getting her things together?'

Dunyashka retorted vexedly, 'Oh, you're just terrible!
How was I to know I ought to have told you? She hasn't
gone for good, has she? She must have gone to visit her
mother. I just can't think what you're crying about!'

Ilyinichna awaited Natalya's return with the greatest
anxiety, but decided not to tell her husband for fear
of his reproaches and scolding.

At sunset the herd came in from the steppe. The brief
summer shadows fell. Lamps were lit here and there in
the village, but still Natalya did not come. The Melekhovs sat down to their supper. Pale with anxiety,
Ilyinichna served the noodle soup, seasoned with onions
fried in sunflower oil. The old man picked up his spoon,
scooped up some crumbs of stale bread, poured them
into his bearded mouth, glanced absent-mindedly round
the table, and asked, 'Where's Natalya? Why don't you
call her to table?'

'She's not at home,' Ilyinichna replied in a voice barely
above a whisper.

'Where is she?'

'She must have gone to see her mother.'

'Well, she's a long time about it. She ought to

541

know our ways by now,' Pantelei muttered grumpily.

As always he ate diligently, with a kind of fanatic zeal; occasionally he would lay his spoon upside down on the table and with an admiring sidelong glance at his grandson, who was sitting beside him, say roughly, 'Turn your head, little laddie, let me wipe your lips. Your mother has gone astray and there's no one to look after you.' And with his big calloused, black palm he would wipe Mishatka's tender pink lips.

They finished their supper in silence and rose from the table. Pantelei commanded, 'Put out the lamp. There's no need to waste oil.'

'Shall I lock the door?' Ilyinichna asked.

'Yes, lock it.'

'What about Natalya?'

'She can knock. Mebbe she'll be gallivanting around till morning? This is a fine fashion... And you let her carry on without a word said, you old witch! Go off visiting at night, would she!... I'll teach her in the morning. She's following Darya's example.'

Ilyinichna went to bed without undressing. She lay for half an hour, turning over and sighing, and was just about to get up and go to Kapitonovna's when she heard faint, uncertain footsteps by the window. The old woman sprang out of bed with an agility that belied her years and hurried out into the porch to open the door.

Natalya, pale as death, slowly climbed the porch steps, clinging to the handrail. The full moon shone brilliantly on her haggard face with its sunken eyes and painfully arched brows. She staggered forward like a badly wounded animal, each footstep leaving a dark spot of blood on the floor.

Ilyinichna hugged her silently and led her into the porch. Natalya leaned against the doorpost and whispered hoarsely, 'Is everyone asleep? Mother, wipe the blood... Look what a trail I've left.'

'What have you done to yourself?!' Ilyinichna exclaimed in an undertone, choking back her tears.

Natalya tried to smile, but a wretched grimace contorted her face.

'Don't make a noise, Mother. Or you'll wake the family... Well, I've freed myself. Now my mind's at rest... But there's so much blood... I'm bleeding like a pig... Give me your hand, Mother... My head's swimming.'

Ilyinichna bolted the front-door and, as though she were in a strange house, groped for a long time in the

542

darkness to find the handle of the inner door. On tiptoe she led Natalya into the big front room, wakened Dunyashka and sent her out, then called Darya and lighted the lamp.

The door into the kitchen was open and Pantelei's steady, powerful snoring could be heard; little Polyushka was smacking her lips sweetly and murmuring in her sleep. How sound the untroubled sleep of a child!

While Ilyinichna was puffing up the pillow and making the bed, Natalya sat down on a bench and laid her head weakly on the edge of the table. Dunyashka wanted to come in, but Ilyinichna said sternly, 'Go away, you shameless creature, and don't show yourself here again! This is no place for you!'

With a frown on her face Darya went out into the porch with a floorcloth. Natalya raised her head with an effort and said, 'Take the clean clothes off the bed and put some sacking down for me... I'll only make it dirty...'

'Be quiet!' Ilyinichna commanded. 'Undress and get into bed. Do you feel bad? Shall I bring you some water?'

'I feel so weak... Bring me a clean nightshirt and some water.'

Natalya rose with an effort and walked unsteadily to the bed. Only then did Ilyinichna notice that her skirt was soaked in blood and clung wetly to her legs. She stared in horror as Natalya wrung out the hem as if she had been caught in the rain and began to undress.

'You've lost so much blood!' Ilyinichna said with a sob.

Natalya took off her clothes and closed her eyes, breathing in short quick gasps. Ilyinichna looked at her once more and then made resolutely for the kitchen. With difficulty she roused Pantelei and said, 'Natalya's ill... And it's very bad, she might die... Harness up at once and go to the stanitsa for a doctor.'

'What's this rubbish you've thought up! What's happened to her? She's ill, you say? She ought to do less gallivanting about at night...'

His wife briefly explained what the matter was. Pantelei sprang out of bed in a frenzy and, buttoning his trousers as he went, made for the front room.

'The scum! The little bitch! What's the idea, eh?! Who forced her to do that!... Now I'll give her a rating, that I will...'

'Are you mad, you devil?! Where're you off to?... Don't go in there! She can't be bothered with you now...

543

You'll wake the children! Get out into the yard and harness up quickly!...' But ignoring his wife, the old man went to the door of the front room and kicked it open.

'So that's what you've done to yourself, you daughter of the devil!' he bellowed, standing on the threshold.

'Oh, you mustn't! Don't come in, Father! For love of Christ, don't!' Natalya shrieked, clasping the shift she had just taken off to her breast.

Cursing and swearing, Pantelei started looking for his coat, cap and harness. He was so long about it that Dunyashka burst into the room and assailed her father with tearful fury.

'Go quickly! What are you rummaging for like a beetle in a dung heap? Natalya's dying and he dithers around for hours getting ready! Call yourself a father! If you don't want to go, say so! I'll harness the horse and go myself!'

'Are you daft! Where did you break loose from? No one cares what you say, you ringworm! Shouting at her own father, the little devil!' Pantelei took a swipe at his daughter with his coat and stomped out into the yard, muttering curses.

After he had gone, the family felt some relief. Darya washed the floors, furiously pushing the chairs and benches aside. Dunyashka, who after the old man's departure had been allowed to enter the room, sat at Natalya's bedside, straightened her pillows and gave her drinks of water; now and then Ilyinichna went to peep at the children sleeping in the side room, and on her return would stand staring at Natalya, cheek in hand and shaking her head sadly.

Natalya lay in silence, rolling her head from side to side on the pillow, her hair wet and dishevelled. She was bleeding to death. Every half hour Ilyinichna lifted her gently, pulled out the sodden undersheet and spread a new one.

As the hours went by Natalya grew steadily weaker. Some time after midnight she opened her eyes and asked, 'Will it soon be light?'

'No sign yet,' the old woman assured her, but to herself she thought, 'That means she won't live! She's afraid she'll go before she sees the children.'

As though to confirm this conjecture, Natalya asked quietly, 'Mother, dear, wake up Mishatka and Polyushka.'

'Whatever for, lovey! Why wake them in the middle of the night? It'll give them such a fright to see you like this, they'll scream the house down... Why should I wake them?'

'I want to see them... I feel bad.'

'God save you, what are you saying? Father will be here any minute with the doctor and he'll help you. Try to sleep now, my poor dear, won't you?'

'How can I sleep?' Natalya replied with a faint irritation in her voice. And then for a long time she was silent and her breathing grew steadier.

Ilyinichna went quietly out into the porch and gave free rein to her tears. She returned to the front room, her face red and swollen, when a faint white streak of dawn appeared in the east. Natalya opened her eyes at the creak of the door and again asked, 'Will it soon be light?'

'It's getting light now.'

'Cover my feet with my coat.'

Dunyashka spread a sheepskin over her feet and tucked in the blanket. Natalya thanked her with a glance, then called Ilyinichna and said, 'Sit down, Mother, and you, Dunyashka, and you, Darya, leave us for a minute, I want to speak to Mother alone... Have they gone?' she asked after a moment, without opening her eyes.

'Yes.'

'Isn't Father back yet?'

'He soon will be. Do you feel worse then?'

'No, about the same... This is what I wanted to say... I'm going to die soon, Mother... I know it in my heart. I've lost so much blood! Tell Darya to light the stove and boil up plenty of water... Wash me yourself, I don't want any strangers...'

'Natalya! How can you, my pet! What are you talking about death for! God is merciful, you'll come through.'

With a weak gesture Natalya bid her mother-in-law to be silent, and said, 'Don't interrupt me... It's hard for me to talk, and I want to say... Oh, my head's swimming again... Did I tell you about the water? I must be strong... Kapitonovna did it for me a long time ago, after dinner, as soon as I got there... She was scared herself, the poor thing... I bled so badly... If only I can last out till morning... Boil up as much water as you can... I want to be clean when I'm dead... Mother dear, dress me in the green skirt, the one with the embroidery on the hem... Grisha liked me in that ... and in the poplin blouse ... it's in the chest, on top, in the righthand corner, under my shawl... And when I'm gone, take the children away to our folk... You would send for Mother, let her come now... I must say goodbye... Take out the sheet, it's all wet...'

With her arm under Natalya's back Ilyinichna pulled the sheet out from under her and spread a fresh one. Natalya managed to whisper, 'Turn me ... over!' then fainted.

A blue dawn peered in through the window. Dunyashka scrubbed out a pail and went to milk the cows. Ilyinichna opened the window wide and the sharp refreshing cool of a summer morning burst into the room, which had grown fetid with the smell of fresh blood and burnt lamp-oil. The breeze sprinkled dewdrops from the cherry leaves on the windowsill; the early voices of the birds, the lowing of the cattle and the juicy crack of a herdsman's whip could be heard.

Natalya opened her eyes, licked her dry, bloodless, yellow lips with the tip of her tongue, and asked for water. She no longer inquired about the children or her mother. Everything was drifting away from her—soon it would be gone forever.

Ilyinichna closed the window and went to the bed. How terribly Natalya had changed in one night! Only the day before she had been like a young apple-tree in blossom—beautiful, strong, healthy, but now her cheeks looked whiter than the chalk of the Donside hills, her nose had tapered, her lips had lost their former vivid freshness, grown thinner and seemed hardly to cover the parted teeth. Only her eyes retained their former brightness, but their expression had changed. Something new, unfamiliar and frightening showed in her gaze when in obedience to some inexplicable urge she raised her bluish lids and scanned the room, letting her eyes rest for a moment on Ilyinichna.

At sunrise Pantelei arrived. The doctor, exhausted by sleepless nights and endless caring for typhus cases and the wounded, climbed out of the tarantass, stretched himself, picked up a bundle from the seat, and went into the house. On the porch he took off his tarpaulin raincoat and, leaning over the rail, soaped his hairy hands at great length, squinting up at Dunyashka, who was pouring water for him from a jug, and even winked at her twice. Then he went into the front room and, having sent everybody out, spent about ten minutes at Natalya's bedside.

Pantelei and Ilyinichna sat in the kitchen.

'Well, how is she?' the old man asked his wife as soon as they left the front room.

'In a bad way...'

'Did she do it of her own accord?'

'It was her own idea...' Ilyinichna avoided giving a direct answer.

'Hot water—quickly!' the doctor ordered, sticking his tousled head round the door.

While the water was being heated, he came out into the kitchen.

In reply to the old man's mute question he made a hopeless gesture.

'She'll be gone by dinner-time. Terrible loss of blood. Nothing can be done! Have you informed Grigory Panteleyevich?'

Without answering, Pantelei limped hurriedly on to the porch and into the yard. Darya saw the old man go behind the mower in the shed, rest his head on a pile of last year's dung bricks, and begin to sob.

The doctor was there for another half an hour. He sat on the porch, dozing in the rays of the rising sun. When the samovar had boiled, he returned to the front room, gave Natalya an injection of camphor, came out again and asked for some milk. Swallowing a yawn with difficulty, he drank two glasses and said, 'You must take me back now. I have sick and wounded to attend to in the stanitsa and it's no good my staying here anyway. It's hopeless. I'd be only too glad to help Grigory Panteleyevich, but, honestly, there's nothing I can do. We're not ambitious. We only heal the sick and we haven't learned yet how to resurrect the dead. Your little woman has been so cut up that she's got nothing to live with... The uterus is torn to shreds. The old woman must have gone at it with an iron hook. It's the price of our benighted ignorance. Can't be helped!'

Pantelei tossed some hay into the tarantass and said to Darya, 'You take him back. Don't forget to water the mare when you get down to the Don.'

He offered the doctor some money, but it was firmly refused.

'You should be ashamed to mention it, Pantelei Prokofievich. You're all our own folk and you push money at me. No, I wouldn't touch it! What have you to thank me for? Don't speak of it! If I'd put your daughter-in-law on her feet, it would be a different matter.'

At about six in the morning Natalya suddenly felt

547

much better. She asked for water to wash her face, combed her hair in front of the glass that Dunyashka held for her and, looking at her family with a new light in her eyes, forced herself to smile.

'Now I'm going to get better! But how frightened I was... I thought it was all up with me... How can those children sleep so long? Go and see if they've woken up, Dunyashka.'

Lukinichna and Agrippina arrived. The old woman burst into tears at the sight of her daughter, but Natalya protested excitedly.

'Why are you crying, Mother! I'm not as bad as all that... Have you come to bury me? How can you cry like this?'

Agrippina gave her mother a nudge and the old woman had the sense to wipe her eyes and say reassuringly, 'That was silly of me, dear. But it wrung my heart to look at you. You've changed so!'

A faint flush appeared in Natalya's cheeks when she heard Mishatka say something and Polyushka laugh in reply.

'Call them in! And do be quick! They can dress later!'

Polyushka was the first to enter. She halted on the threshold, rubbing her sleepy eyes with her fist.

'Your Mummy's ill,' Natalya said with a smile. 'Come up to me, my little darling!'

Polyushka stared in wonder at the solemnly seated grown-ups and, as she approached her mother, asked disappointedly, 'Why didn't you wake me up? And why are they all here?'

'They've come to see me... What need was there to wake you?'

'I'd have brought you some water, I'd have sat with you.'

'Well, go and wash and comb your hair, say your prayers, and then you can come and sit with me.'

'Will you get up for breakfast?'

'I don't know. I don't think so.'

'Then I'll bring it to you in bed, Mummy, Shall I?'

'She's just like her father, but her heart doesn't take after his; it's softer,' Natalya said with a faint smile, letting her head fall back and drawing the blanket round her legs with a shiver.

After an hour she took a turn for the worse. She beckoned the children, hugged them, made the sign of the cross, kissed them and asked her mother to take them home with her. Lukinichna charged Agrippina with the task and herself stayed with her elder daughter.

Natalya closed her eyes and said, as if in oblivion, 'So I shan't see him again...' Then, with sudden recall, rose on her bed. 'Bring back Mishatka!'

A tearful Agrippina pushed the little boy back into the room and went to the kitchen, muttering sorrowfully to herself.

Mishatka, rather sullen, with an unfriendly Melekhov look in his eyes, approached the bed timidly. His mother's deeply changed face made her almost a stranger. Natalya drew her little son towards her and felt his heart beat fast, like a captured sparrow's.

'Bend closer to me, my son! Closer!' she told him.

She whispered something in Mishatka's ear, then pushed him away, looked keenly into his eyes, tightening her trembling lips and with a forced, pitiful smile asked, 'You won't forget? Will you tell him?'

'No, I won't forget...' Mishatka seized his mother's forefinger, squeezed it in his hot little fist, held it for a minute and let it go. He walked away from the bed for some reason on tip-toe, balancing with his arms.

Natalya watched him go, then silently turned away to the wall.

She died at noon.

XVII

Many were the thoughts and memories that passed through Grigory's mind during the two days' journey from the front to his home village. So as not to be left alone in the steppe with his grief, with inescapable thoughts of Natalya, he had taken Prokhor Zykov with him. As soon as they left the village where the squadron was stationed, Grigory started talking about the war, how they had served together in the 12th Regiment on the Austrian front, the march into Romania, the fighting with the Germans. He went on without stopping, recalling all kinds of amusing incidents that had befallen him and the men of his regiment, and laughing over them.

Prokhor, plain man that he was, at first glanced in astonishment at Grigory, marvelling at his unwonted loquacity, but soon he realised that these reminiscences of days gone by were Grigory's way of banishing painful reflections, and took up the conversation with almost too much zeal. While he was relating in every detail the time he had spent in hospital in Chernigov, he happened to glance at Grigory and saw tears running freely down his swarthy cheeks. A sense of delicacy prompted Prokhor to drop behind for a while; after half an hour or so he drew level again and tried to talk about something of no importance, but Grigory would not respond. So they cantered on until midday, neck and neck, in silence.

Grigory was in a desperate hurry. Despite the heat he whipped his horse now into a canter or even a gallop, and only occasionally slowed to a walk. Not until noon when the steeply falling rays of the sun became unbearable did Grigory draw rein in a ravine, unsaddle his horse and let it graze; he himself found a place in the shade, lay down on his face and did not stir until the heat had abated. They did give the horses one feed of oats, but Grigory would not allow the regulation feed times and by the end of the first day even their hard-bitten mounts, which were used to long rides, had deeply sunken flanks and were no longer capable of the unflagging speed they had kept up at first. 'If we go on like this we'll soon ruin the horses,' Prokhor thought to himself irritably. 'Who rides like this? It's all very well for him. He can ride one to death and they'll saddle up another for him right away, but where do I get a new horse from? He'll carry on like this, the devil, and we'll find ourselves walking the rest of the way to Tatarsky, or doing it on a commandeered bone-shaker.'

On the morning of the next day, near Fedoseyevskaya, his impatience got the better of him and he said to Grigory, 'Anyone'd think you'd never been a farmer in your life... Who rides on like this, day and night, without rest? Look what's become of the horses. Let's feed 'em properly at sundown.'

'Keep going,' Grigory replied absently.

'I can't keep up with you, mine's giving up already. What about a halt?'

Grigory said nothing. For another half an hour they cantered on without exchanging a word, then Prokhor declared firmly, 'Let's give 'em a breather! I won't go on any further like this! D'you hear?'

'Push on!'

'How much longer? Till the horse gives up the ghost altogether?'

'Don't talk back!'

'Have a heart, Grigory Panteleyevich! I don't want

to ditch my horse, but that's what we're heading for.'

'All right, may the devil take you! Keep an eye open for some good grass.'

* * *

The telegram had been chasing Grigory round the Khopyor district and had arrived too late... He reached home two days after the funeral. He dismounted at the gate, gave Dunyashka a hug as she ran tearfully out of the house to greet him, and told her frowning, 'Walk the horse well... And don't bawl!' He turned to Prokhor, 'Go home. I'll send for you if you're needed.'

Ilyinichna came out on the porch to meet her son, holding Mishatka and Polyushka by the hand.

Grigory scooped up the pair of them and with a quiver in his voice said, 'No crying now! No tears! My dear little ones! So now you're orphans, eh? Too bad... Mummy let us down...'

Barely able to check his own tears, he walked into the house and greeted his father.

'There was nothing we could do,' Pantelei told him, and at once limped out into the porch.

Ilyinichna took Grigory into the front room and talked to him for a long time about Natalya. She had not intended to tell him everything, but Grigory asked, 'What made her decide not to have the child? D'you know?'

'Yes, I do.'

'Well then?'

'Before that she had been to your, to that... Aksinya told her everything.'

'Uh-huh ... so that was it?' Grigory flushed purple and lowered his eyes.

He came out of the room, looking older and very pale. His quivering bluish lips moved soundlessly as he put the children on his lap. He fondled them for a while, then he took a dusty grey lump of sugar out of his pack, split it in his hand with a knife, and smiled guiltily.

'Here's all the goodies I've brought you... That's the kind of father you've got... All right, out you go into the yard, call Grandad.'

'Will you visit the grave?' Ilyinichna asked.

'A bit later on... The dead don't mind... How did the children take it? Are they all right now?'

'The first day they cried their hearts out, specially Polyushka... Now they never mention her in front of us, but last night I heard Mishatka crying quietly... He had his head under the pillow, so he wouldn't be heard... I went in to him and asked, "What's the matter, dear? Would you like to come into my bed?" "No, Granny," he says, "I must've been dreaming..." Talk to them, be kind to them. The other morning I heard them talking in the porch. Polyushka says, "She'll come back one day. She's young and the young people don't die for ever." They're young and silly themselves, but they feel the pain as much as the grown-ups... You must be hungry, eh? Let me get you something to eat. Why don't you say something?'

Grigory went into the front room. As though entering it for the first time, he scanned the walls, the neatly made bed with its puffed up pillows. This was where Natalya had died, where her voice had uttered its last... He pictured her saying goodbye to the children, kissing them and making the sign of the cross, and once again, just as when he had read the telegram with the news of her death, he felt a sharp, stabbing pain in the heart and a dull ringing in his ears.

Every little thing in the house reminded him of Natalya. His memories of her were ineradicable and agonizing. For some reason he visited every room, then hurried out, almost ran on to the porch. The pain in his heart had grown more intense. Perspiration broke out on his forehead. He walked down the steps, pressing his hand to his left side in fright and telling himself he was not the man he used to be.

Dunyashka was still walking his horse round the yard. Near the barn it refused to go any further, stopped, and sniffed at the ground with its neck outstretched and its upper lip curled back, exposing its strong yellow teeth, then it snorted and bent its forelegs awkwardly. Dunyashka pulled on the rein, but the animal sank stubbornly to the ground.

'Don't let it lie down!' Pantelei shouted from the stable. 'Can't you see, it's still saddled! Why didn't you unsaddle it, stupid?'

Unhurriedly, still keenly aware of what was going on in his chest, Grigory went up to the horse and took off the saddle. With an effort he smiled at Dunyashka.

'Father barks a bit, does he?'

'Same as ever,' Dunyashka smiled responsively.

'Walk him a bit more, sister.'

'He's dry now. Still, I don't mind.'

'Let him have a roll then, don't hinder him.'

'Is it very bad, brother?'

'What would you think?' Grigory answered with a sharp intake of breath.

Moved by a sense of compassion, Dunyashka kissed him on the shoulder, then in sudden embarrassment turned away with tears in her eyes and led the horse into the cattle yard.

Grigory went over to his father, who was busily raking dung out of the stable.

'I'm clearing a place for your mount.'

'Why didn't you tell me? I'd have cleared it myself.'

'Huh, the idea! Think I'm a dodderer now? I'm like an old flintlock, lad! I'll never wear out! And I've still got some kick in me. I'm thinking of reaping the rye tomorrow. You going to be here for long?'

'A month.'

'That's good! Let's go a-reaping, eh? You'll feel better when you're working.'

'That's what I was thinking.'

The old man put down his pitchfork, wiped the sweat from his face and with a confidential note in his voice said, 'Come indoors, you'd better have some dinner. There's no escape from grief. That's just the way it is...'

Ilyinichna laid the table and, when she gave him a clean hand-towel, Grigory thought again, 'It used to be Natalya who served me...' To hide his emotion he tackled his food vigorously. And it was with a feeling of gratitude that he glanced at his father when Pantelei brought up from the cellar a jug of home-brew, plugged with a wisp of hay.

'Let us remember the deceased, God rest her soul,' Pantelei said firmly.

They emptied their glasses. The old man at once refilled them and sighed.

'In just one year our family has lost two souls... Death has taken a fancy to our house.'

'Don't let's talk about that, Dad!' Grigory responded.

He gulped down the second glass and chewed at a lump of fried fish, waiting for the drink to go to his head and stifle the thoughts that pursued him relentlessly.

'There's a fine crop of rye this year! And ours is way ahead of all the rest!' Pantelei boasted. But even in that boastfulness, Grigory sensed a forced note, calculated to distract him.

'What about the wheat?'

'The wheat? It was caught by the frost but not too badly. It'll yield fifteen poods or more to the acre. The folk who sowed *garnovka* have been doing fine, but, as luck would have it, we didn't happen to sow any this year. Still I'm not all that sorry! What can you do with wheat when the country's in such a mess? You can't take it to the elevator at Paramonovo, and you can't keep it in your own barns. As soon as the front moves on a bit, the comrades will come and clean out the lot. But don't you worry, even without this harvest we've got enough wheat to see us through the next two years. Our bins are overflowing, thank the Lord; and that's not all we've got...' The old man winked craftily and said, 'Ask Darya how much we've put away for a rainy day! We filled a pit as deep as you're tall and half as broad again—right up to the top! This damn life we're leading has stripped us down a bit, but we were good farmers once, you know...' The old man laughed tipsily at his own joke, but after a while he stroked his beard in a dignified way and said with sober good sense, 'Mebbe you're thinking of your mother-in-law. Well, I'll tell you this. I didn't forget her. I did what I could to help them in their time of need. The very next day, before she could say a word, I took 'em a whole wagonload of corn without measuring it. Our Natalya, God rest her soul, was real pleased. She even shed a tear when she heard about it... Come on, son, let's have a third. You're the only joy I've got left now!'

At that moment Mishatka sidled timidly up to the table. He climbed on to his father's lap and, putting his left arm awkwardly round his neck, kissed him firmly on the lips.

'What was that for, son?' Grigory asked, deeply moved, as he looked into the boy's tear-misted eyes and held his breath so as not to blow the smell of vodka in his son's face.

Mishatka replied quietly, 'When Mummy was lying in the front room ... when she was still alive, she called me over and told me to tell you this, "When father comes home, give him a kiss from me and tell him to look after you well." And she said something else, but I've forgotten...'

Grigory put down his glass and turned away to the window. An oppressive silence descended on the room.

'Let's drink, eh? Pantelei asked softly.

'I don't want any more.' Grigory put his son off his

lap and hurried out into the porch.

'Wait a bit, son, what about the second course? We've got a boiled chicken and pancakes for you!' Ilyinichna made for the stove, but Grigory had already banged the door.

He roamed aimlessly about the yard, inspecting the cattle pen and the stable. He looked at his horse and thought it could do with a bathe, then he went to the shed. Beside a reaper standing in readiness for the fields, he noticed some pinewood shavings and a cross-cut piece of board. 'That's where Father made Natalya's coffin,' he thought, and strode hastily away to the porch.

Yielding to his son's urgings, Pantelei hurriedly made ready, harnessed the horses to the reaper, filled a water cask, and drove out with him to the fields that night.

XVIII

Grigory was suffering not only because in his own way he had loved Natalya and grown used to her in their six years of married life, but also because he felt he was to blame for her death. If Natalya had carried out her threat, taken the children and gone off to live with her mother, if she had died there, an embittered woman, hating her unfaithful husband and unreconciled with him, Grigory would probably not have felt his loss so keenly and certainly would not have experienced such fierce remorse. But from his mother he had learned that Natalya had forgiven him everything, that she had loved him and remembered him right up to the last minute. This increased his suffering, burdened his conscience with endless reproaches, and forced him to reconsider his past life and behaviour.

At one time Grigory had felt nothing for his wife save a cold indifference and even dislike, but more recently his attitude had changed and the main reason for that change had been the children.

At first Grigory had not experienced the deep paternal feelings that had come to him of late. When returning on short leave from the front he would fondle them almost out of a sense of duty and to please their mother; far from feeling any spontaneous urge to do so, he experienced nothing but a distrustful surprise at the sight of Natalya's outbursts of maternal feeling. He could not understand how anyone could feel such devoted love for these squalling noisy little creatures, and more than once he had said to his wife with some annoyance and derision when she was still nursing the children, 'Why do you jump up like a mad thing? You're out of bed before it even squawks. Let it yell if it wants to, it won't cry our wealth away, you know!' The children had treated him with no less indifference, but as they grew older, their attachment to their father had also grown. The children's love had awakened a response in him, and that feeling, like sparks from a fire, had spread to Natalya.

After the break with Aksinya, Grigory had never seriously considered leaving his wife; never, even when he took up with Aksinya again, had he thought of her as replacing the mother of his children. He wouldn't have minded living with the two of them, loving each in different ways, but after the loss of his wife he suddenly felt an estrangement from Aksinya and then a smouldering anger because she had betrayed their relationship and, in so doing, precipitated Natalya's death.

Try as he would, even out in the fields Grigory could not forget his grief; it was for ever in his thoughts. He wore himself out with toil, riding on the reaper for hours on end, but it was no use; his memory stubbornly went right back into the past, digging up various, often trivial incidents in their life together and scraps of their conversation, and the living, smiling Natalya would arise before him. He would recall her figure, her walk, her way of patting her hair into place, her smile, the intonations of her voice...

On the third day they started reaping the barley. Around noon, when Pantelei had reined in the horses, Grigory climbed down from the rear seat of the reaper, rested his short-handled pitchfork on the cross-bar, and said, 'I want to go home for a bit, Father.'

'What for?'

'I'm missing the children somehow.'

'Well, go then,' the old man agreed willingly. 'And in the meantime I'll do some shooking.'

Grigory at once unharnessed his horse from the reaper, mounted it, and rode off at a walk over the prickly yellow stubble towards the highway. 'Tell him to look after us well!' Natalya's words were ringing in his ears. He closed his eyes, let go of the reins and allowed the horse to make its own way.

In the intensely blue sky a few wind-scattered clouds

hung almost motionless. Rooks were waddling across the stubble. They gathered in families among the shooked grain, the older birds beak-feeding the fledglings, which had only just grown their feathers and were still uncertain on the wing. The reaped acres echoed with their cawing.

Grigory's horse followed the verge of the road, occasionally snapping up a sprig of clover and munching it with a clank of the snaffle. Once or twice it stopped and whinnied at the sight of other horses in the distance, whererupon Grigory opened his eyes and urged it on, staring vacantly at the steppe, the dusty track, the yellow shooks of rye, the greenish-brown strips of ripening millet.

As soon as Grigory reached home, Khristonya appeared, looking sombre and dressed, despite the heat, in a worsted British army tunic and wide breeches. He walked in leaning on a huge freshly stripped ash stick, and boomed a greeting.

'I came to find out how you are. I've heard of your sad loss. So you've buried Natalya Mironovna?'

'How did you get back from the front?' Grigory asked, pretending not to have heard the question and surveying the big Cossack's ungainly and now somewhat bowed figure with satisfaction.

'Convalescent leave after being wounded. Two bullets at once got me in the tummy. And they're still there, must have got stuck in my guts, the damn things. That's why I'm walking with a stick. See?'

'Where did they knock you about like this?'

'At Balashov.'

'Did you capture it? How come you got hit?'

'We were attacking. Ay, they captured Balashov, and Povorino. I was in that too.'

'Well, tell me who you were with, what unit, who was there from our village. Sit down, here's some tobacco.'

Grigory was glad to see a new face and talk about something that had nothing to do with his own personal emotions. Khristonya had the sense to see this, and willingly but in a roundabout way began an account of the capture of Balashov, and how he had been wounded. Puffing at a huge cigarette he had rolled himself, he rumbled in his deep voice, 'Advancing through some sunflowers we were. And they were hammering away at us, I reckon, with machine-guns and artillery, and rifles as well, o'course. Well, I'm a noticeable kind of feller, and when I'm in the line I stand out like a goose among the chickens. No matter how low I crouched, I could still be seen, and that's why the bullets got me. Still, it's a good thing I'm a fair height, if I'd been any shorter they'd have got me in the head, that's for sure! They must have been nearly spent, I reckon, but they gave me such a wallop I got the collywobbles, and both of 'em were hot as hell, as if they'd popped straight out of a stove... I clapped my hand on the spot and I could feel 'em rolling about under my skin, like pebbles, quite close to each other. Well, I gave 'em a squeeze and then, I reckon, I fell down. This is no joke, damn it all, I thought to myself, having something like that inside me! I'd better keep lying down or another one, a bit livelier, might hit and come out t'other side. So there I was, lying on the ground and having a feel at 'em—the bullets, I mean. Still there they were, one next the other. And I got right scared. What'll happen, I thought, if they fall through into my belly, the bastards! They'll be rolling around in my guts and how will the doctors ever find 'em? And it'll be no fun for me either. A man's body, even one like mine, is thin stuff, ye know. So if them bullets get to my main gut, they'll be clattering about inside me like a postman's rattle. Upset everything, that will. So there I lay. I'd pulled the top of a sunflower and started eating the seeds, but I was scared. Our line had gone on ahead. Still, when they'd captured that Balashov place they came and fetched me and put me in the Tishansky hospital. The little doctor there, nimble as a sparrow he was, kept asking me, "Let's have those bullets out, eh?" But I'm not such a fool, you know. "Can they fall through into my belly, Your Honour," I asks him. "No," he says, "they can't." Ah, then I won't have 'em taken out, I thought. I know the way it is! They cut 'em out and before the scar has time to heal, they send you back to your unit. "No, Your Honour," I says. "I won't have it done. It'll be more fun for me to keep 'em. I want to take 'em home and show the wife, and they don't bother me much, they're not all that heavy." So he told me off and gave me a week's leave.'

Grigory listened smiling to this artless tale.

'What regiment were you in?' he asked.

'The Fourth, combined.'

'Anyone from our village with you?'

'Plenty—Anikei, Beskhlebnov, Akim Koloveidin, Syom-ka Miroshnikov, Tikhon Gorbachov.'

'How're the Cossacks? Not complaining?'

'They're fed up with the officers, I reckon. Rotten lot of bastards they landed us with, make you sick. And they're nearly all Russians, no Cossacks amongst 'em.'

While Khristonya was telling his story, he kept pulling down the short sleeves of his English tunic, stroking the knees and staring, as though unable to believe his eyes, at the fine woollen cloth of his English breeches.

'But they didn't have any boots to fit me,' he said thoughtfully. 'There's not a full-sized foot like mine in the whole British Empire... We sow and eat wheat, you know, but out there, I reckon, they live on rye, like in Russia. How could they have such feet? They've fitted out the whole squadron, uniforms, boots and all, even sent us their sweet-smelling cigarettes, but all the same it's bad.'

'What's bad?' Grigory inquired.

Khristonya smiled and said, 'Outside it looks good, but it's bad inside. The Cossacks are grumbling again; they don't want to fight. So nothing'll come of this war. They say they won't go any further than the Khopyor district.'

When he had seen Khristonya off, Grigory decided after a little thought, 'I'll live here for another week, then go back to the front. I'll eat my heart out here.' He stayed at home till evening. Recalling his own childhood, he made Mishatka a windmill out of bulrushes, wove a snare out of horse-hair for catching sparrows, and skilfully built his daughter a tiny carriage with wheels that turned and a pretty painted shaft. He even tried to make her a rag doll, but that proved to be beyond his powers and the doll had to be completed by Dunyashka.

The children, who had never had so much of their father before, at first treated his efforts with distrust, but soon they would not leave his side for a minute. By evening, when Grigory was making ready to go to the fields, Mishatka declared, holding back his tears, 'You're always like that! You come home for a little while, then leave us... Take your snare, your windmill and our rattle, take them all! I don't want them!'

Grigory enclosed his son's little fists in his own big hands and said, 'If that's how it is, let's settle the matter. You're a Cossack now, so come out into the fields with me. We'll reap the barley and stack it, you'll sit on the reaper with Grandad and gee-up the horses. You should see how many grasshoppers there are out there in the grass. How many different birds in the ravines! And Po-

lyushka can stay at home with Granny. She won't mind.
She's a girl, so it's her job to sweep the floors, bring
Granny water from the Don in her little bucket, and all
kinds of other women's business. Will you come?'

'Won't I just!' Mishatka cried delightedly, his eyes
shining in anticipation.

Ilyinichna tried to object.

'Where're you taking him off to? There's no end to
your mad ideas! Where will he sleep? Who will keep an
eye on him? God forbid, he'll get himself kicked by a
horse or bitten by a snake. Don't go with your father,
dear, stay at home!' she appealed to her grandson.

But the little boy's eyes narrowed and flared ominously (just like Grandad Pantelei's, when he got into a fury),
his fists clenched and in a tearful high-pitched voice he
cried, 'Granny, be quiet!... I'm going anyway! Daddy
dear, don't listen to her!'

Laughing, Grigory picked his son up in his arms and
reassured his mother, 'He'll sleep with me. And from here
we'll ride all the way at a walk. I shan't drop him, shall
I? Get his clothes ready, Mother, and don't worry—I'll
look after him and bring him back safe and sound tomorrow night.'

Thus there began the friendship between Grigory
and his little son.

In the two weeks he spent in Tatarsky Grigory saw
Aksinya only three times, and even then it was but a
glimpse. With the intelligence and tact inherent to her
nature Aksinya avoided meeting him, realising that it
would be better to keep out of sight. Her woman's
instinct told her that any careless or untimely expression
of her feelings might set him against her and cast a
shadow on their relationship. She waited for him to make
the advance. This happened the day before he left for
the front. He was driving a load of grain back from the
fields. It was late and in the twilight he met Aksinya at
the end of the lane leading out of the village. She bowed
to him from a distance and smiled faintly. Her smile
was tense and expectant. Grigory returned her bow,
but could not pass by in silence.

'How're you getting on?' he asked, imperceptibly
tightening the rein and checking the briskly stepping horses.

'Not badly, thank you, Grigory Panteleyevich.'

'How is it you're never to be seen?'

'I've been out in the fields... I've got the whole place
on my hands.'

Perhaps because Mishatka was sitting on the load beside him Grigory did not stop the horses or continue the conversation. He drove on a few paces and turned at the sound of her voice. Aksinya was standing by the fence.

'Will you be staying long in the village?' she asked, plucking agitatedly at the petals of a daisy.

'I'm off tomorrow.'

He could see that she wanted to ask something else. But for some reason she left her question unasked, let her hand fall to her side, and hurried out on to the common without a backward glance.

XIX

The sky was blanketed in cloud. Fine rain was sifting down. The young aftergrass in the stubble and the scrub and thorn bushes scattered across the steppe were glistening wetly.

Deeply disappointed by his commander's premature departure from the village, Prokhor rode in silence, not offering a single comment. Beyond the village of Sevastyanovsky they met three mounted Cossacks. They were riding abreast, urging on their horses with their heels and talking animatedly. One of them, elderly with a reddish beard and wearing a grey homespun coat, recognised Grigory from a distance. 'Why, it's Melekhov, lads!' he said loudly to his companions and, as they came up, reined in his tall bay stallion.

'Hullo there, Grigory Panteleyevich!' he greeted Grigory.

'Hullo!' Grigory replied, trying vainly to recall where he had met this red-bearded, surly-looking Cossack.

Evidently the man had been made a junior cornet quite recently and, to avoid being taken for a rank-and-file Cossack, had sewn his new shoulder straps straight on to his homespun coat.

'Don't you know me?' he asked, riding up close and holding out a broad hand covered with fiery-red hair. There was a heavy whiff of vodka on his breath. A smug complacency radiated from the newly promoted junior cornet's face, his small light-blue eyes were twinkling, and his lips under the ginger moustache were parted in a smile.

This homespun officer's absurd appearance tickled Gri-

561

gory's sense of humour. Without hiding his amusement, he replied, 'No, I don't. I must have met you when you were still in the ranks... Have you been a junior cornet for long?'

'Good shot! Only a week since I was promoted. But we met at Kudinov's headquarters, about the time of Annunciation, I think. You got me out of bad trouble then, don't you remember! Hi, Trifon! Ride on for a bit! I'll catch you up!' he called out to the others, who had halted a short distance away.

With an effort Grigory recalled the circumstances of his encounter with the red-bearded junior cornet and even remembered his nickname—'Semak!'—and what Kudinov had said about him, 'He's a fine marksman, the devil, never misses! He can bring down a running hare with a rifle. He's daring in battle and a fine scout, but he's got as much brains as a baby.' Semak, who had commanded a squadron during the rebellion, had committed some offence for which Kudinov had wanted to punish him, but Grigory had interceded and Semak had been pardoned and left in command of the squadron.

'Back from the front?' Grigory asked.

'That's right, I'm on my way from Novokhopyorsk, on leave. We made a detour of about a hundred and fifty versts and called at Slashchevskaya—I've a bunch of relatives there. I remember a good turn, Grigory Panteleyevich! Do me a favour. Let me treat you to a drink, eh? I've got two bottles of neat in my saddle bags, let's drink 'em up?'

Grigory refused point-blank but accepted one of the bottles that was then offered as a present.

'The things that went on there! The Cossacks and the officers loaded 'emselves with booty!' Semak related boastfully. 'I was in Balashov too. When we captured it, the first place we made for was the station. Every siding was packed with trains. Sugar in one wagon, uniforms in another, all kinds of stuff in a third. Some of the Cossacks took forty sets of clothing! And then we went off to clean out the yids. That was a laugh! One smart fellow from my squadron collected eighteen pocket watches, ten of 'em gold; the son-of-a-bitch pinned 'em all across his chest and looked like a proper rich merchant! And the rings he had—more than you could count! Two or three on every finger...'

Grigory pointed to Semak's bulging saddle bags. 'What have you got there?'

'Oh, all kinds of things.'

'So you were looting too?'

'Looting? That's a fine way to talk... It's not loot, I got it lawfully. Our regimental commander, he told us, "If you take the town, it's yours for the next forty-eight hours!" Am I any worse than the rest? I only took the public property that came to hand... Others did worse things.'

'Fine soldiers!' Grigory surveyed the acquisitive cornet with disgust and said, 'You and your kind are only fit for highway robbery, not for fighting! You've turned war into a scramble for loot! You, rotten swine! Found yourselves a new trade! D'you think you and your colonel won't have to pay for this one day?'

'Pay for what?'

'You know what I mean!'

'But who can make us pay?'

'Someone with higher rank.'

Semak smiled derisively and said, 'But they're just as bad themselves! We take the stuff in our saddle bags and wagons, but they send off whole baggage trains.'

'Did you see that?'

'Did I see it! I myself escorted one of 'em as far as Yaryzhenskaya. One wagon was loaded with silver—cups and spoons! Some of the officers jumped on us, wanted to know what we were carrying, but as soon as I said it was general so-and-so's personal property, they'd go off like lambs.'

'What general was that?' Grigory asked, narrowing his eyes and toying nervously with his reins.

Semak gave a crafty smile and replied, 'I've forgotten his name... Now who was it, for God's sake? No, it's gone for good, can't remember! But you needn't swear at me, Grigory Panteleyevich. Everyone does it and that's the honest truth! Compared with others, I'm a mere lamb; I hardly touched anyone, but others stripped people in the street and the way they raped the Jew girls—by the dozen! I didn't go in for that kind o' thing, I've got my own lawful wife, and what a woman she is—more like a stallion! Oh no, you're wrong to take it out on me. Heh, where're you off to?'

Grigory nodded coldly and with a curt 'Follow me!' to Prokhor put his horse into a canter.

On their way they met more and more Cossacks, riding singly and in groups. Quite often they encountered two-horse wagons. Their loads were covered with tarpaulins or sacking and tied down carefully. The wagons were escorted by Cossacks trotting along smartly in new summer tunics and field-green Red Army breeches. Their dusty sunburnt faces were excited and cheerful but, at the sight of Grigory, they rode by in silence, saluting as if by command, and resuming their conversation only when they were at a respectable distance.

'Here come the merchants!' Prokhor would say with a smirk at the sight of horsemen escorting a wagonload of loot.

But not everyone was riding home on leave with a burden of booty. When they stopped to water the horses at a village well, Grigory heard the sound of a song coming from a nearby yard. Judging by the clear, tuneful voices, the singers were young Cossacks.

'Must be seeing off someone into the army,' Prokhor said as he drew a pail of water from the well.

After the bottle of alcohol he had drunk the day before he wouldn't have minded a glass to clear his head, so he hastily finished watering the horses, and suggested with a chuckle, 'Why don't we go and join 'em, Panteleyevich? We might pick up a drink to help us on our way. The house looks rich enough, though it is thatched with rushes.'

Grigory agreed to go and see how the 'bulrush' was being sent off. They tethered their horses to the fence and entered the yard. By the shed stood four saddled mounts. A boy came out of the barn carrying a metal pan filled with oats. He glanced at Grigory and went over to the horses, which neighed in greeting. The song poured forth from behind the house. A quivering young tenor led the verse:

> Along that road, along that road
> No man had ever trod before...

A deep smoke-clogged bass repeated the second half of the line and joined with the tenor, then new voices merged in the harmony and the song flowed majestically, freely and sadly. Not wishing to interrupt the singers, Grigory touched Prokhor's sleeve and whispered, 'Wait, don't show yourself, let them finish their song.'

'It's not a seeing off. The Yelanskaya folk sing that way. That's how they always strike up. A fine harmony they've got there, the devils!' Prokhor commented approvingly, then spat with disappointment;

evidently his hopes of a drink would not be realised.

The gentle tenor told the story of the Cossack's fatal blunder:

> *No trace of foot or hoof it bore.*
> *Then up there came a Cossack force,*
> *Behind there galloped a goodly horse,*
> *Its Circassian saddle all askew,*
> *Across its right ear the bridle new,*
> *About its legs the silken rein,*
> *A young Don Cossack in its train.*
> *To his faithful steed he makes this plea:*
> *'Wait, oh wait, my faithful steed,*
> *'Leave me not in such dire need,*
> *'On foot from Chechen fierce I cannot flee...'*

Carried away by the singing, Grigory stood leaning against the white stone foundation of the house, oblivious of the horses' neighing or the creak of a passing wagon.

When the song was over, one of the singers coughed and said, 'Took it away beautiful, didn't we! Well, we did the best we can. And you, womenfolk, might give us soldiers something for the road. We've eaten well, God bless you, but we haven't a scrap of grub for the road...'

Grigory came out of his reverie and stepped round the corner of the house. Four young Cossacks were sitting on the lower step of the porch, surrounded by a crowd of women, young and old, and their children. The women were weeping and blowing their noses, wiping away their tears with the corners of their kerchiefs. One of the older women, tall and dark-eyed, with traces of an icon-like beauty on her faded face, was talking when Grigory came up to the porch.

'How well you sing, my dears, how touchingly! You've all got mothers, I'm sure, and I'm sure when they think of their sons and how they're getting killed at the war, they weep their hearts out...' The yellowish whites of her eyes flashed in reply to Grigory's greeting and she said with sudden anger, 'And you, Your Honour, lead such young flowers as these to their death? You get them killed off?'

'We're being killed off ourselves, Granny,' Grigory replied somberly.

The Cossacks, embarrassed by the arrival of a strange officer, rose quickly, upsetting the plates with what was left of the food and straightening their tunics, shoulder straps and sword belts. They had sung without even discarding their rifles. The oldest of them looked no more than twenty-five.

'Where are you from?' Grigory asked, surveying the soldiers' young fresh faces.

'From our unit...' one of them, a snub-nosed lad with laughing eyes, replied hesitantly.

'I mean where you were born. What stanitsa? You're not from round here, are you?'

'Yelanskaya. We're going on leave, Your Honour.'

Grigory recognised the song-leader by his voice and asked, smiling, 'Was it you who was leading the song?'

'Yes.'

'You've got a fine voice! What set you off singing? Joy of life, eh? You don't look as if you've been drinking.'

A tall brown-haired lad with a dashingly combed forelock that was grey from the dust, and a deep ruddiness in his dark cheeks, glanced sideways at the old women and with an embarrassed smile replied reluctantly, 'Joy?... It's need makes us sing! They won't feed you in these parts for nothing—just a hunk of bread and that's all. So we've got the idea of singing for our supper. As soon as we start singing, the women gather round to listen; we strike up something touching like and they bring us a chunk of bacon fat or a bowl of milk, or something else to eat...'

'We're like priests, Lieutenant, we sing and pass the plate round!' the song-leader said, winking to his comrades and screwing up his laughing eyes.

One of the Cossacks pulled a greasy slip of paper out of his tunic pocket and held it out to Grigory.

'Here's our leave warrant, Your Honour.'

'What good is that to me?'

'Mebbe you don't trust us, think we're deserters...'

'You can show that when you meet a punitive detachment,' Grigory said vexedly, but before leaving he nevertheless offered them some advice. 'You'd better ride at night and rest up during the day... Your bit of paper isn't worth much and it might land you in trouble... It isn't stamped, is it?'

'The squadron hasn't got a stamp.'

'Well, if you don't want a caning from the Kalmyks, you'd better take my advice!'

Some three versts from the village, just before entering a stretch of woodland, that ran down to the road, Grigory spotted two more horsemen riding towards him. They stopped and looked, then turned away sharply into the wood.

'That pair haven't even got a bit of paper,' Prokhor reasoned. 'See the way they bolted! Why the devil do they have to ride in the daytime!'

At the sight of Grigory and Prokhor several more riders turned off the road and hastily disappeared. One elderly Cossack infantryman, who was quietly making his way home, dived into a patch of sunflowers and crouched there like a hare on a field balk. Prokhor rose in his stirrups as he rode past and shouted, 'Hi there, Cossack, you don't know how to hide! Your head's down but your bum's showing!' And with feigned fury he suddenly barked, 'Now then! Out of it! Show us your papers!'

When the Cossack jumped up and scuttled away through the sunflowers, Prokhor roared with laughter and was about to gallop after the fugitive, but Grigory stopped him.

'Don't play the fool! Let him go to the devil! He'll run himself to death—or die of fright!'

'Don't you believe it! You couldn't catch him with wolfhounds. He'll gallop a good ten versts or more. Didn't you see the way he made off through the sunflowers! It beats me where they get the speed from.'

Prokhor disapproved of deserters on principle.

'They're coming in droves. Like peas out of a sack! If we don't look out, Panteleyevich, we'll soon be the only two left to defend the front.'

The nearer Grigory got to the front, the more apparent became the revolting picture of the disintegration of the Don Army, a process that had begun just when the army, reinforced by the insurgents, had achieved its greatest successes on the Northern Front. Now its units were incapable of developing a decisive offensive and breaking the enemy's resistance, or even standing up to a resolute attack.

In the stanitsas and villages where the first-line reserves were stationed, the officers did nothing but drink; transports of every description were bursting with loot that had not yet been dispatched to the rear; no unit could muster more than sixty per cent of its full strength; the Cossacks absented themselves without leave and the Kalmyk punitive detachments combed the steppe in vain, powerless to stop the wave of mass desertion. In the occupied villages of the Saratov province the Cossacks behaved like conquerors on foreign territory, plundering and raping, destroying stocks of grain and slaughtering cattle. The only replacements for the army were green youngsters or old men of fifty. In the reserve squadrons the Cossacks talked openly of not wanting to fight, and in the units that were being transferred to the Voronezh Front they often refused to obey their officers. Cases of murder of officers in the front line were rumoured to be on the increase.

It was dusk when Grigory stopped for the night in a small hamlet not far from Balashov. The 4th Separate Reserve Squadron, composed of Cossacks in the older age groups and an engineer company of the Taganrog Regiment had taken all the available accommodation. Grigory and his orderly could have spent the night in the open as they usually did, but as darkness fell it began to rain and Prokhor was shivering in one of his regular attacks of malarial fever; they had to find a roof to sleep under. On the edge of the village, near a large house surrounded by poplars, they saw an armoured car that had been wrecked by a shell. As he rode past, Grigory read the scrawled inscription on its green side, 'Death to the White Scum!' and below that the signature, 'Fighting Mad'. In the yard, horses were snorting at the tethering posts and voices could be heard; behind the house a campfire was burning and a canopy of smoke hung over the green crowns of the trees; Cossacks were moving about in the light of the flames. The wind was charged with the smell of burning straw and singed pig bristles.

Grigory dismounted and walked into the house.

'Who's the master here?' he asked, as he entered a crowded low-ceilinged room.

'I am. What d'ye want?' A stockily built man leaning against the stove glanced round at Grigory without changing his position.

'Will you put us up for the night? There are two of us.'

'We're packed as it is, like seeds in a watermelon,' an elderly Cossack lying on a bench grunted.

'I wouldn't mind but we're a bit crowded,' the owner responded half apologetically.

'We'll squeeze in somehow. We can't sleep out in the rain,' Grigory insisted. 'My orderly is sick.'

The Cossack who had been lying on the bench cleared his throat, swung his legs off the bench and, after a closer look at Grigory, said in a different tone of voice, 'Counting the owners, Your Honour, there're fourteen of us here, in two little rooms, and the third is occupied by an English officer with two batmen, and one of our officers as well.'

'Mebbe you could go in with them?' another Cossack with a grizzled beard and the shoulder straps of a senior sergeant suggested.

'No. I'd rather stay here. I don't need much room. I'll bed down on the floor, I won't be in your way,' Grigory took off his greatcoat, smoothed his hair with his hand and sat down at the table.

Prokhor went out to attend to the horses.

Their conversation must have been overheard. About five minutes later a short, stylishly dressed lieutenant came in from the next room.

'Are you looking for somewhere to sleep?' he asked Grigory and, after a quick glance at his shoulder straps, smiled politely and suggested, 'Come in with us, Lieutenant. Lieutenant Campbell, of the British Army, and I invite you to join us. You'll find it more comfortable. My name is Shcheglov. And yours?' He shook hands with Grigory and asked, 'Are you from the front? Oh, just back from leave! Do come in! We shall be glad of your company. You must be hungry and we have some good things to offer you.'

The lieutenant was wearing a tunic of splendid light-green cloth with a St. George cross dangling over the breast pocket. His parting was immaculate, his boots carefully polished, and his brown, clean-shaven cheeks, his trim figure, everything about him smelled of cleanliness and eau-de-Cologne. In the porch he stepped aside to let Grigory pass and said, 'The door's on the left. Be careful, don't trip over the box.'

Grigory was greeted by a tall powerfully built young Englishman with close-set grey eyes and a fluffy black moustache that could not conceal a deep slantwise scar on his upper lip. The Russian lieutenant introduced Grigory and said something in English. The Englishman shook hands and, looking now at his guest, now at the Russian lieutenant, uttered a few phrases and motioned them to sit down.

Four camp-beds had been set up in the middle of the room; boxes, kitbags and leather suitcases were piled in a corner. On a chest standing against the wall lay a light machine-gun of a pattern unknown to Grigory, a field-glasses case, ammunition boxes, and a carbine with a dark weathered stock and a brand-new, untarnished, blue-grey barrel.

The British lieutenant said something in a pleasant husky voice, glancing at Grigory in a friendly manner. Grigory could not understand the unfamiliar foreign speech but guessed it was about him and felt slightly embarrassed. The Russian lieutenant rummaged in one of the suitcases, listened smilingly, and said, 'Mr. Campbell says he has great respect for the Cossacks. He considers them fine cavalrymen and soldiers. Would you like something to eat? A drink perhaps? He says that danger brings men together... Oh, well, he says a lot of silly things!' The Russian lieutenant produced several tins and two bottles of brandy and bent over the suitcase again, still interpreting. 'He says he was very well received by the Cossack officers in Ust-Medveditskaya. They drank a huge barrel of Don wine together, everyone got rolling drunk and they had a very jolly time with some highschool girls. The usual thing! He considers it his pleasant duty to return their hospitality. And you'll have to endure it. Well, I'm sorry for you... Do you drink?'

'Thanks, I do,' Grigory replied, glancing surreptitiously at his hands, which were grimed with dirt from the road and the horse's reins.

The Russian lieutenant set out the tins on the table, opened them skilfully with a knife, and gave a sigh.

'You know, Lieutenant, he's made my life a misery, this English hog! He drinks from morning to night. You've never seen anything like it! I don't mind a drink myself, but not in such Homeric doses. But this fellow,' he glanced smilingly at the Englishman and, to Grigory's surprise, suddenly swore violently, 'drinks all the time, even on an empty stomach!'

The Englisman smiled, nodded and in broken Russian, said, 'Good, *khorosho*... We must drink your health! *Vashe zdoroviye!*'

Grigory laughed and swept the hair back from his forehead. He liked the two young men, and the blandly smiling English officer with his excruciating Russian accent was magnificent.

Wiping the glasses, the Russian lieutenant said, 'I've been arsing around with him for two weeks now!

What d'you think of that? He's instructing our men how to drive the tanks attached to our Second Corps, and I'm his interpreter. I speak fluent English, I have the misfortune, and it's been my downfall... Our people also drink, but not like this. It's weird! You'll soon see what he's capable of! He needs at least four or five bottles of brandy a day for himself alone. He drinks it gradually and never gets drunk. He can still work afterwards. He's exhausted me. My stomach's out of order, I wake up in a terrible mood every day, and I'm so pickled in alcohol that I'm afraid to sit near a lighted lamp... It's the very devil!' While speaking he filled two glasses and poured a small drink for himself.

The Englishman eyed his glass and protested laughingly. The Russian put his hand imploringly to his heart and replied in English with a restrained smile; only for an instant did sparks of anger flare in his dark kindly eyes. Grigory clinked glasses with his hospitable hosts and tossed it back.

'Oh!' the Englishman exclaimed approvingly and, after sipping his glass, looked contemptuously at the Russian lieutenant.

The Englishman sat with his big, workingman's hands motionless on the table, the backs grimy with ingrained grease, the fingers scarred and peeling from frequent contact with petrol, but his face was well-groomed, red and chubby. The contrast between the hands and face was so great that it sometimes seemed to Grigory that the lieutenant was wearing a mask.

'You shall come to my rescue,' the Russian lieutenant said, filling the two tumblers to the brim.

'Why, won't he drink alone?'

'That's the trouble! In the morning he drinks by himself, but not in the evening. Well, here we go!'

'This is strong stuff...' Grigory sipped the brandy and then, with the English officer watching him in surprise, again emptied his glass.

'He says you're a good fellow. He likes the way you drink.'

'I wouldn't mind changing your job for mine,' Grigory said smiling.

'You would run away after a fortnight, I assure you.'

'From a soft job like yours?'

'I shall certainly forgo its attractions.'

'It's worse at the front.'

'This is just as bad. There I may stop a bullet or a

571

shell splinter, but here my assured fate is delirium tremens. Try some of this tinned fruit. Won't you have some ham?'

'Thanks, I've got some already.'

'The British are first-class at this sort of thing. They feed their army better than we do.'

'Do we feed ours? Our army lives off the country.'

'Unfortunately, that's true. But that method won't get us far, particularly if we allow the population to be robbed with impunity.'

Grigory gave the Russian lieutenant a keen look and asked, 'Where are you heading?'

'We're both going the same way, why do you ask?' Meanwhile the Englishman had quietly taken possession of the bottle and filled the Russian lieutenant's glass to the brim.

'Now you'll have to drink bottoms up,' Grigory said with a smile.

'That's started it!' the lieutenant looked at his glass with a groan. His cheeks flushed a delicate pink.

The three men clinked glasses in silence and drank.

'Yes, we're on the same road, but we'll be stopping at different places,' Grigory resumed, frowning and trying vainly to fork the slippery apricot on his plate. 'Some will be getting off soon, others will go on, like in a train...'

'Won't you be travelling all the way?'

'I haven't got enough capital to pay the fare... Have you?'

'Well, I'm in a different position; even if they make me get off, I'll walk the rest of the way!'

'Then good luck to you! Let's drink!'

'I suppose I'll have to. Oh well, the first step's the worst!'

The English lieutenant clinked glasses with Grigory and his Russian companion and drank in silence, scarcely touching the food. His face turned brick-red, his eyes grew lighter, and a deliberate slowness appeared in his movements. Before they had finished the second bottle, he rose heavily, walked straight to the suitcases and returned with three more bottles of brandy. As he put them on the table he smiled with the corners of his mouth and said something in his deep voice.

'Mr. Campbell says we must prolong the pleasure. May the devil take him! How about you?'

'I don't mind,' Grigory assented.

'What a capacity, eh! In that English body lives the

soul of a Russian merchant. I think I'm just about primed.'

'You don't look it,' Grigory said untruthfully.

'Damn it all! I'm as weak as a virgin... But I can still live up to my responsibilities! Yes, and live up to them well!'

The Russain lieutenant had become noticeably fuddled. His dark eyes had an oily gleam in them and were beginning to squint, his face muscles were sagging, his lips were almost out of control, and his smooth brown cheeks had begun to twitch steadily. The brandy had taken devastating effect. His expression was that of a bull that had just been stunned for slaughter.

'You're still in fine form. Now you've got into your stride you needn't worry,' Grigory said, egging him on. Though decidedly tipsy himself, he felt as if he could still drink a lot more.

'You really mean it?' The Russian lieutenant cheered up. 'No, I was a little off colour at first. But now, by all means—any amount! Yes, any amount! I like you, Lieutenant. There's something strong and sincere about you. I like that. Let's drink to the land that fathered this drunken oaf. He's a brutish creature, I admit, but his country's a wonderful place. Rule, Britannia, Britannia, rule the waves! Shall we drink? But not bottoms up. To your proud country, Mr. Campbell!' The lieutenant drank with a desperate grimace and ate a piece of ham. 'I speak of England as enviously as a street urchin with a broken-nosed whore for a mother would speak of a respectable lady, the mother of the looked-after little boy he happens to have made friends with. What a country it is, Lieutenant! You could never imagine it, but I lived there... Well, let's drink!'

'Your own mother's dearer to you than a stranger's.'

'We won't argue about that, let's drink!'

'Let's. But aren't you ashamed to speak of your country like that?'

'This country... Our country needs to have its rottenness scoured out of it with fire and sword, but we're powerless. It turns out we have no country. So to hell with it! Campbell doesn't believe we can beat the Reds.'

'Doesn't he?'

'No, he doesn't. He has a poor opinion of our army and praises the Reds.'

'Has he been in action?'

'Oh, yes! He was nearly captured by the Reds. Damn this brandy!'

'It's strong? Same as neat spirit?'

'Not quite. Campbell was saved by the cavalry, or they'd have got him. It was near the village of Zhukov. The Reds captured one of our tanks... You're looking sad. What is it?'

'My wife died a little while ago.'

'That's terrible! Any children?'

'Yes.'

'Here's to your children! I haven't got any, or perhaps I have. If I have, they're probably selling newspapers in the street... Campbell has a fiancée back in England. He writes to her regularly, twice a week. And I expect he writes a lot of rubbish. I almost hate him. What?'

'I didn't say anything. Why does he respect the Reds?'

'Who said he "respects" them?'

'You did.'

'Impossible! He doesn't respect them, he couldn't respect them, you've got it all wrong! But I'll ask him.'

Campbell listened carefully to the pale, befuddled Russian lieutenant, then began to talk. Before he had finished, Grigory asked, 'What's he babbling about?'

'He's seen their infantry charging tanks with nothing but bast shoes on their feet. Isn't that enough? He says you can't beat the people. He's a fool! Don't you believe him!'

'Why not?'

'Not at all.'

'But why?'

'He's drunk and talking rubbish. What does it mean— you can't beat the people? You can destroy some of them and force the rest into obeisance... What did I say? No, not obeisance— obedience. How many bottles have we drunk?' The lieutenant dropped his head on his arms, knocking over a tin of fruit, and for about ten minutes sat slumped over the table, breathing heavily.

Outside the night was dark. Rain was drumming on the shutters. Now and then there was a distant rumble, and Grigory could not make out whether it was thunder or gunfire. Campbell sat sipping his brandy, wrapped in a blue cloud of cigar smoke. Grigory roused the Russian lieutenant and, rising unsteadily to his feet, said, 'Listen! Ask him why he thinks the Reds will beat us.'

'Go to the devil!' the Russian lieutenant grunted.

'No, you ask him.'

'To the devil! Go to the devil!'

'Ask him, I say!'

For a minute the lieutenant stared dazedly at Grigory, then amid hiccoughs said something to the attentively listening Englishman, and again slumped forward. Campbell looked at him with a contemptuous smile, then touched Grigory's sleeve and made his point in silence. He put an apricot stone in the middle of the table and, as if by way of comparison, placed his massive hand edgewise on the table beside it, then clicked his tongue and brought his hand down on the apricot stone.

'Clever, eh! I know that without you telling me...' Grigory murmured thoughtfully. Swaying unsteadily, he put his arm round the hospitable Englishman's shoulders, made a sweeping gesture at the table, and bowed. 'Thanks for the feast! And goodbye! But you know what I want to tell you? You'd better go home as soon as you can, before someone here knocks your head off. I mean it for your own good. Understand? It's no use meddling in our affairs. Get me? So, please, go, or they'll clout hell out of you!'

The Englishman rose with a nod and began to talk in an animated fashion, glancing helplessly at his sleeping interpreter and clapping Grigory amiably on the back.

Grigory found the door latch with some difficulty and staggered out on to the porch. Fine, driving rain lashed his face. A flash of lightning illuminated the big yard, a wet manger, the glistening leaves of the trees in the orchard. Coming down from the porch, Grigory slipped and fell, and, as he picked himself up, he heard voices.

'Them officers still drinking, eh?' someone asked, striking a match on the porch.

And a hoarse voice replied with a tight-lipped threat, 'They'll drink... They'll drink till it chokes 'em!'

XX

Just as in 1918, the Don Army lost its offensive drive as soon as it crossed the borders of the Khopyor district. The Cossack insurgents of the Upper Don and some of the Khopyor men, too, were unwilling to fight beyond their own borders. Another factor was the increased resistance from the Red units, which had received fresh replacements and were now operating on territory where they had the sympathy of the local people. Again the Cossacks were in a defensive mood and none of the tricks of the Don Army command could make them fight with the determination they had shown in the recent battles within their borders—despite their numerical advantage on this sector. The badly mauled 9th Red Army, which mustered 11,000 bayonets, 5,000 sabres and 52 guns, was facing a Cossack force of 14,400 bayonets, 10,600 sabres and 53 guns.

Most of the action was on the flanks, particularly where units of the Volunteer Kuban Southern Army were engaging the Red forces. While simultaneously driving deep into the Ukraine, a part of the Volunteer Army commanded by General Wrangel was closing in on the 10th Red Army and advancing in the face of fierce resistance towards Saratov. By July 28th the Kuban cavalry was on the outskirts of Kamyshin and had captured most of its defenders. A counter-attack launched by units of the 10th Red Army was repelled. In a bold manoeuvre the Kuban-Terek Combined Cavalry Division threatened to turn the 10th Army's left flank and the Red command was obliged to pull back to the Borzenkovo—Latyshevo—Krasny Yar—Kamenka—Bannoye line. By this time the 10th Army was fielding 18,000 bayonets, 8,000 sabres and 132 guns against the Volunteer Kuban Army's 7,600 bayonets, 10,750 sabres and 69 guns. In addition, the Whites had tank detachments and a considerable number of aircraft, which were used for reconnaissance and also took part in combat operations. But neither the French aircraft nor the British tanks and artillery did Wrangel any good and he got no further than Kamyshin. In this sector the stubborn fighting dragged on, bringing only minor changes in the shape of the front.

At the end of July the Red armies began preparing for a broad offensive along the whole central sector of the Southern Front. The 9th and 10th armies were combined into a strike force under the command of Shorin. Support for this force was to be provided by units transferred from the Eastern Front, namely the 28th Division and a brigade from the former Kazan Fortified Area, and the 25th Division and a brigade from the Saratov Fortified Area. In addition, the Southern Front Command strengthened the strike force with troops from the Front's reserve and the 56th Infantry Division. A supporting attack was to be launched on the Voronezh sector by the 8th Army reinforced with the 31st Infantry Division, which had been transferred from

the Eastern Front, and also the 7th Infantry Division.
The general offensive was to begin between 1 and
10 August. According to the plan drawn up by the Red
High Command, the attack by the 8th and 9th armies
was to be combined with flanking movements. A particularly responsible and difficult task had been assigned
to the 10th Army, which was to fight its way along the
left bank of the Don and cut off the enemy's main forces
from the North Caucasus. Further west a part of the 14th
Army had the task of making an energetic feint in the
direction of the Chaplino—Lozovaya line.

While the 9th and 10th armies were being regrouped,
the White command set about thwarting the offensive
by building up General Mamontov's cavalry corps, with
which it hoped to pierce the opposing front and execute
a deep raid in the rear of the Red armies. The success
of Wrangel's army on the Tsaritsyn sector had made it
possible to extend this army's front leftward, thus shortening the Don Army's front and making some of the
Don Army's mounted divisions available for the raid. On
August 7th 6,000 sabres, 2,800 bayonets and three four-
gun batteries were concentrated in the stanitsa of Uryupinskaya. And on the 10th, General Mamontov's newly
formed corps broke through at the junction between the
8th and 9th armies and from the village of Novokhopyorsk
struck out in the direction of Tambov.

The White command's original concept had been to
use General Konovalov's cavalry corps for the raid as
well as Mamontov's, but owing to the fighting that had
developed on the sector held by Konovalov his corps
could not be spared from the front. This explains the
limited nature of the task assigned to Mamontov, who
was adjured not to overreach himself and not to think
of marching on Moscow. Having destroyed enemy supply lines and communications, he was to rejoin the main
forces, whereas at first both he and Konovalov had been
ordered to hurl the whole mass of their cavalry in a devastating attack on the central Red armies' flanks and
rear and then proceed by forced marches into the heart
of Russia, replenishing their forces from the anti-Soviet
sections of the population and driving on towards Moscow.

The 8th Army succeeded in restoring the situation
on its left flank by bringing in the army reserve. The
9th Army's right flank was thrown into greater disorder.
Shorin, the commander of the main strike force, acted

quickly and succeeded in sealing off the inner flanks of both armies but was unable to hold up Mamontov's cavalry. On Shorin's orders the 56th Reserve Division started out from the area of Kirsanov to meet Mamontov. One of its battalions, which was loaded on to wagons and sent to the station of Sampur, was routed in a head-on clash with one of the side detachments of Mamontov's corps. The same fate befell the cavalry brigade of the 36th Infantry Division, which had been moved up to cover the Tambov—Balashov section of the railway. The brigade ran headlong into the mass of Mamontov's cavalry and after a brief engagement was scattered.

On August 18th Mamontov swooped on Tambov and occupied the city. But this did not prevent the main forces of Shorin's strike force from launching their offensive, although the best part of two infantry divisions had to be withdrawn from the group to deal with Mamontov. Simultaneously an offensive was launched on the Ukrainian sector of the Southern Front.

The front, which in the north and north-east had stretched almost in a straight line from Stary Oskol to Balashov with a bulge in the direction of Tsaritsyn, began to even out. Under the pressure of superior numbers, the Cossack regiments retreated southwards, frequently counter-attacking and holding out on every line. Back on their own soil they recovered their fighting ability; desertion sharply decreased and reinforcements began to flow in from the stanitsas of the Middle Don. The further Shorin's strike force advanced into Don Army territory, the fiercer the resistance became. On their own initiative, at public meetings the Cossacks of the insurgent stanitsas of the Upper Don declared total mobilisation, prayed for victory, and at once set out for the front.

Fighting its way towards the Khopyor and the Don in the face of bitter resistance from the Whites and on territory with a population mostly hostile to the Red forces, Shorin's group gradually lost its offensive momentum. Meanwhile, in the area of Kachalinskaya and Kotluban station the White command had formed a strong and manoeuvrable group consisting of three Kuban corps and the 6th Infantry Division for a thrust at the 10th Army, which had been most successful in developing its offensive.

XXI

In one year the Melekhov family had shrunk to half its size. Pantelei had been right when he said that death had taken a fancy to their house. No sooner had they buried Natalya than the large front room of the house was once again filled with the scent of incense and cornflowers. About ten days after Grigory's departure for the front Darya drowned herself in the Don.

One Saturday, after coming in from the fields, she and Dunyashka went down to the river to bathe. They undressed by the vegetable patches and sat for some time on the soft trampled grass. Ever since morning Darya had been in low spirits and had complained of a headache and feeling ill; several times she had secretly wept.

Before going into the water Dunyashka wound her hair into a knot, tied it with her kerchief and, glancing sideways at Darya, said sympathetically, 'How thin you've got, Darya, all your veins are showing.'

'I'll soon fill out again!'

'Is your headache better now?'

'Yes. Well, let's have a swim, it's getting late.' Darya was the first to enter the water. She took a running dive, came up with a snort, and swam out into midstream. The swift current caught her up and began to carry her downstream.

Watching Darya admiringly as she swam with broad manlike strokes, Dunyashka waded in up to her waist, washed her face, and splashed water on her breasts and sturdy, femininely plump arms. On the neighbouring vegetable patch Obnizov's two daughters-in-law were watering the cabbages. They heard Dunyashka call out laughingly to Darya, 'Come back, Darya! The pike will get you!'

Darya turned back, swam a short distance, then for a second half-rose out of the water, clasping her hands over her head, cried out, 'Goodbye, girls!' and sank like a stone.

A quarter of an hour later Dunyashka ran into the house, pale-faced and wearing only her underskirt.

'Darya's drowned, Mummy!' she burst out, panting.

Only the next day was Darya's body recovered thanks to the hooked lines which Arkhip Peskovatskov, the oldest and most experienced fisherman in the village, had stretched across the river at six points downstream from the spot where Darya had drowned. He and Pantelei rowed out together to check the lines. A crowd of wom-

579

men and children had gathered on the bank with Dunyashka among them. When Arkhip raised the fourth line with the handle of his oar and paddled about twenty yards from the bank, Dunyashka clearly heard him say in a low voice, 'I reckon she's here...' Dunyashka saw him carefully taking in the line, hauling at it with a visible effort as it plunged away into the depths. Something white showed up near the bank. Both old men leaned forward, the boat shipped water, and to the ears of the hushed crowd came the dull thud of a body being heaved into the boat. A sigh ran through the crowd. One of the women gave a sob. Khristonya, who was standing near by, shouted roughly to the children, 'Now then, out of it!' Through her tears Dunyashka saw Arkhip standing in the stern and paddling skilfully and noiselessly towards the bank. Darya was lying with her legs lifelessly bent under her and her cheek pressed to the wet bottom of the boat. Her white body, which had acquired only a slight bluish tinge, bore the deep marks of the fish hooks. A fresh pink scratch showed on the sun-tanned calf of her leg just below a garter that she had evidently forgotten to take off before bathing; it was bleeding. The point of the hook had slipped up the leg, cutting a jagged furrow. Crushing her apron convulsively, Dunyashka stepped out of the crowd and covered the body with a sack that had been slit down the seam. Pantelei briskly rolled up his trousers and began heaving the boat up the beach. Soon a wagon drove up and Darya was carried to the Melekhovs' house.

Overcoming her fear and feeling of revulsion, Dunyashka helped her mother to wash the cold body, which still retained the chill of the deep Don current. There was something unfamiliar and stern in Darya's slightly swollen face, in the dull gleam of the colourless, washed-out eyes. River sand sparkled in her hair like silver, damp strands of waterweed clung greenly to her cheeks, and in the arms hanging limply from the bench there was such frightening repose that after one glance Dunyashka hastily turned away, astonished and horrified that this Darya could be so different from the one who had but recently joked and laughed and loved life so much. And for long afterwards, when she recalled the stony chill of Darya's breasts and belly, the hard resilience of her rigid limbs, Dunyashka trembled and tried to forget it all as quickly as she could. She was afraid the dead Darya would appear to her in her dreams, and for a week she slept with her mother and, before going to bed, prayed to God and implored him in her thoughts, 'Oh, Lord! Don't let me dream of her! Protect me, Lord!'

But for the tale told by the Obnizov women of how they had heard Darya call out, 'Goodbye, girls!' she would have been buried quietly and without any fuss but, on learning of this last shout, which clearly indicated that Darya had deliberately taken her own life, Father Vissarion firmly refused to hold a funeral service for the suicide. Pantelei was outraged.

'Not give her a proper burial service? Why not? She's a Christian, isn't she?'

'I can't bury a suicide, the law doesn't allow it.'

'How d'ye think she should be buried then, like a dog?'

'You ask my opinion? As you wish and where you wish, but not in the cemetery, where honest Christians are buried.'

'Please, you must be merciful!' Pantelei tried persuasion. 'Such a shameful thing has never happened in our family.'

'But I can't. I respect you, Pantelei Prokofievich, as a model parishioner, but I can't. It'll be reported to the bishop and I shall be in trouble,' the priest insisted.

This was a disgrace. Pantelei did all he could to persuade the obstinate priest, promised to pay more and in reliable tsarist currency, and offered him a yearling ewe as a gift, but in the end, seeing that persuasion would not work, he resorted to threats.

'I'm not going to bury her outside the cemetery. She's not just a stray that wandered in from somewhere, she's my own daughter-in-law. Her husband was killed in action against the Reds and had officer's rank, she herself had been decorated with a St. George medal, and you give me this horse-shit? No, Father, you won't have things your way, you'll bury her properly! Let her lie in our front room for the time being and I'll report this to the stanitsa ataman. He'll have a word with you!'

Pantelei stalked out of the priest's house without saying goodbye and slammed the door after him. But the threat had its effect; half an hour later a messenger arrived to say that Father Vissarion would come with his assistant.

Darya was buried properly, in the cemetery, beside Petro. While they were digging the grave, Pantelei chose a place for himself. As he wielded his spade he glanced around and decided that no better spot could be found, and there was no need to look further. Over Petro's grave a recently planted poplar rustled its young branches; autumn had already painted its crown with the sad yellow of decay. Straying through the broken wall, calves had made pathways among the graves; the road past the cemetery led out to the mill; the trees planted by caring relatives of the dead—maple, poplar, locust—and also the wild blackthorn, gave a green and friendly freshness; the bindweed grew riotously among them, the late winter-cress glowed yellow; wild oats and seed-heavy couchgrass waved their spiky ears. The crosses stood wreathed from top to bottom in blue convolvulus. It was indeed a cheerful spot, good and dry...

The old man continued his work, often dropping the spade and sitting down on the damp clayey earth to smoke and think about death. But it so happened that this was not a time when old men could die quietly in their own homes and go to rest where their fathers and grandfathers before them had found their last resting place...

After Darya had been buried, the Melekhovs' house became even quieter. They carted in the corn, worked on the threshing floor, brought home a rich harvest of melons and watermelons. The family yearned for news of Grigory, but not a word had been heard of him since he left for the front. More than once Ilyinichna grumbled, 'He doesn't even send greetings to the children, the wretch! He won't have anything to do with us now his wife's dead...' As time went on, however, more and more serving Cossacks turned up in the village. Rumours got around that the Cossacks had been thrown back on the Balashov front and were retreating towards the Don, so as to have the protection of a water barrier and be able to hold out till winter. But as for what would happen in winter, none of the front-line men made any bones about it, 'As soon as the Don freezes, the Reds'll chase us all the way to the sea!'

Diligently occupied as he was with the threshing, Pantelei seemed not to pay much attention to the rumours that were rife along the Don, but he could not be indifferent to what was happening. More and more often he began to scold his wife and daughter and grew even more irritable when he learned that the front was coming near. He often busied himself, making or mending something for the farm, but as soon as the work went wrong, he would abandon it furiously and stump away, cursing and spitting, to the threshing barn to cool off. Dunyashka witnessed such outbursts more than once. One day he started mending a yoke. Something would not come right and, losing his temper for no reason at all, the old man grabbed an axe and hacked away at the yoke until there was nothing left but chips of wood. The same thing happened when he was mending a horse collar one evening. By the light of the lamp Pantelei waxed some thread and set about sewing up the broken seam of the collar; either the thread was rotten or the old man's hands were jumpy, but the thread broke twice in succession. That was enough. Uttering a terrible blasphemy, Pantelei sprang up, knocked over his stool, kicked it away to the stove and, growling like a dog, tore at the leather cover of the collar with his teeth, then threw it down on the floor and, hopping about like a cockerel, started stamping on it. Ilyinichna, who had gone to bed early, heard the noise and got up in fright but, on seeing what had happened, could not resist reproaching her husband.

'You've gone stark staring mad in your old age, you devil! What had the collar done to upset you?'

Pantelei glared at his wife with frenzied eyes and bellowed, 'Shut up, you—!!!' and, picking up a piece of the collar, hurled it at the old woman.

Choking with laughter, Dunyashka shot out into the porch. But her father, after storming about for a while, calmed down, begged his wife's forgiveness for the strong language he had used in the heat of the moment, and then stood grunting and scratching his head over the remains of the collar, wondering what he could use them for. Such fits of frenzy occurred more than once, but Ilyinichna, learning from bitter experience, adopted a different tactic for intervening. As soon as Pantelei started cursing and wrecking some household item, she would humbly but rather loudly say, 'Go on, knock it about, Prokofievich! Break it! We can always get ourselves another!' And she would even try to help him in the work of destruction. Pantelei would cool down at once, stare at his wife for a minute with uncomprehending eyes, then with shaking hands grope in his pockets for his pouch and sit down shamefacedly in a corner to smoke and soothe his overwrought nerves, cursing himself for his temper and counting up what it had cost him. A three-month-old pig that had ventured into the kitchen garden was the next victim of the old man's ungovernable fury. Pantelei broke its back with a stake from the fence and five minutes later, as he extracted bristles from the dead pig with a nail, he looked guiltily at the frowning Ilyinichna and said, 'It was just a packet of trouble, not a pig... It'd have died anyway. There's a plague around that catches 'em just at this time of year. Now at least we can eat it, or it would have been wasted. Isn't that right, woman? Why are you standing over me like a thunder-cloud? Damn and blast the creature! If it had been a decent pig, but this was just a runt. Why, I could have broken its back by spitting at it! And what a scamp! Rooted up forty potato clusters—that's what it did!'

'There wasn't more than thirty in the whole patch,' Ilyinichna corrected him quietly.

'Well, if there'd been forty, it'd have buggered up all forty—it was that kind of pig! Thank the Lord we've got rid of it, the pest!' Pantelei retorted.

The children were at a loose end now that their father had gone. Ilyinichna was too busy with household matters to give them enough attention and, left to their own devices, they spent their days playing in the orchard or on the threshing floor. One day after dinner Mishatka disappeared and did not come home until sunset. When Ilyinichna asked him where he had been, he replied that he had been playing with some boys down by the Don, but Polyushka gave him away at once.

'He's fibbing, Granny! He was at Auntie Aksinya's!'

'How do you know?' Ilyinichna asked, unpleasantly surprised by the news.

'I saw him climbing over the fence from their yard.'

'Is that where you were? Speak up, dear, what are you blushing for?'

Mishatka looked his grandmother squarely in the eye and replied, 'I didn't tell the truth, Granny... I wasn't down by the Don, I went to see Auntie Aksinya.'

'What made you go there?'

'She asked me in, so I went.'

'Then why did you pretend you'd been out playing with the other boys?'

Mishatka hesitated for a second, but then raised his truthful eyes and whispered, 'I was afraid you'd be cross.'

'Why should I be cross? No, that's not it... Why did she call you in? What did you do while you were there?'

'Nothing. She saw me and called me. So I went over

to her and she took me into the house and sat me on a chair...'

'Well, and what then?' Ilyinichna questioned impatiently, skilfully hiding her alarm.

'She gave me some cold pancakes to eat, and then she gave me this,' Mishatka took a lump of sugar out of his pocket, displaying it proudly, and put it back in his pocket.

'What did she say to you? Did she ask you about anything?'

'She said to come and see her sometimes 'cos she was lonely. She promised me a treat... And she said not to tell anyone I'd been at her place. 'Cos Granny'll be angry, she said.'

'So that's it...' Ilyinichna exclaimed, panting with suppressed indignation. 'But did she ask you to tell her anything?'

'Yes, she did.'

'What did she want to know? Come on, out with it, dear, don't be afraid!'

'She asked if I was missing Daddy? I said I did. And she wanted to know when he'd be coming home or if we'd heard anything. But I said I didn't know, 'cos he was at the war. And after that she took me on her knee and told me a fairy-tale.' Excitement flared in Mishatka's eyes and he smiled. 'A good tale it was too! About a boy called Vanyushka, and how the swans and geese carried him on their wings, and about a witch called Baba-Yaga!'

Ilyinichna listened to Mishatka's confession with pursed lips and said sternly, 'Don't go there any more, little one, and don't take any more of her treats, or Grandad will hear about it and give you a belting. God forbid that Grandad might get to know about it—he'll skin you alive! Don't go there any more, lovey!'

But two days later, despite these strict orders, Mishatka again visited the Astakhovs' house. His grandmother found out from looking at the boy's shirt. The torn sleeve that she had not had time to mend that morning had been skilfully darned, and there was a pearly new button on the collar. Knowing that Dunyashka was too busy with the threshing to mend the children's clothes, Ilyinichna asked reproachfully, 'So you've been round next door again?'

'Yes, I was...' Mishatka muttered in confusion, and added at once, 'I won't do it any more, Granny. Please, don't be cross!'

Ilyinichna then decided to speak to Aksinya and tell her plainly to leave Mishatka alone and stop trying to win his affections with presents or fairy-tales. 'She drove Natalya to her grave, and now she's after the children, the hellcat, just to get her hands on Grigory again. What a snake she is! Her own husband still alive and she's out to catch another... But it won't come off! Surely Grigory would never take her after such a sin?' the old woman thought to herself.

It had not escaped her maternally keen and jealous gaze that when Grigory was at home he had avoided Aksinya. She realised that he had done so not for fear of what people might say but because he blamed Aksinya for his wife's death. Secretly Ilyinichna hoped that Natalya's death would part Grigory and Aksinya for ever and that Aksinya would never become a member of their family.

That evening Ilyinichna noticed Aksinya on the pier down by the Don and called her over.

'Now then, come here a minute, there's something I want to talk to you about.'

Aksinya put down her pails and approached calmly, with a greeting.

'Now listen to me, my dear,' Ilyinichna began, scanning her neighbour's beautiful but hated face. 'What's the idea of snaring other people's children? Why d'you keep asking the boy to your house and making up to him? Who asked you to darn his shirt and give him all these presents? D'you think there's no one to look after him now his mother's gone? That we can't manage without you? Where's your conscience, you brazen hussy!'

'What have I done wrong? Why do you call me such names?' Aksinya asked, flushing.

'Done wrong? What right have you to touch Natalya's child when you yourself drove her to her grave?'

'Who drove her? Be sensible! She did it herself.'

'But it was because of you.'

'That's not for me to know.'

'But I know it!' Ilyinichna burst out with feeling.

'Don't shout, neighbour, I'm not your daughter-in-law, you can't shout at me. I've got a husband for that.'

'I can see right through you! I see what you've set your heart on! No, you're not my daughter, but you want to be! First you want to lure the children, then get Grigory into your clutches?'

'Nothing of the kind! You must be going wrong in the head, Granny! I've got a husband of my own!'

'And you mean to throw him over and get yourself another!'

Aksinya's face paled perceptibly and she said, 'I don't know why you're flying at me like this, trying to shame me... I've never forced myself on anyone and I don't mean to. And as for snaring your grandson, what's so bad about that? I haven't any children of my own, as you know, so I'm happy to see other people's. It's a bit of comfort. That's why I asked him in... Snaring him with presents, you say! What if I did give him a lump of sugar? Is that snaring him? Why should I? It's just a lot of rubbish!'

'You didn't ask him round much when his mother was alive, did you? But just as soon as Natalya's dead, you make yourself his provider!'

'He did come round even when Natalya was alive,' Aksinya said with a faint smile.

'Don't tell lies, you shameless creature!'

'Ask him first, then call me a liar.'

'Well, whatever happened then, don't you dare ask the boy round any more. And don't think it'll make Grigory any more fond of you. You'll never be his wife, so get that into your head and keep it there!'

Her face convulsed with anger, Aksinya said hoarsely, 'That's enough! He won't ask your permission! And don't you interfere in other people's affairs!'

Ilyinichna was about to offer a rejoinder, but Aksinya turned and without another word went back to her pails, hoisted the yoke on to her shoulders and walked away quickly up the path, water splashing as she went.

After that she took to ignoring the Melekhovs. She would walk past, nostrils flaring with satanic pride. But whenever she saw Mishatka, she would look round timidly and, if there was no one about, she would run over to him, bend down, clasp him to her breast, kiss his sunburnt forehead and somber dark, Melekhov eyes, and, laughing and crying at the same time, whisper incoherently, 'Darling little son of Grigory! My bonny boy! See, how I'm missing you! She's a fool is your Auntie Aksinya... What a fool she is!' And for some time afterwards the tremulous smile would linger on her lips and her glistening eyes would shine with girlish happiness.

At the end of August Pantelei was mobilised. All the Cossacks capable of bearing arms left Tatarsky for the front and he went with them. Out of the male population of the village there remained only the disabled, the under-aged and the very old men. It was total mobilisation and no one but the obviously unfit were granted exemption by the medical boards.

On receiving orders from the village ataman to report at the assembly point, Pantelei hastily said goodbye to his wife, grandchildren and Dunyashka, sank down on his knees with a grunt, bowed to the earth twice and, crossing himself before the ikons, said, 'Goodbye, my dears! It looks as if we won't see each other again. The last hour has come. So let this be my behest to you: thresh that grain day and night, try to finish it before the rains come. Hire someone to help you if you have to. If I don't get back by autumn, you must manage without me; plough up as much land as you can, and mind you sow at least a strip of rye. Run the farm well, woman, don't let things slide! Whatever happens to Grigory and me, whether we come back or not, you'll need all the grain you can get. War may be war, but it's a poor sort of life without grain. And may God preserve you!'

Ilyinichna saw the old man off as far as the square, watched him limping along beside Khristonya as they hurried after the wagon, then wiped her swollen eyes with her apron and, without looking back, made her way home. A stack of unthreshed wheat was waiting for her on the threshing floor, the milk was still baking in the stove, the children had not had their breakfast, and she had hundreds of other things to do. So she hurried home, acknowledging the greetings of other women with silent nods, not stopping to chat, and only inclining her head in reply to a sympathetic 'Seen off your soldier, have you?' from any passing acquaintance.

A few days later, after milking the cows at dawn, Ilyinichna drove them out into the lane and was just about to return to the yard when a muffled, persistent rumble reached her ears. She scanned the sky but there was not a cloud in sight. After a while the rumble came again.

'Hear the music, woman?' the old herdsman who was rounding up the cattle asked her.

'What music?'

'The one that's all on the bass notes.'

'I hear it but I can't tell what it is.'

'You soon will. When their stuff starts coming over and landing in the village, you'll know rightaway. That's gunfire, that is! And right now it's mashing up our old men.'

Ilyinichna crossed herself and walked back to her gate in silence.

The boom of guns continued incessantly for four days. It was particularly audible at dawn. But when the wind was from the north-east, the thunder of distant battle could be heard even during the day. For a minute the work on the threshing floors would cease, the women would cross themselves and sigh dolorously, recalling their near ones and whispering prayers, and then the stone rollers would resume their thudding, the boy drivers would urge on the horses and oxen, the winnowers would clatter, and the working day would come into its own again. The end of August was wondrously fine and dry. The wind carried the chaff dust all over the village, the smell of threshed rye straw hung sweetly in the air, and the sun blazed down mercilessly, but in everything there was a feeling of approaching autumn. The faded bluish-grey wormwood showed up whitely on the pastureland, the tops of the poplars on the far side of the Don had turned yellow, the smell of apples in the orchards grew more pungent, the distant horizons became autumnally clear, and the first flocks of migrating cranes began to alight on the deserted fields.

Day after day the wagons carrying ammunition to the fords across the Don rolled eastwards along the Hetman's Highway. Refugees appeared in the Donside villages. They related that the Cossacks were making a fighting withdrawal; some said it was a planned retreat for the purpose of luring the Reds on, then encircling and destroying them. Some of the Tatarsky folk quietly began to make preparations for leaving. They fed up their oxen and horses and at night busied themselves burying grain and chestfuls of their most valuable possessions. After a lull the gunfire broke out again on September 5th with renewed force and became clearly and ominously audible. The fighting was now about forty versts from the Don, to the north-east to Tatarsky. The next day the sound of gunfire could also be heard from upstream, in the west. The front was moving irresistibly towards the Don.

On learning that most of the Tatarsky folk were making ready to leave, Ilyinichna suggested to Dunyashka that they should go too. She felt bewildered and did not know what to do about the farm or the house. Should she abandon everything and flee with the others or should she stay? Before leaving for the front, Pantelei had spoken of the threshing, the autumn ploughing and the cattle, but had not said a word about what to do if the front approached Tatarsky. As a makeshift Ilyinichna decided to send off Dunyashka and the children with someone from the village and stay behind herself, even if the Reds occupied the village.

On the night of September 15th, Pantelei quite unexpectedly arrived home. He had walked all the way from somewhere near Kazanskaya and was utterly exhausted and in a furious temper. After half an hour's rest he sat down at the table and began to eat as Ilyinichna had never in her life seen him eat before; a pot of cabbage soup disappeared as if he had tossed it over his shoulder, then he set about the millet porridge. Ilyinichna threw up her hands in astonishment.

'Lord above, the way you're eating, Prokofievich! It looks as if you hadn't had a bite for three days!'

'Did ye think I had, you old fool? It's three whole days since I touched a morsel.'

'D'you mean to say they haven't been feeding you out there?'

'It's the devil's own way of feeding you!' Pantelei mumbled with his mouth full, purring like a cat. 'You eat what you can grab. And I haven't learnt daylight robbery yet. It's all right for the youngsters, they haven't got a scrap of conscience left... This goddamned war, it's given them such a knack of thieving—real shocked I was until I got used to it. They grab everything they see and walk off with it... It's not a war, it's hell on earth!'

'You'd better not eat so much. You might do yourself some harm. Look how you're swelling, just like a spider!'

'Keep quiet, woman. And bring me some milk, a good big pot!'

Ilyinichna was so overcome at the sight of her famished husband that she burst into tears.

'Are you home for good now?' she asked, when Pantelei had dealt with the porridge.

'That we shall see...' he replied evasively.

'So they've let you, old ones, come home, have they?'

'The hell they have! How could they when the Reds are pushing right through to the Don? I cleared out on my own.'

'Won't you have to answer for that?' Ilyinichna asked apprehensively.

'I may have to, if they catch me.'

'You mean you're going to lie low?'

'Did ye think I'd go gallivanting round the streets or visiting the neighbours? Pah, you dotty old thing!' Pantelei spat in vexation, but his wife was not to be put off.

'Mercy on us! They'll be after you for this and we'll be in more trouble.'

'Well, I'd rather be caught here and put in prison than go tramping about the steppe with a rifle on my back,' Pantelei replied wearily. 'I'm not all that young to be marching forty versts a day, digging trenches, charging the enemy, and crawling around dodging bullets. Let the devil dodge 'em! My old messmate from Krivaya Rechka stopped one just under the left shoulder-blade and didn't even kick once. Nothing very good about that!'

The old man carried his rifle and ammunition pouch outside and hid it in the chaff heap, and when Ilyinichna wanted to know where his coat was, he gave her a grim and reluctant reply.

'I wore it out, I mean I threw it away. They pressed us so hard at Shumilinskaya that we dropped every darn thing and ran like scalded cats. What good was an old homespun! Why, some of us had sheepskins and left them behind... What's my coat to you anyway that you keep talking about it? Mebbe if it had been any good, but it was no better than a beggar's...'

In fact, the coat had been a new one, but anything the old man lost was at once declared by him to be good for nothing. It was a habit he had acquired for comforting himself. Knowing this, Ilyinichna made no demur about the quality of the coat.

That night the family council decided that Ilyinichna and Pantelei and the little ones should stay at home until the last minute to guard their property and bury the threshed grain, while Dunyashka should take a pair of old oxen and drive off with the chests to their relatives, who lived in the village of Latyshev on the Chir.

But these plans were not destined to be fully accomplished. In the morning they saw Dunyashka off, and at noon a punitive detachment of Kalmyk Cossacks from the Sal steppes rode into Tatarsky. One of the villagers must have seen Pantelei making his way home, for within an hour of the detachment's arrival four Kalmyks cantered up to the Melekhov farm. At the sight of the horsemen Pantelei scrambled up into the loft with amazing speed and agility, while Ilyinichna went out to meet the visitors.

'Where your old man?' an elderly but well set-up Kalmyk with senior sergeant's insignia on his shoulderstraps asked as he dismounted and walked past Ilyinichna through the gate.

'At the front. Where else d'you expect him to be?' Ilyinichna replied gruffly.

'Bring me in house, I go to make search.'

'What're you searching for?'

'Your old man. You not ashamed! Old woman like you and live by lies!' the smart-looking sergeant said, shaking his head and showing a row of close-set white teeth.

'Don't grin at me, you unclean creature! I told you he's not here, and he isn't!'

'No more of talk, let go into house! If not, we come in,' the offended Kalmyk said severely and made resolutely for the porch on his bow-legs.

They inspected the rooms thoroughly, conferred together in Kalmyk, then two of them went to search the outbuildings, while one, very short and so dark he looked almost black, with a pock-marked face and flattened nose, hitched up his baggy striped trousers and went into the inner porch. Through the half-open door Ilyinichna saw the Kalmyk jump and get a grip on a rafter then agilely pull himself up. Five minutes later he jumped down with equal agility to be followed by a grunting and coughing Pantelei, all smeared with clay and with a beard full of cobwebs. He gave his stern-lipped wife one look and said, 'They found me, the damned devils! Someone must have reported...'

Pantelei was marched off under escort to be courtmartialled at Karginskaya. Ilyinichna had a cry, then began listening to the renewed roar of gunfire mingled with the distinctly audible chatter of machine-guns on the other side of the Don, and went to the barn to hide at least a little of the grain.

XXII

Fourteen captured deserters were awaiting trial. Judgement was summary and unmerciful. The president of the court, an elderly major, asked the accused his name and rank, and the number of his unit, inquired how long he had been on the run, and exchanged a few muttered remarks with the other members of the court, a one-armed cornet and a moustached and plump-faced sergeant-major, who had grown fat on the flesh-pots of the law. Sentence was then passed. Most of the deserters were condemned to corporal punishment with the birch, which was administered by the Kalmyks in a deserted house specially assigned for the purpose. The valiant Don Army had bred far too many deserters lately for them to be flogged openly and in public, as in 1918.

Pantelei was the sixth to be called. He stood at attention before the judges' table, worried and pale-faced.

'Name?' the major asked without looking at the accused.

'Melekhov, Your Honour.'

'First name and patronymic?'

'Pantelei Prokofievich, Your Honour.'

The major raised his eyes from his papers and stared fixedly at the old man.

'Where are you from?'

'Tatarsky Village, Vyoshenskaya Stanitsa, Your Honour.'

'Are you the father of Lieutenant Grigory Melekhov?'

'Yes, Your Honour.' Pantelei cheered up at once, sensing that the birch was not quite so close to his aged body as it had been.

'Aren't you ashamed of yourself?' the major asked, keeping his piercing eyes fixed on Pantelei's haggard face.

At this Pantelei committed a breach of regulations by placing his left hand on his chest and saying in a quavering voice, 'Your Honour! I'll pray for you for the rest of my life if you wish, but don't order them to flog me! I've got two married sons ... the elder one was killed by the Reds... I've got grandchildren... Surely I don't have to be thrashed, an old man like me?'

'Old men must also be taught to obey. Did you think you'd be decorated for your desertion?' the one-armed cornet intervened. The corners of his mouth were twitching nervously.

'Not decorated, of course... Just send me back to my unit and I promise to serve honestly and well... I don't know what made me desert. The devil must have been at my elbow...' Pantelei rambled on about the unthreshed

593

grain, his lameness and the farm he had been forced to abandon, but the major silenced him with a gesture, leaned towards the cornet and whispered in his ear at great length. The cornet nodded and the major turned to Pantelei.

'Very well. Have you said all you have to say? I know your son and am surprised that he has such a father. When did you desert your unit? A week ago? D'you want the Reds to occupy your village and strip you to the bone? What kind of example are you setting for the young men? By law we should sentence you to corporal punishment but out of respect for your son's rank as an officer I shall spare you that disgrace. Have you always served in the ranks?'

'Yes, Your Honour.'

'With what rank?'

'I was a junior sergeant, Your Honour.'

'Take off your insignia!' the major raised his voice and shouted rudely. 'Go back to your unit at once! Report to your squadron commander that by order of the court martial you have been deprived of your sergeant's rank. Did you have any decorations for this or the last war?... Oh, get out!'

Beside himself with joy, Pantelei left the court, made the sign of the cross at the dome of the local church, and set off straight across the hill—towards home. 'Well, this time I'll hide myself a bit better! I'll be damned if they find me, even if they send out a squadron of Kalmyks!' he thought, limping over the weedy stubble.

After going some distance across country, however, he decided it would be better to keep to the beaten track, so as not to attract the attention of passing troops. 'It might make 'em think I'm a deserter, then I'll get a thrashing without any trial at all,' he reasoned, turning off along a deserted plaintain-covered cart-track. For some reason he no longer thought of himself as a deserter.

The nearer he came to the Don, the more often he met refugees and their wagons. It was a repeat of what had happened in spring during the insurgents' retreat to the left bank of the Don. Wagons loaded with chattels were wending their way in all directions across the steppe. Herds of lowing cattle were trotting along like cavalry on the march, followed by flocks of sheep amid clouds of dust... The creak of wheels, the neighing of horses, human shouts, the rumble of hundreds of hooves, and the wailling of children, filled the calm expanse of the steppe with ceaseless and alarming clamour.

'Where're you going, Grandad? Turn back—the Reds are on our heels!' a Cossack with a bandaged head called out to him from a passing wagon.

'Get along with you! Where are they, these Reds?' Pantelei exclaimed, halting in confusion.

'On the other side. They'll be in Vyoshenskaya now. Is that where you're going?'

His worst fears allayed, Pantelei continued his journey and by evening reached Tatarsky. As he walked down the hill, he scanned the village attentively. It looked surprisingly deserted. There was not a soul in the streets. Houses with closed shutters stood silent and abandoned. Not a human voice or a cow's moo were to be heard; the only sign of people was a bustling crowd on the river bank. As he came nearer Pantelei saw armed Cossacks pulling boats ashore and carrying them up to the village. Clearly Tatarsky had been abandoned by its inhabitants. He cautiously entered his lane and headed for his house. Ilyinichna and the children were sitting in the kitchen.

'Here's Grandad!' Mishatka cried joyfully, flinging his arms round the old man's neck.

Ilyinichna wept for joy and through her tears said, 'I never hoped to see you again! Well, Prokofievich, say what you like, but I'm not staying here any more. Let it all go to the blazes, but I won't guard an empty house. The whole village on the run and me stuck here with the children like a fool! Harness up the mare this minute and let's get away! Did they let you go?'

'Yes.'

'For good?'

'For good as long as they don't catch me...'

'Well, you won't be able to hide here anyway! This morning, when the Reds started shooting at us from the other side, it gave me a real fright! I stayed down in the cellar with the kiddies while it was on. They've only just driven 'em away. The Cossacks came here asking for milk and said we'd better be moving.'

'Are they Cossacks from our village?' Pantelei inquired, carefully examining a fresh bullet hole in the carving round the window frame.

'No, strangers. From the Khopyor, I reckon.'

'Then we'd better go,' Pantelei said with a sigh.

That evening he dug a hole in the fuel heap and

dumped seven sacks of wheat there. He carefully covered them with earth and heaped bricks of dried dung fuel on top, and as soon as it grew dusk he harnessed the mare to a light wagon, loaded it with two winter coats, a sack of flour, some millet, a tied sheep, hitched the two cows to the back and, when Ilyinichna and the children were safely seated, said, 'Well, may God be with us!' and drove out of the yard. Handing the reins to his wife, he went back and closed the gate. All the way to the hill he snuffled and wiped his tears on the sleeve of his tunic as he trudged along beside the wagon.

XXIII

On September 17th units of Shorin's strike force, after a march of thirty versts, reached the Don. In the morning on September 18th the Red batteries began to rumble all along the river from the mouth of the Medveditsa to Kazanskaya stanitsa. After a brief artillery softening-up the infantry captured the left-bank villages and Bukanovskaya, Yelanskaya and Vyoshenskaya stanitsas. By the end of the day a stretch of about hundred and fifty versts along the left bank of the Don had been cleared of Whites. The Cossack squadrons retreated, crossing the Don in good order, to the previously prepared positions. All the available means of ferrying were in their hands, but the bridge at Vyoshenskaya was nearly captured by the Reds. Well beforehand the Cossacks had packed it with straw and poured kerosene over the planking so that it could be set fire to in the event of a retreat, and they were about to do so when a messenger galloped up with the news that one of the squadrons of the 37th Regiment was on its way from the village of Perevozny to the Vyoshenskaya crossing. The lagging squadron galloped headlong up to the bridge when the Red infantry was already on the outskirts. Though harassed by machine-gun fire, the Cossacks managed to cross the bridge and set fire to it, losing more than ten killed and wounded and as many horses.

Until the end of September the 22nd and 23rd divisions of the 9th Red Army held the villages and stanitsas they had captured on the left bank of the Don. The opposing sides were separated by a river that at that time of year was nowhere more than one hundred and sixty yards wide and, in some places, only sixty. The Reds made no determined efforts to force a crossing; here and there they tried the fords, but were driven back. For two weeks a lively exchange of artillery and rifle fire continued along the whole sector. The Cossacks held the commanding heights and kept the enemy concentration on the approaches to the Don under fire, giving the Reds no chance during the day to move up to the bank; but since the Cossack squadrons on this sector were of the lowest calibre (old men and young soldiers between the ages of seventeen and nineteen, they too made no attempt to force the river, push back the Reds, and launch an offensive along the left bank.

After retreating to the right bank, the Cossacks expected to see the houses of the occupied villages go up in flames on the first day, but to their great astonishment not a single column of smoke appeared on the left bank; and on top of this came the news, from fugitives who had crossed the river at night, that the Red Army men were not plundering any property and were paying generously in Soviet money for their food, and even for watermelons and milk. This caused confusion and dismay among the Cossacks. It had been expected that after the rebellion the Reds would raze all the insurgent villages and stanitsas to the ground, and that any of the population that had stayed behind, or at least the male half of it, would be ruthlessly exterminated; but according to reliable information the Reds had not touched any civilians and, to all appearances, had no vengeful intentions.

On the night of the 18th the Khopyor Cossacks in an outpost opposite Vyoshenskaya decided to investigate this strange behaviour on the part of the enemy; a loud-voiced Cossack cupped his hands round his mouth and shouted, 'Hi there, Red bellies! Why aren't you burning our houses? Run out of matches? Swim over here, and we'll give you some!'

From the darkness a raucous voice answered, 'We didn't catch you at home or we'd have burnt you and your houses!'

'Hard up, are you? Nothing to light a fire with?' the Khopyor man persisted defiantly.

He was answered calmly and cheerfully, 'Come over here, you White bastard. We'll put enough fire in your pants to keep you scratching for the rest of your life!'

The outposts exchanged long volleys of abuse and banter, then fired a few shots and quietened down.

In the early days of October the main forces of the Don Army, consisting of two army corps concentrated on the Kazanskaya—Pavlovsk line, took the offensive. The 3rd Don Army Corps with 8,000 bayonets and 6,000 sabres, forced the Don not far from Pavlovsk, drove back the 56th Red Division and began a successsful advance eastwards. Soon after this the 2nd Corps, under Konovalov, crossed the Don. Since it consisted largely of cavalry it was able to penetrate deep into the enemy's lines and strike a number of devastating blows. The 21st Red Infantry Division, which had been kept in reserve, was committed to action and held up the 3rd Corps for a time, but under pressure from the two combined Cossack corps was forced to begin a withdrawal. In a fierce engagement on October 14th the 2nd Corps routed and almost annihilated the 14th Red Infantry Division. By the end of the week the left bank of the Don as far as Vyoshenskaya had been cleared of the Reds. Having gained a broad jumping-off ground, the two Cossack corps pushed the 9th Red Army back to the Luzevo—Shirinkin—Vorobyovka line, forcing its 23rd Division to hurriedly realign its front west of Vyoshenskaya, in the direction of Kruglovsky.

Almost simultaneously with General Konovalov's 2nd Corps, the 1st Don Army Corps forced the Don on its sector, near Kletskaya.

The Reds' 22nd and 23nd divisions on the left flank were threatened with encirclement. In view of this danger, the command of the South-Eastern Front ordered the 9th Army to pull back to a line stretching from the mouth of the River Ikorets through Buturlinovka, Uspenskaya and Tishanskaya, to Kumylzhenskaya. But the army did not succeed in holding this line. The numerous irregular Cossack squadrons mustered under the general mobilisation crossed over from the right bank of the Don and, linking up with the regular troops of the 2nd Corps, forced the 9th Army to make a rapid retreat northwards. Between the 24th and 29th of October the Whites captured Filonovo Station, Povorino and the town of Novokhopyorsk. But great though the successes of the Don Army in October undoubtedly were, the Cossacks lacked the confidence that had inspired them in spring, during their victorious advance to the northern borders of the region. Most of the front-line men realised that this success was temporary, and that they would be unable to hold out longer than the winter.

Soon the situation on the Southern Front changed. The defeat of the Volunteer Army in a general engagement on the Orel—Kromy sector and the brilliant actions of Budyonny's cavalry at Voronezh decided the outcome of the struggle. In November the Volunteer Army fell back southward, exposing the left flank of the Don Army and dragging the Cossack forces with it in its retreat.

XXIV

For two and a half weeks Pantelei lived safely with his family in Latyshev and, as soon as he heard that the Reds had retreated from the Don, made preparations to return home. About five versts from the village he climbed down from the wagon with an air of having made up his mind once and for all.

'I can't go on dawdling like this! And we can't go faster because of these cussed cows. What the devil did we take them with us for? Dunyashka! Hold your oxen! Hitch the cows to your wagon and I'll trot on ahead. Our home may be nothing but ashes by now!'

Overcome by a storm of impatience, he transferred the children from his wagon to Dunyashka's, shifted some of the load as well, and rattled away along the bumpy road in his unburdened wagon. The mare began to sweat before they had gone one verst; never had her master treated her so ruthlessly, wielding the whip without respite.

'You'll drive the mare to death galloping like a madman,' Ilyinichna protested, holding on to the sides of the wagon and wincing painfully as she was thrown about.

'She won't come to weep over my grave anyway... Gee-up, you, godforsaken nag! Sweating, are you!... There may be nothing left of our home but a few stumps in the ground...' Pantelei snarled back.

His forebodings proved unfounded. The house was still standing but nearly all the windows had been knocked out, the door had been torn from its hinges, and the walls were pitted with bullet-holes. The yard was a scene of desolation. The corner of the stable had been sheered away by a shell, a second shell had dug a small crater by the well, shattering the wooden frame and snapping the well-sweep. The war from which Pantelei had fled had visited his farm, leaving its ugly trail of devastation. But even more damage to the farm had been caused by the Khopyor Cossacks who had been stationed in the village. In the cattle yard they had pulled down the fences and dug deep trenches; to save themselves trouble, they had dismantled the walls of the barn and used the logs to make shelters; the stone wall had been pulled apart to make an emplacement for their machine-gun and half a rick of hay had been ruined by horses; fences had been burned and the outdoor kitchen used as a latrine.

Pantelei clutched his head in dismay as he surveyed the house and its outbuildings. For once his eternal habit of dismissing anything lost as valueless forsook him. How in the devil's name could he say that everything he had spent his life building up was worth nothing and good only for demolition? The barn was not a homespun coat and it had been by no means cheap to build.

'We might have never had a barn!' Ilyinichna said with a sigh.

'What kind of a barn was...' Pantelei responded fast enough, but did not finish the phrase and with a despairing flip of his hand walked off to the threshing floor.

The walls of the house, disfigured by bullets and shell-splinters, looked desolate and forbidding. The wind whistled through the empty room, thick dust layered the table and benches. It would take them days to put things straight.

The next day Pantelei rode to Vyoshenskaya and not without difficulty persuaded a medical friend of his to give him a paper certifying that in view of his lame leg Cossack Pantelei Melekhov was incapable of walking and needed treatment. This certificate helped Pantelei to avoid being sent to the front. He presented it to the ataman and, whenever he entered the administration building, leaned heavily on a stick and, to reinforce the impression, limped on both legs in turn.

Never before had life in Tatarsky been at such sixes and sevens as after the return from evacuation. People went from house to house, trying to find the belongings the Khopyor men had spread all over the village. They searched the steppe and the ravines for cows that had strayed from the herd. A flock of three hundred sheep from the upper end of the village had disappeared on the first day, as soon as Tatarsky came under bombardment. According to the shepherd, a shell had exploded in front of the grazing flock, whereupon the sheep had bolted into the steppe and vanished. The flock was discovered a week later forty versts from the village, near Yelanskaya, and when it was driven back to the village and sorted out, the owners found that half the flock were from another district, with strange brandmarks on their ears, while more than fifty of the village sheep were still missing. A sewing-machine belonging to the Bogatiryovs was found on the Melekhovs' vegetable patch and Pantelei traced the roofing iron from his barn to Anikei's threshing floor. The same thing had happened in the neighbouring villages. And for long afterwards folk from villages all along the Don called in at Tatarsky, and often their inquiring voices were heard on the roads. 'Have ye seen a cow, reddish brown, with a white patch on its forehead, and a broken left horn?' or 'You haven't had a yearling bullock stray in here by any chance, a browny?'

No doubt more than one bullock had been cooked in the Cossack squadrons' pots and field kitchens, but hope kept their masters roaming far and wide across the steppe until they finally realised that not everything that is lost can be retrieved.

Having gained his release from military service, Pantelei set to work to put the outbuildings and fences to rights. Unthreshed stacks of grain were still standing on the threshing floor and greedy mice were scurrying all over them, but the old man did no threshing. How could he when the yard was still unfenced, the barn in ruins, and the whole farm in an abominable state of disorder? Besides, the fine autumn weather was still holding, and there was no need to hurry with the threshing.

Dunyashka and Ilyinichna patched up the walls of the house and whitewashed them and lent Pantelei a willing hand with a temporary fence and other jobs. Somehow they found glass and repaired the windows, then cleaned out the outdoor kitchen and the well. The old man went down it himself and must have caught a chill there; he coughed and sneezed for a week afterwards and went about with his shirt damp from perspiration. But two bottles of home-brew and a good sweat over the hot stove put him right again as if by magic.

There was still no news of Grigory, and only at the end of October did Pantelei learn by chance that his son was in good fettle and in action with his regiment somewhere in the Voronezh Province. The information was supplied by a wounded man from the same regiment, who was passing through the village. Pantelei cheered up, celebrated by drinking his last bottle of home-brew, infused with red pepper, and went about for the rest of the day, as vocal and proud as a young cockerel, stopping everyone he met and saying, 'Hear that? Our Grigory's captured Voronezh! We've had word he's been promoted and got command of a division again, mebbe a corps. Ye'd go a long way to find a fighter like him!' The old man piled one fantasy on another in his need to share his joy and have a boast.

'Ay, your son's a hero,' the villagers would reply.

Whereupon Pantelei would wink happily and rattle on, 'Couldn't be anything else with a father like me, could he? I can say without boasting that I was just the same when I was young! My leg's the trouble now, or I'd be showing 'em my mettle now! Mebbe not with a division, but I'd know all right how to handle a squadron! If there was more of us, old men, at the front, we'd have captured Moscow long ago. Just marking time they are, can't deal with a few peasants!'

The last of Pantelei's listeners that day was old Beskhlebnov. As he passed the house, Pantelei had not missed the chance of buttonholing him.

'Hi, wait a minute, Filip Agevich! Good day to you! Come in for a chat.'

Beskhlebnov approached with a greeting.

'Did ye hear of the stunts my Grigory's been up to?' Pantelei asked.

'What's he been up to then?'

'They've given him a division again! That's a monster to be in command of, eh!'

'A division?'

'Yes, a division?'

'You don't say so!'

'Yes, I do! And they wouldn't give that to just anyone, would they now?'

'O'course, they wouldn't!'

Pantelei surveyed his companion triumphantly and took this gratifying discussion a stage further.

'It's a wonder what he's grown into. Medals right across his chest! What d'ye think o'that? And how many times has he been wounded and shellshocked? Any other man would have pegged out long ago, but with him it's like water off a duck's back. No, we've not run out of real Cossacks on the quiet Don!'

'Ay, there're still some around, but it don't seem to

do us much good,' Grandad Beskhlebnov, never a great talker, said thoughtfully.

'Not much good? How's that? Look ye now! They've chased the Reds as far as Voronezh. They're closing in on Moscow!'

'They're taking a long time about it!'

'Ye can't do things in a hurry, Filip Agevich. Ye've got to remember nothing can be done in a hurry at war. More haste less speed. In this job ye've got to go careful, follow the maps and these—what d'ye call 'em?—operation plans. Russia's swarming with peasants, and how many of us Cossacks are there? Just a handful!'

'True enough, but I don't reckon our lads will hold out very long. Come winter, we'd better be expecting guests, that's what folk are saying.'

'If Moscow's not captured now, they'll be down here. That's right.'

'D'ye think they'll capture it?'

'They should do, but who knows what might happen up there. Ye mean our lads won't manage it? All the twelve Cossack armies have risen! Won't they pull it off?'

'Plagued if I know! How about you, done your fighting, eh?'

'What kind of a fighter would I be! If it wasn't for this leg trouble of mine, I'd show 'em how to make short work of the enemy! We, old men, are a hardy lot.'

'They say some o' these hardy old men ran so hard from the Reds on t'other side of the Don that there wasn't a coat left on their backs. They stripped 'emselves well nigh naked and threw it all away. I've heard tell the steppe was all yellow like at tulip time—with sheepskins!'

Pantelei gave Beskhlebnov an injured look and said curtly, 'That's a lot of cock, I reckon! Mebbe someone dropped a few things to make it easier going, but folk will always pile it on thick. What's an old homespun anyway—I mean, a sheepskin! It's not worth giving your life for, is it? And not every old man can run fast in one. In this darn war you've got to have legs like a wolfhound, and where can I get 'em, f'rinstance? Why are you so sorry about those sheepskins, Filip Agevich? What the devil—God forgive me—do you need 'em for? What's it matter about sheepskins or homespuns? The thing is to give the enemy a thorough good beating, how say you? Well, goodbye for now. I've been chatting long enough and there's work to be done. Did you find your calf?

Still looking for it? Not heard a moo, eh? Well, the Khopyor men must have wolfed it, may it choke 'em! And as for the war, you needn't worry. Our men'll beat the muzhiks!' And Pantelei limped away to his porch with an air of dignity.

But it was not so easy to beat the 'muzhiks'. The Cossacks' recent offensive had cost them more than a few lives. An hour later Pantelei's good mood was spoiled by unpleasant news. As he was shaping a beam for the well frame he heard the sound of women's wailing and weeping for the dead. The sound came nearer. Pantelei sent Dunyashka to find out what the trouble was.

'Run and find out who's died,' he said, sinking his axe into the chopping block.

Dunyashka soon returned with word that three Cossacks killed on the Filonovo front had just been brought back to the village. They were Anikei, Khristonya, and a seventeen-year-old lad from the other end of the village. Stunned by the news, Pantelei took off his cap and crossed himself.

'May their souls rest in peace! What a fine Cossack he was!' he said, thinking of Khristonya and recalling how they had so recently set off together for the mustering point.

It was no use trying to work. Anikei's wife was screaming and uttering such lamentations that a lump rose in Pantelei's throat. To get out of range of the woman's heart-rending cries, he went indoors and closed the door firmly behind him. In the front room Dunyashka was pouring out her story to Ilyinichna.

'...I took one look, Mother dear, and Anikei—he's got hardly any head left at all! Just a mush! Terrible it was! And the stink—you could smell it a mile away... Why they brought him back I don't know! And Khristonya was lying on the wagon on his back and his legs were sticking out from under his greatcoat... Clean and white as snow, he was! Only just under the right eye there was a little hole, no bigger than a farthing, and behind his ear—a spot of dried blood.'

Pantelei spat fiercely on the floor, went out into the yard, took his axe and limped away towards the Don.

'Tell Granny I've gone across the Don to cut some brushwood. Did ye hear me, laddie?' he said as he passed Mishatka, who was playing by the outdoor kitchen.

A quiet gentle autumn had settled over the far bank of the Don. Withered poplar leaves were rustling down.

The wild rose bushes looked as though they were wrapped in fire, the red seedpods among their sparse leafage blazed like little tongues of flame. The forest was filled with the bitter, all-pervading scent of rotting oak bark. The ground was thick with brambles and amid the tangle of creeping branches ripe smoky blue clusters of berries hid skilfully from the sun. On the dead grass the dew lingered till noon, threads of gossamer gleamed with its silver. Only the businesslike tapping of a woodpecker and the twitter of thrushes pecking the rowan berries disturbed the stillness.

The silent, austere beauty of the forest had a soothing effect on Pantelei. He roamed about among the bushes, raking up the damp cover of fallen leaves, and thought, 'That's life for you. Only a little while ago they were alive, and now they're being washed for burial. What a fine Cossack has been laid low! And only the other day he came to see us and was standing by the Don when they fished out Darya. Ah, Khristonya! So there was an enemy bullet waiting for you too... And Anikei—what a joker he was, loved a drink and a laugh, and now it's all over—he's a corpse...' Pantelei remembered his daughter's words and with unexpected clarity pictured Anikei's smiling, beardless, eunuch-like face, but the present Anikei—lifeless and with his head crushed beyond recognition—defied imagination. 'I shouldn't have angered God like that, boasting of Grigory,' Pantelei reproached himself, recalling his chat with Beskhlebnov. 'Mebbe Grigory's caught a packet too? God forbid! Who'll take care of us in our old age?'

A brown woodcock flew up from under a bush and startled the old man. Aimlessly he watched the bird's swift slanting flight, then walked on. By a small pond he took a fancy to some clumps of brushwood and started cutting. He worked stubbornly and tried not to think about anything. In one year death had claimed so many of his family and friends that his heart grew heavy at the mere thought and the whole world seemed to be wrapped in a black shroud.

'That bush is just right for fences,' he said aloud to divert himself from dark thoughts.

After a good spell of work Pantelei took off his jacket, sat down on the heap of brushwood he had cut and, drinking in the tart smell of withered leaves, sat gazing at the distant horizon trimmed with a light-blue mist, at the far coppices, threaded with autumn gold and gleaming with their last beauty. Not far away stood a black maple bush. Indescribably beautiful, it glowed in the cold autumnal sunshine, and its outspread branches, draped in purple leaves, were like the wings of some legendary bird about to soar up from the earth. Pantelei admired it for a while, then happened to glance at the pond and noticed in the transparent still water the dark backs of several big carp, swimming so near the surface that he could see their fins and fluttering crimson tails. There were about eight of them. Sometimes they disappeared under the green shields of the water-lilies, then swam out again into clear water to snap at the wet sinking willow leaves. Autumn had almost dried up the pond and it would be no trouble at all to catch those carp. After a brief search Pantelei found a broken basket that someone had left by the next pond. He took off his trousers and, shivering and grunting from the cold, started fishing. Sinking up to his knees in the mud, he waded along the edge of the pond, dragging the basket along the bottom, and then thrusting his hand inside, expecting to find a mighty fish struggling there. His efforts were crowned with success. He managed to trap three carp weighing about ten pounds each. But the cold had given him the cramp in his lame leg and he could not go on. He decided three were enough and climbed out of the pond, rubbed his feet with rushes, pulled on his trousers and cut some more wood to get warm. What a bit of luck! Not everyone has the luck to catch nearly a pood of fish out of the blue like that! The fishing had diverted him and dispelled his gloomy thoughts. He found a safe place for the basket, intending to come back and catch the rest of the fish, then, after a furtive look round to make sure no one had seen him tossing the plump golden carp out on to the bank, he picked up his faggot and the twig on to which he had threaded the fish by their gills and made his way unhurriedly down to the Don.

With a satisfied smile he told Ilyinichna about his fisherman's luck and feasted his eyes yet again on the coppery red carp, but Ilyinichna was no partner for him in his delight. She had been to see the dead men and come back tear-stained and sad.

'Will you go to see Anikei?' she asked.

'No. Haven't I seen dead men? Enough to last me!'

'You ought to go. They'll say he didn't even come to say goodbye!'

'Leave me alone, for Christ's sake! He's no kin of mine, so I don't need to take my leave of him!' Pantelei countered furiously.

Nor did he attend the funeral. That morning he rowed across the Don and spent the whole day there. The tolling of the church bell forced him to take off his cap and cross himself, but then he began to fume at the priest. Why go on ringing like this? One dong for each of 'em would have been enough, but he had to jingle away for an hour or more! What was the good of it all? It only upset people and made them think of death again. And autumn was enough to remind you of that, what with the falling leaves, the calling of the geese as they flew away across the faded blue sky, and the drooping withered grass...

No matter what steps Pantelei took to guard himself against sorrow, he soon had to endure a fresh shock. One day, while they were eating their dinner, Dunyashka looked out of the window and said, 'Here's another dead man back from the front! There's a saddled horse tethered behind the wagon and they're going very slow... One's driving the horses and the dead man's lying under a greatcoat. The driver's got his back to us, I can't see whether he's from our village or not...' Dunyashka strained her eyes and her cheeks went white. 'Oh, but it's ... it's...' she whispered, then burst into a piercing cry. 'They're bringing Grigory!... It's his horse!' and she rushed out into the porch sobbing.

Ilyinichna buried her face in her hands without rising from the table. Pantelei rose heavily and walked to the door, groping like a blind man.

Prokhor Zykov opened the gate, glanced at Dunyashka as she dashed down from the porch, and said cheerlessly, 'Receive your guests... Weren't you expecting us?'

'Brother dear!' Dunyashka moaned, wringing her hands.

And only when he saw her tear-sprinkled face and the silent figure of Pantelei on the steps did Prokhor think of saying, 'Don't be scared! Don't be scared! He's alive. He's got the typhus.'

Pantelei leaned back weakly against the doorpost.

'Alive!!!' Dunyashka cried, laughing and crying at the same time. 'Grisha's alive! Hear that? They've brought him home ill! Go and tell mother! What are you standing there for?!'

'Don't be scared, Pantelei Prokofievich! I've got him

607

here alive but you'd better not ask how well he is,' Prokhor hastened to confirm, leading the horses into the yard.

Pantelei took a few shaky steps forward and sank down on one of the porch steps. Dunyashka rushed past him like a whirlwind to reassure her mother. Prokhor stopped the horses just by the porch and looked at Pantelei.

'What are you sitting there for? Bring out a blanket, we must carry him in.'

The old man sat in silence. Tears were streaming from his eyes, but not a muscle moved in his face. Twice he raised his arm to cross himself, then let it fall, lacking the strength to lift it to his forehead. Something was gurgling in his throat.

'Looks as if you've been scared out of your wits,' Prokhor said sympathetically. 'Why didn't I think of sending someone ahead to warn you? I'm a mutt, a real mutt! Well, up you get, Prokofievich, we've got to carry the sick man in. Where's your blanket? Or shall we take him in our arms?'

'Wait a bit...' Pantelei said huskily. 'My legs... I seem to have lost the use of my legs... I thought he'd been killed... Thank the Lord... I never thought...' He tore open the collar of his faded old shirt and gasped for air.

'Get up, get up, Prokofievich!' Prokhor urged him. 'There's no one else to carry him but us, is there?'

With a noticeable effort Pantelei stood up and walked down the steps, turned back the greatcoat and bent over the unconscious figure of Grigory. The gurgling sound again rose from his throat but he mastered himself and turned to Prokhor.

'Take his legs. We'll carry him.'

They carried Grigory into the front room, took off his boots and clothes and put him into bed. Dunyashka called anxiously from the kitchen.

'Dad! Mother's in a bad way... Come here!'

Ilyinichna was lying on the floor in the kitchen. Dunyashka was kneeling beside her, sprinkling water over her bluish face.

'Run and get Granny Kapitonovna, quick now! She knows how to let blood. Tell her mother needs to get rid of some blood, so she'll bring her 'strument!' Pantelei commanded.

But Dunyashka, now a girl of marriageable age, could not run through the village bareheaded; she snatched up a

kerchief, hurriedly wound it round her head and said,
'Look at the kids! They're frightened to death! Lord,
what a terrible thing to happen!... Look after them, Dad,
and I'll be back in a minute!' Dunyashka may even have
paused to glance at herself in the mirror, but a look from
her father, who had by now come back to life, sent her
headlong out of the kitchen.

As she ran out of the gate she saw Aksinya. Without a
trace of colour in her face she was leaning against the
fence, her arms hanging lifelessly at her sides. No tears
shone in her dark misty eyes, but there was so much
suffering and mute entreaty there that Dunyashka halted for a second and, involuntarily and to her own surprise, said, 'He's alive, alive! He's got typhus.' And she
dashed away down the street, holding her high breasts
to stop them bouncing.

Curious women were hastening towards the Melekhov
farm from all sides. They noticed Aksinya walk unhurriedly away from the gate, then suddenly quicken her
pace, bending forward and covering her face with her
hands.

XXV

It took Grigory a month to recover. He rose from his
bed for the first time towards the end of November and,
like a tall skeleton, walked unsteadily across the room
and stood at the window.

The ground and the thatched roofs of the outhouses
were coated with fresh, dazzlingly white snow. Sledge
tracks showed up in the lane. The bluish hoarfrost trimming the fences and trees glittered irridescently in the
rays of the setting sun.

Grigory gazed through the window, smiling thoughtfully and stroking his moustache with bony fingers. It
was as though he had never seen such a glorious winter.
Everything struck him as unusual, full of novelty and
meaning. Illness seemed to have strengthened his vision,
and he began to see new things in his surroundings and
discover changes in those that had for long been familiar.

He began to show a quite uncharacteristic curiosity
and interest in everything that was going on in the
village and on the farm. Everything in life acquired a new,
hidden meaning, everything attracted his attention. He
looked at this new world with slightly surprised eyes
and an innocent, childlike smile lingered often on his

lips, strangely altering his stern face, the wild-animal look in his eyes, and softening the harsh lines at the corners of his mouth. Sometimes, brows twitching intently, he would examine a household implement he had known since childhood with the air of a man who had recently returned from some distant land and was seeing it for the first time. Ilyinichna was utterly astonished one day when she found him studying a spinning wheel from all angles. As soon as she entered the room, Grigory turned away, looking rather embarrassed.

Dunyashka could not help laughing to see him looking so long and skinny. He walked about the room in only his underclothes, holding up his underpants with one hand, stooping, and moving his long scrawny legs cautiously. When sitting down, he would always hold on to something for fear of falling. The black mop of hair he had grown during his illness began to come out and the grizzled forelock was lank and matted.

With Dunyashka's help he shaved his head and, when he turned to face his sister, she dropped the razor, clutched her belly, and collapsed on the bed, choking with laughter.

Grigory waited patiently for her to recover, then burst out in a shaky high-pitched voice, 'You'll bust yourself one day, and then you'll be sorry. You don't want that, do you?'

'Oh, brother dear! Lovey! I'd better go... I can't bear it! Just look at him! A real scarecrow!' Dunyashka groaned between fits of laughter.

'I'd like to see you after a dose of typhus. Now then, pick up that razor!'

His mother defended him indignantly.

'What are you squawking for, you stupid hussy?'

'But look what he's like, Mummy!' Dunyashka responded, drying her tears. 'His head's all knobbly and round, and as black as his hair... Oh, I just can't!...'

'Give me the glass!' Grigory demanded.

He stared at his reflection in the mirror and himself went off into a long fit of silent laughter.

'Why did you shave it all off, dear, you looked better before,' Ilyinichna grumbled.

'Would you rather have me bald?'

'Well, the way you look now you're not fit to be seen!'

'Oh, get off my back!' Grigory muttered vexedly, whipping up a lather with the shaving brush.

Unable to go outdoors, he played long games with the children. When talking to them, however, he avoided speaking of Natalya. But one day Polyushka cuddled up to him and asked, 'Daddy, won't Mummy ever come back?'

'No, little one. Nobody comes back from there.'

'Where's that? From the cemetery?'

'People don't come back once they're dead.'

'Is she dead forever then?'

'Of course, she is. Forever.'

'But I thought she'd miss us one day and come back...' Polyushka whispered only just audibly.

'Don't think about her, dear, it's better not to,' Grigory said hoarsely.

'But I can't help it! Won't she even come to see us? Just for a little while?'

'No. Now go and play with Mishatka.' Grigory turned away. Illness had weakened his will; there were tears in his eyes and, to hide them from the children, he stayed at the window, pressing his face to the pane.

The war was another subject he preferred not to discuss with the children, but Mishatka was more interested in the war than anything else. He often pestered his father with questions about the fighting and who the Reds were, and how and why they had to be killed. Grigory frowned and tried to change the subject.

'Off you go again! You've got war on the brain! Let's talk about how we'll go fishing in summer. Shall I make you a fishing rod? As soon as I can go outdoors, I'll start making you a line out of horse hair.'

He felt an inward shame when Mishatka asked him about the war and could find no answers to the boy's artless questions. But why? Perhaps it was because he had never found any himself? And it was not so easy to put Mishatka off. He would listen with seeming attention to his father's plans for the summer's fishing, but then got back to his old theme.

'Daddy, did you kill anyone at the war?'

'Keep off, you pest!'

'Aren't you afraid to kill people? Do they bleed when they're killed? Is there a lot of blood? More than from a chicken or a sheep?'

'I told you, stop talking about that!'

Mishatka would be quiet for a minute, then go on thoughtfully, 'I've seen Grandad kill a sheep. I wasn't frightened... Just a little bit, p'raps, but not very.'

'Don't talk to him!' Ilyinichna exclaimed in annoyance. 'Here's a little killer growing up! A regular cutthroat, he is! All you hear from him is war, war, war! He can't talk about anything else. What an idea, my little one, to go on chattering about this damnable—God forgive me—war? Come and have a pancake, and be quiet for a bit.'

But the war made itself felt every day. Cossacks back from the front came to see Grigory and talked about the routing of Shkuro and Mamontov by Budyonny's cavalry, about the unsuccessful actions near Orel, and about the general retreat that had begun. Two more Tatarsky men had been killed in the fighting at Kardail and Gribanovka; Gerasim Akhvatkin was brought home wounded; Dmitry Goloshchokov died of typhus. Grigory counted up the toll of Tatarsky men killed in two wars and it worked out that there wasn't a family in the village that had not felt the touch of death.

Grigory was still confined to the house when the village ataman brought an order from his superiors that Lieutenant Melekhov should be told to report at once to the medical board for reassignment.

'Write back that I'll report without any reminders, when I'm on my feet again,' Grigory responded curtly.

The front was steadily moving towards the Don. Once again there was talk of abandoning the village. Soon an order from the district ataman was read out on the square, commanding all adult Cossacks to join the retreat.

Pantelei came home with the news.

'What should we do?' he asked.

Grigory shrugged.

'What else can we do? We'll have to go. Everyone will go now, orders or no orders.'

'I'm talking about you and me. Will we go together or what?'

'No, we won't. Tomorrow or the day after I'll ride to the stanitsa, find out what units will be passing through Vyoshenskaya and join up with one of 'em. You'll have to go as a refugee. Or d'you want to join an army unit too?'

'Damned if I do!' Pantelei said in alarm. 'I'll pair up with Grandad Beskhlebnov then, he's been asking me to keep him company. He's a steady kind of feller and he's got a good horse. We'll spank along with a pair. My mare's fat as butter. She's been stuffing herself, the dang creature, and the way she kicks—terrible it is!'

'Yes, go with him,' Grigory agreed readily. 'Now let's see where you'll be going. Mebbe we'll be taking the same route.'

Grigory took a map of South Russia out of his map-case and told his father exactly which villages he should go through. He was about to scribble the names down on paper, but the old man, who had at first looked at the map with respect, said, 'Don't write 'em down. You know more about all this than I do, of course, and a map's a great thing, it won't lead you wrong, but how can I keep to it, if it don't suit me? You say I'd better make for Karginskaya. Yes, I know it's more direct that way, but I'll still have to go round about.'

'But why?'

'I'll tell you for why. Because I've got a cousin in Latyshev, and she'll give me food for myself and fodder for the horses that I'd have to buy off strangers. And your map shows I've got to head for Astakhovo, it's more direct, but I'll go through Malakhovsky. I've got relatives there and an old regimental comrade; I'll be able to save some hay there, too, and use other folks'. You can't take a haystack with you, ye know, and in strange parts you mayn't even be able to buy any, let alone have it given to you.'

'You haven't got any relatives across the Don, have you?' Grigory asked sarcastically.

'Yes, I have.'

'Mebbe you'll go over there then?'

'Don't you come that ballyhoo on me!' Pantelei blazed up. 'Talk serious and drop the joking! This is a fine time to joke! Think you're clever, do ye!'

'And it's no time for visiting the family! If you're going to retreat, retreat! It's not Shrovetide!'

'I don't need you to tell me where to go!'

'Well, go your own way then!'

'Why should I follow your plans? Only the crow flies straight, haven't ye heard that? There mightn't be any road there at all in wintertime. What rubbish you talk! And you were in command of a division!'

It was a long argument, but on second thoughts Grigory had to confess there was a lot of sense in the old man's words, and he said appeasingly, 'Don't be cross, Dad, I'm not forcing you. Go any way you like. I'll try to find you on the other side of the Donets.'

'You should've said that long ago!' Pantelei replied joyfully. 'Stuffing me with these maps of yours! They're all very well but horses won't go without fodder—remember that!'

While Grigory was still sick the old man had been quietly preparing for departure. He had fed up the mare, mended the sledge, ordered a pair of new felt boots and soled them himself with leather to stop the damp soaking through; he had also filled several big sacks with his best oats. Even for retreat he prepared with all the care and forethought of a good farmer; anything he might need on his journey was laid in store. An axe and a handsaw. a chisel, cobbling tools, thread, spare soles, nails, a hammer, a bundle of straps, string, a lump of resin—everything, down to the last horse-shoe and nail, was wrapped up in tarpaulin, ready to be loaded on to a sledge at a moment's notice. Pantelei even packed a steelyard and, when his wife asked what he would need it for on the road, he lectured her reproachfully.

'The older you grow the sillier you get. Can't you grasp a simple thing like that? Whether I'll be buying hay or chaff, it has to be weighed, don't it? You can't measure hay with a rod, can you?'

'Has no one else a steelyard but you?'

'Ah, but what kind of scales?' Pantelei boiled up again. 'Mebbe they're all set wrong to trick the likes of us. That's just the point! We know what strangers are! You get thirty pounds of hay and pay good money for forty. So I'd rather take scales with me than be done like that at every stop. It's no trouble! And you can do without; what the devil do ye need scales for? If the army comes through, they'll take the hay without any weighing... They'll be too busy stuffing their sacks with it. I've seen 'em before, the hornless devils, and I know just what they're like!'

At first Pantelei thought of loading a cart on the sledge so as not to spend money on buying one in spring, but further reflection led him to abandon any such disastrous plan.

Grigory also made his preparation. He cleaned his pistol and rifle and sharpened the sabre that had served him so well; when he began to feel stronger, he went out to inspect his horse and at the sight of its glistening crupper realised that his father had done more than care for his own mare. With an effort he mounted the high-spirited stallion, put it through its paces and, on his way home, saw—or was it his imagination?—a white handkerchief waving in the window of the Astakhovs' house.

614

At a village meeting the Tatarsky Cossacks decided to leave all together. For two days the women baked and roasted good things for their menfolk to take with them. The departure was fixed for December 12th. Overnight Pantelei loaded the sledge with hay and oats, and at the crack of dawn put on his big sheepskin, wound a sash round his waist, tucked his mittens into the sash, said his prayers, and took leave of his family.

The train of sledges moved slowly out of the village and up the hill. The women gathered on the outskirts and stood waving their kerchiefs, then a wind sprang up in the steppe and the whirling snowy mist obscured both the slowly moving sledges and the Cossacks tramping along beside them.

Before leaving for Vyoshenskaya, Grigory went to see Aksinya. He called on her in the evening, when the lights were on in the village. Aksinya was spinning. Anikei's widow was sitting with her, knitting a stocking and talking. Grigory said briefly to Aksinya, 'Come outside for a minute. There's something I want to tell you.'

In the porch he put his hand on her shoulder and said, 'Will you come with me in the retreat?'

There was a long silence while Aksinya considered her reply, then she said quietly, 'What about the farm? And the house?'

'Get somebody to look after them. We've got to go.'

'When?'

'I'll call for you tomorrow.'

Smiling in the darkness, Aksinya said, 'Remember, I told you long ago I'd go with you to the end of the world. And I'm still the same. My love is true to you. I'll come, whatever happens! When shall I expect you?'

'Tomorrow evening. Don't take much stuff. Just some clothes and what food you've got. Goodbye for now.'

'Goodbye. Won't you come in?... She'll be going in a minute. I haven't seen you for ages... Grisha dearest, my darling! And I was beginning to think you... No! I won't say it.'

'I can't now. I must go to Vyoshenskaya. Expect me tomorrow.'

For some time after Grigory had left, Aksinya stood in the porch, smiling and rubbing her glowing cheeks with her hands.

$$* \quad * \quad *$$

In Vyoshenskaya the district administration and stores were being evacuated. At the District Ataman's office Grigory inquired about the situation at the front. The acting adjutant, a young cornet, told him, 'The Reds are near Alexeyevskaya. We don't know what units will be passing through here, if any. You can see for yourself that no one knows anything, they're all in a hurry to get away. My advice is don't waste time here, go to Millerovo. You'd be more likely to find out where your unit is there. In any case your regiment will follow the railway. Will the enemy be held up at the Don? I don't think so. Vyoshenskaya will be surrendered without a fight, that's for sure.'

Grigory got home late that night. While she was making supper, his mother said, 'Your Prokhor has turned up. He came round about an hour after you'd left and promised to come again, but there's been no sign of him.'

Much pleased, Grigory ate a hasty supper and went to see Prokhor, who met him with a cheerless smile.

'I thought you'd gone straight off from Vyoshki without me.'

'Where the devil did you spring from?' Grigory asked, laughing and slapping his trusty orderly on the shoulder.

'From the front, of course.'

'Did you desert?'

'God forbid, what are you saying? A fighter like me running away? It was all above board, I didn't want to set off for warmer parts without you. We sinned together so we'd better face Judgement Day together! We're done for—did you know that?'

'Yes, I know. Tell me, though, how was it you got permission to leave your unit?'

'That's a long story, I'll tell you later,' Prokhor replied evasively, and looked even gloomier.

'Where's the regiment?'

'Plagued if I know where it is now.'

'When did you leave it then?'

'A fortnight ago.'

'Where've you been all this time?'

'What a man you are, honestly...' Prokhor grumbled, and shot a glance at his wife. 'Where? How? What for?... I was in a place where I'm not any more. I said I'd tell you later, and I will. Heh, woman! Where's the home-brew? We must have a glass to mark our reunion! Haven't you got any? Well, run out and get some quick! You've forgotten army discipline while your husband's been away! Got right out of hand!'

'What's all the noise about?' Prokhor's wife asked smiling. 'Don't you shout at me, you're not much of a master here, y'know. You're only at home about two days in a year.'

'Everyone shouts at me. And who else can I shout at but you? Wait until I've served to the rank of general, then I'll start bawling at others. But for the time being you'll have to put up with it, so off you go—at the gallop!'

When his wife had dressed and gone out, Prokhor looked reproachfully at Grigory and began to talk.

'Can't you take a hint, Panteleyevich... I can't tell you everything in front of the wife, and you go on asking this and that. Well, have got over your typhus?'

'Yes, I'm all right now, but tell me about yourself. What are you hiding, you son of the devil... Out with it! What have you been up to? How did you give 'em the slip?'

'It was worse than giving 'em the slip... After I'd brought you home sick, back I went to my unit, and got sent to the squadron, in the third troop. And me so keen on fighting! Well, I rode in a couple of charges, and then I thought, "You'll be kicking up the daisies before long at this rate! You'll have to find a loophole, Prokhor, or you'll be done for!" And then the action got so hot and they got such a lock on us, we couldn't even breathe! Wherever there's a gap, in we go! If the line starts to crumble, we have to prop it up. In one week eleven of our Cossacks were wiped out like so many flies! So I got fed up. So fed up I was, I even got lice on me.' Prokhor lighted a cigarette and held out his pouch to Grigory, then went on unhurriedly. 'And just near Lyski I happened to be out on patrol. Three of us was cantering along a ridge keeping a look-out on all sides, when out of a ravine comes a Red with his hands up. So we ride up to him and he shouts, "Cossacks! I'm on your side. Don't cut me down, I want to come over to you!" And then the devil must have jogged my elbow. Something got my rag out and I rode up to him and says, "You, son-of-a-bitch, you've no right to give up once you've started fighting! You're a snake in the grass, you are, I says. Can't you see we're only just holding out as it is? What's the idea of surrendering and giving us reinforcements?!'' And with that I whacked him across the back with the sheath of my sabre. And the other Cossacks with me took the same line. "Is that the way to fight, chopping and changing, now on one side, now on the other? If you all went at it together, the war would soon be over!'' How the devil were we to know this deserter was an officer? But that's just what he was! When I lost my temper and whacked him, he goes all white in the face and says very quiet like, "I am an officer, how dare you strike me! In the old days I was in the hussars and I had to serve with the Reds because I was mobilised. You will take me straight to your commander and I'll tell him all about it.'' "Show us your papers,'' we says. And he answers, proud as a peacock, "I don't wish to speak to you, take me to your commander!'' '

'Why didn't you want to talk about it in front of your wife?' Grigory interrupted in surprise.

'I haven't got to the main part yet, and don't you interrupt me, if you please. We decided to take him back to the squadron, and it was a pity we did... We should have finished him off on the spot, and had done with it. But we brought him in like we was supposed to, and the next day—what do we see?—he's been made commander of our squadron. How d'you like that? And then it started! After a while he calls me in and says, "Is that the way you're fighting for a united and indivisible Russia, you scum? What was it you said to me when you took me prisoner, remember?'' I tried a few excuses, but he wouldn't show me any mercy. And at the thought of the whack I gave him, he started shaking all over. "Do you know,'' he says, "that I'm a captain of a hussar regiment and a nobleman, and you dared to strike me, you lout?'' And so it goes on. He had the troop commander put me on extra sentry duty and all kinds of other duties, shoots 'em at me like peas out of a pail. In a word, he's got it in for me good and proper, the bastard! And it's the same thing with the other two that was with me when we captured him. The lads put up with it for as long as they could, but then they calls me aside and says, "Let's get rid of him, or he'll worry the life out of us!'' Well, I thought it over and decided to complain to the regiment commander, because my conscience wouldn't let me kill him. At the moment when we captured him, I could have cut him down, but afterwards somehow I couldn't do it in cold blood... Even when my wife kills

a chicken, I shut my eyes. And this was downright murder...'

'But you did kill him?' Grigory interrupted again.

'Wait a bit and you'll hear it all. Well, I complained to
the regiment commander—yes, I got that far—but he just
laughs and says, "You've no right to take offence, Zykov,
seeing that you did strike him, and he's quite right to
tighten up discipline. He's only doing his duty as a good
officer should." That's all I got out of him. So I thinks
to myself, "Hang that good officer round your neck
instead of a cross, but I'm not going to serve with him
in the same squadron!" I asked for a transfer but they
wouldn't do it. Then I thought of slipping away from my
unit. But how can you? Well, they brought us back into
the second line for a week's rest, and then the devil
jogged my elbow again... The only thing to do, I thought,
is to pick up a dose of clap that's lying around handy.
Then I'll go sick and meanwhile the retreat will start,
because that's what it looks like doing. So something
happened that had never happened to me before—I
started running after the women and looking out for one
that looked unreliable like. But how can you tell? It's
not written all over her face that she's sick, you have to
guess!' Prokhor spat bitterly and listened for any sound
of his wife's return.

Grigory put his hand over his mouth to hide a smile
and with laughter gleaming from his narrowed eyes
asked, 'Well, did you pick it up?'

Prokhor gave him a watery look. His eyes were sad
and calm, like those of an old dog living out its last
days on earth. After a brief pause he said, 'You think
it was easy to pick up? When you don't need it, it comes
on the breeze. But this time I couldn't find it for love
nor money. It was enough to make you weep!'

Grigory turned away laughing silently, then took his
hand away from his face and said in a weak voice, 'Don't
spin it out, for Christ's sake! Did you get it or not?'

'Of course, you can laugh...' Prokhor said offendedly.
'Any fool can laugh at someone else's troubles.'

'I'm not laughing... What happened next?'

'Next I started courting my landlord's daughter. A
girl of about forty, mebbe a bit younger. Blackheads
all over her face, and what a face—God help us! The
neighbours told me she'd been going to the doctor pretty often like. So I thinks to myself, "This one'll give it
to me, for sure!" So I starts strutting round her like a

619

young cock, puffing up my chest and spouting all kinds of speeches... Where it all came from, I don't know!' Prokhor smiled guiltily, and even seemed to cheer up a little at the memory. 'I promised to marry her, and a lot of other crap... And in the end I talked her round and we was on the brink of sin, when all of a sudden she bursts into tears. I tries to find out what's up. "Mebbe you're sick," I says. "If so, it don't matter. In fact, it's even better." But I was a bit jumpy myself because it was night-time and someone might come out to the chaff shed if they heard a noise. "Don't shout, for Christ's sake!" I says. "And if you're sick, don't worry, I'll agree to anything for love of you." And then she says to me, "Darling Prokhor! I'm not sick at all. I'm a virgin and I'm afraid — that's why I'm crying." You won't believe it, Grigory Panteleyevich, but when she said that I broke out in a muck sweat! Lord Jesus, I thought, that's torn it! This is the last straw!... And in a queer voice I asks, "Why did you keep going to the doctor then, you hussy? Why'd you give folk the wrong idea like this?" "I went to him," she says, "to get some lotion to clean my face." So I clutches my head and says to her, "Get up and go away right now, you goddam ugly anti-Christ! I don't want you pure and I'm not going to marry you!"' Prokhor spat and went on even more bitterly. 'So all my work was for nothing. I went to the house, picked up my things and moved to another billet that very night. After that the lads gave me the tip and I got what I needed from a widow. But this time I came straight to the point. "You sick?" I says. "Just a bit, I am," she says. "Well," I says, "I don't need a ton of it." So I paid her twenty Kerensky roubles for her help and the next day had a look at my achievement and buzzed off to the hospital, and from there straight home.'

'Did you come without a horse?'

'Without a horse? Why? I'm fully mounted and equipped for action. The lads sent my horse along. But that's not the point. Tell me what to say to the wife? Or mebbe I'd better keep out of harm's way and spend the night at your place?'

'No, what the hell for! Stay at home. Say you're wounded. Have you got a bandage?'

'I've got a field dressing.'

'Well, use it then.'

'She won't believe me,' Prokhor said despondently, but he got up, rummaged in his bags, went off into the

620

front room and called softly, 'Keep her talking if she comes in, I won't be a tick!'

Grigory rolled a cigarette and thought about his plans for the journey. 'We'll harness up the horses and drive together on the sledge,' he decided. 'We'd better leave in the evening, so the family don't see Aksinya with me. Though they'll get to know about it anyway...'

'I didn't finish telling you about the squadron commander.' Prokhor limped out of the front room and sat down at the table. 'Our lads knocked him off two days after I'd gone into hospital.'

'You don't say?'

'Honestly! They gave him one in the back, during an attack, and that was the end of it. So I needn't have landed myself in trouble like this after all. That's what riles me!'

'Did they find the one who did it?' Grigory asked absently, taken up with thoughts of the forthcoming journey.

'How could they! The front started moving so fast they didn't have time. Where's my old woman got to? I'll be losing my thirst soon. When do you reckon to be going?'

'Tomorrow.'

'Can't we wait a day?'

'What for?'

'I'd shake off some of these lice. I don't want to take 'em with me.'

'You can shake 'em off on the road. This is no time for hanging about. The Reds are only two days' march from Vyoshenskaya.'

'Do we leave in the morning?'

'No, at night. We only need to get as far as Karginskaya, we'll stop there.'

'Won't the Reds be on our tails?'

'We'll have to be careful. Now listen... I'm thinking of taking Aksinya Astakhova with me. Got anything against it?'

'Why should I care? Take two Aksinyas, if you like... It'll be a bit heavy for the horses.'

'Not all that heavy.'

'Women get in the way on a journey... What the hell d'ye need her for? If there was just the two of us, we'd be well away!' Prokhor gave a sigh and averted his eyes. 'I knew you'd be fetching her along with you. Still up to your fun and games... Ah, Grigory Panteleyevich, the whip's been weeping bitter tears for you for a long time now!'

'That's none of your business,' Grigory said coldly. 'Don't start blabbing to your wife about it.'

'Did I ever blab before? Have a bit of conscience! Who's she going to leave the house with?'

There was a sound of footsteps in the porch. Prokhor's wife came in, snow glittering on her grey fluffy shawl.

'Snowing hard, eh?' Prokhor took some glasses out of the cupboard, then asked, 'Did you bring anything?'

His ruddy-cheeked wife pulled two steamed-up bottles out of her bosom and placed them on the table.

'Now we'll make the road smoother for us!' Prokhor said, livening up. And after a sniff at the vodka, he declared, 'First-rate! And strong as the devil!'

Grigory drank two small glasses and went home, saying he was tired.

XXVI

'Well, the war's over! The Reds have given us such a kick in the pants we'll be rolling back till we reach the sea, till we land up with our backsides in the briny,' said Prokhor, when they had driven up the hill.

Tatarsky lay beneath them, wrapped in dark-blue smoke. The sun was setting behind the snowy pink edge of the horizon. The snow squeaked crisply under the sledge runners. The horses were walking. Grigory was lying in the big two-horse sledge with his back against the saddles they had taken with them. Beside him sat Aksinya in a fleece-lined coat trimmed with fur, her dark eyes sparkling joyfully from under a fluffy white shawl. Now and then Grigory glanced sideways at her and saw her cheek glowing tenderly in the frost, one thick black eyebrow, and the bluishly gleaming white of the eye beneath the curling frost-rimed lashes. She was gazing with lively curiosity at the snow-covered steppe, the glazed road, and the distant horizons sinking into the dusk. Accustomed as she was to being always at home, everything struck her as new and unusual, everything attracted her attention. But sometimes, as she lowered her eyes and felt the pleasant nip of the frost on her eyelashes, she would smile at the thought of how unexpectedly and strangely her dream had at last come true. At last she was going away with Grigory from Tatarsky, from a place, both loved and hated, where she had suffered so much, where she had struggled through half her life with a husband she could not love, where everything was filled with memories that constantly and unbearably came to mind. She smiled because her whole body was aware of Grigory's presence and there was no room for thoughts of the price she had paid for this happiness, or of the future that was wrapped in darkness as enticing as the steppeland horizons that lay before her.

Prokhor happened to look round, and noticed the quivering smile on Aksinya's flushed frost-swollen lips.

'What are you grinning at? Look at her—the bride-to-be! Glad to get away from home, eh?'

'Did you think I wouldn't be!' Aksinya replied in a ringing voice.

'Fine thing to be glad about... You foolish woman! There's no telling how this trip will end, so don't smile too soon! Wipe that grin off your face!'

'Life couldn't be any worse for me.'

'It makes me sick to look at the two of you...' Prokhor swung his whip furiously at the horses.

'Turn away then and stick your finger down your throat,' Aksinya advised, laughing.

'Now you're being daft again! Am I supposed to go on sticking it there all the way to the sea? That's a fine idea!'

'What's made you feel so sick all of a sudden?'

'As if you didn't know! What about your husband? Picked up with another man and heading for the devil knows where! Suppose Stepan turns up in the village? How about that?'

'You know what, Prokhor,' Aksinya retorted, 'you'd better not meddle in our affairs, or you'll be unlucky yourself one day.'

'I'm not meddling in your affairs, why the devil should I! But I can speak my mind, can't I? Or am I to be just a coachman and only talk to the horses? Full of fine ideas, aren't you! No, you can be as cross with me as you like, Aksinya, but what you need is a good hiding, and more of the same if you squeal! And as for luck, you needn't try to scare me, because I've got it with me. Mine's a special kind. It don't crow all that much but it keeps me awake... Giddyup, you dang beasts! They want to walk all the way, they do, the lop-eared devils!'

Grigory listened with a smile, then said in a conciliatory tone, 'Don't start quarrelling when we're hardly out of the village. There's a long road ahead of us, you'll have plenty of time for that later on. What are you getting at her for, Prokhor?'

'I'm getting at her,' Prokhor said unrelentingly, 'because she'd better not try contradicting me. Right now I'm thinking there's nothing in this world that's worse than women! They're a breed of stinging nettles... If you ask me, chum, they're God's worst invention! Women! If I had the chance, I'd do away with the lot of 'em. That's how riled I am with 'em just now! What are you cackling at? Any fool can laugh at another man's trouble! Here, hold the reins and I'll get down for a minute.'

Prokhor walked for a long stretch, then perched himself on the sledge again and refrained from any further conversation.

They spent the night in Karginskaya. After breakfast the next morning they set off again and by nightfall had covered some sixty versts.

Long lines of refugee wagons rolled southwards. The further Grigory went from the Vyoshenskaya district, the harder it became to find somewhere to stay the night. Near Morozovskaya the first Cossack troops began to appear. Cavalry units numbering only thirty or forty sabres went by, the transport columns were endless. By evening every scrap of room in the villages was occupied and there was nowhere even to stable the horses. In one of the Ukrainian settlements, after a fruitless search for accommodation, Grigory had to spend the night in a shed. By morning his clothes, which had got soaked in a snowstorm, were stiff with ice and cracked whenever he moved. The three of them hardly slept at all that night and got themselves warm only in the early hours of the morning, by making a fire of some straw in the yard.

At daybreak Aksinya timidly suggested, 'Maybe we could spend the day here, Grisha? We've had such a terrible night in the cold and didn't get hardly any sleep, can't we have a rest now?'

Grigory agreed. With difficulty he found a place. At dawn the wagons had moved on, but a field hospital with over a hundred wounded and typhus cases had also stayed behind for the day.

About ten Cossacks were sleeping on the dirty earthen floor of the tiny room. Prokhor brought in a mat and a bag of food, spread some straw by the door, grabbed the legs of an old fellow who was fast asleep, pulled him aside and said with rough kindness, 'Bed down here, Aksinya, you've had such a time you don't look yourself any more.'

At nightfall the settlement again filled up with fugitives. Until dawn campfires burned in the yards and the air was alive with the sound of voices, neighing, and the creak of sledge runners. At first light Grigory wakened Prokhor and whispered, 'Harness up. We've got to get moving.'

'Why so early?' Prokhor answered, yawning.

'Listen.'

Prokhor lifted his head from his saddle and heard the distant muffled rumble of gunfire.

They washed, made a breakfast of fatback, and drove out of the already bustling settlement. Long rows of sledges lined the lanes, people were scurrying about. In the morning murk someone shouted hoarsely, 'Bury 'em yourself! It'll be high noon while we're digging a grave for six!'

'Why should we have to do it?' another voice replied calmly in Ukrainian.

'You'll bury 'em all right!' the husky one cried. 'And if you don't want to, let them lie and rot under your noses. It's nothing to do with me!'

'But how can you, Doctor? We've got enough of our own to bury without burying strangers. Won't you bury them yourselves?'

'Go to the devil, you blithering idiot! Do you expect me to surrender the whole hospital to the Reds?'

As they drove round the wagons, Grigory said, 'No one needs the dead...'

'No one's got time for the living, let alone the dead,' Prokhor responded.

The whole northern Don was heading south. Wagonload after wagonload of refugees crossed the Tsaritsyn—Likhaya railway and rolled towards Manych. During his week on the road Grigory often asked about Tatarsky people, but none had been heard of in the villages on his route; most likely they had veered leftward to avoid the Ukrainian settlements and driven through Cossack villages towards Oblivskaya. Not until the thirteenth day did Grigory pick up the trail. When he had crossed the railway he heard in one of the villages that a Cossack from the Vyoshenskaya district was lying sick with typhus in the next house. He went to find out who it was and, on entering the narrow room, found Grandad Obnizov lying on the floor. From him he learned that some Tatarsky people had left the village two days before, that many of them had typhus, that two had already died on the road, and that he, Obnizov, had been left behind at his own request.

'If I come through and the Red comrades have mercy and don't kill me, I'll get home somehow. And if not, I'll die here. What's it matter where you die, it's no picnic anywhere,' the old man said in farewell.

Grigory asked about his father's health, but Obnizov replied that he could tell him nothing because he had been on one of the rear wagons and had not seen Pantelei since Malakhovsky village.

At the next stop Grigory was lucky. At the first house he called at to ask for a night's lodging he met some Cossacks he knew from the Upper Chir. They made room and Grigory found a place by the stove. There were about fifteen refugees lying on the floor, three of them with typhus and one with frost-bite. The Cossacks were making a supper of millet porridge laced with bacon fat and hospitably offered it to Grigory and his companions. He and Prokhor ate hungrily, but Aksinya refused.

'Aren't you hungry?' asked Prokhor, who in the past few days, for no apparent reason, had changed his attitude to Aksinya and treated her roughly but with sympathy.

'I feel kind of sick,' Aksinya put on her shawl and went out into the yard.

'Mebbe she's ill?' Prokhor muttered.

'Who knows?' Grigory left his plate of porridge and went out too.

Aksinya was standing by the porch, her hand pressed to her chest. Grigory put his arm round her and asked worriedly, 'What is it, love?'

'I feel sick and I've got a headache.'

'Come indoors and lie down.'

'You go, I won't be a minute.'

Her voice was flat and lifeless, her movements limp. Grigory eyed her keenly when she entered the overheated room and noticed the feverish flush on her cheeks and the tell-tale brightness of her eyes. His heart contracted with anxiety. Aksinya was obviously ill. He remembered that the day before, too, she had complained of feeling shivery and dizzy, and before dawn had broken into such a sweat that the curls on her neck had become as wet as if she had washed them. He had noticed this when he awoke and had lain for a long time with his eyes fixed on Aksinya, not wishing to rise and disturb her sleep.

Aksinya had bravely born the hardships of the road. She had even tried to cheer up Prokhor, who often complained, 'What the devil of a war is this? Who invented it? You go driving along all day and when you stop there's nowhere to put up for the night, and none of us knows where this trip's going to get us?' But that day even Aksinya gave in under the strain. When they turned in for the night, Grigory thought he heard her crying.

'What is it, dear?' he asked in a whisper. 'Where's the pain?'

'I'm ill... What'll we do now? Will you leave me behind?'

'There's a foolish woman for you! How could I leave you? Don't cry, mebbe it's only a chill and you're scared already.'

'Grisha, darling, it's typhus.'

'Nonsense! There's no sign; your forehead's cool enough. It may not be that.' Grigory tried to comfort her, but in his heart he was sure it was, and his brain was wrestling with the problem of what to do with her if she got too ill to move.

'It's terrible travelling like this!' Aksinya whispered, clinging to him. 'Look how crowded everywhere is at night! We'll be eaten up by the lice, Grisha! There's nowhere even for me to clean myself—men all around... I went out to a shed yesterday and undressed and my petticoat was full of them... God in heaven, I've never seen such horrors! It makes me sick to think of them and I can't eat... And yesterday did you see the old man that was sleeping on the bench, how many he's got? They were crawling all over his coat.'

'Don't think about 'em, that's a fine thing to talk about! They're only lice, no one counts them in the army,' Grigory whispered irritably.

'I'm itching all over.'

'Everybody's itching. What can we do about it? Put up with it. We'll have a bath when we get to Yekaterinodar.'

'It's no good putting on anything clean,' Aksinya said with a sigh. 'They'll be the end of us, Grisha!'

'Go to sleep, we've got to be off early in the morning.'

Grigory was a long time getting to sleep. So was

627

Aksinya. She sobbed once or twice, covering her head with her coat, then tossed about sighing, and fell asleep only when Grigory turned over and took her in his arms. In the middle of the night Grigory was awakened by a fierce knocking. Someone was battering at the door and bawling, 'Now then, open up! Or we'll break the door down! Asleep, eh, you bastards!'

The master of the house, an elderly and peaceable Cossack, went out into the porch and asked, 'Who is it? What d'you want? If it's to spend the night, we're full up in here. There's no room to move as it is.'

'Open up!' came the shouts from the yard.

The door into the front room was flung open and about five armed Cossacks burst in.

'Who's spending the night here?' one of them asked through stiff lips, his face black as iron from the frost.

'Refugees. And who are you?'

Without answering one of them strode into the best room and shouted, 'You lot, here! Sprawling around! Out of it quick! Troops are going to be stationed here. Get up! And look lively or we'll soon shake you out of here!'

'Who are you to be bawling like this?' Grigory asked huskily and rose slowly from his bed.

'I'll show you who I am!' the Cossack stepped towards Grigory and the dim light of the little oil lamp shone dully on the barrel of a revolver.

'Quick on the draw, aren't you...' Grigory said insidiously. 'Now then, show me your toy!' He snatched the Cossack's wrist and squeezed it so hard that the man gasped and let the revolver fall to the floor. It dropped with a soft thud on the mat. Grigory thrust the Cossack away, and, bending quickly, picked it up and slipped it into his pocket. 'Now we can talk,' he said calmly. 'What unit is this? How many of you smart ones are there?'

Recovering from his surprise, the Cossack shouted, 'In here, lads!'

Grigory walked to the door and, standing on the threshold with his back against the door-post, said, 'I'm a lieutenant of the 19th Don Regiment. Quiet there! No shouting! Who's that barking out there? What's all this fighting talk, Cossacks? Who're you going to shake out? Who gave you permission for that? About turn and clear off!'

'Who're you bawling at?' one of the Cossacks said

loudly. 'We've seen plenty of your kind of lieutenants! Are we to spend the night in the yard? Clear the premises! We've got orders to throw all the refugees out of the houses, get that? A fine noise you make! We've seen plenty like you before now!'

Grigory came up close to the speaker and rasped, 'Not like me, you haven't. Shall I make one of you fools into two? I can do! No, don't back away! It's not my revolver, I took it from your man. Here, give it back to him and get out of here, or I'll soon have the hide off you!' With easy strength Grigory swung the Cossack round and pushed him to the door.

'Shall we rough him up?' a stalwart Cossack with his face wrapped in a camel-hair hood said thoughtfully. He was standing behind Grigory and studying him attentively as he stamped his feet in their huge creaking felt boots soled with leather. Grigory turned to face him and clenched his fists, but the Cossack raised his hand and said in a friendly tone, 'Now just listen, Your Honour, or whatever they call you. Hold your horses! We'll go to keep out of trouble. But in times like these you'd better not lean too heavy on the Cossacks. Things are getting serious now, like in 'seventeen. You might run into some hotheads and they'll slice you up good and proper! We can see you're a firebrand and, by the way you talk, I reckon you were one of us once. So watch your step, or you'll run into trouble...'

The man whose revolver Grigory had taken said savagely, 'Cut out the sermons. Let's go next door.' He was the first to leave. With a sidelong look at Grigory he said regretfully, 'We don't want the bother, mister officer, or we'd have christened you!'

Grigory's lips twisted contemptuously.

'You? You ought to christen yourself! Get going, before I take your pants down! Here's a fine christener! Pity I gave you back your revolver. Tough guys like you shouldn't be toting revolvers! You'd do better with a wooden spoon!'

'Come on, lads, to hell with him! Don't touch the stuff and it won't stink!' one of the Cossacks who had not taken any part in the exchange said, laughing good-naturedly.

Cursing and swearing, the Cossacks clumped out into the porch in their frozen boots. Grigory ordered his host sternly, 'Don't dare open the door again! They'll knock and go away. And if they don't, wake me!'

Roused by the rumpus, the men from the Upper Chir were muttering among themselves.

'Discipline's gone to bits!' one of the older men said with a sigh. 'The way they talk to an officer, the sons-of-bitches... What if that had been in the old days, eh? They'd have got hard labour!'

'Talk—that's nothing! They was going to start a fight! "Shall we rough him up?" says one of 'em, that great hulking brute in a hood. That's the mood they're in, the devils!'

'And you're going to let 'em off like that, Grigory Panteleyevich?' one of the Cossacks asked.

As he pulled his greatcoat over him, listening to the talk with a tolerant smile, Grigory replied, 'What can you do with 'em? They've broken away from the rest, they won't obey anyone; they're just a gang, without any command. Who can judge or order them? They'll only obey someone stronger. I reckon they haven't got a single officer left in their lot. I've seen squadrons like them before, they're a bunch of strays! Well, let's get some sleep.'

Aksinya whispered under her breath, 'Why did you have to meddle with them, Grisha? Don't fly at that kind, for goodness sake! They're that crazy, they could kill you!'

'Go to sleep, we'll be up early tomorrow. How d'you feel now? No better?'

'Just the same.'

'Got a headache?'

'Yes. I don't think I can get up...'

Grigory put his hand to her forehead and sighed.

'Like a furnace! Still, never mind! You're a healthy woman, you'll get over it.'

Aksinya said nothing. She was tortured by thirst. Several times she went out to the kitchen, drank some tepid water and, fighting her sickness and dizziness, lay down again on the mat.

Four or five times during the night the house was all but broken into. Passing groups hammered at the door with their rifle butts, forced open the shutters and drummed on the windows and went away only when the master of the house, taking his cue from Grigory, swore at them and shouted from the porch, 'Get out of here! This is brigade headquarters!'

At dawn Prokhor and Grigory harnessed the horses. Aksinya struggled into her clothes and came out. The sun had risen. Dove-grey smoke was rising from the chimneys into the blue sky. Lighted from below by the sun, a small rosy cloud hung high in the heavens. Fences and roofs were thickly coated with hoarfrost. The horses were steaming.

Grigory helped Aksinya into the sledge and asked, 'Wouldn't you like to lie down? You'll find it easier that way.'

Aksinya nodded. She looked at Grigory with silent gratitude as he wrapped up her feet, then she closed her eyes.

At noon, when they stopped at Novo-Mikhailovskoye, some two versts from the highway, to feed the horses, Aksinya could not get out of the sledge. Grigory half led, half carried her into the house and put her into the bed hospitably offered by the mistress of the house.

'Is it very bad, dear?' he asked, bending over her pale face.

With an effort she opened her eyes, looked up at him mistily and again fell into a daze. With shaking hands Grigory removed her shawl. Aksinya's cheeks were as cold as ice, her forehead was burning, and there were little icicles at the temples, where the sweat had frozen. By evening Aksinya was unconscious. Before the swoon came over her, she had asked for water, and whispered, 'Only cold water, from the snow.' After a pause she said, 'Call Grisha.'

'I'm here. What d'you want, love?' Grigory took her hand, and fondled it with a clumsy shyness.

'Don't leave me, Grisha, dearest!'

'Of course, I won't. How can you say it?'

'Don't leave me with strangers... I'll die here.'

Prokhor brought some water. Aksinya pressed her parched lips greedily to the rim of the copper mug, took a few sips, and with a moan let her head fall back on the pillow. Five minutes later she began to ramble incoherently. Only a few words came through to Grigory, who was sitting beside her. 'Must do the washing ... get some blue-bag ... it's too early...' Her mutterings sank to a whisper. Prokhor shook his head and said reproachfully, 'I told you not to take her with you! What'll we do now? It's a trial, this is! Well, do we stay here for the night? Are you deaf, or what? Do we stay the night or move on?'

Grigory said nothing. He sat with his shoulders hunch-

ed, his eyes fixed on Aksinya's pale face. The mistress of
the house, a hospitable, kindly woman, glanced at Aksinya and asked Prokhor quietly, 'Is she his wife? Have
they got children?'

'Yes, they have. We've got everything, except luck,'
Prokhor mumbled.

Grigory went outside and sat on the sledge, smoking.
Aksinya had to be left in the village. Any further travel
might be the death of her. That was clear. Grigory went
back into the house and sat down by the bed again.

'Will we stay the night?' Prokhor asked.

'Yes. And mebbe tomorrow too.'

It was not long before the master of the house appeared—a small, puny-looking fellow with shifty eyes.
With his wooden leg tapping (his own had been cut off
at the knee), he limped briskly up to the table, took
off his coat, gave Prokhor a hostile look, and asked, 'So
the Lord has brought us guests? Where from?' And
without waiting for an answer, he ordered his wife, 'Give
me something to eat and be quick about it. I'm as hungry as a wolf!'

He ate greedily and at great length. His shifty gaze
rested often on Prokhor and the prostrate Aksinya.
When Grigory came out of the front room and greeted
him, he nodded silently, then said, 'Retreating, eh?'

'That's right.'

'Had enough fighting, Your Honour?'

'Looks like it.'

'Who's that—your wife?' the man nodded towards
Aksinya.

'Yes.'

'Why did you put her in the bed? Where are we to
sleep?' he said, addressing his wife.

'She's ill, Vanya. I felt sorry for her.'

'Sorry! You can't be sorry for all of 'em, look at the
hordes that keep coming! You're crowding us out,
Your Honour...'

There was an unusual note of pleading, almost entreaty
in Grigory's voice when he appealed to his hosts, hands
clasped to his chest.

'Good people! Help me in my trouble, for the sake of
Christ. I can't take her any further, she'll die on the
road. Kindly allow me to leave her with you. I'll pay
anything you ask for looking after her and I'll remember
your kindness for the rest of my life... Don't refuse me,
please!'

The master of the house at first refused outright on the grounds that he had no time to look after a sick woman, that she would be in the way but, when he had finished his dinner, he said, 'Well, stands to reason, who would go to the trouble of looking after her for nothing? How much would you pay for care and attendance? How much is our labour worth to you?'

Grigory took all the money he had out of his pocket and offered it to his host. The man took the wad of Don bank notes and counted them, licking his fingers.

'Haven't you got any tsarist money?'

'No.'

'Mebbe you've got some Kerenskies? This stuff is a bit too unreliable...'

'I haven't got any of that either. I'll leave you my horse, if you want it.'

The man pondered, then replied thoughtfully, 'No. I'd take the horse, of course. There's nothing we need more than a horse on a farm, but these days it won't do. If the Whites don't grab it, the Reds will, and we'll never get a chance to use it. I've got a knock-kneed old mare in the stable, but I never know if someone won't put a halter on her and haul her away.' He paused reflectively and, half-apologetically, added, 'Don't think I'm so terrible mean and greedy, God forbid! But judge for yourself, Your Honour. She'll be in bed for a month or more. That means a lot of fetch and carry, and then there's feeding her. She'll want bread, milk, an egg or two, meat. And all that costs money, ye know, don't it? And we'll have to wash her clothes and wash her, and all the rest... My wife would have been looking after the home, but now she'll have to spend time looking after a sick woman. That's no easy matter! Now don't hold your purse-strings, add something to make up the price. I'm a cripple, only one leg, as you see. What good am I for earning or working? We live on what God sends us, hand to mouth like...'

Burning with stifled impatience, Grigory said, 'I'm not grudging you anything, you kind soul. I've given you all the money I've got, I'll get by without any. What else d'you want of me?'

'All your money? Given it all to me?' the man sniggered mistrustfully. 'With a salary like yours, you must have sacks of it.'

'Tell me straight,' Grigory said, turning pale. 'Will you keep her or not?'

'No, if you grudge the money, there's no sense in leaving her with us.' The man's voice was resentful. 'That's a tricky business too... The wife of an officer and all that. The neighbours will find out, then the comrades will be coming along after you; they'll find out too and start badgering me... No, in that case you'd better take her with you. Mebbe one of the neighbours will agree to have her.' With apparent regret he returned Grigory's money, took out his pouch and started making himself a cigarette.

Grigory put on his greatcoat and said to Prokhor, 'Stay here with her and I'll go and look for somewhere else.'

His hand was on the door-latch, when the master of the house stopped him.

'Wait a bit, Your Honour. What's the hurry? D'you think I'm not sorry for the poor woman? I'm very sorry, that I am. I've been a soldier myself and I respect your title and rank. But couldn't you add a little something to that money?'

At this juncture Prokhor exploded. Purple with indignation, he roared, 'What more can we give you, you one-legged viper?! Break off your last leg, that's what we ought to do with you! Grigory Panteleyevich! Allow me to make mincemeat of him, then we'll put Aksinya aboard and get going, and may he burn in hell!'

Their host listened to Prokhor's tirade without a single interruption. When it was over, he said, 'You're wrong to insult me like this, soldiers! It's all a matter of give and take, so there's no reason for us to swear at each other. Why did you fly at me like that, Cossack? Was I talking about money? I didn't mean that at all! What I meant was that you might have some spare weapons, like, say, a rifle or a revolver of sorts... It's all the same to you whether you keep 'em or not. But for us, in times like these, they're worth a fortune. You've got to have a gun in the house! That's what I've been driving at. Give me the money you offered before and add a rifle, then it's a bargain! Leave your sick wife with us and we'll look after her like one of our own, by the holy cross!'

Grigory looked at Prokhor and said quietly, 'Give him my rifle and cartridges, then go and harness up. Aksinya will have to stay... God be my judge, but I can't drive her to her death!'

XXVII

The days dragged by, grey and cheerless. After leaving Aksinya behind, Grigory lost all interest in his surroundings. In the morning he would get into the sledge and drive across the boundless snow-covered steppe; in the evening, when he had found a haven for the night, he would go straight to bed. And so it went on day after day. All he knew or cared about the front was that it was retreating southwards. He realised that any serious resistance was over, that most of the Cossacks had lost the urge to defend their homeland, that the White armies were, by all accounts, at the end of their last campaign and, having failed to hold out on the Don, would fare no better on the Kuban.

The war was nearing its end. The final events unfolded swiftly and inevitably. The Kuban men abandoned the front in their thousands and went home. The men of the Don were broken. Bled white by the fighting and by typhus, having lost three-quarters of its strength, the Volunteer Army had no muscle to resist the pressure of the Red Army in the full flush of victory.

Among the refugees the word was that on the Kuban General Denikin's brutal reprisals against the members of the Kuban parliament were causing great indignation. It was said that the Kuban was preparing an uprising against the Volunteer Army, and that the unhindered passage of Soviet forces into the Caucasus was already being negotiated with representatives of the Red Army. Persistent rumours suggested that the Cossacks of the Kuban and the Terek were as hostile to the Don Cossacks as to the Volunteers, and that the first big clash between a Don division and the Kuban unmounted forces had already taken place somewhere near Korenovskaya.

During halts Grigory listened attentively to the talk and every day grew more convinced of the Whites' inevitable defeat. And yet from time to time he entertained the hope that danger would force the disintegrating, demoralised and quarrelling White forces to unite, to make a stand and rout the victoriously advancing Reds. But the surrender of Rostov dashed even this hope and he treated with suspicion the rumour that the Reds had retreated after stubborn fighting around Bataisk. Tormented by inaction, he would have liked to join up with any military unit, but when he proposed this to Prokhor, the answer was a firm refusal.

'Grigory Panteleyevich, you must be stark staring mad!' he declared indignantly. 'Why the devil should we nose into that hell-fire? The game's up, you can see that for yourself, so why throw our lives away for nothing? Or did you think the two of us could help 'em out of it? We've got to get out of harm's way as fast as we darn well can, before someone recruits us by force, and you come out with such a daft idea! Now no more of that and let's keep retreating like peaceable old men. You and me, we've done all the fighting we need in five years, so let the others try it! Did I pick up a dose of clap just to go begging to be sent to the front again? No, thanks! Very kind of you, I must say! I've had such a bellyful of this war that I want to throw up whenever I think of it! Go yourself if you want to, but not me! I'll get myself into hospital, I've had enough!'

After a long silence Grigory said, 'Have it your way. We'll head for the Kuban, and then we'll see.'

Prokhor stuck to his guns. At every place of any size he sought out a doctor and asked for powders or medicine, but showed no zeal in taking them. When Grigory asked why, after taking one powder, he destroyed the rest by trampling them carefully into the snow, he explained that he only wanted to hold down the disease, so that in the event of his being re-examined it would be easier for him to escape enlistment. At Velikoknyazhe-skaya a Cossack with experience in such matters advised him to treat himself with a decoction made of duck's feet. From then on, whenever he came to a village or a stanitsa, Prokhor would ask the first person he met, 'Could ye kindly tell me now, do ye keep any ducks around here?' And when the bewildered villager replied in the negative, referring to the fact that with no water near by there was no sense in breeding ducks, Prokhor would respond with withering scorn, 'You live like a lot of savages! I reckon you've never heard a duck quack in your lives! You steppeland blockheads!' Then turning to Grigory, he would add with profound regret, 'Looks like someone's laid a curse on us! We never get any luck! Now, if they had some ducks here, I'd buy one right away, at any price, or steal one, and then I'd be on the way to getting better. Right now it's going from bad to worse! First it was just a game, only kept me from dozing on the road, but now, of all the poxy things, it's a real torture! It's got me hopping out o' the sledge every five minutes.'

Encountering no sympathy from Grigory, Prokhor would lapse into a long silence and sometimes drive for hours without uttering a word, looking very ruffled.

The days of driving from place to place seemed desperately long, but even longer were the interminable winter nights. Grigory had all the time in the world to think about the present and recall the past. He would leaf through the years of his life, which had taken such a strange, unhappy course. Sitting in the sledge with his misty gaze fixed on the snowy vastness of the deathly still steppe, or lying at night with closed eyes and clenched teeth in a suffocatingly crowded little room, he would think all the time only of Aksinya, sick and unconscious, abandoned in that nameless little village, and of the family he had left in Tatarsky... Out there, on the Don, the Soviets had taken over, and Grigory was constantly assailed by the nagging thought, 'Surely they won't make mother and Dunyashka suffer because of me?' And at once he would try to soothe himself by recalling the talk he had heard on the road that the Red Army marched through peacefully and treated the people of the occupied villages well. His anxiety would gradually abate and the idea that his aged mother would have to answer for him seemed unbelievable, monstrous, a mere fantasy. Memories of the children wrung his heart. He was afraid they would not escape the typhus. And yet, dearly though he loved them, he felt that nothing could equal the grief he had felt after Natalya's death...

At one of the winter-stabling villages near the Sal he and Prokhor lived for four days to give the horses a rest. They often discussed their plans. On the first day Prokhor asked, 'Will our lot hold the front on the Kuban or fall back to the Caucasus? What d'you think?'

'I don't know. What d'you care anyway?'

'That's a fine idea! Of course, I care! The way we're going they'll chase us into Turkey. What do we do there—drink gall?'

'I'm not Denikin. It's no good asking me where they'll chase us to,' Grigory retorted.

'Why I'm asking is that I heard a rumour they'd make a stand on the River Kuban and in spring strike out for home.'

'Who's going to make a stand?' Grigory said derisively.

'The Cossacks and the Cadets—who else?'

'That's a lot of bunk! Are you so gormless you can't

637

see what's going on around you? Everyone wants to clear out! Who's going to make a stand?'

'Ay, lad, I can see for myself we're up the creek, but I still can't believe it somehow...' Prokhor sighed. 'But what about if we have to take ship to foreign lands or crawl there on all fours, how about you? Will you go?'

'Will you?'

'The way I look at it is this: where you go, there go I. I can't stay behind alone, if everyone's going.'

'That's what I think. We've been wandering like sheep so we'd better follow the rams.'

'Rams can take you the devil knows where in their foolishness... Drop that yarn! Talk sense!'

'Leave me alone, please! We'll see when we get there. Why start fortune-telling!'

'All right then—amen! I won't bother you any more,' Prokhor agreed.

But the next day, when they went to clean out the horses, he brought up the subject again.

'Have you heard of the Greens?' he asked tentatively, examining a three-pronged hay fork with studied care.

'I've heard of 'em. Now what?'

'What are these Greens that have turned up all of a sudden? Who are they fighting for?'

'For the Reds.'

'Why'd they call themselves Greens then?'

'Darned if I know, because they hide in the woods, I suppose.'

'Mebbe we ought to go green too?' after long consideration Prokhor suggested timidly.

'I don't want to somehow.'

'Well, aren't there any others besides these Greens we could join up with to get home soon? It's all the same to me—green, blue, or egg-yellow. I'll paint myself any colour as long as they're agin the war and want to send the boys home.'

'That kind may turn up one day, if you wait long enough,' Grigory advised.

At the end of January, in a misty, thawing noon Grigory and Prokhor drove into the settlement of Belaya Glina. About fifteen thousand refugees had crowded into the settlement and a good half of them had typhus. Cossacks in short British greatcoats, sheepskins and Caucasian beshmets roamed about in search of lodgings for themselves, and fodder for their horses; the streets were full of riders and transports going in various directions. Scores of emaciated horses stood at the mangers in the yards, miserably munching straw; the lanes were littered with abandoned sledges, wagons and caissons. As he was driving down one of the streets, Prokhor noticed a tall bay horse tethered to the fence.

'That's cousin Andrei's horse! There must be some folk from our village here,' he exclaimed, and in a moment he was off the sledge and walking up to the house to find out.

A few minutes later Andrei Topolskov came out of the house with his greatcoat draped over his shoulders. He was a cousin and neighbour of Prokhor's. Accompanied by Prokhor, he walked up to the sledge with some dignity and held out a black grimy hand that stank of horse sweat.

'Are you with the village transports?' Grigory asked.

'Ay, we're all in the same boat.'

'What kind of journey did you have?'

'You know what it's like... We leave someone behind after every stop, and horses too...'

'How's my old man? Still fit?'

Looking past Grigory, Topolskov drew a deep breath.

'Bad, Grigory Panteleyevich. Things are bad... Pray for your father, yesterday evening he gave up his soul to God. He's passed away...'

'Have they buried him?' Grigory asked, turning pale.

'I couldn't say. I haven't been there today. Drive on and I'll show you the house... Keep to the right, cousin, it's the fourth house from the corner, on the right-hand side.'

When they reached the big iron-roofed house, Prokhor stopped the horses by the fence, but Topolskov advised him to drive into the yard.

'It's a bit crowded here too, about twenty people in the house, but you'll squeeze in somehow,' he said, and jumped off the sledge to open the gate.

Grigory was the first to enter the overheated room. Several people he knew from his village were lying or sitting on the floor. One or two of them were mending boots or harness. Three, including old Beskhlebnov, Pantelei's sledge companion, were sitting at the table, eating soup. At the sight of Grigory the Cossacks rose to their feet and chorused a reply to his brief greeting.

'Where's my father?' Grigory asked, taking off his cap and looking round the room.

'It's a great grief to us... Pantelei Prokofievich has

passed on,' Beskhlebnov replied quietly and, wiping his mouth with his sleeve, put down his spoon and crossed himself. 'He gave up the ghost last night, may his soul be blessed in heaven.'

'I know. Have you buried him?'

'Not yet. We were going to today, but he's still here now. We took him out into the cold room. Come with me,' Beskhlebnov opened the door into the next room and said, almost apologetically, 'The Cossacks didn't want to spend the night with a dead man. It's the smell. And anyway it's better for him out here... They don't heat in here.'

The large front room smelled strongly of hemp seed and mice. One corner was taken up with heeps of millet and hemp; tubs of flour and butter stood in a row on a bench. Pantelei was lying on a mat in the middle of the room. Grigory stepped past Beskhlebnov, entered the room and halted beside his father.

'He was ill for a fortnight,' Beskhlebnov said in a low voice. 'The typhus took him back at Mechetka. So this is where your dear father breathed his last... That's life...'

Grigory bent forward and looked at his father. How disease had changed that dear face, it was like a stranger's. The pale sunken cheeks were covered with a grey stubble, the moustache drooped low over the sunken mouth, the eyes were half closed and the bluish enamel of the whites had lost their former sparkling verve and brilliance. The old man's sagging lower jaw was tied up with a red neckerchief and against the red the curly grey beard seemed even more silvery and white.

Grigory knelt to look for the last time and remember, but an involuntary shudder of horror and revulsion passed through him. Lice were crawling all over the old man's grey waxed face, filling the eye-sockets, the furrows in the cheeks, swarming in the beard, scurrying over the eyebrows, and massing greyly on the high collar of his blue Circassian coat...

* * *

Grigory and two other Cossacks used crow-bars to hack out a grave in the frozen iron-hard loam. Prokhor knocked together a coffin out of odds and ends of boards. At the close of the day they carried Pantelei out and buried him in the alien Stavropol soil. An hour later, when the lamps had been lit in the settlement, Grigory drove out in the direction of Novopokrovskaya.

At their next stop, Korenovskaya, he began to feel ill. Prokhor spent half the day looking for a doctor. He eventually found a half-tipsy army surgeon and with much difficulty persuaded him to come to their lodgings. Without taking off his greatcoat the surgeon examined Grigory, felt his pulse, and stated confidently, 'Recurrent typhus. I advise you to end your travels, Lieutenant. Otherwise you'll die on the road.'

'And wait here for the Reds?' Grigory asked, making a wry face.

'Well, the Reds are still a long way off.'

'They'll get closer.'

'I don't doubt it. But you'd do better to stay. Of the two evils I'd choose the lesser.'

'No, I'll slog along somehow,' Grigory said resolutely, and started pulling on his tunic. 'Will you give me some medicine?'

'Go on then, it's your affair, not mine. My duty was to advise you, but it's up to you whether you take it. As for medicine, the best is peace and quiet and proper attention. I could prescribe something for you but the medical supplies have been evacuated. I've got nothing here but chloroform, iodine and alcohol.'

'At least give me some alcohol!'

'Gladly! You'll die on the road anyway, so a drop of alcohol won't change anything. Tell your orderly to come with me. I'll let you have a thousand grammes. I'm a kind man.' The surgeon saluted and walked out with uncertain steps.

Prokhor came back with the alcohol, found a two-horse wagon somewhere, harnessed up the horses, and with gloomy irony reported as he entered the room, 'The carriage is waiting, Your Honour!'

And once again the despondent, dreary days dragged on.

From the foothills of the Caucasus the swift southern spring swooped on the lands of the Kuban. On the flat steppeland the snow melted fast. Patches of greasy black earth appeared, the spring torrents babbled with silvery voices, the road grew blotchy, the distant light-blue horizons were truly springlike and the broad skies were tinged with a deeper, warmer blue.

After a couple of days the winter wheat revealed itself

to the sun and white mists rose over the fields. The horses squelched along the bare road, sinking up to their fetlocks in mud, getting stuck in the dells, arching their backs with the strain, and streaming with sweat. Prokhor tied up their tails and often got off the wagon, wading along in the mud and muttering, 'This isn't mud, it's tar, honest to God it is! The horses sweat all the way from one stop to the next.'

Grigory lay silent and shivering under a big sheepskin. But Prokhor could not be without someone to talk to, so he would nudge Grigory's foot or sleeve and say, 'The mud here—see how thick it is! Just try and get off! What did you want to go and get ill for!'

'Go to hell!' Grigory responded in a barely audible whisper.

Whenever they met someone, Prokhor would ask, 'Is the mud thicker further on, or about the same?'

He would receive a joking reply and, content to have exchanged a word with a living soul, would walk on for a while in silence, often stopping the horses and mopping the big beads of sweat from his brown forehead. If anyone on horseback overtook them, he could not resist stopping him with a greeting and asking where they were heading for, where they came from, and in the end he would say, 'You're making a mistake to go on. It's impossible. Why? Because of the mud. People coming the other way tell me the horses are up to their bellies in it, the wagon wheels won't turn and any short man just goes under and gets drowned. No kidding! Why do we keep going? We've got no choice, you see. I've got a sick archbishop here and he couldn't live with the Reds, not on no account...'

Most of the horsemen swore good-naturedly at Prokhor and rode on, but some would study him carefully before taking the road again and say, 'Are all the fools retreating from the Don too? Is everyone like you up there?'

It might be some other gibe, but no less offensive. Only one Kuban Cossack, who had fallen behind his group, lost his temper with Prokhor for detaining him with his foolish talk and was about to lash out at him with a whip, but Prokhor leapt on to the wagon with amazing agility, pulled his carbine out from under the matting, and laid it across his knees. The Kuban man rode away swearing while Prokhor, roaring with laughter, bawled after him, 'That's not like hiding in the corn at

Tsaritsyn! Heh, you thick-head with your floppy sleeves! Come back, you hominy hogger! Bumped into the wrong man, eh! Pick up your skirts or you'll get 'em all muddy! You wing-flapping chicken-eater! Heh, bacon bum! I don't want to waste a bullet on you or I'd give you swiping at me! Drop that whip, d'ye hear!'

Bored silly, Prokhor did his best to amuse himself.

Since the day he fell ill, Grigory had been living in a dream. From time to time he lost consciousness, then came to again. One day when he awoke from a long oblivion, he saw Prokhor bending over him.

'Still alive?' he asked, looking sympathetically into Grigory's bleary eyes.

The sun was shining overhead. Flocks of dark-winged wild geese were crossing the sky, now in bunches now in a broken velvety black line, their cries echoing in the intense blue. The smell of the warm earth and the young grass was stupefying. Grigory gulped the reviving spring air into his lungs and his chest heaved. He barely heard Prokhor's voice and everything around him seemed unrealistically, unbelievably small and remote. From behind them came the muffled rumble of gunfire. Not far away iron-rimmed wheels were clicking regularly, horses were snorting and neighing, and the sound of voices, the pungent scent of baked bread, hay and horse sweat invaded his senses. But it all reached Grigory's clouded consciousness as if from another world. With a great effort of will he listened to Prokhor's voice and managed to understand what he was saying.

Prokhor was asking, 'Can you drink some milk?'

Barely able to move his tongue, Grigory licked his parched lips and felt a thick cold liquid with a familiar fresh taste being poured into his mouth. After a few gulps he clenched his teeth. Prokhor stoppered the flask and bent over Grigory again. More by the movement of Prokhor's wind-chapped lips than by anything else Grigory guessed what he was saying.

'Shall I leave you here? Too hard for you, is it?'

Grigory's face expressed suffering and alarm. Once again he screwed up his will and whispered, 'Take me on—till I die.'

From Prokhor's face he guessed that he had heard, then he closed his eyes calmly, accepting oblivion as a relief, sinking into the intense darkness of forgetfulness, escaping from all the noise and shouting of this world.

XXVIII

All the way to Abinskaya only one thing left a trace on Grigory's memory. During a pitch-dark night he was awakened by the fiercely penetrating cold. Wagons were moving along the road, several abreast. Judging by the sound of voices and the ceaseless murmur of wheels, the baggage train was huge. The wagon carrying Grigory was somewhere in the middle of it. The horses plodded on at a walk. Prokhor would click his tongue and occasionally urge them on with a husky shout and a flourish of his whip. Grigory would hear the thin whistle of the leather lash and the creak of harness as the horses strained harder at the traces and the wagon picked up speed, sometimes bumping its shaft against the back of the wagon ahead.

With an effort Grigory pulled up the sheepskin and lay back. Swirling heavy clouds were flying southward across the black sky. At rare intervals a lonely star would gleam momentarily like a yellow spark through a gap, then the steppe would again be wrapped in impenetrable gloom, the wind would whistle despondently in the telegraph wires and fine rain would sprinkle down.

A column of cavalry was coming along the road in marching order. Grigory heard the familiar steady jingle of well-fitting Cossack equipment and the muffled but also steady squelching of hooves in the mud. No less than two squadrons had passed, but the sound of hooves could still be heard; it must be a regiment that was passing. And suddenly the brave, rather harsh voice of a song-leader soared up like a bird over the steppe:

Ah, how it was on the river, on the River Kamyshinka,
In the glorious steppes, the steppes of Saratov...

Hundreds of voices lifted the old Cossack song zestfully, and highest of all rose a tenor descant of astonishing power and beauty. While the vibrant heart-catching tenor still soared somewhere in the darkness, overriding the basses, the song-leader began another line:

There the Cossacks lived, good men and free,
All of the Don, the Greben and the Yaik countries...

Something seemed to snap inside Grigory... A sudden fit of sobbing shook his body and a spasm seized his throat. Swallowing his tears, he waited eagerly for the leader to begin again, and soundlessly whispered after him the words he had known since adolescence:

> *Their Ataman was Yermak, son of Timofei,*
> *Their captain was Astashka, son of Lavrenty...*

As soon as the song sounded forth, the murmur of talk from the wagons died away and the shouts of the drivers ceased, and the whole thousand-strong line of transports moved on in silence; only the creak of the wheels and the squelching of hooves through the mud could be heard at the moments when the song-leader, uttering every word distinctly, came out with the verse. An old Cossack song that had survived the centuries lived and ruled over the dark steppe. In artlessly simple words it told of the Cossacks' free ancestors, who had fearlessly attacked and routed the tsar's armies, who had plied the Don and the Volga in their light pirate barks, who had plundered the tsar's ships, who had 'plucked' the merchants, boyars and voivodes, who had subdued distant Siberia... And in gloomy silence the mighty song was listened to by the descendants of the free Cossacks, descendants who had been defeated and were retreating in an inglorious war against the Russian people...

The regiment rode past. The singers overtook the wagon train and rode on far ahead. But for a long time the wagons rolled on in an enchanted silence, and not a word of talk or a shout at the weary horses was heard. But from far away in the darkness the song still reached them, spreading ever farther like the Don at floodtime:

> *One thought alone they all did share:*
> *Brothers, soon the summer's warmth must end*
> *And winter come with freezing air.*
> *Where then shall we the winter spend?*
> *To the Yaik to march will be too far,*
> *On the Volga all men count us thieves,*
> *If to Kazan we go, the tsar is there,*
> *A tsar most terrible, Ivan Vasilyevich...*

Even when the chorus could no longer be heard, the descant still rang out, falling and rising again. It was listened to in the same tense and brooding silence.

...And there was something else Grigory remembered.

He had awoken in a warm room and, without opening his eyes, felt in every limb the pleasant freshness of clean bed linen and his nostrils had caught the astringent smell of medicines. At first he thought he was in a field hospital, but from the next room came an explosion of male laughter, a clatter of crockery and the sound of tipsy voices. A familiar voice was booming, 'There's a clever feller for ye! You should've found out where our unit was and we'd have helped you. Here, drink, what the devil are ye gaping at?!'

In a weeping tipsy voice Prokhor replied, 'But for Lord's sake, how was I to know? D'you think it was easy for me to nurse him? I fed him with chewed bits, like a little baby, and gave him milk to drink, by all that's holy! I'd chew up some bread and stuff it in his mouth, honestly! Had to part his teeth with my sword... And once when I poured some milk into his mouth he choked and nearly died... Think of that!'

'Did you wash him yesterday?'

'Sure I did and cut his hair with the clippers, and spent all my money on milk and grub... Not that I grudge it, to the devil with it! But think of chewing the stuff and feeding him by hand? Was that easy? Don't you dare say it was or I'll bash you and not give a damn for your rank!'

Grigory's room was suddenly invaded by Prokhor, Kharlampy Yermakov, Petro Bogatiryov, red as a beetroot, with his lambskin busby on the back of his head, Platon Ryabchikov, and two other Cossacks, both strangers.

'He's opened his eyes!!!' Yermakov bellowed wildly, staggering towards Grigory.

The merry, swashbuckling Platon Ryabchikov, half weeping and waving a bottle, bawled, 'Grisha! My love! Remember the drinking we did on the Chir! And the fighting? What's become of all our valour!! What are the generals up to? What are they doing with our army?! Damn their eyes! Alive again? Here, have a drink, and you'll perk up rightaway! This is pure spirits!'

'We thought we'd never find you!' Yermakov mumbled, his dark oily eyes shining gladly, and plumped himself down on the bed, leaning on Grigory with all his weight.

'Where are we?' Grigory asked in a barely audible voice, forcing his eyes to take in the familiar faces.

'We've taken Yekaterinodar! Soon we'll be trotting

on a bit further! Drink! Grigory Panteleyevich! Dear man! Get up, for God's sake, I can't bear to see you lying down!' Ryabchikov collapsed on Grigory's feet, but Bogatiryov, smiling silently and evidently more sober than any of the others, gripped his belt, picked him up without much difficulty and carefully lowered him to the floor.

'Take the bottle away from him! It'll get spilt!' Yermakov exclaimed in alarm, and with a broad tipsy grin said to Grigory, 'D'you know what we're celebrating? It's been just a long run of bad luck, but for once the Cossacks have struck lucky on foreign soil... They've plundered a wine store to stop it falling into Red hands... The things that went on there... Better than in a dream! They shot up a tank with their rifles and it started spurting pure spirits. Filled it full of holes they did and at every hole someone stood with a cap or a pail or a bottle, or just cupping his hands and drinking on the spot... They cut down the two Volunteers that were guarding the store, got inside and had a fine time. While I was there one Cossack got up atop of the tank and wanted to fill a horse's drinking pail, but he fell in and drowned. The floor was cement and soon the liquor was up to their knees. They just waded about in it, bending down and drinking, then lying down in it... It's wrong of course, but you can't help laughing. More than one will drown to death there. And we got some pickings too. We don't need much. We rolled out a barrel holding about ten pailfuls and that'll do us. Let's have our fling! The quiet Don's finished anyway! Platon nearly got drowned there. They knocked him over and started treading on him. He went under twice and was ready to die. I only just managed to pull him out...'

They all reeked of liquor, onion and tobacco. Grigory felt slightly sick and dizzy and closed his eyes with a forced smile.

In Yekaterinodar he kept to his bed for a week in a flat belonging to a doctor friend of Bogatiryov's. Slowly he recovered from his illness, and then, as Prokhor put it, he started 'perking up', and at Abinskaya mounted his horse for the first time since the retreat had begun.

                              *   *   *

Novorossiisk had become a port of evacuation. Ships
were sailing for Turkey with the money-bags of Russia,
the landowners, the families of generals, influential
statesmen and politicians. At the wharves loading continued day and night. Officer cadets worked as gangs of
stevedores, filling the holds with military equipment
and the trunks and suitcases of high-born refugees.

The Volunteer Army had outstripped the Don and
Kuban Cossacks in retreat, reached Novorossiisk first
and begun to embark on the transports. The staff had
prudently taken refuge aboard the British dreadnought
Emperor of India, which had anchored in the harbour.
Fighting was going on around Tonnelnaya. Tens of
thousands of refugees thronged the streets of the city.
Military units continued to arrive. The turmoil on the
quayside was indescribable. Herds of abandoned horses
in their thousands roamed the limestone hill-sides around
the city. Cossack saddles, equipment and military stores
were piled high in the streets adjoining the wharves.
No one needed them any more. Rumours had spread
through the city that only the Volunteer Army would
be taken aboard and the Don and Kuban Cossacks would
have to march on to Georgia.

In the morning on March 25th, Grigory and Platon
Ryabchikov went to the port to find out whether any
units of the 2nd Don Corps were being embarked because
the day before the word had gone round among the
Cossacks that General Denikin had given the order that
all Don Cossacks who still had their arms and horses
were to be transported to the Crimea.

The wharves were crowded with Kalmyks from the Sal
district. With droves of horses and camels from the Manych
and the Sal they had towed their wooden caravans all the
way to the sea. Almost stifled by the reek of mutton fat,
Grigory and Ryabchikov pushed their way through the
crowd to the gangway of a big transport tied up at the
wharf. The gangway was guarded by a strong squad
of officers of Markov's Division. A crowd of Don Army artillerymen was waiting nearby to be embarked. Tarpaulin-
covered guns were mounted in the stern of the ship. Squeezing his way forward, Grigory asked a dashing black-
moustached sergeant-major, 'What battery is this, Cossack?'

The sergeant-major squinted at Grigory and replied
reluctantly, 'The 36th.'

'Kargin's?'

'That's right.'

'Who's in charge of embarkation here?'

'There he is by the rails, some colonel or other.'

Ryabchikov touched Grigory's arm and said furiously, 'Let's get out of here, and to hell with 'em! D'you think you'll get anywhere with this lot? When there was fighting to be done, they needed us, but now we're in the way.'

The sergeant-major winked at the artillerymen lined up in the queue.

'You're lucky, gunners! They aren't even taking officers.'

The colonel, who was in charge of the loading, came smartly down the gangway; he was followed by a bald official, hurrying and stumbling in the skirts of an expensive fur coat. He held his sealskin hat clasped imploringly to his chest. His perspiring face and short-sighted eyes expressed such abject entreaty that the colonel turned away in disgust and said roughly, 'I've told you already! Stop accosting me like this, or I'll have you put ashore! You must be mad! How the devil can we take your chattels? Are you blind? Don't you see what's going on here? Really! Yes, complain by all means, to General Denikin himself, if you choose! I've said I can't and I can't, don't you understand the Russian language?'

When he had got rid of the pestering official and stepped down on to the wharf, Grigory stood in his path, saluted and asked agitatedly, 'Can officers count on getting aboard?'

'Not on this ship. There's no room.'

'What ship will take us then?'

'Find out at the evacuation office.'

'We've been there, no one knows anything.'

'I don't know either, let me pass!'

'But you're taking the 36th Battery! Why have you no room for us?'

'Let—me—pass, I tell you! I'm not an information desk!' The colonel tried gently to push Grigory aside but to no avail. Bluish sparks flared in Grigory's eyes.

'So you don't need us any more? But you did before, didn't you? Hands off, you won't push me away!'

The colonel looked into Grigory's eyes and glanced over his shoulder; the Markov men at the gangway had crossed their rifles and were holding back the crowd with difficulty. Looking past Grigory, the colonel asked wearily, 'What unit are you from?'

649

'I'm from the 19th Don Cossack Regiment, the rest are from other regiments.'

'How many of you altogether?'

'About ten.'

'I can't do it. No room.'

Ryabchikov saw Grigory's nostrils quiver as he said in a low voice, 'What's the game, you bastard? You rear rat! Let us through, or else...'

'Now Grisha will cut him down!' Ryabchikov thought with gleeful anticipation, but noticing two Markov men hurriedly boring their way through the crowd with their rifle butts to rescue the colonel, he touched Grigory's sleeve warningly.

'Don't bother with 'em, Panteleyevich! Let's go...'

'You're an idiot! And you'll answer for your behaviour!' Pale-faced, the colonel turned towards the approaching Markov men and pointed at Grigory. 'Gentlemen! Deal with this epileptic! We must have order here! I have an urgent matter to discuss with the commandant, and I have to listen to all kinds of compliments from such...' And he slipped hurriedly past Grigory.

A tall Markov man with a neatly trimmed English-style moustache and lieutenant's shoulder straps on his blue uniform coat came up to Grigory.

'What do you want? Why are you causing this disturbance?'

'A place on the ship, that's what I want!'

'Where is your unit?'

'I don't know.'

'Your papers?'

The second member of the guard, a young full-lipped fellow with a pince-nez, said in a wobbling bass, 'Better take him to the guard-house. Don't waste your time, Vysotsky!'

The lieutenant studied Grigory's papers attentively and returned them.

'Go and find your unit. I advise you to keep away from here and not interfere with the loading. We have orders to arrest anyone behaving in an undisciplined manner and hindering embarkation, regardless of rank.' The lieutenant compressed his lips, waited a few seconds and, with a sidelong glance at Ryabchikov, leaned towards Grigory and whispered, 'My advice to you is to talk to the commander of the 36th Battery, then get in their queue and you'll go aboard.'

Ryabchikov, who had heard the lieutenant's whispered advice, said joyfully, 'Go and see Kargin and I'll run and fetch the lads. Any stuff of yours you want besides your kitbag?'

'Let's go together,' Grigory said indifferently.

On the way back to their quarters they met a Cossack they knew from the village of Semyonovsky. He was driving a huge covered wagonload of bread. Ryabchikov hailed him.

'Fyodor, hi there! Where're you heading?'

'Ah, Platon, Grigory Panteleyevich, good health to you! We're supplying our regiment with bread for the journey. Could hardly get it baked. Otherwise we'd have had to make do with boiled stuff...'

Grigory went up to the wagon and asked, 'Has your bread been weighed? Or counted?'

'Who the devil would count it? Why, d'you need some bread?'

'Yes.'

'Take some!'

'How much can we have?'

'As much as you can carry. We've got plenty!'

Ryabchikov stared in surprise as Grigory took loaf after loaf. Unable to restrain his curiosity any longer, he asked, 'What in hell's name d'you want all that bread for?'

'We need it,' Grigory answered curtly.

He begged two sacks off the driver, put the loaves in them, thanked the man for his kindness and told Ryabchikov to help him carry them.

'You're not thinking of spending the winter here, are you?' Ryabchikov asked ironically, heaving a sack on to his shoulder.

'It's not for me.'

'Who's it for then?'

'My horse.'

Ryabchikov promptly dropped the sack, looking bewildered.

'Are you joking?'

'No, I mean it.'

'So you ... what's the idea, Panteleyevich? You want to stay behind? Is that it?'

'That's right. Now pick up that sack and come on. I've got to feed my horse, it's chewing up its manger. A horse may come in useful, I'm not going to serve on foot...'

All the way back to their quarters Ryabchikov said

nothing, merely grunting and heaving the sack higher on his back.

At the gate he asked, 'Will you tell the lads?' and, without waiting for a reply, said with a shade of resentment in his voice, 'This is a fine idea you've got hold of... What about us?'

'That's up to you,' Grigory replied with feigned indifference. 'They won't take us, there's no room for everybody. All right then, we'll do without! Why the hell should we go begging to them! We'll stay here and try our luck. Come on, what are you stuck in the gate for?'

'It's enough to make anyone stuck, the way you talk... I can't see the bloody gate. What a mess! You've bowled me over, Grisha, that ye have! Knocked me silly. I was wondering, what the devil does he want all that bread for? The lads will be proper upset when they get to know about it.'

'And what about you? Won't you stay?' Grigory inquired.

'No fear!' Ryabchikov exclaimed in alarm.

'Think it over.'

'No need to think! I'll go like a shot if there's room for me. I'll tack on to Kargin's battery and sail with them.'

'You're making a mistake.'

'Well, strike me! I value my own skin, chum! I don't feel like letting the Reds try out their swords on it.'

'You'd better think hard, Platon! It's a big thing to decide...'

'I'll say it is! I'm going.'

'Well, just as you like. I'm not trying to persuade you,' Grigory said curtly, and was the first to mount the stone steps of the porch.

None of the other Cossacks were in the lodging. The landlady, an elderly stooped Armenian, said they had gone out, promising to be back soon. Without taking off his coat, Grigory cut some loaves into thick slices and went out to the shed where the horses were stabled. He divided the bread equally between his own horse and Prokhor's and was just about to fetch a pail of water when Ryabchikov appeared in the doorway. He was carrying several big hunks of bread in the hem of his greatcoat. His horse, sensing its master's approach, gave a brief neigh. Ryabchikov walked silently past the quietly smiling Grigory, tipped the bread into the manger and, without looking up, said, 'You needn't grin! If that's the way things are, I'll have to feed my horse too... D'you think I want to go away? I'd have to take myself by the scruff of the neck and throw myself aboard that goddamned ship! It's fear that does it... I've only got one head on my shoulders, haven't I? God forbid, but if I get it cut off, I won't grow another before Christmas.'

Prokhor and the other Cossacks did not return till evening. Yermakov brought in a huge bottle of surgical spirit and Prokhor a sackful of hermetically sealed jars containing a murky yellow liquid. Yermakov explained, 'An army doctor we ran into wanted us to carry his medicines from the stores to the wharf. The dockers won't work and only the cadets were carrying stuff, so we lent a hand. The doctor paid us in spirit and Prokhor pinched these jars—God punish me if I'm lying!'

'What's in them?' Ryabchikov inquired.

'This is stronger stuff than spirit!' Prokhor shook a jar, held it up to the light and, watching the thick liquid bubbling under the dark glass, concluded complacently, 'This, lads, is the most expensive foreign wine that's made. They only give it to the sick, so a young cadet told me that knows the English language. We'll get aboard ship, drown our sorrows, strike up with "Dear Land of Our Fathers", drink all the way to the Crimea and chuck the jars away into the sea.'

'Hurry up and get aboard then, they're holding up the ship because of you. "Where's Prokhor Zykov?" they keep asking, "He's such a great hero, we can't sail without him." ' Ryabchikov said sarcastically. And after a pause, he pointed a yellow, smoke-stained finger at Grigory, 'He's changed his mind about going. And so have I.'

'You don't say?' Prokhor gasped, and nearly dropped the jar in surprise.

'What's this? What's the big idea?' Yermakov asked, eyeing Grigory with a frown.

'We've decided not to go.'

'Why?'

'Because there's no room for us.'

'If there isn't today, there will be tomorrow,' Bogatiryov said confidently.

'Have you been down to the wharves?'

'Well?'

'Know what's going on there?'

'So what?'

'So what! If you know, what's the use of talking? They'd only take the two of us, Ryabchikov and me, and even then we'd have had to get in line with Kargin's battery. That's the only way.'

'Has that battery gone aboard yet?' Bogatiryov asked with sudden interest.

On learning that the artillerymen were still queuing up for embarkation, he at once started packing underclothes, spare trousers and a tunic into his kitbag. He added a loaf of bread and took his leave.

'Stay with us, Petro!' Yermakov advised. 'It's better to stick together.'

Bogatiryov held out a sweaty hand without replying. At the door he nodded again and said, 'Goodbye and good health! God willing, we may meet again!' and ran out of the house.

A long and awkward silence followed his departure. Yermakov went to the kitchen, brought back four glasses and filling them with liquor, put a big copper kettle of cold water on the table, cut some slices of bacon fat and, still without uttering a word, sat down, leaned his elbows on the table, and for several minutes stared dully at his feet, then he drank some water straight from the spout of the kettle and said hoarsely, 'On the Kuban all the water stinks of kerosene. Why is that?'

No one replied. Ryabchikov wiped the damp blade of his sabre with a clean rag. Grigory started rummaging in his box. Prokhor stared absently out of the window at the bare hillsides dotted with herds of horses.

'Sit down and have a drink.' Without more ado Yermakov tossed back half a tumbler of spirit, washed it down with water and, as he chewed a piece of pink bacon fat, looked at Grigory with more cheerful eyes and asked, 'Won't the Red comrades send us to kingdom come?'

'They can't kill us all. There'll be thousands staying behind here,' Grigory replied.

'I'm not talking about all,' Yermakov said with a laugh. 'It's my own skin I'm worried about.'

After a fair amount had been drunk, the talk grew more animated. A little while later Bogatiryov, frowning and blue with cold, reappeared. He dumped a bale of brand-new British greatcoats on the threshold and took off his coat in silence.

'Welcome back!' Prokhor greeted him sarcastically, with a bow.

Bogatiryov gave him a furious look and said with a sigh, 'Even if all the Denikins and the other buggers besides begged on their bended knees, I wouldn't go! I stood in that queue, perishing with cold, and all for nothing. It stopped at me. One of the two in front of me got through but not the other. Half the battery was left behind. What d'you make of that, eh?'

'That's how they deal with the likes of you!' Yermakov said with a chuckle, filling a glass until it overflowed. 'Here, drown your sorrows with this! Or will you wait till they come and ask you aboard? Look out of the window. Isn't that General Wrangel coming for you right now?'

Bogatiryov drank without replying. He was in no mood for joking. But Yermakov and Ryabchikov, themselves half tipsy, plied their landlady with drink until she could barely toddle, and talked of going in search of an accordion-player.

'Better go to the station,' Bogatiryov advised, 'they're emptying the trucks there. They've got a whole trainload of equipment for the taking.'

'What the hell do we need your equipment for!' Yermakov bawled. 'These greatcoats you brought will do for us. And they won't let us keep that much. Petro, you old snitch! We're thinking about going over to the Reds, understand? We're Cossacks, aren't we? Or what? If the Reds will spare our lives, let's go and serve ' em! We're Don Cossacks! Thoroughbreds without a drop of alien blood! It's our job to use our sabres. You know how I can slash? To the root! Stand up and I'll try it on you! Can't stand, eh? It's all the same to us who we cut down as long as we can use our sabres. That's right, isn't it, Melekhov?'

'Leave me alone!' Grigory said, with a weary flip of his hand.

Squinting with bloodshot eyes, Yermakov reached out for his sabre, which was lying on the chest. Bogatiryov pushed him back good-naturedly and said, 'Cool down, you warrior brave, or I'll cool you. Drink with dignity, man, you've got officer's rank, ye know.'

'Shit on that rank! I need it like a hole in the head. Don't remind me! You're the same yourself. Lemme cut off your shoulder straps? Petro, me old chum, it won't take a sec...'

'We'll have time for that later on,' Bogatiryov chuckled, warding off his riotous friend.

They drank till dawn. In the evening some Cossacks from another regiment turned up, one of them with an accordion. Yermakov danced until he dropped. They carried him to a corner and he went off to sleep at once on the bare floor, legs wide apart, head thrown back awkwardly. The dreary carousal went on till morning. 'I'm from Kumshatskaya!... Ay, the very same! We used to have oxen so tall you couldn't reach their horns! Our horses were like lions! But now what's left on the farm? One mangy bitch! And that'll soon peg out because there's nowt to feed her on...' an elderly Cossack, one of the chance acquaintances who had come in for the drink-up, proclaimed, sobbing drunkenly. A Cossack from the Kuban in a tattered Circassian coat asked the accordion-player for a Caucasian dance and with his arms pictur-esquely outspread glided round the room with such astonishing light-footedness that to Grigory his feet seemed not even to touch the filthy, bootmarked floor.

At midnight one of the Cossacks brought in from no one knew where two tall earthenware pitchers. Time-darkened half rotten labels showed on their sides, the corks were coated in sealing wax, and massive leaden seals dangled from under the cherry-red wax. Prokhor held one of the pitchers, moving his lips painfully as he tried to understand the foreign inscription on the label. Yermakov, who had just woken up, took it away from him, put it on the floor and bared his sabre. Before Prokhor could bat an eyelid, Yermakov lopped off the neck of the pitcher with a slanting stroke, and shouted, 'Bring your glasses!'

The thick, strangely aromatic and astringent wine was consumed in a few minutes and for a long time after-wards Yermakov clicked his tongue and mumbled, 'That was not wine, but the holy sacrament! That's a wine to be drunk only before death, and not by everybody, but only by those that never played cards, never smoked tobacco, and never touched women... An archbishop's drink, to put it in one word!' At this point Prokhor remembered the jars of medicinal wine he had in his sack.

'Just a minute! Platon, go easy on the praise! I've got some better wine than that! That's just shit, but the wine I got from the stores, that the real stuff! Incense and honey, mebbe even better! Not archbishop's wine, chum, but the tsar's! And no doubt about it! The tsars used to drink it, and now it's our turn!' he boasted, opening one of the jars.

Ryabchikov, who had never been known to refuse a drink, gulped down half a glassful of the muddy yellow liquid, turned pale and stared with bulging eyes.

'That's not wine, it's carbolic!' he gasped in fury, splashing the dregs out on to Prokhor's shirt, and staggered out into the corridor.

'He's lying, the snake! This is English wine! Top grade! Don't you believe him, lads!' Prokhor roared, trying to make himself heard above the babble of tipsy voices. He drank his glass in one gulp and turned even whiter than Ryabchikov.

'Well, how d'you like it?' Yermakov inquired, twitching his nostrils and staring into Prokhor's glazed eyes. 'How's the tsar's wine? Strong enough? Sweet enough? Speak, you hobgoblin, or I'll break this jar on your head!'

Prokhor shook his head, suffered in silence, then with a great hiccough jumped to his feet and dashed out after Ryabchikov. Choking with laughter, Yermakov winked conspiratorially at Grigory and went out into the yard. A minute later he returned to the room and his booming laughter drowned all the other voices.

'What's up with you?' Grigory asked wearily. 'What are you hee-hawing about, you mutt?'

'Go and see the way they're turning their insides out, m'boy! D'you know what they've been drinking?'

'What?'

'English lice-killer!'

'No?!'

'Honest to God! When I was at the stores, I thought at first it was wine, then I asked the doctor what it was. It's a drug, he says. Is it one that'll cure all our sorrows, I asks. Has it got any booze in it? God forbid, he says, it's what the Allies sent us, it's a lotion against lice. Strictly for external use, you mustn't swallow it!'

'Why didn't you tell them, you villain?' Grigory said, frowning.

'Let them purge themselves before surrendering, it won't kill 'em!' Yermakov wiped the tears from his eyes and added not without malice, 'And they won't drink so much. The way they go at it, you hardly have time to grab a glass. That'll teach these guzzlers! Well, what about you and me, shall we drink? Or shall we wait? Let's drink to our destruction, eh?'

Just before dawn Grigory went out on to the porch, rolled himself a cigarette with trembling hands, lit it, and stood leaning against the fog-dampened wall.

From the house came a ceaseless hubbub of tipsy shouts, the wheezy notes of the accordion, and a wild cascade of whistles; the dancers had got the bit between their teeth... A breeze from the bay carried the deep muffled roar of ships' sirens; the babble of voices from the wharves merged into a steady drone, interrupted only by loud shouts of command, the neighing of horses, and the hoots of locomotives. Somewhere in the direction of Tonnelnaya fighting was going on. Heavy guns rumbled and in the intervals between the shots the chatter of machine-guns could be heard. A flare soared high over the Markhotka Pass and spurted shimmering light. For a few seconds the humpbacked mountains showed up in the green phantasmal radiance, then again the clinging darkness of the March night enfolded the mountains, and the artillery volleys grew louder and more frequent, almost merging with one another.

XXIX

A cold salt-laden wind was blowing from the sea. It smelled of the unknown, of foreign lands. But for the men of the Don not only the wind but everything else in this dreary draught-ridden seaport town was alien and hostile. They stood on the harbour mole, huddled together, waiting for embarkation... Frothy green waves foamed up the beach. A sun that was without warmth peered through a cloud. British and French destroyers stood in the roads with smoking funnels; a dreadnought towered menacingly above the water, canopied with a black cloud of smoke. The wharves were wrapped in an ominous silence. Where the last transport had recently rocked at its moorings the water was now littered with officers' saddles, suitcases, blankets, overcoats, red plush-covered chairs, and other odds and ends, tossed overboard at the last moment from the gangways.

Grigory went down to the wharves first thing in the

morning. Leaving his horse with Prokhor, he mingled with the crowd, looking for acquaintances and listening to the snatches of harrassed talk. He was standing by the gangway of the *Svyatoslav* when an elderly colonel of the reserve who had been refused a place on the ship shot himself.

A few minutes before this the colonel, a small fussy man with grey stubble on his cheeks and puffy tearful eyes, had been clutching at the belt of the commander of the guard, babbling pitifully, blowing his nose and wiping his nicotine-stained moustache, his eyes and trembling lips with a grubby handkerchief, and then he seemed suddenly to make up his mind... No sooner had the shot been fired than a light-fingered Cossack snatched the gleaming nickel-plated Browning from the dead man's hand. The body in its pale-grey officer's greatcoat was kicked aside like a log, the fighting round the gangway rose in fury, and the hoarse, embittered voices of the refugees howled even more savagely.

When the last ship heaved away from the wharf, the sound of weeping women's voices, hysterical screams and shouts of abuse rose from the crowd. Before the short deep blast of the ship's siren had died away, a young Kalmyk in a big fox-fur hat jumped into the water and swam out after the ship.

'Must be keen to go!' one of the Cossacks said with a sigh.

'Couldn't stay behind,' said a Cossack standing beside Grigory. 'That one must have done the Reds a lot of harm.'

Grigory gritted his teeth as he watched the swimming Kalmyk. The strokes of his arms began to falter, the shoulders sank deeper into the water as the sodden coat dragged him down. A wave swept away the fox-fur hat.

'He'll drown, the blighted heathen!' an old man in a Caucasian coat said pityingly.

Grigory turned away sharply and went back to his horse. Prokhor was talking animatedly to Ryabchikov and Bogatiryov, who had just ridden up. At the sight of Grigory, Ryabchikov shifted impatiently in his saddle, dug his heels into his horse's flanks and shouted, 'Hurry up, Panteleyevich!' And without waiting for Grigory to reach him, he added, 'Let's get going before it's too late. We've got half a squadron of Cossacks here and we're thinking of heading for Gelenjik, then on into Georgia. What about you?'

Grigory walked up with his hands thrust deep into his greatcoat pockets, pushing his way through the aimless mob of Cossacks on the wharf.

'Are you coming or not?' Ryabchikov persisted, riding up to him.

'No.'

'There's a lieutenant-colonel wants to come with us. He knows the road like the back of his hand. I could lead you to Tiflis with my eyes closed, he says. Let's go, Grisha! And from there to the Turks, eh? We've got to get away somehow! This is the end, and you're like a sleepy fish.'

'No, I won't go with you,' Grigory took the reins from Prokhor, and climbed heavily, like an old man, into the saddle. 'I won't go. It's no use. And besides, it's a bit too late... Look!'

Ryabchikov glanced over his shoulder and with a furious gesture tore the sword-knot off his sabre. Lines of Red Army men were pouring down the hillsides. Machine-guns stuttered wildly near the cement works. The guns on an armoured train let off a volley at the advancing enemy. The first shell exploded by the Aslanidi Mill.

'Let's go back to our quarters, lads, follow me!' Grigory said more cheerfully, seeming to brace himself up.

But Ryabchikov seized Grigory's horse by the bridle and shouted in fright. 'No, don't go there. Let's surrender as we are here... It's better to face death in the open.'

'To hell with that, let's go! What death? What are you blathering about?' Grigory said something else in his annoyance, but his voice was drowned by a thunderous roar from the sea. Before quitting the shores of its Russian ally, the *Emperor of India*, had turned round and let loose a broadside from its twelve-inch guns. Covering the transports as they steamed out of the bay, it shelled the lines of the Red and Green forces that were approaching the outskirts, then transferred its fire to the top of the pass, where Red batteries had appeared. The British shells screamed over the heads of the Cossacks huddled on the wharves. Keeping a tight rein on his frightened horse, Bogatiryov shouted above the roar of the firing, 'Those British guns can bark! But what's the use of bashing the Reds now! It won't do any good. It's just a lot of noise.'

'Let them bash away. It's all the same to us now.'

With a smile Grigory gave his horse a flick of the reins and rode off down the street.

Six horsemen with drawn swords rounded a corner and came flying towards him at a mad gallop. The red ribbon on the chest of the leader showed up like a bleeding wound.

PART EIGHT

I

For two days a warm wind blew from the south. The last snow vanished from the fields. The foaming spring torrents played themselves out. At dawn on the third day the wind dropped and heavy mists gathered over the steppe; the clumps of last year's feather grass were silvered with moisture, and the barrows, the ravines, the villages, the spires of the bell-towers, and the soaring crowns of the poplars were all wrapped in an impenetrable whitish haze. A blissfully blue spring had come to the broad steppelands of the Don.

One misty morning Aksinya stepped out to the porch for the first time since her recovery and stood for a long time, intoxicated by the winy sweetness of the fresh spring air. Overcoming a slight nausea and dizziness, she walked to the well in the orchard, put down her pail and sat down on the wooden well frame.

The world seemed a different place, wondrously renewed and seductive. With shining eyes she looked around her excitedly, childishly arranging and rearranging the folds of her dress. The mist-enfolded distance, the apple-trees half submerged in thaw water, the damp fence and the road beyond with the deep washed-out ruts of the previous autumn—everything seemed to her unbelievably beautiful, everything bloomed in intense and gentle colours, as though illuminated by sunlight.

A patch of clear sky that showed through the mist

dazzled her with its cold blue sheen; the smell of rotted straw and thawing black-earth was so familiar and pleasing that she took a deep breath and a faint smile appeared on her lips; the artless song of a lark somewhere in the misty steppe awakened an unconscious sadness. So familiar, yet so far from home, it made her heart beat faster and forced two meagre tears from her eyes.

Thoughtlessly rejoicing in the life that had returned to her, she felt an enormous desire to touch everything with her hands, to look at everything. She wanted to fondle a damp-blackened currant bush, to press her cheek to an apple bough covered with dove-grey velvet fuzz, she wanted to step over a broken hurdle and roam across the muddy common to where, on the other side of a broad hollow, a lovely green field of winter wheat merged with the misty distance.

Aksinya waited for several days, expecting Grigory to appear, but then she learned from the neighbours who called on her host that the war was not over, that many Cossacks had sailed from Novorossiisk for the Crimea, and that those who had stayed behind had either joined the Red Army or been sent to the mines.

At the end of the week Aksinya made up her mind to return home and almost at once a travelling companion came along. One evening a little hunchbacked old man entered the cottage without knocking. He bowed silently and began to unbutton the muddy tattered British greatcoat that hung baggily on his bony frame.

'What's this, good sir? You don't even say good evening before you start making yourself at home?' the master of the house inquired, staring in astonishment at his uninvited guest.

The newcomer deftly discarded his greatcoat, shook it out on the threshold, hung it up carefully on a hook and, smoothing down his clipped grey beard, said with a smile, 'Forgive me, for the Lord's sake, dear sir, but it's these present times that have taught me first to take off my coat and then ask permission to stay the night, otherwise no one will let you in. People have grown hard these days, they don't welcome guests.'

'But where are we to put you? See how crowded we are?' the master said more agreeably.

'I need no more room than a pixy's nose. Just here by your doorstep I'll roll myself up and go to sleep.'

'Who are ye then, Grandad? A refugee?' the housewife wanted to know.

'Ay, that's it, a refugee, that's what I am. I was looking for a refuge and went all the way to the sea without finding one, and now I'm trotting quietly back again because I'm tired of looking,' the garrulous old fellow replied, squatting down by the threshold.

'But where are you from?' the master pursued the inquiry.

The old man took a pair of big tailor's scissors out of his pocket, waggled them in his hand, and with the same persistent smile on his lips said, 'Here it is, my certificate of rank. It's brought me all the way from Novorossiisk. But my place of birth is a long way from here, I'm from Vyoshenskaya. And that's where I'm going, after my dose of sea water.'

'And I'm from Vyoshenskaya too, Grandad,' Aksinya said, flushing with joy.

'You don't say so!' the old man exclaimed. 'There's a fine place to meet a fellow coutrywoman! Though in our times it's no great wonder. We're like the Jews nowadays, we've been scattered over the face of the earth. That's how it is on the Kuban now. If you throw a stick at a dog, you'll hit a Don Cossack. All over the place they are—more than you could count. And there's even more buried underground. I've seen plenty, good folk, in the course of this retreat. The misery people have suffered, it's beyond telling! The day before yesterday I was sitting in a station and next to me there was a noblewoman. Wearing spectacles she was, and through her spectacles she was searching her clothes for lice. Walking all over her they were. She picks them off with her fingers and screws up her face as if she'd bitten a crab apple. Then she starts squeezing that poor little louse and she frowns even more, till she's nearly frowned her face inside out, it's so horrible for her! But some folk are so hard they can kill a man without even wincing. I myself saw one such bravo cut down three Kalmyks. Then he wipes his sabre on his horse's mane, takes out a cigarette, lights it and rides up to me and asks, "What are you goggling at, old gaffer? Want me to cut your head off?" "God bless you, son," I says. "If you cut my head off, what shall I chew bread with?" So he laughed and rode away.'

'For some who've had plenty of practice it's easier to kill a man than to crush lice. Human life has cheapened since the revolution,' the master of the house said gravely.

'Only too true!' his guest agreed. 'Human beings are not cattle, they can get used to anything. Well, I asks this noble woman who she is. "By your dress," I says, "you don't look like a commoner." And she looks at me and washes her face in tears. "I'm the wife of Major-General Grechikhin," she says. There's a general for you, I thinks, there's a major, and as many lice as fleas on a mangy cat! And I says to her, "Your Excellency, if you go on crushing your—beg pardon—your creepy crawlies like that, you'll be busy till Intercession. And you'll break all your fingernails. Why don't you settle 'em all at once!" "But how can I?" she asks. So I gives her a bit of advice. "Take off your clothes," I says, "spread 'em out on some firm ground and go at them with a bottle." And what do I see? Off goes my general's wife behind the water tower and there she is lamming into her petticoat with a green glass bottle, as if she's been doing it all her life! Well, I stood admiring her for a bit and I thinks to myself, "God's got a lot of everything. He's let loose the creepies on the noble folk too, let the lice suck their sweet blood as well. Why should they be drinking the working man's blood all the time... God—he's no fool! He knows his job. And sometimes he gets kinder to people and arranges things just right, so you couldn't think of anything better." '

Chattering away without stopping and seeing that his hosts were listening with great attention, the tailor hinted adroitly that he had a lot more interesting things to tell, but hunger was making him sleepy.

After supper, when he was making up his bed on the floor, he asked Aksinya, 'Do you mean to stay here much longer, neighbour?'

'I want to go home, Grandad.'

'Then come with me, it'll be more cheerful like together.'

Aksinya gladly agreed to his proposal and the next morning, after saying goodbye to their hosts, they walked out of the lonely little steppeland village of Novo-Mikhailovsky.

* * *

Twelve days later they arrived in Milyutinskaya and knocked at the door of a large, rich-looking house. The next morning Aksinya's companion told her he had decided to stay on for a week in the stanitsa to have a rest and give his blistered feet time to heal. He could walk no further. There was some tailoring to be done in the house where they had spent the night and the old man, tired of having no application for his skill, quickly perched himself by the window, took out his scissors and a pair of spectacles on a string, and began deftly unpicking a tattered garment.

When parting with Aksinya, the old man made the sign of the cross over her and unexpectedly shed a tear, but he quickly brushed it away and with his customary jocularity said, 'Need's no mother but it makes us care for one another... And now I'm sorry to see you go... Still, it can't be helped. Go on alone, girlie, your guide has gone lame on both feet at once, they must have fed him on barley somewhere... Still we've done a good march together, you and me, a bit too good for my three score and ten. If you have the chance, tell my old woman that her old lover-boy is safe and sound. Put him through the mill good and proper, they did, but he's still alive, making trousers for good folk while he walks, and before long he'll be turning up at home... And tell her this too: her stupid old fool has given up retreating and is now advancing homewards, he just can't wait to be lying up warm and cosy on the stove-bed.'

Aksinya spent a few more days on the road, but in Bokovskaya she got a lift to Tatarsky on a passing wagon. Late in the evening she reached home, entered the wide-open gate, glanced at the Melekhovs' house next door, and gasped for breath as a sudden spasm gripped her throat. In the empty, unlived-in kitchen she wept out all her pent-up tears, then went down to the Don for water, lit the stove, and sat down at the table with her hands in her lap. She became so lost in thought that she did not hear the creak of the door and raised her eyes only when Ilyinichna came in and said quietly, 'Hullo, neighbour dear! You've been gone a long time away in foreign lands...'

Aksinya gave her a startled look and rose to her feet.

'Why d'you stare at me like that and say nothing? Or have you brought bad news?' Ilyinichna came up slowly to the table, and sat down on the end of the bench, her eyes still searching Aksinya's face.

'No, what news could I have... I wasn't expecting you and you startled me so when you came in...' Aksinya replied confusedly.

'You're so thin, all skin and bones.'

'I've had typhus.'

'How about our Grigory? How's he?.. Where did you part with him? Is he alive?'

Aksinya told her briefly. Ilyinichna listened without a word, and finally she asked, 'When he left you, was he ill then?'

'No, he wasn't.'

'And you haven't heard anything since?'

'No.'

Ilyinichna sighed with relief.

'Well, thanks for your good news. But there's all kinds of talk going on about him in the village.'

'What are they saying?' Aksinya asked in a whisper.

'It's just talk... You can't listen to everyone. Only one of our men has come back—Ivan Beskhlebnov. He saw Grisha in Yekaterinodar and he says he was sick. I don't believe any of the others!'

'But what do they say, Granny?'

'We've heard tell of a Cossack from Singin who says that Grisha was cut down by the Reds in Novorossiisk. So I walked all the way to Singin— a mother's heart can't wait—and found that Cossack. He denied it. He didn't see it and hasn't heard of it, he says. And another rumour was that he'd been put in prison, and died there of typhus...'

Ilyinichna lowered her eyes and sat for a long time, staring at her knotted heavy hands. Her ageing face was calm, her lips sternly compressed, but suddenly a deep flush appeared in her dark cheeks and her eyelids quivered. She looked at Aksinya with dry, frenziedly burning eyes and said hoarsely, 'I don't believe it! It can't be that I've lost my last son. There's no cause for God to punish me so... I have only a little while left to live and I've known enough grief without that!.. Grisha's alive! My heart has no forebodings, so he must be alive, my dearest!'

Aksinya turned away without speaking.

There was a long silence in the kitchen, then the wind blew open the front door and they heard the muffled roar of the thaw water in the poplars on the other side of the Don and the anxious call of the wild geese on the flooded reaches.

Aksinya closed the door and leaned against the stove.

'Don't grieve for him, Granny,' she said quietly. 'How could any sickness take a man like him? He's as hard as iron. His kind don't die. He rode the whole way in such fierce frosts without any gloves on.'

'Did he mention the children?' Ilyinichna asked wearily.

'Yes, he spoke of you and of the children. Are they well?'

'Yes, what could happen to them! But our Pantelei Prokofievich died during the retreat. We're all alone now...'

Aksinya crossed herself, marvelling at the calmness with which the old woman had spoken of her husband's death.

Leaning on the table, Ilyinichna rose with an effort.

'I've been sitting too long, it's dark outside already.'

'Stay a while, Granny.'

'Dunyashka's all alone, I must go.' As she adjusted her kerchief, she surveyed the kitchen and frowned. 'The chimney's smoking. You ought to have let someone live here while you were gone. Well, goodbye to you!' And as she grasped the door handle, without looking round she said, 'When you're settled in, come and see us. Let us know if you hear anything about Grigory.'

From that day on the relationship between the Melekhovs and Aksinya changed abruptly. Anxiety for Grigory's life seemed to bring them together and make them kin. The next morning Dunyashka, seeing Aksinya in the yard, called to her, came up to the fence and putting her arm round Aksinya's thin shoulders, smiled with simple affection.

'How thin you've grown, Aksinya dear! You're nothing but skin and bones.'

'It's enough to make anyone thin,' Aksinya said smiling back, and not without some inward envy scanning the girl's rosy face, fresh with the bloom of a mature beauty.

'Did Mother come and see you yesterday?' Dunyashka asked, for some reason in a whisper.

'Yes.'

'I thought she would. Did she ask about Grisha?'

'Yes.'

'And she didn't cry?'

'No, she's a brave old soul.'

With a trustful look at Aksinya Dunyashka said, 'It'd have been better if she'd cried, she'd have felt easier... You know, Aksinya, she's got kind of funny this winter, she's not her old self any more. When she heard about Father, I thought her heart would break and I was terribly frightened, but she didn't even shed a tear. All she said was, "May his soul rest in peace, his sufferings are over, the poor dear..." And all day till evening she wouldn't say a word to anyone. I tried talking to her of this and that, but she would say nothing, just waved me aside. Oh, what a terrible day that was! And in the evening I saw to the animals and, when I came in, I said, "Mummy, what are we going to have for supper?" And then her heart let up and she spoke...' Dunyashka heaved a sigh and, looking thoughtfully over Aksinya's shoulder, asked, 'Is our Grigory dead? Are the rumours true?'

'I don't know, dear.'

Dunyashka gave Aksinya a searching glance and sighed even more deeply.

'Mother's just pining away for him! She never calls him anything but "my youngest". And she just can't believe he's not among the living. You know, Aksinya, if she finds out for sure that he's dead, she'll die herself of heartbreak. Her life's ebbing anyway. She's only got one thing to hang on to, and that's Grigory. She's even lost interest in her grandchildren, and she's no heart at all for work... Just think of it, in one year four of our family...'

Moved by compassion, Aksinya reached out over the fence, hugged Dunyashka, and kissed her firmly on the cheek.

'Get your mother busy with something, my dear, don't let her grieve too much.'

'But how can I?' Dunyashka wiped her eyes with the corner of her kerchief and asked, 'Come in and talk to her, it'll help her. There's no need for you to keep away from us!'

'I will come, I promise!'

'Tomorrow I'll have to go out to the fields with Anikei's wife. We want to sow a few acres of wheat. Are you going to sow anything?'

'A fine sower I'd make,' Aksinya smiled ruefully. 'I haven't got anything to sow with, and why should I? I don't need much while I'm alone, I'll get by without.'

'Heard anything of Stepan?'

'Nothing,' Aksinya replied indifferently, and to her own surprise said, 'I'm not missing him much.' The sudden disclosure made her flush and, hiding her confusion, she said hurriedly, 'Well, goodbye, dear, I'll be going indoors to clear up.'

Pretending not to have noticed Aksinya's confusion, Dunyashka said, 'Wait a bit, I wanted to ask you, won't you give us a hand with the work? The soil's drying out, I'm afraid we won't manage in time. There's only two men left in the whole village, and they're cripples.'

Aksinya agreed willingly and Dunyashka went indoors to make ready for the fields.

All day she was busy preparing for the fieldwork. With the help of Anikei's widow she sorted the seed, put the harrow right somehow, greased the wagon wheels, and adjusted the seeder. And in the evening she put some of the sifted wheat in her kerchief, took it to the cemetery and sprinkled it on the graves of Petro, Natalya and Darya, so that in the morning the birds should gather on that dear spot. In the simplicity of her heart she believed that their merry chirping would be heard by the dead and bring them joy.

* * *

Not until dawn did a hush fall upon the banks of the Don. The water in the flooded woodlands murmured softly as it lapped the pale-green trunks of the poplars and gently swayed the submerged tops of oak saplings and young aspens; in the flooded lakes the tassels of the bulrushes rustled as they bent with the current; on the wide reaches and in remote creeks, where the thaw water stood in a bewitched stillness, reflecting the glimmering light of the starry sky, the barnacle geese called faintly to one another, the teal whistled sleepily, and once in a while the voices of migrant swans spending the night on the open water resounded like silver trumpets. Sometimes a fish would splash as it pursued its prey in the broad expanse; wavelets spread wide across the gold-spangled water and the warning quacking of alarmed birds could be heard. Then once again the stillness would settle on Donside. But at dawn, as soon as the chalky spurs of the hills glowed pink, a ground wind sprang up. Dense and powerful, it blew against the current. Choppy waves rose on the Don, the woodland waters swirled turbulently, and the trees moaned as they swayed to and fro. The wind roared all day and died down only in the small hours. Such weather lasted for several days.

A lilac mist hung over the steppe. The soil was drying out, the grass had stopped growing and cracks had appeared in the ploughland. The soil was losing its moisture hour by hour, yet there was hardly a soul to be seen on the Tatarsky fields. Only a few decrepit old men were left in the village; the Cossacks who had returned from the retreat were sick and frostbitten and unfit for work, and only women and children were toiling in the fields. The wind drove the dust through the deserted village, banged the shutters, and plucked at the thatching on the barns. 'We'll go hungry this year,' the old folk said. 'No one but women to work the land and only one in three households are sowing. Soil without seed won't give you nothing.'

Just before sunset Aksinya drove the oxen down to the pond. It was her second day out in the fields. By the dyke, holding the reins of a saddled horse, stood the Obnizovs' ten-year-old boy. The horse was munching its lips, its grey, velvety muzzle was dripping, and the dismounted rider was amusing himself by throwing chunks of dry clay into the pond and watching the circles spread across the water.

'Where're you making for, Vanyatka?' Aksinya asked.

'Just brought some grub out for Mum.'

'What's been happening in the village?'

'Nothing much. Old Gerasim caught a whacking big carp last night in his net. And Fyodor Melnikov's back from the retreat.'

Standing on tiptoe, the boy bridled the horse, clutched a braid of its mane and with impish agility leapt into the saddle. He rode away from the pond at a sensible walking pace but, after going a little way, looked back at Aksinya and dashed off at such a gallop that the faded blue shirt swelled up like a bubble on his back.

While the oxen were drinking, Aksinya lay down on the dyke and soon made up her mind to return to the village. Melnikov was a serving Cossack and he ought to know something about Grigory's fate. She told Dunyashka of her intention as soon as she had driven the oxen back to the camp. 'I'll be back early tomorrow.'

'Something to attend to?'

'Yes.'

Aksinya returned the next morning. Dunyashka was harnessing the oxen. Aksinya approached, carelessly waving a switch, but her brows were drawn together in a frown, and there were sad lines at the corners of her lips.

'Fyodor Melnikov is back. I went to ask him about Grigory. He doesn't know anything,' she said briefly and, turning on her heel, walked off towards the seeder.

After the sowing, Aksinya set about putting the farm in order. She planted watermelons, smeared fresh clay on the walls of the house and whitewashed them, and did her best to rethatch the roof of the shed with what was left of the straw. Her days were full of toil, but anxiety for Grigory never left her for a minute. She thought only reluctantly of Stepan, and for some reason it seemed to her that he would not come back, but when any of the Cossacks returned to the village she would first ask, 'You didn't see my Stepan, did you?' and then, carefully and little by little, would try to find out something about Grigory. The whole village knew of their liaison and even the scandal-loving housewives had stopped gossiping about them, but Aksinya was ashamed to show her feelings and only occasionally, when some taciturn soldier failed to mention Grigory, would she ask, screwing up her eyes in embarrassment, 'You didn't happen to meet our neighbour, Grigory Panteleyevich, did you? His mother's real worried about him, she's pining away...'

None of the village Cossacks had seen either Grigory or Stepan since the Don Army's surrender in Novorossiisk. Only at the end of June did a friend of Stepan's from the village of Kolundayevsky call on Aksinya on his way home across the Don. 'Stepan sailed for the Crimea,' he told her, 'I'll say that for sure. I saw him going aboard the ship. The place was too crowded to get a word with him.' To her question about Grigory he replied evasively, 'I saw him on the wharf, he was still wearing his shoulder straps, but there was no sign of him later. A lot of officers were taken off to Moscow. Who knows where he is now?'

But a week later a wounded Prokhor Zykov turned up in the village. He had been transported from Millerovo on a requisitioned wagon. As soon as she heard of his arrival, Aksinya stopped milking, put the calf to the cow and, adjusting her kerchief as she went, hurried off, almost running, to the Zykovs'. 'Prokhor must know, he's bound to! But what if he says Grigory's dead? What then?' she thought on the way and slowed her pace, clasping her hand to her heart in fear of hearing the dread news.

Prokhor met her in his front room, smiling broadly and trying to hide the stump of his left arm behind his back.

'Hullo there, mess-mate! Glad to see you still alive! We thought you'd kicked the bucket in that little village. You were in a bad way... Well, how's a spot of typhus for making us even prettier, eh? Look at the way the White Poles have carved me up, drat their eyes!' Prokhor pointed to the knotted sleeve of his army tunic. 'When the wife saw it, off she goes into tears and crying, and I says to her, "Don't howl, you fool! Others get their head chopped off and don't make a fuss, but what's an arm! Nowadays they fit you out with wooden ones. It don't feel the cold and if you cut it, it won't bleed." The only pity is, my girl, that I haven't learnt to fix things proper with one hand. I just can't button my trousers! I came all the way from Kiev with my fly open. What a disgrace, eh! So you just mustn't mind if you happen to notice anything about me not quite in order... But come in now and sit down, be our guest. Let's have a talk before the wife comes back. I've sent her off for some liquor, the hussy. Her husband comes home with an arm missing and she's got nothing to welcome him with. You're all the same while your husbands are away, I know you sloppy creatures inside out, that I do!'

'But tell me...'

'I know, I'll tell you. He ordered me to bow like this.' Prokhor made a jesting bow, raised his head and twitched his eyebrows in astonishment. 'There now! What're you crying for, you silly woman? You women, you're all topsy-turvy. You cry if we're killed and you cry if we stay alive. Wipe your eyes, woman, what's all the blubbering about? I tell you he's safe and sound, and real fat in the face! In Novorossiisk we both joined Comrade Budyonny's Cavalry Army, the 14th Division. Our Grigory Panteleyevich took command of a squadron, and I, o'course, was with him and off we marched to Kiev. Oho, girl, we gave them White Poles a pasting! On the way there Grigory Panteleyevich says to me, "I've cut down Germans and tried my sword on all kinds of Austrians. Surely the Poles' skulls aren't any harder? I reckon it'll be easier hacking them than our own Russian ones, what d'ye think?" And he winks at me with a big grin. He's changed since he joined the Red Army, looks quite cheerful, and sleek as a gelding. But, o'course, we couldn't do without a little family quarrel... One day

I rides up to him and says joking like, "Time to call a halt, Your Honour—Comrade Melekhov!" And you should have seen his eyes flash! "Just you drop those jokes of yours, or you'll come to a bad end," he says. And that evening he called me over about something and the devil tempted me to Your Honour him again... Out comes his pistol! All white in the face he was and snarling like a wolf. And he's got a mouth full of teeth, not less than a hundred, I reckon. I ducked away under my horse's belly. But he nearly killed me. That's the kind of hobgoblin he is! Well, we got into the Ukraine and had a go at them Polish fellers. Some warriors they are! Stuffed up to the arse with pride, but they run fast enough when you push 'em.'

'Might he be coming home on leave...' Aksinya ventured.

'Not a hope!' Prokhor cut her short. 'He says he's going to serve till he's made up for his past sins. And he'll do it—you don't have to be clever to play a mug's game... At one place he led us in an attack. With my own eyes I saw him cut down four of their Uhlans. He's a left-hander by birth, the devil, so he can get at 'em from both sides... After the battle Budyonny himself shook hands with him in front of the troops and a message of thanks was handed out to the squadron and him. That's the kind of capers he's cutting out there, your Panteleyevich!'

Aksinya listened as if in a trance. She came to herself only at the Melekhovs' gate. In the porch Dunyashka was straining milk. Without raising her head, she asked, 'Have you come for the rennet? I promised to bring it over but I forgot.' But when she saw Aksinya's eyes wet with tears and shining with happiness, she understood everything without any words.

Pressing her burning face to Dunyashka's shoulder, Aksinya whispered, 'Alive and well... Sent his greetings... Go! Go and tell your mother!'

II

By summer about thirty of the Cossacks who had joined in the retreat returned to Tatarsky. Most of them were old men and reservists. Apart from the sick and wounded, there were no young or middle-aged Cossacks among them. Some were in the Red Army; the rest had been enlisted in Wrangel's regiments and were biding their time in the Crimea, preparing for a fresh march on the Don.

A good half of those who had retreated were to remain for ever in foreign lands. Some had died of typhus, others had fallen in the final battles on the Kuban, a few had lost their way and frozen to death in the steppes beyond Manych, two had been captured by the Red-Greens and had not been heard of since. Tatarsky had lost many of its Cossacks. The women passed their days in tense and anxious expectation, and every evening when they came out to take in their cows from the returning herd they would stand with their hands to their eyes, watching and waiting for a belated traveller to appear out of the lilac twilight haze on the highway.

When a tattered, lice-ridden, half-starved but long-awaited husband did appear, the house would be filled with joyful fuss and bustle. Water would be heated to wash the grime-blackened soldier, the children would vie with each other in attending on their father and anticipating his every wish, and the wife, beside herself with joy, would dart to and fro, now to lay the table, now to take some clean underclothes for her husband from the chest. But the underclothes, as luck would have it, would turn out to be unmended, and with her trembling hands she would be quite unable to thread a needle... At such happy moments even the watch-dog, which had recognised its master from afar and run at his heel all the way home, licking his hands, would be allowed to enter the house; the children would not get into trouble for breaking things or spilling milk, and any offence would pass unpunished. Before the master of the house had bathed and changed his clothes, the house would be full of women inquiring about their dear ones. They would hang timidly on every word the soldier uttered. And before long one of them was sure to go out into the yard with her hands pressed to her streaming eyes and stagger blindly down the lane, and in one of the houses a new widow would weep and wail, accompanied by the thin voices of her children. That was how Tatarsky lived in those days. The joy that entered one home brought unending, remorseless grief to another.

The next morning the master, clean shaven and looking years younger, rises at first light and inspects his house and farm, noting what has to be attended to at once. After breakfast he goes to it. Merrily the plane thrusts or the axe taps somewhere in a shed, in the cool, as if to tell everyone there is a man here with skilled hands, ready and eager for work. But a stunned silence hangs over the house and yard where the day before they learned of the death of the husband and father. The mother, exhausted by grief, now lies silent, surrounded by a huddle of orphaned children, grown older in one night.

On hearing of the return of one of the villagers, Ilyinichna would say, 'But when will our man come back! The others keep coming but there's not a word about ours.'

'They don't let the young Cossacks go, Mother! Can't you understand!' Dunyashka would retort vexedly.

'Don't let them go? What about Tikhon Gerasimov? He's a year younger than Grisha.'

'But he's wounded, Mother!'

'Wounded! Why, only yesterday I saw him at the forge, skipping around like a youngster. That's no wounded man for you!'

'He was wounded and now he's getting better.'

'Hasn't our boy been wounded enough? His whole body is covered in scars. Don't you think he needs time off to recover?'

Dunyashka would do all she could to persuade her mother there was no hope of Grigory's returning just now, but the old woman was not easily convinced.

'Be quiet, you fool!' she would command her daughter. 'I know as much as you do, and you're too young to teach your mother. I say he will come soon, so he will. Now be off with you, I won't waste any more breath on you!'

The old woman longed for her son's return and never missed a chance of mentioning him. If Mishatka ever disobeyed her, he could be sure of a warning, 'Just you wait, you little demon, I'll tell your father when he comes home and you'll catch it from him!' Whenever she saw a wagon go by with fresh ribs on its sides, she would sigh and say, 'You can see at once that their man's at home, but ours can't seem to take the homeward road...' Ilyinichna had never liked tobacco smoke and had always turned any smokers out of the kitchen, but of late she had changed in this respect too. 'Go and call Prokhor over,' she would often say to Dunyashka. 'Let him smoke a cigarette in here. This place stinks of the dead. When our Grisha comes home, that's when the house will smell again of a living Cossack...' Every day she would cook an extra helping of everything and after dinner she always put a pot of cabbage soup in the oven. And she would be very surprised when Dunyashka asked the reason, 'But what else d'you expect? Our soldier may be home today and he'll have a hot meal waiting for him. He won't want to wait while I warm things up. He'll be hungry, I'm sure...' One day, when she came in from the melon field, Dunyashka noticed a cap with a faded band and an old coat of Grigory's hanging from a nail in the kitchen. She glanced inquiringly at her mother and with a rather pitiful little smile Ilyinichna said, 'I got it out of the chest, Dunyashka. It cheers me up a bit when I come indoors... As if he's here himself...'

Eventually Dunyashka grew tired of listening to this endless talk of Grigory.

'Don't you ever get fed up with rambling on about the same thing all the time, Mother? You've got everyone down with it. The only thing we ever hear from you is Grisha this, Grisha that...'

'Fed up with talking about my own son? Have children yourself, then you'll know...' Ilyinichna replied quietly.

She took Grigory's cap and coat out of the kitchen and hung them in her own room and for a few days said nothing about her son. But not long before the mowing, Dunyashka was told, 'You get cross when I mention Grigory, but how'll we get along without him? Have you ever thought of that, stupid? It'll soon be mowing time and we haven't got anyone even to make a rake for us... We'll never manage by ourselves. A farm's no good without a master...'

Dunyashka let that pass. She knew perfectly well that her mother was not really much concerned about the problems of the farm, and that her warnings were no more than a pretext to talk about Grigory and relieve her feelings. She was missing her son more than ever and could not hide the fact. That evening she refused her supper and, when Dunyashka asked if she felt poorly, she received the reluctant reply, 'I'm getting old... My heart aches for Grisha... It aches so bad that there's no joy in life and it pains me to look upon the world.'

But it was not Grigory who came back to run the Melekhov farm... Before the mowing began, Mikhail Koshevoi turned up in the village. He spent the night with some distant relatives and the next morning paid a

677

visit to the Melekhovs. Ilyinichna was busy with the cooking when her visitor, after politely knocking at the door and receiving no answer, entered the kitchen, took off his shabby soldier's cap and smiled at Ilyinichna.

'Hullo there, Auntie Ilyinichna! You weren't expecting me, eh?'

'Hullo. What are you to me that I'd be expecting you? Second cousin to our doorpost?' Ilyinichna replied rudely, staring indignantly at Koshevoi's hated face.

Not in the least abashed by this reception, Koshevoi said, 'Come, that's no way to talk... We used to know each other.'

'And no more.'

'No more would be needed for me to pay you a call. I've not come to live with you.'

'I should think not,' Ilyinichna remarked and, ignoring the visitor, busied herself with the cooking.

Not to be put off, Koshevoi surveyed the kitchen and said, 'I just dropped in to find out how you're getting on... We haven't seen each other for more than a twelve-month.'

'We didn't miss you much,' Ilyinichna snapped, furiously clattering the pots on the stove.

Dunyashka was clearing up in the front room. At the sound of Mikhail's voice her face paled and she silently clasped her hands. She sank down on a bench and listened breathlessly to the conversation in the kitchen. At first a deep flush spread over her face, then her cheeks grew so pale that two white lines appeared at the sides of her high-bridged nose. She heard Mikhail stride firmly across the kitchen, heard the creak of a chair as he sat down on it, and the scrape of a match being struck. The smell of cigarette smoke floated into the front room.

'The old man's died, they say?'

'Yes, he has.'

'What about Grigory?'

Ilyinichna was a long time answering, then with obvious reluctance replied, 'He's serving with the Reds. He's pinned a star on his cap like the one you've got.'

'He ought to have done that long ago.'

'That's his business.'

More than ordinary concern sounded in Koshevoi's voice when he asked, 'How is Yevdokiya Panteleyevna?'

'She's tidying up. You're a precious early guest. Decent folk don't come visiting at this hour in the morning.'

'Can't help that. I wanted to come, so I came. What's the sense in picking a time.'

'Ah, Mikhail, you shouldn't anger me so...'

'What have I done to anger you, Auntie?'

'You know what!'

'Tell me?'

'The way you talk!'

Mikhail's sigh was too much for Dunyashka. She jumped up, straightened her skirt, and stepped into the kitchen. Mishka, sallow-faced and unbelievably thin, was sitting by the window, finishing his cigarette. At the sight of her his lacklustre eyes brightened and a faint flush appeared on his face. Rising hastily, he gave her a husky greeting.

'Hullo!' Dunyashka replied almost inaudibly.

'Go and fetch some water,' Ilyinichna ordered at once with a quick glance at her daughter.

Mikhail waited patiently for her return. Ilyinichna said nothing. Mikhail was also silent, then he stubbed out his cigarette and asked, 'What are you so fierce with me for, Auntie? Have I crossed you in some way?'

Ilyinichna swung round from the stove as though she had been stung.

'Aren't you ashamed to come here, you brazen creature?!' she said. 'You dare to ask me that?! You're a murderer...'

'Me? A murderer?'

'Indeed, you are! Who killed Petro? Wasn't it you?'

'Yes.'

'Well, then! Think what that means! And you come here ... and sit down as if...' Ilyinichna broke off choking, but quickly recovered her breath and went on, 'Am I his mother or what? How can you look me in the face?'

Mikhail paled noticeably. He had been expecting this. Stammering a little in his agitation, he said, 'Why shouldn't I? Suppose Petro had caught me, what would he have done? You think he'd have kissed me on the topknot? He'd have killed me the same. We didn't clash on those hills just to nursemaid each other! That's what war's about.'

'And our kinsman Grishaka? Killing a peaceable old man—is that war too?'

'Why not?' Mikhail said in surprise. 'Of course, it's war! I know these peaceable ones! A peaceable one like him sits at home holding up his trousers, but he does more harm than many a man in the fighting line... It was old men like Grandad Grishaka who set the Cossacks against us. They started this war! Who spread all that agitation against us? They did, these peaceable ones. And you call me a murderer... A fine murderer I'd make! There've been times when I couldn't even kill a lamb or a pig, and I know I couldn't kill one now. I can't lift my hand against an animal. When others do it, I stick my fingers in my ears and get away so as not to hear or see them.'

'But when it came to our kinsman, you could...'

'You've got that kinsman of yours on the brain!' Mikhail interrupted exasperatedly. 'We had as much good out of him as milk from a he-goat. But he did a lot of harm. I told him to get out of the house, but he wouldn't, so that was where he finished up. I've got a big grudge against old devils like him! I can't kill an animal, or mebbe only in anger, but as for such filth—excuse me for saying so—as your kinsman and others like him, I can kill as many as you like! My hand's firm enough when it comes to dealing with enemies that are not needed in this world!'

'It must be your firmness that's made you so skinny,' Ilyinichna said maliciously. 'Your conscience must be pricking you...'

'Not one bit!' Mikhail smiled good-naturedly. 'As if my conscience would prick me because of rubbish like that old stick. I've had malaria and it's knocked the stuffing out of me. Or else, Mum, I'd have...'

'I'm no mum of yours!' Ilyinichna blazed. 'Call a bitch your mother!'

'Don't you bitch me!' Mikhail said in a low voice, and narrowed his eyes ominously. 'No one's paying me to take everything you throw at me. I'm talking sense to you, woman. Don't bear me a grudge for Petro. He got what he was asking for.'

'You're a murderer! A murderer! Get out of here, I can't bear the sight of you!' Ilyinichna persisted stubbornly.

Mikhail lighted another cigarette and asked calmly, 'What about Mitka Korshunov—another kinsman of yours—isn't he a murderer? And Grigory? You don't say anything about your own son, but he's a murderer all right!'

'Don't tell lies!'

'I stopped telling lies yesterday. What is he then in your view? D'you know how many of our men he's killed? That's just it! If you're going to give that name to everyone who's been in the war, then we're all murderers. The thing is what the killing's for, and who you kill,' Mikhail concluded significantly.

Ilyinichna let that pass but, seeing that her guest had no intention of leaving, she said severely, 'That'll do! I've no time for talking to you, you'd better go home.'

'A fine home I've got,' Mikhail smiled wrily, and stood up.

No, not for anything would he be put off by such talk! He was not so thin-skinned as to pay attention to an angry old woman's insults. He knew Dunyashka loved him and nothing else mattered, including this old woman.

The next day he called again, said good morning as if nothing had happened, and sat down by the window, following Dunyashka's every movement with his eyes.

'You're here a lot,' Ilyinichna snapped without replying to Mikhail's greeting.

Dunyashka blushed scarlet, flashed a glance at her mother and dropped her eyes without saying a word. With a smirk Mishka replied, 'I don't come to see you, Auntie Ilyinichna, you needn't fly at me.'

'It'd be better if you forgot the way to our house altogether.'

'Where am I to go then?' Mikhail asked more seriously. 'Thanks to your kinsman Mitka, I'm on my own now, I can't sit all the time in an empty house, like a lone wolf in its den. I'll be visiting you, whether you like it or not, Auntie,' he concluded and seated himself more comfortably, planting his legs wide apart.

Ilyinichna eyed him closely. It wouldn't be easy to turn him out of the house. There was an ox-like stubbornness in Mishka's thick-set figure, in the tilt of his head, and the firmly compressed lips.

After he had gone, Ilyinichna sent the children out into the yard and said to her daughter, 'He's not to set foot in this house again. D'you hear?'

Dunyashka looked at her mother unblinkingly, and something of the Melekhov nature flashed in her frenziedly narrowed eyes as she said, as though biting off every word, 'No! He will come! You won't forbid him! He will come!' Overcome by her feelings, she buried her face in her apron and ran out into the porch.

Ilyinichna sank down by the window, breathing heavily, and sat there for a long time, shaking her head and staring with unseeing eyes far away into the steppe, where a silvery sunlit fringe of young wormwood divided earth and sky.

That evening Dunyashka and her mother, unreconciled and not speaking, were busy mending a fence that had fallen down on the vegatable patch by the Don. Mikhail came up, took the spade that Dunyashka was holding, and said, 'You don't dig deep enough. Your fence will be down again as soon as there's a puff of wind.' He set about deepening the holes for the posts, then helped them to lift the hurdles, fixed them to the posts, and walked away. The next morning he came to the house with two new handles, for a rake and a fork, and propped them against the Melekhovs' porch; after greeting Ilyinichna, he asked in a businesslike manner, 'D'you reckon to mow in the meadow? Other folk have crossed the Don already.'

Ilyinichna said nothing, and Dunyashka answered for her mother.

'We haven't got anything to get across on. The boat's been lying in the shed since autumn, it's all dried out.'

'You should've floated it in spring,' Mikhail reproached her. 'Mebbe I'll caulk it? You'll be in a bad way without a boat.'

Dunyashka looked submissively and expectantly at her mother. Ilyinichna went on kneading her dough in silence, as if the conversation had nothing to do with her.

'Got any hemp?' Mikhail asked, smiling faintly.

Dunyashka went to the storeroom and brought back an armful of hemp.

By dinner-time Mikhail finished caulking the boat and came round to the kitchen.

'Well, the boat's in the water, let it soak. You'd better chain it to a stump or someone may nick it.' And again he asked, 'Well, Auntie, how about the mowing? Mebbe I could help you. I'm at a loose end right now.'

'Ask her.' Ilyinichna nodded at Dunyashka.

'I'm asking the mistress.'

'Looks as if I'm not the mistress any more.'

Dunyashka burst into tears and went out into the front room.

'Then I'll have to lend you a hand,' Mikhail proclaimed decisively. 'Where d'you keep your tools? I want to make a rake for you. Your old one's no good, I reckon.'

He went off to the shed and, whistling to himself, started shaping teeth for a rake. Little Mishatka hung about round him, looking up imploringly into his eyes and begged, 'Uncle Misha, make me a little rake 'cos I haven't got anyone to make me one. Granny can't and Auntie can't... You're the only one who can and you're good at making them!'

'All right, laddie, I'll make you one, but stand back a bit or you might get a chip of wood in your eye,' Mikhail urged him, laughing and thinking to himself, 'How like his father he is... A real chip of the old block! Eyes and brows, the same way of lifting his upper lip... Fine job of work!'

He started making a child's rake, but before he could finish it, his lips turned blue and a bitter but resigned expression appeared on his yellow face. He stopped whistling, put down his knife and gave a shiver.

'Now then, Mishatka, bring me a bit of sackcloth or something and I'll lie down,' he said.

'What for?' Mishatka wanted to know.

'I'm going to be ill.'

'But why?'

'What a sticker you are, eh? A regular pest... It's time for me to be ill, that's all! Hurry up!'

'What about my rake?'

'I'll finish it later.'

Mikhail began to shake all over. With his teeth chattering he lay down on the sacking Mishatka had brought, took off his cap and covered his face with it.

'Are you ill already?' Mishatka asked disappointedly.

'Good and proper.'

'Why are you shaking?'

'It's the fever.'

'Why are your teeth chattering like that?'

Mikhail looked out from under his cap with one eye at his persistent little namesake, smiled briefly, and stopped answering his questions. Mishatka gave him a scared look and ran off to the house.

'Granny! Uncle Misha is lying in the shed and he's shaking all over something terrible!'

Ilyinichna looked out of the window, went back to the table and stood there for a long time in silence, thinking.

'Why don't you say something, Granny?' Mishatka asked impatiently, tugging at her sleeve.

Ilyinichna turned to him and said firmly, 'Get a blanket, dear, and take it out to him, the godless creature. Let him cover himself with that. It's the fever that's shaking him, a kind of illness. Can you carry a blanket?' She went to the window again, looked out and said hurriedly, 'Stop! Don't take it, it's not needed.'

Dunyashka was covering Koshevoi with her sheepskin coat and bending over to say something to him.

After the attack Mikhail went on with his preparations for the mowing and worked until dusk. He was noticeably weaker. His movements had become sluggish and unsure, but he managed to make the rake for Mishatka.

In the evening Ilyinichna made the supper, sat the children down at table and, without looking at Dunyashka, said, 'Go and call in that ... fellow of yours ... for supper.'

Mikhail sat down at the table without crossing himself, his shoulders hunched wearily. His sallow face with its grimy traces of dried sweat showed his exhaustion, his hand trembled when he lifted his spoon. He ate only a little and without appetite, occasionally looking up indifferently at the family. But to her own surprise Ilyinichna noticed that the 'murderer's' lacklustre eyes burned with fresh life when they rested on little Mishatka, sparks of delight and affection flared in them for a moment and died away, and a barely perceptible smile lingered at the corners of his mouth. Then he would shift his glance and a stolid indifference would again take possession of his face.

Ilyinichna started watching Koshevoi furtively and only then did she notice how terribly thin he had grown during his illness. Under his dusty grey tunic, the collar bones stood out like arches, the broad shoulders were sharp and angular, and the Adam's apple with its stubble of gingerish hair protruded strangely from the boyishly thin neck... The longer Ilyinichna examined the 'murderers' bowed figure and waxen face, the more uncomfortable and inwardly divided she felt. And all at once an unbidden pity for this man whom she hated—that overpowering maternal pity that subdues even the strongest women—awakened in Ilyinichna's heart. Unable to resist this new feeling, she pushed a plate full of milk towards Mikhail and said, 'Eat a bit more, for God's sake, do! You're so thin it makes me sick to look at you... A fine suitor you make!'

III

The word got around in the village about Koshevoi and Dunyashka. A woman who happened to meet Dunyashka by the pier asked sneeringly, 'Have you hired Mikhail as a farmhand? He always seems to be at your place.'

Despite all her daughter's pleadings Ilyinichna remained adamant, 'No, and you needn't ask. I won't let you marry him! You shan't have my blessing!' And only when Dunyashka declared that she would go and live with Koshevoi, and started packing her things there and then, did Ilyinichna change her mind.

'Come to your senses, girl!' she exclaimed in fright. 'What will I do here with the children all alone? What'll become of us?'

'That's up to you, Mother, but I'm not going to be the laughing-stock of the village,' Dunyashka said quietly, and went on tossing her dowry out of the chest.

Ilyinichna could only move her lips soundlessly, then she walked heavily to the ikon corner.

'Well, daughter,' she whispered, taking down an ikon. 'If that's what you've decided, come here and God bless you.'

Dunyashka promptly dropped to her knees, Ilyinichna blessed her and said with a quiver in her voice, 'My mother blessed me with this ikon... What if your father saw you now... Don't you remember what he said about your chosen one? God be my witness, but it makes me sad...' And without another word she turned and went out into the porch.

Mikhail argued and pleaded with his bride to dispense with the wedding ceremony, but the obstinate young woman got her way. Mikhail had to swallow his objections and agree. Inwardly cursing the world and all things in it, he preapared for his wedding as if he were going to the scaffold. That night Father Vissarion quietly joined them in holy matrimony in an empty church. After the ceremony he congratulated the young couple, and said didactically, 'So there you are, young Soviet comrade, that's how it is in life. Last year you burnt down my house with your own hands, committed it to the flames, so to speak, and today I have to marry you. Don't spit in the well, they say, because you may need to drink from it one day. But all the same I'm glad, sincerely glad, that you have come to your senses and found the road to Christ's church.'

That was too much for Mikhail. Burning with shame and reproaching himself for his weakness, he had held his peace in church, but at this he gave the unforgiving priest a sidelong glance and in a whisper, so that Dunyashka should not hear, replied, 'It's a pity you ran away from the village at the time or I'd have burned the house down with you in it! Get me?'

Staggered by the unexpected reply, the priest stood blinking at Mikhail while the bridegroom tugged at his young wife's sleeve and with a stern 'Come on!' marched off to the door, stamping his army boots.

At this dreary wedding no one drank home-brewed vodka and no songs were bawled in tipsy voices. Prokhor Zykov, who had been best man, spent most of the next day complaining to Aksinya and spitting in disgust.

'Well, my girl, that was a fine wedding, that was! At church Mikhail said something to the reverend that made the old boy's jaw drop! And at supper what a spread they had? A fried chicken and sour milk... Couldn't they have put a drop of home-brew on the table, the devils! What if Grigory Panteleyevich had seen how they married off his sister!.. He'd have had a fit! No, my girl, I've had enough. No more of these new-fangled weddings for me! It's more fun at a dogs' wedding. At least the dogs make the fur fly and there's plenty of noise, but here there was nothing to drink and not even a fight. May they roast in hell, the measly lot! You won't believe it, but I was so upset after that wedding I didn't sleep all night. I lay there tossing and scratching as if someone had slipped a handful of fleas down my shirt.'

The farm's affairs took a new turn once Koshevoi had installed himself with the Melekhovs. In next to no time he mended the fence, carted the hay in from the steppe and stacked it on the threshing floor, topping the well-made stack with professional skill. In preparation for the harvest he renovated the sails and box of the reaper, carefully cleared up the barnyard, repaired the old winnower and put the horse harness in order because he was secretly hoping to barter a pair of oxen for a horse and had told Dunyashka more than once, 'We've got to get a horse. Driving these cloven-hoofed apostles is a pain in the neck.' In the storeroom he came across a pail of whitewash and some ultramarine and at once decided to paint the grey shutters. All of a sudden the Melekhovs' house looked years younger as it surveyed the world with bright-blue eyes.

Mishka turned out to be a keen farmer. Despite his illness, he put his back into the work. Dunyashka helped him in everything.

In the short spell that she had been married her looks had noticeably improved; she seemed to have filled out in the shoulders and hips. There was a new expression in her eyes, something new in her walk, and even in the way she patted her hair. All her former gawkiness had gone and, with it, her girlish way of doing everything in fits and starts. Smiling and content, she looked at her husband with loving eyes and saw nothing else that was going on around her. Young happiness is blind...

But every day Ilyinichna grew more painfully aware of the loneliness that was closing in on her. She had become unwanted in the house where she had lived nearly all her life. Dunyashka and her husband had set to work as if they were building their nest out of nothing. They never consulted her about anything or asked her consent when deciding household matters; they never even had an affectionate word for the old soul. Only when sitting at table would they pass a few meaningless remarks and when the meal was over Ilyinichna would again be left with her unhappy thoughts. She could take no joy in her daughter's happiness, and the presence of a stranger in the house—for such her son-in-law had remained—made her miserable. After losing so many of her loved ones in the space of a single year, she lived a broken life, aged and pitiful. She had suffered so much grief, perhaps too much. She no longer had the strength to bear it, and her heart was full of superstitious forebodings that death, which had so often visited the Melekhov family of late, would again cross their threshold, and more than once. Having reconciled herself to her daughter's marriage, Ilyinichna had only one desire, to live to see Grigory's return, to hand over the children to him, and then to close her eyes for ever. In the course of her long and difficult life surely she had endured enough to deserve repose.

The long summer days dragged on endlessly. The sun blazed down. But its stinging rays seemed to have lost their warmth. Ilyinichna would sit for hours on the steps of the porch, in the full heat of the day, motionless and indifferent to her surroundings. This was not the busy and zealous housewife of former days. She had no desire to do anything. It all seemed useless and not worth the trouble, and besides she was not strong enough to work as she had in the old days. Often she would stare at her hands, misshapen by years of toil, and say to herself, 'Yes, my old hands have done their job... Time they had a rest... I've lived long enough... If only I could see my Grisha again...'

Only once did the joy she used to take in life return. Prokhor came by on his way back from the stanitsa and, while still at a distance, shouted, 'Stand us a drink, Granny Ilyinichna! I've got a letter for you from your son!'

The old woman turned pale. In her eyes a letter could mean nothing but fresh misfortune. But when Prokhor read her the brief letter, half of which consisted of greetings to relatives, with only a postscript at the end to say that he, Grigory, would try to get some leave in autumn, Ilyinichna was speechless for joy. Small bead-like tears rolled down the deep furrows in her brown face. Head bowed, she wiped them with her sleeve and her rough hand, but still they flowed down her cheeks, falling on to her apron and spotting it like warm rain-drops. Prokhor had no liking for women's tears. In fact, he couldn't bear them. So, frowning with annoyance he said, 'What a mess you've made of yourself, Granny! How much wetness have you women got inside you! You ought to be jumping for joy, not crying. Well, I'm off, goodbye for now! It's no pleasure to look at you.'

Ilyinichna came to herself just in time and stopped him.

'For such a message, my dear boy... How could I now... Just a minute, I've got something here for you...' She mumbled rummaging in the chest for a bottle of home-brew that she had been keeping for many a long day.

Prokhor sat down and stroked his moustache.

'You'll have one with me to celebrate, won't you?' he asked. And at once the alarming thought crossed his mind, 'There I go again with my big mouth! I'll have to share with her, and there may be only a drop of liquor in that bottle.'

Ilyinichna refused. She folded the letter carefully and put it behind the ikon, then seemed to change her mind, took it down again, held it in both hands for a moment, then tucked it into her bosom, and pressed it firmly to her heart.

Dunyashka came in from the fields, read the letter several times, and sighed smilingly.

'Oh, if only he'd come soon! You're not yourself these days.'

Ilyinichna jealously took the letter away from her, tucked it into her bosom again and, smiling at her daughter with radiant, half-closed eyes, said, 'I'm what I am, no one bothers about me these days, but my youngest son, he's remembered his mother! The way he writes, eh! With such respect, not just Mother but Ilyinichna! My kindest regards to you, dear Mother, and to the dear children, he writes, and he didn't forget you either... What are you laughing at? You're a fool, Dunyashka, just a silly young fool!'

'Oh, Mother, mayn't I even smile! Where are you off to now?'

'I'm going to the vegetable garden, to hoe the potatoes.'

'I'll do it tomorrow myself. Why don't you stay at home? First you complain of being ill, and then you're off to work.'

'No, I'll go... I've had good news, I want to be alone for a bit,' Ilyinichna confessed, putting on her kerchief with a youthful sprightliness.

On the way to the vegetable patch she called on Aksinya, and for decency's sake began by talking about other things, then produced the letter.

'Our boy's sent a letter, given joy to his mother, and he's hoping to come home on leave. Here, good neighbour, read it and I'll listen to it again.'

From that day on Aksinya often had to read out the letter. Ilyinichna would come round in the evening, take the yellowed envelope out of the kerchief in which it was carefully wrapped, and ask with a sigh, 'Read it to me, Aksinya dear, I feel so down at heart today. In a dream I saw him as a little boy, just as he was when he was going to school...'

As time went by, the words scrawled in indelible pencil, grew blurred, and many of them became illegible, but Aksinya had read the letter so often that she knew it by heart. And even later on, when the thin paper was in tatters, she could recite the whole message down to the last line.

Two weeks later, when Dunyashka was busy with the threshing, Ilyinichna began to feel very ill. She did not want to interrupt her daughter's labours but the cooking was too much for her.

'I can't get up today. You'll have to manage by yourself,' she told her daughter.

'What's the trouble, Mummy?'

Ilyinichna straightened the frills of her old and faded

blouse and, without raising her eyes, replied, 'Everything... I feel as if something's broken inside me. When he was young, your late father, he'd get so angry and start beating me... And his fists were like lumps of iron... I'd be laid up for a week, more dead than alive. And that's how it feels now. Everything aches, as if I'd been beaten.'

'Should I send Mikhail for the doctor?'

'What do I need him for! I'll get over it somehow.'

The next day Ilyinichna did rise from her bed and took a little walk in the yard, but by evening she was in bed again. Her face was slightly swollen and there was a puffiness under her eyes. During the night she often raised herself with her arms from the high pillows and gasped for breath. Then the feeling of suffocation would pass and she was able to lie comfortably on her back and even get out of bed. For a few days she lived in a state of quiet resignation and peace. She wanted to be alone and, when Aksinya came in to see her, she answered her questions briefly and sighed with relief when she left. She was glad the children spent most of the day outdoors and that Dunyashka seldom came in to bother her with her questions. She no longer needed anyone's sympathy or comforting. The time had come when her great need was to be alone and remember many things in life. Her eyes half closed she would lie for hours, without movement, only her slightly swollen fingers toying with the folds of the blanket, and in those hours her whole life passed before her.

It was surprising how brief and poor that life now turned out to be and how much sorrow and pain there had been that she did not want to remember. For some reason her thoughts and memories turned most often to Grigory. Perhaps it was because her anxiety for him had been with her all these years since the outbreak of war and all her present ties with life were now bound up with him, and him alone. Or perhaps her anguish for her elder son and husband had been blunted by time, for she remembered them less and could see them only through a grey misty haze. She felt little inclination to recall her youth, her married life. It was all so unnecessary and so far away and brought her neither joy nor consolation. Returning to the past in these last memories, she remained stern and honest. But her 'youngest' came to her with an almost tangible clarity. And as soon as she remembered him, her heart beat faster. Then came suffocation, her face darkened and she would lie for a long time unconscious, but when her breathing was steady she would again think of him. How could she forget her last son...

One day Ilyinichna was lying in the front room. The noonday sun was shining brightly outside. Majestic white clouds were billowing across the dazzling blue of the southern horizon. The deep silence was broken only by the monotonous, soporific buzzing of the grasshoppers. Just under the window a few clumps of half-withered goosefoot mixed with foxtail and quitch that had not yet been burnt up by the sun still clung to the foundations and this was where the grasshoppers had found their refuge and were pouring out their song. Ilyinichna listened to their ceaseless trilling, sensed the barely perceptible smell of sun-warmed grass in the room, and for a moment she had a vision of the sun-scorched August steppe, a field of golden wheat stubble, and a burning blue sky wrapped in a dove-grey haze.

She clearly perceived the oxen grazing on a wormwood-covered bank, the wagon with a tarpaulin spread over it, heard the piercing chatter of the grasshoppers, and breathed in the bitter-sweet scent of the wormwood. And she also saw herself—young, tall and beautiful... She was walking, hurrying towards a field camp. The stubble was rustling under her feet, pricking her bare calves, the hot wind was drying the sweat-soaked back of the blouse that she was wearing tucked into her skirt and burning her neck. Her face was glowing, the blood singing in her ears. She had crooked her arm to steady her heavy, taut, milk-filled breasts and, at the sound of a baby's choking little cries, she quickened her pace and unbuttoned her blouse as she walked.

Her weathered lips trembled and smiled as she picked the little brown baby out of the cradle hanging from the wagon. Holding in her teeth the damp string of the crucifix, she hurriedly gave him her breast and through clenched teeth whispered, 'Hungry are you, little son, my dear little boy? Ooh, aren't you handsome! Has your mummy been starving you?' And little Grisha, still whimpering offendedly, sucked the nipple, biting it painfully with his tiny teeth. Near by stood Grisha's father, young and with a thick black moustache, honing his scythe. From under her lowered lashes she could see his smile and the bluish whites of his slightly mocking eyes. The heat grew intolerable, the sweat rolled down

23*

her forehead and tickled her cheeks, she could hardly breathe, and gradually the vision faded.

She opened her eyes, passed her hand over her face, which was wet with tears, then lay for a long time, tortured by attacks of breathlessness and sometimes fainting.

In the evening, when Dunyashka and her husband had gone to sleep, she summoned up her last strength, rose from her bed and went out into the yard. Aksinya, who had been out late looking for a cow that had broken away from the herd, noticed her as she was walking home. Slowly Ilyinichna made her way to the threshing floor. 'Why has she gone there if she's ill?' Aksinya wondered and, cautiously approaching the fence between the two yards, looked over it into her neighbour's barnyard. The moon was full, and a gusty wind was blowing from the steppe. A dense shadow from a rick of straw stretched across the hard-packed earth of the threshing floor. Ilyinichna was holding on to the fence with both hands and looking out into the steppe, where a mowers' campfire was glittering faintly like a distant star. Her puffy face was illumined by the blue moonlight, and a grey lock of hair had slipped from under her black shawl.

Ilyinichna stood gazing into the shadowy blueness of the steppe, then quite softly, as though he were just beside her, called, 'Grisha dear! My dearest!' She was silent for a while, then in a different, low and choking voice she said, 'Blood of my heart!'

Overcome by an inexplicable feeling of anguish and fear, Aksinya shuddered violently and, drawing back quickly from the fence, hurried indoors.

That night Ilyinichna realised that she would soon die, that death was at her bedside. At dawn she took one of Grigory's shirts out of the chest, folded it and placed it under her pillow; she also prepared the clothes that she was to be dressed in after she had breathed her last.

In the morning, Dunyashka came in as usual to see her mother. Ilyinichna took Grigory's neatly folded shirt from under her pillow and silently held it out to her daughter.

'What is it?' Dunyashka asked in surprise.

'Grisha's shirt... Give it to your husband, let him wear it. He'll have sweated his old one to bits by now...' Ilyinichna replied, almost inaudibly.

Dunyashka looked at the chest and saw a black skirt

and blouse and a pair of slippers—all the things that accompany the dead on their last journey—and her face paled.

'Mummy dear, what's all this black for? Put them away, do, for the Lord's sake! God bless you, it's too early for you to think about dying yet.'

'No, my time is near,' Ilyinichna whispered. 'It's my turn now... Look after the children, watch over them till Grisha comes home... I won't live to see him... Not now I won't!'

To hide her tears Ilyinichna turned away to the wall and covered her face with her kerchief.

Three days later she died. Some village women of her age washed her body, dressed her for burial and laid her out on the table in the front room. In the evening Aksinya came to pay her last respects. Only with difficulty did she recognise in the little dead woman's austerely tranquil face the features of the former proud and courageous Ilyinichna. As she pressed her lips to the cold yellow forehead, Aksinya noticed that familiar grey lock of hair, which had now slipped out from under a white kerchief, and the small round ear, just like a girl's.

Dunyashka let Aksinya take the children home with her. Both of them were very quiet and frightened by this new death. She fed them and took them to bed with her. It was a strange experience for her to be hugging the two little children of the man she loved, who now nestled quietly, one on either side of her. To take their minds off their dead grandmother, she told them some of the fairy-tales she remembered from her own childhood. In a soft, crooning voice she came to the end of the tale about the poor orphan Vanyushka:

> *Geese and swans,*
> *Lift me up*
> *On your white wings.*
> *Carry me away*
> *To my own,*
> *My native land...*

And before she could finish the tale she heard the sound of the children's steady, even breathing. Mishatka was lying on the edge of the bed with his cheek pressed to her shoulder. Aksinya moved her shoulder carefully, easing his head into a more comfortable position, and suddenly she felt such relentless, burning anguish in her heart that a spasm seized her throat. She wept bitterly, shaking with the sobs that coursed through her body, but she could not even wipe away her tears! Grigory's children were sleeping in her arms and she didn't want to wake them.

IV

It might have been expected that after Ilyinichna's death Koshevoi, now the sole and undisputed master of the house, would set about rebuilding the farm with even greater zeal, but no such thing happened. Every day Mikhail showed less enthusiasm for work. He would take himself off for days on end, and in the evenings sit on the porch until late, smoking and pondering certain thoughts of his own. Dunyashka quickly noticed the change in her husband. She was often astonished to see Mikhail, who had previously worked with such zest, suddenly abandon his axe or plane and sit down to rest in a corner. It was the same in the fields, when they were sowing the winter rye; Mikhail would go up and down the field once or twice, then stop the oxen, make himself a cigarette and slump down on the ground, smoking and frowning.

Dunyashka, who had inherited her father's practical bent, thought anxiously to herself, 'He hasn't lasted long... Either he's sick or he's lazy. I'll soon be in trouble with a husband like him! Anyone would think he was working for strangers. Half the day smoking, the other half lolling about, and no time at all for work... I'll have to put a word in his ear, gentle like, so as not to make him cross. If he goes on like this we'll be up to our necks in poverty.'

One day she asked cautiously, 'What's come over you, Misha? Or are you ailing again?'

'Ailing! I'm fed up!' Mikhail replied irritably and, whipping up the oxen, marched off after the seeder.

Dunyashka thought she had better not ask any more questions; after all, it was not for a woman to teach her husband. The discussion went no further.

But Dunyashka was mistaken in her conjectures. The only impediment to Mikhail's zeal was his growing conviction that he had settled down too early. 'I've been in too much of a hurry to take up farming,' he thought regretfully, as he read reports from the fronts in the local paper or listened of an evening to the tales of Cossacks

694

demobilised from the Red Army. But the thing that worried him most was the mood of the villagers. Some of them openly declared that winter would see the collapse of Soviet power, that Wrangel had marched from the Crimea, joined forced with Makhno and was approaching Rostov, and that the Allies had landed a huge expeditionary force in Novorossiisk. Rumours spread through the village, one more absurd than the next. The Cossacks who had returned from concentration camps and mines got their strength back on home provender during the summer and remained aloof, drinking heavily at night and talking things over among themselves. If they happened to meet Koshevoi, they would ask with a show of indifference, 'You read the newspapers, Koshevoi. Tell us now, will they soon put an end to Wrangel? Are the Allies out to give us another pasting? It isn't true, is it? Just a pack of lies, eh?'

One Sunday evening Prokhor Zykov came round. Mishka had just returned from the fields and was washing himself by the porch. Dunyashka was pouring water on to his hands and looking with a smile at her husband's thin sunburnt neck. Prokhor greeted them and sat down on the bottom step of the porch.

'Have you heard anything about Grigory Panteleyevich?'

'No,' Dunyashka replied. 'He doesn't write.'

'Are you missing him then?' Mikhail wiped his face and looked unsmilingly into Prokhor's eyes.

Prokhor sighed and adjusted his empty shirt sleeve. 'Of course, I am. We did all our army service together.'

'And you're reckoning to carry on again?'

'Carry on what?'

'Your war service.'

'We've done our bit.'

'And I was thinking you couldn't wait to get back on active service,' Mikhail went on, still without a smile. 'To fight the Soviets again.'

'There's no need to talk like that, Mikhail,' Prokhor said offendedly.

'Why not? I've heard some of the talk that's going on in the village.'

'You heard me say such a thing? Where?'

'Not you, but others like you and Grigory, who are waiting for their lot to come back.'

'I'm not waiting for any lot. The way I see it, we're all alike.'

'That's just the trouble. That you think we're all alike. Come indoors. Don't get your back up, I was only joking.'

Prokhor mounted the steps reluctantly and, as he entered the porch he said, 'Your jokes aren't very funny, chum... It's time to forget the past. I've made up for mine.'

'Not all the past can be forgotten,' Mikhail said drily, sitting down at the table. 'Sit down and have supper with us.'

'Thanks. No, you can't forget everything, of course. Take me, I lost an arm. I'd be only too glad to forget that, but it won't let me. It keeps on reminding me.'

As she laid the table, Dunyashka asked, without looking at her husband, 'Are all the men who were with the Whites never to be forgiven then? Is that how you look at it?'

'What did you think?'

'I always thought that he shall be blinded who remembereth old wrongs.'

'Well, mebbe, that's what the Gospel says,' Mikhail responded coldly. 'But if you ask me, a man must always answer for what he's done.'

'The authorities don't say anything about that,' Dunyashka replied quielty.

She was reluctant to argue with her husband in front of a stranger but she felt inwardly offended with Mikhail for what seemed to her his tactless joke against Prokhor and for the hostility towards her brother that he openly displayed.

'The authorities don't say anything to you because it's none of your business, but the ones who served with the Whites will have to answer under Soviet law.'

'So I'll have to answer too, will I?' Prokhor asked.

'You're small fry; you needn't worry. Orderlies don't count. But when Grigory comes home, he'll have to answer. We'll want to know about his part in the uprising.'

'Who will? You?' Dunyashka's eyes flashed as she put down a bowl of milk on the table.

'I for one,' Mikhail replied calmly.

'It's nothing to do with you... There'll be plenty of others pointing their fingers at him without you. He's earned his pardon in the Red Army.'

Dunyashka's voice trembled. She sat down at the table, toying nervously with the hem of her apron. Seemingly unaware of his wife's feelings, Mikhail went on as calmly as before, 'I, for one, will be interested to know. And as for his pardon, that'll have to wait a bit... First we'll see if he's really earned it. He spilled a lot of our blood. We'll have to reckon up whose blood is worth more.'

It was the first moment of discord in their married life. There was a long awkward silence. Mikhail supped his milk and said nothing, occasionally wiping his lips with a towel. Prokhor smoked, watching Dunyashka out of the corner of his eye, then started talking about farming matters. He stayed for another half an hour or so and, before leaving, said, 'Kirill Gromov's back. Did you hear?'

'No. Where's he come from?'

'From the Reds. He was in the First Cavalry Army too.'

'And before that he'd been with General Mamontov?'

'That's right.'

'A great fighter he was,' Koshevoi said sarcastically.

'And how! Biggest looter of the lot. It came easy to him.'

'They say he didn't think twice about cutting down prisoners. Killed 'em for their boots. Just boots and nothing else.'

'That's what they say,' Prokhor confirmed.

'Must we forgive him too?' Mishka asked softly. 'God forgives his enemies and so must we, is that it?'

'Well, who can say... What can you do with him now?'

'I'd do something...' Koshevoi narrowed his eyes. 'I'd do so much to him that he'd croak! And that's what he'll get anyway. The Don Emergency Commission is in Vyoshenskaya, they'll take care of him.'

Prokhor smiled and said, 'Well, it's true that only the grave will straighten a hunchback. He came back from the Red Army with all kinds of loot too. His wife was bragging to mine about the fur coat he'd brought her, and all the dresses and other stuff. He was in Maslak's brigade and came home from there. I'll bet he's a deserter, he's got his weapons with him.'

'What weapons?' Mikhail inquired.

'What'd you think? A sawn-off carbine, a revolver, and something else besides maybe.'

'Has he been to the Soviet to register, d'you know?'

Prokhor gave a laugh and dismissed the idea with a wave of his hand.

'Wild horses wouldn't drag him there! The way I see it, he's on the run. Today or tomorrow he'll off and away. Ay, by the look of it Kirill does still want a fight, and you were blaming me. No, chum, I've done my fighting, I've had a bellyful and it's more than enough.'

Soon after Prokhor left, Mikhail went out into the yard. Dunyashka fed the children and was just about to go to bed when Mishka came in, carrying something wrapped in sackcloth.

'Where did you go rushing off to?' Dunyashka asked ungraciously.

'For something I've been keeping in my bottom drawer,' Mikhail replied with a good-natured smile.

He unwrapped a carefully packed rifle, a bulging bag of cartridges, a revolver, and two hand grenades, set it all out on a bench, then poured some kerosene into a saucer.

'Where does it come from?' Dunyashka indicated the weapons with a twitch of her eyebrow.

'It's mine, from the front.'

'Where've you been hiding it?'

'Wherever it was, I kept it safe.'

'What a one you are for hiding things! And didn't say a word about it. Not even to your own wife?'

Obviously trying to make up to his wife, Mikhail smiled tolerantly, and said, 'What good would it do you, Dunya? It's not a woman's business. Let this property of mine stay where it is, lass, it won't do us any harm.'

'But why did you bring it into the house? You keep talking about the law, you know everything... Won't the law make you answer for this?'

Mishka's face grew stern.

'You're just a fool, woman! If Kirill Gromov comes home with a gun, that means trouble for the Soviets. But any weapons I bring can do the government nothing but good. Can't you see that? Who could I have to answer to? God knows what you're talking about. Get into bed and go to sleep!'

He had drawn what seemed to him the only correct conclusion. If the White scum were coming back with weapons, he would have to watch out. He carefully cleaned the rifle and revolver, and the next morning, at daybreak, set out on foot for Vyoshenskaya.

As Dunyashka was putting some food into his field bag, she exclaimed bitterly and with some annoyance, 'You're not being straight with me! Can't you say if you're going away for long and what for? What kind of a life is it for me! He gets himself ready to go away and

698

won't say a word!.. Are you a husband or a lodger?'

'I'm going to Vyoshenskaya, to the Commission. What more can I tell you? When I come back, you'll know everything.'

Steadying his field bag with his hand, Mikhail walked down to the Don, got into the boat and rowed it swiftly over to the other side.

* * *

In Vyoshenskaya, the doctor who examined Mikhail told him briefly, 'You're not fit for service in the Red Army, comrade. Your malaria has taken it out of you. You'd better have some treatment or you'll be in trouble. The Red Army doesn't need men in your state.'

'Not needed after serving two years? Who do they need then?'

'We need healthy people. You'll be needed when you're fit again. Take this prescription and the chemist will give you some quinine.'

'So that's the way it is!' Koshevoi pulled his tunic on as if he were putting a collar on a restive horse, freed his head with some difficulty, buttoned his trousers when he was in the street and marched straight off to the office of the district Party Committee.

He returned to Tatarsky as chairman of the village Revolutionary Committee.

After a hasty greeting, he said to his wife, 'Now we'll see!'

'What are you on about now?' Dunyashka asked in surprise.

'The same thing.'

'But what?'

'I've been appointed chairman. Is that clear?'

Dunyashka clasped her hands in dismay. She was about to say something but Mikhail was not listening; he adjusted the folds of his faded field-service tunic, straightened the belt and strode off to the Soviet.

Since the previous winter the chairman of the Revolutionary Committee had been an old man named Mikheyev. Shortsighted and rather deaf, he found his duties too much for him, and great was his joy when he learned that Koshevoi was to take over.

'Here's the papers, laddie, here's the village seal, take 'em for the Lord's sake,' he said with unfeigned satisfaction, crossing himself and rubbing his hands. 'I'm in my seventies and I'd never held any post before till I got landed with this one in my old age... This is your young man's job, it's not for me! I'm hard o'hearing and hard o'seeing... It's time I was praying to God and they make me chairman.'

Mikhail glanced through the orders and instructions from the Vyoshenskaya Revolutionary Committee and asked, 'Where's the secretary?'

'Whad'ye say?'

'Hell! Where is the secretary, I said?'

'The secretary? He's out sowing rye. He don't show up here more than once a week, devil take him! All these messages and instructions that have got to be read, and you couldn't find him with bloodhounds. An important paper can lie here for days without being looked at. I'm not much of a man of letters, that I'm not! It's hard for me to sign my name and I can't read a word. All I can do is use the rubber stamp...'

With knitted brows Koshevoi inspected the shabby office of the Revolutionary Committee, which was graced by only one fly-blown poster.

The old man was so delighted by his unexpected release that he even ventured to make a jest. When he handed over to Koshevoi the office stamp, wrapped up in a piece of rag, he said, 'Here's all your office property, no funds or anything of that kind, and under Soviet power you're not supposed to have an ataman's staff of office. If you want one, I can lend ye this old stick o'mine.' And smiling toothlessly, he held out an ash walking-stick that much handling had given a good polish.

But Koshevoi was in no mood for jokes. Once again he surveyed the dingy room, frowned and said with a sigh, 'All right, Grandad, we'll consider you've handed over the office affairs to me. And now get to blazes out of here,' and he flashed his eyes expressively at the door.

Then he took his seat at the desk, planted his elbows wide apart and sat for a long time in solitude, gritting his teeth and sticking out his lower jaw. God, what a son-of-a-bitch he'd been all this time, grubbing in the dirt and never lifting his head to take any real notice of what was going on around. Furious with himself and everything in the vicinity, Mikhail rose from the desk, straightened his tunic and, staring into space, said aloud through clenched teeth, 'I'll show you what Soviet power means, my dovies!'

He closed the door firmly behind him and fastened it with a chain, then set off for home across the square. Near the church he met young Andrei Obnizov, gave him a casual nod and walked on, but second thoughts turned him round.

'Hi, Andrei! Wait! Come here a minute!'

The shy fair-haired lad came up to him without speaking. Mikhail offered him his hand as if he were an adult and asked, 'Where were you heading for? This way? Ah, so you're just out for a walk, eh? Or is it work? Now here's what I wanted to ask you. You went to higher elementary school, didn't you? You did? That's fine. Know anything about office work?'

'What kind?'

'The usual kind. Know anything about incomings and outgoings?'

'What are you talking about, Comrade Koshevoi?'

'Well, about the various papers that have to be dealt with. D'you know about that? There's some that are outgoing like, and others,' Mikhail waggled his fingers vaguely and, without waiting for a reply, said firmly, 'If you don't know, you'll soon learn. Right now I'm chairman of the village Revolutionary Committee and I'm appointing you, as a lad who knows his letters, to be secretary. So off you go to the Revolutionary Committee office and look after things there. They're all on the desk, and I'll be back soon. Get me?'

'But comrade Koshevoi!'

Mishka brushed the objection aside and said impatiently, 'We'll talk about that later. Go and take over.' And he went off down the street at a slow, steady pace.

At home he put on his newest trousers, pushed his revolver into his pocket and, having carefully adjusted his cap in front of the mirror, said to his wife, 'I've got to go off somewhere on business. If anyone wants to know where the chairman is, say he'll soon be back.'

The position of chairman carried certain obligations. Mikhail walked at a slow and dignified pace; this style of walking was so unusual for him that some of the villagers who met him stopped in their tracks and stood staring after him with smiles on their faces. Prokhor Zykov, who bumped into him in a side lane, backed away to the fence in mock respect and asked, 'Is it you, Mikhail? All dolled up in your best on a week-day and march-

701

ing along like you were on parade... You're not going to woo another bride, are ye?'

'Something like that,' Mikhail replied, compressing his lips significantly.

As he approached the gates of the Gromov farm, he groped in his pocket for his tobacco pouch and carefully scanned the big yard, its scattered outbuildings, and the windows of the house.

Kirill Gromov's mother had just come out on the porch.

Leaning back, she was carrying a large bowl of chopped pumpkins for feeding the animals. Koshevoi gave her a respectful greeting and walked up the steps.

'Is Kirill at home?'

'Ay, he's at home, you can go in,' the old woman said, making way for him.

Koshevoi entered the dark inner porch and groped for the door-handle. Kirill himself opened the door into the front room, and stepped back a pace. Clean-shaven, smiling and slightly tipsy, he gave a brief inquiring glance and said easily, 'Another soldier back from the wars! Come in, Koshevoi, sit down and make yourself at home. We're just having a drink or two.'

'Thanks for your hospitality and may the cup be sweet.' Koshevoi shook hands with his host, surveying the guests at the table.

His arrival was clearly untimely. A broad-shouldered Cossack he had never seen before, who was lounging in the corner under the ikons, shot a quick questioning glance at Kirill and moved his glass aside. Semyon Akhvatkin, a distant relative of the Korshunovs, frowned at the sight of the newcomer and deliberately looked away.

The host asked Mikhail to the table.

'Thanks for the invitation.'

'Come on, sit down. Don't give us the cold shoulder, have a drink.'

Mikhail sat down at the table. As he took the glass from his host, he nodded and said, 'Here's to your homecoming, Kirill Ivanovich!'

'Thanks. Have you been out of the army long?'

'Yes. I've had time to settle down.'

'Settled down and got married, they say?.. Heh, what's the idea? Why're you dodging? Come on, bottoms up!'

'I don't feel like it. There's something I want to talk to you about.'

702

'Oh, no! None of that! I'm not going to talk business today. Today I'm enjoying myself with my friends. If you want to talk business, come tomorrow.'

Koshevoi stood up and, smiling calmly, said, 'It's only a piddling little thing, but it can't wait. Let's go outside for a minute?'

Kirill stroked his carefully twisted black moustache and said nothing for a while, then he stood up.

'Mebbe you'll say it here? Why break up the party?'

'No, let's go outside,' Koshevoi said quietly but insistently.

'Go out and talk to him, what're you haggling for?' said the strange Cossack with the big shoulders.

Kirill reluctantly led the way into the kitchen. To his wife, who was busy at the stove, he whispered, 'Go outside, Katerina!' then sat down on a bench and asked curtly, 'What's your business?'

'How many days have you been at home?'

'Why?'

'How long have you been at home, I said.'

'This'll be the fourth, I reckon.'

'Have you been to the Revolutionary Committee?'

'No, not yet.'

'Will you be reporting to Vyoshenskaya, to the military commissariat?'

'What are you driving at? Talk business, if that's what you've come for.'

'That's what I am doing.'

'Then go to the devil! Who the hell d'you think you are? Why should I report to you what I do?'

'I'm the chairman of the Revolutionary Committee. Show me the warrant you got from your unit.'

'So that's it!' Kirill drawled, and his sharp, suddenly sober eyes drilled into Koshevoi's. 'So that's what you're up to!'

'Right. Show me you papers!'

'I'll come to the Soviet today and bring 'em.'

'I want to see them now.'

'I've put 'em away somewhere.'

'Find them.'

'Not now. Go home, Mikhail, keep out of trouble.'

'You won't give me much trouble.' Mikhail slipped his hand into his righthand pocket. 'Put on your coat!'

'Chuck it, Mikhail! You'd better keep off me.'

'Come on, I said.'

'Where to?'

'The Revolutionary Committee.'

'I don't feel like it somehow,' Kirill had turned pale but he spoke with a derisive smile.

Koshevoi side-stepped quickly to the left, pulled the revolver out of his pocket, and cocked it.

'Will you come or not?' he asked quietly.

Without answering, Kirill made for the front room, but Mikhail stood in the way and with his eyes indicated the door into the porch.

'Heh, boys!' Kirill called out in a deliberately casual tone. 'I've been kind of arrested! Drink up the vodka without me!'

The door of the front room swung open and Akhvatkin was about to step over the threshold, but at the sight of the revolver aimed at his chest, hastily drew back behind the doorpost.

'Get going,' Koshevoi ordered Kirill.

Kirill strolled swaggeringly to the door, pulled lazily at the handle and suddenly, in one bound, darted across the porch, slammed the front door madly behind him and sprang down from the steps. While he ran crouching across the yard to the orchard, Mikhail fired twice and missed. Resting the barrel of the revolver in the crook of his left arm and planting his feet wide apart, he aimed carefully. After the third shot Kirill seemed to stumble, but then recovered and leapt lightly over the fence. Mikhail ran down from the porch. From the house behind him a rifle went off with a dry, harsh crack. The bullet snicked a bit of clay out of the whitewashed wall of a shed in front of him and sang away, scattering splinters of stone on the ground.

Kirill was running with easy rapid strides. His crouching figure showed up intermittently between the green shapes of the apple-trees. Mikhail jumped over the fence, dropped down and fired twice from a lying position at the fleeing figure, then turned to look at the house. The front door was wide open. Kirill's mother was standing on the steps with her hand shading her eyes, looking at the orchard. 'I should've shot him on the spot, without any talk,' Mikhail thought dully. He lay for a few more minutes by the fence, watching the house and steadily, almost mechanically scraping the mud off his knees, then rose, climbed awkwardly over the fence and, lowering his revolver, made for home.

V

Akhvatkin and the strange Cossack Koshevoi had seen at the Gromovs' disappeared along with Kirill. That night two more Cossacks went into hiding. A small detachment from the Don Emergency Commission arrived in the village. A few Cossacks were arrested and four who had come back from their units without the necessary papers were sent to Vyoshenskaya to serve in a punishment company.

Koshevoi spent his days at the Revolutionary Committee, came home at dusk, placed a loaded rifle beside the bed and his revolver under the pillow and went to bed without undressing. On the second day after Gromov's escape he said to Dunyashka, 'Let's sleep in the porch.'

'Whatever for?' Dunyashka exclaimed.

'They might shoot through the window. The bed's by the window.'

Without a word Dunyashka shifted the bed into the porch, but in the evening she asked, 'Is this the kind of hole-and-corner life we're going to have from now on? Come winter, we'll still be sleeping in the porch?'

'Winter's a long way off yet, but we'll have to put up with it for the time being.'

'How long will that be?'

'Until I've got Kirill.'

'As if he'd give you the chance!'

'One day he will,' Mikhail said confidently.

But he was wrong. Kirill Gromov, who had gone into hiding with his friends somewhere on the other side of the Don, heard that Makhno was approaching the district, recrossed the Don and headed for Krasnokutskaya, where the advance detachments of Makhno's band were reported to be. Under cover of night he visited the village, happened to meet Prokhor Zykov in the street, and ordered him to tell Koshevoi that he sent his regards and could be expected as a guest. Prokhor told Mikhail in the morning.

'Let him come. He got away once but he won't give me the slip again. He's taught me how to treat him and his lot. I must thank him for that,' Mikhail said, when he had heard Prokhor's story.

Makhno did, in fact, appear in the Upper Don District. In a brief engagement near the village of Konkov he smashed an infantry battalion that had been sent to meet him from Vyoshenskaya, but instead of striking at the heart of the district he turned towards the station at Millerovo, crossed the railway to the north of it and withdrew towards Starobelsk. The most active White Guard Cossacks joined up with him, but the majority stayed at home, biding their time.

Koshevoi remained on his guard, keeping a careful eye on all that happened in the village. And life in Tatarsky was rather shabby these days. The Cossacks were heartily cursing the Soviet government for all the shortages they were experiencing. The little shop of the recently organised United Consumers' Co-operative had practically nothing on its shelves. All such necessaries as soap, sugar, salt, kerosene, matches, tobacco, and cart grease, were out of stock and the bare shelves were graced only by a few packets of expensive Asmolov cigarettes and bits of hardware that usually lay for months without being sold.

Instead of kerosene the villagers burned boiled butter and fat in their wick-lamps. Home-grown tobacco replaced the commercial brand. For lack of matches, wide use was made of flints and steel strikers hastily produced by the village blacksmiths. Tinder was boiled in a mixture of water and sunflower ash to make it more inflammable, but without practice it was still difficult to get a light. Quite often, when Mikhail was on his way home in the evening he would notice a bunch of smokers gathered in a side lane, all trying to strike a spark from their flints and spitting curses as they muttered, 'Come on, Soviet power, give us a light!' Eventually somebody's spark would fall on a bit of dry tinder and catch fire. Everyone would blow together on the smoky flame and, when they had got their fags going, they would squat down on their haunches and share the latest news. There was not enough paper for cigarettes. All the record books were stolen from the churchyard lodge and, when these had been used up, the home supplies of paper were ransacked, including even the children's exercise books and old men's holy texts.

Prokhor Zykov, who came round to the former Melekhov farm fairly often, begged some paper for smoking off Mikhail and said sorrowfully, 'The lid of the wife's chest was papered inside with old newspapers. I ripped 'em out and smoked 'em. We had a New Testament, a holy book like that, but I used that too. Then I smoked the Old Testament. But the saints didn't write enough of these testaments... The wife used to have a birthday book—all our relations were in it, dead or alive, but I smoked that too. What am I supposed to do now—smoke cabbage leaves or try making paper out of burdock? No, Mikhail, say what you like, but gimme a newspaper. I can't do without a smoke. On the German front I'd sometimes swap my bread ration for a handful of baccy.'

It was a dreary life in Tatarsky that autumn... The ungreased wheels of wagons and farm implements squeaked and squealed, leather harness and boots dried out and cracked without tar, but the worst misery of all was the lack of salt. The Tatarsky folk exchanged a well-fed sheep for five pounds of salt in Vyoshenskaya and drove home, cursing Soviet power and the general disruption. The shortage of salt gave Mikhail a lot of trouble... One day some of the village elders appeared at the Soviet. They greeted the chairman in a dignified manner, took off their caps, and sat down on the benches.

'There be no salt, m'lord chairman,' said one of them.

'We don't have lords any more,' Mikhail corrected him.

'Excuse me, I said it out of habit... We can live without lords, but not without salt.'

'Well, what were you wanting, Elders?'

'You're the chairman, it's your job to see to it that they bring us some salt. You can't expect us to cart it from Manych with oxen.'

'I've reported that to district headquarters. They know all about it. They ought to be bringing some soon.'

'We've heard that before,' said one of the old men, staring at his feet.

Mikhail flushed and stood up behind his desk. Purple with anger, he turned out his pockets.

'I haven't got any salt. Don't you see? I don't carry it about with me and I can't suck it out of my finger for you. Is that clear, Elders?'

'Where's it all got to, this salt?' Chumakov, a one-eyed old fellow, asked after a while, looking round in surprise with his solitary eye. 'Under the old government no one ever thought about it, there was heaps of the stuff everywhere, but now there's not a pinch to be found.'

'It's nothing to do with our government,' Mikhail said more calmly. 'There's only one government to blame, and that's your old Cadet government! It's caused such disruption everywhere that there's nothing to de-

707

liver salt with! All the railways are smashed up, trucks and all...'

Mikhail gave the old men a long account of how the Whites during their retreat had destroyed state property, blown up factories and set fire to warehouses. He had seen some of it himself during the war, he had heard some from other people, and the rest he invented with the sole aim of diverting the discontent from his own cherished Soviet government. To protect it from reproaches he lied and dodged without ill intent, thinking to himself, 'It won't do all that much harm if I slander those bastards a bit. They're bastards anyway, so they won't be any the worse for it, but it'll do us some good...'

'You think that these bourgeois are just stuffed dummies? Oh, no! They're a crafty lot! They carted away all the stocks of sugar and salt, thousands of poods of it, from all over Russia, and dumped it in the Crimea beforehand. And now they've loaded it on board ship and taken it away to other countries to sell it,' Mikhail proclaimed, eyes gleaming.

'You mean to say they've taken all the cart-grease as well?' Chumakov asked, blinking his one eye unbelievingly.

'What did you think, Grandad? They'd leave some for you? Why worry about you or any of the working folk? They'll find someone to sell that cart-grease to as well! They'd have taken everything, if they could, so that we'd all starve.'

'Ay, that's true,' one of the old men agreed. 'The rich are all greedy guts. The richer a man is, the greedier he gets. One of the merchants in Vyoshenskaya, when the first retreat started, put everything he'd got on his wagons, every little thing. The Reds were quite close but there he was in his fur coat running about the house pulling nails out of the walls with pincers. "I won't leave those devils a single nail," he says. So it's no wonder they've taken all the cart-grease away with 'em.'

In the end, another old fellow, Makeyev, asked good-naturedly, 'But what are we going to do without salt anyhow?'

'Our workers will soon mine some fresh salt, but in the meantime you send some wagons to Manych,' Mikhail advised cautiously.

'Folk don't want to go there. The Kalmyks are making trouble, they won't let us take salt from the lakes and they grab our oxen. A friend o' mine came back with nothing but his whip. During the night, near Veliko-knyazheskaya, three armed Kalmyks rode up to him, took his oxen, and pointed to his throat, "Keep quiet, Father," they says, "or you'll die a nasty death..." How can we go there!'

'Ay, we'll have to wait a bit,' Chumakov said with a sigh. Mikhail managed to pacify the old men, but at home, and again because of the salt, he had high words with Dunyashka. In general, something seemed to have gone awry in their relationship.

It had all begun on that memorable day when in Prokhor's presence he had brought up the subject of Grigory. That small disagreement had not been forgotten. One evening Mikhail said at supper, 'Your soup's not salted, missus. Or do you think too little is better than too much?'

'There'll never be too much with this government. D'you know how much salt we've got left?'

'How much?'

'Two handfuls.'

'That's bad,' Mikhail sighed.

'Sensible folk drove to Manych for salt in summer, but you never have time to think of such things,' Dunyashka said bitterly.

'What could I drive? I can't very well harness you up in the first year of marriage, and the bullocks aren't strong enough...'

'Save your jokes for another time! When you have to eat unsalted food, that'll be the time to joke!'

'What are you getting at me for? Where d'you want me to fetch your salt from? You, women... Give, give, give, even if I have to cough it up with my guts. What if there is no salt, God damn it?'

'Other people have been to Manych and back with bullocks. They'll have salt and all they need while we chew everything unsalted and sour.'

'We'll manage somehow, Dunyashka. It won't be long now before they bring us some salt. The country must have plenty of the stuff.'

'You've got plenty of everything.'

'Who d'you mean by "you"?'

'The Reds.'

'What are you then?'

'I'm what I am. And the way you bragged! "We'll have plenty of everything, we'll all live equal and rich." Here are your riches then—nothing to salt our soup with!'

Mikhail gave his wife a frightened look and turned pale.

'How can you, Dunyashka? What're you saying? Is that the way to talk?'

But Dunyashka had got the bit between her teeth; she too was pale with indignation and anger, and her voice rose to a shout.

'Ay, that's the way! What're you staring for? D'you know, my fine chairman, that people are getting swollen gums from not having salt? D'you know what people are eating instead of salt? They're taking earth from the salt marshes, they go out beyond Nechayev Mound for it and put that earth in their soup... Have you heard that?'

'Now steady on, don't shout. Yes, I've heard... What else?'

Dunyashka spread her arms.

'What else?!'

'We've got to put up with it somehow, haven't we?'

'Well, put up with it then!'

'I'll put up with it, but how about you... It's the Melekhov breed coming out in you.'

'What breed is that?'

'Counter-revolutionary, that's what!' Mikhail said huskily, and rose from the table. Not looking at his wife, he fixed his eyes on the floor, and his lips were quivering when he said, 'If you speak like that again, we won't be living together any more, remember that! That's enemy talk, that is...'

Dunyashka was going to retort, but Mishka's eyes flashed and he raised his clenched fist.

'Be quiet!...' he muttered.

Dunyashka looked at him without fear and with unconcealed curiosity. A little later she said calmly and cheerfully, 'Oh, all right then, why the devil did we have to start talking about it anyway... We'll get along without salt!' She was silent for a moment, then with the quiet smile that Mikhail loved so much she said, 'You mustn't take it to heart so, Misha! If you take everything we women say to heart, your heart won't last long. We can say all kinds of things when we're in a bad temper... Well, d'you want some stewed fruit or shall I get you some milk?'

Despite her youth Dunyashka had learned enough worldly wisdom to know when to persist in a quarrel and when to give in.

About a fortnight later a letter arrived from Grigory. He wrote that he had been wounded on the Wrangel front and that, when he recovered, he would probably be demobbed. Dunyashka told her husband and asked guardedly, 'He'll be coming home, Misha. How'll we manage then?'

'We'll move to my place. Let him live here alone. We'll share out the property.'

'We can't all be together. It looks as if he'll marry Aksinya.'

'Even if we could, I wouldn't live under the same roof as your brother,' Mikhail declared fiercely.

Dunyashka raised her brows in astonishment.

'Why not, Misha?'

'You know why not.'

'Because he served with the Whites?'

'Right.'

'You don't like him, do you... You used to be friends!'

'Why the hell should I like him! We used to be friends, but that friendship's over.'

Dunyashka was sitting at the spinning wheel and it was humming steadily. Suddenly the thread broke. She stopped the wheel with her hand and, as she joined the thread, asked without looking at her husband, 'When he comes back, what'll happen to him for serving with the Cossacks?'

'He'll be tried. The tribunal will try him.'

'What might they sentence him to?'

'That's not for me to know, I'm not a judge.'

'Might they sentence him to be shot?'

Mishka looked at the bed where Mishatka and Polyushka were sleeping and listened to their steady breathing. Lowering his voice, he said, 'They might.'

Dunyashka asked no more questions. In the morning, as soon as she had milked the cow, she went to see Aksinya.

'Grisha will soon be home. I thought you'd be glad to know.'

Aksinya put the pot of water she had been holding down on the stove and clasped her hands to her chest. Looking at her flushed face, Dunyashka said, 'Don't be too glad though. My man says he'll be put on trial. God knows what the sentence might be.'

A flash of fear showed in Aksinya's moist radiant eyes.

'For what?' she asked abruptly, though a belated smile still hovered on her lips.

711

'For the uprising, for everything.'

'Rubbish! They won't try him. Your Mikhail doesn't know what he's talking about. A fine adviser you've got there!'

'Maybe they won't.' Dunyashka was quiet for a moment, then suppressing a sigh, she said, 'He's real bitter against my brother. It upsets me so—more than I can say! I'm right sorry for my brother! He's been wounded again... What a mixed-up life he's had.'

'If only he gets back! We'll take the children and go away somewhere,' Aksinya said excitedly.

For some reason she had pulled off her kerchief. She put it on again and started, aimlessly moving the pots about the stove, trying vainly to fight down her excitement.

Dunyashka noticed that Aksinya's hands were shaking when she sat down on the bench and tried to smooth the folds of her shabby apron.

Something clutched at Dunyashka's throat. She suddenly wanted to go away into a corner and cry.

'Mummy never lived to see him back,' she said quietly. 'Well, I'll be going. I must light the stove.'

In the porch Aksinya gave her a hurried, awkward kiss on the neck, then caught her hand and kissed that.

'Are you glad?' Dunyashka asked in a gritty little voice.

'Yes, just a little, the tiniest bit,' Aksinya replied, trying to hide with a joke, with a trembling smile the tears that were about to flow.

VI

At Millerovo Station Grigory was treated as a demobilised Red commander and provided with a requisitioned wagon. In every Ukrainian settlement on his way home he changed his horses and after a day's driving reached the border of the Upper Don district. In the first Cossack village the chairman of the Revolutionary Committee, a young Red Army man, just back from the army, said, 'You'll have to make do with oxen, Comrade Commander. There's only one horse left in the whole village, and that's only got three legs. All the horses were left behind on the Kuban during the retreat.'

'Mebbe I could ride it home?' Grigory asked,

drumming on the table with his fingers and looking closely into the merry eyes of the tough young chairman.

'You couldn't. Even if you rode for a week! Don't worry, we've got some good sturdy oxen and we'll have to send a wagon to Vyoshenskaya anyway with some telephone wire. It got left behind here after this war. That's the wagon for you and you won't have to change it, it'll take you all the way home.' The chairman closed his left eye and, smiling slyly, added, 'We'll give you the best oxen and a fine driver—a young widow, she is... Ay, we've got a young saucepot here, you couldn't dream of a better! With her you'll be home before you know where you are. I've been in the army myself. I know a man's wartime needs.'

Grigory thought it over. It would be foolish to wait for a passing wagon to give him a lift and the distance was much too great to walk. He would have to agree to ox-drawn transport.

An hour later the wagon appeared. The wheels of the ancient hay wain squeaked complainingly, only a few broken fragments were left of the backboard, and wisps of the carelessly spread hay were draped over the sides. 'So this is what we've come to!' Grigory thought, staring in disgust at the miserable equipage. The driver was striding along beside the oxen, waving her whip. She was indeed a fine buxom woman. Her figure was slightly spoiled by her disproportionately massive chest, and a scar across her well-rounded chin made her young pinkish brown face look older and hard-boiled; the bridge of her nose was sprinkled with golden freckles, as small as millet grains.

Adjusting her kerchief, she narrowed her eyes and surveyed Grigory attentively.

'Are you the one I've got to take?'

Grigory rose from the porch and pulled his great-coat round him.

'That's right. Have you loaded the wire?'

'I'll be damned if I will!' was the shrill reply. 'Driving and working all the hours that are made! What do they think I am? They'll load up that wire themselves, and if they don't I'll go empty!'

She heaved the coils of wire on to the wagon, scolding the chairman volubly but without malice and occasionally shooting an appreciative glance at Grigory. The chairman stood chuckling to himself and gazing at the young widow in candid admiration. Now and then he'd wink at Grigory, as much as to say, 'See what wenches we've got! And you wouldn't believe me!'

The brown faded autumn steppe stretched away beyond the village. From the ploughland a bluish stream of smoke reached out across the track. The ploughmen were burning the dry tangle of stalks on the melon fields. The smell of the smoke roused sad memories in Grigory. Time was when he had gone out to plough in the hushed autumn steppe, looked up at the black sky glittering with stars, and listened to the call of the wild geese as they flew over high above... He turned over restlessly on the hay and glanced at the driver.

'How old are you, lass?'

'Getting on for sixty,' she replied coquettishly, smiling with only her eyes.

'No, I mean without joking.'

'Twenty.'

'And a widow?'

'Yes.'

'What did you do with your husband?'

'He got killed.'

'Long ago?'

'More than a year now.'

'During the uprising, was it?'

'After, just before autumn.'

'How are you getting along?'

'Somehow.'

'Lonely?'

She studied him for a moment and pulled her kerchief up over her lips to hide a smile. Her voice became deeper and there was a new lilt in it when she said, 'No time to be lonely at work.'

'I mean lonely without a husband?'

'I'm living with my mother-in-law, there's plenty to do to keep the place going.'

'But how d'you make out with no husband?'

She turned to face Grigory. A flush played on her brown cheeks and tiny reddish sparks flared and died in her eyes.

'What are you getting at?'

'What d'you think?'

She pulled the kerchief away from her lips and drawled, 'Oh, there's plenty of *that*! There's still a few kind folk in the world...' And after a pause she went on, 'When my husband was alive, I didn't have the chance to taste of being a woman. We'd only lived a month together

714

when he was called up. I can get by without him. It's
easier now the young Cossacks have come back to the
village; but it was pretty bad before. Gee-up, Baldy!
Gee-up! That's how it is, soldier! That's the life I
lead.'

Grigory fell silent. What was the good of leading her
on like this?

The big well-fed oxen plodded on at the same steady
pace. One of them had a broken horn that had mended
and now grew downwards over its forehead. Grigory
lay on the wagon, propping himself on his elbows and
keeping his eyes closed. Memory recalled the oxen he
had worked with as a boy and, later on, as a grown man.
They had all been different in colour, build and character, even their horns had been of different shapes. The
Melekhov farm had once had a bullock with just such a
crazy crumpled horn as this one. Fierce and cunning,
it was always squinting sideways with its red-veined eyes,
trying to kick anyone who approached it from behind,
and during the working season, when the oxen were let
out to graze at night, it would always stray homewards,
or—worse still—disappear into the forest or some distant ravine. Often Grigory had ridden the steppe for a
whole day until at last he found the beast at the very
bottom of a ravine among dense thorn thickets or in the
shadow of some gnarled old crab-apple tree. That one-
horned devil knew how to slip its halter, toss the fastening off the cattle-yard gate with its horn, swim across the
Don, and roam far away across the meadows. Yes, it
had given him plenty of trouble in its time...

'That bullock of yours, the one with the crumpled
horn, is it obedient?' Grigory asked.

'He's all right. Why d'you ask?'

'I was only thinking of something.'

'Only's a fine word if you've got nothing else to say,'
the driver said scornfully.

Grigory let it pass. He felt comforted by memories
of peacetime, of work, of anything that was not connected with the war. He was sick and tired of this war that
had dragged on for seven years, and the mere thought
of it or any episode connected with his service in the
army made his gorge rise.

He had done with fighting. He'd had enough. He was
going home, so that at last he could get down to work,
live with his children and with Aksinya. While still at
the front he had decided to have Aksinya to live with

him and be a mother to his children. Yes, he must fix that, and the sooner the better.

Grigory relished the thought of casting off his army greatcoat and boots, putting on easy leather shoes, tucking his trousers Cossack-style into white woollen socks, and driving out into the fields with a homespun coat over his warm jacket. It would be good to get his hands on the plough handles and follow it along the moist furrow, drinking in the damp fresh smell of crumbling soil and the bitter aromas of the turf sliced by the ploughshare. In foreign lands the soil and the grass had a different smell. Many a time in Poland, the Ukraine and the Crimea he had rubbed a grey sprig of wormwood between his palms, sniffed it and thought nostalgically, 'No, it's not the same, it's not ours...'

But his driver was bored. She wanted to talk. She stopped urging on the bullocks, made herself more comfortable and, toying with the leather tassel of her whip, quietly studied Grigory, the intent expression on his face, and his half-closed eyes. 'He's not so old despite his grey hairs. But there's something strange about him,' she thought. 'Keeps screwing up his eyes. Why does he do that, I wonder. He looks so fagged out, as if he'd been hauling wagons himself... But he's not a bad looker. Too much grey hair though, and his moustache is nearly all grey too. But not bad otherwise. What's he thinking about? At first he seemed to be out for some fun, then he simmered down and asked about the bullock. Hasn't he got anything to talk about? Or is he shy? Doesn't look it. His eyes are steady. No, he's a good Cossack, but there's something funny about him. All right then, you round-shouldered devil, keep quiet if you want to! As if I needed you! I can keep quiet myself! On his way home to his wife and can't wait to get there. Well, keep quiet then and good luck to you!'

She leaned back against the ribs of the wagon and broke into a quiet song.

Grigory raised his head and looked at the sun. It was still quite early. The shadows from the withered thistles guarding the road like gloomy sentinels were no more than half a pace long; it was probably only about two o'clock.

The steppe was deathly still, as though bewitched. The sun gave only a meagre warmth. A light breeze stirred the reddish withered grass. There was not a sound of a bird or a suslik. No kites or eagles hovered in the cold

light-blue sky. Only once a grey shadow slithered across
the road and, without raising his head, Grigory heard
the beat of broad wings, as an ash-grey bustard, its
white underfeathers gleaming in the sun, flew over and
alighted by a distant mound, whose shadow merged with
the murky lilac of the horizon. Only in late autumn had
Grigory observed such a sad and profound silence, when
you could almost hear the rustling of the tumbleweed
among the withered grass as, propelled by the wind, it
rolled on and on across the steppe.

The road seemed endless. It wound along a hillside,
dipped into a ravine, and once again climbed to the top
of a ridge of hills. All around, as far as the eye could
see, it was the same, the remote dreary vastness of the
steppe.

Grigory took a fancy to a bush of Tatarian maple
growing on the side of a ravine. Seared by the first frosts,
its leaves glowed a smoky purple, like the ash-sprinkled
embers of a dying fire.

'What's your name, love?' the driver asked, giving
Grigory's shoulder a gentle dig with the handle of her whip.

He started and turned towards her. She was not looking at him.

'Grigory. What's yours?'

'Call me something sweet.'

'Can't you be quiet for a bit, Something Sweet.'

'I'm tired of keeping quiet! I haven't said a word
since morning, it's given me a dry mouth. Why are you
so gloomy, Grigory?'

'What have I got to be glad about?'

'You're going home, you ought to be glad.'

'My glad years have gone by.'

'Pooh, what a poor old man. What made you so grey
when you're still young?'

'You must know everything, mustn't you?.. It's the
easy life I've had that did it.'

'Are you married, Grigory?'

'Yes, I'm married. You get married too, as soon as
you can, Something Sweet.'

'Why must it be soon?'

'You're a lot too playful.'

'Is that bad?'

'It can be. I knew a playful one, she was a widow
too, and she went on playing and playing until her nose
fell in.'

'Ooh, how you frightened me!' she exclaimed in mock

dismay, then added in a matter-of-fact tone, 'With us widows it's a case of don't go into the woods if you're afraid of the wolves.'

Grigory glanced at her. She was laughing soundlessly, her small white teeth clenched. Her upper lip was quivering and from under lowered lashes her eyes gleamed challengingly. Grigory smiled despite himself and put his hand on her warm round knee.

'Poor Something Sweet,' he said sympathetically. 'Only twenty years old and look what life has done to you.'

In the twinkling of an eye her merriness was gone. She thrust his hand away severely and flushed so violently that the little freckles round the bridge of her nose disappeared.

'Pity your wife when you see her, I can get all the pity I want!'

'Now don't be cross, wait a bit!'

'Oh, to hell with you!'

'I only said it out of kindness.'

'You can take your kindness and—' She swore as skilfully and habitually as any man and her eyes flashed darkly.

Grigory raised his eyebrows and grunted with embarrassment.

'You know how to let fly! You're a real wildcat!'

'And what are you? A saint in a lousy greatcoat, that's what you are! I know your kind! Get married and all the rest! How long is it since you've been such a righteous man?'

'Not so long,' Grigory said, chuckling.

'Then why're you preaching at me? I've got a mother-in-law for that.'

'Come off it now, what are you fuming about, you daft woman? I only said it in passing,' Grigory assured her placatingly. 'Look, you've let the bullocks roam off the road.'

As he settled himself more comfortably on the hay, Grigory glanced at the merry widow and noticed tears in her eyes. 'Here comes trouble! These women, they're always like that,' he thought, feeling inwardly embarrassed and annoyed.

He soon fell asleep, lying on his back, his face covered with the lapel of his greatcoat. It was nearly dusk when he awoke. The pale evening stars had come out and there was a fresh and joyous smell of hay in the air.

'The oxen need to be fed,' said his driver.

'Let's stop then.'

Grigory himself unhitched the oxen, took a tin of meat and some bread out of his pack, collected an armful of withered scrub, and made a fire not far from the wagon.

'Come and have supper, Something Sweet, you've been cross long enough.'

She sat down by the fire and silently shook out of her bag a hunk of bread and a lump of rusty-looking bacon fat. They had a peaceful supper, chatting about nothing in particular, then she made her bed on the wagon, while Grigory threw some dried ox dung on the fire to keep it going, and bedded down beside it army fashion. He lay for a long time with his head on his pack, gazing up at the glittering starry sky and thinking vaguely of the children and Aksinya, then dozed off. He was awakened by a woman's voice, low and inviting.

'Are you asleep, soldier? Asleep, are you?'

Grigory raised his head. His companion was leaning out of the wagon. Her face, illuminated from below by the shifting light of the dying fire, was pink and fresh, her teeth and the lace edging of her kerchief were a dazzling white. As though there had been no tiff between them, she was smiling again and making little movements with her eyebrows.

'I'm afraid you'll get frozen out there. The ground must be cold. Come in with me if you feel chilly. My coat's ever so warm! Won't you come?'

Grigory thought for a moment and answered with a sigh, 'Thanks, girl, but I don't feel like it. A year or two ago mebbe... I reckon I won't freeze to death by the fire.'

She also gave a sigh and said, 'Well, it's up to you,' and pulled her coat over her head.

A little while later Grigory rose and gathered his things together. He had decided to walk the rest of the way and be in Tatarsky by morning. A commander returning from active service couldn't arrive home on an ox-drawn wagon in broad daylight. The talk and jesting at his expense would have been too much to bear.

He wakened the driver.

'I'm going to walk it. Not scared to be left alone in the steppe, are you?'

'No, I'm not the scary kind. Besides, there's a village near by. What's the matter? Can't you wait?'

'No, I can't. Well, goodbye, Something Sweet, don't think badly of me.'

Grigory walked out on the road, and turned up his collar. The first white flake fell on his lashes. The wind had swung round to the north and in its cold breath Grigory thought he felt the familiar cherished smell of snow.

* * *

Koshevoi returned from his trip to the stanitsa in the evening. Dunyashka was watching from the window as he drove up to the gate. She covered her head quickly and went out to meet him.

'Grigory came home this morning,' she said at the gate, casting a worried, expectant look at her husband...

'Congratulations,' Mikhail replied quietly, and with some irony.

He walked into the kitchen, lips tight, jaw muscles quivering. Grigory had Polyushka on his lap, dressed-up in a clean frock by her aunt. Grigory gently put the child down on the floor and came forward to meet his brother-in-law, smiling and holding out a big brown hand. He was about to embrace Mikhail but, seeing the coldness and hostility in his unsmiling eyes, checked himself.

'Well, hullo, Mikhail!'

'Hullo.'

'It's a long time since we saw each other! Seems like a hundred years!'

'Ay, it's been a long time. Welcome home.'

'Thanks. So we're kinsmen now?'

'We have to be... What's that blood on your cheek?'

'Just a scratch. I shaved in a hurry.'

They sat down at the table and eyed each other in silence, estranged and embarrassed. They knew they would have to have it out, but that was impossible at the moment. Mikhail had enough self-control to talk calmly about farm matters and the changes that had taken place in the village.

Grigory looked out of the window at the fields covered with the first light-blue snow of winter, at the bare branches of the apple-trees. This was not how he had imagined his reunion with Koshevoi.

After a while Mikhail went out into the porch. As he sharpened a knife carefully on a whetstone, he said to Dunyashka, 'I want to get someone round to slaughter a sheep. We ought to give the master of the house a proper welcome. Run and get some home-brew. No, just a minute. Go to Prokhor's and tell him to get some, even if it kills him. He'll do it better than you. Ask him to supper.'

Dunyashka beamed with joy and gave her husband a look of silent gratitude... 'Perhaps they'll sort it out. After all, they've done their fighting, what more have they got now to quarrel over? Please, God, make them see reason!' she thought hopefully as she went to fetch Prokhor.

In less than half an hour Prokhor arrived, panting for breath.

'Grigory Panteleyevich!.. My old chum!.. I never thought I'd see you again!' he burst out with tears in his voice and, tripping over the doorstep, nearly dropped the huge pitcher of home-brew he was carrying.

As he hugged Grigory he gave a sob, wiped his eyes with his fist and smoothed down his tear-wet moustache. Something quivered in Grigory's throat but he controlled himself and, deeply moved, he slapped his faithful orderly roughly on the back, and tumbled out his greetings.

'So we've met again... I'm glad to see you, Prokhor, real glad! What are you weeping for, old man? Got a bit weak in the withers, have you? Screws coming loose? How's the arm? Your wife hasn't pulled off your other one yet, has she?'

Prokhor blew his nose loudly and took off his sheep-skin.

'We get on like a couple of turtle-doves these days. My other arm's as good as ever, see? And this one that the White Poles snatched off me is beginning to grow again, believe me! In a year's time it'll have a hand and fingers,' he declared with his customary cheerfulness, waggling his empty shirt-sleeve.

War had taught them to hide their true feelings beneath a smile and add a big pinch of salt to both their food and their conversation; so Grigory continued his questions in the same jocular vein.

'How's life, you old he-goat? How d'you jump these days?'

'Like an old man—I look before I leap.'

'Did you pick up anything else while I was away?'

'What kind of thing?'

'The kind of bird you were carrying around last winter.'

721

'God forbid, Panteleyevich! How could I afford such a luxury? And what kind of catcher would I be with only one arm? That's your job, a young bachelor like you ... it's time for me to turn in my equipment to the old woman—a good gadget for greasing the frying pans with.'

They feasted their eyes on each other, two old comrades of the trenches, laughing and overjoyed to be seeing each other again.

'Home for good?' Prokhor asked.

'Yes, for good and all.'

'What rank did you finish up with?'

'Second-in-command of the regiment.'

'Why'd they let you go so early?'

Grigory's face darkened and he answered briefly, 'They didn't need me any more.'

'How was that?'

'I don't know. Because of the past, I suppose.'

'But you got through that commission of the Special Department that was screening the officers, didn't you? How can the past count now?'

'In plenty of ways.'

'Where's Mikhail?'

'In the yard. Cleaning out the cattle shed.'

Prokhor moved closer and lowered his voice.

'They shot Platon Ryabchikov a month ago.'

'You don't mean it?'

'God's truth!'

The door of the porch creaked.

'We'll talk later,' Prokhor whispered and then, on a louder note, 'So here we are, Comrade Commander, let's drink to this great joy, eh? Shall I go and call Mikhail?'

'Ask him in.'

Dunyashka laid the table. She could not think of enough ways of pleasing her brother. She put a clean towel across his knees, placed the plate of salted watermelon slices within easy reach and wiped his glass five times over. Grigory noticed with a smile how respectful her manner of addressing him had become.

At table, to begin with, Mikhail maintained a stubborn silence, listening attentively to everything Grigory said. He drank only a little and reluctantly. Prokhor, on the other hand, tossed back glass after glass, merely growing redder in the face and smoothing down his straw-coloured moustache with his fist more often.

When she had fed the children and put them to bed, Dunyashka placed a big plate of boiled mutton on the table and whispered to Grigory, 'Brother dear, I'll run and fetch Aksinya. You won't mind, will you?'

Grigory nodded silently. He thought no one had noticed the suspense he had been in all the evening, but Dunyashka had noticed him stiffen at every sound resembling a knock and shoot a guarded, listening glance at the door. Nothing escaped the watchful eye of that young woman.

'Is Tereshchenko still commanding a troop?' Prokhor asked, gripping his glass as if he were afraid someone would take it from him.

'He was killed at Lvov.'

'God rest his soul. He was a fine cavalryman!' Prokhor crossed himself hurriedly and sipped at his glass, not noticing Koshevoi's malicious smile.

'And that one with the queer name? He used to be our right marker. Now what was his name, damn it— Mai-Boroda? Ukrainian, fat and jolly, the one who cut a Polish officer in half at Brody—is he safe and sound?'

'Like a stallion! They've put him in a machine-gun squadron.'

'Who did you hand over your horse to?'

'I had another one by that time.'

'What did you do with Whitey?'

'It was killed by a shell splinter.'

'In battle?'

'We were in a little town and they started shelling us. It was hit at the tethering post.'

'Ah, what a pity! It was a fine horse!' Prokhor sighed, and raised his glass again.

The door latch rattled in the porch. Grigory gave a start. Aksinya stepped across the threshold, uttered a barely audible 'Good evening to you!' and untied her kerchief, breast heaving, radiant eyes fixed on Grigory. She walked to the table and sat down beside Dunyashka. Snowflakes were melting on her brows and lashes, and on her pale face. Closing her eyes, she wiped her face with her hand, took a deep breath and then, recovering herself, again fastened her fervent gaze on Grigory.

'Mess-mate! Aksinya, love! We retreated together, we fed the lice together... We had to leave you behind on the Kuban, but what else could we do?' Prokhor held out a glass, splashing liquor on the table. 'Drink to Grigory Panteleyevich! Drink to his homecoming... I told you he'd come back safe and sound, and here he is. You can have him for a song! And he's in perfect condition!'

'He's loaded already, neighbour, don't listen to him.' Grigory looked laughingly at Prokhor.

Aksinya bowed to Grigory and Dunyashka and raised the glass only a little above the table. She was afraid they would see her hand shaking.

'Welcome home, Grigory Panteleyevich. Here's to your happy event, Dunyashka!'

'And what is it to you? A grief?' Prokhor chortled, poking Mikhail in the ribs.

Aksinya flushed deeply and even the small lobes of her ears turned a transparent pink, but with a steady angry look at Prokhor she replied, 'It's a joy to me too... A great joy!'

Prokhor was disarmed and delighted by such candour.

'Drink up then, to the last drop,' he begged. 'For Lord's sake! You can speak straight, so drink straight! It breaks my heart to see people leave their liquor.'

Aksinya did not stay long, just a long as she felt was decent. Only a few times, and swiftly, did she glance at her beloved. She forced herself to look at the others and avoided Grigory's eyes because she could not have feigned indifference and did not wish to show her feelings before strangers. Grigory caught only that one direct glance from the threshold, full of love and devotion, but it told him everything that mattered. He went out to see Aksinya to the gate. Prokhor, by now quite tipsy, shouted after them, 'Don't be too long! We'll drink it all!'

In the porch Grigory silently kissed Aksinya on the forehead and on the lips.

'Well, how are things, Aksinya?'

'Oh, there's too much to tell... Will you come tomorrow?'

'Yes.'

She hurried home as though some urgent task awaited her, slowing her pace only as she approached the porch and mounted the creaking steps. She wanted to be alone with her thoughts, with the happiness that had come so unexpectedly.

She threw off her jacket and kerchief and, without lighting the lamp, went into the front room. The deep violet glow of the night poured in through the unshuttered windows. A cricket was trilling behind the stove.

Out of habit Aksinya glanced into the mirror and, although she could not see her reflection in the darkness, she patted her hair into place and smoothed the frills of her muslin blouse. Then she went to the window and sank down wearily on a bench.

She had been disappointed in her hopes and desires so many times, and perhaps for this reason the joy she had recently experienced gave way to the anxiety that was always lurking in the back of her mind. How would life work out for her now? What did the future hold? Had the bad luck that had dogged her for so long changed too late?

Exhausted by the emotional excitement of the evening, she sat for a long time, pressing her cheek to the frosty windowpane and gazing calmly and a little sadly into the darkness, illuminated only by a glimmer of light from the snow.

* * *

Grigory sat down at the table, filled his glass from the jug and drank it in one gulp.

'Good stuff?' Prokhor inquired.

'Couldn't say. It's a long time since I drank.'

'As good as Tsar's vodka, by God it is!' Prokhor said with conviction and, lurching sideways, flung his arm round Mikhail's shoulders. 'You know less about such things, Mikhail, than a calf does about cattle swill. But I know what I'm talking about when it comes to drink! The wines and liqueurs I've tasted in my time! There's one wine that foams like a mad dog as soon as you take the cork out. God knows I wouldn't tell a lie! In Poland, when we broke through the front with Comrade Budyonny and started lashing the White Poles, we swooped on a big estate. The house had two storeys or more, the sheds were chock-full of cattle, all kinds of birds strutting about the yard, no room to spit even. In a word, that landowner must have lived like a tsar. When our troop arrived, some officers were feasting with the owner. They hadn't been expecting us, you see. Well, we sabred the lot, some in the orchard, others on the staircase, but we took one of 'em prisoner. Fine-looking officer he was, but as soon as we got hold of him, his moustache dropped and he started shaking with fear. Grigory Panteleyevich was summoned urgent to headquarters and we were left in charge of the place. Well, we went into the downstairs rooms and there was a huge table with all kinds of eats on it! Lovely sight it was, but we were scared to eat the stuff, though we were dying of hunger. What if it's all poisoned, we thought? And there was our prisoner looking daggers at us. So we says to him, "Eat!" And he ate, not very willingly, but he ate. "Drink!" we says. And he drinks. We made him take a big helping from every dish, and a glassful from every bottle. There he was, the devil, swelling up with grub before our very eyes, and we were so hungry our mouths were watering. Well, when we saw that this officer wasn't dying, we tucked in. Ay, we stuffed ourselves and drank that foaming wine till it was up to our nostrils, and what do we see next—the officer's being sick all over the place. "Now we're done for!" we thought. "The bastard ate poisoned food himself to trick us." So we come at him with our sabres and he flaps his arms and legs at us. "Good sirs, it's only because I had too much to eat, by your kindness. Don't worry, the food's quite wholesome!" So back to the wine we went! All you have to do is push the cork and it goes off like a rifle. And the way the foam comes spouting out, it's terrible to watch! After that wine I fell off my horse three times in one night! As soon as I got in the saddle, off I came again, as if the wind had blown me. Ay, if only I could have a glass or two of that wine on an empty stomach every day, I'd live to be a hundred, but I'll never last out otherwise. Take this stuff here, d'ye call that a drink? The poisonous muck! It's enough to make a man peg out before his time...' Prokhor nodded at the jug of home-brew and promptly filled his glass to the brim.

Dunyashka went to sleep with the children in the front room, and soon afterwards Prokhor, too, rose from the table. Swaying to and fro, he threw his sheepskin over his shoulders and said, 'I won't take the jug. It goes agin the grain to carry an empty jug around... When I get home, the old woman'll pitch into me. She's good at that! Where she gets all these spiteful words from, I dunno! When I come home a bit tipsy, she starts on me, f'rinstance, like this, "You drunken one-armed dog, you this and that, you—" And I says to her quietly, in a calm and reasonable way, "Where have you, you devil's whore, you bitch's udder, ever seen a drunken dog, and with one arm missing at that?! There's no such thing on earth."

But as soon as I knock down one of her lies, up she comes with another. As soon as I've dealt with that, up she comes with a third, and that's how it goes on all night till break of day... Sometimes I get so fed up with listening to her, I go and sleep outside. But at other times, when I've had a drink or two, she won't open her mouth, not even to swear at me, and then I can't get to sleep, by God I can't! There seems to be something missing and I get itchy all over and just can't sleep at all! But then I give my better half a dig and off she goes at me again till I'm seeing sparks! She's a whelp of the devil, is my old woman, but why complain? Let her rave at me—it'll only make her work harder, won't it? Well, I'll be going, so goodbye all! But mebbe I'll spend the night in a manger, so as not to disturb her just now?'

'Can you walk home?' Grigory asked, laughing.

'I'll make it, even if I have to crawl backwards like a crayfish! I'm a Cossack, ain't I, Panteleyevich? That's an insulting thing for me to hear from you.'

'God bless you, then!'

Grigory saw his friend as far as the gate, then returned to the kitchen.

'Well, shall we talk, Mikhail?'

'All right.'

For a time they sat facing each other over the table in silence. At last Grigory said, "Something has come between us! I can tell by the way you look at me! Are you sorry to see me back? Or am I wrong?'

'No, you're right—I am sorry.'

'Why?'

'More trouble.'

'I reckon I'll be able to feed myself.'

'I didn't mean that.'

'What did you mean then?'

'We're enemies.'

'We were once.'

'It looks as if we still are.'

'I don't get you. Why?'

'You're not trustworthy.'

'You shouldn't say that. That's not true.'

'Yes, it is. Why did they demob you at a time like this? Out with it!'

'I don't know.'

'You know well enough, but you won't tell me! They didn't trust you, did they?'

'If they hadn't trusted me, they wouldn't have given me a squadron.'

'That was at the beginning, but if they wouldn't keep you in the army, it's clear what the trouble was, chum!'

'Do you trust me?' Grigory asked, looking straight into the other's eyes.

'No! You can feed a wolf but it'll still hanker after the forest.'

'You've had too much to drink, Mikhail.'

'Don't come that on me! I'm no more drunk than you are. They didn't trust you over there, and back here they won't trust you either, you can count on that!'

Grigory said nothing. Listlessly he took a piece of salted cucumber from his plate, chewed it and spat it out.

'Did the wife tell you about Kirill Gromov?' Mikhail asked.

'Yes, she did.'

'I was sorry to see him back too. As soon as I heard about it, the very same day, I...'

Grigory turned pale and his eyes bulged with fury.

'You think I'm the same as Kirill Gromov?!'

'Don't shout. In what way are you better?'

'Now, look here...'

'There's nothing to look at. I've looked already. And a bit later Mitka Korshunov will turn up. Should I be glad to see him? No, you'd have done better not to come back to the village.'

'Better for you?'

'For me and for everyone, more peaceful.'

'Don't lump me with them.'

'I've told you already, Grigory, and it's no good getting your back up: you're not better than them, you're a lot worse, more dangerous.'

'How? What are you blathering about?'

'They're just the rank-and-file, but you started the whole uprising.'

'I didn't start it, I was the commander of a division.'

'Wasn't that enough?'

'Enough or too much—that's not the point. If the Red Army men hadn't tried to kill me at that party, I might never have taken part in the uprising.'

'If you hadn't been an officer, no one would have touched you.'

'If I hadn't been called up for the service, I wouldn't have been an officer... That' a long story!'

'Long and rotten.'

'It can't be changed now, it's too late.'

They lighted cigarettes in silence. Flicking the ash off with a fingernail, Koshevoi said, 'I know about your heroic deeds, I've heard all that. You killed a lot of our men, and that's why I don't want to have you in my sight... It's not something you can easily forget.'

Grigory smiled wrily.

'What a long memory you've got! You killed my brother Petro, but I don't remind you of that... If we remember everything, we'll have to live like wolves.'

'All right, I killed him, I don't deny that! If I'd caught you then, I'd have made short work of you too!'

'But I, when Ivan Alexeyevich was taken prisoner in Ust-Khopyorskaya, hurried back here because I was afraid you were with him, I was afraid the Cossacks would kill you... It seems I needn't have hurried.'

'What a kind man, eh! I'd like to see how you'd be talking to me now if the Cadets were in power, if you'd come out on top. You'd have torn the skin off my back in strips, I reckon! It's only now you're so kind.'

'Someone might have done that, but I wouldn't have dirtied my hands on you.'

'So we're different people... I've never been squeamish about dirtying my hands on enemies and I won't flinch now, if I have to dirty 'em again.' Mikhail poured the rest of the liquor into the glasses, 'Want a drink?'

'Let's have one. We've got a lot too sober for this kind of talk.'

They clinked glasses in silence and drank. Grigory leaned forward over the table and looked at Mikhail with narrowed eyes, twisting the tip of his moustache.

'What is it you're afraid of, Mikhail? That I'll rebel against the Soviets again?'

'I'm not afraid of anything, but I think that if there was a flare-up, you'd soon nip over to the other side.'

'I could have gone over to the Poles, don't you think? One of our units did desert to them in a bunch.'

'And you missed your chance?'

'No, I didn't want to. I've served long enough and I don't want to serve in any more armies. I've done enough fighting to last me a lifetime and it's taken all the heart out of me. I'm sick of everything—revolution and counter-revolution. Let it all go to... To hell with it all! I want to live with my children and work the farm, and that's all. Believe me, Mikhail, I say that from the bottom of my heart!'

But none of his assurances could convince Koshevoi.

Grigory realised this and broke off. For a moment he felt bitterly annoyed with himself. Why the devil had he made excuses, tried to argue? What was the use of going on with this drunken wrangle, listening to Mikhail's damnfool preaching? To hell with it. Grigory stood up.

'It's no good talking like this! I've had enough! There's only one last thing I want to tell you: I won't go against the government unless it grabs me by the throat. But if it does, I'll defend myself! Whatever happens, I'm not going to pay for the uprising with my head, like Platon Ryabchikov did.'

'What have you got in mind?'

'What I said. Let 'em take into account my service in the Red Army and the wounds I got while I was doing it. I'm ready to go to prison for the uprising, but if they want to shoot me for it—no thanks! That's a bit too much!'

Mikhail's lips twisted scornfully.

'Listen to him! The Revolutionary Tribunal or the Emergency Commission won't ask you what you want or don't want, and they won't do any trading with you. If you've done wrong, you'll take what's coming to you—and some. Old debts have to be paid in full!'

'We'll see about that.'

'Sure we will.'

Grigory took off his belt and shirt and with a grunt began to pull off his boots.

'Are we going to share the property?' he asked, studying the loose sole of his boot with exaggerated attention.

'Our sharing won't take long. I'll put my place to rights and move out.'

'Ay, let's keep away from each other. We won't get on living together.'

'No, we won't,' Mikhail agreed.

'I didn't think you had such an opinion of me... But what's the good of arguing?'

'I told you straight. I told you what I think. When will you be going to Vyoshenskaya?'

'One day, fairly soon.'

'Not one day. You've got to go tomorrow.'

'I've just walked nearly forty versts, I'm dead beat. I'll rest up tomorrow and go for registration the day after.'

'The order says registration at once. Go tomorrow.'

'I need a day's rest, don't I? I won't run away.'

'How the devil do I know? I don't want to answer for you.'

'What a bastard you've become, Mikhail!' Grigory said, scanning his former friend's hard-set face with some surprise.

'Don't you "bastard" me! I'm not used to it...' Mikhail took a breath and raised his voice. 'You'd better drop these officer's ways of yours, you know! Get cracking tomorrow, and if you won't got of your own accord, I'll send you under escort. Is that clear?'

'Now everything's clear...' Grigory glanced with hatred at Mikhail's back as he walked out of the room, then lay down on the bed without undressing.

So, everything had happened as it was bound to happen. What other welcome could he, Grigory, have expected? What reason had there been to think that his brief honourable service in the Red Army would atone for all his past sins? And perhaps Mikhail was right when he said that not everything could be forgiven and that old debts would have to be paid in full?

...In a dream Grigory saw a broad stretch of steppe and a regiment drawn up in attack formation. From far away came the long drawn-out command, 'Squad-ron!...' And just then he remembered that his saddle girths were loose. He thrust hard on the stirrup with his left foot and the saddle skewed sideways. Overcome with shame and dismay, he jumped off his horse to tighten the girth and at that moment heard a sudden thunder of hooves, which just as suddenly died away.

The regiment had charged without him.

Grigory turned over restlessly and, as he awoke, heard himself give a hoarse groan.

Daybreak was glimmering through the window. The wind must have opened the shutter during the night and through the frost-coated pane he could see the green glittering shape of the waning moon. Grigory groped for his tobacco pouch and made a cigarette. His heart was still thumping loudly. He turned over on his back and thought with a smile, 'What devil's nonsense you can see in a dream! So I missed a battle...' Little did he know at that daybreak hour how many more times yet he would ride into battle in both dream and reality.

VII

Dunyashka got up early, to milk the cow. Grigory was moving quietly about the kitchen, coughing now and then. Dunyashka tucked in the children and dressed quickly. When she entered the kitchen, Grigory was buttoning his greatcoat.

'Where're you off to so early, brother?'

'I want to take a walk round the village, to see what it looks like.'

'Have some breakfast first, then...'

'I don't feel like it. I've got a headache.'

'Will you be back for breakfast? I'm just going to light the stove.'

'No need to wait for me. I may be quite a while.'

Grigory walked out into the lane. Morning had brought a thaw. The wind was blowing from the south, moist and warm. The mush of snow and earth caked on his heels. As he trudged towards the square, Grigory scanned the houses and outbuildings he had known since childhood as if he were in a strange place. All round the square stood the charred remains of the merchants' houses and shops that Koshevoi had burned down the year before; there were yawning gaps in the churchyard wall. 'Someone needed bricks for his stove,' Grigory thought indifferently. The church was still standing; it seemed smaller, as if it had sunk into the earth. Its long-unpainted roofs gleamed rustily, the walls were blotched and streaky, and red brick showed through where the plaster had peeled off.

There were not many people about. Grigory met two or three sleepy-looking women near the well. They bowed silently, as though to a stranger, and only when he had passed did they stop to stare after him.

'I ought to visit Mother's and Natalya's graves,' he thought and turned off the road towards the cemetery, but after a few paces he stopped. He felt depressed enough without that. 'I'll go another time,' he decided and turned his steps towards Prokhor's. 'It's all the same to them whether I come or not. They're at peace now. It's all over. Their graves are covered with snow. But it must be cold down there, underground... How quickly they lived their lives, like in a dream. There they lie all together, side by side—my wife, my mother, Petro and Darya... The whole family's moved and come together again. They're lucky, but Father, he's all alone in a strange land. He must be homesick among strangers...'

By now Grigory had lost interest in his surroundings. He walked with his eyes on the ground, on the white thaw-moistened snow, which was so soft that he could hardly feel it or hear it squeaking under his boots.

His thoughts turned to his children. They were unnaturally restrained and silent for their age, not like they had been when their mother was alive. Death had robbed them of too much. They were frightened. Why had Polyushka burst into tears yesterday when she saw him? Children didn't usually cry when they met somebody. What had she been thinking of? And why that gleam of fear in her eyes when he had picked her up? Perhaps she had believed all this time that her father was dead and would never come home, and his sudden appearance had frightened her? Anyway, he had never done them any harm. But he must tell Aksinya to be kind to them and do everything to make up for the loss of their mother... They'd probably take well to their stepmother. She was kind and affectionate. Out of love for him she would love the children.

But there was little comfort in these thoughts. It would not be as easy as that. Life was not so simple as he had imagined only recently. Foolishly as a child he had thought he could just come home, change his army greatcoat for a ploughman's homespun and everything would go according to plan; no one would say a word against him, there would be no reproaches, things would settle down, and he would live the life of a peaceful farmer and perfect family man. But no, real life was a different matter.

Grigory cautiously pushed open the sagging gate of the Zykovs' farmyard. Prokhor in a pair of shapeless down-at-heel felt boots and a floppy fur hat tilted over his eyes was walking towards the porch, carelessly swinging an empty milking pail. The white drops of milk splashed invisibly over the snow.

'Had a good night, Comrade Commander?'

'Praise the Lord.'

'We'd better take a hair of the dog that bit us. My head feels as empty as this pail.'

'That sounds a good idea, but why's the pail empty? Did you milk the cow yourself?'

Prokhor tilted his fur cap on to the back of his head, and it was only then that Grigory noticed the gloomy expression on his friend's face.

'Will the devil milk her for me, if I don't? I milked her, the hag. Hope she don't get tummy trouble after my milking!' Prokhor threw down the pail furiously and concluded briefly, 'Come inside.'

'Where's your wife?' Grigory asked hesitantly.

'Stewing in hell by now, I hope! At some unearthly hour in the morning she ups and drives off to Kruzhilinsky for sloes. She pounced on me as soon as I got home from your place! The sermons she gave me! Then up she gets and it's "I'm going to get the sloes! The Maksayev women are going today and I'll go with 'em!" "Go for pears, if you like, and good riddance!" I says. So I got up, lighted the stove, and went out to milk the cow. That was a milking, that was! You think a man can do that job with one arm?'

'Why didn't you ask one of the women to help you, you chump?'

'A lamb's a chump, it sucks its mother when she's dry. But I'm no chump and never have been. I thought I could manage on my own! Some managing! There I was, crawling under that cow on my hands and knees, and she, the hell-born hag, wouldn't stand still, stamping all over the place, she was. I even took my cap off so as not to frighten her. But it didn't help. My shirt was soaking by the time I'd milked her, and then I just put my hand out to pick up the pail, and—she kicks it over! The pail goes one way and me the other. That's how I milked her. It's not a cow, it's the devil incarnate with horns on! I spat in her face and off I went. I can get by without milk. Now then, what about that hair of the dog?'

'Have you got any?'

'One bottle. Stashed away.'

'Good enough.'

'Come in, then, and be my guest. Like some fried eggs? I can do that for you in a jiffy.'

Grigory cut the bacon fat and helped his host light the stove. They watched in silence as the lumps of pink fat sizzled and melted and went sliding about the frying pan. Then Prokhor reached up behind the ikon and produced a dusty bottle.

'That's where I hide my secrets from the old woman,' he explained briefly.

They ate their meal in the little well-heated room, drank the liquor and talked in low tones.

Who else was there for Grigory to confide in, if not Prokhor. He sat at the table, his long muscular legs planted wide apart, and talked without raising his husky bass much above a whisper.

'While I was in the army and all the way home I was

thinking how I'd live on the land, enjoy a bit of family life and take a rest from this hellish mess. Just think of it—I haven't been out of the saddle for more than seven years! Nearly every night I have the same lovely dream: either I'm killing someone or someone's killing me... But it looks as if I won't get what I want, Prokhor... Other men will plough the soil and till it.'

'Did you have a talk with Mikhail yesterday?'

'Ay, some sweet words were spoken.'

'What's he got against you?'

Grigory made a cross with two fingers.

'It's all up with our friendship. He's against me for serving in the Whites. He thinks I've got a grudge against the new government, that I want to stab it in the back. He's afraid I'll start an uprising. But why the devil I'd do a thing like that, he doesn't know himself, the fool.'

'That's what he told me.'

Grigory gave a cheerless laugh.

'When we were on our way across the Ukraine into Poland, a Ukrainian asked us for arms to defend his village with. They'd been plagued with bandits robbing them and killing their cattle. The commander of our regiment—I was present at the time—says to him, "If we give you arms, you'll go and join a band yourselves." And this Ukrainian, he laughs and says, "Just you arm us, comrade, and we'll keep the bandits out of the village, and your lot as well." And that's the way I feel, like that Ukrainian. It'd be fine to keep both the Whites and the Reds out of Tatarsky, if only we could. As I see it, one's no better than the other. What's the difference between my brother-in-law Mitka Korshunov, say, and Mikhail Koshevoi. He thinks I'm so devoted to the Whites I can't live without 'em. Bloody nonsense! Like hell I'm devoted! Not so long ago, when we were closing in on the Crimea, I was in a skirmish with a Kornilov officer—smart little colonel, moustache trimmed like an Englishman's, two little strips under his nostrils like snot—and I gave him such a wallop it did my heart good! Half his head and half his cap was all that poor colonel had left, and the white cockade fell off... That's how devoted I am! They've played me enough dirty tricks. I won this blasted officer's rank with my own blood, but among the other officers I stood out like a white crow. They never treated me like a human being, the bastards. They wouldn't even shake hands. As if I'd have anything to do with 'em after that... No bloody fear! It makes me sick to talk about it! Me? Get those bastards back into power? Did I invite the Fitzhelaurovs to take over? One taste of that had me choking for a year afterwards. Now I know better, I've had a bellyful!'

Dipping his bread in the hot fat, Prokhor said, 'There won't be any uprising. For one thing, there's only a few Cossacks left and they've learnt their lesson. Our bunch have had so much blood let out of 'em and they've got so good and well-behaved, you couldn't drag 'em into a mutiny with wild horses. And besides, folk are hungry for a peaceful life. You should have seen the way everyone worked last summer. Great ricks of hay, all the corn harvested to the last grain. Wheezing with the strain some of 'em were, but they went on ploughing and sowing as if they meant to live to be a hundred! No, there couldn't be any uprising. That's just daft talk. Although, you can never tell what the Cossacks might get up to.'

'What can they get up to? What are you hinting at?'

'Our neighbours've got up to something.'

'What?'

'As if you didn't know! There's been an uprising in Voronezh Province, somewhere beyond Boguchar.'

'That's just a yarn!'

'Some yarn! I heard it yesterday, off a militiaman I know. He thinks they'll be sent there to deal with it.'

'Where exactly?'

'In Monastyrshchina, Sukhoi Donets, Paseka, Old and New Kalitva, and a few other places besides. It's a huge uprising, they say.'

'Why didn't you tell me this yesterday, you old goose?'

'I didn't want to mention it in front of Mikhail. Besides what's the pleasure in talking of such things? I don't want to hear about that kind o'thing for the rest of my life,' Prokhor replied grumpily.

Grigory's face clouded. After a thoughtful silence he said, 'That's bad news.'

'It's nothing to do with you. Let the Tufties worry. They'll get a good tanning on their behinds, then they'll know how to rebel. It's nothing to do with us. I'm not sorry for 'em.'

'It'll make things a bit difficult for me.'

'In what way?'

'What way? If the district authorities take the same view of me as Koshevoi, I'm for the cooler. They've got an uprising next door, and here's a former officer, and an insurgent at that... Get me?'

Prokhor stopped chewing and looked thoughtful. No such idea had occurred to him. Befuddled by drink, his mind worked slowly and circuitously.

'How do you come into it, Panteleyevich?' he asked perplexedly.

Grigory frowned irritably and said nothing. He was clearly alarmed by the news. Prokhor offered him another glass, but he pushed it aside and said resolutely, 'No more drink for me.'

'Let's have just one more, eh? Drink, Grigory Panteleyevich, till you're black in the face. Life's so cheerful nowadays the only thing to do is drown it in home-brew.'

'Get black in the face by yourself. Your head's thick enough as it is and drink'll make you thicker. I've got to go off to Vyoshenskaya today to get registered.'

Prokhor looked hard at him. Grigory's weathered, sunburnt face was flushed with a deep ruddy glow and soft white skin showed only at the very roots of his combed-back hair. He was calm, this seasoned warrior with whom war and misfortune had bound Prokhor with a bond of kinship. There was a look of grim weariness in his gloomy, slightly puffy eyes.

'Aren't you afraid they'll, er... put you in the clink?' Grigory livened up suddenly.

'That's just what I am afraid of, boy! I've never been in prison before and I fear it worse than death. But it looks as if I'll have to taste some of that too.'

'You shouldn't have come home,' Prokhor said regretfully.

'Where was I to go then?'

'You could have hung about in town somewhere and waited till things settled down, then come home afterwards.'

Grigory brushed the idea away with a laugh.

'That's not for me! Hanging about's worse than anything. Where could I go and leave the kids behind?'

'What about the kids! They've lived long enough without you, haven't they? You could've picked 'em up later, and your lady fair as well. Oh, I forgot to tell you! The masters of the place where you were with Aksinya before the war have both passed on.'

'The Listnitskys?'

'Right. My cousin Zakhar was batman to the young Listnitsky during the retreat and he told me. The old general died in Morozovskaya of typhus, and the young one got as far as Yekaterinodar, and there his wife got in a tangle with General Pokrovsky. That was too much for him and he shot himself.'

'To hell with them,' Grigory said indifferently. 'I'm sorry, for the good people who've suffered, but no one will miss them.' He rose and pulled on his greatcoat, and with his hand on the door said thoughtfully, 'Though, the devil knows, I've always envied men like the young Listnitsky or our Koshevoi... Everything was clear to them from the start, and to me even now nothing is clear. They've both got their own straight roads, their own goals, but ever since 1917 I've been swinging this way and that staggering along like a drunk... I left the Whites but didn't stick to the Reds, so here I am, floating about like dung in an ice hole... You see, Prokhor, I should have been in the Red Army all the way through, then things might have worked out all right for me. To start with—as you know—I served the Soviets heart and soul, but then all that fell apart... With the Whites, for their command anyway, I was a stranger, always under suspicion. How else could it be? A farmer's son, an uneducated Cossack—how could they treat me as one of them? They didn't trust me! And then the same thing happened with the Reds. I'm not blind, I saw the kind of looks the commissar and the Communists in the squadron were giving me... In battle they watched me every step and probably they were thinking, "That White bastard, he's a Cossack officer, watch him or he'll let us down." I noticed what was going on and it took the heart out of me right away. I couldn't stand any more of that suspicion. Even a rock will crack in the heat. It was just as well they did demob me. It brings the end nearer...' He cleared his throat huskily, paused for a moment and, without looking round at Prokhor, said in a quite different voice, 'Thanks for your hospitality. I'll be going. Look after yourself. This evening, if I come back, I'll drop in. Put that bottle away or your wife will break the pot-lifter on your back when she comes home.'

Prokhor saw him to the front door and in the porch whispered, 'Take care, Panteleyevich, mind you don't get locked up.'

'I'll mind,' Grigory replied briefly.

Without going home, he walked down to the Don, untied a boat that was hitched to the pier, scooped the water out of it with his hands, broke a stake out of a

fence, cleared the ice along the bank and paddled over
to the other side.

Dark-green waves with white caps whipped up by the
wind were rolling westward up the Don. In the quiet
inlets they broke up the frail transparent ice and swayed
the green tresses of the water weeds. The silvery tinkle
of breaking ice could be heard all along the banks
mingling with the soft rustle of wave-lapped shingle,
but out in the fast water, Grigory could hear only the
dull splash and gurgle of the waves crowding against the
gunwale and the low incessant murmur of the wind in
the Donside forest.

When he had pulled the boat up the bank, Grigory
sat down, took off his boots and wound his footcloths
afresh to make himself comfortable for a long walk.

By noon he was in Vyoshenskaya.

The office of the District Military Commissariat was
crowded and noisy. Telephones buzzed sharply, doors
slammed, armed men walked in and out, and from the
rooms came the curt clatter of type-writers. In the corridor a score of Red Army men were gathered round a
shortish individual in a waisted half-length sheepskin,
talking volubly and roaring with laughter. As Grigory was
walking down the corridor two Red Army men hauled
a heavy machine-gun out of the end room. Its wheels
bumped softly on the chipped wooden floor. One of the
machine-gunners, a big burly fellow, called out jestingly,
'Now then, make way, punishment company, or I'll
run you over!'

'Looks as if they're really going out to put down that
uprising,' Grigory thought to himself.

His registration did not take long. After hurriedly
marking his papers, the secretary said, 'Go and see the
Political Bureau of the Don Emergency Commission.
As a former officer, you've got to be listed with them.'

'I'll do that,' said Grigory and saluted, betraying no
sign of the anxiety that had seized him.

Out in the square his thoughts brought him to a halt.
He would have to go to the Political Bureau, but his
whole being protested agonisingly against it. 'They'll
lock me up!' an inner voice told him, and he trembled
with fear and revulsion at the thought. He stood by the
school fence, staring with unseeing eyes at the trampled
ground and saw himself with his hands tied, walking
down a dirty staircase into a cellar, and behind him, a
man firmly gripping the butt of a revolver. Grigory

clenched his fists and looked at the swollen veins. And these hands would be tied? The blood rushed to his face. No, he wouldn't go there today! Tomorrow by all means, but now he would go back to the village, spend the day with the children, see Aksinya, and come back to Vyoshenskaya in the morning. Never mind his leg that was hurting him when he walked. He'd only go home for a day and then come back, without fail! Let it all happen tomorrow, but not today!

'Ah, Melekhov! It's ages since I saw you...'

Grigory swung round. It was Yakov Fomin, who had served in the same regiment as Grigory and later commanded the mutinous 28th Regiment of the Don Army.

But this was not the old Fomin, the bearlike carelessly dressed rebel chief that Grigory had once known. In two years he had changed a lot. He was wearing a well-fitting cavalry greatcoat, his carefully groomed moustache had a dapper twist, and his whole figure, his deliberately smart bearing and complacent smile testified to a sense of his own superiority and distinction.

'What brings you here?' he asked, shaking Grigory's hand and looking hard into his face with his wide-spaced light-blue eyes.

'I've been demobbed. I've just called at the Military Commissariat...'

'Been here long?'

'Since yesterday.'

'I often remember your brother Petro. A fine Cossack he was and he died a stupid death... We used to be great pals. You shouldn't have rebelled like you did last year, Melekhov. You made a mistake there!'

Some reply was needed. Grigory said, 'Yes, the Cossacks made a mistake.'

'What unit have you been serving in?'

'The First Cavalry Army.'

'What as?'

'Squadron Commander.'

'Oh, is that so! I'm commanding a squadron myself now. The one here, in Vyoshenskaya, our security squadron.' He glanced round and, lowering his voice, suggested, 'Let's take a stroll. Walk with me for a bit. We can't talk with all these people around.'

They walked down the street together. With a sidelong glance at Grigory, Fomin asked, 'Are you going to settle down at home now?'

'Where else? At home, of course.'

'Farming?'

'That's right.'

Fomin shook his head regretfully and sighed.

'You've picked a bad time, Melekhov. Very bad... You shouldn't have turned up here for another year or two.'

'Why not?'

Bending forward and taking Grigory by the elbow, Fomin whispered, 'There's trouble brewing in the district. The Cossacks are real sore about the food requisitioning. There's been an uprising in the Boguchar area. We're going off today to put it down. You'd better clear out, lad, and quick about it. Petro and me, we were great friends, that's why I'm giving you this tip: clear out!'

'I've nowhere to go.'

'Well, see for yourself! I'm telling you this because the Political Bureau has started arresting officers. This week they brought in three cornets from Dudarevka, one from Reshetovka, and on this side of the Don they're rounding 'em up in bunches. They've even started clamping down on the rank-and-file Cossacks. So figure it out for yourself, Grigory Panteleyevich.'

'Thanks for the tip but I'm not clearing out,' Grigory said stubbornly.

'That's up to you.'

Fomin started talking about the situation in the district, his relations with the district authorities and the district military commander Shakhayev. Absorbed in his own thoughts, Grigory listened inattentively. They had walked three blocks when Fomin halted.

'I've got to call on somebody now. See you later.' He put his hand to his cap, said goodbye coldly, and walked off down sidelane with his new leather equipment creaking, very erect and absurdly pompous.

Grigory watched him go and turned back. As he climbed the stone steps of the two-storey Political Bureau building, he thought, 'If this is the end, let's get it over! You were good at making trouble, Grigory, now show us how you can answer for it!'

VIII

At about eight in the morning Aksinya raked out the stove and sat down on a bench, wiping her flushed perspiring face with her apron. She had risen before dawn to get her cooking over and done with. She had made a chicken soup with noodles, baked some pancakes, and put some dumplings liberally smeared with cream on the frying pan. She knew that Grigory was fond of well-fried dumplings and had prepared a feast in the hope that her beloved would come and eat with her.

She was longing to go to the Melekhovs on some pretext and spend a few minutes there, just to catch a glimpse of Grigory. It was unbearable to think that he was so close and yet not be able to see him. But she managed to conquer the desire and stayed at home. After all, she was not a girl. She could not act thoughtlessly at her age.

She washed her hands and face more carefully than usual, put on a clean blouse and a new embroidered underskirt, then stood for some time over the open chest wondering what to wear. It would look odd to be dressed up on a weekday, but she did not want to stay in her plain working clothes. Unable to make up her mind, she frowned as she looked through the well-ironed skirts. In the end she chose a dark-blue skirt and a light-blue blouse trimmed with black lace that she had hardly ever worn. It was the best she had. After all, did it matter what the neighbours might think? For them it might be just an ordinary day, but for her it was the day of days. She dressed hurriedly and went up to the mirror. A faint smile of surprise crossed her lips at the sight of the pair of young, zestful eyes that were studying her with merry attention. Aksinya examined her face sternly, then gave a sigh of relief. No, her good looks had not faded yet! More than one Cossack yet would stop when she approached and watch her pass with yearning eyes.

As she straightened her skirt in front of the mirror, she said aloud, 'Well, Grigory Panteleyevich, look out!' And feeling herself blush, broke into a low restrained laugh. All of this, however, did not prevent her finding a few grey hairs at her temples and plucking them out. Grigory should see nothing that might remind him of her age. For him she wanted to be just as young as she had been seven years ago.

Until dinner-time she managed to stay at home, but eventually her patience gave out and she threw a white goatswool shawl over her shoulders and went round to the Melekhovs. Dunyashka was alone in the house. Aksinya greeted her and asked, 'Haven't you had dinner yet?'

'How can you have dinner on time with stay-outs like them! My husband's at the Soviet and Grisha has gone off to Vyoshenskaya. I've fed the children and I'm still waiting for the men.'

Outwardly calm, Aksinya did not reveal by a word or a gesture how disappointed she was. She said, 'And I thought you must be all together. When will Grisha ... Grigory Panteleyevich be back? Today?'

Dunyashka gave her dressed-up neighbour a quick glance and said shortly, 'He's gone to get registered.'

'When did he promise to be back?'

Tears gleamed in Dunyashka's eyes; and she burst out reproachfully, 'You picked a fine time to dress up... Don't you know he may never come back!'

'Not come back?'

'Mikhail says he'll be arrested in Vyoshenskaya!...' Dunyashka wept a few angry tears and, as she wiped her eyes with her sleeve, cried, 'Oh, curse this rotten life! When will it all end? He goes off and the children start making such a fuss, they won't let me move. "Where's Daddy gone? When will he come back?" But how should I know? I turned them out into the yard, but I'm all upset myself... What a cursed rotten life this is! Never any peace, it's enough to make you howl!'

'If he doesn't come back tonight, I'll go to Vyoshenskaya tomorrow and find out.' Aksinya spoke in such an unconcerned voice, as if it were some everyday matter that was not worth bothering about.

Marvelling at her composure, Dunyashka said with a sigh, 'It looks as if it's no good waiting. He walked into trouble when he came back here.'

'It's too early to say yet! Stop crying, dear, or the children will wonder... Goodbye now!'

* * *

Grigory returned late in the evening. After spending a little while at home, he went to Aksinya's.

The anxiety in which she had spent the whole long day took some of the joy out of their meeting. By evening Aksinya had begun to feel as if she had worked all day without unbending her back. Exhausted and depressed by the suspense of waiting, she lay down on the bed and dozed off, but at the sound of footsteps by the window sprang off the bed like a girl.

743

'Why didn't you say you were going to Vyoshki?' she asked, hugging Grigory and unbuttoning his greatcoat.

'There wasn't time, I was in a hurry.'

'We've both had a good cry over you, Dunyashka and me; we thought you wouldn't come back.'

Grigory smiled wryly.

'It's not as bad as that.' He was silent for a moment, then added, 'Not yet!'

He limped over to the table and sat down. The door of the front room was open, revealing the broad wooden bed in the corner, the chest with its tarnished copper corner-pieces. Everything here was just as it had been when he used to come here in Stepan's absence as a lad; he could see hardly any change; even the smell was the same—the tang of fresh hops mingled with that of newly washed floors and the faint, barely perceptible scent of withered mother-of-thyme. It seemed but a short while since he had left this house at dawn. But how long ago it was in reality...

He suppressed a sigh and unhurriedly began making himself a cigarette, but for some reason his hands shook and he spilled the tobacco in his lap.

Aksinya laid the table hastily. But what about the soup? It was cold and would have to be warmed up. Pale and out of breath, she ran to the shed for kindling to light the stove. While she puffed at the spluttering chips of wood, she stole a glance at Grigory sitting hunched over the table and smoking.

'How did it go with you there? Did you settle everything?'

'It was all right.'

'What made Dunyashka so sure you'd be arrested? She scared me to death.'

Grigory frowned and threw away his cigarette in annoyance.

'Mikhail put the idea into her head. It's all his talk, calling down trouble on me.'

Aksinya came up to the table. Grigory took her hands.

'You know what,' he said, looking up into her eyes, 'things don't look too good for me. I myself thought I wouldn't be coming out again when I went to that Politbureau. After all, I was in command of a division during the uprising, I have the rank of lieutenant... That's just the kind they're clamping down on.'

'What did they say to you?'

'They gave me a list of questions to fill in, a kind of

form, where you have to put down all your service record. And I'm no good at writing. I've never had to write so much in my life. I sat there for about two hours, describing all the things I've done. Then two other men came into the room and asked me all about the uprising. Not bad fellows, quite polite. The senior one asks, "Would you like some tea? Only it's with saccharine." As if I wanted tea! All I want, I thought, is to get out of here alive.' Grigory paused and contemptuously, as if about someone else, said, 'A bit weak in the knees I turned out to be when it came to paying the price. Real scared I was.'

He was angry with himself for having taken fright, for being unable to fight his fears. And it was doubly humiliating that they had proved groundless. Now the panic he had experienced looked absurd and shameful. He had reflected on this all the way home, and for this reason, perhaps, told the whole story, ridiculing himself and somewhat exaggerating his fears.

Aksinya listened attentively, then gently freed her hands and went to the stove. While she was tending the fire, she asked, 'What will happen now?'

'I've got to report there in a week's time.'

'D'you think they'll arrest you, after all?'

'It looks like it. Sooner or later they will.'

'What shall we do? How can we live like this, Grisha?'

'I don't know. Let's talk about it later. Have you some water for me to wash with?'

They sat down to supper and once more Aksinya experienced the full-blooded happiness that she had known in the morning. Grigory was here, at her side; she could gaze at him endlessly, without thinking that others might be watching her glances, she could say everything she wanted to say with her eyes, hiding nothing and feeling no embarrassment. Oh God, how she had missed him, how her body had yearned and pined for those big, rough hands. She scarcely touched her food; leaning forward a little, she watched Grigory chewing hungrily, and with her misty gaze caressed his face, the brown neck enclosed by the high stiff collar of the tunic, the broad shoulders, and the hands resting heavily on the table... She drank in his smell, the mingled smell of astringent male sweat and tobacco, a smell that she knew so well and that was his and only his. Even blindfolded, she could have picked out Grigory from a thousand other men by that smell alone... A deep flush burned in her cheeks, her heart beat fast and resonantly. That evening she could not be an attentive hostess because she had no eyes for anything but Grigory. But he demanded no attention; he cut the bread for himself, scanned the room and spotted the salt-cellar on the stove, and gave himself a second helping of soup.

'I'm as hungry as a wolf,' he said with an apologetic smile. 'I haven't had a bite to eat since morning.'

Only then did Aksinya remember her duties and jumped hastily to her feet.

"Oh, how stupid of me! I'd forgotten all about the pancakes and dumplings! Eat some more chicken, please! Make a real good meal, my dearest! I'll have it all ready in a minute.'

But how he ate! Taking so long about it! As if he hadn't been fed for a week. There was no need whatever to press food on him. Aksinya waited patiently but in the end even her patience gave out; she moved up beside him, pulled his head towards her with her left hand, took a clean towel in her right and wiped his greasy lips and chin and, narrowing her eyes till they glittered like orange sparks in the darkness, pressed her lips breathlessly to his.

At bottom, it takes very little to make a person happy. At any rate, Aksinya was happy that evening.

IX

Grigory found it difficult to be with Koshevoi. Their relationship had crystallised on the first day, and they had nothing more to say to each other. In all probability Mikhail found no pleasure in seeing Grigory either. He hired two carpenters, who made hurried repairs to his little cottage; they replaced some rafters, pulled down and rebuilt one of the sagging walls, put in new door and window frames, and new doors.

After his return from Vyoshenskaya Grigory went to the village Revolutionary Committee, showed Koshevoi his military papers endorsed by the Military Commissariat, and left without a word. He had moved in with Aksinya and taken the children with him and some of the family property. Dunyashka wept when she saw him off to his new home.

'Don't hold it against me, brother. It's not my fault,' she said, looking up at him imploringly.

'Hold what, Dunyashka? Of course, I won't,' Grigory assured her. 'Come and see us sometimes... I'm the only one left of your family. I've always been fond of you and I still am... Your husband though, that's a different matter. But we're not going to break up our friendship.'

'We'll soon be moving out, don't be angry.'

'I'm not angry!' Grigory said vexedly. 'Stay in the house till spring if you like. You're not in my way and there's plenty of room at Aksinya's for me and the children.'

'Will you marry her, Grisha?'

'We'll have time for that later on,' Grigory replied vaguely.

'Make her your wife, brother, she's a good woman,' Dunyashka said decidedly. 'Our mother said she was the only wife for you. She took a real liking to her in her last months and often went to see her before she died.'

'Sounds as if you're trying to persuade me,' Grigory said, smiling. 'Who else should I marry but Aksinya? Not Granny Andronikha, eh?'

Andronikha was the oldest woman in Tatarsky. She was well over a hundred. Dunyashka burst out laughing at the thought of her tiny bent figure.

'The things you say, brother! I was only asking. You don't tell me anything, so I asked.'

'Don't worry, I'll invite you to the wedding if I invite anyone!' Grigory patted his sister's shoulder jokingly and left his father's house with a light heart.

To be honest, he didn't mind where he lived as long as he could live in peace. But peace was just what he could not find. For a few days he lived in a state of oppressive idleness. He tried to do a few jobs in Aksinya's yard but at once felt that there was nothing he could put his hands to. Nothing appealed to him. The uncertainty tortured him and made life unbearable; the thought was constantly on his mind that he might be arrested, and, at best, be thrown into prison. But he was just as likely to be shot.

When she woke during the night, Aksinya would see that he was not asleep. Usually he lay with his hands behind his head, staring up into the shadowy gloom, his eyes cold and angry. She knew what he was thinking about, but could do nothing to help him. It made her suffer to see his suffering and to think that her hopes of their living together would once again come to nothing. She asked him no questions. Let him decide for himself. Only once, when she awoke during the night and saw the purple glow of his cigarette did she ask, 'Grisha, still awake?.. Perhaps you'd better get out of the village while this is on? Or couldn't we go off together somewhere and hide?'

With loving care he tucked in the blanket round her feet and answered reluctantly.

'I'll think about it. Go to sleep.'

'We could come back when things settled down, couldn't we?'

But again he replied vaguely, as if unable to make up his mind, 'We'll see how things work out. Go to sleep, love,' and with a gentle tenderness he put his lips to her bare, silkily cool shoulder.

But, in fact, he had already reached a decision. He would not report to Vyoshenskaya any more. The man from the Politbureau who had received him last time would wait in vain. He had sat at the table then with his greatcoat over his shoulders, stretching himself indulgently and pretending to yawn as he listened to Grigory's story of the uprising. He would hear no more. Everything had been told.

On the day when he was to report, Grigory would disappear from the village, if necessary for a long time. Where to, he did not yet know himself, but he had firmly decided to go. He didn't want to die or be locked up. Yes, he had made his choice but there was no need to tell Aksinya at once, spoil the last few days for her; they were not all that cheerful anyway. He would have to break it to her on the last day. But now let her sleep peacefully, with her face almost buried in his armpit. She had often said during those nights, 'I like sleeping under your wing.' Well, let her sleep for the time being. She wouldn't have long, poor thing, to nestle up to him.

In the mornings Grigory played with the children, then roamed aimlessly round the village. He felt better with people around him.

One day Prokhor suggested getting together at Nikita Melnikov's for a drink with the young Cossacks who had been in the army with them. Grigory refused pointblank. He knew from the talk in the village that there was discontent over the food requisitioning. The subject was bound to come up during a drinking party and he did not want to put himself under suspicion. Even when meeting acquaintances he avoided any political discussion. He had had enough of politics; they had done him enough harm already.

Caution was all the more necessary because surplus

grain was being surrendered reluctantly, in view of which three old men had been taken as hostages and sent off to Vyoshenskaya with an escort of two requisitioners.

The next day, near the little cooperative shop that had been set up in the village Grigory met the former artilleryman Zakhar Kramskov, recently back from the Red Army. He was thoroughly drunk and swaying on his feet, but as he came up to Grigory he fastened all the buttons of his mud-stained jacket and said huskily, 'Good health to you, Grigory Panteleyevich!'

'Hullo,' Grigory grasped the massive hand that was offered to him. The stocky artilleryman was as tough as an elm.

'Recognise me?'

'Of course.'

'Remember last year at Bokovskaya how our battery saved you? Without us your cavalry would have had a rough time. The number of Reds we wiped out then, eh! First we'd give 'em an H.E., then a shrapnel... Gunlayer on the first gun! That's me!' Zakhar thumped his broad chest with his fist.

Grigory glanced around. Some Cossacks not far away were looking at them and listening. Grigory's lips twitched at the corners and his firm white teeth showed in an angry snarl.

'You're drunk,' he said in a low voice, grinding out the words through his teeth. 'Go and sleep it off and keep your big mouth shut.'

'I'm not drunk!' the tipsy gunner proclaimed loudly. 'Mebbe I am tho' —from grief! I've come home and what do I find? This is no life, it's a foggin mess! There's nothing for Cossacks to live for, and no more Cossacks either! A levy of forty poods of grain. What d'you call that? Did they sow it, the ones who tax us? Do they know what it takes to grow grain?'

He stared with bleary, bloodshot eyes and, lurching forward suddenly, gave Grigory a bear hug and breathed vodka fumes in his face.

'Why're you wearing trousers without stripes? Written yourself off as a muzhik, eh? We won't let you! M'darling boy, Grigory Panteleyevich! We've got to fight it all over again! We'll say like we did last year: down with the communes and long live Soviet power!'

Grigory pushed him away violently and whispered, 'Go home, you drunken swine! D'you know what you're saying?!'

Kramskov held up his hand with the nicotine-stained fingers extended like a fan and muttered, 'Very sorry, if I said anything wrong. Forgive me, please, but I'm telling you the truth, as my commander... You're our commander, a father to us, and I'm telling you this: we've got to fight it out all over again!'

Grigory turned away without answering and walked home across the square. Until evening he remained under the impression of the absurd encounter and, as he recalled Kramskov's tipsy utterances and the sympathetic silence and smiles of the Cossacks, he thought, 'No, I've got to get out quick! No good can come of this.'

He would have to report to Vyoshenskaya on Saturday. That meant that in three days' time he would have to quit the village. But on Thursday night, when he was just about to go to bed, someone knocked urgently at the door. Aksinya went out into the porch. Grigory heard her asking who was there. The reply was inaudible but, roused by a vague sense of alarm, he got up and went to the window. The door latch rattled. Dunyashka entered the room. Grigory saw her pale face and, without asking any questions, picked up his greatcoat and cap from the bench where he had left them.

'Brother, dear...'

'What is it?' he asked quietly, pushing his arms into the sleeves of his greatcoat.

Dunyashka poured out her story breathlessly, 'You must go away at once! We've got four horsemen, come here from the stanitsa. They're in the front room right now... They spoke in whispers but I heard what they were saying... I stood by the door and heard everything... Mikhail says you've got to be arrested... He's telling them about you... Go away now!'

Grigory stepped forward and hugged her, kissing her firmly on the cheek.

'Thank you, sister! Go back now or they'll notice you're not there. Goodbye!' He turned to Aksinya, 'Bread! Hurry! Just a hunk, not a whole loaf!'

So his only too brief peaceful life was over... He acted as he did in battle—hastily but with assurance; he went into the front room, kissed the sleeping children gently, so as not to wake them, and took Aksinya in his arms.

'Goodbye, love! I'll soon send a message, Prokhor will let you know. Look after the children. Bolt the door. If they ask, tell them he's gone to Vyoshenskaya. Well, goodbye, don't be sad, Aksinya love!' As he kissed her he felt the warm salty moisture of tears on her lips.

There was no time to comfort her or listen to her helpless babble. He gently released himself from her embrace, stepped into the porch, listened and with a sudden jerk opened the outer door. The wind from the Don splashed cold air over his face. He closed his eyes for a second, to accustom himself to the darkness.

Aksinya heard the sound of his feet crunching through the snow and every step stabbed pain into her heart. The footsteps died away and the fence creaked. Then all was quiet again, but for the wind murmuring in the forest across the Don. Aksinya strained her ears for some other sound besides that of the wind, but there was nothing. Feeling cold, she went into the kitchen and put out the lamp.

X

In the late autumn of 1920, when food-requisitioning detachments were set up to deal with the situation created by failures to deliver grain under the surplus food procurement regulations, a muffled discontent began to brew among the Cossack population of the Don. In the Upper Don stanitsas—Shumilinskaya, Kazanskaya, Migulinskaya, Meshkovskaya, Vyoshenskaya, Yelanskaya, Slashchevskaya and elsewhere—armed bands made their appearance. This was the reply of the well-to-do Cossacks to the setting up of the food-requisitioning detachments, to the more energetic measures that the Soviets were taking to enforce the delivery of food surpluses.

Most of the bands, which varied in strength from five to twenty-five bayonets, consisted of local Cossacks who had in the past been active White Guards. They included men who had served in the punitive detachments in 1918 and 1919 and sergeants, sergeants-major and junior cornets of the old Don Army who had escaped the September mobilisation of non-commissioned officers, and former insurgents who had won a reputation for their exploits or for the shooting of Red Army prisoners during the uprising on the Upper Don in the previous year—in a word, men whose road was not that of the Soviets.

They attacked food-requisitioning detachments in the villages, turned back transports carting grain to the delivery points, killed the Communists and the non-Party

Cossacks supporting Soviet power, and put up a fight whenever they could.

The task of getting rid of these bands was assigned to the garrison battalion of the Upper Don District, which was stationed in Vyoshenskaya and the village of Bazki. But all efforts to destroy the bands, which were scattered over a vast area, proved fruitless—first, because the local population supported the bandits, kept them supplied with food and information on the movements of the Red Army units, and also hid them if needs be, and, secondly, because the commander of the battalion, one Kaparin, a former captain of the tsarist army and a Socialist-Revolutionary, had no desire to destroy the counter-revolutionary forces that had recently sprung up on the Upper Don and did all he could to hinder operations against them. Only occasionally, under pressure from the chairman of the District Party Committee, did he undertake brief expeditions, quickly returning to Vyoshenskaya on the grounds that he could not disperse his forces and be so irresponsible as to risk leaving Vyoshenskaya with its district administration offices and stores undefended. The battalion, which numbered about four hundred bayonets and fourteen machine-guns, was mainly engaged in garrison duties. The men guarded prisoners, carted water, felled timber in the forest, and as a contribution to the nation's labour effort gathered gallnuts in the oak woods for making ink. The battalion kept all the numerous district institutions and offices well supplied with ink and firewood, while the number of small insurgent bands in the district swelled to threatening proportions. And only in December, when a big revolt broke out on the territory of the neighbouring Boguchar district did the wood-felling and collection of gallnuts come to a sudden end. On the orders of the Commander-in-Chief of the Don Region the battalion, consisting of three companies and a machine-gun platoon, together with the garrison cavalry squadron, the 1st Battalion of the 12th Food Procurement Regiment and two small security detachments, were sent to crush the revolt.

In an engagement on the approaches to the village of Sukhoi Donets the Vyoshenskaya squadron under Yakov Fomin attacked the insurgent lines from the flank, overran them and put them to flight, cutting down about a hundred and seventeen men in the pursuit with a loss of only three of its own men. All but a few of the squadron were Cossacks from the Upper Don, and here, too, they remained faithful to ancient Cossack tradition. After the battle, despite the protests of the squadron's two Communists, nearly half the squadron changed their old greatcoats and wadded jackets for warm well-made sheepskin coats taken off the insurgents.

A few days after the suppression of the revolt the squadron was withdrawn to Kazanskaya. To compensate for the burdens of army life Fomin took what amusement he could find in the stanitsa. An incorrigible ladies' man and a cheerful and sociable tippler, he would disappear for nights on end and turn up at his quarters only at dawn. When his men, with whom Fomin was on back-slapping terms, saw their commander in the street in well-polished boots, they would wink to each other and say, 'Off he goes to the grass widows, our stallion! Now only the dawn will flush him out.'

Unbeknown to the commissar and the political organiser, Fomin also visited the quarters of his cronies in the squadron if he heard there was some hard liquor going. And his visits were not infrequent. But it was not long before the dashing commander became discouraged and gloomy and almost forgot his former pastimes. In the evenings he no longer polished his smart top-boots with the same zeal, he stopped shaving every day, and though he still occasionally dropped in for a drink on the men of his village who were serving in the squadron, he showed little inclination to talk on these social occasions.

The change in Fomin's character coincided with a message the detachment commander had received from the Political Bureau of the Don Emergency Commission in Vyoshenskaya, informing him that in Mikhailovka, a village of the neighbouring Ust-Medveditskaya District, the garrison battalion commanded by Vakulin had mutinied.

Vakulin had been a regimental comrade and friend of Fomin's. They had at one time served under Mironov. Together they had marched from Saransk to the Don, and together they had laid down their arms in the same heap when Mironov's rebellious corps had been surrounded by Budyonny's cavalry. Fomin and Vakulin had remained on friendly terms until quite recently. Not long ago, at the beginning of September, Vakulin had come to Vyoshenskaya, and even then he had been grinding his teeth and complaining to his old friend about 'having the screws put on us by commissars who're ruining the farmers with their food requisitioning and leading the country to destruction'. Inwardly Fomin shared Vakulin's views but he acted cautiously, with the cunning that had often made up for his lack of natural intelligence. On the whole, he was a cautious man. He never hurried and never said yes or no at once. But soon after he learned of the mutiny of Vakulin's squadron, his habitual caution deserted him. One evening, before the squadron was due to return to Vyoshenskaya, one of the troop commanders, Alferov, held a party. A huge horse bucket of home-brew stood on the table. The talk grew animated. Fomin listened in silence and without comment scooped liquor from the bucket. But when one of the men recalled the charge they had made at Sukhoi Donets, Fomin interrupted the speaker and, twirling his moustache, said, 'Ay, we didn't do badly chopping up the Tufties, but let's hope we don't get into trouble ourselves soon... What if we get back to Vyoshenskaya and find that the food detachments have grabbed all the grain our families stocked up? The folk here are pretty sore with these food detachments. They're sweeping the bins clean as a whistle.'

A hush fell on the room. Fomin surveyed his men and, forcing a smile, said, 'I was just joking... Mind you don't blab it around or they'll make the devil knows what out of a mere joke.'

On his return to Vyoshenskaya, Fomin set off for his home village of Rubezhny, accompanied by a half troop of Red Army men. In the village he dismounted without riding into his yard, tossed the reins to one of the men and walked to the house.

He nodded coldly to his wife, made a low bow to his aged mother, greeted her respectfully, and embraced his children.

'Where's Dad?' he asked, seating himself on a stool and planting his sabre between his knees.

'He be gone off to the mill,' the old woman replied and, looking up at her son, commanded sternly, 'Take your hat off, infidel! Who sits under the ikon in his hat? Mark my words, Yakov, you'll come to a bad end.'

Fomin smiled reluctantly, and removed his round Kuban cap, but not his coat.

'Why don't you take your coat off?'

'I've only dropped in for a minute to see you. My duties don't leave me any time to myself.'

'We know all about your duties,' the old woman said

severely, alluding to her son's dissolute life and woman-chasing in Vyoshenskaya.

Rumours of that had long since made the rounds of Rubezhny.

Fomin's wife, prematurely aged, pale and down-trodden, shot a scared look at her mother-in-law and withdrew to the stove. In an attempt to please her husband in some way, to win his favour and be granted just one glance of affection, she took a cloth from under the stove, knelt down and with her back bowed began to clean the thick mud off Fomin's boots.

'What a fine pair of boots you've got there, Yasha... And how muddy they are... But soon I'll make them clean again, it won't take a minute!' she whispered almost inaudibly, not daring to raise her head as she grovelled before her husband.

He had given up living with her long ago and now experienced no feeling for the woman he had loved as a young man other than a rather contemptuous pity. But she had always loved him and, secretly hoping that one day he would return to her, forgave him everything. Year after year she had run the farm, brought up the children, and done all she could to please her harsh-tempered mother-in-law. All the burden of the field work rested on her thin shoulders. The back-breaking work and an illness that had begun after the birth of her second child had sapped her health as the years went by. She had lost weight and all the colour had gone out of her face.

Premature age had carved a web of wrinkles in her cheeks. Her eyes had acquired the expression of fright-ened submission that one finds in sick intelligent ani-mals. She herself had not noticed how quickly she was ageing, how her health was declining, and, still cherish-ing a forlorn hope, she gazed at her handsome husband, on the rare occasions when they met, with a timid love and admiration.

Fomin looked down at his wife's pitifully bent back with its thin shoulder blades jutting out under the blouse, at her big trembling hands diligently scraping the mud off his boots and thought, 'What a beauty, I must say! And I used to sleep with this hag... My God, she's aged... How much older she looks!'

'Leave it! I'll soon get 'em dirty again,' he said irri-tably, freeing his feet from his wife's hands.

She straightened her back with an effort and stood up.

755

A slight flush had appeared in her sallow cheeks. There was so much love and doglike devotion in the moist gaze she directed at her husband that he turned away and asked his mother, 'Well, how are you getting on here?'

'The same as usual,' the old woman replied morosely.

'Has the food detachment been in the village?'

'Only yesterday they went off to Lower Krivskaya.'

'Did they take any of your grain?'

'Yes. How much did they cart away, Davydka?'

A lad of fourteen, very much like his father, with the same widely spaced light-blue eyes, replied, 'Grandad was there, he knows. Ten sacks, I think.'

'I see...' Fomin rose, shot a brief glance at his son, and adjusted his sword belt. His face had paled. 'Did you tell 'em whose grain they were taking?' he asked.

The old woman let her hand cleave the air and smiled, not without malice.

'Your name don't mean much to them! Their top man, he says, "Everyone without no exception has got to give in any grain they have to spare. He can be Fomin or the District Chairman, but we'll still take his surplus grain!" And off they went to our corn bins.'

'I'll pay them back for that, Mother! I'll get even with 'em!' Fomin muttered and, after a hasty farewell, left the house.

After his visit home, he began cautiously sounding out the men in his squadron and without much difficulty discovered that the majority disapproved of the grain requisitioning. Their wives and near and distant relatives came in from the villages with tales of how the food-detachment men made searches and carted off all the grain, leaving only enough for seed and feeding the family. The result of all this was that at the end of January, at a garrison meeting in Bazki, during a speech by Military Commissar Shakhayev, the men of the squadron protested openly.

'Get rid of the food detachments!'

'No more of this grain business!'

'Down with the food commissars!'

The Red Army men of the security company shouted back, 'Contras!' and 'Disband this scum!'

The meeting was long and stormy. One of the few Communists in the garrison turned anxiously to Fomin, 'You speak to them, Comrade Fomin! Listen to the way your men are carrying on!'

Fomin smiled into his moustache.

'But I'm a non-Party man, they won't listen to me!'

He made no contribution to the discussion and left, long before the meeting was over, with Kaparin, the battalion commander. On the way to Vyoshenskaya they talked things over and very soon found they understood each other. A week later, in a confidential meeting between the two of them at Fomin's quarters, Kaparin told him, 'Either we act now or we'll never act. You've got to realise that, Yakov Yefimovich! We've got to seize the chance. This is a good moment. The Cossacks support us. Your prestige in the district is high. The mood of the population couldn't be more favourable. Why are you holding back? Come to a decision!'

'What is there to decide?' Fomin drawled slowly, looking up from under lowered brows. 'It's all decided. Only we've got to work out a plan that'll work without a hitch. That's what we've got to talk about.'

The suspicious friendship between Fomin and Kaparin did not pass unnoticed. Some of the Communists in the battalion started keeping a watch on them and reported their suspicions to Artemyev, head of the Political Bureau of the Don Emergency Commission, and Shakhayev, the Military Commissar.

'Once frightened twice shy,' Artemyev said, laughing. 'That Kaparin is a coward. D'you think he'd ever dare to start anything? We'll watch Fomin, we've had an eye on him for some time, but I shouldn't think even Fomin would risk any action. It's a lot of bunk,' he concluded firmly.

But it was too late for watching; the plotters had laid their plans already. The revolt was to begin on March 12th at eight in the morning. On that day Fomin was to lead his squadron out for its morning exercises fully armed, then launch a sudden attack on the machine-gun platoon, capture the guns, and help the garrison company to 'purge' the district institutions.

Kaparin was worried that he might not have the support of the whole battalion and confided his doubts to Fomin, who listened attentively and said, 'It'll be all right as long as we grab the machine-guns. We'll soon bring your battalion to heel after that.'

Careful surveillance of Fomin and Kaparin produced no results. If the two men ever met, it was only in the course of their duties. Not until one night at the end of February did a patrol spot them together in the street. Fomin was leading his saddled horse by the bridle and

Kaparin was walking beside him. When challenged, Kaparin called back 'Friends'. They went into Kaparin's quarters. Fomin tethered his horse to the porch. No lamp was lighted in the room. It was after three in the morning when Fomin reappeared, mounted his horse and rode to his own quarters. This was all that could be established.

In a coded telegram to the Commander-in-Chief of the Don Region, District Military Commissar Shakhayev reported his suspicions concerning Fomin and Kaparin. A few days later he received a reply sanctioning the removal of both men from their posts and their arrest.

At a meeting of the District Party Bureau it was decided to tell Fomin that by order of the District Military Commissariat he had been summoned to Novocherkassk to place himself at the disposal of the Commander-in-Chief and that he should hand over the squadron to his second-in-command Ovchinnikov: the same day the squadron was to be sent to Kazanskaya on the pretext that a band had appeared in the area, after which the conspirators would be arrested during the night. The decision to get the squadron out of Vyoshenskaya was prompted by fears that it might mutiny if it knew of Fomin's arrest. Tkachenko, a Communist and commander of the second company of the garrison battalion, was given the task of warning the battalion's Communists and company commanders of the possibility of a mutiny and alerting the company and machine-gun platoon that were stationed in Vyoshenskaya.

The next morning Fomin received the order.

'All right then, you take over the squadron, Ovchinnikov. I'm going to Novocherkassk,' he said calmly, 'Do you want to see the records?'

Troop Commander Ovchinnikov, a non-party man, who had been given no warning and suspected nothing, started poring over the squadron's record books.

Fomin seized the opportunity and scribbled a note to Kaparin: 'We attack today. I'm being dismissed. Get ready.' In the porch he handed the note to his orderly and whispered, 'Put this note in your cheek and ride at a walk—at a walk, understand?—to Kaparin's. If anyone stops you on the way, swallow it. As soon as you've delivered, come back here.'

On receiving the order to proceed to Kazanskaya, Ovchinnikov drew up the squadron in marching order on the square in front of the church. When he had done so, Fomin appeared and rode up to him.

'Allow me to say goodbye to the squadron.'

'By all means. But keep it short.'

Reining in his restive mount in front of the squadron, Fomin addressed the troops.

'You know me, comrades. You know that I have always been a fighter. I've always been with you. But what I won't stand for is when they rob the Cossacks, rob those who till the soil and grow the grain. And that's why I've been dismissed from my command. I know what they'll do to me. So I want to say goodbye to you...'

For a second the uproar in the squadron interrupted Fomin's speech. He rose in his stirrups and raised his voice sharply.

'If you want to put a stop to this robbery, kick the food detachments out of here, smash the procurement commissars, and military commissars! They've come here to the Don...'

Shouting drowned Fomin's concluding words. He waited for the right moment, then bellowed his order.

'By the right, in threes, quick—march!'

The squadron obediently responded. Ovchinnikov, dumbfounded by what had happened, charged up to Fomin.

'Where're you going, Comrade Fomin?'

Without turning his head, Fomin replied derisively, 'We'll just take a ride round the church.'

Only then did Ovchinnikov realise what had been happening in the past few minutes. He broke away from the column; the political organiser, the assistant commissar and only one Red Army man followed him. Fomin noticed their absence when they had ridden about ten paces. Turning his horse, he shouted, 'Ovchinnikov, halt there!'

The four horsemen went from a trot into a gallop, scattering clots of half-melted snow on all sides.

Fomin commanded, 'To arms! Catch Ovchinnikov!.. First troop! After him!'

Scattered shots rang out. About sixteen men of the First Troop rode in pursuit. Meanwhile Fomin broke the rest of the squadron into two groups. One of them, led by the commander of the Third Troop, was sent to disarm the machine-gun platoon, while he himself led the other to the quarters of the garrison company, which was stationed on the northern outskirts of the stanitsa, in the old stud-farm stables.

The first group charged down along the main street,

firing in the air and brandishing their sabres. After cutting down four Communists they happened to meet, the mutineers formed up hurriedly on the edge of the stanitsa and silently, without cheering, rode forward to attack the men of the machine-gun platoon, who had come running out of their quarters.

The house where the platoon was billeted stood by itself. The distance between it and the last houses in the stanitsa was not more than two hundred paces, but when they encountered point-blank machine-gun fire, the mutineers swung their horses round and rode back. Three of them were hit before they reached the nearest lane. The attempt to take the machine-gunners by surprise had failed. No second attempt was undertaken. Chumakov, the commander of the Third Troop, got his group under cover and, without dismounting, took a cautious look from the corner of a stone shed.

'They've rolled out a couple more Maxims,' he reported, then wiped his sweating forehead with his lambskin cap and turned to his men. 'Let's go back, lads!.. We'll leave the machine-gunners to Fomin. How many are lying there on the snow—three? Well, let him try it himself.'

As soon as the firing started on the eastern edge of the stanitsa, Tkachenko, the commander of the garrison company, ran out of his quarters, pulling on his coat as he ran, and headed for the barracks. About thirty Red Army men were already lined up outside the building. They greeted their commander with bewildered questions.

'Who's shooting?'

'What's going on?'

Without replying, Tkachenko formed up the rest of the men who had run out of the building. A few Communists who worked in the district administration dashed up at about the same time and fell in with the others.

Rifle fire crackled in various parts of the stanitsa. Somewhere on the western outskirts a hand grenade went off with a boom. At the sight of fifty mounted men with bared sabres galloping in the direction of the barracks, Tkachenko unhurriedly drew his revolver. There was no time to give orders. His men stopped talking and got into position with their rifles.

'But they're our lot! That's our battalion commander Comrade Kaparin!' one of them burst out.

The attackers rode out of the street and, all together, as if at a word of command, crouched over their horses' necks and galloped flat out for the barracks.

'Stop 'em!' Tkachenko yelled.

A volley crashed out, drowning his voice. At a hundred paces from the company's ranks four riders came off their horses. The rest scattered in disorder and rode back. A flurry of shots followed them. One rider, evidently slightly wounded, slid out of his saddle, but managed to keep hold of the reins. For about twenty paces he was dragged along by the galloping horse, then found his feet, grasped a stirrup and the cantle of the saddle and in a flash was back on his horse. With a fierce tug at the reins he swung round at full gallop and disappeared into the nearest lane.

The men of the First Troop, after a fruitless pursuit of Ovchinnikov, returned to the stanitsa. A search for Commissar Shakhayev yielded no results. He was not to be found in the deserted offices of the Military Commissariat or at his quarters. When the shooting broke out, he had run down to the Don and across the ice into the forest, and from there to the village of Bazki. By the next day he was fifty versts from Vyoshenskaya, in Ust-Khopyorskaya.

The majority of the leading functionaries managed to go into hiding. It was not very safe to search for them because the Red Army men of the machine-gun platoon, armed with light machine-guns, had occupied the centre of the stanitsa and were covering all the streets adjoining the main square.

The mutineers abandoned their search, rode down to the Don and galloped to the church square, where they had begun their pursuit of Ovchinnikov. Soon the whole of Fomin's squadron had assembled there. They formed up again. Fomin mounted guard posts and ordered the rest of the men to go back to their quarters but keep their horses saddled.

Fomin and Kaparin and the troop commanders withdrew to one of the houses on the outskirts.

'The game's up!' Kaparin exclaimed in despair, sinking exhaustedly on to a bench.

'Ay, we didn't capture the stanitsa, so we can't hold out here,' Fomin said quietly.

'We'd better take a ride round the district, Yakov Yefimovich. What's the odds? We won't die before we're dead anyhow. We'll rouse the Cossacks, and then we'll get the stanitsa back,' Chumakov proposed.

Fomin eyed him in silence, and turned to Kaparin.

'Upset, Your Honour? Wipe the snot off your nose! We started together, so we'll have to get on with it together... What d'you think—should we leave the stanitsa or have another try?'

Chumakov interrupted sharply.

'Let others do the trying! I'm not going to charge machine-guns head on. It's a dead loss, that is.'

'I'm not asking you, so shut up!' Fomin snapped, and gave Chumakov a look that made the Cossack drop his eyes.

After a brief pause Kaparin said, 'No, there's no sense in starting all over again. They have a superiority in arms. Fourteen machine-guns, and we have none. And they've got more men too... We'll have to withdraw and start organising the Cossacks for an uprising. Before reinforcements arrive, we can have the whole district up in arms. That's our only hope!'

After a long silence Fomin said, 'Well, that's what we'll have to do then. Troop commander! Go and check the equipment and count each man's ammunition. It's a strict order that not one bullet is to be wasted. The first man to disobey will be cut down by me personally. Tell 'em that.' He paused and thumped angrily on the table with his huge fist. 'Damn those machine-guns! But it's all your fault, Chumakov! Couldn't you have got at least four of 'em! Now, of course, they'll drive us out of the stanitsa... Well, off you go! If they don't attack us, we'll spend the night here and march out at dawn. We'll make a tour of the district.'

The night passed calmly, with the mutinous squadron at one end of Vyoshenskaya and the garrison company and the Communists and Young Communists who had joined it, at the other. Only two blocks divided the opposing forces, but neither side ventured to launch a night attack.

In the morning the mutinous squadron withdrew without a fight and rode off in a south-easterly direction.

XI

For the first three weeks after leaving the village Grigory lived in Upper Krivsky, near Yelanskaya, with a Cossack of his old regiment. After that he went on to Gorbatovsky and lived there for a month, with a distant relative of Aksinya's.

He lay for days on end on his bed, going outside only

at night. It was all very much like a prison. Grigory suffered desperately from home-sickness and the enforced idleness and felt irresistibly drawn towards home, the children and Aksinya. Time and again during those sleepless nights he pulled on his greatcoat with the firm intention of returning to Tatarsky, but each time he changed his mind, took off his coat and flung himself down on the bed with a groan. In the end it was more than he could bear. His host, an uncle, once removed, of Aksinya's, sympathised with Grigory but could not shelter such a guest for ever. One day, when he had gone to his room after supper, Grigory heard hosts talking. The man's wife was asking in a voice shrill with hatred, 'When will all this end?'

'What? What're you talking about?' her husband's deep voice replied.

'When will you get rid of this sponger?'

'Be quiet, woman!'

'No, I won't be quiet! We've got precious little grain left for ourselves, and you keep that hunchbacked devil here, feeding him every day. How much longer will it go on, I ask you? What if the Soviet gets to know about it? They'll have our heads, orphan our children!..'

'Be quiet, Avdotya!'

'I won't be quiet! We've got children! There's no more than twenty poods of grain left, and you go on feeding this sponger. What relation is he to you? Your own brother? A cousin? He's nothing to do with your family! He's nobody to you, and you keep him and feed him, and give him our milk to drink! Shut up, you bald devil! Or tomorrow I'll go to the Soviet myself and tell them what a nice customer you've got in the house!'

The next day the master of the house came into Grigory's room and, staring at the floor, said, 'Grigory Panteleyevich! Think what you like of me, but you can't live in my house any more... I respect you, and I knew and respected your late father, but right now it's too much for me to give you bed and board... And I'm afraid the authorities may find out about you. Go where you like. I've got a family, I can't risk my neck for your sake. Forgive me, for the Lord's sake, but spare us that.'

'All right then,' Grigory said curtly. 'Thanks for your hospitality, for sheltering me. Thanks for everything. I can see I'm a burden to you, but where am I to go? All roads are closed to me.'

'That's up to you.'

'All right. I'll leave tonight. Thank you, Artamon Vasilyevich, for everything.'

'It was nothing.'

'I won't forget your kindness. Mebbe one day I'll be able to help you.'

Deeply moved, his host slapped him on the shoulder.

'Say no more! If it was up to me you could stay on another couple of months, but my old woman won't have it. She's been ranting at me every day, the bitch! I'm a Cossack and you're a Cossack; we're both against the Soviets and I'll help you out. Make for the village of Yagodny. I've got a cousin who lives there, he'll take you in. Tell him from me: Artamon says you're to treat me like his own son, feed me and keep me for as long as you can manage it. I'll settle with him later. But mind you go away tonight. I can't keep you here any longer. On the one hand there's the wife pitching into me, and on the other I'm afraid the Soviet may find out... You've had a good spell with us, Grigory Panteleyevich, so let's call it a day. I value my life, too, ye know...'

Late that night Grigory left the village and had barely reached the windmill on the hill when three horsemen appeared from nowhere and challenged him.

'Stop, you son-of-a-bitch! Who are you?'

Grigory's heart sank. He halted without answering. It would have been senseless to run. On either side of the road there was not a ditch or a bush, nothing but bare, deserted steppe. He wouldn't have got far.

'You a Communist? Back you go, curse your mother! Now then, look lively!'

Another horseman rode down on Grigory and ordered, 'Hands out of your pockets! Out with 'em, or I'll slash your head off!'

Grigory silently took his hands out of the pockets of his greatcoat and, still wondering what had happened to him and what kind of men his captors were, asked, 'Where am I to go?'

'Back to the village. Turn round.'

One rider escorted him into the village. The other two left them on the outskirts and rode off towards the highway. Grigory walked on in silence. In the village he slowed down a little and asked, 'Who are you?'

'Keep going! No talking! Hands behind your back, d'ye hear?'

Grigory obeyed, but a little further on he asked again, 'Now, look here, who are you?'

'Orthodox.'

'I'm not an Old Believer myself.'

'Thank your lucky stars then.'

'Where're you taking me?'

'To the commander. Keep moving, scum, or I'll...'

The escort gave Grigory a prick with his sabre. The well-sharpened point touched Grigory's bare neck, just between the collar of his coat and his cap; terror flared up in him for a moment, to be followed at once by helpless anger. Turning up his collar, he twisted his head to glance at his escort and said through clenched teeth, 'Don't fool around! D'ye hear? Or I might get that thing away from you...'

'Go on, you bastard, stop talking! I'll show you get away! Hands behind your back!'

Grigory took another couple of paces in silence, then said, 'I've not been talking, so stop cursing me. What a shit, eh!'

'Don't look round!'

'I'm not looking round.'

'Shut up and get a move on!'

'Mebbe you want me to trot?' Grigory asked, wiping snowflakes off his eyelashes.

Without replying, the escort flicked his horse with the reins. The animal's chest, clammy with sweat and the nocturnal damp, cannoned into Grigory's back and a hoof squelched into the melting snow just by his foot.

'Careful!' Grigory shouted, clutching at the horse's mane.

His escort raised his sabre to head level and said quietly, 'Get moving, you bastard, and stop your gob, or I won't take you all the way. I've got a light touch. Shut up! Not another word out of ye!'

No more was said for the rest of the way. At the first farmstead the rider reined in his mount and said, 'Go in through that gate.'

Grigory entered the open gate. A large house with an iron roof loomed up at the back of the yard. Horses were snorting and champing loudly under the overhang of a shed. About six armed men were standing round the porch. The escort sheathed his sabre and said as he dismounted, 'Go inside, straight up the steps, first door on the left. Go in and don't look round. How many more times have I got to tell ye, damn your eyes and guts!'

Grigory climbed the steps of the porch slowly. A man in a Budyonny helmet and long cavalry greatcoat standing by the rail asked, 'Just caught, eh?'

'Ay, picked him up by the windmill,' the familiar husky voice of Grigory's escort answered.

'Group secretary or what?'

'Darned if I know. Some bastard or other, but we'll soon find out who he is.'

'Either this is a band or it's the Emergency Commission men from Vyoshenskaya, playing their tricks. I've walked right into it, like a fool,' Grigory thought, lingering in the porch deliberately as he tried to gather his thoughts.

The first person he saw when he opened the door was Fomin. He was sitting at a table surrounded by several men in uniform, all of them strangers to Grigory. Greatcoats and sheepskins were heaped on the bed, carbines were stacked against a bench, which was piled with sabres, cartridge belts, pouches and saddle-bags. The men, the coats and their equipment stank of horse sweat.

Grigory took off his hat and said quietly, 'Hullo there!'

'Melekhov! Well, it's a small world! So we meet again! Where did you spring from? Take your coat off and sit down.' Fomin rose from the table and walked up to Grigory, holding out his hand. 'What are you doing around here?'

'I had some business to deal with.'

'What business? You're a long way from home...' Fomin eyed Grigory curiously. 'Out with it now—were you in hiding here?'

'That's the whole truth,' Grigory said, forcing a smile.

'Where did my lads pick you up?'

'Near the village.'

'Where were you making for?'

'Nowhere in particular.'

Fomin gave Grigory another keen look and smiled.

'I see you think we've caught you and are going to take you back to Vyoshenskaya? No, matey, that road's barred to us... Don't be scared! We've stopped serving the Soviets. We didn't get on together.'

'Ay, we've got a divorce,' an elderly Cossack who was smoking by the stove, remarked.

One of the men at the table gave a loud laugh.

'Have you heard anything about me?' Fomin asked.

'No.'

'Well, sit down and we'll have a talk. Soup and meat for our guest!'

Grigory did not believe a word of what Fomin was saying. Pale and reserved, he took off his coat and sat down at the table. He felt badly in need of a cigarette, but remembered that he had run out of tobacco two days ago.

'Got anything to smoke?' he asked Fomin.

Fomin obligingly offered him a leather cigarette case. He noticed that the fingers with which Grigory took the cigarette were trembling slightly, and smiled again into his flowing ginger moustache.

'We've risen against the Soviets. We're for the people and against the food requisitioning and the commissars. They've fooled us long enough, now we're going to fool them. Understand, Melekhov?'

Grigory lighted up and took several hurried pulls without replying. He felt dizzy and rather sick. He hadn't had much to eat for the past month, and only now did he realise how weak he had become. He stubbed out his cigarette and tackled the food hungrily. Fomin told him briefly about the mutiny and their first days of roaming round the district, bombastically describing their furtive wanderings as a 'raid'. Grigory listened in silence and swallowed down the bread and greasy, badly cooked mutton almost without chewing.

'You've got bloody thin while you've been visiting,' Fomin said, chuckling good-naturedly.

'I wasn't living with my mother-in-law,' Grigory muttered, with a belch.

'You don't look like it. Tuck in, man, put away as much as you can. We don't grudge the grub here.'

'Thanks. Now I feel like a smoke.' Grigory took the cigarette that was offered him, went up to an iron pot standing on a bench, lifted the wooden lid and scooped out some water. It was icy cold and slightly salty. He gulped down two big mugfuls, after which he smoked with pleasure.

'The Cossacks aren't all that glad to see us,' Fomin went on with his story, taking a seat beside Grigory. 'They had a proper shake-up last year during the uprising... But some of them volunteer. We've had about forty join us. We've set our sights higher than that though. We want to rouse the whole district and get the neighbouring districts to help us. Then we'll be able to have it out, heart to heart, with this Soviet government!'

A noisy discussion was going on at the table. While Grigory listened to Fomin, he quietly observed the men with him. Not a single familiar face! No, Fomin was not to be trusted, he must be up to something. Caution promted Grigory to hold his tongue, but he couldn't be silent all the time.

'If you mean what you say, Comrade Fomin, what is it you want to do? Start a new war?' he asked, fighting the drowsiness that had assailed him.

'I've told you what we want.'

'To change the government?'

'Right.'

'What will you put in its place?'

'Our own, Cossack government!'

'The atamans?'

'Well, it's a bit too soon to talk about atamans. We'll set up a government elected by the people. But that won't be just yet. Anyway I'm not so hot on politics. I'm a military man, it's my job to destroy commissars and Communists, and as for the government, Kaparin, my chief of staff, will tell you about that. He's the big brain on all such matters. Knows his stuff, he does. Educated man!' Fomin leaned towards Grigory and whispered, 'Used to be a captain in the tsarist army. A real bright lad! Right now he's asleep in the front room. He's feeling poorly. Guess he's not used to the long marches we're making.'

From the porch came the sounds of a scuffle, a groan, more scuffling and a muffled shout, 'Give him one!' The talk at the table died away at once. Fomin shot a wary glance at the door. Someone jerked it open and a white cloud of steam flowed downwards into the room. A tall man, hatless and wearing a wadded jacket and grey felt boots, propelled by a heavy blow on the back, staggered into the room and struck his shoulder hard on the corner of the stove. From the porch someone shouted cheerfully, before slamming the door, 'Here y'are, take another one!'

Fomin rose and straightened the belt round his tunic.

'Who are you?' he asked sternly.

Breathing heavily, the man in the jacket ran his hand through his hair and winced with pain as he tried to move his shoulder blades. The blow, evidently with a rifle butt, must have touched his spine.

'Why don't you speak? Lost your tongue? Who are you, I said?'

'I'm in the Red Army.'

'What unit?'

'Twelfth Food Regiment.'

'Ah, here's a find!' said one of the men at the table, smiling.

Fomin continued his interrogation.

'What are you doing here?'

'Defence detachment. They sent us to...'

'Yes, I know. How many of you here in the village?'

'Fourteen.'

'Where are the rest?'

For a moment the Red Army man said nothing, then with an effort he parted his lips. A gurgle rose from his throat and a thin stream of blood trickled from the left corner of his mouth. He wiped his lips with his hand, looked at the palm and rubbed it clean on his trousers.

'That bastard ... of yours...' he croaked, swallowing blood, 'damaged my lungs.'

'Never mind! We'll cure you!' a stocky Cossack said derisively, rising from the table and winking at the others.

'Where are the rest?' Fomin asked again.

'They've gone off to Yelanskaya with the transports.'

'Where're you from? Where were you born?'

The Red Army man looked at Fomin with feverishly bright blue eyes, spat out a clot of blood, and replied in a deep clear voice, 'Pskov Province.'

'Pskov, Moscow... We've heard of your kind before,' Fomin said mockingly. 'You came a long way, lad, to grab other folk's grain.. Well, let's get it over, eh? What'll we do with you?'

'You should let me go.'

'You're a straightforward lad, aren't you!.. Or mebbe we'll let him go, boys? What d'ye say?' Fomin turned to the men at the table, chuckling into his moustache.

Grigory, who had been watching the whole scene closely, noticed the comprehending smiles on the brown weather-beaten faces.

'Take him on for a couple of months, then we'll let him go home to his woman,' said one of Fomin's men.

'Mebbe you'll serve with us?' Fomin asked, vainly trying to hide a smile. 'We'll give you a horse, a saddle, and instead of that felt crap you've got on your feet, a pair of new top-boots... A rotten outfit your commanders give you. D'you call them boots? The snow's melting and there are you with felt on your feet. Why don't you join us, eh?'

'He's a muzhik, he's never ridden a horse in his life,'

one of the Cossacks squeaked in a high-pitched voice, clowning.

The Red Army man said nothing. He leaned back against the stove, surveying the company with clear, no longer feverish eyes. Sometimes he winced with pain, opening his mouth a little when he found it hard to breathe.

'Well, will you stay with us?' Fomin asked once more.

'Who are you?'

'Who are we?' Fomin raised his eyebrows sharply, and stroked his moustache. 'We're fighters for the working people. We're against the tyranny of the commissars and Communists, that's what we are.'

And then Grigory suddenly saw a smile on the Red Army man's face.

'So that's what you are... And I was wondering,' the prisoner smiled, showing his blood-stained teeth, and spoke as though he were pleasantly surprised at the news he had just heard, but there was something in his voice that put his listeners on their guard. 'So the way you look at it, you're fighters for the people? But the way we look at it, you're just bandits. And you expect me to serve with you? You're some jokers, I must say!'

'You're a cheerful feller yourself, from what I've seen of you.' Fomin narrowed his eyes and asked curtly, 'You a Communist?'

'No, I don't belong to any party.'

'It doesn't sound like it.'

'Honestly, I'm a non-Party man.'

Fomin cleared his throat, and then turned to the table. 'Chumakov! Get rid of him.'

'You've got no reason to kill me,' the Red Army man said quietly.

He was answered by a silence. Chumakov, a stocky handsome Cossack in a British jerkin, rose unwillingly from the table and smoothed down his already smoothly combed light-brown hair.

'I'm fed up with this job,' he said cheerfully, pulling a sabre out of the pile on the bench and testing the blade with his thumb.

'You don't have to do it yourself. Tell the lads in the yard,' Fomin advised.

Chumakov eyed the Red Army man coldly, from head to foot, and said, 'Get moving, son.'

The prisoner lurched away from the stove, hunched his shoulders, and walked slowly to the door, leaving wet marks on the floor from his sodden felt boots.

'You might have wiped your feet first! Coming in here, spoiling our floor like this!.. You dirty feller!' Chumakov pretended to grumble as he followed the prisoner.

'Tell 'em to take him out in the street or to the threshing floor. Don't do it by the house. The owners don't like it!' Fomin shouted after him.

He went over to Grigory and sat down beside him. 'We try 'em quick, don't we?' he said.

'Yes, you do,' Grigory replied, avoiding his glance.

Fomin drew a deep breath.

'Nothing else you can do. That's how it's got to be now.' He was about to say something else, but there was a scuffle on the porch, someone shouted, and a single shot rang out.

'What are they mucking about at there!' Fomin exclaimed in annoyance.

One of the men at the table jumped up and kicked the door open.

'What's the matter there?' he shouted into the darkness.

Chumakov came in and said excitedly, 'The lively bugger! Jumped off the top step and ran for it. I had to waste a bullet. The boys are finishing him off...'

'Tell 'em to dump him in the lane.'

'I've told 'em already, Yakov Yefimovich.'

For a minute there was a hush in the room, then someone asked, 'How's the weather, Chumakov? Not clearing up yet, is it?'

'Some big clouds about.'

'If it rains, it'll wash the last snow away.'

'So what?'

'I don't like riding about in slush.'

Grigory went over to the bed and picked up his hat. 'Where're you off to?'

'I want to go outside.'

Grigory went out on to the porch. The moon gleamed faintly through a cloud. The big yard, the roofs of the outbuildings, the bare pointed crests of the pyramid poplars, the horses with blankets over their backs were all illuminated by the ghostly bluish radiance of midnight. The murdered Red Army man lay a few paces from the porch with his head in a gleaming puddle of thaw water. Three Cossacks were bending over him, talking quietly and fumbling about.

'He's still breathing, honestly he is!' one of them grumbled. 'Why didn't you finish him off proper, you cack-handed devil? I told you to go for his head! You clod!'

A husky-voiced Cossack, the one who had escorted Grigory, replied, 'He'll peg out in a minute! He'll kick for a bit and peg out... Lift his head, can't you! I can't get this thing off. By the hair, that's right. Now hold him.'

There was a squelch. One of the men standing over the body straightened up. The husky-voiced Cossack grunted as he pulled off the dead man's jacket. A little later he said, 'I've got a light touch. That's why he didn't croak yet. At home sometimes I'd be killing a hog... Keep hold, don't drop him! Oh, shit!.. Ay, I'd slash that hog's throat, I would, right through to the wind-pipe, and then the cussed animal would get up and go running round the yard. Keep running it would, all covered in blood and wheezing like a bellows. Nothing to breathe, but still it wouldn't die. That's because of my light touch. All right then, drop him... Still breathing, eh? What d'ye think of that? And I went through nearly the bone...'

A third Cossack held up the dead man's jacket at arm's length and said, 'We've bloodied the left side... It's all sticky. Ugh!'

'It'll dry and rub off. It's not grease,' the husky one said calmly and squatted down again. 'It'll dry or wash off. That don't matter.'

'What now? You want to take his trousers off?' the first man grumbled.

The husky voice said sharply, 'If you're in such a hurry, go to the horses. We'll manage without you! Can't let good stuff go begging, can we?'

Grigory turned away and went into the house.

Fomin met him with a brief sizing-up look and rose. 'Let's go into the front room and have a chat. There's too much noise in here.'

The large overheated front room smelled of mice and hemp seed. A shortish man in a service tunic was asleep on the bed with his arms flung out. His thin hair was tousled and full of fluff and feathers. He lay with one cheek pressed into a dirty pillow that had no pillow-case. The lamp hanging from the ceiling shone on his pale, unshaven face.

Fomin woke him and said, 'Get up, Kaparin. We have a guest. This is our man—Melekhov, Grigory—a former lieutenant, for your information.'

Kaparin swung his legs off the bed, rubbed his face with his hands, and stood up. With a slight half-bow he shook hands with Grigory.

'How d'ye do? Captain Kaparin.'

Fomin cordially offered Grigory a chair and himself sat down on the chest. He had probably noticed that the treatment of the Red Army man had made a bad impression on Grigory, so he said, 'Don't think we're so tough on everyone we capture. That was a food-procurement worker, you chump. We show no mercy on them and commissars, but we pardon the rest. Yesterday, for example, we caught three militiamen; we took their horses, saddles and weapons, and let them go. What the devil do we need to kill them for?'

Grigory said nothing. He sat with his hands on his knees, thinking his own thoughts, and Fomin's voice came to him as if in a dream.

'...So that's how we've been fighting,' Fomin went on. 'We reckon we'll rouse the Cossacks. This government of Soviets can't live. We've heard rumours that there's war everywhere. Rebellions everywhere—Siberia, the Ukraine, and even in Petrograd itself. The whole fleet has mutinied in that fortress, what do they call it now...'

'In Kronstadt,' Kaparin prompted him.

Grigory raised his head and with vacant, unseeing eyes looked at Fomin, then at Kaparin.

'Here, have a smoke,' Fomin held out his cigarette case. 'So they've got Petrograd already and they're on the march to Moscow. Things are stirring everywhere! So why should we slumber? We'll rouse the Cossacks, shake off the Soviet government, and then, if the Cadets give us a hand, we'll have it all our own way. Let their learned men set up a government and we'll help 'em.' He paused, then asked, 'What d'you think, Melekhov? If the Cadets fight their way back from the Black Sea and we join up with 'em, won't it count in our favour that we were the first to rise in the rear? Kaparin says it's bound to. Surely they won't hold it against me that in 1918 I led the 28th Regiment away from the front and served the Soviets for a couple of years?'

'So that's what he's after! The man's a fool, but he's cunning...' Grigory thought, smiling despite himself. Fomin waited for a reply. Evidently the question had been weighing on his mind.

Grigory said reluctantly, 'That's a long story.'

'Of course,' Fomin agreed readily. 'I said that just by

the way. Time will tell. But right now we've got to act and smash the Communists here, in the rear. We won't let 'em live! They've put their rotten infantry on wagons and think they can catch us... Let 'em try. We'll have the whole district up on its hindlegs before they get a cavalry unit here.'

Once again Grigory sat staring at his feet, thinking. Kaparin excused himself and lay back on the bed.

'I get very tired. We keep doing these mad marches and get so little sleep,' he said, smiling listlessly.

'Time we had a rest too.' Fomin stood up and let his heavy hand rest on Grigory's shoulder. 'Good for you, Melekhov, that you took the advice I gave you that day in Vyoshki! If you hadn't gone into hiding then, they'd have had you up against a wall. You'd be lying among the Vyoshenskaya sand hills with your finger-nails rotting... I've got an eye for that kind of thing. Well, have you made up your mind? Speak up and then we'll go to bed.'

'What d'you want me to tell you?'

'Will you join us or what? You can't spend your whole life hiding away in other people's sheds.'

Grigory had been expecting this question. He had to choose. Either he went on roaming around the villages, living a homeless, hungry life and eating his heart out with homesickness, until one of his hosts betrayed him to the authorities, or he could give himself up to the Political Bureau, or he could join Fomin. And he made his choice. For the first time that evening he looked Fomin straight in the eye and, twisting his lips, said, 'I've got a choice like the one in the tale of the knights of old: turn left and you'll lose your horse, turn right and you'll lose your head... Three roads and not one worth taking...'

'Cut out the fairy tales.'

'I've nowhere to go, so I've chosen.'

'Well?'

'I'm joining your band.'

Fomin frowned and bit his moustache.

'Don't use that word any more. Why is it a band? The Communists call us that to insult us, but you mustn't. We're rebels. Short and to the point.'

His dissatisfaction was only momentary. He was clearly delighted by Grigory's decision and unable to hide the fact. Rubbing his hands cheerfully, he said, 'We've got a good reinforcement! Hear that, Captain? We'll give you a troop, Melekhov, and if you don't want to command a troop, you can take a staff job with Kaparin. I'll give you my own horse. I've got a spare one.'

XII

At dawn there was light frost. The puddles were coated with a bluish crust of ice. The snow had hardened, and squealed underfoot. The horses' hooves left crumbling round imprints on the clean patches of granular snow, and even where it had been melted by yesterday's thaw the bare earth and dead matted grass only gave a little under the hooves and responded with a dull mutter.

Fomin's troops formed up outside the village. Six horsemen who had been sent ahead as an advance guard showed up on the distant highway.

'Here's my army!' Fomin said, smiling as he rode up to Grigory. 'You could break the devil's horns with these boys!'

Grigory scanned the column and thought sadly, 'If you'd fallen foul of my Budyonny squadron with this army of yours, we'd have made mincemeat of you in half an hour.'

Fomin waved his whip and asked, 'How do they look?'

'Not bad for cutting down prisoners and stripping the dead, but what they're like in action, I wouldn't know,' Grigory replied drily.

Turning his back to the wind, Fomin lighted a cigarette and said, 'You'll see 'em in action soon. Most of 'em have been in the army, they won't let you down.'

Six two-horse transports with ammunition and provisions were positioned in the middle of the column. Fomin cantered forward and gave the order to march. On the hill he again rode up to Grigory and asked, 'Well, how d'ye like my horse? Does he suit you?'

'He's a good horse.'

They rode on together for some time in silence, then Grigory asked, 'D'you reckon to be in Tatarsky?'

'Missing your family?'

'I'd like to see them.'

'Mebbe we'll look 'em up. Just now I'm thinking of heading for the Chir to rouse the Cossacks there a bit.'

But the Cossacks were not very willing to be 'roused', as Grigory discovered in the next few days. When Fomin occupied a village or stanitsa, he would call the citizens to a meeting. Usually he did the talking, but sometimes Kaparin did it for him. They urged the Cossacks to take up arms, talked of the 'burdens placed on the farmers by the Soviet government' and of the 'inevitable ruin that will follow unless the Soviet government is over-thrown'. Fomin did not speak so fluently and correctly as Kaparin, but at greater length and in a language the Cossacks understood. He usually ended his speech with the same stock phrases, 'From this day forward we free you of grain deliveries. You needn't take any more grain to the reception points. It's time to stop feeding the Communist spongers. They're getting fat on your grain, but the squeeze is over. You are free men! Arm yourselves and give our government your support! Cossacks, hurrah!'

The menfolk stared at the ground and maintained a sullen silence, but the women gave free rein to their tongues. Malicious questions and shouts rose from their tight ranks:

'Has your good government brought us any soap?'

'Where d'you keep it, this government o'yours. In your saddle-bags?'

'Whose grain are you eating yourselves?'

'You'll be coming round begging in a minute, won't you?'

'They've got sabres. They won't ask us before they chop the chickens' heads off!'

'What d'ye mean—don't deliver any more grain? You're here today and gone tomorrow, and we'll be here to take the rap.'

'We won't give you our husbands! Do your own fight-ing!'

And much else was blurted out with great bitterness by the women, who had been disillusioned by years of war, feared the outbreak of a new conflict, and clung to their husbands with the tenacity of desperation.

Fomin listened unconcernedly to their clamour. He knew what it counted for. When silence was restored, he appealed to the men. Their answers were brief and reasonable.

'Don't try to force us, Comrade Fomin, we've had enough of fighting.'

'We tried it once, didn't we? We rebelled in 'nine-teen!'

'We've got nothing to rebel with and what's the good? There's no reason to yet.'

'It'll be seed-time soon. We've got to sow, not fight.'

One day a shout came from the back rows, 'You're talking sweet now! But where were you in 'nineteen, when we rebelled?' You've woken up too late, Fomin!'

Grigory saw Fomin's face change, but he restrained himself and said nothing in reply.

For the first week Fomin listened calmly enough to the Cossacks' reasoning and their brief refusals to support his campaign; even the women's shouts and abuse failed to rattle him. 'Don't worry, we'll persuade 'em!' he declared complacently, smiling into his moustache. But when he realised that the majority of the Cossack population were against him, he suddenly changed his tactics. He no longer dismounted before making his speech and began to rely on threats rather than persuasion. But the results were the same. The Cossacks on whose support he had counted listened in silence, and as silently dispersed.

In one of the villages where he spoke a Cossack woman made a speech in reply. A widow, tall, broad-boned and buxom, she spoke in a deep masculine voice and with a man's brisk and forceful gestures. Her broad pockmarked face was full of fierce determination and her big protruding lips kept twisting in a scornful smile. Pointing her plump red hand at Fomin, who was sitting stiffly in his saddle, she spat out the barbed, stinging words.

'What are you stirring up trouble here for? Where d'you want to push our Cossacks now? What hole d'you want to get them into? Hasn't this rotten war made enough widows? Haven't we got enough orphans? Bring fresh trouble on our heads, would ye? Who's this tsar-liberator that has come to us from Rubezhny village? Why don't you put your own house in order and get over these shortages, and after that you can teach us how to live, what government we should have and what we shouldn't. Back home your own wife never gets her neck out of the yoke, that we know for sure! And here are you, with your big moustache, riding around on a horse, stirring up trouble. Look to your own farm—if the wind didn't hold it up, your own house would have tumbled down long ago. A fine teacher you are! Why don't you say something, ginger mug? Or isn't it the truth?'

A rustle of laughter passed through the crowd, and died away. Fomin's left hand, which was resting on the pommel of his saddle, fumbled slowly with the reins and his face darkened with suppressed anger, but he maintained a stubborn silence, racking his brains for a dignified way out of his predicament.

'What's this government of yours that you want us to

support?' the widow persisted, ramming home her advantage.

Arms akimbo, she advanced slowly towards him, swinging her massive hips. The Cossacks made way for her, hiding their smiles and lowering their laughing eyes. They formed a circle, as if for a dance, jostling each other to make room.

'Your government's just a shadow,' the widow boomed in her deep voice. 'It tags along behind you and you don't stay in one place more than an hour! "Today you're riding high, tomorrow you'll be squashed like a fly!" That's what you are and what your government is too!'

Fomin dug his heels into his horse's flanks and rode into the crowd. It drew back, leaving only the widow in the middle of a wide circle. She had seen much in her time, so she looked up imperturbably at the horse's bared teeth and the furious face of its rider.

As he bore down on her, Fomin raised his whip.

'Quiet, you pock-marked harpy!... What's this agitation you're carrying on!?'

The horse's snarling muzzle towered over the head of the fearless widow. A pale-green clot of froth dropped from the snaffle and fell on the widow's black kerchief, and from there on to her cheek. She brushed it away and took a step back.

'Do we have to keep quiet while only you speak?' she cried, looking up at Fomin with round, furiously gleaming eyes.

Fomin did not strike. Brandishing his whip, he bawled, 'You Bolshevik plague carrier! I'll have my men pull your skirts up and give you a good thrashing with cleaning rods, then you'll know better!'

The widow retreated another two paces and all of a sudden turned her back on Fomin, bent down and flung up her skirt, 'And have you seen this, you great warrior?' she exclaimed and, straightening up with astonishing agility, turned to face Fomin again. 'Thrash me, would you? Not a snotty nose like you!'

Fomin spat furiously and tightened the reins to hold his backing horse.

'Keep your skirt down, horsey-face! Showing off your fat bottom, are you?' he roared, wheeling his horse and trying vainly to maintain a stern expression.

A muffled, half-suppressed burst of laughter rose from the crowd. In an attempt to save his commander's honour one of Fomin's men ran up to the widow and brandished the butt of his carbine, but a burly Cossack, a couple of heads taller, shielded her with a broad shoulder and said quietly but menacingly, 'Hands off!'

Three more of the village Cossacks came up and stood in front of the widow. One of them, a young fellow with a thick forelock, whispered to Fomin's man, 'What are you shaking your gun for? It's easy to hit a woman, but just you show your valour out there on the hill. You can all be brave in your own back yard.'

Fomin walked his horse to the fence and rose in the stirrups.

'Cossacks! Have a good think now!' he shouted, addressing the slowly dispersing crowd. 'Today we're asking for volunteers, but in a week's time we'll be back and it'll be a different story!'

For some reason he suddenly brightened up and, as he reined in his caracoling horse, he shouted laughingly, 'We're not the scary kind! You won't scare us with these female... (there followed several unprintable expressions). We've seen pock-marked ones and all the other kinds! We'll come back and if there aren't any volunteers, we'll mobilise all the young Cossacks by force. Mark my words! We've no time to play around soft-talking you!'

The crowd halted for a minute and there was animated talk and laughter. Still smiling, Fomin commanded, 'To horse!'

Purple in the face with suppressed laughter, Grigory cantered over to his troop.

Fomin's detachment rode in a straggling column up the muddy road on to the hill and the unhospitable village disappeared from view, but Grigory still caught himself smiling and thought to himself, 'It's a good thing we Cossacks are cheerful folk. We'd rather have a joke to keep us company than grief, God forbid, if we kept serious about all we do, this life would be enough to make you hang yourself!' His cheerful mood stayed with him for some time, and it was only when they halted for the night that he reflected with alarm and bitterness that there was little chance of rousing the Cossacks and Fomin's whole scheme was doomed to inevitable failure.

XIII

Spring was on the way. There was more warmth in the sun. On the southern slopes of the hills the snow had melted and at noon the earth, now a rusty-red with last year's grass, gave off a translucent lilac haze. In the sunnier spots on the ancient mounds, from under boulders sunk deep in the loamy soil the first bright green blades of lungwort appeared. The land that had been ploughed in autumn was free of snow. The rooks moved from the deserted winter tracks to the threshing floors and the thaw-flooded fields of winter wheat. In the gullies and ravines the snow was blue and saturated with moisture; the air that rose from them was still grimly cool, but already spring torrents, invisible to the eye, were singing softly in the bottoms, and in the woods and copses the poplars were green with the tender, barely perceptible flush of spring.

The working season was approaching and every day Fomin's band melted. In the morning, after the night's rest they would always be a man or two short, and one night nearly half a troop disappeared; eight men with all their equipment had ridden off to Vyoshenskaya to surrender. There was ploughing and sowing to be done. The earth was calling, urging men to work, and many of the band, realising that the struggle was hopeless, quietly slipped away and made for home. Only the desperate ones remained, those for whom there could be no return, whose offence against Soviet power was too great for any hope of pardon.

By the early days of April Fomin could field no more than eighty-six sabres. Grigory had also stayed with the band. He lacked the courage to go home. He was firmly convinced that Fomin's was a lost cause and that sooner or later the band would be smashed. He knew they would be routed in their first encounter with any regular cavalry unit of the Red Army. But still he stayed on as Fomin's righthand man, secretly hoping to be able to last out till summer, then snatch two of the band's best horses, make a dash for Tatarsky at night, and from there head southwards with Aksinya. The Donland steppes stretched far and wide, and there were plenty of unfrequented tracks across them; in summer they would all be open and there would be no lack of shelter. His plan was to abandon the horses and make his way with Aksinya on foot to the Kuban, to the foothills of the Caucasus, and there find a place where he could lie low through this time of troubles. There seemed to be no other way out.

On Kaparin's advice Fomin had decided to cross to the left bank of the Don before the ice broke up. On the thickly wooded border of the Khopyor district he hoped to be able to shake off any pursuit that might be offered.

The band crossed the Don above the village of Rybny. Here and there, where the current was swift, the ice was already breaking up. Under the bright April sun the water looked as if it were covered with glittering silver scales; but the beaten track that now rose two or three feet above the level of the surrounding ice remained impregnable. The men put down fences in the shallows near the bank, led the horses across one by one, formed up on the other side and, having sent out a patrol, rode off in the direction of Yelanskaya.

The next day Grigory happened to meet a man from his village, old one-eyed Grandad Chumakov. He was on his way to see relatives in Gryaznovsky and ran into the band not far from the village. Grigory took the old man aside and questioned him eagerly.

'How are my little ones? Are they safe and well, Grandad?'

'Ay, that they are, Grigory Panteleyevich, God protects them.'

'I have a great favour to ask of you, Grandad. Give my best regards to them and to my sister, Yevdokiya Panteleyevna, and also to Prokhor Zykov, and tell Aksinya Astakhova to be expecting me soon. But don't let anyone else know that you've seen me. Right?'

'Don't worry, son. I'll do just as you say.'

'What's the news in the village?'

'Nothing new, we're still going on in the same old way.'

'Is Koshevoi still the chairman?'

'He is.'

'They're not harming my family, are they?'

'Not as I've heard, so they can't be. Why should they harm 'em? They're not to blame for what you do.'

'What are they saying about me in the village?'

The old man blew his nose, slowly wiped his moustache and beard with a red neckerchief, then replied evasively.

'God knows... They're saying all kinds o' things, whatever they can think of. Will you soon be making your peace with the Soviet authorities?'

What answer could Grigory give? Holding back his horse, which was straining impatiently to follow the others, he smiled and said, 'I don't know, Grandad. Nothing's clear yet.'

'Not clear? We fought the Circassians, we fought the Turks, but there had to be peace in the end. And here you are, all our own folk, yet you can't come to an agreement... It's wrong, Grigory Panteleyevich. Upon my word, it is! The merciful God, he sees everything, he won't forgive you all for this, believe me! Ay, it's beyond me! Russians, true Christians, going for each other like this and there's no pulling you apart. You could have had a bit of a scrap and it wouldn't have been so bad, but this is the fourth year you've been at it. To my old man's way of thinking it's time to have done with it!'

Grigory said goodbye to the old fellow and galloped off to catch up with his troop. Old Chumakov stood leaning on his stick and wiping a rheumy tear from his empty eye-socket with his sleeve. With his one, youthfully keen eye he watched Grigory ride away, admired his jaunty riding posture, and whispered softly to himself, 'He's a good Cossack. A fine hand at everything but he's a ne'er do well... He's lost his way! He'd be just the man for fighting the Circassians, but what has he taken into his head to do! Why, in the name of plague, does he have to worry about this government? What are they thinking of, these young Cossacks? Of course, you couldn't expect anything else from Grishka. They always were a wayward lot, the whole breed... Pantelei, when he was alive, was just as wild, and I remember the grandfather, Prokofy... He was another maverick, he was, not like one of us... But what these other Cossacks are thinking about, it beats me, so help me God!'

* * *

Fomin gave up holding public meetings when he occupied villages. He saw that agitation was useless. It was all he could do to keep the men he had, let alone recruit others. He had grown noticeably gloomier and less talkative, and begun to seek solace in the village home-brew. Wherever they stopped for the night a sombre drinking bout took place. The men drank too. Discipline collapsed and looting increased. The houses of people working in the Soviet administration, who went into hiding as soon as the band approached, were stripped of everything that could be carried away on horseback. Many saddle packs swelled to an enormous size. One day Grigory saw a man in his troop with a sewing-machine.

He had looped the reins over the pommel of his saddle and was holding it under his left arm. Grigory had to use his whip to make the man part with his acquisition. That evening he decided to have it out with Fomin. They were alone together. Fomin, his face bloated from drinking, sat at the table while Grigory strode up and down the room.

'Sit down, man, stop flitting about in front of me,' Fomin said irritably.

Ignoring his remark, Grigory went on pacing up and down the little room for some time.

Eventually he said, 'I'm fed up with this, Fomin! You've got to stop this looting and boozing!'

'Been having bad dreams lately?'

'Cut the funny stuff... People are beginning to speak badly of us!'

'You know I can't do anything with the lads,' Fomin said reluctantly.

'But you aren't even trying!'

'You can't teach me! And these people you think so much of aren't worth talking about. It's for their sake, the scum, that we're suffering, and they... I'm going to look after myself from now on.'

'You don't even do that. You're too busy boozing. You haven't been sober for four days now, and the others do nothing but soak. Even at night, on sentry duty. What d'you want? For us to be caught napping and slashed to bits in one of these villages?'

'You think it'll never happen to us?' Fomin laughed drily. 'We've all got to die one day. The jug carried water for a long time, but in the end... Know that saying?'

'Then let's ride to Vyoshenskaya tomorrow and put up our hands, tell 'em we're surrendering.'

'No, we'll enjoy ourselves a bit longer yet.'

Grigory halted in front of the table, planting his feet wide apart.

'If you don't put your lot in order, if you don't stop this looting and drinking, I'll break away from you and take half your men with me,' he said quietly.

'Just you try,' Fomin drawled menacingly.

'I won't have to try!'

'You... you'd better not threaten me!' Fomin put his hand on his revolver holster.

'Hands off that holster! I'll slash you across the table first!' Grigory said quickly, turning pale and half drawing his sabre from its sheath.

Fomin put his hands on the table and smiled.

'What are you getting at me for like this? My head's splitting as it is, and you come round with your daft questions. Put your sabre back! Can't I even have a little joke with you? Oh, aren't we touchy! Just like a girl of sixteen...'

'I've told you what I want, so get it into your head and make it stay there. We're not all of the same mind as you.'

'I know.'

'Well, remember it then! Order everyone to empty their packs tomorrow. This is a cavalry unit, not a baggage train. Drum that into 'em! And they call themselves fighters for the people! They're weighed down with loot. They trade the stuff at every village they come to like a bunch of peddlers in the old days... It makes me writhe with shame! Why the hell did I ever take up with you?' Grigory spat and turned away to the window, pale with indignation and anger.

Fomin laughed and said, 'The cavalry hasn't been after us yet... When a wolf with a full belly is being chased, it throws up everything it's eaten as it runs. And my bastards will do the same—they'd chuck away everything if they were hard pressed. Never mind, Melekhov, don't get sore. I'll put matters right! I've been just a bit down-hearted lately and slackened the reins, but I'll tighten them again! We can't split up, we'd better face the music together.'

Their conversation was interrupted. The mistress of the house came in with a steaming bowl of cabbage soup and was soon followed by a bunch of Cossacks led by Chumakov.

But what had been said had its effect. The next morning Fomin gave orders to empty the saddle packs and himself checked to see that the order was carried out. One of the worst looters, who refused to part with his booty and offered resistance, was shot down on the spot by Fomin himself.

'Get rid of that carcass!' he said calmly, kicking the body aside. He surveyed the ranks and raised his voice, 'You've done enough rummaging in the family chests, you sons-of-bitches! That's not what I roused you against the Soviet government for! From a slain enemy you can take everything, even his dirty pants if you're not fussy, but leave the families alone! We're not fighting the women. And anyone who don't obey will get the same treatment!'

A murmur passed through the ranks and died away.

Discipline seemed to have been restored. For about three days the band ranged along the left bank of the Don, destroying small detachments of the local defence forces in brief engagements.

In Shumilinskaya Kaparin suggested transferring operations to the Voronezh Province. His idea was that they would gain wide support among the population, which had recently rebelled against the Soviets. But when Fomin proposed this to the Cossacks, they were unanimous in their opposition. 'We're not going to leave our own territory!' Protest meetings were held and the decision had to be withdrawn. For the next four days the band headed steadily eastward, avoiding battle with the cavalry group that had been tailing them since they left Kazanskaya.

It was not easy to cover their tracks because the spring field work was in full swing and there were people about everywhere, even in remote corners of the steppe. They often rode at night but as soon as they halted in the morning to feed their horses, the enemy's patrols would appear, harrass them with bursts from a light machine-gun, and Fomin's men would have to bridle their horses under fire. Outside the village of Melnikovo, not far from Vyoshenskaya, Fomin managed to trick the enemy with a skilful manoeuvre and broke away from the pursuit. From his own reconnaissance he had learned that the cavalry group was commanded by Yegor Zhuravlyov, a Cossack from Bukanovskaya, who was both aggressive and knowledgeable in the art of war. He also knew that the group outnumbered his band by almost two to one and had six light machine-guns and fresh horses, which had not been exhausted by long marches. All this forced Fomin to avoid battle in order to give his men and horses a chance to rest, hoping that when the chance came, not in open battle but by a surprise attack, he would give the group a trouncing and thus rid himself of his pursuers. He also hoped to make a good haul of the enemy's machine-guns and rifle ammunition. But his plans failed. What Grigory had been afraid of happened on April 18th, on the edge of the Slashchevsky Oak Forest. The night before, Fomin and most of his men had been drinking heavily in the village of Sevastyanovsky. They rode out at dawn. Hardly any of them had slept that night and some now dozed off in the saddle. At about nine in the morning they halted for a rest near the village of Ozhogin. Fomin posted sentries and ordered the horses to be fed.

A strong gusty wind was blowing from the east. A brownish cloud of sandy dust veiled the horizon. The steppe was wrapped in a dense haze. The sun barely penetrated the swirling murk. Greatcoats, horses' tails and manes flapped in the wind. The horses turned their backs to the blast and looked for shelter by the scattered hawthorn bushes on the fringe of the forest. The prickly sand dust stung the men's eyes and it was hard to make out anything at a distance.

Grigory wiped his horse's muzzle and damp eye sockets with his usual care, hitched on the nose-bag and went over to Kaparin, who was feeding his horse from the hem of his greatcoat.

'What a place to choose for a halt!' he said, pointing his whip at the forest.

Kaparin shrugged.

'I told that fool but what's the use!'

'We ought to have halted in the steppe or on the edge of a village.'

'You think we can expect an attack from the forest?'

'Yes.'

'The enemy's far away.'

'They may be very close by now, they're not infantry.'

'The trees are bare. We'd probably spot them.'

'No one's keeping a look-out, they're nearly all asleep. I'm afraid the sentries are too.'

'They could hardly stay on their feet after yesterday's boozing, you won't wake them now.' Kaparin frowned as if in pain, and said in a low voice, 'We'll come to grief with this man leading us. He's as thick-headed as they come and stupid, indescribably stupid! Why don't you take over command? The Cossacks respect you. They'd gladly follow you.'

'That's not for me, I won't be staying with you much longer,' Grigory replied drily and returned to his horse, regretting the careless admission he had made.

Kaparin tipped out the rest of the oats on to the ground and followed him.

'Look here, Melekhov,' he said, breaking off a branch of hawthorn and pinching off the taut swollen buds. 'I think we won't hold out much longer if we don't merge with some big anti-Soviet unit—Maslak's brigade, for example. He's roaming around somewhere in the south of the district. We've got to get through to them, otherwise we'll all be wiped out one fine day.'

'The Don's flooding right now. You can't get across.'

'Not now, but when the flood subsides we must get away from here. Don't you think so?'

After a little thought Grigory replied, 'You're right. We've got to get away from here. It's no good staying.'

Kaparin livened up. He began to talk at length about the hope of support from the Cossacks having failed and the need to persuade Fomin not to go on roaming aimlessly around the district but to agree to merge with a more powerful group.

Grigory grew tired of listening to the man's chatter. He was keeping his eye on his horse and as soon as the nose-bag was empty he took it off, put on the bridle and tightened the saddle girths.

'We won't be moving for some time yet, there's no need to hurry,' Kaparin said.

'You'd better go and saddle your horse, you mayn't have time later,' Grigory replied.

Kaparin gave him a quick glance and went over to his horse, which was standing by one of the transports.

Leading his horse by the bridle, Grigory walked up to Fomin. Fomin was sprawling on a sheepskin cloak, lazily picking at the wing of a boiled chicken. He moved over and gestured to Grigory to join him.

'Sit down and eat with me.'

'We've got to get away from here, not waste time eating,' Grigory told him.

'We'll move when we've fed the horses.'

'We can feed them later.'

'What's all the hurry for?' Fomin threw away the bone and wiped his hands on the cloak.

'They'll take us by surprise. It's just the place for that.'

'Like hell they will! Our patrol has just come in, they say there's no one on the hill. Zhuravlyov must have lost us or he'd be on our tail right now. There's nothing to worry about from Bukanovskaya. The military commissar there is Mikhei Pavlov. He's a fighter, but he's short of men; he won't take us on. We'll rest up for a bit and wait for this wind to die down, then make for Slashchevskaya. Sit down and have some chicken. What are you hovering over me for? You're getting rather jumpy, Melekhov. Soon you'll be giving every bush a wide berth. Think what a long way you'll have to ride!' Fomin made a sweeping gesture and roared with laughter.

Grigory swore angrily and walked away. He tethered his horse to a bush and lay down beside it, shielding his face from the dust with his greatcoat. Lulled by the sound of the wind and the faint melodious rustle of the tall withered grass nodding over him, he fell into a doze.

A long burst of machine-gun fire brought him to his feet. Before the burst ended, he had untied his horse. Fomin's bellow drowned all the other voices, 'To horse!' Two or three more machine-guns opened up on the right, from the forest. As soon as he was in the saddle Grigory grasped the situation. On the right, near the edge of the forest about fifty Red Army men, barely visible through the dust, had lined up for the charge and were attacking in a direction that cut off retreat across the hill. In the dim light of the sun their sabres glinted above their heads with a cold and only too familiar bluish gleam. From a bushy hillock in the forest itself machine-guns were hammering away with feverish haste, emptying disk after disk. From the left, too, half a squadron of Red Army men were charging silently, brandishing their sabres and spreading out to lock the ring of encirclement. The only hope of escape was to break through the thin line of attackers on the left and make a dash for the Don. Grigory shouted to Fomin, 'Follow me!' and set off at a gallop, drawing his sabre.

After about forty paces he looked round. Fomin, Kaparin, Chumakov and a few others were going flat out, about twenty paces behind him. The machine-guns in the forest were silent except for one on the extreme right that was letting off vicious bursts at the men scrambling round the baggage wagons. But then that gun, too, fell silent and Grigory realised that the Red horsemen had reached the halting place and were at work with their sabres. The desperate muffled screams and the occasional scattered firing of the defenders told him what was happening. He had no time to look back. As he dashed towards the charging cavalry, he chose his target. A Red Army man in a short sheepskin jacket was galloping towards him. He was riding a grey not very fast horse. As if by a flash of lightning Grigory saw the horse with its white foam-flecked breastband, the rider with his red, flushed young face, and the broad sombre steppe stretching down to the Don behind him... In a moment he would have to evade a blow and make his thrust. Ten paces from his adversary Grigory swung sharply to the left, heard the biting whir of the sabre over his head and, straightening up in the saddle, reached out and with only the point of his sabre touched the head of the rider as he went past. Grigory's hand scarcely felt the impact but, as he glanced back, he saw the Red Army man droop and slide slowly out of the saddle, blood streaming down the back of his yellow jacket. The grey horse stumbled out of its gallop and broke into a canter, rearing its head and twisting sideways, as if frightened by its own shadow.

Grigory crouched over his horse's neck. Bullets were whining overhead. The horse's flattened ears were quivering and beads of sweat had appeared on their tips. Grigory could hear only the whine of the bullets and the panting of his horse. He looked round again and saw Fomin and Chumakov. About a hundred paces behind them was a lagging Kaparin and, further behind, only one of the Second Troop, the lame Sterlyadnikov, was fighting to get away from two Red Army pursuers. All the rest of the eight or nine men who had followed Fomin had already been cut down. With their tails flying in the wind the riderless horses were trotting away in different directions and being rounded up by the Red Army men. Only one, a tall bay that had belonged to a member of the band, was galloping neck and neck with Kaparin's horse, snorting and dragging its dead rider, whose foot had caught in the stirrup when he fell.

As soon as he had cleared the sandy summit, Grigory reined in his horse, and returned his sabre to its sheath. Only a few seconds were needed to make the horse lie down, a simple trick that Grigory had taught it in the first week. From behind this cover he emptied his magazine, but his aim was hasty and only his last shot dismounted a Red Army rider. This enabled the fifth member of the band to get away from his pursuers.

'Get up! You'll be caught!' Fomin shouted as he came up with Grigory.

* * *

The band was utterly routed. Only five men survived. They were chased as far as Antonovsky and the pursuit was abandoned only when the five fugitives plunged into the woods surrounding the village.

Throughout the chase not one of the five had uttered a word.

As it was about to cross a stream Kaparin's horse collapsed and could not be roused. The other horses were staggering under their riders, dropping thick flecks of foam in their wake.

'You ought to be minding sheep, not commanding a detachment!' Grigory said as he dismounted, not looking at Fomin.

Fomin heaved himself off his horse without replying. He began to unsaddle it but, abandoning the task, walked away and sat down on a fern-covered tussock.

'We'll have to leave the horses behind,' he said, looking round in a scared fashion.

'What then?' Chumakov asked.

'Cross to the other side without 'em.'

'Where to?'

'We'll lie low in the woods till nightfall, then cross the Don and hide away for the time being in Rubezhny. A lot of my folk live around there.'

'More stupidity!' Kaparin burst out furiously. 'You imagine they won't look for you there? That's just where they'll be waiting—in your own village! What's your head made of?'

'Well, where are we to go?' Fomin asked in confusion.

Grigory emptied his cartridges and a hunk of bread out of his saddle-bags.

'Are you going to have a long argument about it? Come on! Tether the horses and unsaddle them and let's get going, or they'll catch us while we're hanging about here.'

Chumakov threw down his whip, stamped it into the mud, and said in a shaking voice, 'Now we're foot-sloggers... And all our lads killed... Mother of God, how they cut us up! I never thought I'd get away alive... Death was staring me in the face...'

They unsaddled the horses in silence, tethered all four to one alder-tree and in single file, stepping in each other's tracks like wolves, made for the Don, carrying their saddles and trying to keep to the denser thickets.

XIV

In spring, when the Don bursts its banks and the flood waters cover the surrounding meadows, a small stretch of the high left bank opposite Rubezhny village remains unsubmerged.

From the Donside hills in spring the island can be seen from afar, densely overgrown with young osiers, oaks and branchy bluish-grey bushes of bay willow.

In summer the trees there are wrapped to their crowns in wild hops and the ground below is covered with impassable thickets of prickly blackberry; pale-blue bindweed curls and creeps over the bushes and in the few clearings the tall, thick grass, lavishly fed by the fat soil, grows higher than a man.

In summer the woods are quiet, dark and cool even at noon. The silence is broken only by the orioles and by cuckoos that vie with one another in counting the years someone has yet to live. And in winter these woods are utterly bare and deserted, locked in a deathly stillness. The jagged tree-tops stand out blackly against the whitish winter sky. Year after year only the she-wolf and her cubs find a safe refuge in the thickets and spend their days lying low among the snow-clogged scrub.

It was on this island that Fomin, Grigory Melekhov and the other survivors of the band took shelter. It was a rough life. They fed themselves on the meagre supplies that Fomin's cousin ferried to them at night. They often went hungry, but at least they slept to their heart's content, with their saddle cushions for pillows. At night they took it in turns to stand guard. No fires were lighted for fear that someone might notice their presence.

The flood water swirled southward, washing the shores of the island. It growled menacingly as it broke through the chain of old poplars that barred its path, then murmured songfully as it stirred the tops of the submerged bushes.

Grigory soon grew accustomed to the ceaseless sound of the water so close at hand. He would lie for hours on the steep bank gazing across the wide watery expanse at the chalky spurs of the Donside hills bathed in a lilac sunny haze. Out there, beyond that haze was his home village, Aksinya, the children... To them his cheerless thoughts took wing. For a moment when he recalled his family, his heart would flare and burn with regret, and a fierce hatred of Mikhail, but he suppressed these feelings, trying not to look at the Donside hills and save himself the pangs of recall. There was no point in giving rein to cruel memory. He was unhappy enough as it was. Even without that his chest was racked with such pain that he sometimes felt as if his heart had been flayed and was not beating but bleeding. Evidently his wounds, the hardships of war and the typhus had done their work, and every minute he was aware of the unwelcome thumping of his heart. Sometimes the searing pain in the left side of his chest became so acute that his lips would dry instantly and he could scarcely restrain a groan. But he found a sure means of relieving the pain. He would lie down, pressing his left side to the damp earth, or soak the front of his shirt in cold water, and the pain would gradually, almost reluctantly leave his body.

The days waxed fair and windless. Only now and then would a few small white clouds, tousled by the upper winds, float across the clear sky while their reflections glided over the flood waters like a flock of swans and disappeared as they touched the far bank.

It was good to watch the rapids swirling round the island, to listen to the varied voices of the water and think of nothing that would awaken suffering, or try not to. Grigory would stare for hours at the whimsical and infinitely varied curlicues of the current. Their shape changed every minute. Where recently a steady stream had carried the broken stems of bulrushes, crumpled leaves and roots of grass, a fantastic eddy would suddenly form and greedily suck in everything that came floating by, and a little later, where the eddy had been, the water would boil up and seethe murkily, belching forth now a blackened root or sedge, now a limp oak leaf, now a wisp of straw carried from no one knew where.

In the evenings cherry-red sunsets burned in the west. The moon rose from behind a tall poplar, and its light flowed across the Don like a cold white flame, intermittently bright and dark where the wind had ruffled the water. At night the sounds of the water merged with the unceasing cries of countless flocks of wild geese flying northward over the island. Fearing no disturbance, the birds would often land on its eastern shore. In the still waters of the flooded forest the teal cackled invitingly, the ducks quacked and the geese gaggled and called softly to one another. And one night, as he silently approached the shore, Grigory saw a large flock of swans not far from the island. The sun had not yet risen. The dawn was blazing beyond a distant ridge of forest. In its reflected light the water looked pink, and so did the big majestic birds on its still surface, their proud heads turned towards the east. Hearing a rustle from the shore they took off with strident trumpeting and as they soared above the forest Grigory was dazzled by the marvellous snow-white gleam of their plumage.

Fomin and his men each found their own ways of passing the time. The thrifty Sterlyadnikov would settle himself in a comfortable position for his lame leg and get busy mending his clothes and boots and carefully cleaning his weapons; Kaparin, who had not done himself any good sleeping on the damp ground, lay all day in the sun with his sheepskin over his head, giving occasional muffled coughs; Fomin and Chumakov played indefatigably with makeshift cards; Grigory roamed about the island and sat for long hours by the water. They spoke little among themselves—everything had long ago been said—and assembled only for meals and in the evenings, when they were expecting Fomin's cousin. They were plagued with boredom and only once during their whole stay on the island did Grigory see Chumakov and Sterlyadnikov, in a sudden surge of high spirits, grab each other for a wrestle. They grappled for a long time, grunting and shooting jokes at each other, and sinking ankle-deep in the loose white sand. The lame Sterlyadnikov was obviously the stronger of the two, but Chumakov was the more agile. They wrestled in Kalmyk style, holding each other's belts, thrusting their shoulders forward and keeping a close watch on each other's feet. Their faces grew pale with concentration, their breathing laboured. Grigory watched the bout with interest. He saw Chumakov seize his chance and fall back, pulling his opponent with him, then with a thrust of his bent legs throw him over his head. The next moment, lithe and agile as a polecat, Chumakov was lying on top of his adversary, pressing his shoulders into the sand, and the panting and laughing Sterlyadnikov was bellowing, 'What a bastard you are! We said—no head throws!'

'Look at 'em, scrapping like a couple of young cockerels! That's enough or you'll be having a real fight,' Fomin said.

But no, they had no intention of fighting. Quite peaceably, with their arms round each other's shoulders they sat down on the sand and Chumakov in his husky but pleasant bass struck up a fast-moving jig:

> *Oh, you frosts! You frosts!*
> *You fierce Epiphany frosts!*
> *You've frozen the grey wolf in the rushes*
> *And chilled the maiden in her bower...*

Sterlyadnikov took up the song in a thin, high tenor and they began singing in harmony and unexpectedly well:

> *Then the maiden on the porch appeared*
> *With a black fur-coat upon her arm,*
> *Her sergeant on his horse she wrapped up warm...*

Then Sterlyadnikov let himself go. He jumped up and, snapping his fingers and scuffing the sand with his lame leg, started to dance. Still singing, Chumakov drew his sabre, dug a little hole in the sand and said, 'Wait a minute, you lame devil! You've got one leg shorter than the other, you can't dance proper on the level... What you need is a slope or a hole. Here stick your long leg in the hole and you'll see what a fine job you make of it... Come on now!'

Sterlyadnikov wiped the sweat from his brow and obediently planted his sound leg into the hollow Chumakov had dug.

'Ay, it's easier for me like this,' he said.

Choking with laughter, Chumakov clapped his hands and rattled off some more of the song:

> *Call on me, love, when you're riding by,*
> *Oh, how I'll kiss you if you come...*

And Sterlyadnikov, setting his face in the serious expression of all dancers, performed some quite skilful steps and even tried kicking out his legs.

The days passed, one much like the other. With the coming of darkness they waited impatiently for Fomin's cousin. All five of them would gather on the shore, talking in low voices, smoking and concealing their cigarettes under the hem of their greatcoats. It was decided that they should live for another week on the island, then cross to the right bank by night, rustle up some horses and make their way south. Maslak's band was said to be still roaming about somewhere in the south.

Fomin had instructed his relatives to find out in which of the neighbouring villages there were suitable riding horses, and to keep him daily informed about what was happening in the district. The reports they brought were not encouraging. The hunt had spread to the left bank of the Don; Red Army men had been in Rubezhny, but had left as soon as they had searched Fomin's house.

'We've got to get away from here soon. Why the devil should we hang on? Let's make a break for it tomorrow?' Chumakov suggested one day at breakfast.

'We'd better find out about the horses first,' Fomin said. 'Why should we hurry? If only they'd bring us a bit more grub, I wouldn't give up this spot till winter. Look how beautiful it is all around! We'll have a good rest, then get down to business again. Let them go on looking for us, but we're not going to walk into their arms. It was my stupid fault they smashed us up, I admit, and it's a great pity, of course, but this isn't the end. We'll get some more men together! As soon as we're mounted again, we'll ride round the local villages and in a week we'll pick up a good fifty, if not a hundred. We'll muscle up again, honestly we will!'

'Rubbish! Idiotic complacency!' Kaparin said irritably. 'The Cossacks have betrayed us. They didn't follow us then and they won't now. You've got to have the courage to face the truth, not comfort yourself with vain hopes.'

'They won't follow us? Why not?'

'Because they won't. They didn't then and they won't now.'

'Well, we'll see about that!' Fomin burst out defiantly. 'I'm not going to lay down arms!'

'It's all just empty talk,' Kaparin said wearily.

'You bloody creep!' Fomin burst out furiously. 'What's all the panic for? I'm sick and tired of your moaning and groaning! What was all the fuss about in the first place? Why did we have to rebel? Why did you come in if you haven't got the guts for it? You got me into this, and now you're quitting? Why don't you speak?'

'I have nothing to discuss with you and you can go to hell, you fool!' Kaparin shouted hysterically and walked away, wrapping his greatcoat round him with a shiver and turning up his collar.

'They're all so thin-skinned, these noble folk. Just say a word to him and he turns green about the gills,' Fomin said with a sigh.

For a time they sat in silence, listening to the steady swishing of the water. A duck pursued by two drakes flew overhead, quacking wildly. A twittering flock of starlings swooped over the clearing but at the sight of people soared up again and swept round like a black whiplash.

After a while Kaparin came back.

'I want to go over to the village today,' he said, and

looked at Fomin, blinking rapidly.

'What for?'

'That's a strange question! Can't you see that I'm so ill I can hardly stand?'

'So what? D'ye think you'll get better in the village?' Fomin asked, showing no sign of concern.

'I've got to have a few nights in a warm place.'

'You're not going anywhere,' Fomin said firmly.

'Am I to die here then?'

'That's up to you.'

'But why can't I go? These nights out in the cold are killing me!'

'Suppose you're nabbed in the village? Did you think of that? Then we'll all be done for. You think I don't know you? You'd give us away at the first interrogation! Or even before, on the road to Vyoshenskaya.'

Chumakov laughed and nodded approvingly. He shared Fomin's opinion. But Kaparin stood his ground.

'I must go. Your witty assumptions have not convinced me to the contrary.'

'And I'm telling you to stay put and keep out of trouble.'

'But try to understand, Yakov Yefimovich—I can't go on living like an animal! I have pleurisy and perhaps even pneumonia!'

'You'll get over it! Lie out in the sunshine and it'll make you better.'

Kaparin declared sharply, 'I'm leaving today. You have no right to keep me here. I'm going!'

Fomin looked at him with suspiciously narrowed eyes, and with a wink at Chumakov rose to his feet.

'It looks as if you really are ill, Kaparin... You must have quite a fever, I reckon... Now then, let me feel it—is your head very hot?' He took a few steps towards Kaparin, holding out his hand.

Kaparin sensed the threat in Fomin's face and backed away with a shout.

'Keep off!'

'Don't shout! What's the shouting for? I only want to feel your forehead. What are you scared of?' Fomin stepped forward and grabbed Kaparin by the throat. 'Surrender, would you, you bastard?!' he muttered in a choking whisper and braced himself in an effort to throw Kaparin to the ground.

Grigory had to use all his strength to separate them.

After the midday meal Kaparin came up to Grigory

while he was hanging out some clothes to dry, and said, 'I want a word with you alone... Let's sit down.'

They sat down on the rotting brown trunk of a poplar that had been uprooted by a storm.

Kaparin gave a chesty cough and asked, 'What d'you think of that idiot's behaviour? I'm sincerely grateful to you for your intervention. You acted nobly, as an officer should. But this is terrible! I can't go on like this. We're like wild animals... How many days is it since we had a cooked meal? And this sleeping out on the damp ground... I've caught a chill and there's a dreadful pain in my side. I probably have pneumonia. I'm longing to be able to sit by a fire, sleep in a warm room, change my underwear... I dream of a clean shirt, a sheet... No, I can't stand any more of it!'

Grigory smiled.

'You want a nice comfortable war, eh?'

'How can you call this war?' Kaparin responded quickly. 'This is not war! We're just roaming endlessly from place to place, murdering an official here and there, and then running away. It would be war if we had the support of the people, if there was an uprising, but as it is—this is no war!'

'What else can we do? We can't surrender, can we?'

'No, but what's the alternative?'

Grigory shrugged. He said what had often come into his head while he had been resting on the island.

'A bad freedom is better than a good prison. You know the saying, "Prisons are well built but who wants to live in them?"'

Kaparin traced figures in the sand with a stick and after a long silence said, 'We don't necessarily have to surrender, but we must find some new forms of struggle against the Bolsheviks. We've got to get shot of this scum. You're an educated person!..'

'Me? Educated?' Grigory laughed drily. 'I can hardly pronounce the word.'

'You're an officer.'

'That was an accident.'

'No, joking apart, you're an officer, you've been in the company of other officers, you've seen real people, you're not a Soviet upstart like Fomin, and you must realise that there's no point in our staying here. It's suicide. He exposed us to attack in that oak wood, and if we make common cause with him any longer he'll expose us again. He's just a lout, and a violent one at that! We'll end up badly with him!'

'So what you mean is we don't surrender, but we leave Fomin? And go where? To Maslak?' Grigory asked.

'No. That would be the same kind of gamble, only on a bigger scale. Now I see things differently. We must get away and go not to Maslak...'

'But where then?'

'To Vyoshenskaya.'

Grigory shrugged irritably.

'That's a dead loss. It won't do for me.'

Kaparin looked at him with a sudden gleam in his eyes.

'You didn't understand me, Melekhov. Can I trust you?'

'All the way.'

'On your word of honour as an officer?'

'On my word of honour as a Cossack.'

Kaparin glanced in the direction of Fomin and Chumakov and, although they were a good distance away and could not possibly hear him, he lowered his voice.

'I know what your relationship is with Fomin and the others. You're as out of place among them as I am. I'm not interested in the reasons that prompted you to turn against the Soviets. If I understand them correctly, it's your past and the fear of arrest. Isn't that so?'

'You said the reasons didn't interest you.'

'Quite so. That was by the way. Now a few words about myself. In the past I was an officer and a member of the Socialist Revolutionary Party. Later I completely revised my political views. Only a monarchy can save Russia. Only a monarchy! Providence itself points to this path of salvation for our country. The emblem of the Soviets is the hammer and sickle, is it not?' Kaparin's twig traced the words *molot* and *serp* in the sand, then he fixed his feverishly gleaming eyes on Grigory's face. 'Now read them in reverse. You have? Do you understand? The revolution and the power of the Bolsheviks will end only *prestolom*— with the throne! When I found that out, you know, I was seized by a mystical sense of awe! I was utterly shaken because that is, so to speak, the finger of God pointing to the end of all our waverings...'

Kaparin grew breathless with excitement and fell silent. His sharp eyes had a flicker of madness in them as they stared at Grigory. But Grigory was not a bit shaken and experienced no mystical awe whatever on hearing of this revelation. He had always taken a sober, everyday view of things, so he said in reply, 'That's no finger. Were you at the front in the German war?'

Puzzled by the question, Kaparin was slow to reply. 'Why do you ask? No, I wasn't actually at the front.'

'Where did you spend the war then? In the rear?'

'Yes.'

'All the time?'

'Yes, well, not quite all the time, but most of it. But why do you ask?'

'I've been at the front from 1914 right up to now, with a few short breaks. So about this finger of yours... How can it be God's finger, when there is no God? I stopped believing in that nonsense long ago. Way back in 'fifteen, after I'd had a real look at war, I decided there is no God. None at all! If there was, he'd have no right to allow such a mess. We, front-line men, abolished God and left him for the old men and the women. Let them console themselves with him. So there's no finger of God and there can't be any monarchy either. The people have put an end to that once and for all. And this stuff you're showing me, these letters turned the other way round, that—if you'll excuse me—is just a kid's game, and no more. And I don't quite get what you're driving at. Make it simpler and shorter. I wasn't in none of your cadet colleges and I'm not all that learned, though I was an officer. If I was a bit more educated, mebbe I wouldn't be stuck here with you on this island, cut off by the floods like a lone wolf,' he concluded with a clear undertone of regret in his voice.

'That doesn't matter,' Kaparin said hastily. 'It doesn't matter whether you believe in God or not. That's a question of your own personal belief, your own conscience. Nor does it matter whether you're a monarchist or a supporter of the Constituent Assembly, or simply a Cossack who stands for self-government. What matters is that we are united by a common attitude to the Soviet regime. Don't you agree with me?'

'Go on.'

'We banked on a general uprising of the Cossacks, didn't we? But our card was trumped. Now we've got to get out of this predicament. We can fight the Bolsheviks later, and not only under the leadership of a Fomin. What we've got to do now is save our lives, so I'm proposing a pact.'

'What pact? Who against?'

'Against Fomin.'

'I don't get you.'

'It's quite simple. I'm inviting you to be my accomplice...' Kaparin was agitated and breathed heavily as he spoke. 'You and I will kill this trio and go to Vyoshenskaya. You understand? That will save us. That service to the Soviets will save us from punishment. We shall live! You understand, we'll survive!... We'll save our lives! It stands to reason, of course, that in the future, when the chance presents itself, we shall oppose the Bolsheviks. But only when it's a serious opportunity and not mere adventurism, as it was with this wretched Fomin. Don't you agree? Remember, this is the only way out of our hopeless predicament, and a brilliant way out at that.'

'But how can we do it?' Grigory asked, inwardly shuddering with indignation, but striving to hide his feelings.

'I've thought it all out. We'll do it at night, with our sabres. The next night that Cossack who keeps us supplied with food will come over and we'll get across the Don. That's all. Brilliantly simply and no clever tricks!'

With feigned affability, Grigory said, 'That's fine! But tell me, Kaparin, this morning when you wanted to go to the village to get warm... Did you mean to go to Vyoshenskaya? Did Fomin guess right?'

Kaparin looked attentively at Grigory's smiling face and smiled himself, rather sadly and with some embarrassment.

'Quite frankly, yes. When you have to save your own skin, you don't worry much about the means you employ.'

'Would you have betrayed us?'

'Yes,' Kaparin confessed honestly. 'But I would have tried to shield you personally from the consequences if you had been caught here on the island.'

'But why didn't you kill us all alone? It would have been easy enough at night.'

'There was a risk. After the first shot the others...'

'Give up your arms!' Grigory said quietly, snatching out his revolver. 'Give them up or I'll kill you on the spot! Now I'm going to get up and stand between you and Fomin, and you'll drop your revolver at my feet. Well? Don't think of shooting! I'll get you at the first movement.'

Kaparin turned deathly pale.

'Don't kill me!' he whispered, barely moving his white lips.

'I won't do that. But give me your gun.'

'You will give me away...'

Tears streamed down Kaparin's unshaven cheeks. Grigory frowned with revulsion and pity, and raised his voice, 'Drop your gun! I won't give you away, though I ought to! What a twister you've turned out to be! What a twister!'

Kaparin dropped the revolver at Grigory's feet.

'And the Browning? Give me the Browning as well. It's in your tunic, in the breast pocket.'

Kaparin took out the gleaming nickel-plated Browning and dropped that, then covered his face with his hands. He was shaken by violent sobbing.

'Stop that, you scum!' Grigory said sharply, fighting a desire to strike the man.

'You'll give me away... I'm finished.'

'I've told you I won't. But as soon as we leave the island, clear out. No one needs a man like you. Find your own shelter.'

Kaparin took his hands from his face. His wet purple face with its puffy eyes and shaking lower jaw was hideous.

'Then why... Why did you disarm me?' he stammered.

Grigory said reluctantly, 'So you won't shoot me in the back. There's no telling what you learned folk will do next... And the way you talked about this finger, about the tsar and God... What a snake you are.'

Without another glance at Kaparin Grigory walked back to the camp, spitting involuntarily.

Sterlyadnikov was sewing up his saddle with tarred thread, whistling softly to himself. Fomin and Chumakov were lying on a horse blanket, playing cards as usual.

Fomin glanced briefly at Grigory and asked, 'What did he say to you? What was it all about?'

'Just bellyaching... The way he talked...'

Grigory kept his promise and did not betray Kaparin. But in the evening he quietly removed the bolt from Kaparin's rifle and hid it. The devil knows what he might do during the night, he thought as he made his bed.

In the morning he was awakened by Fomin. Bending over him, Fomin asked, 'Did you take Kaparin's weapons?'

'What? What weapons?' Grigory raised himself on one elbow and straightened his shoulders with an effort.

He had not fallen asleep until just before dawn and the morning cold had chilled him to the bone. His greatcoat, hat and boots were wet with the mist that had fallen at sunrise.

'We can't find his weapons. Did you take 'em? Wake up, Melekhov!'

'Yes, I did. What's up?'

Fomin walked away without replying. Grigory rose and brushed down his greatcoat. Chumakov was making breakfast. He rinsed out the only bowl the camp possessed and, holcing a loaf of bread to his chest, cut off four equal slices, then he poured some milk into the bowl and crumbled a lump of boiled millet into it. He looked round at Grigory.

'You're a long time abed, Melekhov. Look where the sun is!'

'A man with a clear conscience always sleeps well,' said Sterlyadnikov, wiping the wooden spoons he had washed on the hem of his greatcoat. 'But Kaparin, he couldn't sleep all night, tossing and turning he was...'

Fomin smiled silently and looked at Grigory.

'Sit down and have breakfast, you brigands!' Chumakov proposed.

He was the first to take a spoonful of the milk, biting off a big piece of the bread. Grigory picked up his spoon, surveyed the others, and asked, 'Where's Kaparin?'

Fomin and Sterlyadnikov ate in silence. Chumakov eyed Grigory closely and said nothing either.

'What've you done with Kaparin?' Grigory asked again, half guessing what had happened during the night.

'Kaparin's a long way off by now,' Chumakov replied, smiling serenely. 'He's floating down to Rostov. Must be bobbing along somewhere near Ust-Khopyor by now... There's his coat hanging on the tree, see it?'

'You mean you've killed him?' Grigory asked with a glance at Kaparin's sheepskin.

There was no need to ask questions. It was clear what had happened without that, but for some reason he did ask. The answer did not come at once and he repeated his question.

'Ay, we killed him,' said Chumakov, and let his lashes droop over his grey, femininely beautiful eyes. 'I killed him. That's my job—killing people.'

Grigory looked at him attentively. Chumakov's brown

ruddy clear-skinned face was calm, even cheerful. His pale gold-tinted moustache stood out on his sunburnt face, setting off the darker shade of his eyebrows and combed back hair. He was truly handsome and good to look at, this meritorious executioner for Fomin's band... He put his spoon down on the tarpaulin, wiped his moustache with the back of his hand, and said, 'You'd better thank Yakov Yefimovich, Melekhov. He was the one who saved your sweet life. Otherwise you'd be floating in the Don along with Kaparin.'

'But why?'

Chumakov explained in slow deliberate phrases. 'By the look of it Kaparin wanted to surrender. Yesterday he had a very long talk with you... So Yakov Yefimovich and me, we thought we'd better put him out of harm's way. Can I tell him everything?' Chumakov looked questioningly at Fomin.

Fomin nodded and Chumakov, crunching the half-boiled millet with his teeth, continued his story.

'In the evening I made myself a club out of oak and I says to Yakov Yefimovich, "I'll finish off the pair of 'em, Kaparin and Melekhov, tonight." But he says, "Finish off Kaparin, but don't harm Melekhov." And that's how we settled it. I kept watch until Kaparin went to sleep and I could hear you were asleep too, snoring a bit. Then I crept up and hit him on the head with my club. And our captain, he didn't give so much as a kick! He just stretched himself like he was enjoying it and took leave of this life... We searched his pockets quietly, then picked him up by his arms and legs, carried him down to the bank, took off his boots, tunic and coat—and into the water with him. And there was you, still fast asleep, dead to the wide... Ay, death was very close to you, Melekhov, last night! Standing right over your head it was. Although Yakov Yefimovich said I shouldn't touch you, I thought to myself, "What could they have been talking about this afternoon? It's a bad business when two out of five keep apart from the others, having secrets..." So I crept over to you and was going to give you a real good wallop, but then I thought, he's a tough nut, if I hit him, he may jump up and start shooting, if I don't knock him out in one go... But Fomin again put me off my stroke. He comes up and whispers, "Don't touch him, he's our man, you can trust him." And what with one thing and another we couldn't figure out where Kaparin's weapons had got to. So I let you be. You slept well that night, I can tell you, never dreamed of the danger you were in!'

Grigory said calmly, 'You'd have been wrong to kill me, you fool! I never made any deal with Kaparin.'

'Then how come you've got his weapons?'

Grigory smiled.

'I got them away from him yesterday afternoon, and in the evening I took the bolt of his rifle and hid it under my saddle cloth.'

He recounted his conversation with Kaparin and the proposal that had been made.

Fomin asked gruffly, 'Why didn't you tell us about it yesterday?'

'I was sorry for him, the slob,' Grigory confessed frankly.

'Ah, Melekhov, Melekhov!' Chumakov exclaimed, sincerely surprised. 'Put your pity away where you hid the bolt of Kaparin's rifle—under the saddle cloth, or it'll bring you to no good!'

'I don't need you to teach me,' Grigory replied coldly.

'Why should I teach you? But what if I'd sent you off to the other world last night because of your pity—what about that?'

'It would be good riddance,' Grigory replied after a little thought. And more to himself than to the others he added, 'The living fear death when they're awake, but in sleep it must be easy enough...'

XV

At the end of April they rowed across the Don at night. On the bank near Rubezhny a young Cossack named Alexander Koshelev, from the village of Lower Krivsky, was waiting for them.

'I want to join you, Yakov Yefimovich. I'm sick of life at home,' he said to Fomin.

Fomin nudged Grigory with his elbow and whispered, 'There I told you... We've hardly left the island and here they are, waiting for us! I know this lad—he's a fighting Cossack. This is a good sign! We'll pull something off this time!'

There was a smile in Fomin's voice. Clearly he was much encouraged by the appearance of a new recruit. The successful crossing and the fact of having someone join them on the spot had raised his spirits and inspired him with new hope.

'Why, besides your rifle and revolver you've got a sabre and field glasses, eh?' he said approvingly, peering in the darkness and feeling Koshelev's weapons. 'That's a Cossack! You can see at once he's a real Cossack! The right breed!'

Fomin's cousin drove down to the bank in a wagon drawn by a little cob.

'Put the saddles in the wagon,' he said in a low voice. 'And hurry up, for Christ's sake. It'll soon be morning and we've got a long way to go.'

He was nervous and kept hurrying Fomin, but now that he had left the island and felt the firm ground of his own village underfoot, Fomin was in the mood to spend an hour or two at home and look up some of his old friends.

Just before dawn they spotted a herd of horses near the village of Yagodny, picked out the best and saddled them. To the old man who was minding the herd Chumakov said, 'Don't grieve too much over the horses, Grandad. They're not worth a kind word, and we'll only ride 'em for a bit. As soon as we find something better, we'll send these back to their owners. If they want to know who took the horses, tell 'em it was the militia from Krasnokutskaya. Let the owners go there about it... We're pursuing a band, tell 'em!'

When they reached the highway they said goodbye to Fomin's cousin and turned left and the five of them headed south-west at a brisk trot. The word was that Maslak's band had appeared somewhere near Meshkovskaya, and Fomin had decided to join him.

* * *

In search of Maslak's band they spent about three days combing the steppeland tracks of the right bank, avoiding the big villages and stanitsas. In the Ukrainian settlements around Karginskaya they changed their poor nags for fast well-fed Ukrainian mounts.

On the morning of the fourth day, not far from the village of Vezhi, Grigory was the first to spot a column of cavalry coming over a distant pass between two hills. Not less than two squadrons were moving along the road with reconnaissance patrols ranging ahead and on both sides.

'Either that's Maslak, or it's...' Fomin put his field-glasses to his eyes.

'Mebbe it's rain, mebbe snow, what's to come we'll never know,' Chumakov said derisively. 'Take a good look, Yakov Yefimovich, because if it's the Reds we'd better turn round and be quick about it.'

'How the devil can I see from here!' Fomin grumbled.

'Look! They've spotted us! Their patrol's heading this way!' Sterlyadnikov exclaimed.

They had been sighted. The patrol on the right flank swung round and came trotting towards them. Fomin hurriedly pushed his glasses into their case, but Grigory leaned over smiling and gripped Fomin's horse by the bridle.

'Don't be in such a hurry! Let 'em come a bit nearer. There're only a dozen. We'll have a proper look at 'em and we can still get away if need be. We've got fresh horses under us—what are you scared of? Use your glasses!'

The twelve riders approached, looming larger every minute. They stood out clearly against the green young grass on the hillside.

Grigory and the others watched Fomin impatiently. The hands holding the field-glasses to his eyes were trembling, and he was staring so intently that a tear crept down his sunlit cheek.

'Reds! They've got stars on their caps!' he gasped, and wheeled his horse.

The race began. Occasional shots sounded behind them. Over about four versts Grigory galloped beside Fomin, glancing back from time to time.

'So this is how we join forces!' he said mockingly.

Fomin maintained a gloomy silence. Curbing his horse, Chumakov shouted, 'We've got to keep away from the villages! Let's head for the Vyoshenskaya grazing range. Nothing there!'

A few more versts at this gruelling pace and the horses would give up. Frothy sweat had broken out on their straining necks and deep grooves had appeared between the muscles.

'We'll have to ease up! Hold your horses!' Grigory commanded.

Only nine of the twelve riders were still in the pursuit, the others had dropped behind. Grigory measured the distance by eye and shouted, 'Halt! Let's have a shot at them!'

All five slowed down to a trot, dismounted while still moving and slung their rifles off their shoulders.

'Hold the rein! At the man on the far left, rapid—fire!'

They emptied their magazines, killed the horse under one of the Red Army men, and galloped on. The zest went out of the chase. Their pursuers fired a few volleys from a long distance, then gave up.

'The horses need a drink, there's a pond!' Sterlyadnikov said, pointing with his whip to where a steppeland pond showed up blue in the distance.

They had reduced their pace to a walk and were scanning every dell and ravine, making use of any cover they could find.

At the pond they watered the horses, and then pushed on, first at a walk, then at a trot. At noon they stopped to feed the horses on the side of a deep ravine that cut jaggedly across the steppe. Fomin ordered Koshelev to climb the nearest hill on foot and keep watch from there. If any riders appeared, he was to signal at once and make a dash for the horses.

Grigory hobbled his horse and let it graze while he himself lay down on a dry spot on the hillside.

The young grass on the sunny side of the ravine was taller and thicker. The fresh smell of the sun-warmed soil could not suppress the subtle aroma of the fading steppeland violets. They were growing nearby on a strip of abandoned tillage, among the dry stalks of last year's sweet-clover. They made a bright hem along an ancient field balk, and even on the flint-hard virgin land their blue, childishly clear eyes peeped out at the world from among the withered grass of the year before. The violets were living out their appointed term in this remote and vast steppe, and to replace them the magic glow of tulips had appeared on the side of the ravine and on the salty patches. They lifted their scarlet, yellow and white cups to the sun and the wind mingled the different scents, carrying them far away across the steppe.

Hard-packed snow, oozing moisture, still lay in the shadow of the steep northern side. It chilled the air but its cold breath only enhanced the aroma of fading violets, a faint and melancholy fragrance, like a memory of something dear and long since past.

Grigory lay on his stomach with his legs wide apart, resting on his elbows, and gazing at the steppe in its curling wisps of sunlit mist, at the sentinel mounds, dark-blue on the distant ridge of the horizon, at the quivering opalescent haze on the edge of the ravine. For a moment he closed his eyes and listened to the song of the larks, near and far, the light tread and snorting of the grazing horses, the clink of the snaffles and the murmur of the wind in the young grass... A strange feeling of detachment and peace came over him as he lay with his whole body pressed to the hard ground. He knew it of old. It always came to him after a spell of alarm, and at such times he saw all his surroundings with new eyes. His vision and hearing seemed to grow sharper, and everything that had passed unnoticed before now caught his attention. With equal interest he watched the whirring slantwise flight of a hawk pursuing a tiny bird, the slow progress of a black beetle laboriously covering the distance between his two elbows, and the light swaying of a crimson-black tulip, stirred gently by the wind and glowing with a vivid virginal beauty. The tulip was growing quite nearby, on the edge of a crumbling marmot mound. Grigory had only to reach out to pick it, but he lay still, gazing in silent admiration at the flower and the taut leaves of the stem, which still husbanded a few rainbow drops of morning dew in their folds. Then he shifted his gaze and for a long time lay thoughtlessly watching an eagle gliding above the horizon, over a dead village of abandoned marmot burrows.

About two hours later they saddled their horses again and set off in the hope of reaching the Yelanskaya villages by nightfall.

The Red Army patrol had probably telephoned ahead about their movements. As they rode into Kamenka they were greeted by a crackle of rifle fire from across the stream. The hum of bullets turned Fomin away. They galloped along the edge of the village under fire and soon rode clear into the Vyoshenskaya grazing lands. Near Boggy Ravine a small detachment of militia tried to intercept them.

Fomin proposed making a detour to the left.

'We'll attack,' Grigory said resolutely. 'It's only nine of them against five of us. We'll break through!'

He was supported by Chumakov and Sterlyadnikov. Drawing their sabres, they put their weary horses into gallop. The militiamen opened rapid fire without dismounting, but then rode aside without accepting the challenge.

'They're a poor lot. Good at writing reports but no

guts for fighting!' Koshelev shouted contemptuously.

Returning the fire when the pursuing militiamen began to overtake, the fugitives headed eastwards like wolves harried by borzoi hounds, occasionally snapping back and hardly ever stopping. During one of the exchanges Sterlyadnikov was wounded. A bullet pierced the calf of his left leg and touched the bone. He gasped with pain and turned pale.

'They've got me in the leg... My lame leg again... The bastards!'

Chumakov leaned back and roared with laughter. He laughed so hard that tears came to his eyes. He was still shaking with laughter when he helped Sterlyadnikov to mount his horse.

'How did they manage to pick on that leg? They must have aimed special like. They saw a cripple come galloping along and they thinks to 'emselves, let's knock that leg of his for good... Oho, Sterlyadnikov! You'll be the death of me!... You'll have to have another quarter off that leg of yours... How'll you dance now? I'll have to dig an even deeper hole for your other leg.'

'Shut up, big mouth, I can't be bothered with you now! Keep quiet, for Christ's sake!' Sterlyadnikov begged, wincing with pain.

Half an hour later, when they rode out of one of the innumerable ravines he asked them to stop. 'Let's wait a bit... I've got to plug this leg somehow, my boot's full of blood.'

They halted. Grigory held the horses. While Fomin and Koshelev kept up a desultory fire at the militiamen lurking in the distance Chumakov helped Sterlyadnikov to pull off his boot.

'There sure is a lot of blood here,' Chumakov said frowning and poured the sticky red liquid out on to the ground.

He wanted to slit the sodden steaming trouser leg, but Sterlyadnikov wouldn't let him.

'These are good trousers, I don't want 'em ripped up,' he said, and leaning back on his elbows, lifted his wounded leg. 'Pull 'em off, but be careful.'

'Got a bandage?' Chumakov asked, feeling in his pockets.

'What the hell do I need a bandage for? I can manage without that.'

Sterlyadnikov studied the exit hole of the wound, then pulled the bullet out of a cartridge case with his teeth, tipped the gunpowder into the palm of his hand and mixed it thoroughly with some earth, which he had moistened with spit. He plastered both sides of the wound with the mixture and observed with satisfaction, 'That a sure remedy! It'll dry up in a couple of days and heal like a dog.'

They did not stop till they reached the Chir. The militiamen remained at a safe distance and fired only occasional single shots. Fomin frequently looked back.

'They're keeping tabs on us,' he said. 'Mebbe they're expecting help from somewhere? They're not holding back for nothing.'

At the village of Visloguzovsky they forded the Chir and walked their horses up a long rise. The horses were exhausted. Downhill they could manage a trot but up-hill the men had to lead them by the bridle, scraping the quivering flecks of foam off their wet flanks with their hands.

Fomin had guessed right. About five versts from Visloguzovsky the chase was taken up by seven riders on fresh fast horses.

'If they keep passing us along like this, we're done for!' Koshelev said gloomily.

They rode off across the open steppe, taking it in turns to shoot back at their pursuers. While two, lying in the grass, kept up the fire, the others rode on for about four hundred paces, then dismounted and kept the enemy under fire while the first two withdrew and rode on another four hundred metres ahead, then dismounted in their turn and prepared to shoot. They killed or badly wounded one militiaman and brought down the horse under another. Soon Chumakov's horse was also killed. He ran beside Koshelev, holding his stirrup.

The shadows lengthened as the sun went down. At Grigory's suggestion they stopped shuttling and rode on together at a walk. Chumakov kept up with them on foot. After a while they spotted a wagon drawn by two horses on the crest of a hill, and made for the road. The bearded old Cossack driver put his horses into a gallop but their warning shots brought him to a halt.

'I'll cut you down, you old bugger! I'll teach you to run away,' Koshelev snarled through his teeth, lashing his horse fiercely and getting ahead.

'Don't touch him, Sashka, I forbid it!' Fomin cautioned him, and while they were still at a distance, shouted to the old man to take his horses out of the shafts. 'Unhitch your horses, Grandad, if you want to stay alive.'

Ignoring the old man's tearful pleadings, they unhitched the traces, removed the collars and breechbands, and saddled the horses at once.

'Can't you leave me just one of yours to make up for 'em!' the old man begged weeping.

'D'you want a kick in the teeth, you old devil?' Koshelev asked. 'We need the horses ourselves! Thank the Lord you're still alive...'

Fomin and Chumakov mounted the fresh horses. The six riders pursuing them were soon joined by three more.

'We've got to keep moving! Come on, lads!' Fomin said. 'If we get to the Krivsky ravines by nightfall, we'll be safe.'

He lashed his horse and galloped ahead. His second horse ran at his side on a short rein. The scarlet tops of the tulips slashed by their hooves scattered on all sides, like splashes of blood. Grigory who was riding behind him, looked at the red splashes and closed his eyes. He felt suddenly dizzy and a familiar stab of pain went through his heart.

The horses were at the end of their tether. The men too were exhausted by the endless hard riding and lack of food. Sterlyadnikov was swaying in his saddle, his face as white as a sheet. He had lost a lot of blood, and was tortured by thirst and nausea. When he ate a little stale bread, he was sick at once.

In the twilight, not far from the village of Krivsky, they rode into the middle of a herd of horses returning from the steppe. They fired a few last shots at their pursuers and saw with joy that the chase was being abandoned. The nine riders assembled in the distance, seemed to consult about something, and turned back.

* * *

They spent two days in Krivsky at the house of a Cossack acquaintance of Fomin's. Their host was well off and looked after them. Stabled in a dark shed, the horses could hardly eat all the oats they were given and by the end of the second day had thoroughly rested from their mad gallop. The men took turns in minding them, slept together in a cool cobweb-draped chaff shed and stuffed themselves with food, making up for all the hungry days they had spent on the island.

They could have left the village on the second day but they were delayed by Sterlyadnikov. His wound had begun to fester. In the morning it was red round the edges and by evening the leg swelled up and he fainted. He was tortured by thirst. All night, whenever consciousness returned, he begged for water and drank in great thirsty gulps. During the night he drank nearly a pailful of water but could not get up even with help; every movement caused him acute pain and he urinated where he lay, groaning continuously. They carried him to the far corner of the shed so that his groans would not be so audible, but it was no use. Some were very loud and when he fainted he would rave deliriously.

Now they had the added duty of watching over him. They brought him water, moistened his burning forehead and covered his mouth with their hands or caps when he cried out too loud or was raving.

After two days he recovered consciousness and said he felt better.

'When are you leaving?' he asked Chumakov, beckoning to him.

'Tonight.'

'I'll ride with you. Don't leave me here, for Christ's sake.'

'How can you ride?' Fomin said in a low voice. 'You can't even move.'

'Can't I? Look!' Sterlyadnikov stood up with an effort, then lay down again at once.

His face was burning and tiny beads of perspiration had broken out on his forehead.

'We'll take you,' Chumakov said firmly. 'Don't worry, we'll take you! And wipe your tears—you're not a woman.'

'It's sweat,' Sterlyadnikov whispered, and pulled his cap over his eyes.

'We'd be glad to leave you here, but the owner won't let us. Don't get scared, Vasily! Your leg'll soon heal up and we'll have a wrestle and dance together again. Come on, where's your spirit now? It'd be different if it was a bad wound, but that's just a scratch!'

Always rough and inconsiderate in his treatment of others, Chumakov said this so affectionately and with such winning, gentle notes in his voice that Grigory stared at him in surprise.

They rode out of the village not long before daybreak. They had lifted Sterlyadnikov into the saddle with some difficulty but he kept slipping sideways, so Chumakov rode beside him with one arm round his shoulder.

'He's going to be a drag on us... We'll have to dump him,' Fomin whispered as he came up with Grigory, shaking his head despondently.

'Finish him off?'

'What else? Make eyes at him? How can we go on like this?'

They rode for some time in silence. Grigory took over from Chumakov, and was then relieved by Koshelev.

The sun rose. Below them the Don was still wrapped in swirling mists, but from the hill the steppeland vistas were transparently clear and every minute the blue of the heavens deepened, leaving only a few fluffy clouds hanging motionless at the zenith. Heavy dew covered the grass like silver brocade and the horses traced a dark stream-like trail as they passed. Only the larks disturbed the great and blissful stillness of the steppe.

Sterlyadnikov, his head nodding listlessly in time with the horse's gait, said quietly, 'Aw, this is too hard for me!'

'Quiet!' Fomin interrupted him roughly. 'It's no picnic for us either looking after you!'

As they were nearing the Hetman's Highway a bustard shot up from under the horses' feet. The whir of its wings roused Sterlyadnikov from his oblivion.

'Let me down off the horse, lads,' he requested.

Koshelev and Chumakov lifted him carefully out of the saddle and laid him down in the wet grass.

'Let me have a look at your leg. Now then, unbutton your trousers,' Chumakov said, squatting down beside him.

Sterlyadnikov's leg was grotesquely swollen and filled the whole baggy trouser, making it so tight that not a single crease remained. Right up to the hip the dark violet skin was shiny and covered with blotches that felt like velvet to the touch. Similar blotches, of a lighter shade, had appeared on the dark sunken belly. Already a foul, putrid smell rose from the wound and the blood that had dried brown on the trouser, and Chumakov held his nose as he examined his friend's leg, only just managing to stop himself from vomiting. He stared hard at the sick man's lowered blue eyelids and exchanged glances with Fomin.

'Looks as if the gangrene's got him... Ay, you're in a bad way, Vasily Sterlyadnikov... It's a sorry state you're in! Ah, Vasily, how could you let this happen to you?...'

Sterlyadnikov was breathing in short gasps and made no response. Fomin and Grigory dismounted as if at a word of command and approached the sick man from the windward side. He lay there for a little longer, then struggled into a sitting position, and looked round at the others with dull but sternly resigned eyes.

'Brothers! Put me to death... I'm no good for this world any more... I've had enough of this torture, I'm done for, I guess.'

He lay back and closed his eyes. Fomin and the others had known the request would come and had been waiting for it. Fomin gave Koshelev a quick glance and turned away. Without demur Koshelev slung his rifle off his shoulder. 'Shoot him!' he saw Chumakov's lips move as he stepped aside, and read the words rather than heard them. But Sterlyadnikov opened his eyes again and said firmly, 'Aim here,' he raised his hand and pointed at the bridge of his nose. 'So the light goes out at once... If you're in my village, tell the old woman what happened... So she won't wait for me.'

Koshelev was a suspiciously long time fiddling with the bolt of his rifle and Sterlyadnikov closed his eyes and managed to finish what he wanted to say.

'I've only got a wife ... no kiddies... She only gave me one, and that was born dead... We never had no more...'

Koshelev lifted his rifle twice and lowered it again, pale-faced. Chumakov shoved him aside furiously and snatched the rifle.

'If you can't do it, don't try, you pup's liver,' he shouted hoarsely and, taking off his cap, smoothed down his hair.

'Hurry up!' Fomin demanded, one foot in the stirrup.

Groping for the right words, Chumakov said slowly and quietly, 'Vasily! Goodbye and forgive us all, for Christ's sake! We'll meet again in the next world and they'll judge us there... We'll tell your wife what you said.' He waited for an answer but Sterlyadnikov said nothing and grew paler as he awaited death. Only his sun-scorched lashes quivered, as if stirred by the wind, and the fingers of his left hand moved gently as they tried to fasten a broken button on the front of his tunic.

Grigory had seen many deaths but he did not wait to see this one. He strode away hurriedly, pulling his horse by the bridle. He waited for the shot as though he himself were about to receive a bullet between his shoulder blades. His heart counted each second, but when the shot crashed out, his legs sagged and he could scarcely hold his rearing horse.

For about two hours they rode on without a word being spoken. At the next halt Chumakov broke the silence. Covering his eyes with his hand, he said huskily, 'Why the hell did I shoot him? I could've left him there in the steppe and not taken another sin on my soul. He's there, before me now...'

'Can't you get used to it?' Fomin asked. 'All the men you've killed in your time and you've not used to it yet? You must have a lump of rusty iron instead of a heart...'

Chumakov turned pale and gave Fomin a savage look.

'Let me alone, Yakov Yefimovich!' he said quietly. 'Don't rub me on the raw or I might slug you one too... Just like that!'

'Why'd I want to rub you on the raw? I've got troubles enough of my own,' Fomin said in a conciliatory tone and lay back, screwing his eyes up in the sunshine and stretching his limbs with pleasure.

XVI

Contrary to Grigory's expectations, some forty Cossacks joined the band in the space of about ten days. These were the remnants of various small bands that had been routed in battle. After losing their leaders, they had been roaming about the district and were glad to join up with Fomin. It was all the same to them who they served or who they killed as long as they could pursue their free, nomadic life and rob anyone who happened to cross their path. They were a desperate lot, and one day as he surveyed their ranks Fomin said contemptuously to Grigory, 'Well, Grigory, it's the driftwood that floats our way... Look at 'em—gaol-birds, to a man!' Inwardly Fomin still regarded himself as a 'champion of the working folk' and he would still sometimes say, though not as frequently as he used to, 'We're liberators of the Cossacks...' He clung stubbornly to absurd hopes. Once again he had started turning a blind eye to the plundering practiced by his men. He believed that this was an unavoidable evil, that he would eventually get rid of the looters and sooner or later become the commander of a rebel force, not merely the ataman of a tiny band.

But Chumakov did not mince words. He called all Fomin's men 'brigands' and went on till he was hoarse, telling Fomin that he, too, was no better than a highwayman. Fierce arguments broke out between them when there was no one else about.

'I'm against the Soviets on principle!' Fomin would shout, going purple in the face. 'And you swear at me! Don't you realise, you fool, that I'm fighting for an idea!'

'Don't give me that!' Chumakov would shout back. 'You can't fool me! I wasn't born yesterday! Fighting for an idea, are you! You're nothing but an out-and-out brigand. Why you're scared of that word, I just can't understand!'

'Why insult me like this? Who do you say these things, may they choke you?! I've rebelled against the government and I'm fighting it, I've taken up arms. How can I be called a brigand?'

'That's just why you are a brigand, because you're going against the government. Brigands have always been against the government, from way back. Whatever this Soviet government may be, it's the government, it's held out since 1917, and anyone who goes against it is a brigand.'

'You blockhead! What about General Krasnov or Denikin—were they brigands?'

'What else were they then? Except that they had epaulettes on their shoulders. But an epaulette don't count for much. We could wear some ourselves if we wanted to.'

Fomin would thump the table with his fist, spit on the floor and, unable to find any more persuasive arguments, give up the futile dispute. It was no use trying to convince Chumakov.

Most of the newcomers to the band were well armed and equipped. They nearly all had good horses, which had got used to the endless marches and had no difficulty in covering as much as a hundred versts a day. Some of them had two horses, one for the saddle, while the other travelled light, at the rider's side. If necessary, by changing from one mount to another and letting each rest in turn, the two-horse rider could do as much as two hundred versts between one dawn and the next.

One day Fomin said to Grigory, 'If we'd had two

horses each to start with, we'd never have been caught! The militia or the Red Army aren't allowed to take horses from the local people and they don't like doing it, but with us anything's allowed! We must all get ourselves a spare horse and then we'll never be caught! The old folk used to say that was how the Tatars went out raiding, with a couple of horses, and even three sometimes. Who could catch 'em? That's what we ought to do. I like the sound of this Tatar wisdom, that I do!'

They soon rustled up the horses they needed, and this did make them uncatchable for a time. The mounted militia group that had again been marshalled in Vyoshenskaya pursued them in vain. The spare horses made it easy for Fomin's small band to steal marches on the enemy and avoid dangerous clashes.

In the middle of May, however, a force outnumbering the band by almost four to one managed to hem them in along the Don not far from the village of Bobrovsky, near Ust-Khopyorskaya. But after a brief engagement the band broke out along the bank, losing eight of its men killed or wounded. Soon after this Fomin offered Grigory the post of chief of staff.

'We need someone who can read, so that we can go by the map, or one day they'll corner us and give us another bashing. You take on the job, Grigory Panteleyevich.'

'We don't need a staff to catch militiamen and split their skulls,' Grigory replied somberly.

'Every unit must have its staff. Don't talk crap.'

'Give Chumakov the job, if you can't do without a staff.'

'Why don't you want it?'

'I don't know anything about such things.'

'Does Chumakov?'

'No, he doesn't either.'

'Then why the hell are you foisting him on me? You're an officer, you ought to have some idea. You know about tactics and all that kind of thing.'

'I was as much good as an officer as you are at commanding this detachment! And our tactics are always the same: keep going across the steppe and look back all the time,' Grigory said mockingly.

Fomin winked at him and wagged his finger.

'I can see right through you! You're still trying to stay in the shade, aren't you? In the background? It won't save you, mate! Whether you're a troop commander or chief of staff, it comes to the same thing. D'you think they'll let you off lightly if they catch you? You've got some hopes.'

'I'm not thinking of anything like that. Your guessing's all wrong,' Grigory said, studying the hilt of his sabre. 'I just don't want to take on something I know nothing about.'

'Well, it's up to you, you can take it or leave it. We'll get along somehow without you, I reckon,' Fomin assented huffily.

The situation in the district had changed radically. The well-to-do Cossack farmers, who had once entertained Fomin with great hospitality, now bolted their gates against him and slipped away into their orchards and poplar groves as soon as the band appeared in a village. At the trials held in Vyoshenskaya a visiting Revolutionary Tribunal had passed severe sentences on many Cossacks who had welcomed Fomin. Word of this had spread and had its impact on those who had once supported the bandits.

In two weeks Fomin had made a wide sweep along the Upper Don. The band now numbered nearly one hundred and thirty sabres, and it was no longer pursued by a hastily formed mounted group, but by several squadrons of the 13th Cavalry Regiment, which had been brought up from the south.

Many of the bandits who had joined Fomin in the past few days hailed from afar and they had reached the Don in different ways. Some were lone fugitives from exile, from prison or labour camps, but the main reinforcement came in the shape of a fair-sized group that had broken away from Maslak's band and also the remnants of Kurochkin's band, which had been routed. Maslak's men willingly split up and there were some in every troop, but Kurochkin's refused to be separated. They formed a whole troop and held themselves aloof from the others. Whether fighting or resting they acted together and stood up loyally for each other, and when they had looted some village shop or store they would pool everything and then share it out fairly in strict observance of the principle of equality.

A few Cossacks from the Terek and the Kuban, in their tattered Circassian tunics, two Kalmyks from Veliko-knyazheskaya, a Lett in hunting boots that came up to his thighs, and five anarchist sailors in sun-faded pea-jackets and striped vests lent additional colour to Fomin's already motley band.

'Well, will you still make out that you're not brigands but—what d'you call 'em?—fighters for an idea?' Chumakov asked Fomin one day, looking back along the straggling ranks of the column. 'All we need is an unfrocked priest and a pig in trousers to make up the holy family in full array...'

Fomin let that pass in silence. His only desire now was to gather as many men around him as he could. He accepted volunteers quite indiscriminately, asking them a few questions and concluding with a brief, 'You'll do. Go to my chief of staff Chumakov. He'll tell you what troop you're in and give you your weapons.'

In a village near Migulinskaya a swarthy, curly-headed lad, very well-dressed, was brought before Fomin. He stated his wish to join the band. From his answers to Fomin's questions it transpired that he was from Rostov, had recently been sentenced for armed robbery, but had escaped from a Rostov gaol and, on hearing about Fomin, had made his way to the Upper Don.

'What blood are you? Armenian or Bulgarian?' Fomin asked.

'I'm a Jew,' the young man faltered.

Fomin was taken aback and for a time could find nothing to say. He did not know what to do in such a contingency. After racking his brains for a bit, he heaved a sigh and said, 'Well, if you're a Jew you're a Jew. We don't turn up our noses even at them. We can always do with an extra man. Can you ride? No? You'll learn! We'll give you a quiet little mare to start with, and you'll learn. Go and see Chumakov, and he'll tell you what troop you're in.'

A few minutes later Chumakov galloped up to Fomin in a fury.

'Are you daft or just joking?' he shouted as he reined in his horse. 'What the hell did you send me that yid for? I won't take him! Tell him to get out!'

'Take him. It adds to our numbers,' Fomin replied calmly.

But Chumakov foamed at the mouth and shouted, 'I won't have him! I'd rather kill him on the spot! The Cossacks are grumbling already. Go and deal with 'em yourself.'

While they were arguing and swearing at each other, the young Jew was taken over to a baggage cart, and stripped of his embroidered shirt and flared woollen trousers. As he tried on the shirt, one of the Cossacks said, 'See that clump of scrub over there, just outside the village? Well, get there quick and stay there till we've gone, then you can go where your fancy takes you. But don't come near us any more or we'll kill you. You'd better go home to Mummy in Rostov. Fighting's not a Jew's game. The Lord God taught you to trade, not to fight. We'll manage without you and take what's coming to us.'

The Jew was not accepted, but on the same day a new recruit—the half-wit Pasha, known all over Vyoshenskaya—was enlisted in the Second Troop amid much laughter and cracking of jokes. The Cossacks had picked him up in the steppe, brought him back to the village, solemnly fitted him out in the uniform of a Red Army man they had killed, shown him how to handle a rifle and were now engaged in teaching him to use a sabre.

Grigory was on his way to tend his horses at the tethering posts but turned towards the crowd that had gathered. An explosion of laughter made him quicken his pace, and in the silence that followed he heard a didactic voice giving instructions.

'No, not like that, Pasha! Who cuts a man down like that? That's how you chop wood, not a man. This is how you do it, see? First you catch him, then you tell him to kneel down, because you'll find it awkward while he's standing up... When he's down on his knees, you have a good slash at his neck like this, from behind. Try not to make a straight cut, but slanting like, with a pull at the end of the stroke...'

Surrounded by bandits, the half-wit was standing at attention and gripping the hilt of a bared sabre in both hands. As he listened to the instructions of one of the Cossacks, he smiled and blissfully screwed up his protruding grey eyes. The corners of his mouth were white with foam, like the jaws of a horse, and spit was running freely down his coppery-red beard. He licked his dribbling lips and mouthed disjointed phrases.

'I understand, lovey, I understand... Tha's wha' I'll do... Make him kneel, the slave of God, and slash his neck in half... Slash it right through, that I will! You given me a shirt and boots... Only I haven't got no coat... Fit me up with a coat. Please, gimme a coat, and I'll do all you say! Try real hard I will!'

'If you kill a commissar, you'll have a coat. And now,

why don't you tell us how they married you off last year,' one of the Cossacks proposed.

The half-wit's bleary eyes became dilated with animal fear. He uttered a stream of curses and began his story amid general laughter. It was all so revolting that Grigory shuddered and hurried away. 'That's the kind of people I'm tied up with now,' he thought, overcome by regret, bitterness and anger with himself, with this life that had gone sour on him.

He lay down by the tethering posts and tried not to listen to the shouts of the half-wit and the booming guffaws of the Cossacks. 'I'm getting out of here tomorrow. It's time!' he decided, looking at his sleek horses, which were now in fine condition. He had prepared carefully and deliberately for leaving the band. From a militiaman who had been cut down in a skirmish he had taken papers in the name of Ushakov and sewed them into the lining of his greatcoat. He had started grooming his horses for a short but fast gallop two weeks before. He watered them regularly and kept them cleaner than he had ever kept his army mounts. By fair means or foul he obtained grain for them at night and his horses looked better than any of the others, especially the Ukrainian dapple-grey. Its glossy coat gleamed in the sun like Caucasian nielloed silver.

On such horses he could be confident of throwing off any pursuit. He rose to his feet and walked to the nearest house. Respectfully he asked of the old woman sitting on the steps of the barn if she had a scythe.

'I did have one somewhere. Plagued if I know where it is now. What d'you want it for?'

'I wanted to cut a bit of your grass for the horses. Could I?'

The old woman pondered for a while before answering, then she said, 'When are you going to get off our necks? It's nothing but give us this, help us with that. First they come demanding grain, then another lot comes and wants some more, and they take everything they set eyes on. No, I won't give you the scythe! Not for anything I won't!'

'Surely you don't grudge me a bit of grass, godly woman that you are?'

'D'you think grass grows just anywhere? What am I going to feed my cow on?'

'Isn't there plenty of grass in the steppe?'

'Well, ride out there and cut it, my young falcon, there's plenty in the steppe.'

Grigory said irritably, 'You'd better give me that scythe, Granny. I'll only mow a little and the rest will be yours. But if we let the horses in there, it'll all be spoilt!'

The old woman looked hard at Grigory and turned away.

'Go and get it yourself. It must be hanging up in the shed.'

Grigory found an old, badly chipped scythe beneath the overhang of the shed roof and, as he walked past the woman, distinctly heard her say, 'Will we never be rid of you, bloodsuckers!'

This was nothing new for Grigory. He had long been aware of the attitude to them in the villages. 'And they're quite right,' he thought, as he mowed carefully, trying to cut the grass as cleanly as he could. 'Why in the devil's name should they need us? No one needs us, we're just stopping everyone from working and living in peace. It's time to end it all. I've had enough!'

Lost in his own thoughts he stood watching the horses munching eagerly with their black velvety lips at the wisps of tender young grass. He was roused from his meditations by a youthfully unsteady bass.

'That's a real fine horse! Just like a swan!'

Grigory glanced round at the speaker. A young Cossack from Alexeyevskaya who had only just joined the band was looking at the grey and shaking his head in admiration. He walked round it several times, gazing enchantedly at the animal and clicking his tongue.

'Is he yours?'

'What's that to you?' Grigory replied gruffly.

'Let's swap! I've got a bay, a pure Don thoroughbred. It can take any hurdle! And what a gallop! Like lightning!'

'Go to the devil,' Grigory said coldly.

The lad was silent for a moment, sighed disappointedly and sat down not far away. He studied the grey at some length, then said, 'That horse of yours has got the heaves. He can't breathe out properly.'

Grigory silently picked at his teeth with a straw. He was beginning to like the naive youngster.

'Won't you swap then, Uncle?' the lad asked quietly, looking at Grigory with beseeching eyes.

'No, I won't. Even if you offer yourself as a make-weight.'

'Where did you get him?'

'Out of my own head.'

'No, tell me true!'

'Through the same gate as all the others. A mare foaled him.'

'What's the use of talking to such a fool,' the lad said huffily and walked away.

The village was deserted; it looked dead. There was not a soul about except for Fomin's men. The wagon left standing in a sidelane, the chopping block in a yard with an axe hurriedly buried in it, and an unshaped board beside it, the yoked oxen lazily nibbling at the stunted grass in the middle of the street, the overturned bucket by the well—all suggested that the peaceful course of life in the village had been unexpectedly disturbed, that the farmers had left their work unfinished and gone into hiding.

Grigory had seen the same desolation, the same signs of hasty departure when the Cossack regiments had been riding through East Prussia. Now he was seeing it in his home country... The looks that the Germans had given him then had been as sullen and filled with hate as those that he now received from the Cossacks of the Upper Don. He remembered his conversation with the old woman and looked about him wistfully, unbuttoning the collar of his shirt. Again that damned pain was stabbing at his heart.

The sun was burning into the ground. The lane smelled faintly of dust, goosefoot and horse droppings. Rooks were cawing from the shaggy nests scattered among the tall willows. A steppeland stream, fed by pure springs somewhere at the top of the ravine, flowed slowly through the village, dividing it into two halves. From both sides the orchards of the Cossack farmsteads stretched down it in a profusion of cherry-trees that screened the windows of the houses and branching apple-trees, all green with leafage and the ovaries of young fruit upturned to the sun.

With misted eyes Grigory gazed at a yard overgrown with plaintains, at a straw-thatched dwelling with yellow shutters, at the tall well-sweep beside it. On one of the stakes of the fence round the threshing floor there hung a horse's skull, bleached by the rain and with gaping black eye sockets. The green trailer of a pumpkin plant had spiralled to the top of the stake and was clutching with its shaggy tendrils at the protuberances of the skull and the dead teeth, while its suspended tip, seeking support, was already reaching out to the branch of a guelder-rose near by.

Was it in his dreams or in far-off childhood that Grigory had seen all this? Seized by a sudden desperate yearning, he lay down, buried his face in his hands, and rose again only on hearing the distant call 'Saddle up!'

While they were on the march that night he rode out of the ranks as if to change his saddle to the other horse and stood listening to the slowly receding clip-clop of hooves until it was inaudible, then sprang into the saddle and plunged away from the road at a fast gallop.

For about five versts he rode his horses hard without stopping, then slowed to a walk and listened for any sounds of pursuit. The steppe was quiet. The only sounds were the plaintive calling of the sandpipers on the hummocks and the barking of a dog somewhere very far away.

In the black sky, a goldmine of glittering stars. In the steppe, silence and a gentle breeze steeped in the dear and bitter scent of wormwood... Grigory rose in his stirrups and drew a full, deep breath of relief.

XVII

Long before dawn he rode into the meadow on the far bank opposite Tatarsky. A little further downstream, where the river was shallower, he stripped naked, tied his clothes, boots and weapons to the horses' heads and, holding his cartridge pouch in his teeth, started to swim the river. The water seared him with its unbearable cold. In an effort to get warm he struck out vigorously with his right arm, holding the tied bridles in his left hand and quietly encouraging the groaning, snorting horses.

On reaching the bank he dressed hurriedly, tightened the saddle girths and, to warm the horses, set off at a gallop towards the village. The wet greatcoat, wet saddle flaps and wet shirt chilled his body. His teeth chattered, shivers coursed down his spine and he began to shake in every limb, but the fast riding soon warmed him and he approached the village at a walk, looking round on all sides and listening intently. He decided to leave the horses in a ravine and as he made his way down to the bottom their hooves clattered sharply on the stones and fiery sparks flew out from under the shoes.

Grigory tethered the horses to a withered elm he had known since childhood and walked into the village. Here it was, the old Melekhov farmstead, the dark shapes of the apple-trees, the well-sweep pointing up at the Great Bear... Panting with agitation, Grigory walked on towards the Don, cautiously climbed the fence of the Astakhovs' yard and went up to the unshuttered window. He could hear only the pounding of his heart and the dull roar of blood in his head. He tapped quietly on the window frame, so quietly that he himself barely heard the sound. Aksinya came silently to the window and peered out. He saw her clasp her hands to her breast and heard the faint moan that broke from her lips. He signed to her to open the window and slung the rifle off his shoulder. She threw open both frames.

'Quiet! Don't open the door, I'll come in through the window,' he whispered.

He climbed on to the coping. Her bare arms twined round his neck. Those dear arms, they trembled and throbbed so violently on his shoulders that he began to tremble with them.

'Wait, love ... take the rifle,' he muttered, barely able to speak.

With one hand steadying his sabre, he stepped in over the windowsill and closed the window.

He was about to take her in his arms, but she sank heavily to her knees, clasped his legs and pressed her face to his wet greatcoat, while her whole body shook with suppressed weeping. He lifted her up and seated her on a bench. Aksinya silently pressed her face to his chest, shaking convulsively and biting the lapel of his greatcoat so as not to waken the children with her sobbing.

So even Aksinya, strong though she was, had cracked under the strain. Life must have been hard for her in these last months... Grigory fondled the hair that had fallen loose down her back, stroked her hot, damp forehead. He let all her tears come, then asked, 'Are the children well?'

'Yes.'

'And Dunyashka?'

'Dunyashka... Yes, she's all right.'

'Is Mikhail at home? Give over now! Stop crying, my shirt's soaked in your tears. Aksinya! Darling! That's enough! We've no time for crying. Is Mikhail at home?'

She wiped her face and pressed Grigory's cheeks between her wet hands. Smiling at him through her tears, unable to take her eyes off her beloved, she said quietly, 'I won't cry any more... I'm not crying now... Mikhail's away. He's been in Vyoshenskaya for more than a month now, serving in some unit or other. Go and look at the children! We never expected to see you, that we didn't!'

Mishatka and Polyushka were fast asleep. Grigory bent over the bed and looked at them for a while, then tiptoed away and sat down silently beside Aksinya.

'But what about you?' she asked in an excited whisper.

'How did you get here? Where have you been all this time? Suppose they catch you?'

'I've come for you. They won't catch me! Will you come with me?'

'Where to?'

'With me. I've left the band. I was with Fomin. You heard about that?'

'Yes. But where can we go?'

'South. To the Kuban or farther. We'll manage somehow. We won't starve, will we? I won't jib at any work. That's what my hands need—work, not fighting. I've been eating my heart out these last months. But we'll talk about that later.'

'What about the children?'

'We'll leave them with Dunyashka, then see what happens. We can fetch them later. Well? Will you come?'

'Grisha... Grisha darling...'

'No tears! That's enough now! We'll do our crying together later on, when there's time. Get yourself ready, my horses are waiting in the ravine. Well? Are you coming?'

'What would you think?' Aksinya burst out, then glanced at the children, pressing her hand to her lips in fright.

'What would you think?' she repeated in a whisper. 'D'you think it's been easy for me here alone? I'll come, Grisha, my love! I'd walk, I'd crawl after you, but I won't stay here alone any more! There's no life for me without you... Better kill me than leave me again!'

She hugged Grigory with all her strength. He kissed her and glanced at the window. The summer nights were short. They must hurry.

'Won't you rest for a bit?' Aksinya asked.

'What!' he exclaimed. 'It'll soon be light, we've got to go now. Put your clothes on and call Dunyashka. We'll decide about the children. We must make Dry Dell while it's still dark. We'll hide in the woods there for the day, then go on at night. Can you ride a horse?'

'Goodness, I'd ride anything! I keep wondering if this is a dream or is it really happening. I've often dreamed about you and you're always different...' Aksinya combed her hair hurriedly as she spoke, holding the pins in her teeth, and her voice was barely audible. She dressed quickly and walked to the door.

'Shall I wake the children? You'll see what they're like.'

'No, don't,' Grigory said firmly.

He took his pouch out of his cap and started making a cigarette, but as soon as Aksinya had gone out he stepped quickly to the bed and lavished kisses on the children, then he recalled Natalya and a lot more from his ill-fortuned life and gave way to tears.

Straight from the threshold Dunyashka burst out, 'Well, hullo, brother dear! So you're home at last! After all your roaming...' And she went off into a long lament. 'So this is the father the children have waited for so long! Orphans with a living father...'

Grigory embraced her and said sternly, 'Be quiet, you'll wake the little ones! Drop that, sister! I've heard it all before! I've enough tears and sorrow of my own... That's not what I called you in for. Will you take the children and look after them?'

'And you? Where are you going?'

'I'm going away and taking Aksinya with me. Will you take the children? When I get work, I'll come and fetch them.'

'Well, of course, I will. If both of you are going, I'll have to. They can't be left out in the street and given to strangers.'

Grigory silently kissed Dunyashka, then said, 'I'm deeply grateful to you, sister! I knew you wouldn't refuse.'

Dunyashka sat down on the chest without replying.

'When are you leaving? Now?' she asked.

'Yes.'

'What about the house? The farm?'

Aksinya answered uncertainly. 'It's up to you. Take in some lodgers, do what you think best. Anything that's left of the clothes or household things you can move over to your own place.'

'But what shall I tell people? What shall I say when they ask what's become of you?'

'Say you don't know and that's all there is to it.'
Grigory turned to Aksinya. 'Hurry up and get ready,
love. Don't take much. Just a warm jacket and a few
skirts, whatever underwear you've got, and food for the
first few days. That's all.'

Day was just breaking when they came out on the
porch after saying goodbye to Dunyashka and kissing
the children, who were still asleep. They walked down to
the Don and made their way along the bank to the ravine.

'We went off to Yagodnoye like this,' Grigory said.
'Only then your bundle was bigger, and we were younger.'

Full of a joyful excitement, Aksinya glanced sideways
at him.

'I'm still afraid this may be a dream. Give me your
hand to touch, I can't believe it.' She laughed softly
and leaned on Grigory's shoulder as they walked.

He saw her tear-swollen eyes shining with happiness
and her cheeks, pale in the twilight, and with a wry but
tender smile on his hips he thought, 'There's a fine
woman for you. She got ready and came as if she was
going to a party. Nothing frightens her!'

And as if in answer to his thoughts, Aksinya said, 'See
what kind of a woman I am! You had only to whistle
me like a dog and I came running after you. It's love
and pining for you, Grisha, that've done this to me...
I'm only sorry for the little ones, I don't care a rap for
myself. I'd go anywhere to be with you, even to death!'

At the sound of their footsteps the horses neighed
quietly. Dawn was rushing upon them. A strip of sky on
the eastern fringe was already faintly pink. The mist
over the Don had risen off the water.

Grigory untethered the horses and helped Aksinya to
mount. The stirrups were rather too long for her. Reproaching himself for his lack of foresight, he shortened
them and mounted the second horse.

'Keep up behind me, Aksinya! When we get out of the
ravine, we'll gallop. It won't jog you so much. Don't
ride with a loose rein. The horse you've got doesn't like
that. Mind your knees. He's troublesome at times, tries
to snap at your knee. Well, off we go!'

It was about eight versts to Dry Dell. They covered
the distance rapidly and by sunrise they were approaching the forest. Grigory dismounted on the edge and
helped Aksinya out of the saddle.

'Well? Riding's hard when you're not used to it, eh?'
he asked with a smile.

Flushed from the gallop, Aksinya answered him with her dark eyes.

'It's fine! Better than walking. Only my legs...' She smiled in confusion. 'Turn away, Grisha, and I'll have a look. The skin's tingling... I must have rubbed them sore.'

'That's nothing, it'll go off,' Grigory assured her. 'Walk about a bit, your legs are trembling.' And he screwed up his eyes in an affectionately mocking smile. 'Call yourself a Cossack woman!'

He chose a clearing at the lower end of the dell, and said, 'This is where our camp will be. Make yourself comfortable, love!'

He unsaddled the horses, hobbled them and hid the saddles and weapons in the bushes. The heavy dew had turned the grass a bluish grey. On the slopes, where the morning darkness still lingered it looked almost blue. Orange bumble-bees were dozing in the half-open cups of the flowers. Larks were trilling high above the steppe, and from the wheat and the dense sweet-smelling steppeland grass came the steady piping of quails: 'Sleep now! Sleep now!' Grigory flattened the grass under a young oak bush and lay back, resting his head on one of the saddles. The steady piping of the quails, the drowsy song of the larks, the warm wind blowing across the Don from the sands that had not cooled during the night, all invited him to sleep. And surely it was time. He had not slept for several nights running. Lulled by the quails, he gave in to drowsiness and closed his eyes. Aksinya sat beside him in silence, thoughtfully pulling the purple petals off a sprig of fragrant lungwort with her lips.

'Grisha, mightn't someone find us here?' she asked softly, touching Grigory's bearded cheek with the stem of the flower.

He dragged himself out of drowsy oblivion and said huskily, 'There's no one about in the steppe. This is the quiet season. I'll have a sleep, love, and you mind the horses. Then you'll have a sleep. I'm so sleepy... Haven't slept for three days... We'll talk later.'

'Sleep, my dearest, sleep well.'

Aksinya bent over Grigory, drew aside the lock of hair that had fallen over his forehead, and pressed her lips gently to his cheeks.

'Grisha, darling, how many grey hairs you have now,' she whispered. 'You must be getting old? Not long ago you were just a lad.' And with a sad smile she gazed into his face.

He was sleeping with his lips slightly parted and breathing steadily. His black eyelashes, sun-bleached at the tips, were quivering slightly and his upper lip stirred, revealing firmly clenched white teeth. Aksinya's gaze grew more attentive and only now did she notice how much he had changed in the months since they had parted. There was something harsh, almost cruel in the deep furrows between his brows, in the folds round his mouth, in the jutting cheekbones. And for the first time it struck her that he must be terrible in battle, on horseback, brandishing a bared sabre. Her eyes dropped to his big knotty hands and for some reason she sighed.

After a while she rose quietly and crossed the clearing, lifting her skirt high to keep it out of the dew-drenched grass. Somewhere not far away a stream was babbling over stones. She went down to the bottom of the dell, which was paved with mossy green boulders, drank the cold spring water, washed her face and rubbed some colour back into her cheeks with her kerchief. All the time a gentle smile hovered on her lips and her eyes were shining. Grigory was with her again! Once again she had felt the lure of the unknown with its phantasmal vision of happiness. The tears she had shed through all her sleepless nights, the grief she had suffered in these past few months. Only the day before, when the women weeding their potatoes on the vegetable patch next to hers had struck up a sad song, her heart had contracted painfully.

> Come home, grey geese, come home,
> Time your swimming was done,
> And time my crying was done—
> Woman, crying alone...

a woman had begun the lament in a high-pitched voice, and Aksinya had been unable to restrain her tears. She had tried to work and bury the despair that was eating at her heart, but the tears had misted her eyes and dripped steadily on the green potato leaves, on her helpless arms, and she could neither see nor work. She had dropped the hoe, and flung herself down with her face in her hands, letting the tears flow freely.

Only yesterday she had cursed her life, and everything around her had seemed dull and joyless as a cloudy day, but today the world was jubilant and bright, as after a refreshing summer shower. 'We'll find our share of happiness one day,' she thought, gazing thoughtfully at the patterned oak leaves as they caught the slanting rays of the rising sun.

Round the bushes and on the sunny patches there was a wealth of colourful sweet-scented flowers. Aksinya gathered an armful, sat down quietly beside Grigory and, remembering her youth, began to weave a wreath. In turned out well. Aksinya sat admiring it, then added a few pink sweetbriar blossoms and placed it at Grigory's head.

At about ten o'clock Grigory was awakened by the neighing of the horses. He sat up in fright, groping for his weapons.

'There's no one about,' Aksinya said quietly. 'Don't be afraid!'

Grigory rubbed his eyes and smiled sleepily.

'I've learned to live like a hare, I keep one eye open even when I'm asleep, and jump at every little sound. You can't get out of the habit so easily, girl. Have I slept for long?'

'No. Perhaps you'll sleep some more?'

'I'd have to sleep all day to make up for what I've missed. Let's have breakfast. The bread and the knife are in my saddle bags. You find them while I go and water the horses.'

He stood up, took off his greatcoat and worked his shoulders. The sun was hot now. A breeze stirred the leaves of the trees, and their rustle drowned the melodious murmur of the spring.

Grigory went down to the water, made a dam out of twigs and stones, and dug up some soil with his sabre to fill in the chinks. When the water had risen in his pond, he fetched the horses and let them drink, then took off their bridles and again put them out to graze.

Over breakfast Aksinya asked, 'Where shall we be going from here?'

'To Morozovskaya. We'll ride as far as Platov, then walk.'

'What about the horses?'

'We'll leave them.'

'What a pity, Grisha! They're such good horses. The grey's a beauty! Must we leave them? Where did you get them?'

'I got them...' Grigory smiled wryly. 'I robbed a Ukrainian.'

After a slight pause he said, 'Pity or not, we've got

831

to leave them behind. This is no time for us to be horse trading.'

'And why are you carrying arms? What good are they to us? God forbid, but if someone sees them, we'll be in trouble.'

'Who'll see us at night? I kept them just in case. I feel a bit scared now without them... When we leave the horses, we'll leave the arms. They won't be needed any more then.'

After breakfast they lay down on Grigory's great-coat. He fought vainly against sleep while Aksinya, leaning on her elbow, told him how she had lived and what she had been through in his absence. Through an overpowering drowsiness he heard her steady voice but his heavy eyelids just would not stay open. At times her voice seemed to die away altogether, and then he would give a sudden start and wake up, only to close his eyes again after a few minutes. Weariness was stronger than both desire and will.

'...they missed you, they kept asking, where's Daddy? I tried to be as kind as I could. They got used to me and stopped going in to see Dunyashka so often. Polyushka is a quiet little girl, and obedient. All I had to do was make her a few rag dolls, and she would sit with them under the table busy as can be. But Mishatka came running in from the street one day, trembling all over. "What's the matter?" I asked him. And he burst out crying, and so bitterly. "The other boys won't play with me. Your father's a bandit, they say. Mummy, is it true? What are bandits like?" So I told him, "Your father's no bandit. He's just ... just unlucky." And then he kept on at me with his questions: Why is he unlucky, what does unlucky mean? How could I explain it to him?.. They started calling me Mother of their own accord, Grisha. Don't think I taught them. Mikhail was all right to them, he was kind. He wouldn't even say hullo to me though, just turned his head away and walked past, but twice he brought them some sugar from the stanitsa. Prokhor grieved for you. That man, he's done for, he said. Last week he came in to talk to me about you and burst into tears... They searched my place, looking for weapons. They looked everywhere—under the eaves, in the cellar, everywhere...'

Grigory fell asleep without hearing the rest of the story. The leaves of a young elm growing near by were whispering in the breeze. Yellow blobs of light glided over his face. Aksinya lavished kisses on his closed eyes, and then she herself dozed off, resting her cheek on Grigory's arm and smiling in her sleep.

* * *

They left the dell late at night, when the moon had risen. After two hours' riding, they came out on a slope above the River Chir. The corncrakes were screeching in the meadows, frogs were croaking fit to burst in the rushy backwaters, and from far away came the muffled moans of a bittern.

There were orchards all along the bank, dark and unfriendly in the mist.

Not far from a small bridge, Grigory halted. Silence reigned over the village. Grigory touched his horse with his heels and turned aside. He had felt a sudden reluctance to cross the bridge. This stillness was suspicious, and he feared it. On the edge of the village they forded the stream and had just turned into a narrow lane, when a man rose from the roadside ditch. The next moment three more appeared.

'Halt! Who goes there?'

Grigory recoiled from the shout as if he had been struck in the face, and reined in his horse. Recovering himself instantly, he responded loudly, 'Friends!' and as he wheeled his horse sharply, he managed to whisper to Aksinya, 'Turn back! Follow me!'

The four sentries from a grain-requisitioning detachment that had just taken up its quarters in the village advanced silently towards them. One stopped to light a cigarette. He struck a match. Grigory brought his whip down hard on Aksinya's horse. It leapt forward and broke straight into a gallop. Crouching over his horse's neck, Grigory galloped after it. The silence lasted a few long, agonising seconds, then a ragged volley crashed out like a clap of thunder and spurts of fire pierced the darkness. Grigory heard the hot whine of bullets and a long-drawn shout.

'To arms!'

Some two hundred paces from the stream Grigory caught up with the grey horse that was swinging along with great strides and as he drew level, shouted, 'Keep your head down, love! Keep low!'

Aksinya was pulling at the reins and slipping sideways.

Grigory managed to hold her or she would have fallen.

'Are you wounded?! Where? Speak!' Grigory asked hoarsely.

She said nothing, only leaning more and more heavily on his arm. Holding her close as they galloped, Grigory whispered panting, 'For the Lord's sake! Just a word! What is it?!'

But not a word or a groan came from her silent lips.

About two versts from the village Grigory turned sharply off the track, rode down to a ravine, dismounted and, taking Aksinya in his arms, laid her gently on the ground.

He took off her warm jacket, tore the light cotton blouse and her shift from her breast, and felt for the wound. The bullet had entered her left shoulder, smashed the shoulder blade and come out under the right collarbone. With bloodied, trembling hands Grigory rummaged in the saddle bags for a clean undershirt and a field dressing. He lifted Aksinya, placed his knee under her back and bandaged the wound, trying to staunch the blood that was gushing from under the collar-bone. The strips of cloth and bandage were soon soaked black. Blood was also flowing from Aksinya's half-open mouth, gurgling in her throat. With mortal horror gripping his heart Grigory realised that it was all over, that the most terrible thing that could have happened in his life had already happened.

He walked carefully down the steep slope of the ravine, along a path sprinkled with sheep's droppings, carrying Aksinya in his arms. Her head lay helplessly on his shoulder. He heard her whistling, choked breathing and felt the blood leaving her body and flowing out of her mouth on to his chest. The two horses followed him down into the ravine. Snorting and jingling their bridles, they began to crop the rich grass.

Aksinya died in Grigory's arms not long before dawn. Consciousness never returned. He silently kissed her on lips that were cold and salty with blood, lowered her gently to the ground and stood up. An unknown force struck him in the chest. He staggered and fell over on his back, but sprang to his feet again in terror. And once again he fell, striking his bare head painfully on a stone. Then, without rising from his knees, he drew his sabre from its sheath and began to dig a grave. The earth was damp and yielding. He tried to hurry, but his throat tightened till he almost choked and, gasping for breath, he tore his shirt open. The early morning freshness cooled his sweating chest and now it was not so hard for him to work. He scooped out the soil with his hands and cap, not resting for a minute, but it took him a long time to make a grave waist-deep.

He buried his Aksinya by the bright light of morning. As she lay in the grave he folded her brown, but now deathly pale arms on her chest and covered her face with her kerchief, so that the earth should not fall into her half-open eyes that gazed motionlessly at the sky and were already beginning to fade. He bid her farewell, firmly believing that they would not be parted for long...

With his hands he carefully pressed down the damp yellow clay on the grave mound and for a long time knelt beside it, his head bowed, swaying to and fro.

No need to hurry now. This was the end.

The sun rose over the ravine in the dusty murk of a dry wind. Its rays silvered the thick strands of grey on Grigory's bared head and glided over his pale and frighteningly set face. As though awakening from a horrible dream, he raised his head and saw above him a black sky and a blindingly bright black disk that was the sun.

XVIII

In the early spring, when the snow has gone and the grass crushed by winter has dried out, the spring fires begin. The flames driven by the wind stream across the steppe, devour the dry timothy, leap up the tall stalks of the thistle, slither over the brownish tops of the mugwort, and spread out over the hollows. And for long afterwards the steppe smells acridly of the scorched, cracked earth. All around the young grass grows merrily green, the countless larks flutter in the blue sky above it, the passing geese feed on the lush herbs, and the bustards that have come for the summer build their nests there. But where the fires have passed the charred earth lies black and ominous. No birds nest there, the wild animals shun it, and only the swift-winged wind sweeps across and carries the grey-blue ash and dark bitter dust far away.

Black as the fire-scorched steppe was Grigory's life now. He had lost everything he held dear. Ruthless death had taken all, destroyed all. Only the children were left.

And yet he still clung convulsively to the earth, as though his broken life were still of some value to himself and others...

After burying Aksinya, he roamed aimlessly about the steppe for three days, but he went neither home, nor to Vyoshenskaya to surrender. On the fourth day he left his horses in a village near Ust-Khopyorskaya, crossed the Don and set off on foot for the Slashchevskaya oak forest, where Fomin's band had suffered its first defeat in April. He had heard then that some deserters had a permanent camp in the forest, and now, not wishing to go back to Fomin, he had decided to join them.

For several days he roamed about the huge forest. Though tortured by hunger, he hesitated to approach any house or village. With the death of Aksinya he had lost both his native wit and his former daring. The snap of a breaking branch, a rustle from the thickets, the cry of a bird at night, everything plunged him into fear and confusion. For food he had only the wild strawberries that were not yet ripe, some tiny mushrooms, and the leaves of the hazel nut. He grew gaunt and haggard. Towards the end of the fifth day some of the deserters came across him and took him to their dug-out.

There were seven of them. All local men, they had been living in the forest since the previous autumn, when mobilisation had begun. They had made a proper home for themselves in the roomy dug-out and hardly lacked for anything. They often went to see their families at night and came back with fresh supplies of bread, rusks, millet, flour and potatoes. Meat they obtained without much difficulty in other villages, sometimes stealing cattle.

One of the deserters, who had once served in the 12th Cossack Regiment, recognised Grigory and he was accepted without much wrangling.

* * *

Grigory lost count of the dreary, endless days. Until October he put up with life in the forest, but when the autumn rains set in, and then the frosts, his longing for the children, for his native village revived with fresh and unexpected force.

To while away the time he would spend days on end carving wooden spoons and bowls, and skilfully fashioning figures of people and animals out of the softer woods. He tried not to think about anything, to seal his heart against the poison of grief. In the day-time he succeeded but during the long winter nights he was overcome by the anguish of recall. He would toss and turn on the wooden bed, unable to fall asleep. During the day none of his companions heard a word of complaint from him, but at night he would often wake up trembling and pass his hand over his face to find his cheeks and the thick beard that had grown in these six months, wet with tears.

He often dreamed of the children, of Aksinya, his mother and other dear ones who were no longer among the living. His whole life was in the past, and the past seemed but a brief and oppressive dream. 'If only I could go back home just once more, just to see the children, then I could die as I must,' he often thought to himself.

In early spring Chumakov made an unexpected appearance in the camp. He was wet to the waist but as cheerful and restless as ever. When he had dried his clothes by the stove and warmed himself, he sat down beside Grigory on the bunk.

'Well, we've done a lot of roaming since you left us, Melekhov! We've been as far as Astrakhan and in the Kalmyk steppes... Ay, we've seen a lot of the wide world! And the blood we've shed! They took Fomin's wife hostage and grabbed all his property. That got him real mad and he ordered us to cut down anyone who served Soviet power. So we started doing just that: teachers, doctors, agronomists—the whole bloody lot! And not long ago they mopped us up,' he said, with a sigh and a sudden shiver. 'First they routed us at Tishanskaya and a week ago they did it again at Solomny. During the night they surrounded us on three sides and left only one way out, up the hill. And there the snow was real deep, up to the horses' bellies... At daybreak they opened up with their machine-guns, and that was it... They mowed down the lot of us. I and Fomin's little son were the only two that got away. You see, Fomin had been carting his boy Davydka round with him ever since autumn. Fomin himself was killed... I saw it with my own eyes. The first bullet got him in the leg and smashed the knee-cap, the second snicked his head. Three times he fell off his horse. We'd stop and lift him into the saddle, but he'd ride on for a bit then fall again. The third bullet finished him, hit him in the side... Then we had to leave him. I galloped on a bit further, and when I looked back, two horsemen were slashing him where he lay...'

'It was bound to end like that,' Grigory said indifferently.

Chumakov spent the night with them but in the morning started taking his leave.

'Where're you going?' Grigory asked.

Smiling, Chumakov answered, 'To find myself an easy life. Mebbe you'll come with me?'

'No, go your own way.'

'This is no life for me. Your trade, Melekhov—carving these spoons and bowls—wouldn't suit me,' Chumakov said mockingly, doffing his cap and bowing. 'Thank you, peaceable brigands, for your hospitality and shelter. May the good God give you a cheerful life because it's pretty glum here with you. You live in the woods and pray to your stolen goods—d'you call that life?'

After Chumakov's departure Grigory lived in the forest for another week, then made ready for the road.

'Going home?' one of the deserters asked him.

And for the first time since he came to the forest Grigory gave a faint smile.

'Yes.'

'Why don't you stay on till spring. Come May Day, they'll promise us an amnesty, then we'll all go home.'

'No, I can't wait,' Grigory replied and said goodbye all round.

Next morning he reached the Don opposite the village of Tatarsky. For a long time he stood gazing at his own home, pale with a joyous excitement. Then he slipped his rifle and field bag off his shoulder and took out the hussif, the hemp waste, and the bottle of gun oil, and for some reason counted the cartridges. There were twelve clips and twenty-six lying loose.

At the steep cliff the ice had drifted away from the bank. The clear green water was lapping round it, breaking the needles of ice along the edge. Grigory dropped his rifle and revolver into the water, then tipped out the cartridges and carefully wiped his hands on his greatcoat.

Downstream from the village he crossed the dark-blue ice of March, which was already porous and pitted by a sudden thaw, and strode on towards the house. From a distance he saw little Mishatka on the slope above the pier and could barely restrain himself from running towards him.

Mishatka was breaking off the icicles dangling from a rock, throwing them, and studiously watching the blue fragments rolling away down the hill.

Grigory reached the slope and, panting for breath, called out hoarsely, 'Mishatka!... Son!'

The little boy gave him a frightened look and lowered his eyes. He had recognised his father in this bearded terrible-looking man.

All the fond and tender words that Grigory had whispered through the long nights in the forest when recalling his children now fled from his memory. He kneeled and kissed his son's pink cold little hands and in a choking voice could repeat only one word, 'Son ... son...'

Then he picked the boy up in his arms and gazing with dry, frenziedly burning eyes into his face, asked, 'How are you all here? How is Auntie, and Polyushka? Are they alive and well?'

Still not looking at his father, Mishatka replied, quietly, 'Auntie Dunya is well, but Polyushka died last autumn... Of dip ... diphtheria. And Uncle Mikhail is in the army.'

And so it had come about, the one small thing Grigory had longed for through his sleepless nights. He was standing at the gate of his own home and holding his son in his arms.

This was all he had left, all that still made him kin with the earth and with the whole huge world around him, glittering under the cold sun.

The End.

AFTERWORD

A BOOK ABOUT REVOLUTION
AND HUMAN BEINGS

A few years ago the literary journals celebrated a notable date—the fiftieth anniversary of Sholokhov's *Quiet Flows the Don.* Fifty is the age of maturity, an age when many of life's roads are behind us.

In 1927 Alexander Serafimovich, one of the founding fathers of Soviet literature, the author of the famous *Iron Flood* made a prophetic statement. He had just read a manuscript a young writer from the distant stanitsa of Vyoshenskaya had submitted to the magazine *Oktyabr,* of which Serafimovich was the editor. The decision had been taken to start publishing the novel in 1928. On the eve of the new year the veteran author was entertaining Henri Barbusse, Martin Andersen Nexö, and Beiá Illés. He took a bulky folder down from its shelf, held it in his hands for a moment, and with a touch of solemnity in his voice said, 'Dear friends! Just you remember this title—*Quiet Flows the Don.* And remember the name of the author—Mikhail Sholokhov... Take my word for it: that name will soon be known all over Russia, and in two or three years, all over the world.'

He was right. The year 1928 saw two large new editions of the novel in the *Roman Gazeta* and the *New Books of Proletarian Literature* series. There was a tremendous response, not just from professional critics but from ordinary readers, workers and country folk. And before two years had passed, the book was translated into French, German, Swedish, Spanish, Czech and Dutch; soon it appeared in Austria, in the French colonies, then in Japan, Britain, China, Poland, the United States...

Mikhail Sholokhov was only 22 when the first book of the novel was published, but he already had a substantial working life behind him. He had taught at an elementary school for adults, kept the books at a food-procurement office, and worked as a brick-layer and a stevedore. The most memorable passage in his biography tells us of his service in a food-procurement detachment, which he joined at the age of fifteen to help requisition the hoarded grain that was needed to feed starving Russia. 'From 1920 I knocked about the Don country doing various jobs,' he wrote. 'I chased the bands that ruled the Don up to 1922, and the bands chased me. Everything went as it should. I got into some tight corners, but nowadays one tends to forget these things.'

But Sholokhov did not forget his interrogation by the anarchist leader Makhno, when he escaped being shot 'only because I was too young', or the fighting against the band led by Fomin, where the hero of his novel Grigory Melekhov ends his fighting days. On the contrary, inspiration led the young writer to probe deeper and deeper into the events and lives he had witnessed around him. By the time his early stories appeared in book form he had already conceived and set down on paper the characters of his great and tragic epic *Quiet Flows the Don*.

The appearance of the first book of *Quiet Flows the Don* in 1928 was a big event for the young Soviet literature. Maxim Gorky read it and said of its author, 'He writes as a Cossack who loves the Don, Cossack life, nature...'

Love is an active emotion, and Sholokhov's filial attitude to his homeland turned out to be exceptionally fruitful, not only for Russian, but for world literature. The Don itself became as inseparable from the name of Sholokhov, as the Dnieper was from Gogol's, Ryazan from Yesenin's, and the Volga from Gorky's.

But there was a time, in the early years of Soviet power, when any mention of the Don or the Don Cossacks evoked feelings of apprehension or puzzlement among the reading public.

What did people know about the Cossacks? On the one hand, they were the descendants of those men of daring who as early as the 15th century had claimed their right to freedom and got what they wanted even in the abominable conditions of Russian serfdom, they were the runaway serfs and rebels who marched under the banners of Stepan Razin and Yemelyan Pugachov... On the other hand, the word 'Cossacks' suggested something menacing and cruel. The Cossacks were the soldiers who in tsarist times had lashed students with their whips, broken up May Day meetings, and helped to crush the revolution of 1905.

But the Cossacks were also the legendary First Cavalry Army, that glory and bastion of Soviet power! Budyonny himself, its commander, was a Cossack from the Cossack village of Kozyurin. So what kind of people were they, these Cossacks, in reality?

This question is answered by the novel. Sholokhov makes the reader a long-standing guest of a Cossack household, brings him to table with his hosts, takes him out to the fields to build hay ricks, to fish, to thresh grain. He sees the Cossack not only booted, on horseback with his lance and sabre, but in leather slippers, with a rake in his hands, or a child on his lap, or out walking with his girl-friend... Sholokhov wrote about a life that was hard and contradictory. His characters are rough open-hearted people, proud but in many ways tied by class prejudices. Like any other class society, theirs is stratified, internally divided by contradictions and due for energetic historical development and advance.

Quiet Flows the Don is of enormous value to the historian, the political economist, the philosopher and the sociologist. But the greatest of its revelations is the artist's insight into the human heart. Only by knowing the Cossacks' character, their habits, vitality and aspirations, individually at first hand, as well as collectively, can we fully understand how such different individuals as Pyotr and Grigory Melekhov, or Mitka the executioner and the loving Natalya, could grow up under one roof; why some of the Cossacks followed Budyonny and others joined Denikin.

Quiet Flows the Don tells us in the language of art with immortal authenticity about the victory of the socialist revolution in Russia.

The novel is often described as an epic. In my view, this description applies to the work as a whole, including the first book, although its events are, in a sense, 'local' and the 1917 Revolution, the main

842

object of the author's attention, is still a long way off.

...Grigory Melekhov, a young Cossack is sleeping at dawn. There he is for all the world to see, arms thrown out, still wrapped in the dreams of youth.

We can examine him unhurriedly, a handsome fellow, with his thick forelock, hooked nose and high cheekbones covered with brown ruddy skin. Yes, what a fine lad he is, vibrant and ready for all the joys that life in the village of Tatarsky has to offer!

His days follow an unusually calm and uncomplicated course. Horse racing with the other lads of the village or mowing the meadow with his family, enjoying the colourful sight of the festively attired women in fields, or the misty radiance of the sunset beyond the distant hills. His feet leave only a wavy trace in the grass, his scythe swishes through the crisp stalks.

At first sight, there doesn't seem to be very much in these first chapters—just a description of everyday life. We feel the dew on our bare feet. Everything seems ordinary and natural. Even what happens between Grigory and Aksinya suggests nothing that could disturb the peaceful passage of time, so unpretentious and uneventful is this affair from the social point of view.

But this is in fact the story of the people at grass roots, of society and individuals. We are already beginning to get a picture of the Cossacks' moral world and perhaps that of the whole Russian people on the eve of the first imperialist war with its intimations of the great revolution that was to follow.

The social elements in the life of the main character are organically woven into his personal life, forming a single turbulent stream. In Grigory Melekhov's social behaviour there is much that is typical of the Cossacks in those times, and yet everything that happens to him is unique. No other life, no other character can exactly repeat Grigory's, if only because it contains twice or three times as many contradictions. Not for nothing is he known as the 'Turk', the grandson of Prokofy Melekhov, long remembered in the village of Tatarsky for his headstrong decisions and daring defence of human dignity.

On the other hand, the story of the love between Grigory and Aksinya seems rather remote from any social questions. But if we give it a moment's thought, we see that even this love depends on the unfolding of social events and battles, on the abrupt turns in Grigory's political alignments, and in general on his long and painful search for the true path in life.

Inevitably the realities of revolution colour all of Melekhov's destiny. The tension of its powerful magnetic field does not weaken from beginning to end.

There are over 600 characters in *Quiet Flows the Don* and they are all needed to give us a truly profound understanding and appreciation of the complex character of this man of the people, who with such pain is seeking his place in the revolution. Grigory is linked with every one of them in some way or another, even with those he never directly meets amid the turbulent flood of events.

The whole epic canvas of *Quiet Flows the Don* asks the question that Grigory asks himself and the world: Who and what are the Communists? Why are most of the Cossacks attracted to them? Even the intense, searching looks that Grigory gives such men as Bunchuk or the fearless commissar Likhachov add depth to our knowledge of the Bolsheviks portrayed in the novel. Sholokhov makes us see them as they are seen by Grigory, a man who is convinced that they are his enemies and yet cannot fail to admire their courage and the strength of their faith.

Only against this backcloth of six hundred living characters (particularly such characters as Bunchuk and Mikhail Koshevoi) can one understand Grigory's own biography, the profound meaning the author imparts to this splendid image.

Quiet Flows the Don is a story about how the process of revolution takes irresistible possession of a person, no matter how complex and contradictory his own attitude to it may be. As Academician Khrapchenko writes, 'the entry of Melekhov, a man brought up in the patriarchal mould, into the orbit of the October Revolution, constitutes one of the vital moments that gives the questing and mental conflict of this character world significance.'

But can we fully understand him? Though I use the phrase myself, I feel how difficult it is to get to the bottom of Grigory's character, to find an all-embracing formula for something so big, intricate, spun out of human suffering. The history of fifty years' research on *Quiet Flows the Don* by literary scholars, the many interpretations of Grigory's character and destiny that have appeared and are still appearing indicate how baffling is the problem, how easily that 'all-embracing formula' escapes both scholars and critics.

All Soviet art from the outset has worked on the theme of the revolution, the destiny of the people of the new, socialist society, the fate of the land and the people who till it. *Quiet Flows the Don* is one of many artistic answers to these vital questions. Sholokhov's genius absorbed and refracted the wealth of thought, observation and moral questing that the young Soviet literature had accumulated. It may be said that Sholokhov's art is truly flesh of the flesh of the art of socialist realism.

As the years go by, Sholokhov's novel reveals new strata of thought, themes and conflicts, hitherto unperceived by the critics. The controversies that began as soon as *Quiet Flows the Don* was published in 1928 continue to this day; it is still the same book, but the questions that have come up in the discussions of different decades differ in tone and substance.

To some it seems that *Quiet Flows the Don* gives a convincing and comprehensive picture of the distribution of class forces in the revolution and the civil war, and that the main thing the author tells us about is the attitude of the middle peasant, always a key figure in any popular revolution. And indeed, one has no difficulty in finding grounds for such an interpretation in the novel's general scheme. The class set-up is certainly quite obvious. On one side we have the poorest Cossacks (Knave, Khristonya, Prokhor Zykov, Koshevoi), on the other are the rural exploiters (Mokhov, Listnitsky, to some extent Korshunov), and in between there are the Melekhovs, personifying the middle peasant both socially and morally.

Other scholars, following the same narrowly sociological path, have no difficulty in finding evidence for the conclusion that Sholokhov felt it most important to show that not only individual participants in the revolution but even large masses, a significant section of the people, could make historical mistakes and be attracted by a cause that was both unjust and contradictory to their interests, as happened in the Vyoshenskaya rebellion. While some critics interpret the hero's path as one of error, others regard it as one of guilt, the guilt of an individual who refused to heed the truth, learned through experience and suffering, which brought the majority of the Cossacks on to the only true, revolutionary path.

In my view, one can find much convincing evidence

in Sholokhov's work to support the version that the essential thing in *Quiet Flows the Don* is the disposal of the idea that there can be a third path during a revolution. After all, why did Grigory abandon the Red camp, although he hated the Whites, the soft-handed aristocrats, with all the fury of his rebellious soul? He is not a greedy or cowardly egoist, his mental make-up is not exclusively one of a small property owner. On the contrary, he is always in the thick of the fighting, with no thought for his own safety. And he's there because he wants to find the best solution for his people, for whose sake he suffers all the torments, so vividly described by the author.

But Grigory's misfortune is that for him the people are only the Cossacks. He can see no further than the Don; beyond its borders there are only 'muzhiks', 'peasants', 'Russia'. Not that he wants to fight Russia. His programme for the Cossacks is simple enough: let the Whites and the Reds fight it out and we'll find a path in the revolution that will bring us to neither one side nor the other... Everything that befalls Sholokhov's her and many of other characters in the novel shows us what such a philosophy leads to at times of great revolutionary change.

In any revolution, in any social tempest there will always be people who try to deceive themselves with this apparently innocent idea of political neutralism. But how many has this idea brought to the brink of disaster, how many has it hurled to destruction! *Quiet Flows the Don* shows the danger of an ambivalent position in a life-and-death struggle, the fatal mistake of looking for a third path between truth and falsehood, good and evil, light and darkness, revolution and counter-revolution, progressive and reactionary ideology. To the many interpretations of Sholokhov's famous novel one may therefore add yet another: it is about the way in which socio-political ideas take hold of people, huge masses of people, and about the meaning of such ideas for living people, for a particular family, a particular village. The sad fate of Grigory Melekhov, the destruction of nearly everyone in his circle—such is the real price of the 'third path' in a revolution. At the same time *Quiet Flows the Don* is a book about the great Leninist idea of rebuilding the world on new, Communist principles. Not for nothing does the author put into the mouth of the Bolshevik Mikhail Koshevoi the crucial words of the whole novel, 'A man must always answer for what he does.'

But this interpretation is only one of many, none of which can fully embrace the wealth of ideas contained in the novel. As Academician Khrapchenko has remarked, the true greatness of Sholokhov's art 'lies in the astonishing depth of his characters, their universal human significance'. Great though the sweep of the novel, Sholokhov pays astonishingly acute attention to every person that comes withing his field of vision, in both their everyday affairs and at times of crucial turns of fate.

A remarkable feature of Sholokhov's art is his ability to get inside the mind of his hero. The reader involuntarily begins to experience the same emotions and to see the world with his eyes (Lev Tolstoy regarded this ability to 'infect' the reader with the feelings of one's characters as the decisive criterion of literature—'If there is no infection there is no art.')

A remark Sholokhov once made in conversation with some French writers helps us to understand what interests Sholokhov in the life of the individual and humanity as a whole: 'I am interested in people in the grip of social and national cataclysms... It seems to me that their characters crystallise at such moments.'*

The tremendous concentration of pain and drama that one finds in the Sholokhov's conflicts and characters is impressive. The book is indeed about great social cataclysms, about the most dramatic moments in the history of the whole people, the whole country. And yet, taken as a whole, Sholokhov's work strikes one as something radiantly optimistic, as something strong and morally healthy, as firm and solid ground to stand on.

But if the main thing for Sholokhov, as he himself explained, is the individual facing the test of historical cataclysms, does not such a definition contradict another, later statement of Sholokhov's when he explained that his dearest wish in portraying the central character of *Quiet Flows the Don* had been to show 'human charm'? And this is about Grigory Melekhov, broken by life, returning home destroyed physically and mentally, his appearance so awesome, that even his own son is frightened. Where, then, is the 'charm'?

But in the final analysis these different goals do in

_____

*V. Krupin, "On a Visit to Sholokhov"—in *Sovetskaya Rossiya*, 25 August 1967.

fact converge, giving us the unity of Sholokhov's conception of man on earth, a humanistic conception which, like the keystone of an arch, holds together all the other specific interpretations of the novel. What is perhaps the deepest and most painfully sought message of the novel reaches our consciousness: remember the human being! Always, at all times, and in any global social upheaval or conflict. The message comes from the writer who created Grigory and Aksinya, Podtyolkov and Bunchuk, Ilyinichna and Darya Melekhova. But Sholokhov is not content to inspire kind feelings for people in trouble, to arouse understanding and sympathy. He wants the characters he has created to awaken energy, to urge us to make active efforts to help. Sholokhov not only puts man to the test of the time in which he lives; he puts the time to the test of man.

The provisions of the Nobel Prize require that a laureate should make a speech expressing in concise form his views on life and art, on the duty of the artist. Sholokhov had this to say about himself: 'I should like my books to help people to become better, more honest with themselves, to awaken love of humanity, the desire to work actively for the ideals of humanism and human progress.'

This is perhaps the key to understanding the author of *Quiet Flows the Don* as an artist and a humanist.

THE DON COSSACKS

The story of *Quiet Flows the Don* begins with the words: 'During the last but one campaign against the Turks the Cossack Prokofy Melekhov had returned to the village...'

The theme of the Don Cossacks, their history, the customs and traditions that had taken shape in the course of centuries, their role in the moulding of the Russian nation, the Russian state, thus emerges on the very first page of Sholokhov's novel. Tales of Cossack valour come readily to the lips of the old men at Grigory Melekhov's wedding; Grigory's father Pantelei often refers to Cossack tradition; the history of the Cossacks is a highly relevant subject both for the poorest Cossacks who gather of an evening at the house of the revolutionary Stokman, and for the aristocratic officers, who argue fiercely in their frontline dug-out about the past and future of the Don

848

country... It is to this land, 'steeped in the blood of our ancestors' that Grigory Melekhov, Mikhail Koshevoi and Bunchuk will often devote long and painful meditations. Of special interest are the author's thoughts on Cossack history at the beginning of the second and sixth parts of the novel, especially the publicistic digression concerning the socio-political difference between the Cossacks of the northern (Upper Don) lands and those nearer the Sea of Azov, the Lower Don Cossacks: '...the less prosperous Cossacks of the northern districts not blessed with the rich soils of the Azov littoral, its vineyards, abundant hunting and fishing grounds, would at times break away from Cherkassk and take to raiding the Great Russian lands, while providing a safe and reliable stronghold for all rebels, from Razin to Sekach.

'Even in later times, when most of the Don was writhing silently under the imperious hand of the central power, the Upper Don Cossacks rose openly and, led by their own atamans, shook the foundations of the throne, fighting the crown forces, plundering the caravans of barges on the Don, ranging as far as the Volga and inciting the subjugated Cossacks of Zaporozhye to rebellion.'

This passage pinpoints the main thing about the Cossacks, that unique ethnic and social formation, forged in the crucible of Russian history.

The rise of the Don Cossacks dates back to the 15th century, when an unusual type of community began to take shape in the steppes of South Russia that stretched on both sides of the River Don. It consisted mainly of serfs who had fled from the central parts of the country to escape feudal exploitation. The very word 'Cossack' (of Turkic origin) means *free man*. These free men formed independent military communities that were outside the control of the tsar and ruled themselves, at first on a democratic basis. Forced to defend their independence from the tsar and his generals, from the raids of savage nomad tribes, and from foreign invaders attracted by the rich lands of the steppe—Tatars, Turks, Poles—the Cossacks organised their lives, founded their townships (called 'stanitsas') and villages, engaged in breeding animals, particularly horses, in fishing, hunting and trade, literally without laying down their arms. Similar processes took place not only on the Don but in other outlying parts of Russia, where such communities arose as the Zaporozhye Cossacks, on the River Dnieper, the Greben Cossacks in the North Caucasus, and other

849

groups in the Urals and Siberia. The life and customs of the 'Zaporozhye Sich' may be familiar to the reader from Gogol's famous novel *Taras Bulba*.

Little by little, however, the tsar's government succeeded in establishing control over the free Cossack communities and enlisting their services. The autonomy of the Don Cossacks was eroded and instead of having their own atamans, democratically elected by the Cossack Council, they were ruled by the so-called *nakazny* (vice) *atamans* appointed by the tsar. Gradually the Cossacks developed into an elite military caste, supplying irregular troops controlled by the central government. These troops were used to guard borders, patrol newly annexed territories and eventually, in the 20th century, to suppress the revolutionary movement in Russia.

The smallest administrative unit in the Don country was the *stanitsa*, which often comprised a whole group of villages. For 'loyal service' to the tsar the Cossacks were granted privileges that were denied to the rest of the oppressed Russian peasantry and even to those peasants who lived on the Don but had not acquired Cossack status (Ukrainians, 'outsiders', and so on). A Cossack was exempt from several state taxes and had the use, in perpetuity, of as much as 70 acres of land. On the other hand, he was bound by many obligations. A Cossack had to report for military service with his own horse of a certain size and standard, with his own sabre and equipment, and his own uniform (*viz.* Grigory's problem after he has left home and the time comes for him to report for military service). A Cossack was considered to be serving in the army from the age of 18 to 36, during which time he passed through various categories. In his first year he was 'in training', then followed various grades of service 'in the line', and even when living at home in his native village, he was compelled to spend some of his time in camp (such a camp, where Petro Melekhov and Stepan Astakhov are training, is described in the first part of the novel). Besides mounted units the Cossack army also had foot soldiers, (the 'foot-sloggers' with whom Pantelei has to serve in his old age). A squadron of Cossack cavalry consisted of four troops, each troop having two sections; at various times in their careers Petro and Grigory Melekhov command troops, squadrons and regiments (four or five squadrons). A Cossack brigade consisted of two or three regiments.

THE COSSACKS IN THE FIRST WORLD WAR

At the first signal of the outbreak of war, an 'alert' was called on the Don, and the Cossacks were duty bound to take up arms. As a militarised community they were directly affected by any international crisis. And in any war the tsarist government relied heavily on Cossack troops with their strict discipline, combat experience, thorough training and ancient warlike traditions. So not surprisingly, the Cossacks took part in nearly all Russia's wars: in the Russo-Turkish conflicts which continued sporadically through the 17th to 19th centuries, in the Seven Years' War of 1756 to 1763, in the Patriotic War of 1812, and in the Crimean campaign of 1853-56.

None of these wars, however, took such a heavy toll of the Cossacks as the First World War, in which tsarist Russia fought on the side of the Allies (France, Britain, etc.) against the countries of the Triple Alliance led by Germany. Tsarism pushed Cossack troops into the most dangerous and disastrous gaps in the front and this led to enormous losses, (one recalls Sholokhov's monologue in the novel): 'Many of the Cossacks were missing, scattered across the fields of Galicia, Bukovina, East Prussia, the Carpathians and Romania, and their bodies had rotted to the funereal music of the guns...'

Many of the desperate battles in which the Cossacks took part are described in Sholokhov's novel with great authenticity. The fighting in Galicia in the autumn of 1914, when the Russian army launched a broad offensive against the Austro-Hungarian forces (this is where Grigory Melekhov kills a man for the first time); the battles in East Prussia in the spring of 1915 (Grigory saves Stepan Astakhov from death); the Brusilov breakthrough in the summer of 1916 (Grigory saves a howitzer battery); the fighting on the Romanian front (Grigory is wounded in the arm). 'Although I did not take part in the war, no military expert has ever found any mistakes or inaccuracies in my descriptions,' Sholokhov was to write later (in 1934) when speaking of the many years he had devoted to research in the archives and libraries of Rostov-on-Don and Moscow. In a newspaper interview Sholokhov revealed a little of the mechanics of his preparatory work: 'The work of preparing material for *Quiet Flows the Don* proceeded in two directions: first, the collection of reminiscences, eye-witness accounts, facts, and details supplied by living participants in the imperialist and civil wars, conversations and inquiries, the checking of my own concepts and notions; and second, the painstaking study of specialised military literature, the analysis of military operations, numerous memoirs and study of foreign and even White Guard sources.'

Historians and students of the novel have established what sources the author of *Quiet Flows the Don* used in describing various events. It is a long list, from the most impressive historical documents to pamphlets, newspapers, leaflets and orders issued by the military authorities of the time.

As most people know, by 1917 revolutionary outbreaks had taken place among the troops on both sides of the front. These protests were directed against a world war that was a totally unnecessary and ruinous ordeal for the people. The 'maggoty soup' mutiny described in the novel, the fierce argument between Bunchuk and the monarchist officers, the scene of fraternisation between Russians and Germans are all based on real episodes of the anti-war movement that had gripped the front. Despite their former privileged position, the Cossack forces were no less explosive material than other troops. It was here that the revolutionary qualities of such men as Podtyolkov, Bunchuk, Mikhail Koshevoi, Kotlyarov, Knave, and others developed.

War strips away pretence and sharpens all relationships. The legend that all Cossacks, rich or poor, were united and 'above class' was exposed in the flames of military conflict. The social contradictions between them, the difference in their interests and ways, everything that later, during the revolutions, was to divide them irreconcilably came boiling to the surface.

'I was attracted by the task of showing the Cossacks in the revolution.'

The quotation is from what Sholokhov has told us about his original idea for *Quiet Flows the Don*. Among other things he said: '...At first I did not intend to develop it so broadly... I began with the participation of the Cossacks in Kornilov's march on Petrograd.' '...I wrote some quite long pieces and then saw that this was not what I should have begun with and put the manuscript aside... And when the first book of *Quiet Flows the Don* was finished and I started on the next, about Petrograd and Kornilov's abortive putsch, I returned to my first manuscript and used it for the second book.'

Sholokhov's novel recreates many events from the turbulent history of the Russia of those days, including the crucial moment of the collapse of tsarism in Russia. The abdication of Nicholas II and the victory of the bourgeois-democratic revolution in February 1917, when power passed to the Provisional Government, are echoed in the lives of various characters in the novel. We are given graphic pictures of how the news of the 'overthrow' comes to the front (the brigade commander's speech to the Cossack regiments), how it reaches the village of Tatarsky, and what response it evokes on the Listnitsky estate.

As the story unfolds we see that the bourgeois Provisional Government had no intention of carrying out the will of the exhausted Russian people, including the Cossacks, who wanted Russia to be taken out of the war. On the contrary, the Provisional Government threw itself enthusiastically into fulfilling its 'duty to the Allies' and mounted an offensive that was foredoomed to failure. In August 1917, General Kornilov, whom the Provisional Government had appointed Supreme Commander-in-Chief of the Russian Army, staged a counter-revolutionary mutiny for the purpose of setting up a bourgeois-landlord military dictatorship and restoring the monarchy. Army units, including some Cossack divisions were ordered to march on Petrograd. But under the influence of Bolsheviks like Ilya Bunchuk these units, far from suppressing the popular movement, played an important part in bringing about the collapse of the whole Kornilov venture. The general himself, having 'escaped' from arrest (Sholokhov shows us just how this actually happened) set about organising the counter-revolutionary White Guard Volunteer Army on the River Kuban. He was killed in action in the fighting near Yekaterinodar (now Krasnodar) in March 1918.

After showing the dramatic effect of the Kornilov venture on the history of the Don Cossacks, Sholokhov panoramas the subsequent events that took place on Cossack territory. In June 1917, a few months before the Socialist Revolution, the tsarist general Alexei Kaledin, a monarchist and counter-revolutionary, had become Ataman of the Don Army. When the October Revolution brought the workers' and peasants' Soviets to power, he refused to obey them and incited the Army to mutiny. Under his leadership Cossack units waged an active struggle against the forces of the revolution. In December

1917, he captured Rostov-on-Don and attempted to occupy the Donbas coal region, but was defeated by Red Guard detachments. Realising that he had failed, Kaledin shot himself in February 1918.

His successor as Ataman of the Don Army, Pyotr Krasnov, also a former tsarist general, had been in command of the Cossack forces who were thrown against revolutionary Petrograd at the end of 1917. On becoming ataman, he showed himself to be an active enemy of Bolshevism and a true friend of Kaiser Germany, which had taken advantage of the revolution in Russia to occupy Russian territory even though it had concluded a peace treaty with the Bolsheviks. With the support of the German occupying forces, Krasnov stepped up military operations against the Soviets and twice organised attacks on the city of Tsaritsyn. But with his credibility weakened by many setbacks he abandoned his command and fled abroad. (During the Second World War Krasnov collaborated with the Nazis, was captured by Soviet troops and condemned to death by court martial.) The remnants of the Don Army which he had commanded later became part of the 'Volunteer Army'.

This army, which had been set up in South Russia by former tsarist generals Kornilov, Denikin and Alexeyev, was a hotchpotch of the most active counter-revolutionaries. Most of them were officers of the former tsarist army. In the summer of 1919 the Volunteer Army launched its march on Moscow and having linked up with the Vyoshenskaya insurgents, developed an offensive that took it as far as Orel and Voronezh. Here, however, it was defeated by the Red Army and fell back southwards, retreating all the way to the port of Novorossiisk on the Black Sea. From there, in March 1920, the remnants of the defeated army fled to the Crimea where they took refuge under the wing of General Wrangel. In the novel, Grigory Melekhov, Aksinya and Prokhor, his orderly, retreat with the routed forces of the Volunteer Army. Left behind on the warves of Novorossiisk with many other Cossacks, Grigory then joins the First Cavalry Army commanded by Semyon Budyonny. This army, which had taken part in defeating Denikin's forces, continued its legendary march westwards, crushing the forces of Wrangel, the White Poles and others. (It is one of these engagements that Grigory has in mind when he relates, '...When we were getting near the Crimea, I had a scrap with a Kornilov officer...')

THE BOLSHEVIK COSSACKS
PORTRAYED IN THE NOVEL

The second book of *Quiet Flows the Don* has a scene describing how in November 1917 Grigory happened to meet a Cossack, who was to play a significant part in the history of the revolution on the Don—Fyodor Podtyolkov.

We meet many other characters in the novel who come from the Bolshevik camp—underground Communists, Red Guards, commissars, members of food-requisitioning detachments. But even among these Fyodor Podtyolkov is outstanding because here we have not just one of the heroic historical figures but a fully developed character embodying a dramatic theme which lends colour to the whole story. The portrayal of Podtyolkov in the novel testifies to Sholokhov's rare gift for weaving actual historical personages into the texture of his narrative.

Fyodor Podtyolkov (1886-1918) was born in the family of a poor Cossack and took part in the First World War, in which he was awarded two Crosses of St.George for valour. Podtyolkov worked to establish Soviet power on the Don. In Kamenskaya, the centre of the Red Cossack movement, a revolutionary committee was set up under his leadership in 1917, and in the following January he became chairman of the Don Cossack Military-Revolutionary Committee.

Closely associated with him was Mikhail Krivoshlykov (1894-1918), also one of the leaders of the Don Military-Revolutionary Committee.

Krivoshlykov grew up in the family of a Cossack blacksmith. His father managed to give his son an education and, after training at an agricultural school, Mikhail worked for a time as an agronomist. During the war against Germany he had commanded a squadron and when the revolutionary movement spread to the army, the men of his regiment elected him chairman of their regimental committee. Krivoshlykov's gift for organisation revealed itself strikingly in the days of the revolution, when the 'Bolshevised' squadrons were transferred from the front to the Don. Here Krivoshlykov and Podtyolkov and other Bolshevik leaders did a great deal to repulse the advance of the White forces under General Popov and later the forces of Denikin, who had attacked the Red Don Republic from the Kuban. In 1918, when

Rostov-on-Don was threatened by the German occupation forces and the White Guard troops, and the Don Republic was in grave peril, it was decided to organise a special expedition to rouse the Cossacks in defence of the Don. The expedition fell into a trap. The Red Cossacks were tricked, disarmed and shot near the village of Ponomaryov, and the leaders of the expedition, Podtyolkov and Krivoshlykov, were hanged. Their heroic behaviour in the hour of death became one of the most vivid movements in the revolutionary history of the Cossacks. Today an obelisk stands on the spot where the Podtyolkov and his men were executed and many streets and squares in the cities and stanitsas of the Don are named after Podtyolkov and Krivoshlykov.

THE VYOSHENSKAYA RISING OF 1919

The events of this revolt form one of the most dramatic pages in the history of the Civil War in Russia. By the spring of 1919, with the active support of the imperialist powers of the Entente, the counter-revolution succeeded in surrounding the young Soviet Republic with a ring of fire. In the east, in Siberia, the Red Army was compelled to fight the forces of Admiral Kolchak, in the north the forces of Yudenich were advancing, in the south, the republic was threatened by the combined forces of the Don and Volunteer armies under the command of Denikin. In this mortal struggle against the White Guards and the intervention forces, who represented all the major capitalist powers of that time, the Land of Soviets was stretched to the limit of its resources. Its already weakened industry was further strained by the unbearable military burden. The food situation had become desperate, and the young Soviet republic was compelled to pass a law on food requisitioning. The amount of grain and fodder that the peasant farmer had to supply to the state was laid down in each specific case by the authorities. All surplus grain that there was in the countryside had to be brought in to save the cities, industry, and the army. Although the authorities emphasised the temporary nature of this emergency measure (after two years, food requisitioning was replaced by a stable food tax, which allowed the peasant to dispose of his surplus grain as he saw fit), the introduction of food requisitioning was fiercely opposed by some sections of the peasantry, particularly the well-to-do upper crust, the kulaks, whose grain stores were the main target for requisitioning.

On the Don, where the Cossack farmers lived better than the rural population in other parts of Russia, this discontent was exacerbated by such additional factors as the restriction of the Cossacks' former privileges in the ownership of land, and so on. The young, inexperienced personnel of the Soviet local administrations (people like Mikhail Koshevoi, the chairman of the Tatarsky village Soviet) made a good many tactical mistakes. There were also some communist leaders who believed on principle that the Don was 'dangerous', that it had to be 'de-Cossackised', that everything to do with Cossack privileges had to be 'burned out with hot iron', that there was no need to stand on ceremony with the Cossacks, rich or poor. *Quiet Flows the Don* contains many expressive and authentic incidents illustrating the Cossacks' growing discontent, which ultimately broke out in open rebellion. A vivid story is related by a Cossack who is driving Stokman and his companions to their regiment in his wagon. He tells them of the behaviour of the Red commissar Malkin in one of the Cossack stanitsas. Blinded by his sense of power and hatred of Cossacks, Malkin mocks and persecutes the old men and invents all kinds of new restrictions.

Naturally such actions by the advocates of 'de-Cossackisation' were a source of alarm to all true Bolsheviks, and particularly to the party leadership. In Lenin's *Collected Works* we find the text of a telegram sent from Moscow to the leaders of the Revolutionary Military Council of the Southern Front on 3 June 1919, in which Lenin speaks with great concern of the shameful highhandedness of local administrators who were abolishing the very concept of the 'Cossack stanitsa', forbidding Cossacks to wear the traditional red stripes on their trousers, to hold fairs, and so on. Lenin warned: 'We draw attention to the need to be particularly careful in interfering in such small everyday matters, which have no significance in general policy and at the same time irritate the population. Take a firm line on the main questions...'

The actions of people like Malkin did irreparable harm to the revolution and alienated the Cossack masses. The counter-revolutionary forces, which, for historical reasons, were particularly powerful on the Don, were quick to take advantage of the situation created by the Cossacks' dissatisfaction with food requisitioning and the ham-fisted behaviour of the Malkins. The Vyoshenskaya uprising occurred in the rear of the Red Army at the most critical moment, when the Southern Front was threatened by the crack troops of Denikin's Volunteer Army, which were poised for a new thrust. Sholokhov shows very convincingly how this 'stab in the back' was delivered, how step by step the White Guard leadership carried out their scheme for turning 'spontaneous' rebels who had risen under the slogan of 'For the Soviets but against the Communists' into the spearhead of the counter-revolution.

It is generally considered that the uprising which spread through the Vyoshenskaya and Kazanskaya stanitsas began on 14 March, 1919. Its final collapse came in the spring of 1920, when the remnants of the insurgents headed for Novorossiisk along with the rest of Denikin's forces. The Cossack revolt was doomed to failure because an independent 'Cossack realm' existing between the Reds and the Whites was an illusion and because, when faced with the realities of the revolt, the majority of the Cossacks soon realised the futility of opposing themselves to the entire Russian people led by the Soviet government.

It must be acknowledged that this government was humane in its treatment of those who had taken part in the uprising. It pardoned the majority of working Cossacks and helped them to return to peaceful labour, even those who had fled abroad (including some prominent leaders of the uprising) were ultimately granted unrestricted return to their country.

Lenin's tactics in relation to the working Cossacks were successful on a country-wide scale. A special decision 'On the Question of the Cossacks', passed in 1925, stated: 'The party's general line in relation to the countryside should be pursued, in the conditions of Cossack life, with particularly careful and constant attention to local features and traditions in a way that will help to erase the differences between Cossacks, peasants, and the former oppressed nationalities in these areas. Moreover, it should be regarded as completely impermissible to ignore the specific features of Cossack life and to apply forcible measures in combating the vestiges of Cossack traditions.'

THE CHARACTERS AND THEIR PROTOTYPES

Although it is clear to everyone that such characters as Grigory Melekhov or Aksinya, or the old Melekhov couple, are the fruit of the author's imagination from the first moment of the appearance of *Quiet Flows the Don* and to this day scholars have been trying to establish who it was that the author 'used as a model' for his characters, who suggested to him this or that situation in life, or some particularly authentic detail.

Much has been written about the possible prototype of the character of Grigory Melekhov. The favourite candidate is one Kharlampy Yermakov, a Cossack cornet born in the village of Bazki, not far from Vyoshenskaya. Like Sholokhov's hero, Yermakov fought in the world war and won three Crosses of St. George for valour. He was wounded 14 times and suffered shell-shock; he also had Grigory's rare ability of wielding his sabre with both his right and left arms. The author of the novel says on this subject: 'A real person did, in fact, serve as a prototype for Grigory Melekhov. There was a Cossack living on the Don... But I must emphasise, I used only his military biography: the period of his service, the German war, the Civil War.' (Significantly, the name Kharlampy Yermakov appears episodically on the pages of the novel devoted to the uprising.)

In *Quiet Flows the Don* there is also a category of characters who actually existed and are portrayed by the author under their real names. Here we have the White Guard generals: Kornilov, Kaledin, Krasnov, Krymov, Denikin, Fitzhelaurov, and Lukomsky. The Red commanders also figure under their own names. Besides Podtyolkov and Krivoshlykov, whom we have already mentioned, there were Shchadenko, Lagutin, and others. There was also a real person on the Don called Yakov Fomin (in the novel he becomes the leader of the band in which Grigory Melekhov did his last 'service'). In the years when the young Mikhail Sholokhov was fighting in a detachment that helped to clear the Don of bandits, a squadron that had risen against the Soviets and was led by Yakov Fomin, was operating in the Vyoshenskaya area. This squadron soon became a ruthless band of thugs and robbers. The author knew the story of this band at first hand and it gave him rich material not only for *Quiet Flows the Don* but also for his early stories, many of which depict the struggle against the counter-revolutionary remnants on the Don (*viz. The Birthmark, Food Commissar, Another Breed, Shibalok's Seed,* and *Chairman of the Revolutionary Military Council of the Republic*).

The prototypes of such characters as Knave and Ivan Kotlyarov (the latter was Ivan Serdinov, a Bolshevik who was ruthlessly done to death during the Vyoshenskaya uprising) have been discovered among local people on the Don. Even Darya Melekhova has an 'analogue', in Maria Drozdova, the widow of a Cossack officer who was related to Serdinov and bayoneted him when he was a disarmed prisoner. Real people also provided models for the commanders of the Serdobsk regiment and the machine-gunner Garanzha, whom Grigory meets in hospital.

With some humour the writer Anatoly Kalinin, who has devoted part of his memoirs to Sholokhov under the title 'Born Amid the Saffron Sands...' writes about the problem of prototypes in *Quiet Flows the Don:*

'The old woman from whom you are bying milk will tell you, "Grisha Melekhov's my nephew." Only his name was Yermakov and Mikhail got to know all about him and printed it. Got to know about every little thing he did."

'You soon begin to realise that other Vyoshenskaya people have a claim to close kinship with the characters of Sholokhov's books. One of them turns out to be a brother of Grigory Melekhov, another has no objection to calling himself his brother-in-law. We also meet 'sisters' of Aksinya. The cleaner at Collective Farmers' House assured me: "I may be a cousin, and that's almost the same as a sister. She died of typhus in 1920."

'...While I was travelling from Vyoshenskaya to Millerovo in the back of a lorry with about 15 other passengers one of them turned up the collar of his sheepskin and with a firmness that ruled out any objection stated, "Pantelei Melekhov was a cousin of mine."

'You have to get used to this kind of thing.'

These naive claims from the readers of Sholokhov's books to actual 'kinship' with his characters contain more than a grain of truth. They confirm the veracity of the artist's portrayal, they show us how wholeheartedly people accept Sholokhov's characters. Ultimately they are yet another proof that *Quiet Flows the Don* has won enormous popularity among the mass readership and become a book that is truly of the people.

V. Litvinov

REQUEST TO READERS

Raduga Publishers would be glad to have your opinion of this book, its translation and design and any suggestions you may have for future publications.

Please send all your comments to 17, Zubovsky Boulevard, Moscow, USSR.